OVER

MY

DEAD

BODY

OVER MY DEAD BODY

SWEENEY BOO

An Imprint of HarperCollinsPublishers

By the pricking of my thumbs,
Something wicked this way comes.

--*Macbeth* by William Shakespeare, 1606

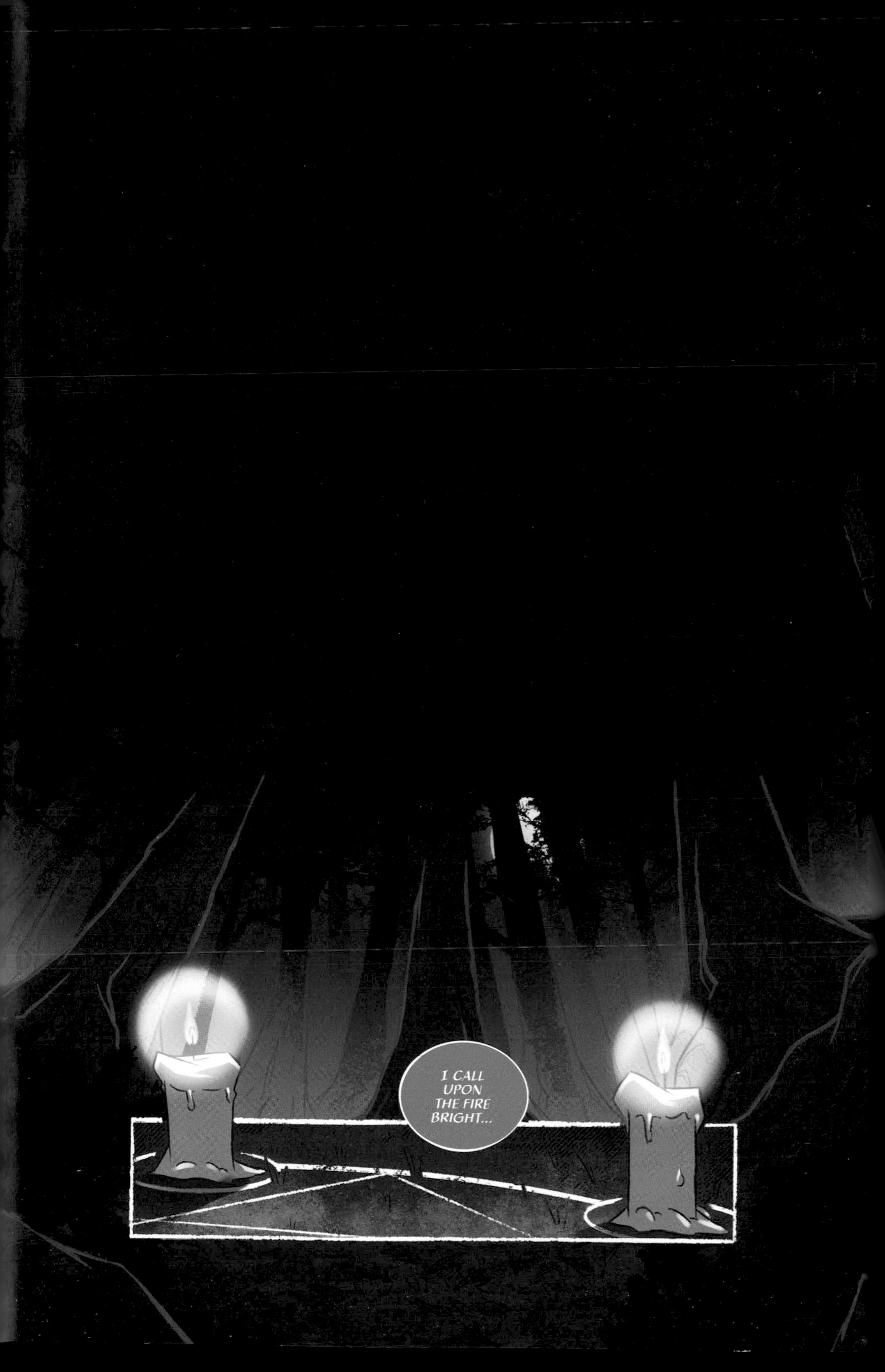
I CALL UPON THE FIRE BRIGHT...

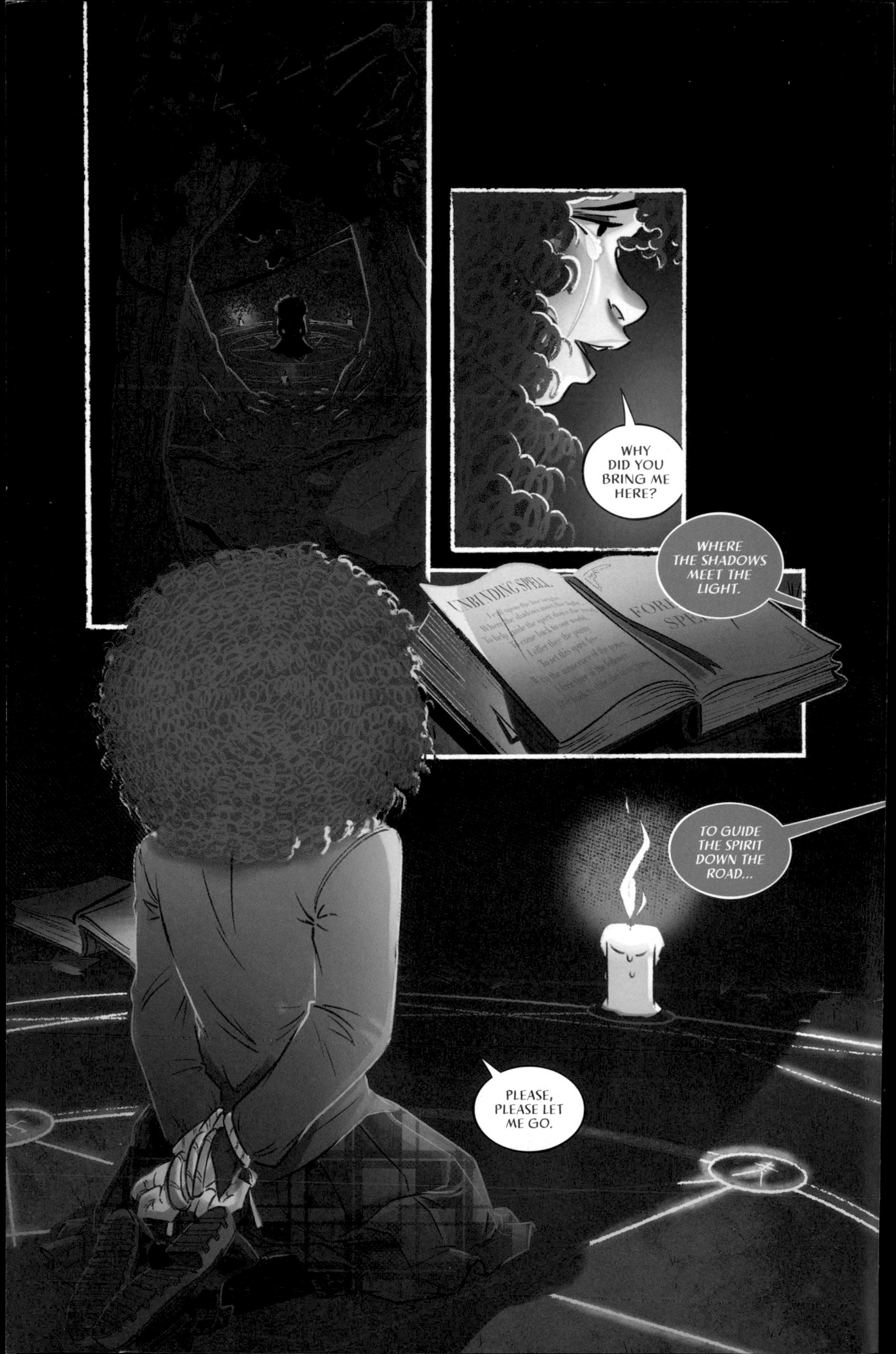
WHY DID YOU BRING ME HERE?
UNBINDING SPELL
WHERE THE SHADOWS MEET THE LIGHT.
TO GUIDE THE SPIRIT DOWN THE ROAD...
PLEASE, PLEASE LET ME GO.

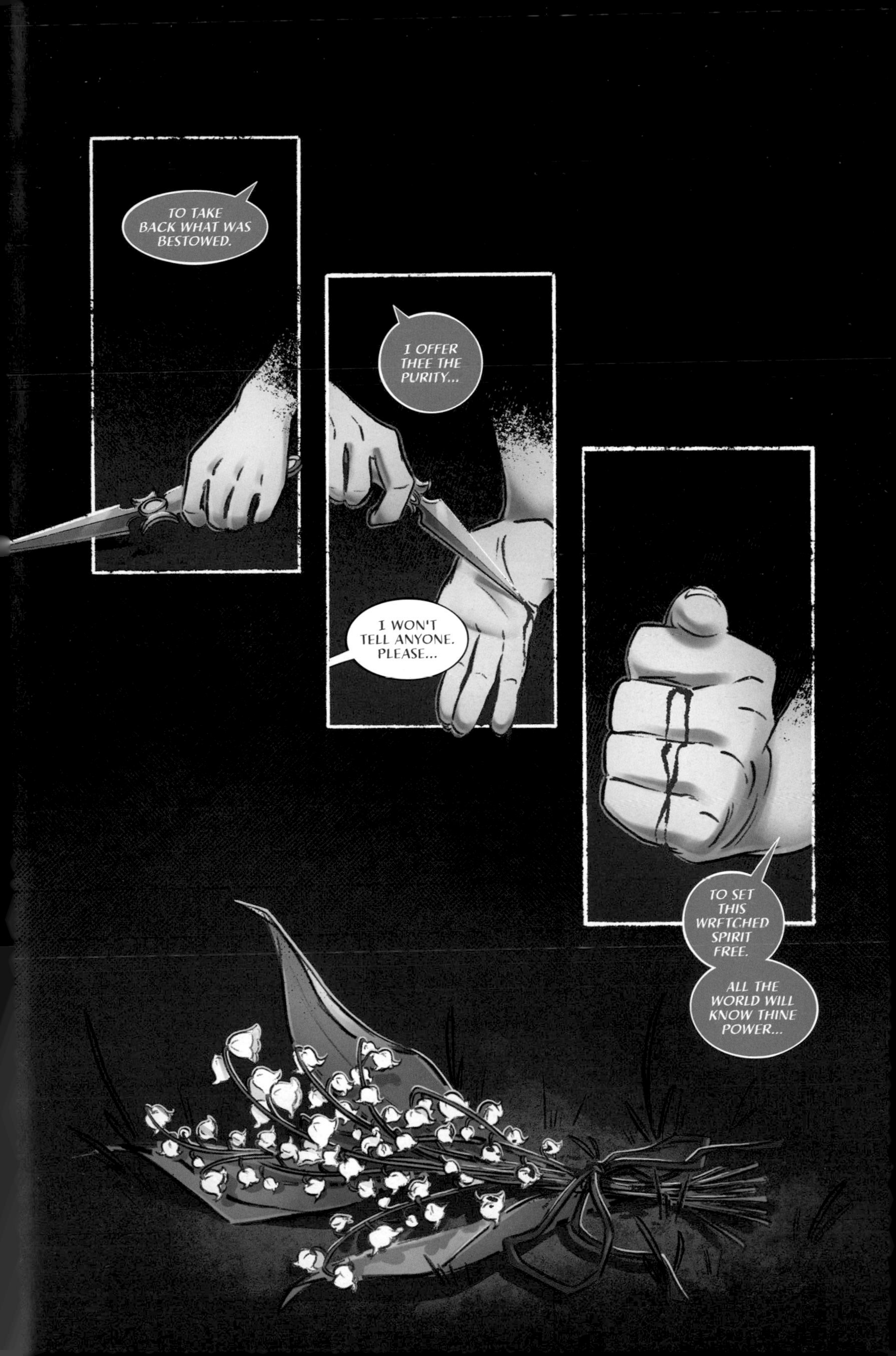
TO TAKE BACK WHAT WAS BESTOWED.
I OFFER THEE THE PURITY...
I WON'T TELL ANYONE. PLEASE...
TO SET THIS WRETCHED SPIRIT FREE.
ALL THE WORLD WILL KNOW THINE POWER...

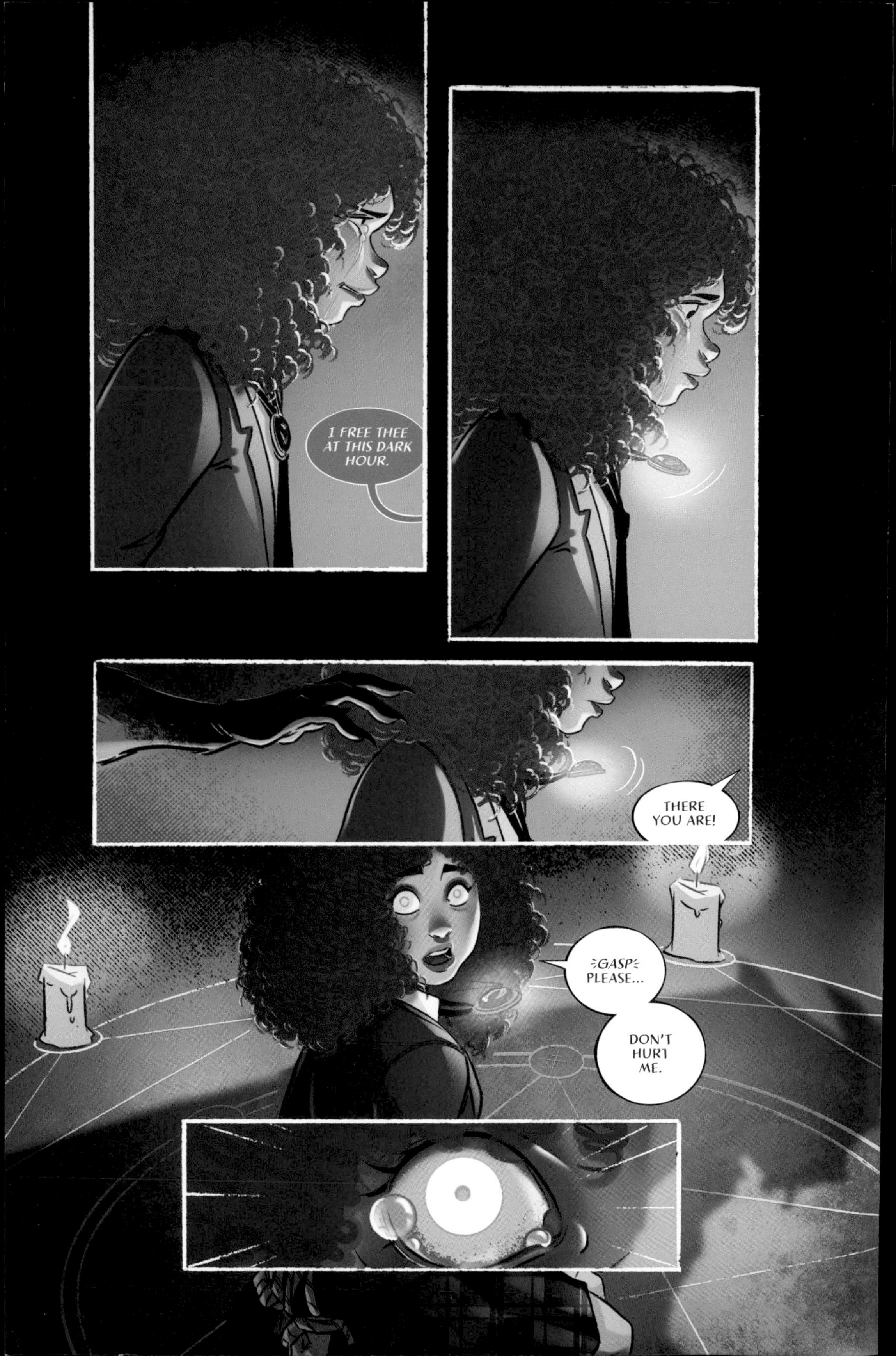
I FREE THEE AT THIS DARK HOUR.
THERE YOU ARE!
GASP PLEASE...
DON'T HURT ME.

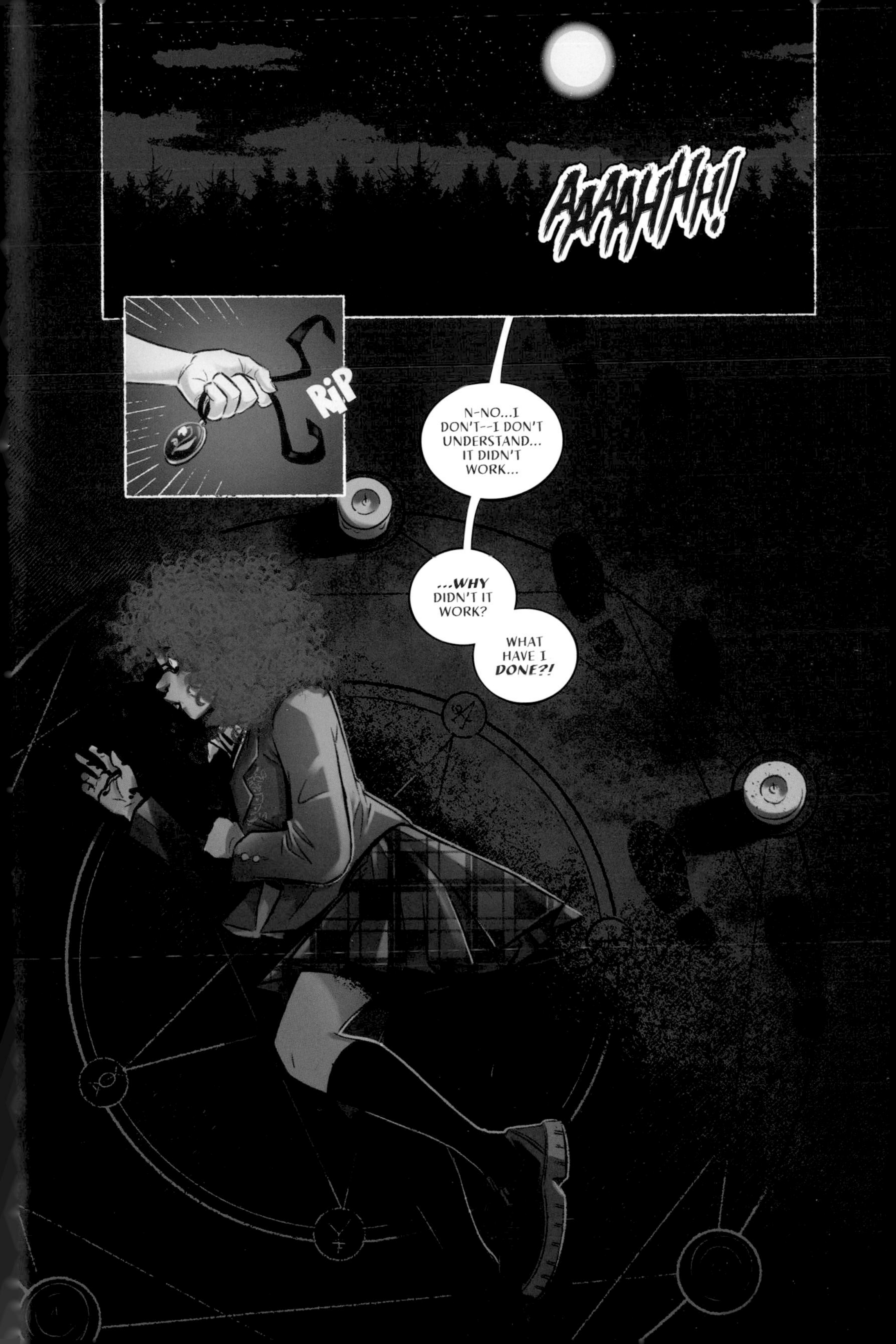
AAAAHHH!
RIP
N-NO...I DON'T--I DON'T UNDERSTAND... IT DIDN'T WORK...
...WHY DIDN'T IT WORK?
WHAT HAVE I DONE?!

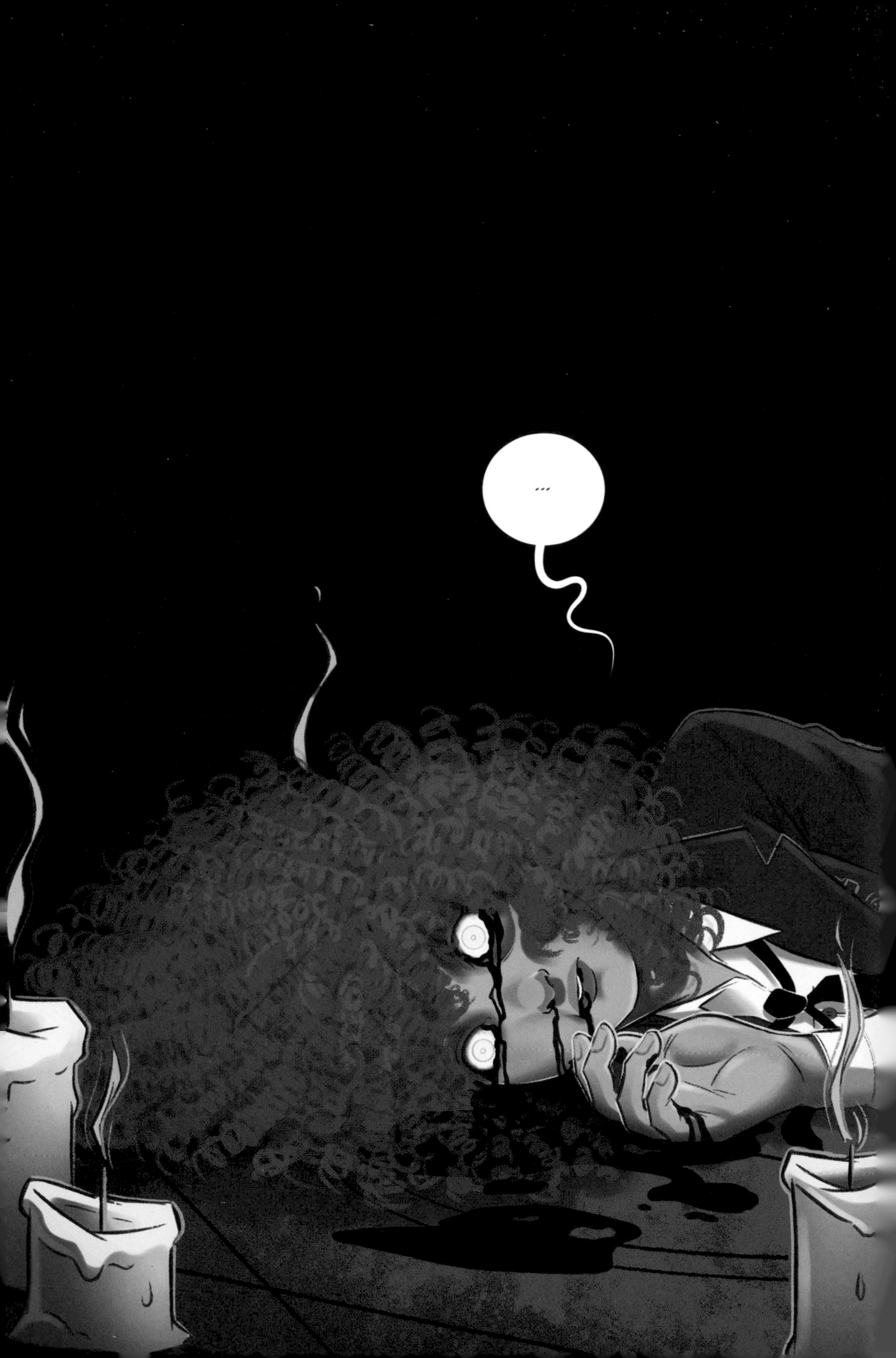
...

CHAPTER I

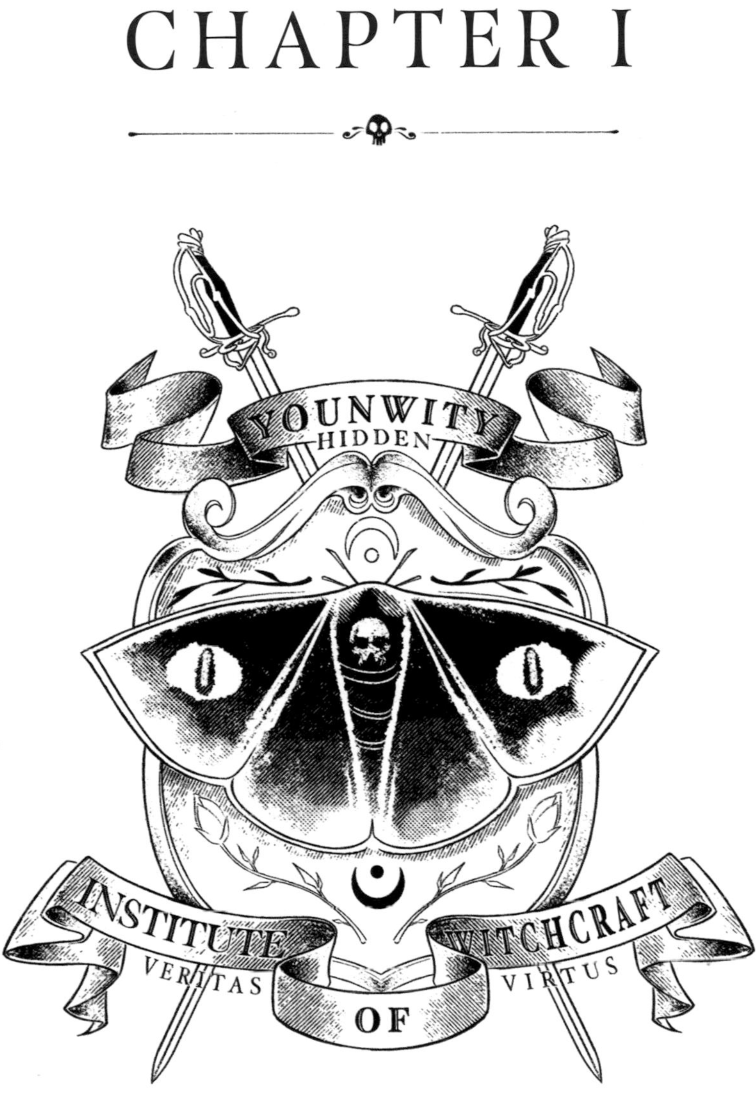
YOUNWITY
HIDDEN
INSTITUTE
OF
WITCHCRAFT
VERITAS
VIRTUS

From childhood's hour I have not been
As others were -- I have not seen
As others saw -- I could not bring
My passions from a common spring --

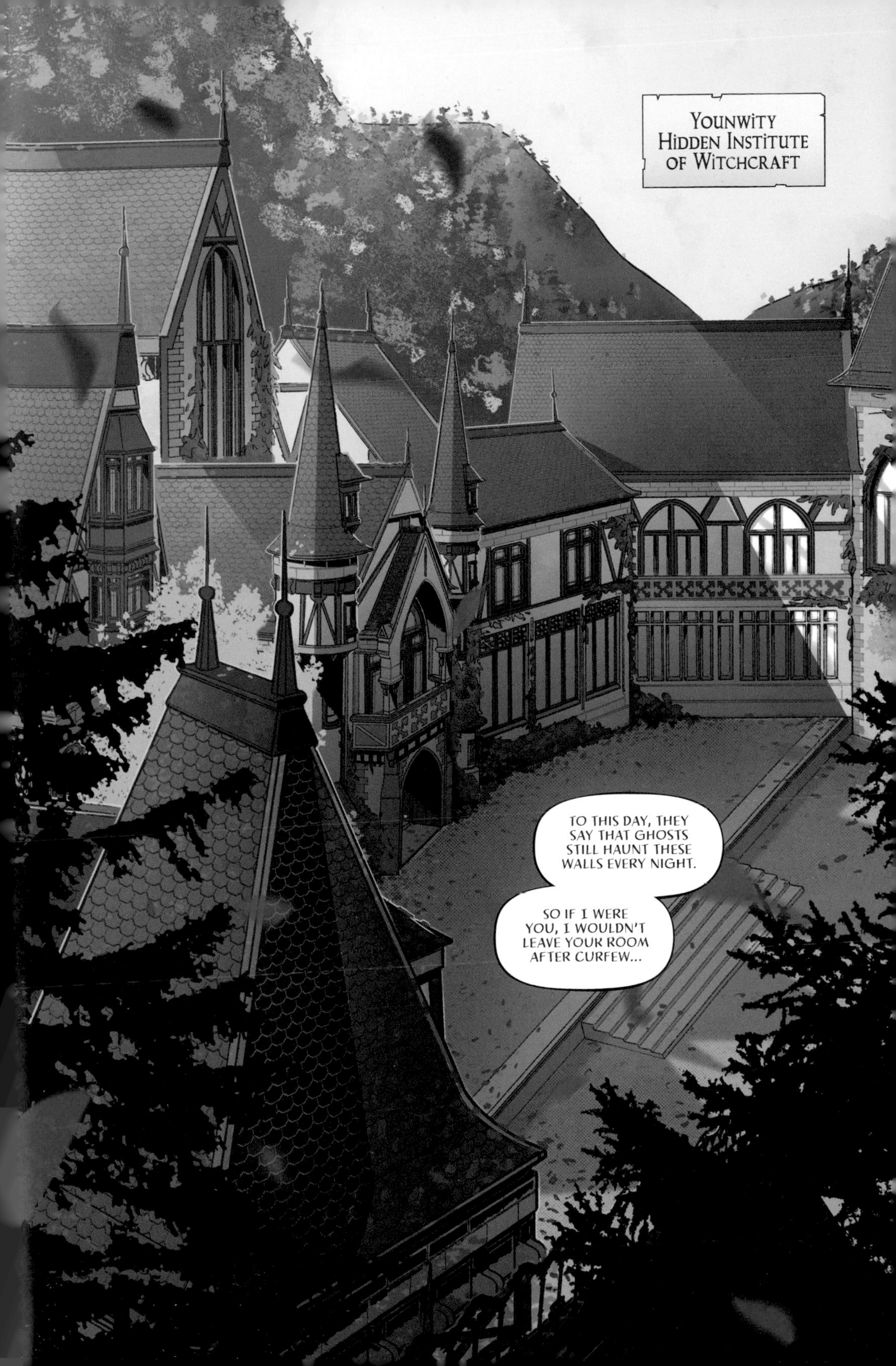
YOUNWITY HIDDEN INSTITUTE OF WITCHCRAFT
TO THIS DAY, THEY SAY THAT GHOSTS STILL HAUNT THESE WALLS EVERY NIGHT.
SO IF I WERE YOU, I WOULDN'T LEAVE YOUR ROOM AFTER CURFEW...

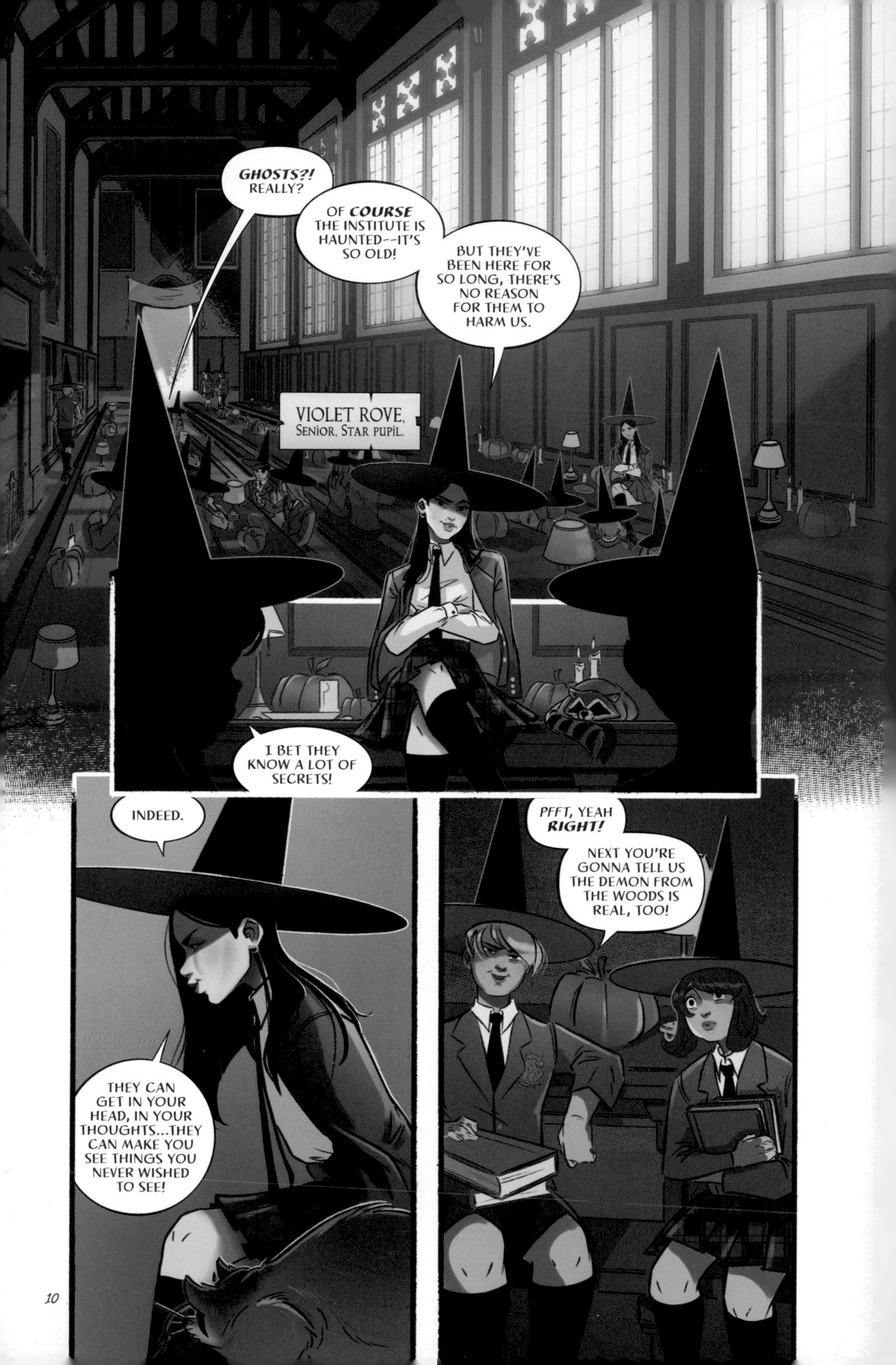

GHOSTS?! REALLY?
OF COURSE THE INSTITUTE IS HAUNTED--IT'S SO OLD!
BUT THEY'VE BEEN HERE FOR SO LONG, THERE'S NO REASON FOR THEM TO HARM US.
VIOLET ROVE, SENIOR, STAR PUPIL.
I BET THEY KNOW A LOT OF SECRETS!
INDEED.
THEY CAN GET IN YOUR HEAD, IN YOUR THOUGHTS...THEY CAN MAKE YOU SEE THINGS YOU NEVER WISHED TO SEE!
PFFT, YEAH RIGHT!
NEXT YOU'RE GONNA TELL US THE DEMON FROM THE WOODS IS REAL, TOO!

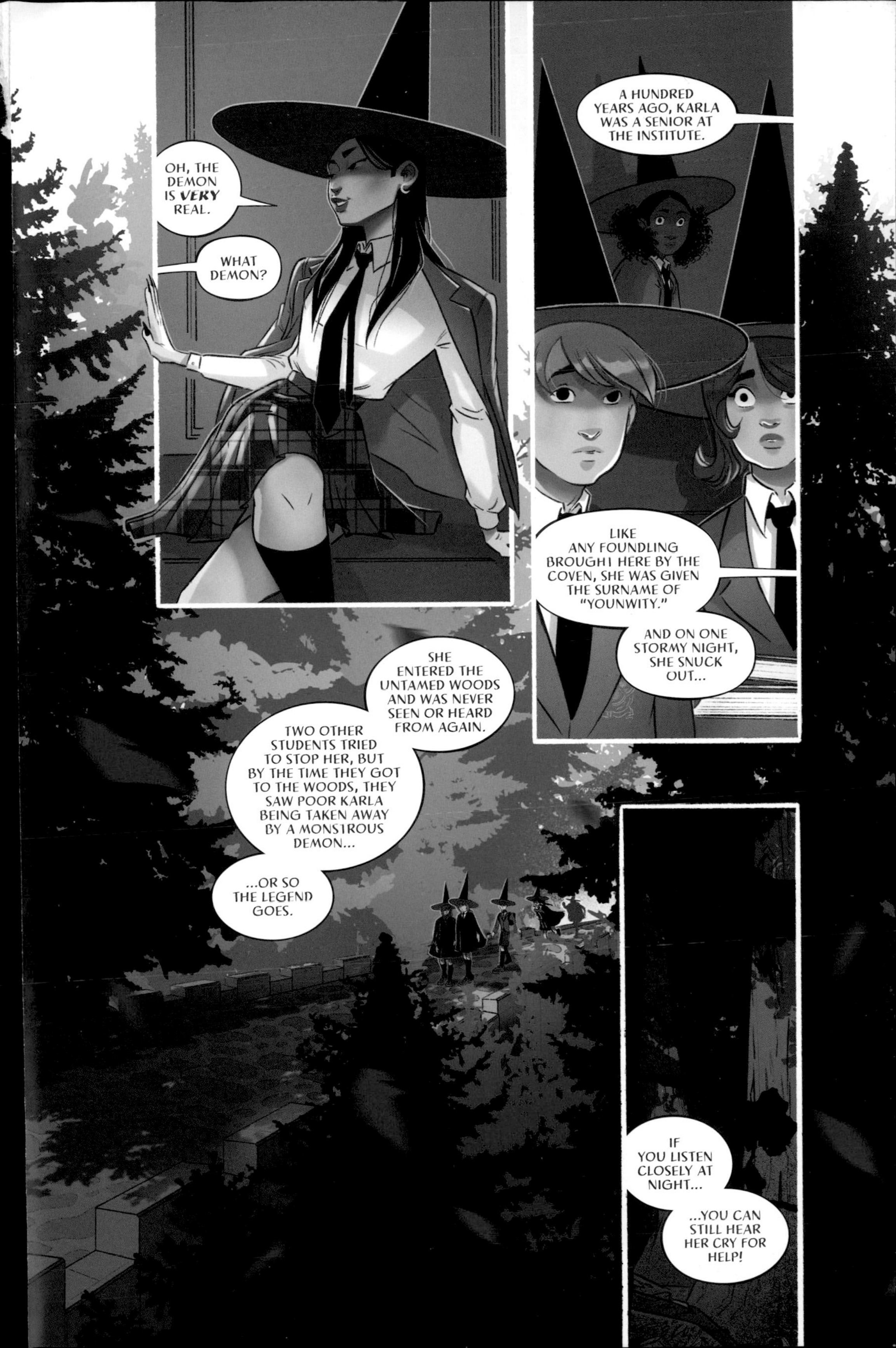
OH, THE DEMON IS VERY REAL.
WHAT DEMON?
A HUNDRED YEARS AGO, KARLA WAS A SENIOR AT THE INSTITUTE.
LIKE ANY FOUNDLING BROUGHT HERE BY THE COVEN, SHE WAS GIVEN THE SURNAME OF "YOUNWITY."
AND ON ONE STORMY NIGHT, SHE SNUCK OUT...
SHE ENTERED THE UNTAMED WOODS AND WAS NEVER SEEN OR HEARD FROM AGAIN.
TWO OTHER STUDENTS TRIED TO STOP HER, BUT BY THE TIME THEY GOT TO THE WOODS, THEY SAW POOR KARLA BEING TAKEN AWAY BY A MONSTROUS DEMON...
...OR SO THE LEGEND GOES.
IF YOU LISTEN CLOSELY AT NIGHT...
...YOU CAN STILL HEAR HER CRY FOR HELP!

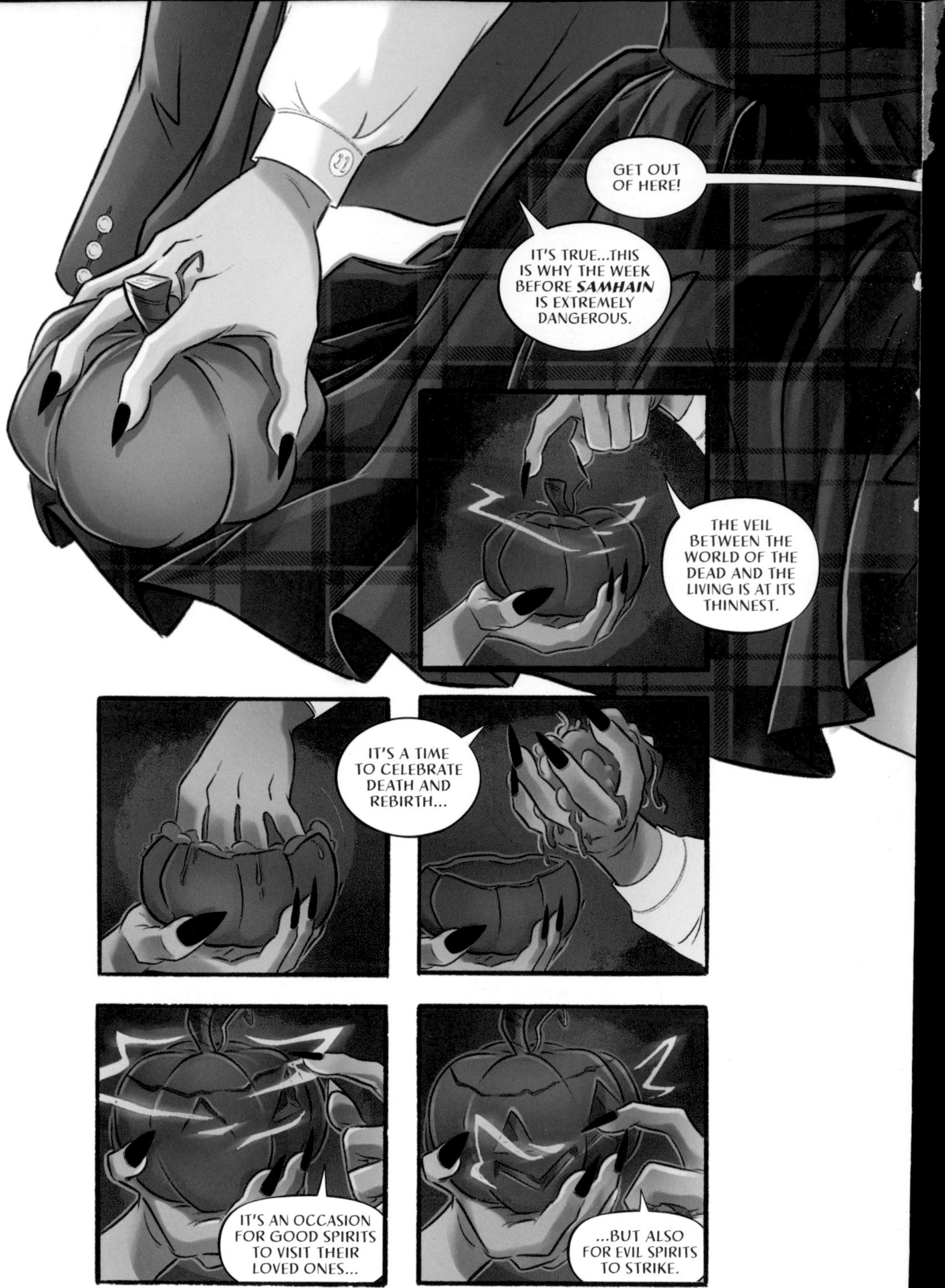
GET OUT OF HERE!
IT'S TRUE...THIS IS WHY THE WEEK BEFORE ***SAMHAIN*** IS EXTREMELY DANGEROUS.
THE VEIL BETWEEN THE WORLD OF THE DEAD AND THE LIVING IS AT ITS THINNEST.
IT'S A TIME TO CELEBRATE DEATH AND REBIRTH...
IT'S AN OCCASION FOR GOOD SPIRITS TO VISIT THEIR LOVED ONES...
...BUT ALSO FOR EVIL SPIRITS TO STRIKE.

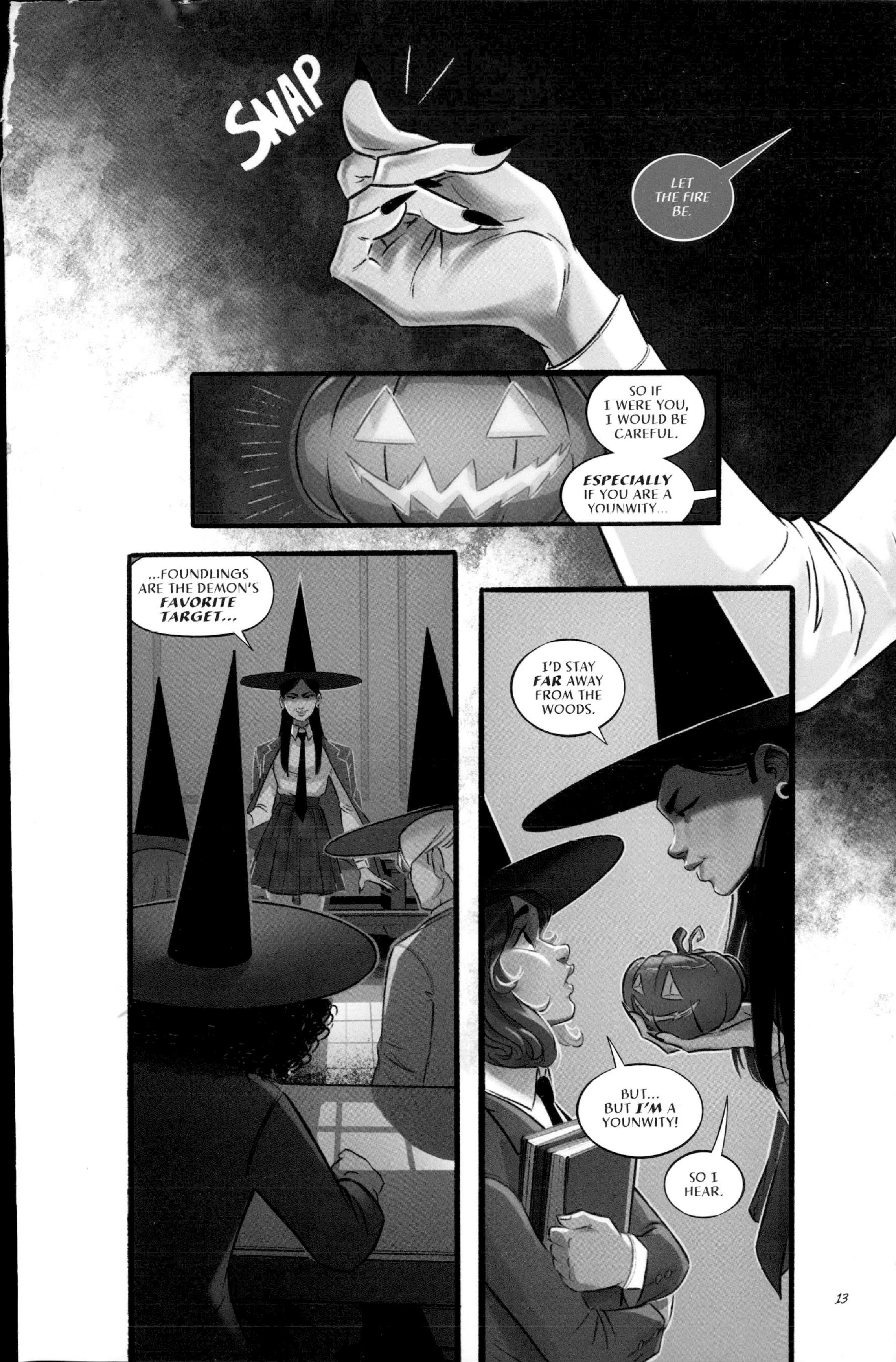
SNAP
LET THE FIRE BE.
SO IF I WERE YOU, I WOULD BE CAREFUL.
ESPECIALLY IF YOU ARE A YOUNWITY...
...FOUNDLINGS ARE THE DEMON'S FAVORITE TARGET...
I'D STAY FAR AWAY FROM THE WOODS.
BUT... BUT I'M A YOUNWITY!
SO I HEAR.

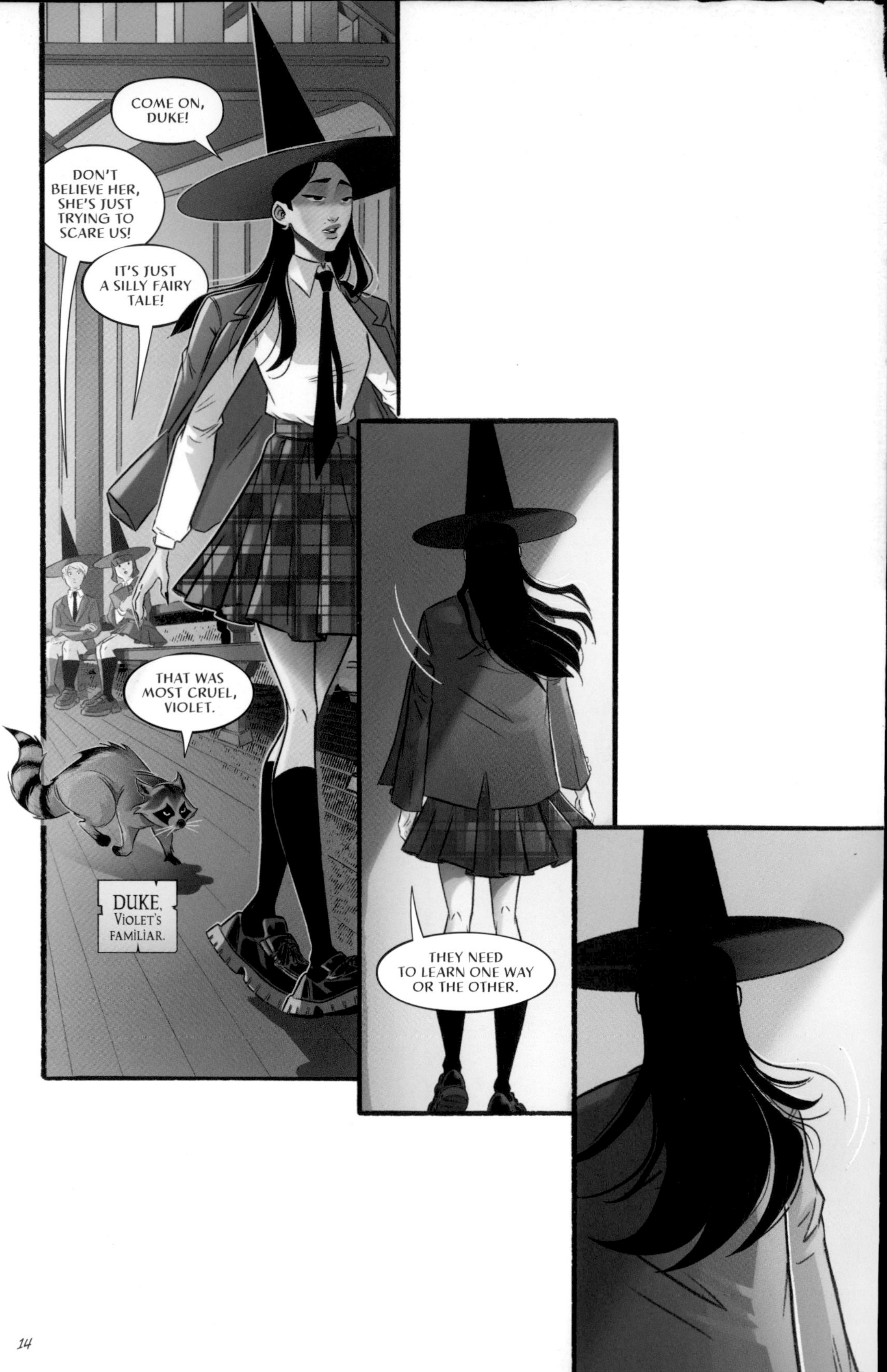

COME ON, DUKE!
DON'T BELIEVE HER, SHE'S JUST TRYING TO SCARE US!
IT'S JUST A SILLY FAIRY TALE!
THAT WAS MOST CRUEL, VIOLET.
DUKE, VIOLET'S FAMILIAR.
THEY NEED TO LEARN ONE WAY OR THE OTHER.

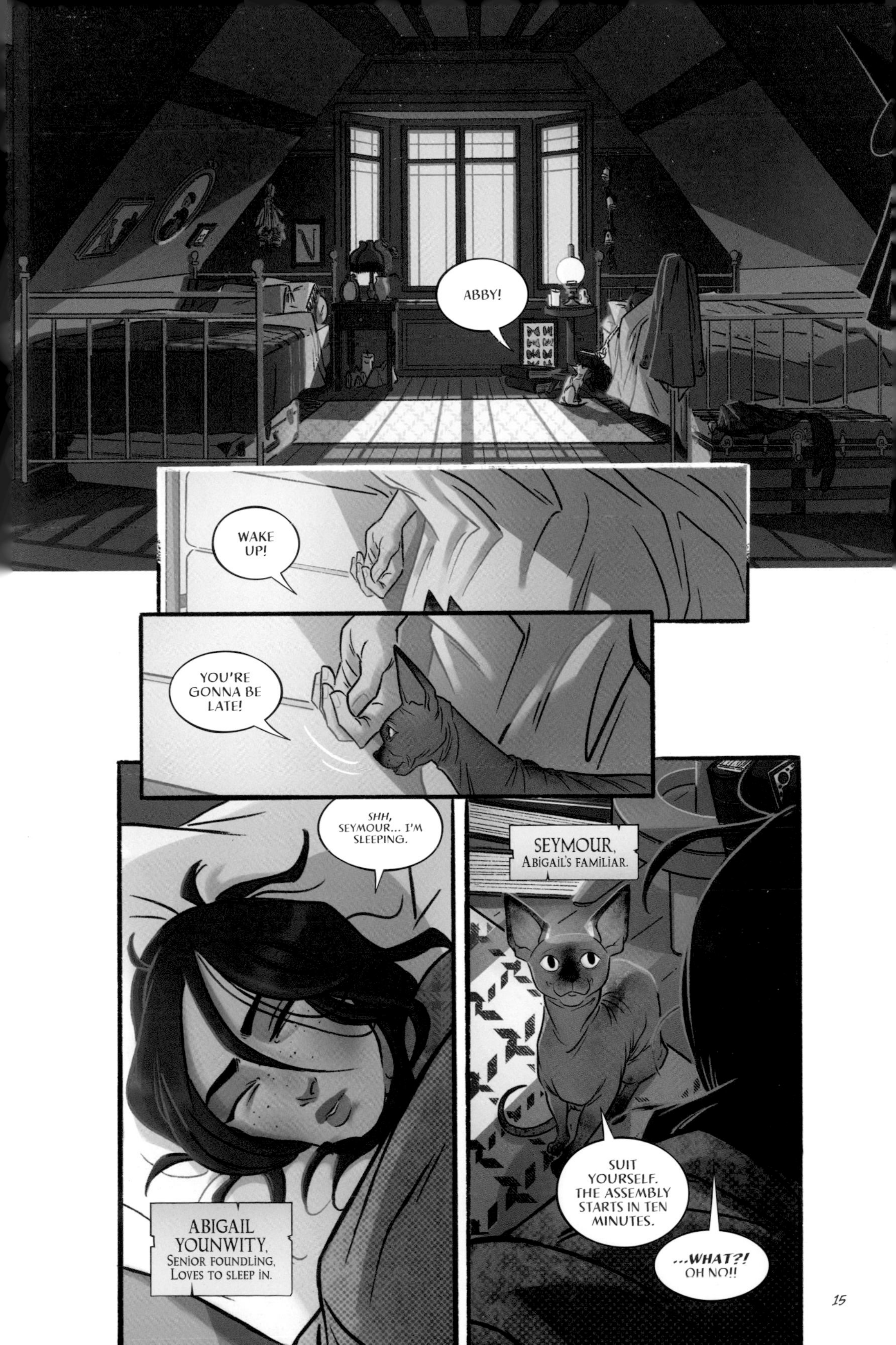
ABBY!
WAKE UP!
YOU'RE GONNA BE LATE!
SHH, SEYMOUR... I'M SLEEPING.
ABIGAIL YOUNWITY, Senior foundling. Loves to sleep in.
SEYMOUR, Abigail's familiar.
SUIT YOURSELF. THE ASSEMBLY STARTS IN TEN MINUTES.
...WHAT?! OH NO!!

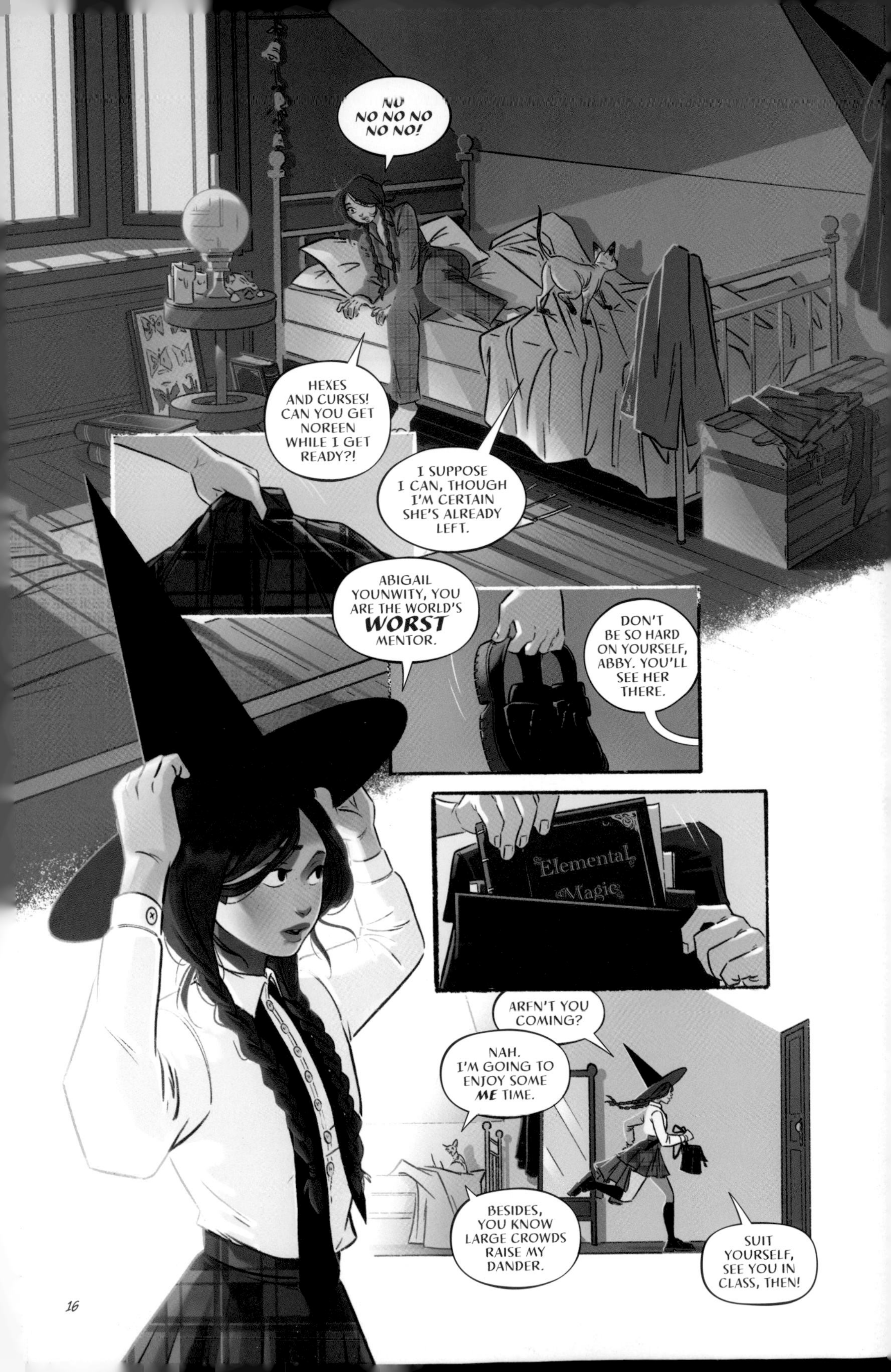
NO
NO NO NO
NO NO!
HEXES AND CURSES! CAN YOU GET NOREEN WHILE I GET READY?!
I SUPPOSE I CAN, THOUGH I'M CERTAIN SHE'S ALREADY LEFT.
ABIGAIL YOUNWITY, YOU ARE THE WORLD'S WORST MENTOR.
DON'T BE SO HARD ON YOURSELF, ABBY. YOU'LL SEE HER THERE.
Elemental Magic
AREN'T YOU COMING?
NAH. I'M GOING TO ENJOY SOME ME TIME.
BESIDES, YOU KNOW LARGE CROWDS RAISE MY DANDER.
SUIT YOURSELF, SEE YOU IN CLASS, THEN!

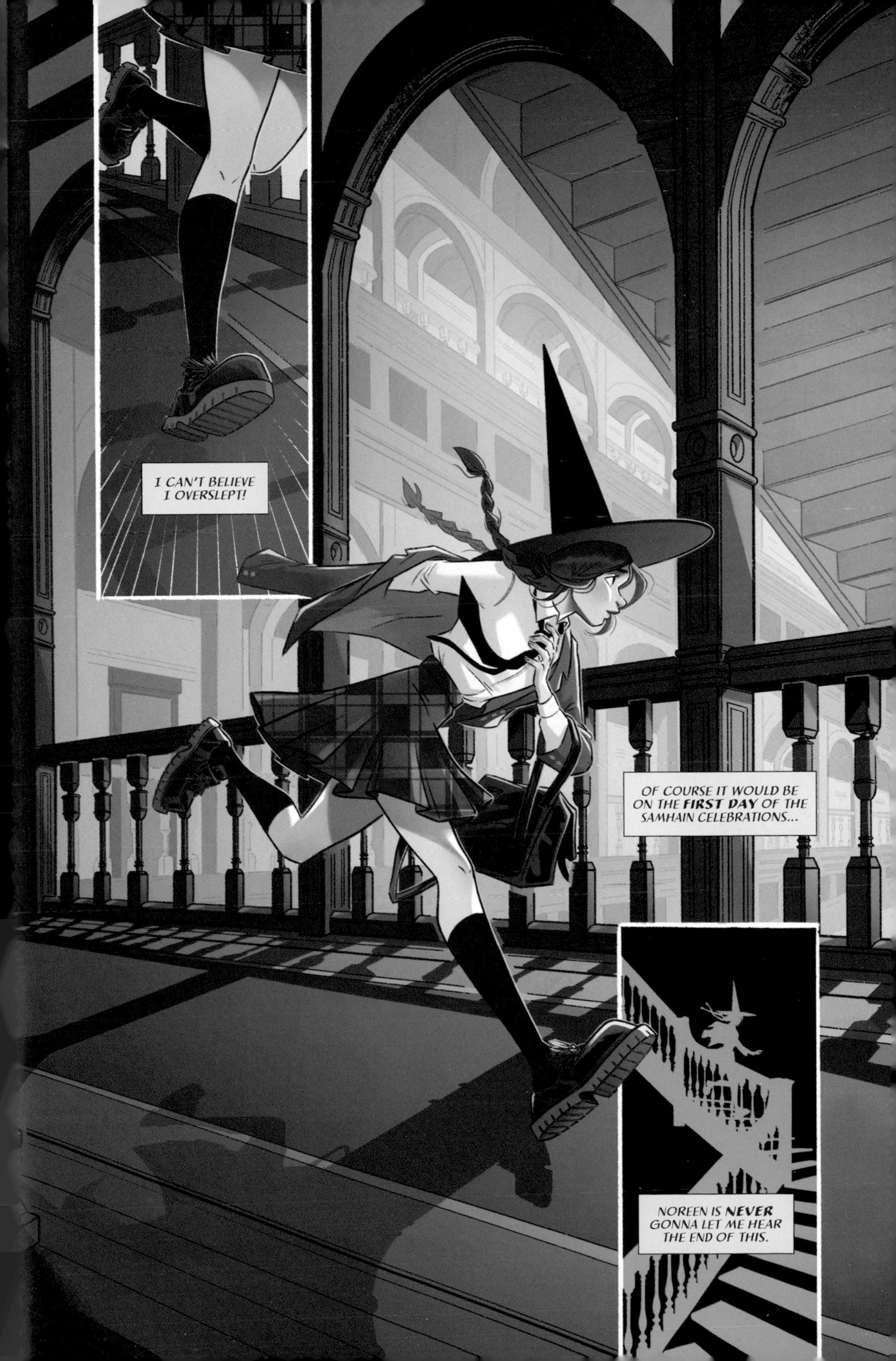
I CAN'T BELIEVE I OVERSLEPT!
OF COURSE IT WOULD BE ON THE **FIRST DAY** OF THE SAMHAIN CELEBRATIONS...
NOREEN IS **NEVER** GONNA LET ME HEAR THE END OF THIS.

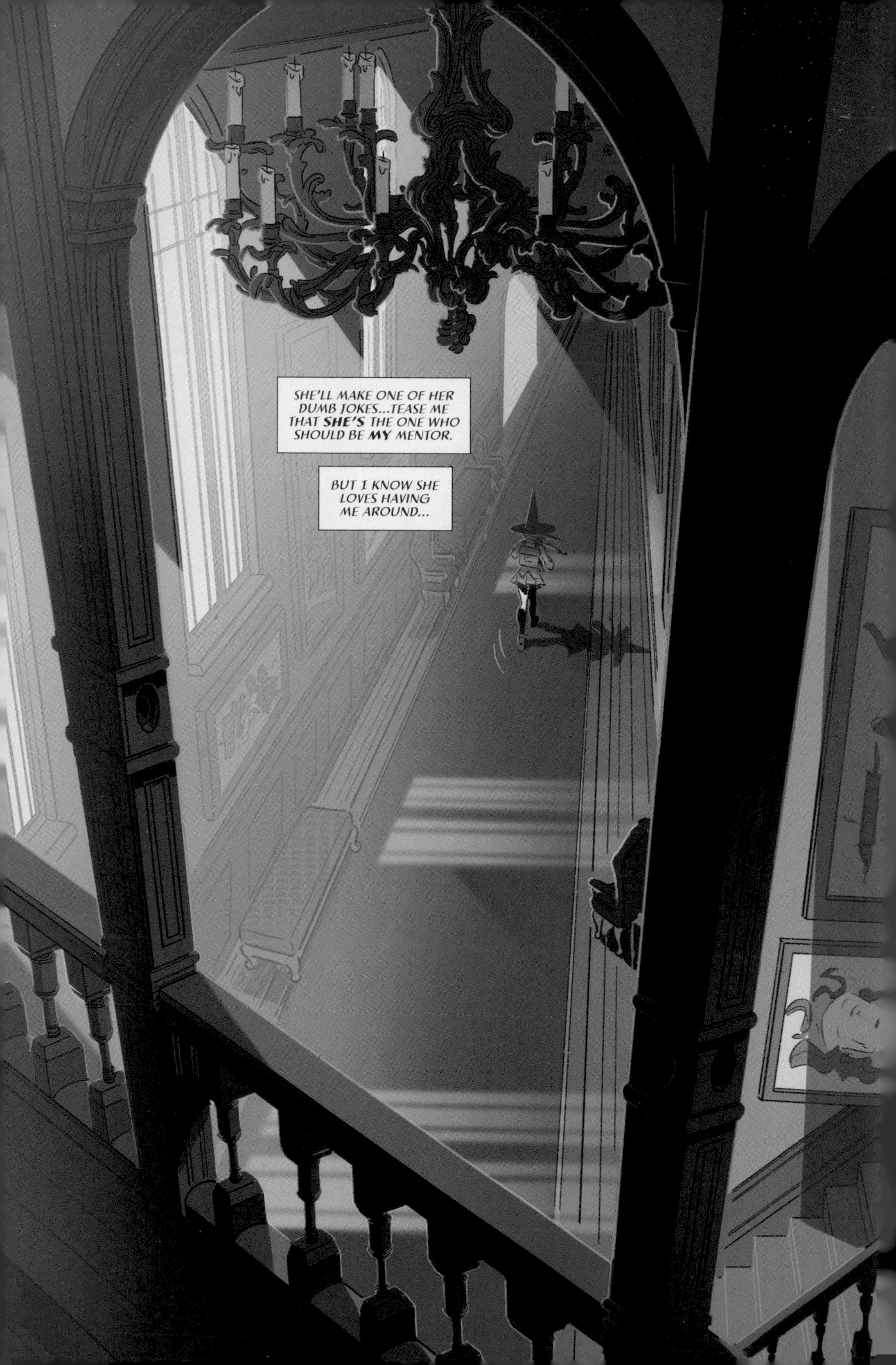
SHE'LL MAKE ONE OF HER DUMB JOKES...TEASE ME THAT **SHE'S** THE ONE WHO SHOULD BE **MY** MENTOR.
BUT I KNOW SHE LOVES HAVING ME AROUND...

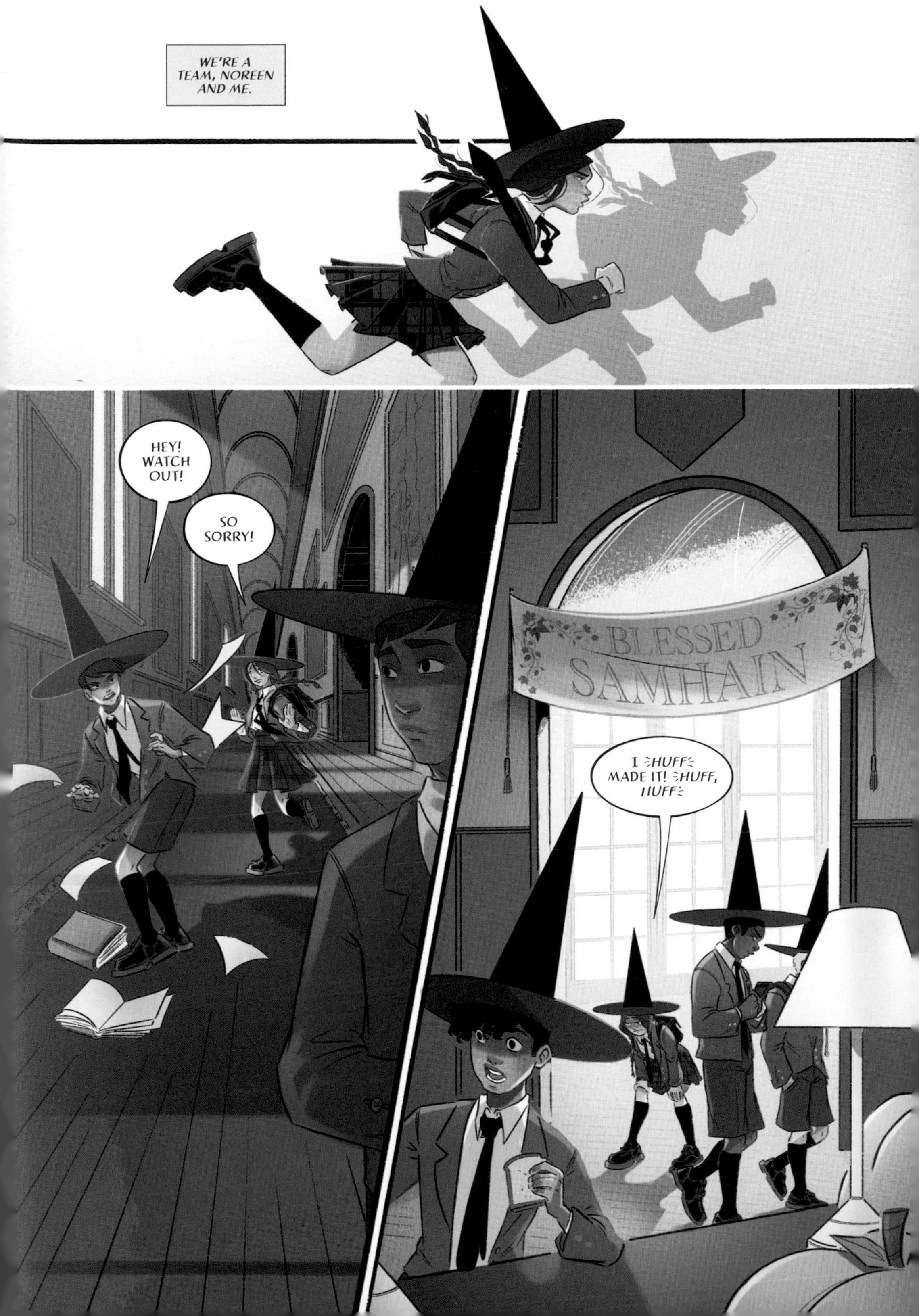
WE'RE A TEAM, NOREEN AND ME.
HEY! WATCH OUT!
SO SORRY!
BLESSED SAMHAIN
I ⋮HUFF⋮ MADE IT! ⋮HUFF, HUFF⋮

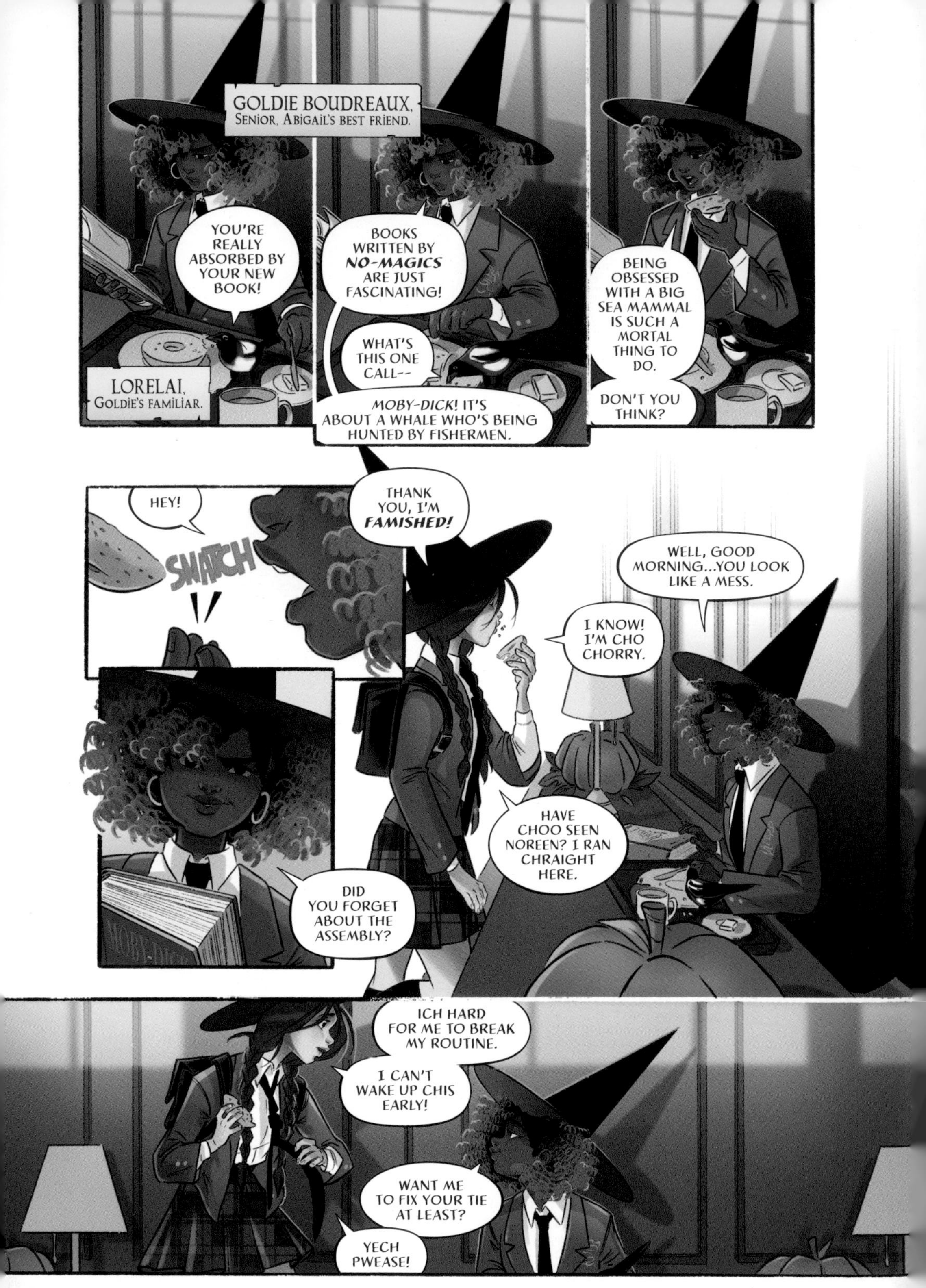

GOLDIE BOUDREAUX, SENIOR, ABIGAIL'S BEST FRIEND.
YOU'RE REALLY ABSORBED BY YOUR NEW BOOK!
LORELAI, GOLDIE'S FAMILIAR.
BOOKS WRITTEN BY *NO-MAGICS* ARE JUST FASCINATING!
WHAT'S THIS ONE CALL--
MOBY-DICK! IT'S ABOUT A WHALE WHO'S BEING HUNTED BY FISHERMEN.
BEING OBSESSED WITH A BIG SEA MAMMAL IS SUCH A MORTAL THING TO DO.
DON'T YOU THINK?
HEY!
SNATCH
THANK YOU, I'M ***FAMISHED!***
WELL, GOOD MORNING...YOU LOOK LIKE A MESS.
I KNOW! I'M CHO CHORRY.
HAVE CHOO SEEN NOREEN? I RAN CHRAIGHT HERE.
DID YOU FORGET ABOUT THE ASSEMBLY?
MOBY-DICK
ICH HARD FOR ME TO BREAK MY ROUTINE.
I CAN'T WAKE UP CHIS EARLY!
WANT ME TO FIX YOUR TIE AT LEAST?
YECH PWEASE!

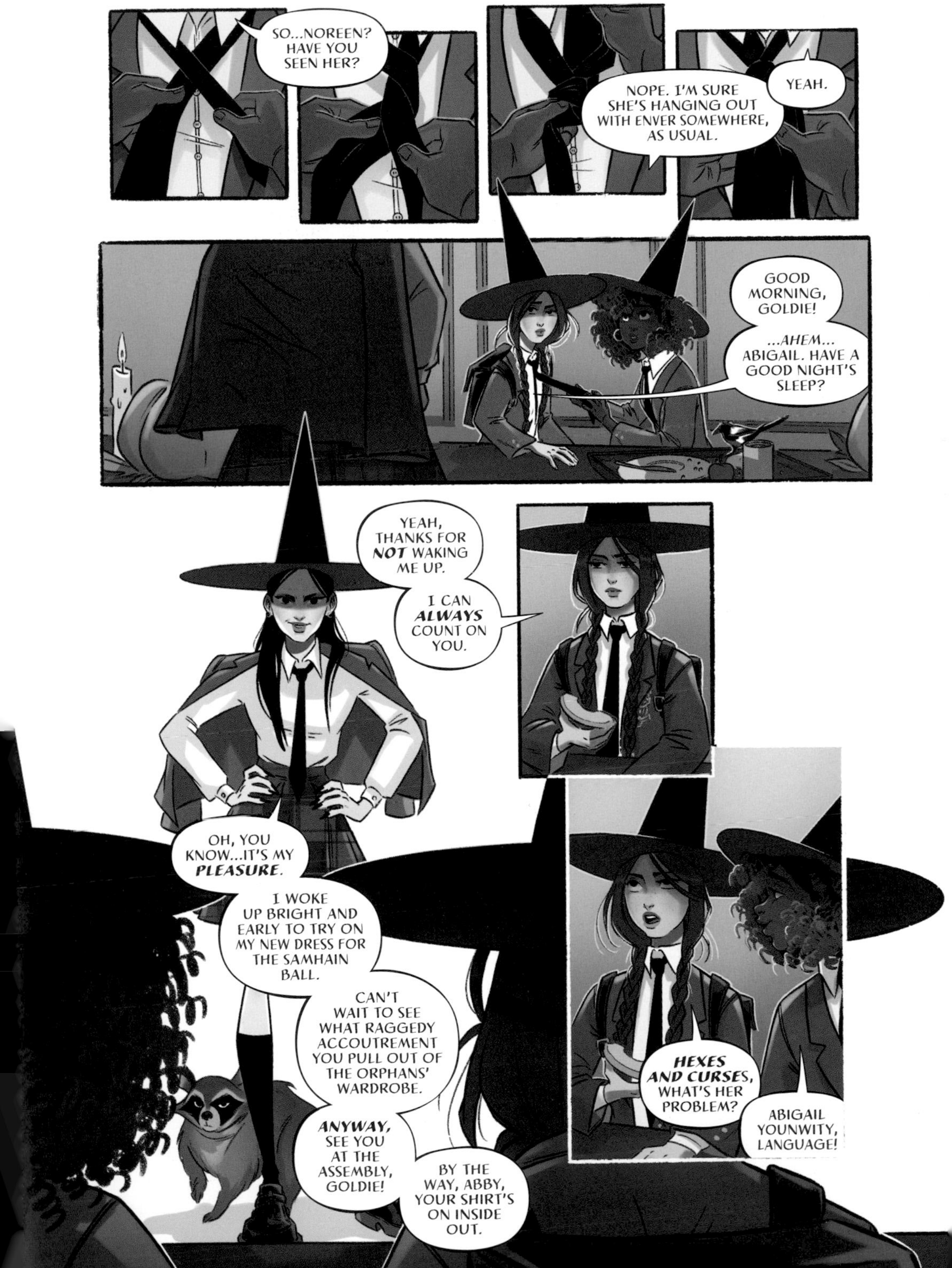
SO...NOREEN? HAVE YOU SEEN HER?
NOPE. I'M SURE SHE'S HANGING OUT WITH ENVER SOMEWHERE, AS USUAL.
YEAH.
GOOD MORNING, GOLDIE!
...AHEM... ABIGAIL. HAVE A GOOD NIGHT'S SLEEP?
YEAH, THANKS FOR NOT WAKING ME UP.
I CAN ALWAYS COUNT ON YOU.
OH, YOU KNOW...IT'S MY PLEASURE.
I WOKE UP BRIGHT AND EARLY TO TRY ON MY NEW DRESS FOR THE SAMHAIN BALL.
CAN'T WAIT TO SEE WHAT RAGGEDY ACCOUTREMENT YOU PULL OUT OF THE ORPHANS' WARDROBE.
ANYWAY, SEE YOU AT THE ASSEMBLY, GOLDIE!
BY THE WAY, ABBY, YOUR SHIRT'S ON INSIDE OUT.
HEXES AND CURSES, WHAT'S HER PROBLEM?
ABIGAIL YOUNWITY, LANGUAGE!

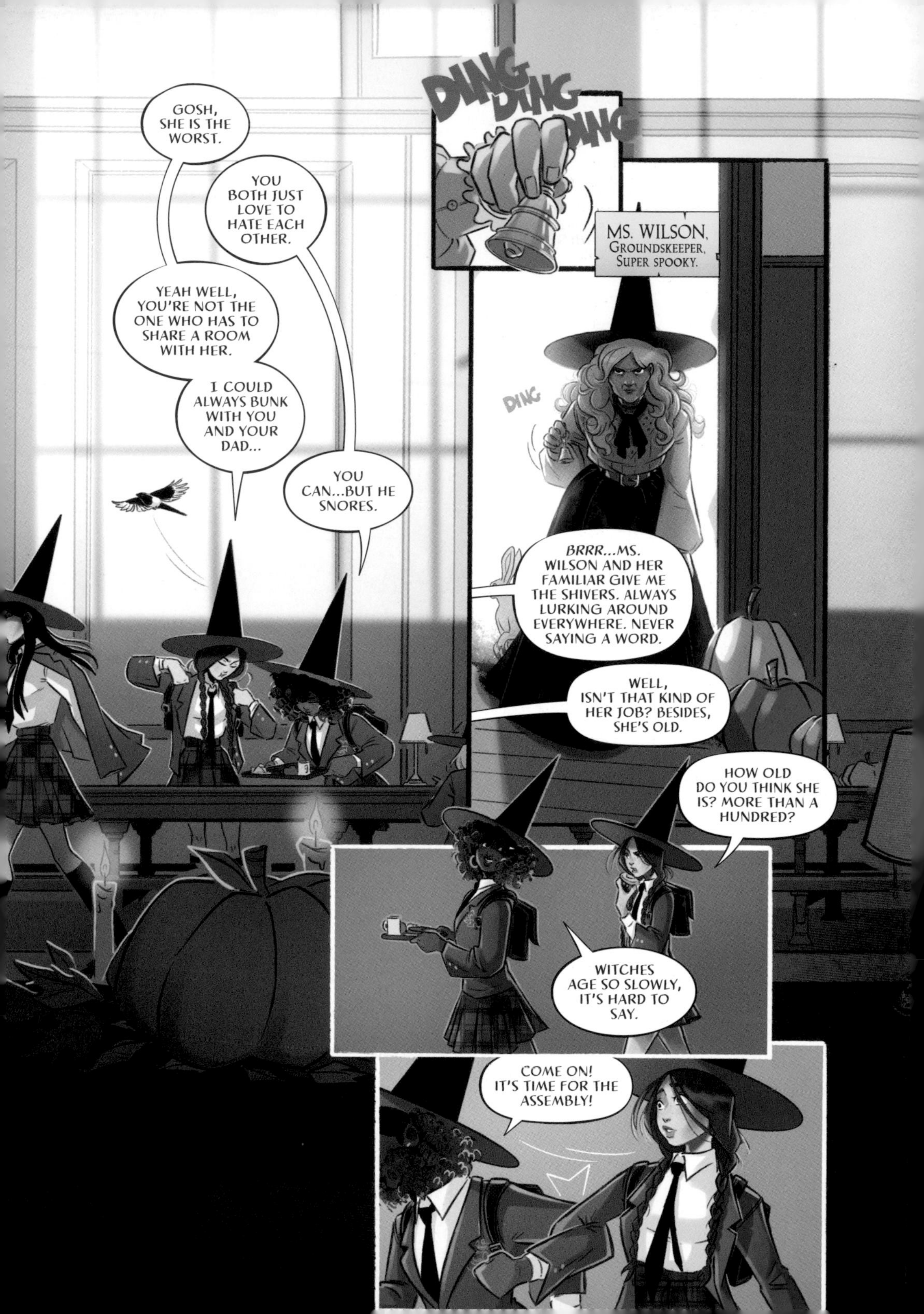
GOSH, SHE IS THE WORST.
YOU BOTH JUST LOVE TO HATE EACH OTHER.
YEAH WELL, YOU'RE NOT THE ONE WHO HAS TO SHARE A ROOM WITH HER.
I COULD ALWAYS BUNK WITH YOU AND YOUR DAD...
YOU CAN...BUT HE SNORES.
DING DING DING
MS. WILSON, GROUNDSKEEPER, SUPER SPOOKY.
DING
BRRR...MS. WILSON AND HER FAMILIAR GIVE ME THE SHIVERS. ALWAYS LURKING AROUND EVERYWHERE. NEVER SAYING A WORD.
WELL, ISN'T THAT KIND OF HER JOB? BESIDES, SHE'S OLD.
HOW OLD DO YOU THINK SHE IS? MORE THAN A HUNDRED?
WITCHES AGE SO SLOWLY, IT'S HARD TO SAY.
COME ON! IT'S TIME FOR THE ASSEMBLY!

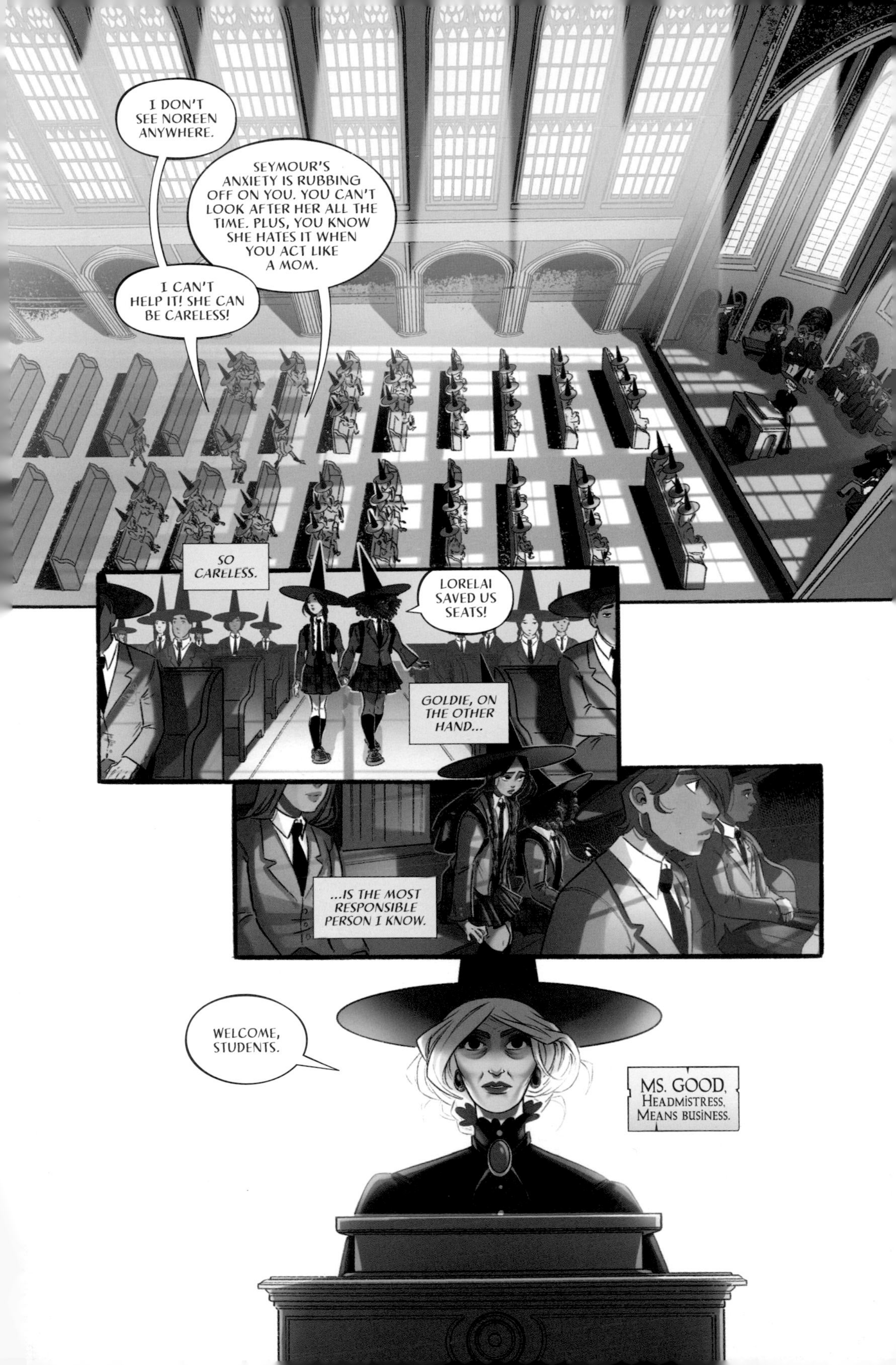
I DON'T SEE NOREEN ANYWHERE.
SEYMOUR'S ANXIETY IS RUBBING OFF ON YOU. YOU CAN'T LOOK AFTER HER ALL THE TIME. PLUS, YOU KNOW SHE HATES IT WHEN YOU ACT LIKE A MOM.
I CAN'T HELP IT! SHE CAN BE CARELESS!
SO CARELESS.
LORELAI SAVED US SEATS!
GOLDIE, ON THE OTHER HAND...
...IS THE MOST RESPONSIBLE PERSON I KNOW.
WELCOME, STUDENTS.
MS. GOOD, HEADMISTRESS, MEANS BUSINESS.

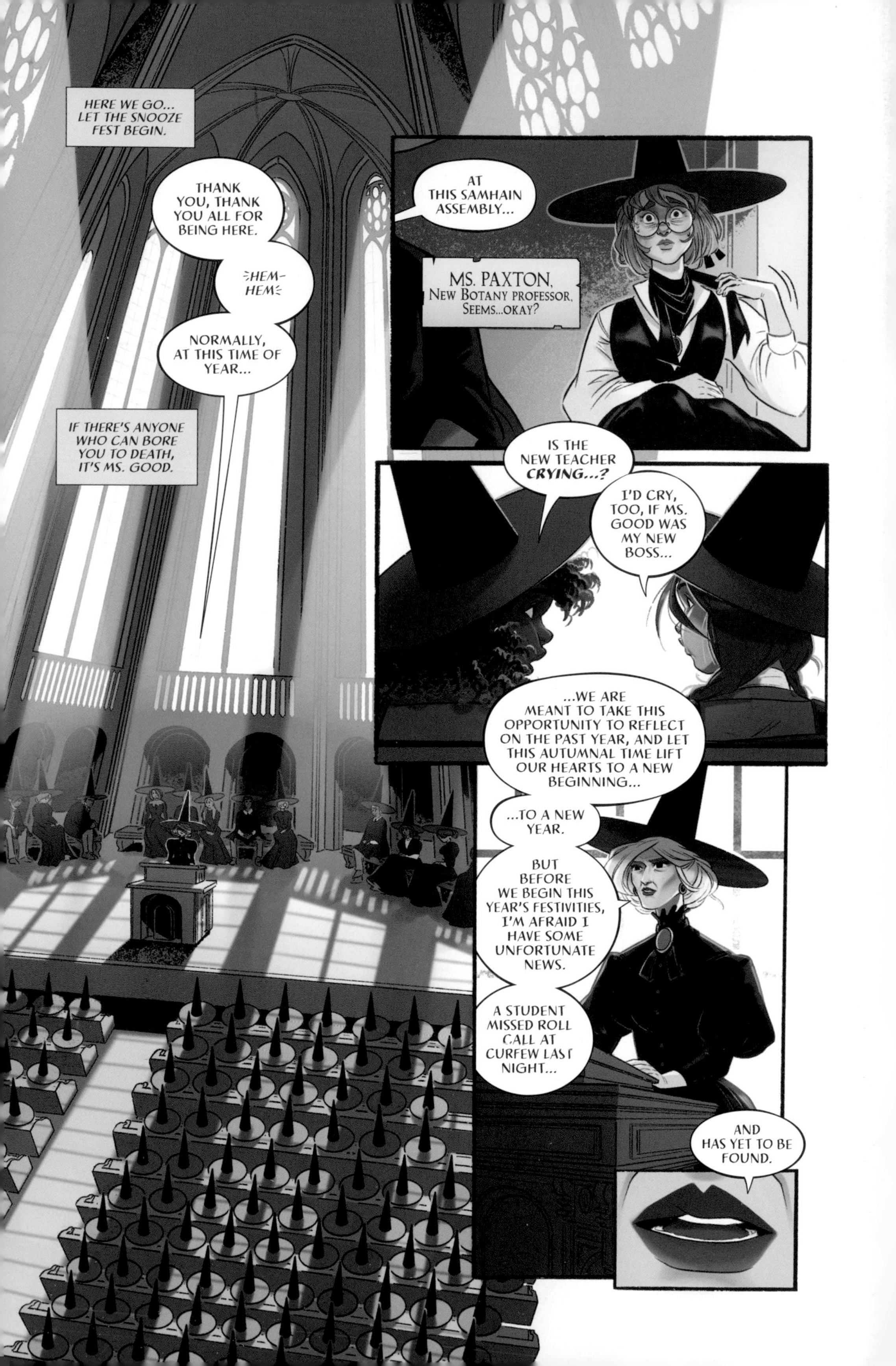
HERE WE GO... LET THE SNOOZE FEST BEGIN.
THANK YOU, THANK YOU ALL FOR BEING HERE.
HEM-HEM
NORMALLY, AT THIS TIME OF YEAR...
IF THERE'S ANYONE WHO CAN BORE YOU TO DEATH, IT'S MS. GOOD.
AT THIS SAMHAIN ASSEMBLY...
MS. PAXTON, NEW BOTANY PROFESSOR, SEEMS...OKAY?
IS THE NEW TEACHER CRYING...?
I'D CRY, TOO, IF MS. GOOD WAS MY NEW BOSS...
...WE ARE MEANT TO TAKE THIS OPPORTUNITY TO REFLECT ON THE PAST YEAR, AND LET THIS AUTUMNAL TIME LIFT OUR HEARTS TO A NEW BEGINNING...
...TO A NEW YEAR.
BUT BEFORE WE BEGIN THIS YEAR'S FESTIVITIES, I'M AFRAID I HAVE SOME UNFORTUNATE NEWS.
A STUDENT MISSED ROLL CALL AT CURFEW LAST NIGHT...
AND HAS YET TO BE FOUND.

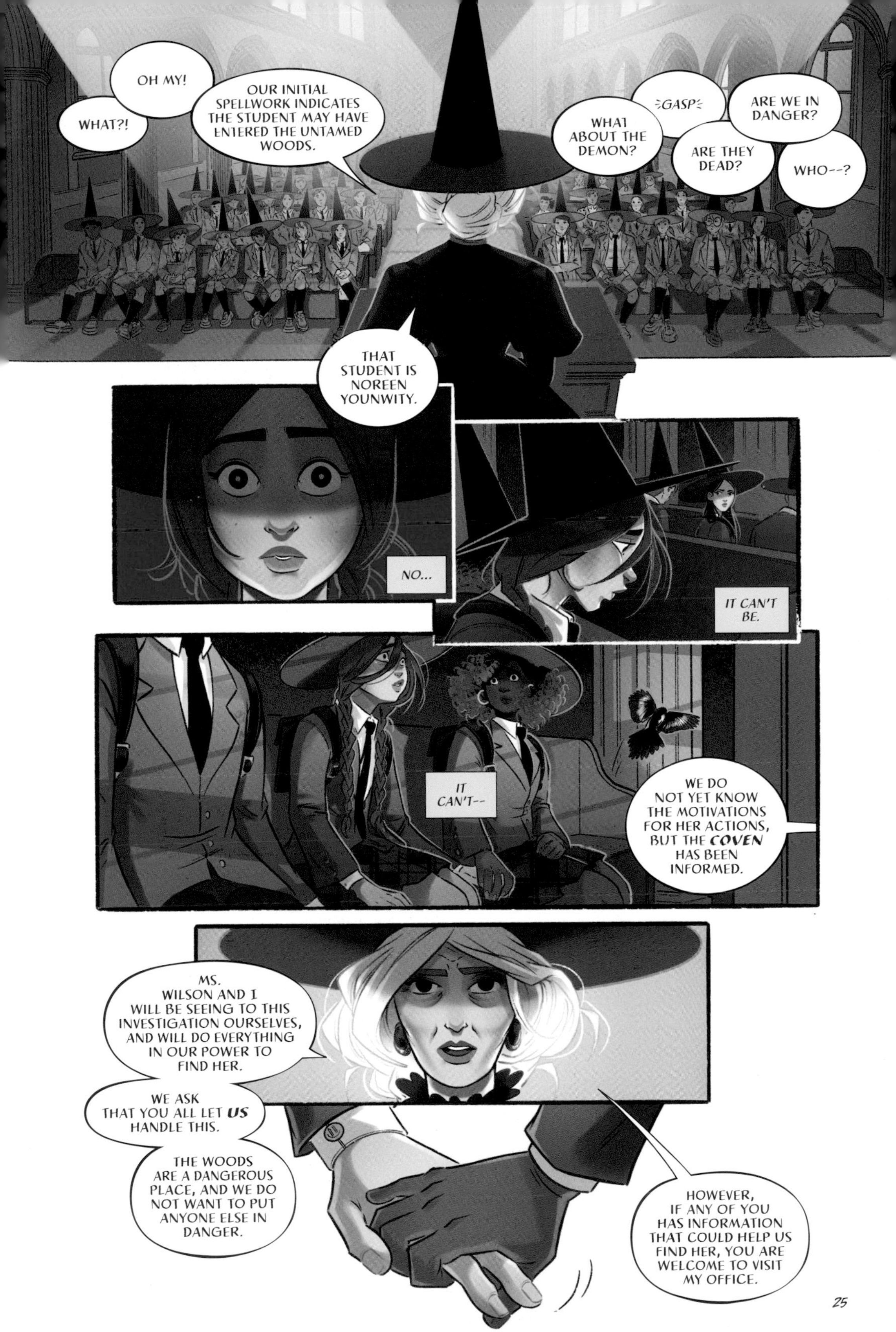
WHAT?!
OH MY!
OUR INITIAL SPELLWORK INDICATES THE STUDENT MAY HAVE ENTERED THE UNTAMED WOODS.
WHAT ABOUT THE DEMON?
GASP
ARE THEY DEAD?
ARE WE IN DANGER?
WHO--?
THAT STUDENT IS NOREEN YOUNWITY.
NO...
IT CAN'T BE.
IT CAN'T--
WE DO NOT YET KNOW THE MOTIVATIONS FOR HER ACTIONS, BUT THE COVEN HAS BEEN INFORMED.
MS. WILSON AND I WILL BE SEEING TO THIS INVESTIGATION OURSELVES, AND WILL DO EVERYTHING IN OUR POWER TO FIND HER.
WE ASK THAT YOU ALL LET US HANDLE THIS.
THE WOODS ARE A DANGEROUS PLACE, AND WE DO NOT WANT TO PUT ANYONE ELSE IN DANGER.
HOWEVER, IF ANY OF YOU HAS INFORMATION THAT COULD HELP US FIND HER, YOU ARE WELCOME TO VISIT MY OFFICE.

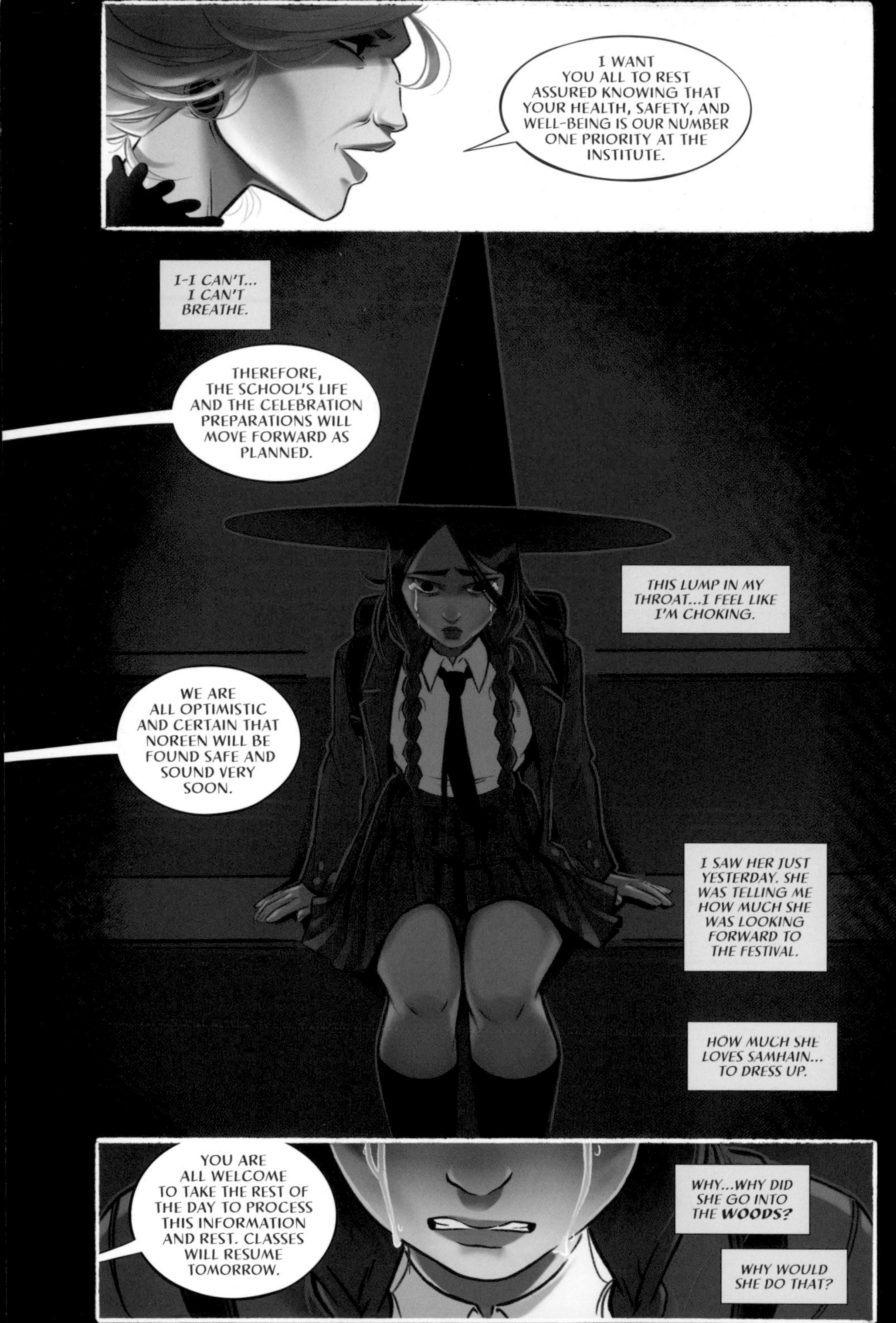
I WANT YOU ALL TO REST ASSURED KNOWING THAT YOUR HEALTH, SAFETY, AND WELL-BEING IS OUR NUMBER ONE PRIORITY AT THE INSTITUTE.
I-I CAN'T... I CAN'T BREATHE.
THEREFORE, THE SCHOOL'S LIFE AND THE CELEBRATION PREPARATIONS WILL MOVE FORWARD AS PLANNED.
THIS LUMP IN MY THROAT...I FEEL LIKE I'M CHOKING.
WE ARE ALL OPTIMISTIC AND CERTAIN THAT NOREEN WILL BE FOUND SAFE AND SOUND VERY SOON.
I SAW HER JUST YESTERDAY. SHE WAS TELLING ME HOW MUCH SHE WAS LOOKING FORWARD TO THE FESTIVAL.
HOW MUCH SHE LOVES SAMHAIN... TO DRESS UP.
YOU ARE ALL WELCOME TO TAKE THE REST OF THE DAY TO PROCESS THIS INFORMATION AND REST. CLASSES WILL RESUME TOMORROW.
WHY...WHY DID SHE GO INTO THE **WOODS?**
WHY WOULD SHE DO THAT?

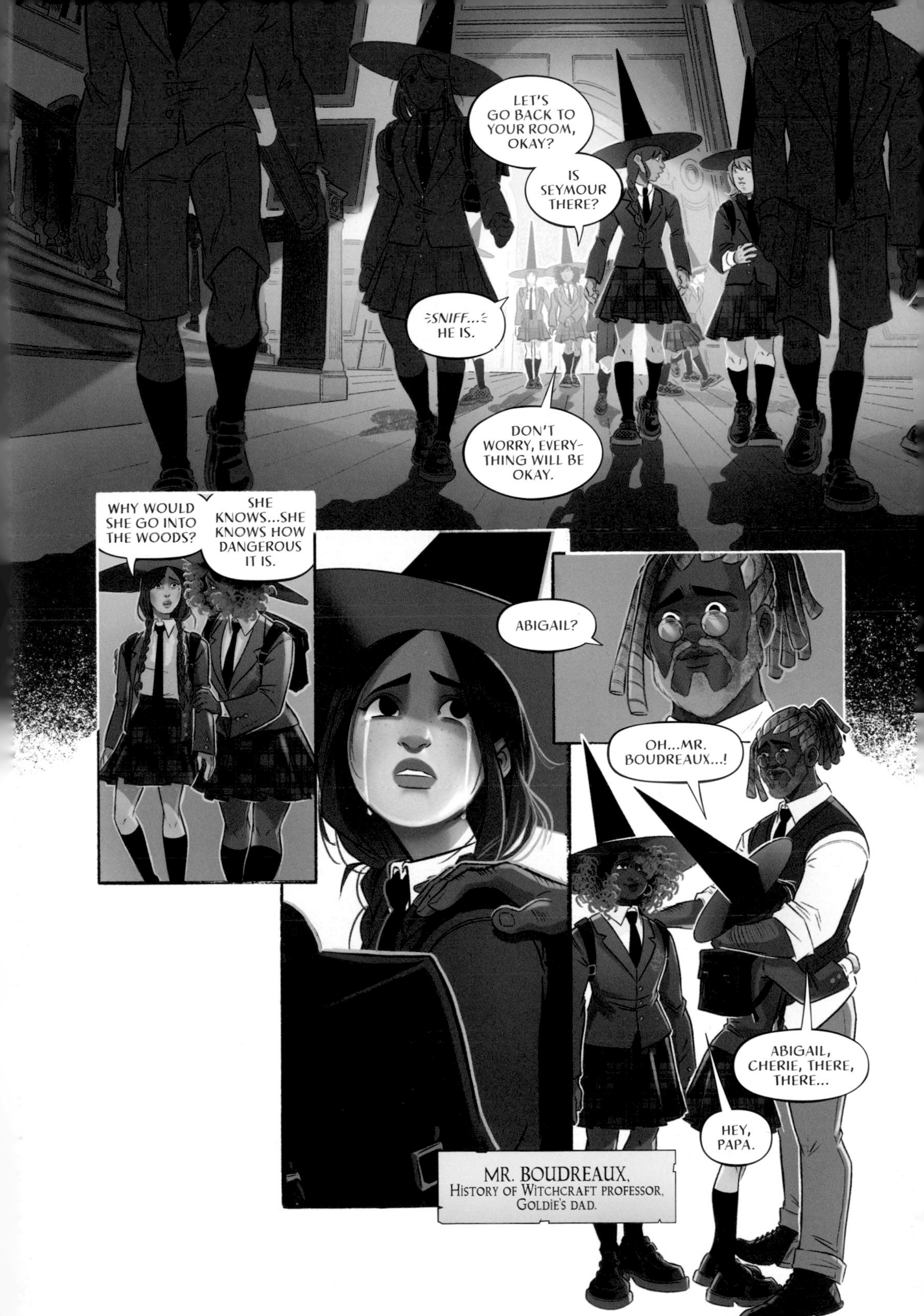
LET'S GO BACK TO YOUR ROOM, OKAY?
IS SEYMOUR THERE?
SNIFF... HE IS.
DON'T WORRY, EVERYTHING WILL BE OKAY.
WHY WOULD SHE GO INTO THE WOODS?
SHE KNOWS...SHE KNOWS HOW DANGEROUS IT IS.
ABIGAIL?
OH...MR. BOUDREAUX...!
ABIGAIL, CHERIE, THERE, THERE...
HEY, PAPA.
MR. BOUDREAUX,
HISTORY OF WITCHCRAFT PROFESSOR,
GOLDIE'S DAD.

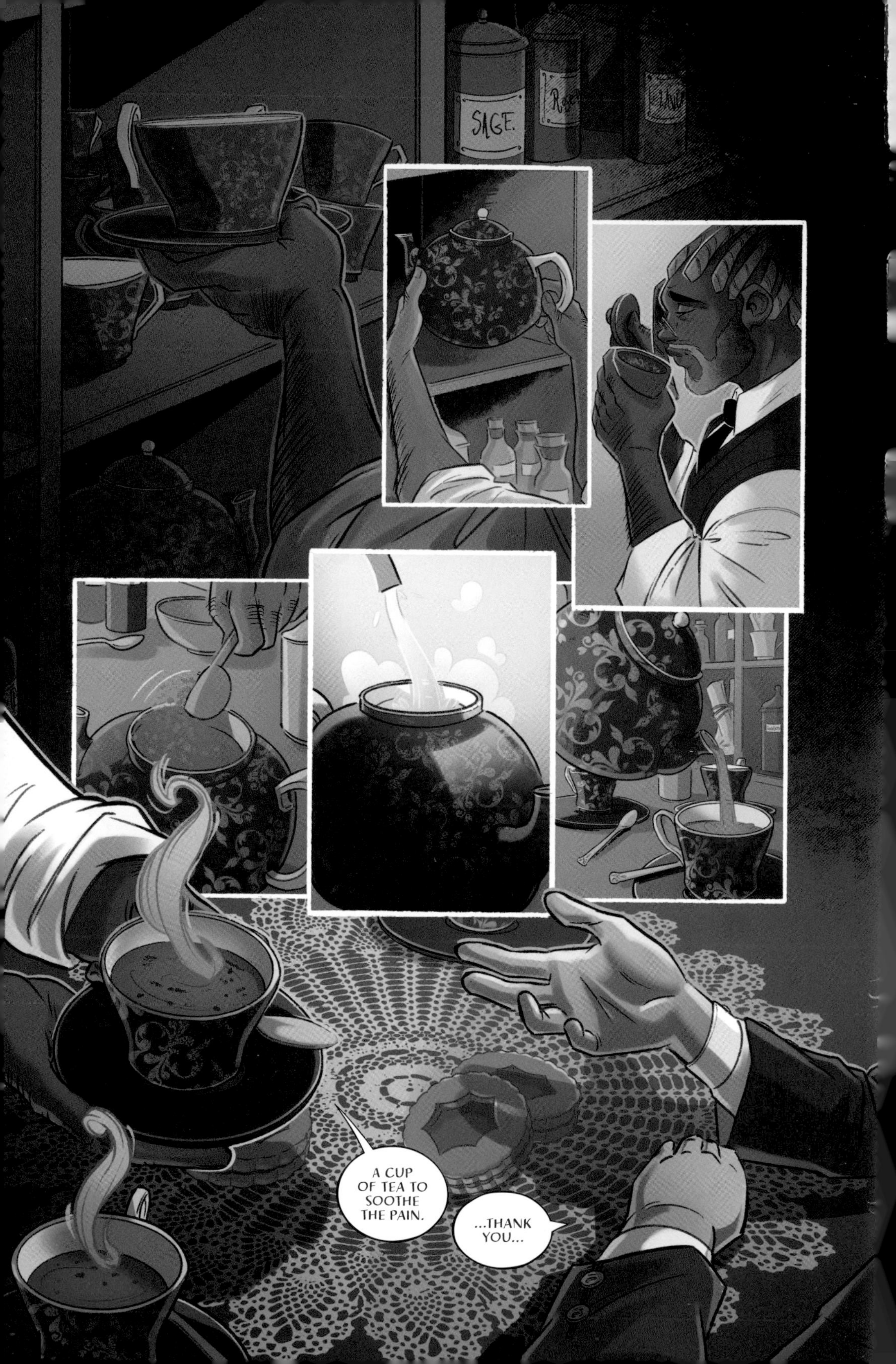
SAGE.
A CUP OF TEA TO SOOTHE THE PAIN.
...THANK YOU...

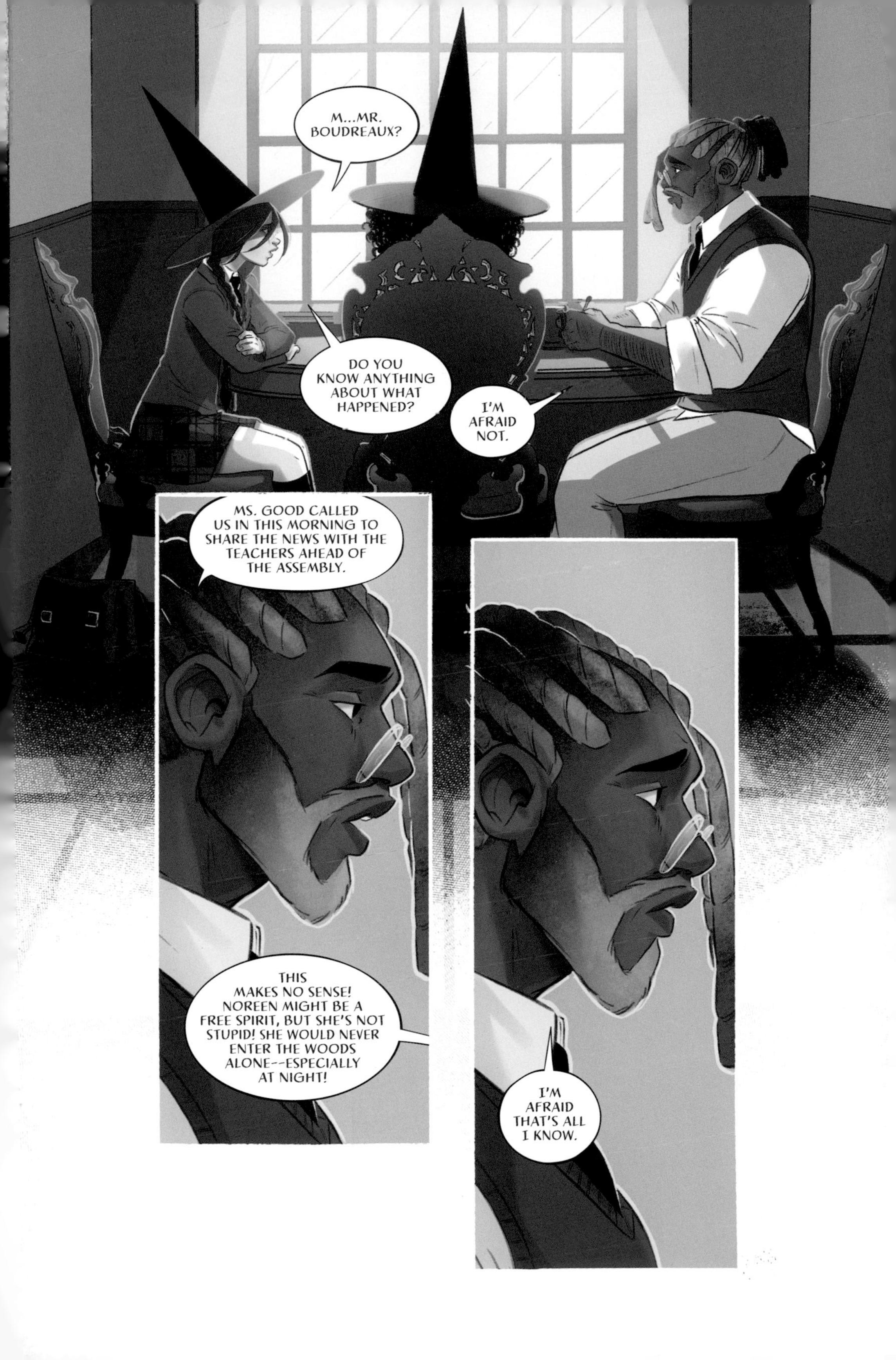
M...MR. BOUDREAUX?
DO YOU KNOW ANYTHING ABOUT WHAT HAPPENED?
I'M AFRAID NOT.
MS. GOOD CALLED US IN THIS MORNING TO SHARE THE NEWS WITH THE TEACHERS AHEAD OF THE ASSEMBLY.
THIS MAKES NO SENSE! NOREEN MIGHT BE A FREE SPIRIT, BUT SHE'S NOT STUPID! SHE WOULD NEVER ENTER THE WOODS ALONE--ESPECIALLY AT NIGHT!
I'M AFRAID THAT'S ALL I KNOW.

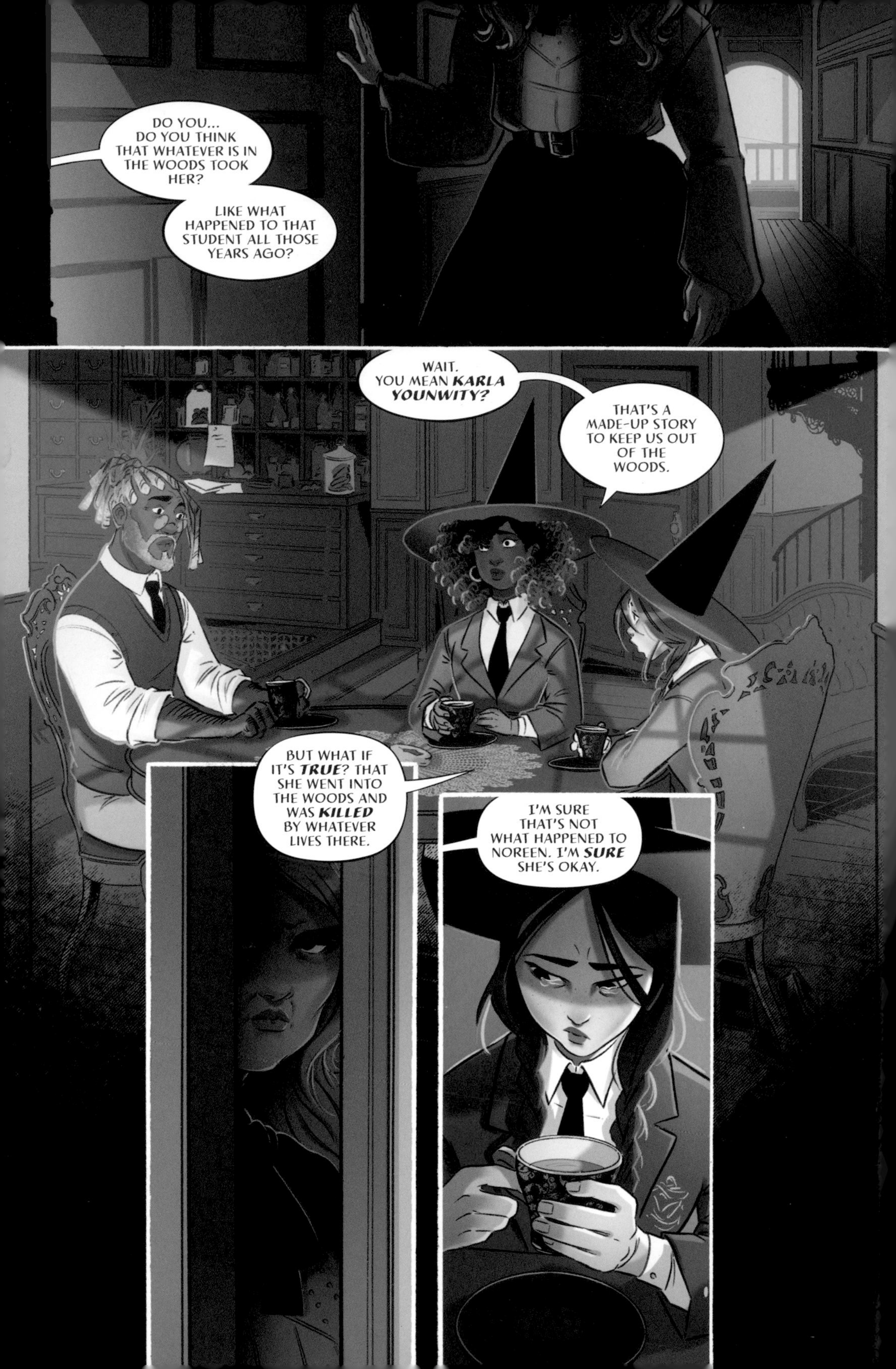
DO YOU... DO YOU THINK THAT WHATEVER IS IN THE WOODS TOOK HER?
LIKE WHAT HAPPENED TO THAT STUDENT ALL THOSE YEARS AGO?
WAIT. YOU MEAN *KARLA YOUNWITY?*
THAT'S A MADE-UP STORY TO KEEP US OUT OF THE WOODS.
BUT WHAT IF IT'S *TRUE*? THAT SHE WENT INTO THE WOODS AND WAS *KILLED* BY WHATEVER LIVES THERE.
I'M SURE THAT'S NOT WHAT HAPPENED TO NOREEN. I'M *SURE* SHE'S OKAY.

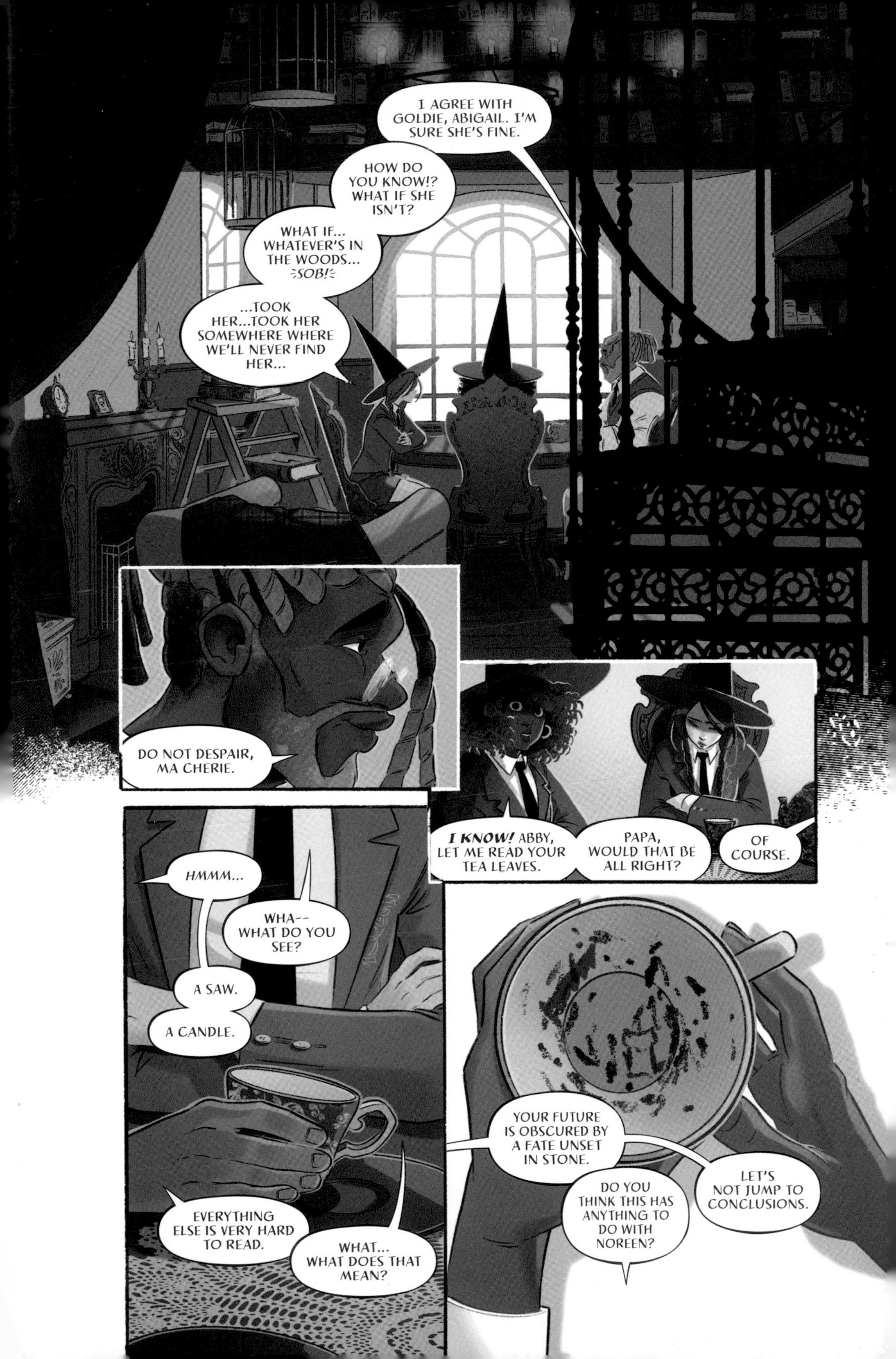
I AGREE WITH GOLDIE, ABIGAIL. I'M SURE SHE'S FINE.
HOW DO YOU KNOW!? WHAT IF SHE ISN'T?
WHAT IF... WHATEVER'S IN THE WOODS... SOB!
...TOOK HER...TOOK HER SOMEWHERE WHERE WE'LL NEVER FIND HER...
DO NOT DESPAIR, MA CHERIE.
I KNOW! ABBY, LET ME READ YOUR TEA LEAVES.
PAPA, WOULD THAT BE ALL RIGHT?
OF COURSE.
HMMM...
WHA-- WHAT DO YOU SEE?
A SAW.
A CANDLE.
EVERYTHING ELSE IS VERY HARD TO READ.
WHAT... WHAT DOES THAT MEAN?
YOUR FUTURE IS OBSCURED BY A FATE UNSET IN STONE.
DO YOU THINK THIS HAS ANYTHING TO DO WITH NOREEN?
LET'S NOT JUMP TO CONCLUSIONS.

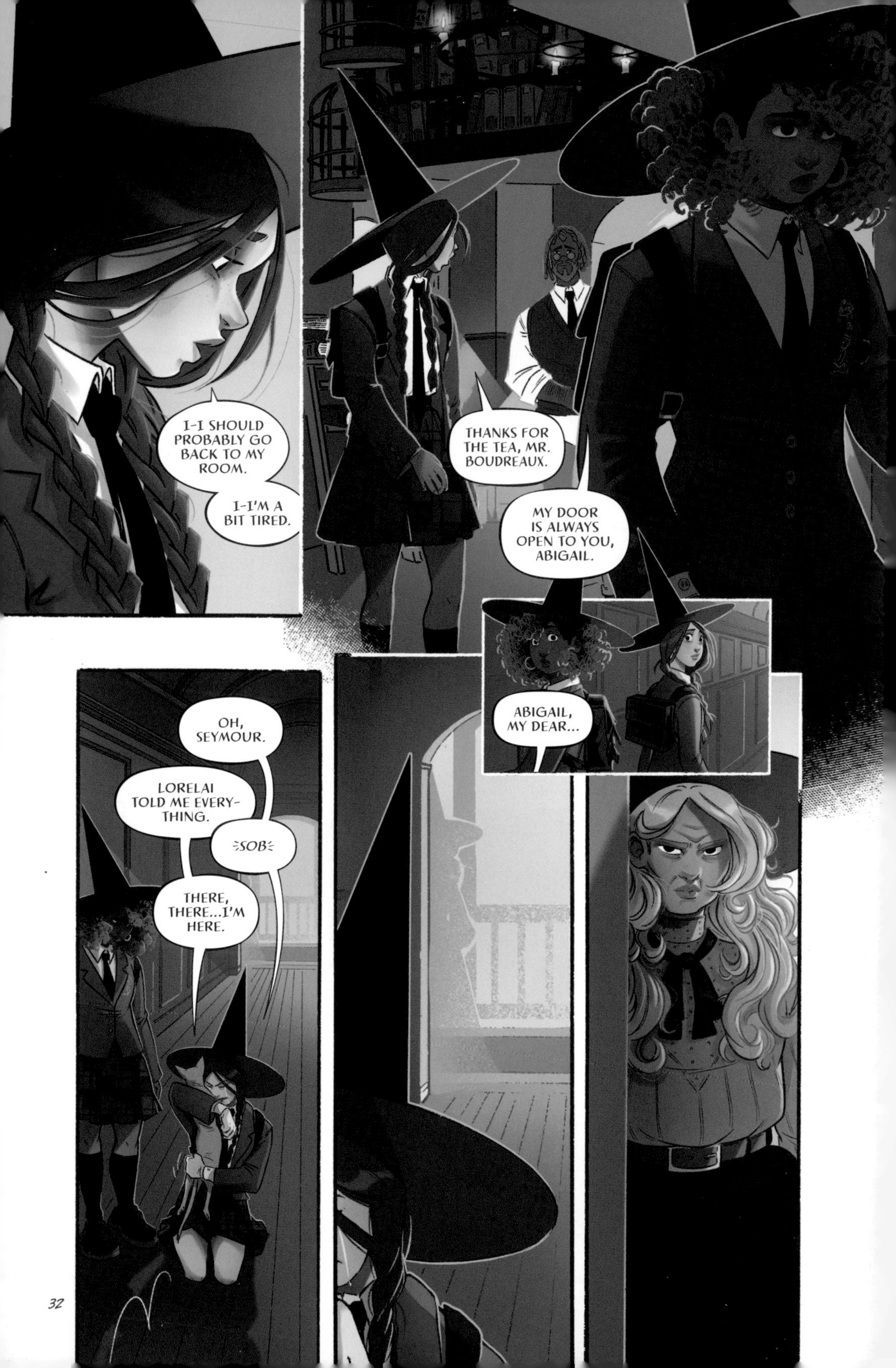
I-I SHOULD PROBABLY GO BACK TO MY ROOM.
I-I'M A BIT TIRED.
THANKS FOR THE TEA, MR. BOUDREAUX.
MY DOOR IS ALWAYS OPEN TO YOU, ABIGAIL.
ABIGAIL, MY DEAR...
OH, SEYMOUR.
LORELAI TOLD ME EVERY-THING.
SOB
THERE, THERE...I'M HERE.

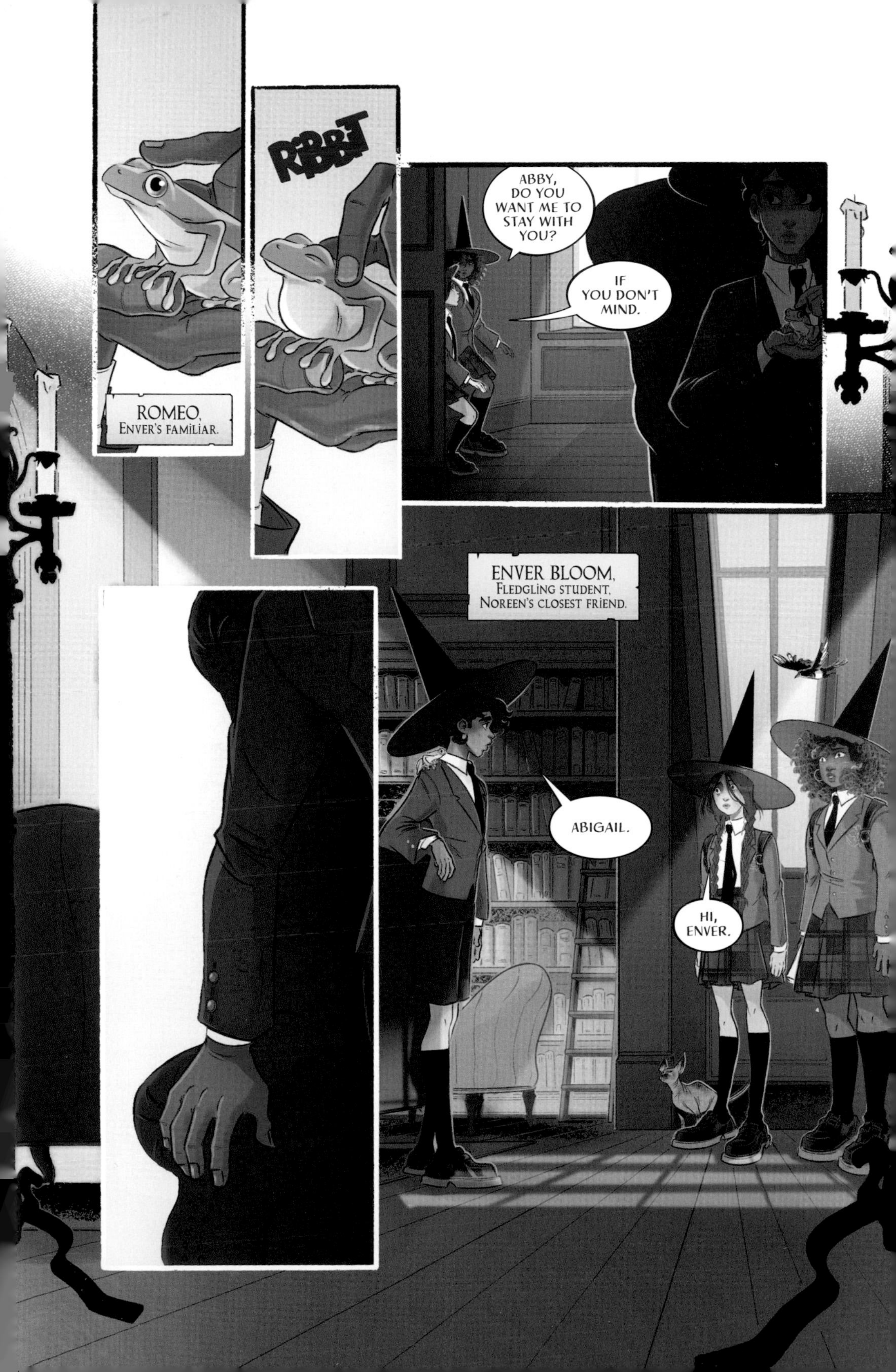
ROMEO,
Enver's familiar.
RIBBIT
ABBY, DO YOU WANT ME TO STAY WITH YOU?
IF YOU DON'T MIND.
ENVER BLOOM,
Fledgling student,
Noreen's closest friend.
ABIGAIL.
HI, ENVER.

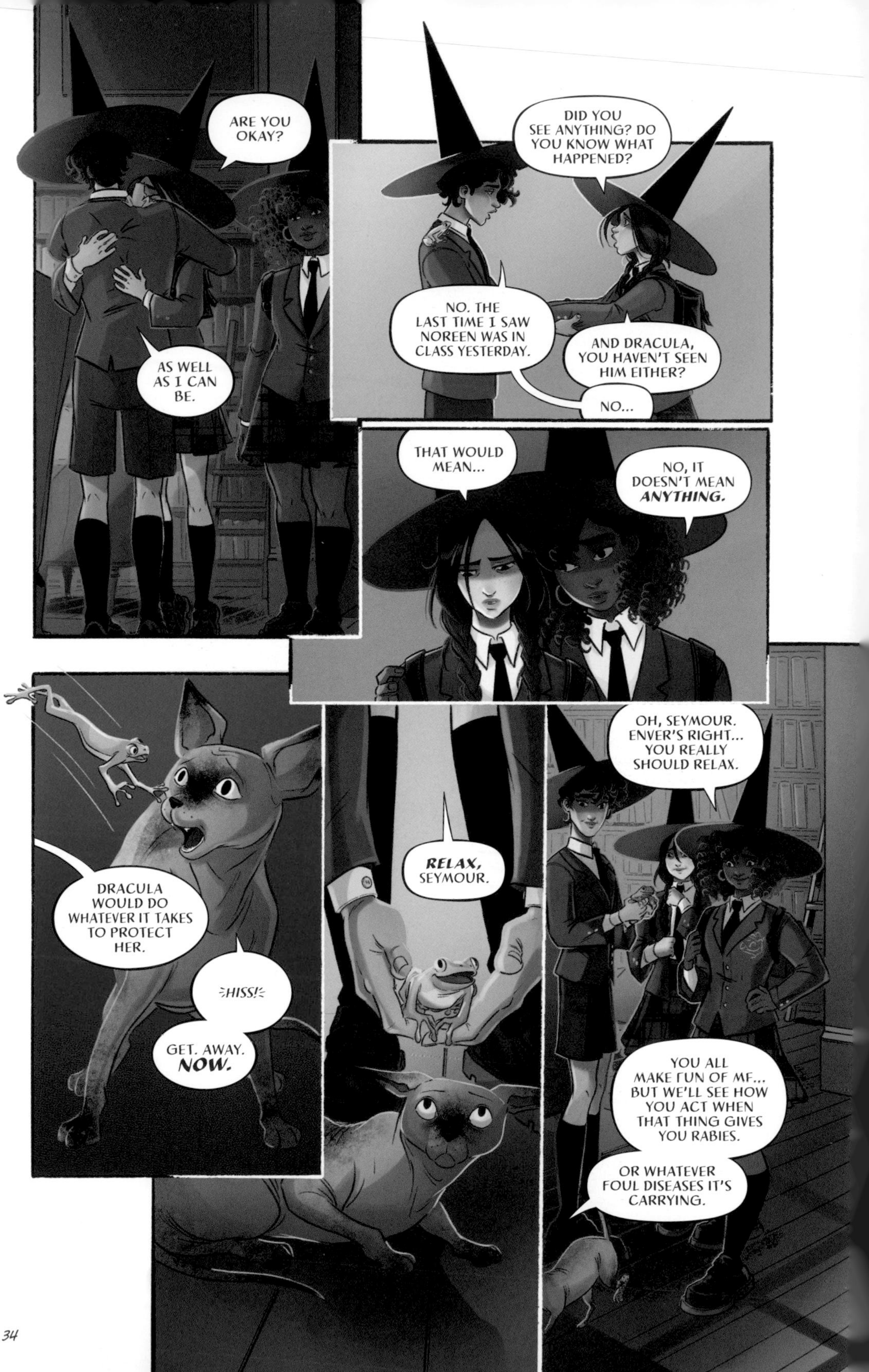
ARE YOU OKAY?
AS WELL AS I CAN BE.
DID YOU SEE ANYTHING? DO YOU KNOW WHAT HAPPENED?
NO. THE LAST TIME I SAW NOREEN WAS IN CLASS YESTERDAY.
AND DRACULA, YOU HAVEN'T SEEN HIM EITHER?
NO...
THAT WOULD MEAN...
NO, IT DOESN'T MEAN ANYTHING.
DRACULA WOULD DO WHATEVER IT TAKES TO PROTECT HER.
HISS!
GET. AWAY. NOW.
RELAX, SEYMOUR.
OH, SEYMOUR. ENVER'S RIGHT... YOU REALLY SHOULD RELAX.
YOU ALL MAKE FUN OF ME... BUT WE'LL SEE HOW YOU ACT WHEN THAT THING GIVES YOU RABIES.
OR WHATEVER FOUL DISEASES IT'S CARRYING.

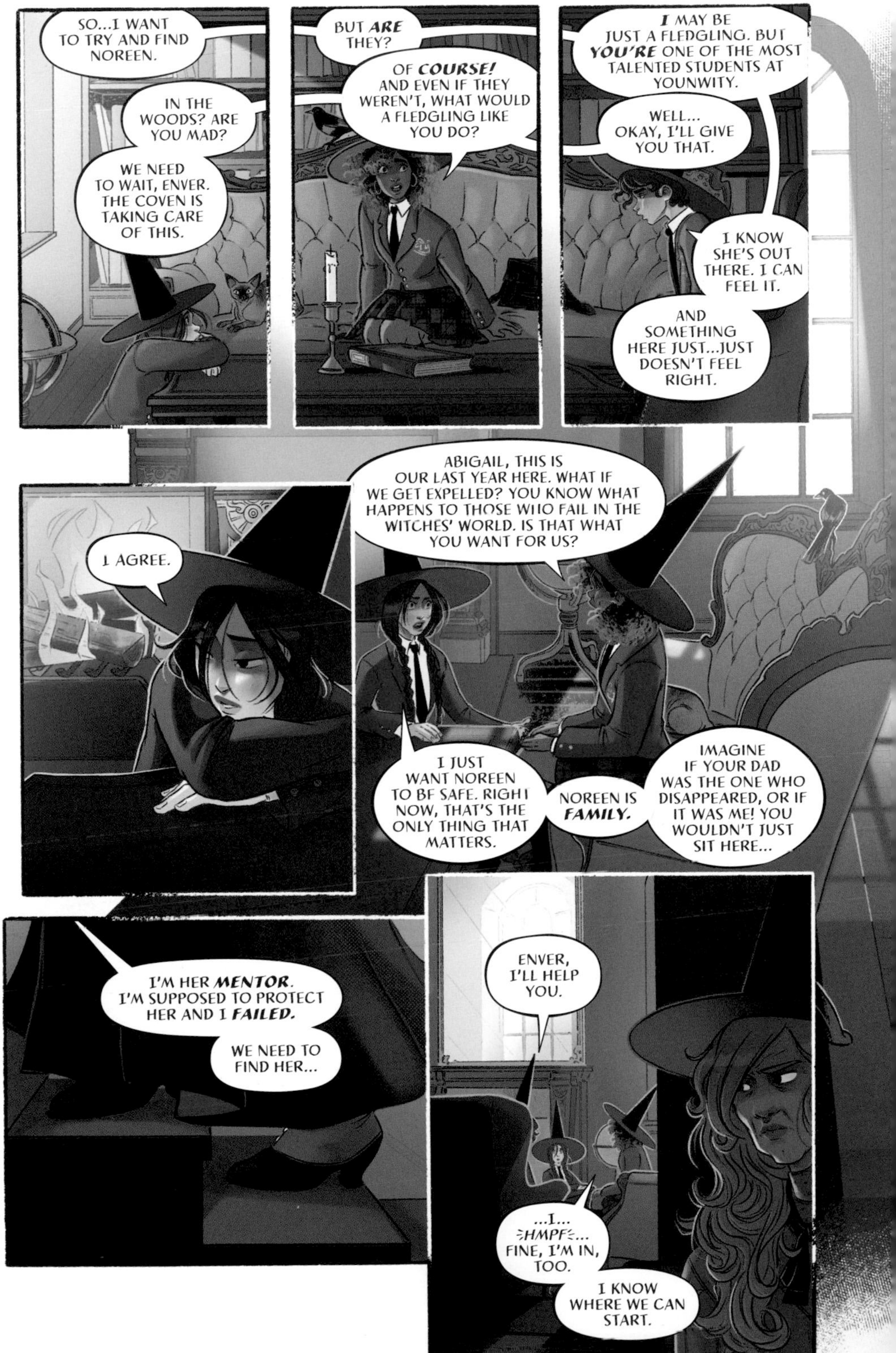
SO...I WANT TO TRY AND FIND NOREEN.
IN THE WOODS? ARE YOU MAD?
WE NEED TO WAIT, ENVER. THE COVEN IS TAKING CARE OF THIS.
BUT *ARE* THEY?
OF *COURSE!* AND EVEN IF THEY WEREN'T, WHAT WOULD A FLEDGLING LIKE YOU DO?
I MAY BE JUST A FLEDGLING. BUT *YOU'RE* ONE OF THE MOST TALENTED STUDENTS AT YOUNWITY.
WELL... OKAY, I'LL GIVE YOU THAT.
I KNOW SHE'S OUT THERE. I CAN FEEL IT.
AND SOMETHING HERE JUST...JUST DOESN'T FEEL RIGHT.
I AGREE.
ABIGAIL, THIS IS OUR LAST YEAR HERE. WHAT IF WE GET EXPELLED? YOU KNOW WHAT HAPPENS TO THOSE WHO FAIL IN THE WITCHES' WORLD. IS THAT WHAT YOU WANT FOR US?
I JUST WANT NOREEN TO BE SAFE. RIGHT NOW, THAT'S THE ONLY THING THAT MATTERS.
NOREEN IS *FAMILY.*
IMAGINE IF YOUR DAD WAS THE ONE WHO DISAPPEARED, OR IF IT WAS ME! YOU WOULDN'T JUST SIT HERE...
I'M HER *MENTOR*. I'M SUPPOSED TO PROTECT HER AND I *FAILED.*
WE NEED TO FIND HER...
ENVER, I'LL HELP YOU.
...I... *HMPF*... FINE, I'M IN, TOO.
I KNOW WHERE WE CAN START.

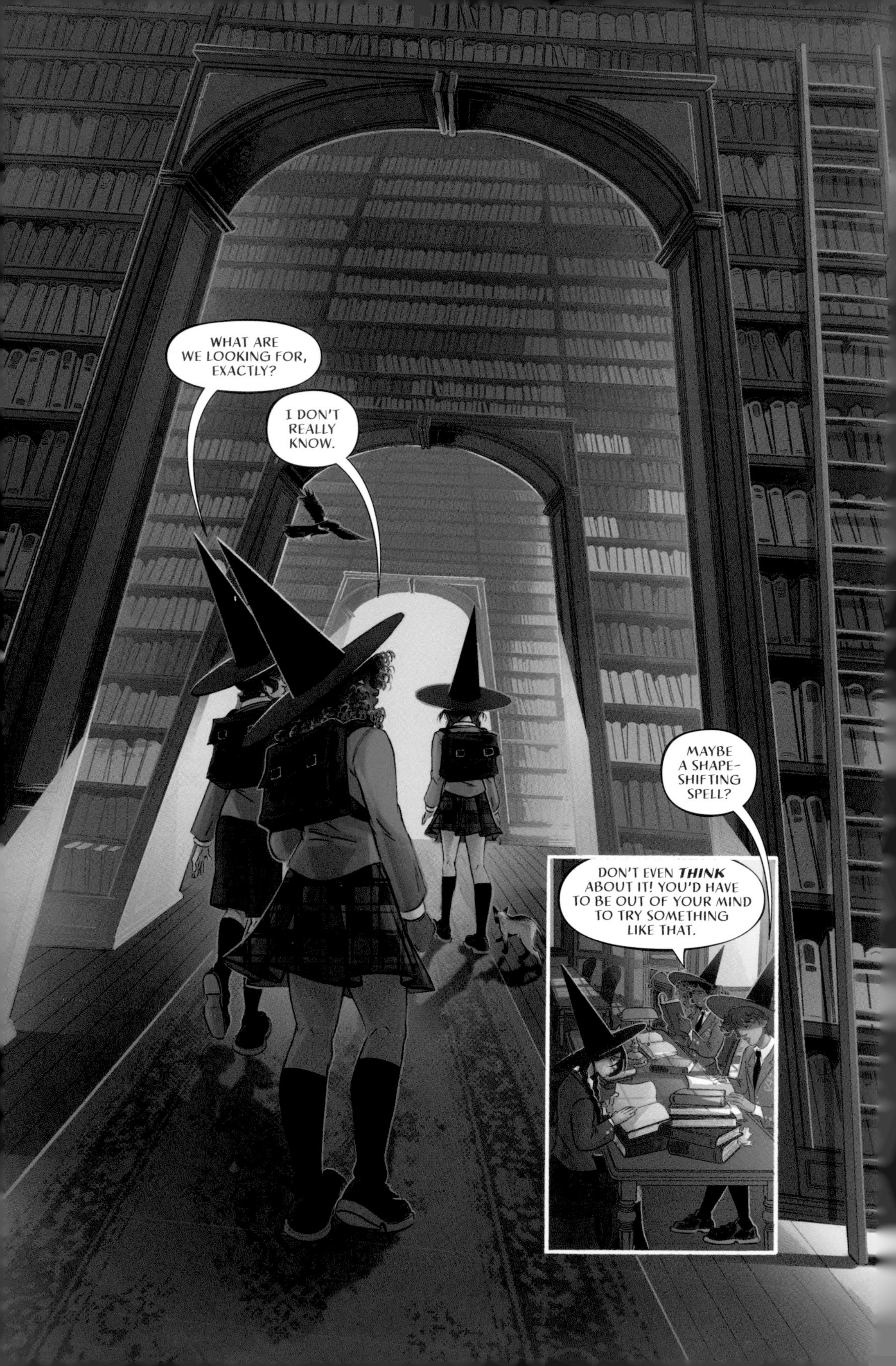
WHAT ARE WE LOOKING FOR, EXACTLY?
I DON'T REALLY KNOW.
MAYBE A SHAPE-SHIFTING SPELL?
DON'T EVEN **THINK** ABOUT IT! YOU'D HAVE TO BE OUT OF YOUR MIND TO TRY SOMETHING LIKE THAT.

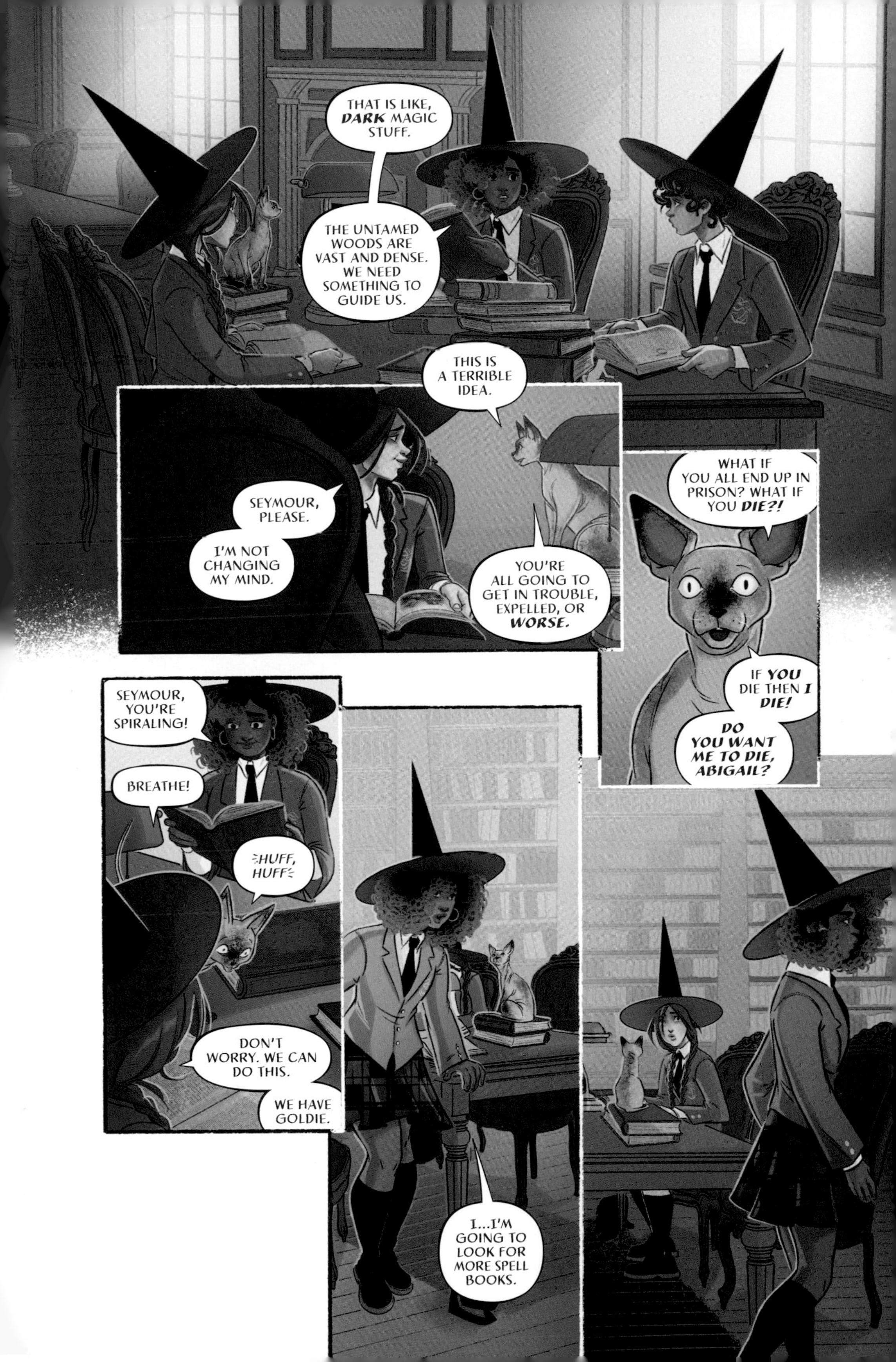
THAT IS LIKE, DARK MAGIC STUFF.
THE UNTAMED WOODS ARE VAST AND DENSE. WE NEED SOMETHING TO GUIDE US.
THIS IS A TERRIBLE IDEA.
SEYMOUR, PLEASE.
I'M NOT CHANGING MY MIND.
YOU'RE ALL GOING TO GET IN TROUBLE, EXPELLED, OR WORSE.
WHAT IF YOU ALL END UP IN PRISON? WHAT IF YOU DIE?!
IF YOU DIE THEN I DIE!
DO YOU WANT ME TO DIE, ABIGAIL?
SEYMOUR, YOU'RE SPIRALING!
BREATHE!
HUFF, HUFF
DON'T WORRY. WE CAN DO THIS.
WE HAVE GOLDIE.
I...I'M GOING TO LOOK FOR MORE SPELL BOOKS.

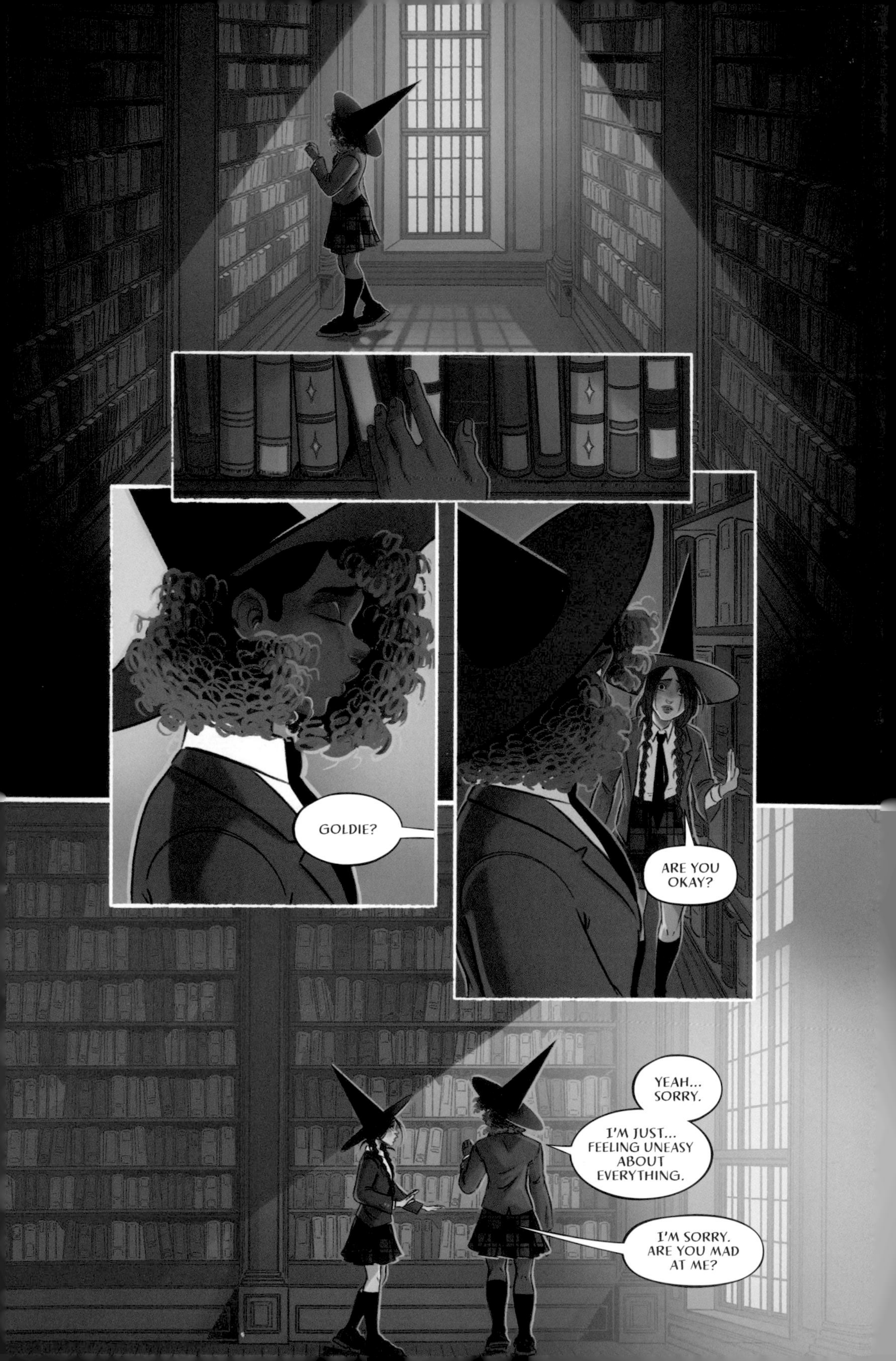
GOLDIE?
ARE YOU OKAY?
YEAH... SORRY.
I'M JUST... FEELING UNEASY ABOUT EVERYTHING.
I'M SORRY. ARE YOU MAD AT ME?

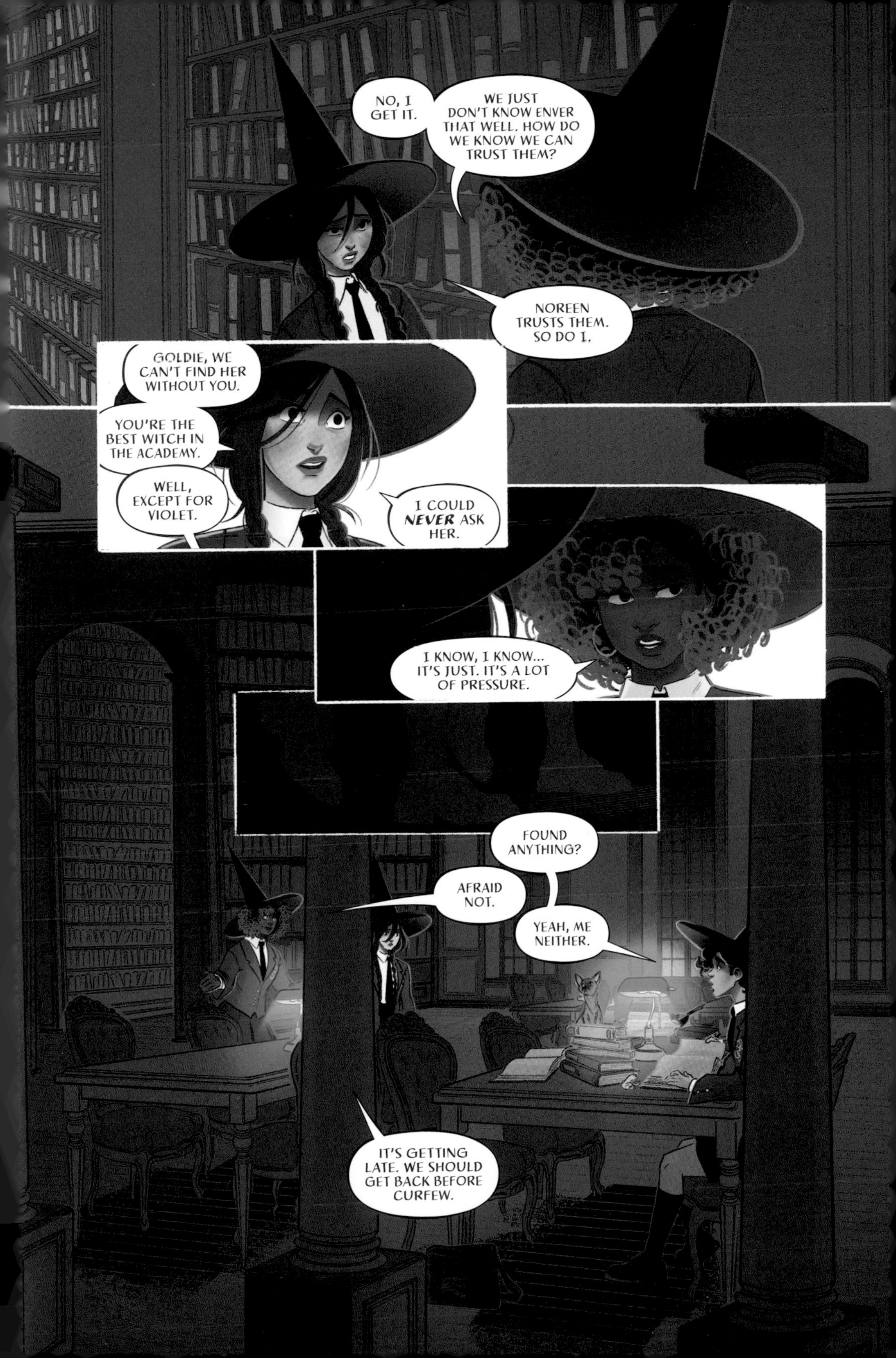
NO, I GET IT.
WE JUST DON'T KNOW ENVER THAT WELL. HOW DO WE KNOW WE CAN TRUST THEM?
NOREEN TRUSTS THEM. SO DO I.
GOLDIE, WE CAN'T FIND HER WITHOUT YOU.
YOU'RE THE BEST WITCH IN THE ACADEMY.
WELL, EXCEPT FOR VIOLET.
I COULD NEVER ASK HER.
I KNOW, I KNOW... IT'S JUST. IT'S A LOT OF PRESSURE.
FOUND ANYTHING?
AFRAID NOT.
YEAH, ME NEITHER.
IT'S GETTING LATE. WE SHOULD GET BACK BEFORE CURFEW.

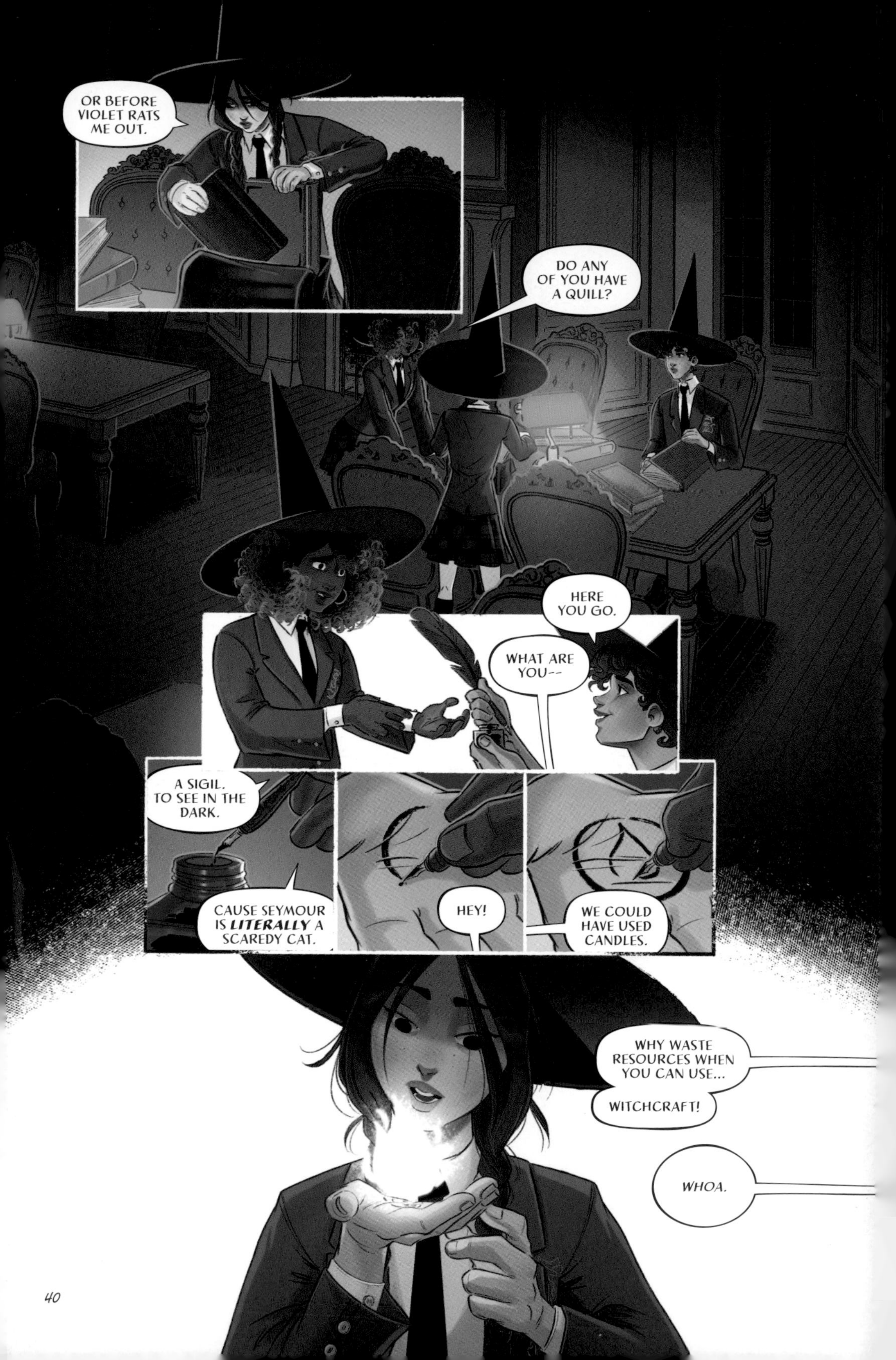
OR BEFORE VIOLET RATS ME OUT.
DO ANY OF YOU HAVE A QUILL?
HERE YOU GO.
WHAT ARE YOU--
A SIGIL. TO SEE IN THE DARK.
CAUSE SEYMOUR IS ***LITERALLY*** A SCAREDY CAT.
HEY!
WE COULD HAVE USED CANDLES.
WHY WASTE RESOURCES WHEN YOU CAN USE...
WITCHCRAFT!
WHOA.

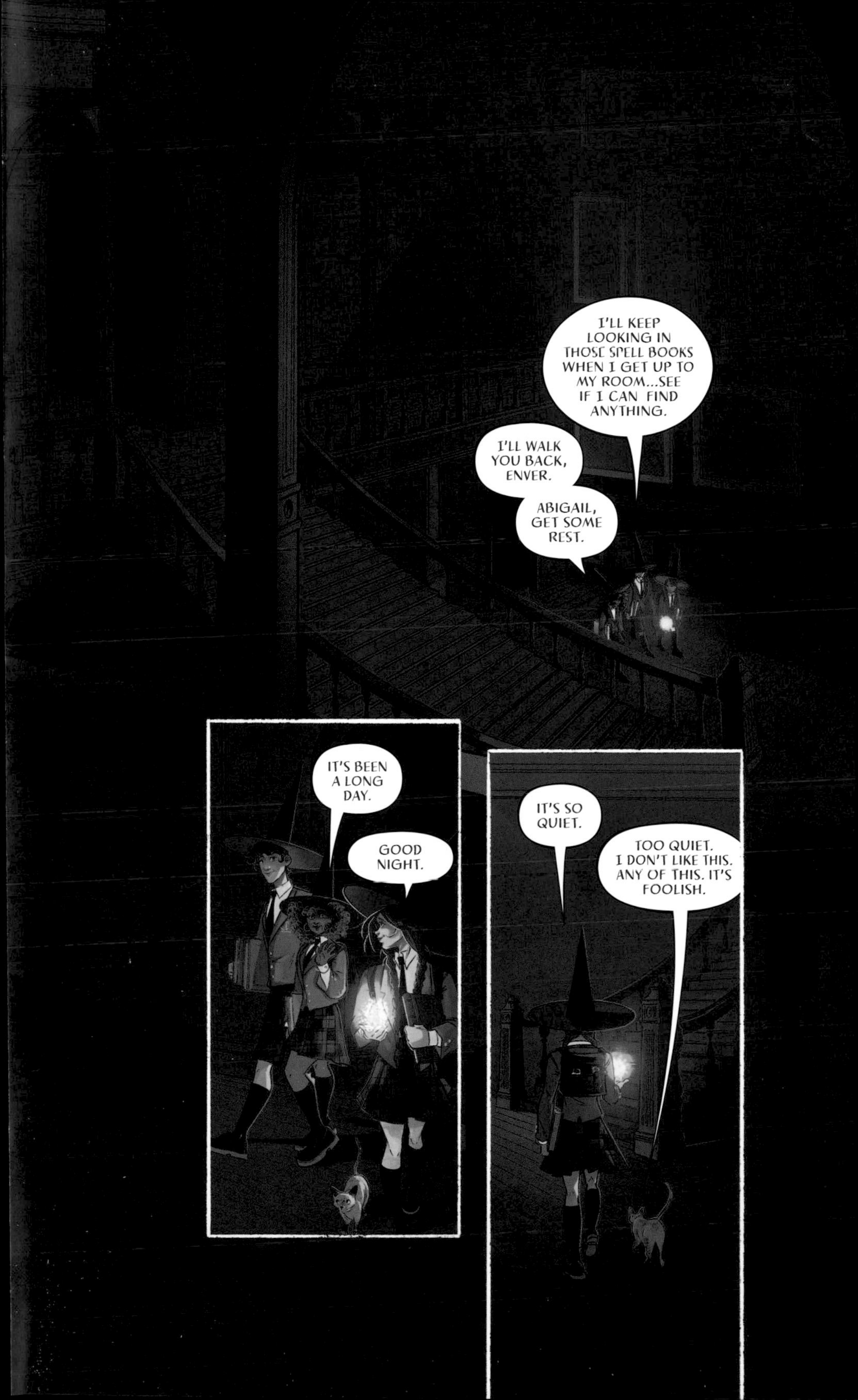
I'LL KEEP LOOKING IN THOSE SPELL BOOKS WHEN I GET UP TO MY ROOM...SEE IF I CAN FIND ANYTHING.
I'LL WALK YOU BACK, ENVER.
ABIGAIL, GET SOME REST.
IT'S BEEN A LONG DAY.
GOOD NIGHT.
IT'S SO QUIET.
TOO QUIET. I DON'T LIKE THIS. ANY OF THIS. IT'S FOOLISH.

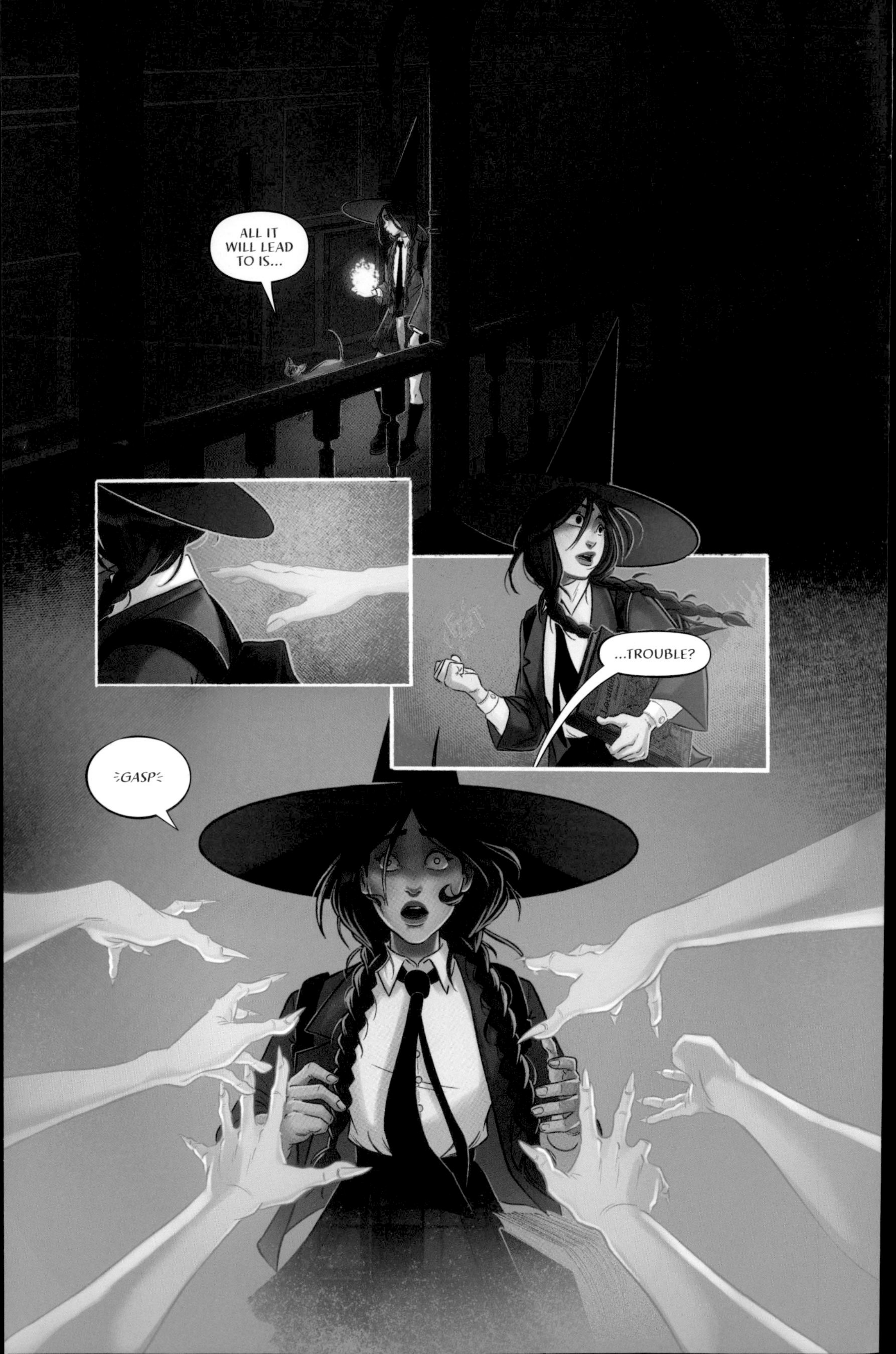
ALL IT WILL LEAD TO IS...
...TROUBLE?
GASP

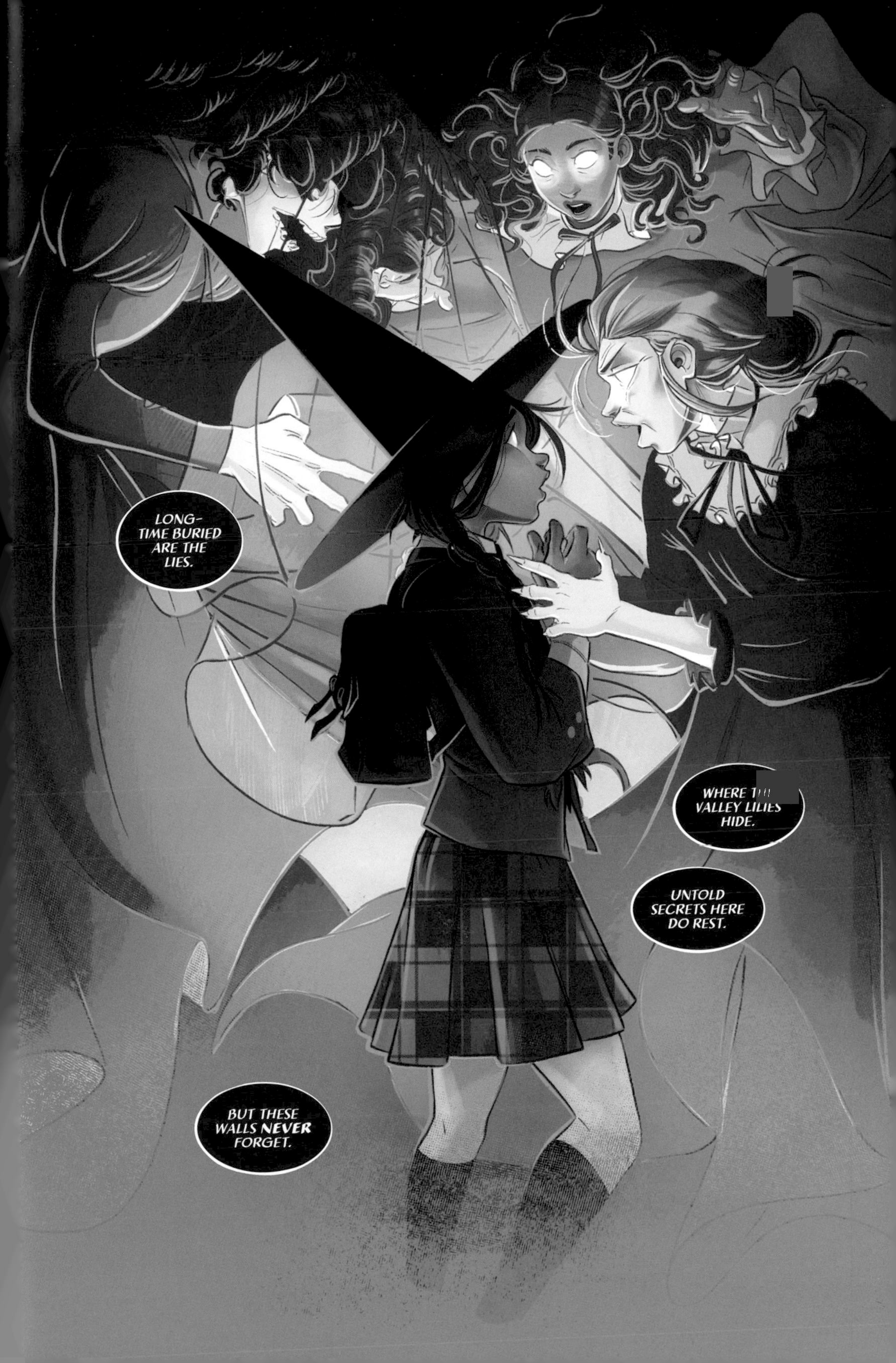
LONG-TIME BURIED ARE THE LIES.
WHERE T[redacted] VALLEY LILIES HIDE.
UNTOLD SECRETS HERE DO REST.
BUT THESE WALLS **NEVER** FORGET.

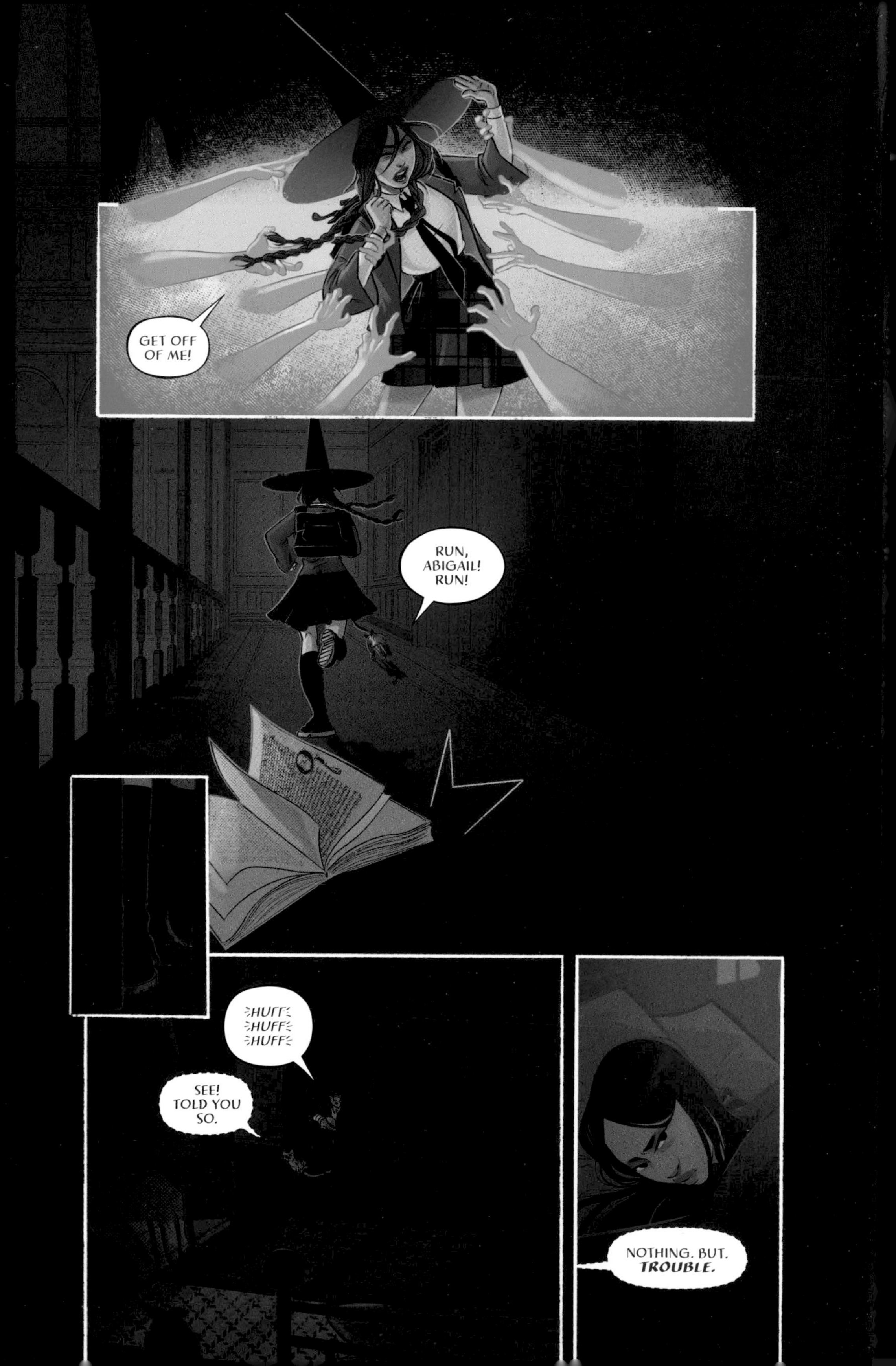

GET OFF OF ME!
RUN, ABIGAIL! RUN!
HUFF HUFF HUFF
SEE! TOLD YOU SO.
NOTHING. BUT. TROUBLE.

CHAPTER II

From the same source I have not taken
My sorrow -- I could not awaken
My heart to joy at the same tone --
And all I lov'd -- *I* lov'd alone --

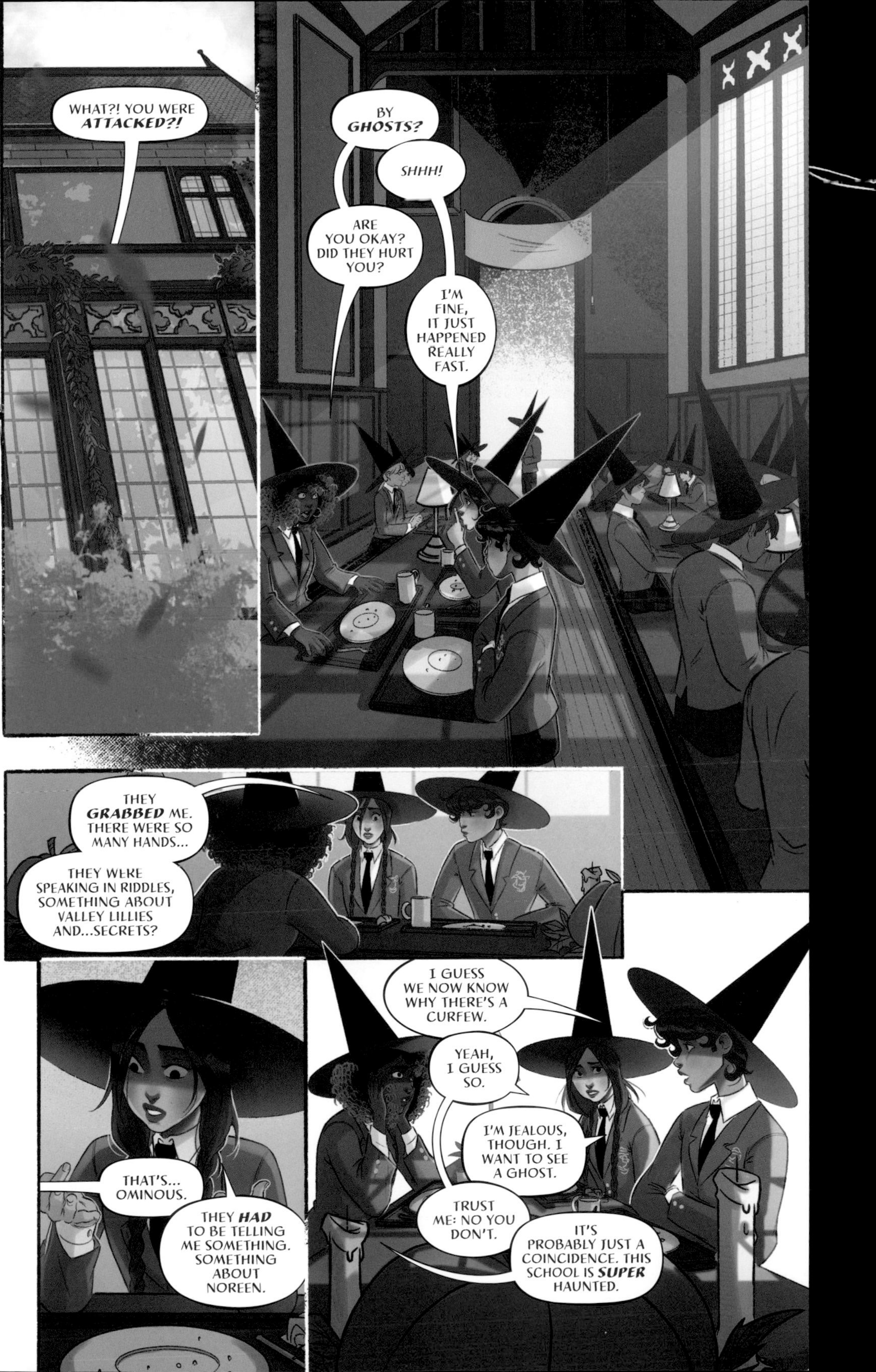
WHAT?! YOU WERE *ATTACKED?!*
BY *GHOSTS?*
SHHH!
ARE YOU OKAY? DID THEY HURT YOU?
I'M FINE, IT JUST HAPPENED REALLY FAST.
THEY *GRABBED* ME. THERE WERE SO MANY HANDS...
THEY WERE SPEAKING IN RIDDLES, SOMETHING ABOUT VALLEY LILLIES AND...SECRETS?
THAT'S... OMINOUS.
THEY *HAD* TO BE TELLING ME SOMETHING. SOMETHING ABOUT NOREEN.
I GUESS WE NOW KNOW WHY THERE'S A CURFEW.
YEAH, I GUESS SO.
I'M JEALOUS, THOUGH. I WANT TO SEE A GHOST.
TRUST ME: NO YOU DON'T.
IT'S PROBABLY JUST A COINCIDENCE. THIS SCHOOL IS *SUPER* HAUNTED.

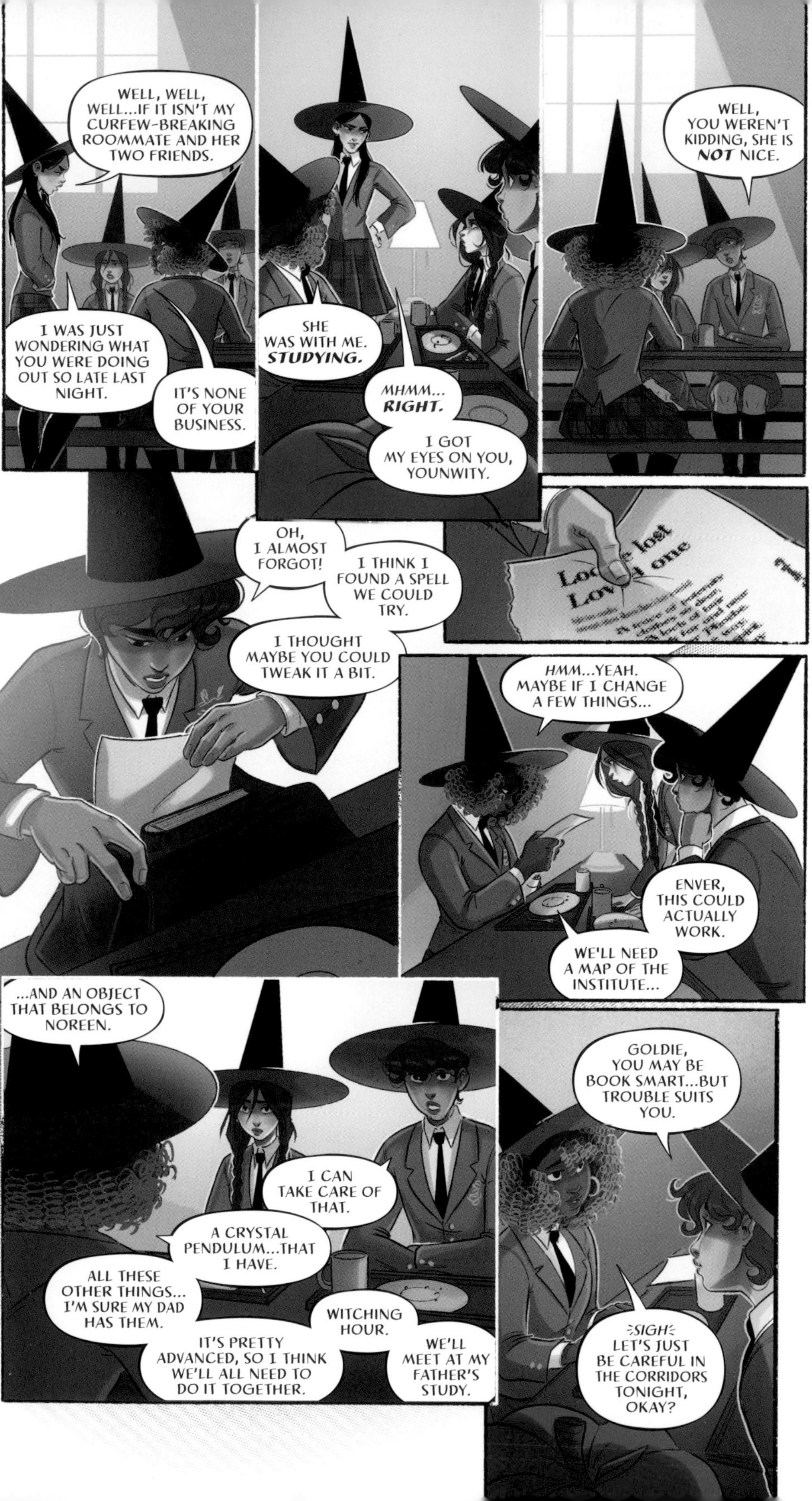
WELL, WELL, WELL...IF IT ISN'T MY CURFEW-BREAKING ROOMMATE AND HER TWO FRIENDS.
I WAS JUST WONDERING WHAT YOU WERE DOING OUT SO LATE LAST NIGHT.
IT'S NONE OF YOUR BUSINESS.
SHE WAS WITH ME. **STUDYING.**
MHMM... ***RIGHT.***
I GOT MY EYES ON YOU, YOUNWITY.
WELL, YOU WEREN'T KIDDING, SHE IS ***NOT*** NICE.
OH, I ALMOST FORGOT!
I THINK I FOUND A SPELL WE COULD TRY.
I THOUGHT MAYBE YOU COULD TWEAK IT A BIT.
*HMM...*YEAH. MAYBE IF I CHANGE A FEW THINGS...
ENVER, THIS COULD ACTUALLY WORK.
WE'LL NEED A MAP OF THE INSTITUTE...
...AND AN OBJECT THAT BELONGS TO NOREEN.
I CAN TAKE CARE OF THAT.
A CRYSTAL PENDULUM...THAT I HAVE.
ALL THESE OTHER THINGS... I'M SURE MY DAD HAS THEM.
IT'S PRETTY ADVANCED, SO I THINK WE'LL ALL NEED TO DO IT TOGETHER.
WITCHING HOUR.
WE'LL MEET AT MY FATHER'S STUDY.
GOLDIE, YOU MAY BE BOOK SMART...BUT TROUBLE SUITS YOU.
SIGH LET'S JUST BE CAREFUL IN THE CORRIDORS TONIGHT, OKAY?

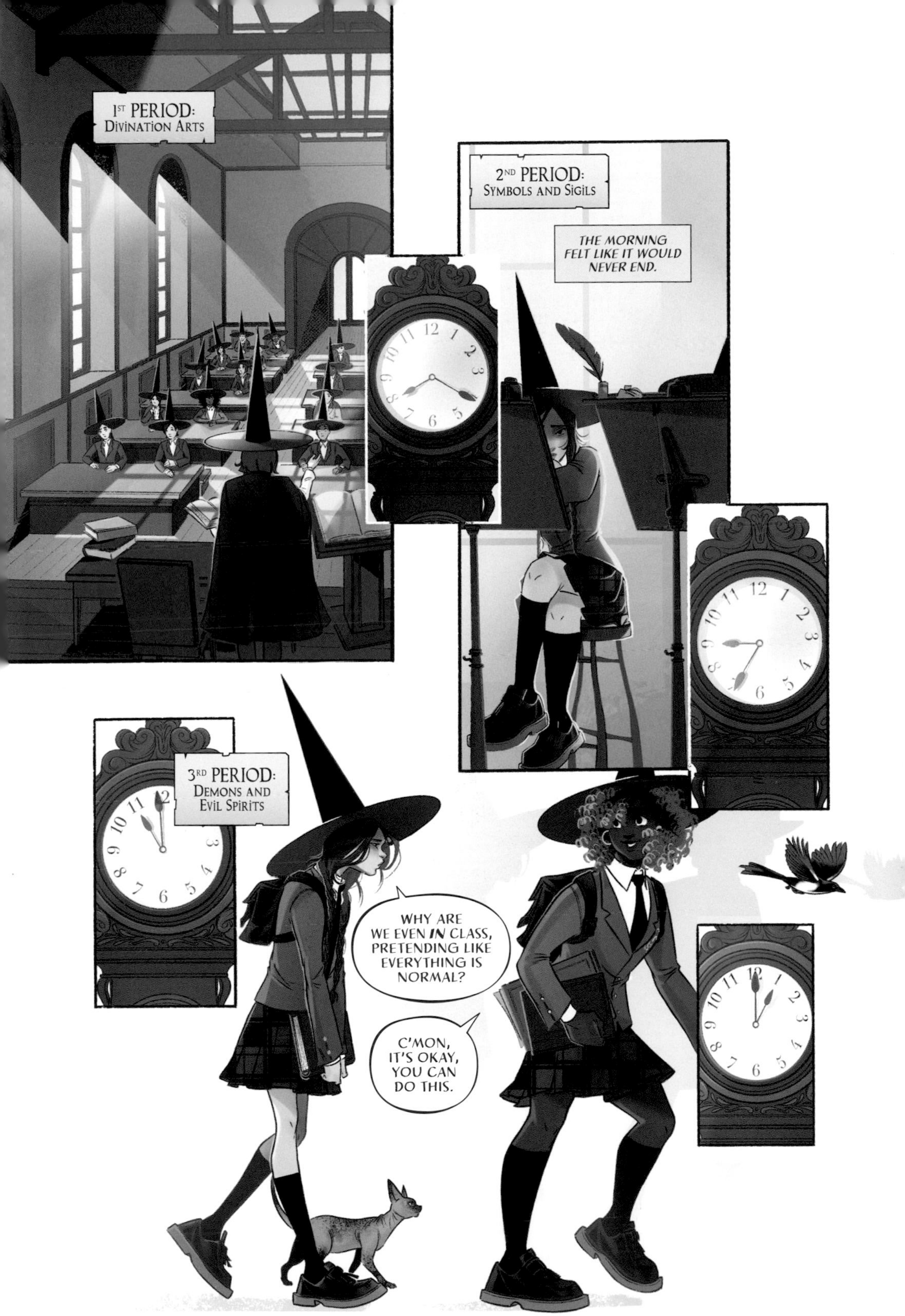

1ST PERIOD: DIVINATION ARTS
2ND PERIOD: SYMBOLS AND SIGILS
THE MORNING FELT LIKE IT WOULD NEVER END.
3RD PERIOD: DEMONS AND EVIL SPIRITS
WHY ARE WE EVEN IN CLASS, PRETENDING LIKE EVERYTHING IS NORMAL?
C'MON, IT'S OKAY, YOU CAN DO THIS.

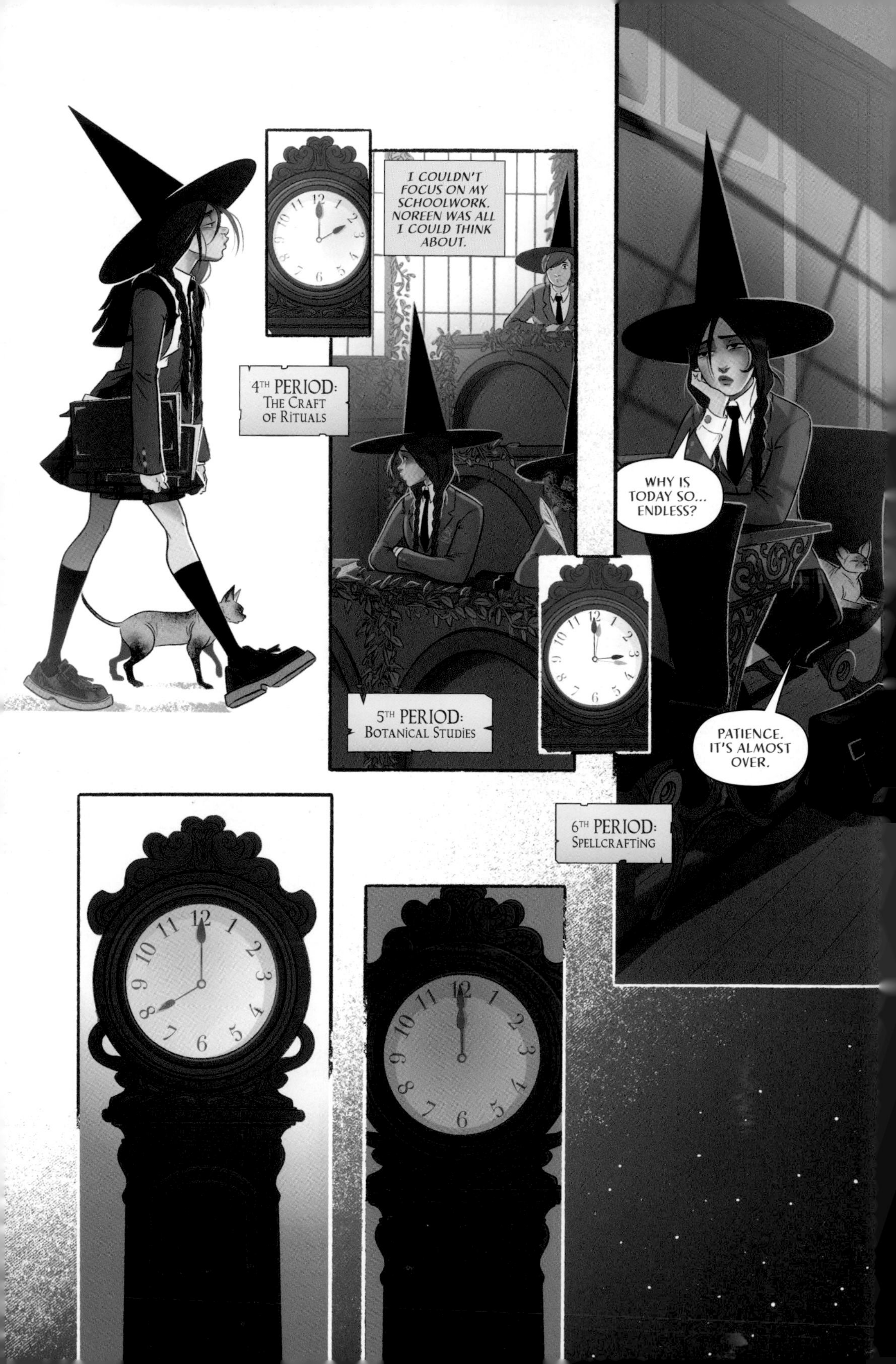
4TH PERIOD:
THE CRAFT OF RITUALS
I COULDN'T FOCUS ON MY SCHOOLWORK. NOREEN WAS ALL I COULD THINK ABOUT.
5TH PERIOD:
BOTANICAL STUDIES
WHY IS TODAY SO... ENDLESS?
PATIENCE. IT'S ALMOST OVER.
6TH PERIOD:
SPELLCRAFTING

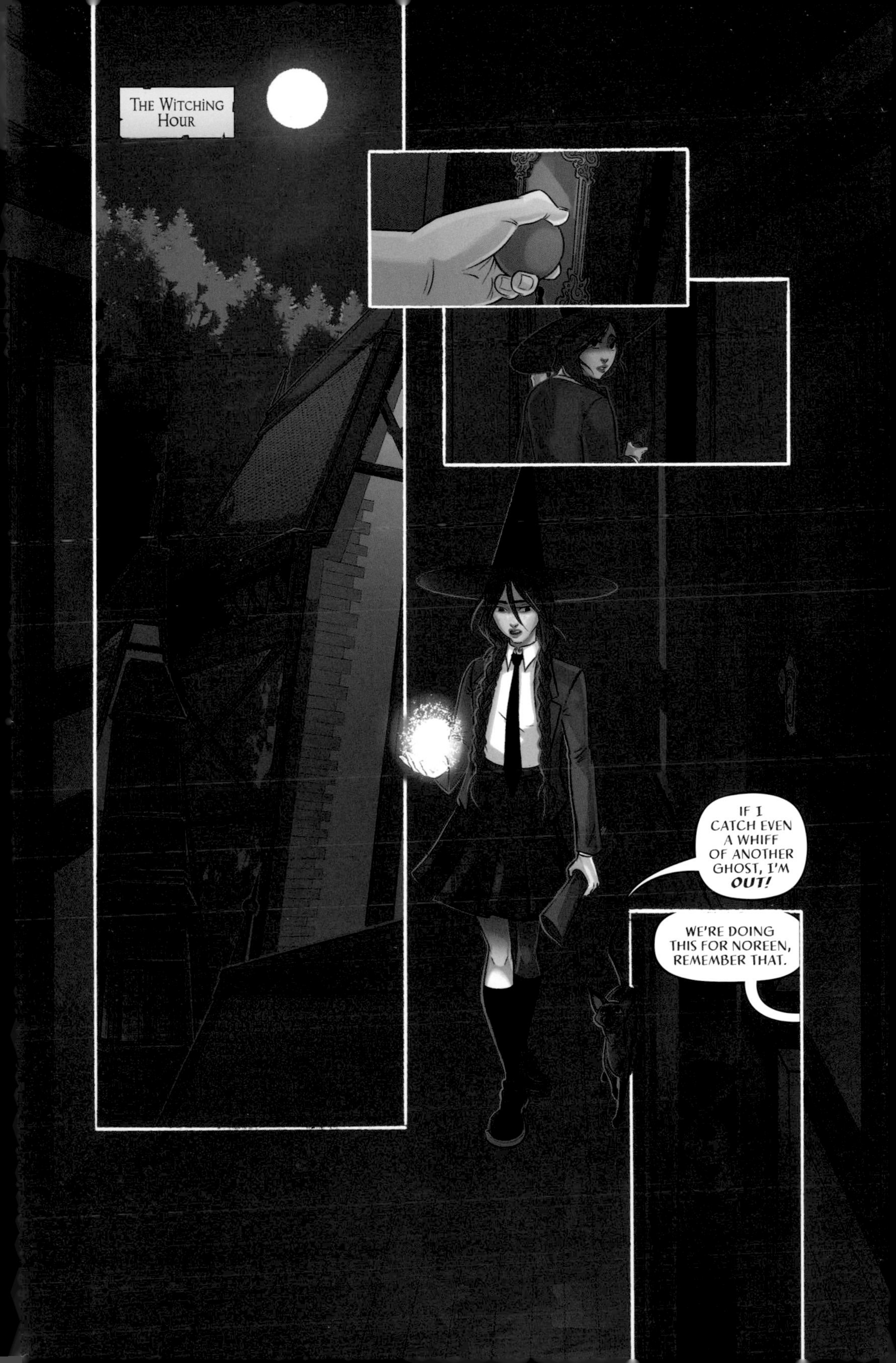
THE WITCHING HOUR
IF I CATCH EVEN A WHIFF OF ANOTHER GHOST, I'M OUT!
WE'RE DOING THIS FOR NOREEN, REMEMBER THAT.

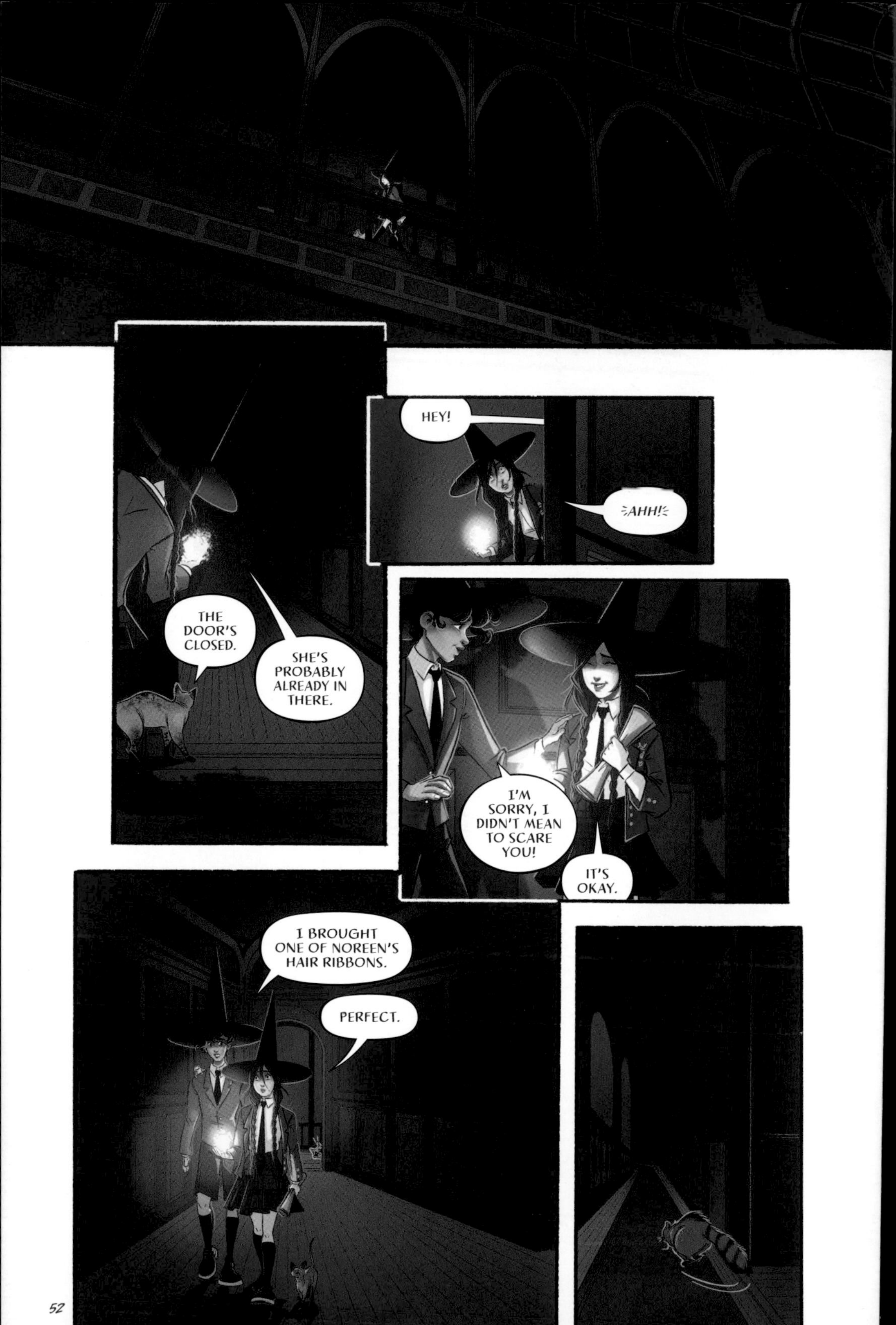
HEY!
AHH!
THE DOOR'S CLOSED.
SHE'S PROBABLY ALREADY IN THERE.
I'M SORRY, I DIDN'T MEAN TO SCARE YOU!
IT'S OKAY.
I BROUGHT ONE OF NOREEN'S HAIR RIBBONS.
PERFECT.

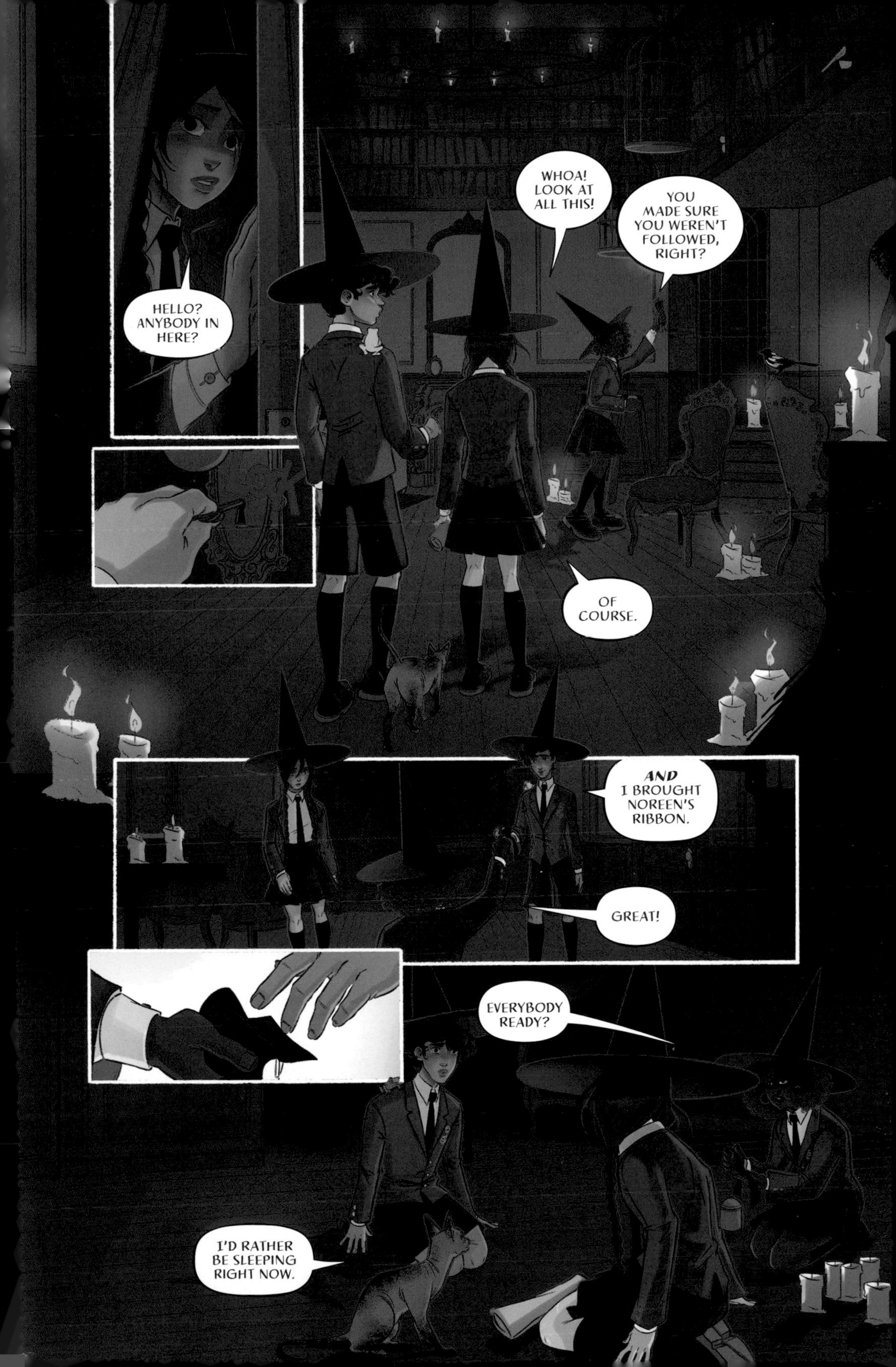
HELLO? ANYBODY IN HERE?
WHOA! LOOK AT ALL THIS!
YOU MADE SURE YOU WEREN'T FOLLOWED, RIGHT?
OF COURSE.
AND I BROUGHT NOREEN'S RIBBON.
GREAT!
EVERYBODY READY?
I'D RATHER BE SLEEPING RIGHT NOW.

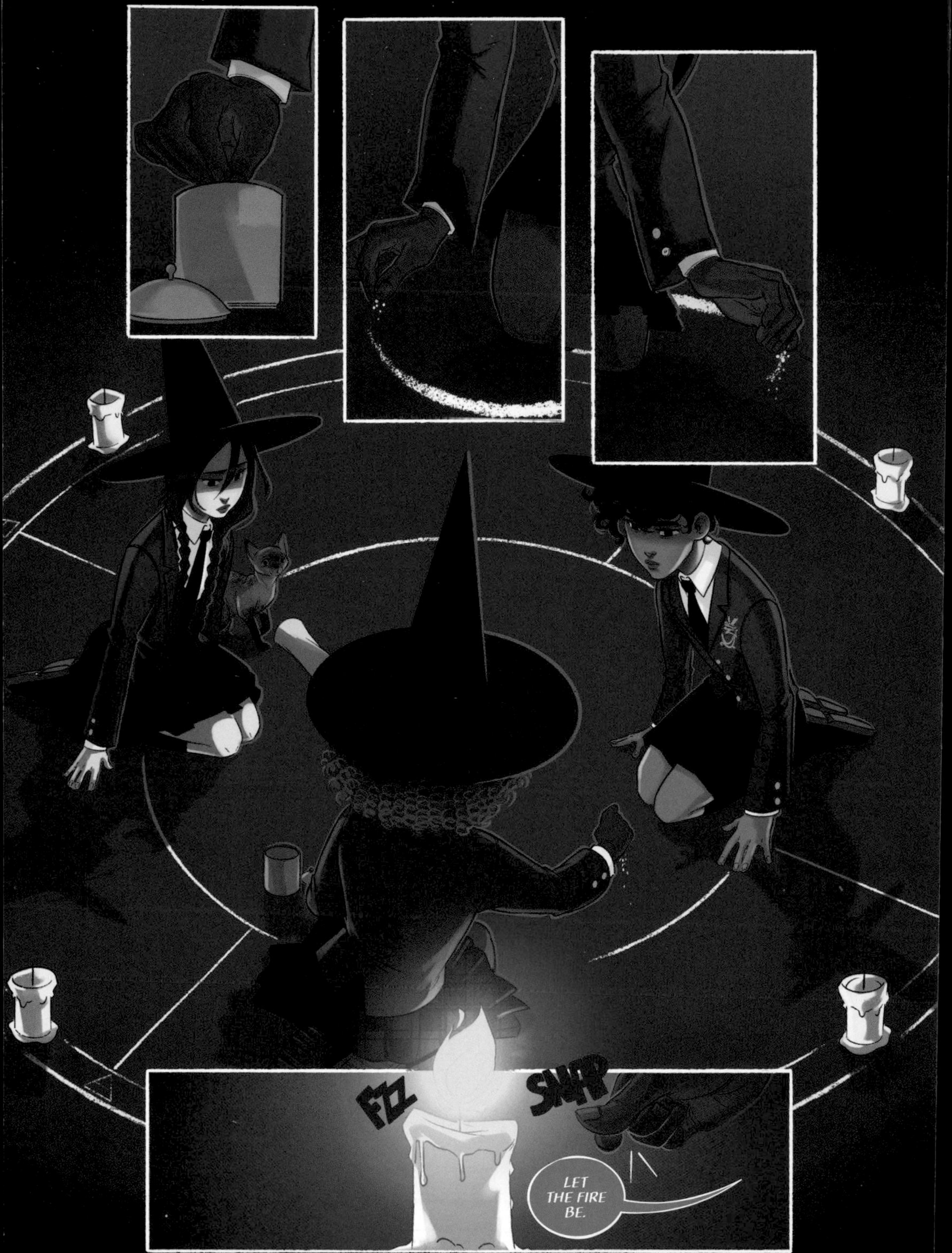
FZZ
SNAP
LET THE FIRE BE.

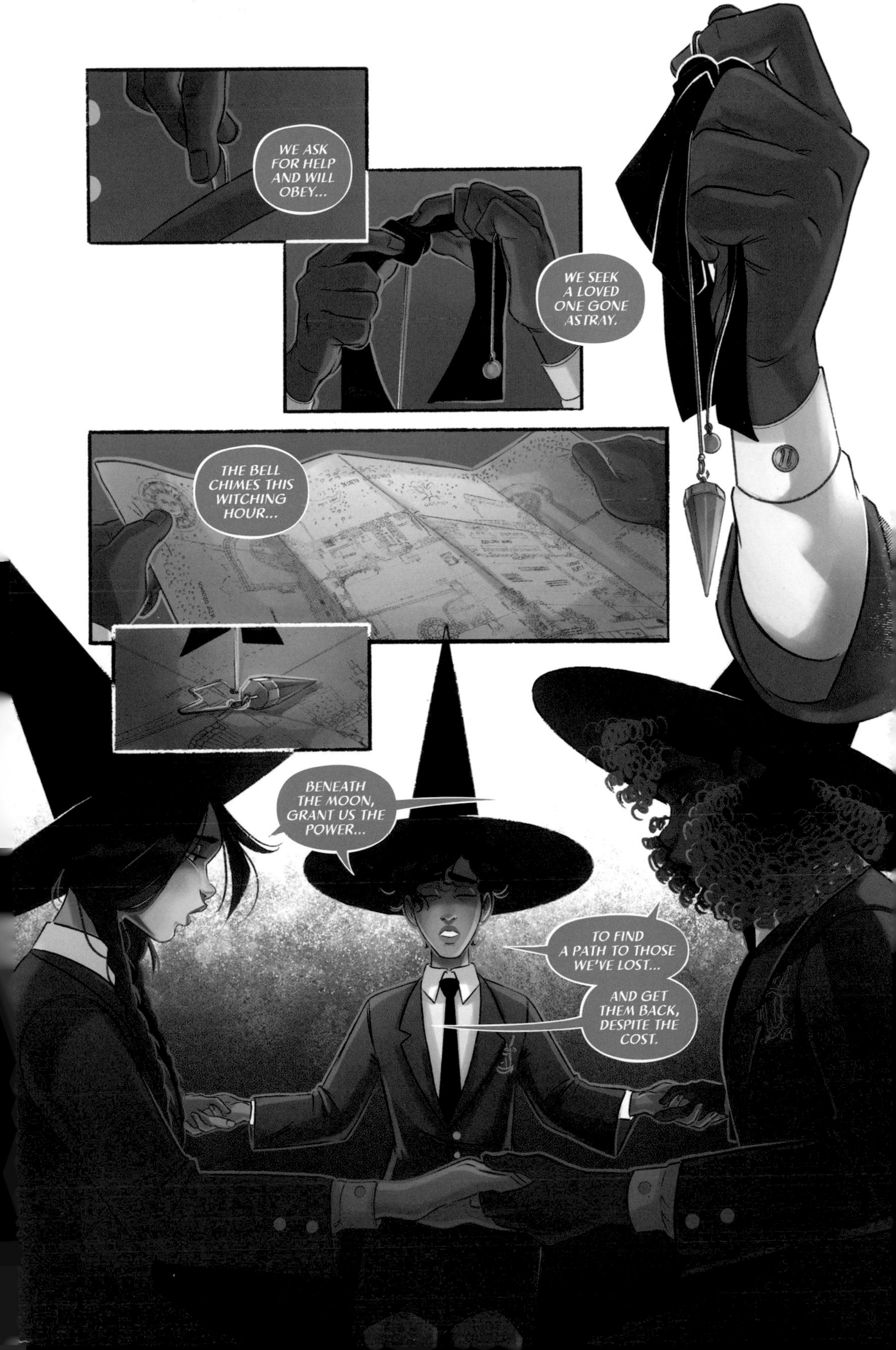
WE ASK FOR HELP AND WILL OBEY...
WE SEEK A LOVED ONE GONE ASTRAY.
THE BELL CHIMES THIS WITCHING HOUR...
BENEATH THE MOON, GRANT US THE POWER...
TO FIND A PATH TO THOSE WE'VE LOST...
AND GET THEM BACK, DESPITE THE COST.

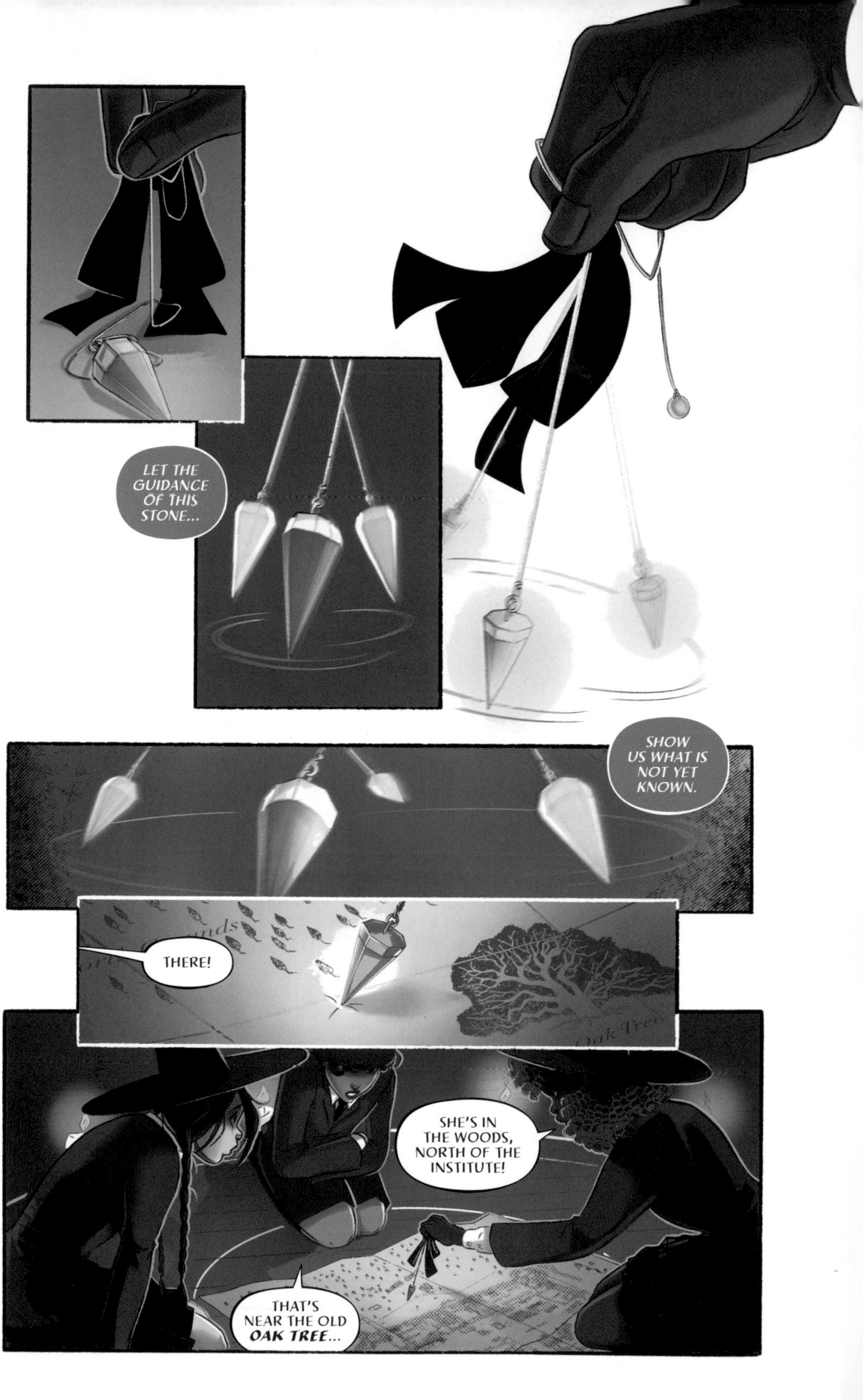
LET THE GUIDANCE OF THIS STONE...
SHOW US WHAT IS NOT YET KNOWN.
THERE!
Oak Tree
SHE'S IN THE WOODS, NORTH OF THE INSTITUTE!
THAT'S NEAR THE OLD **OAK TREE**...

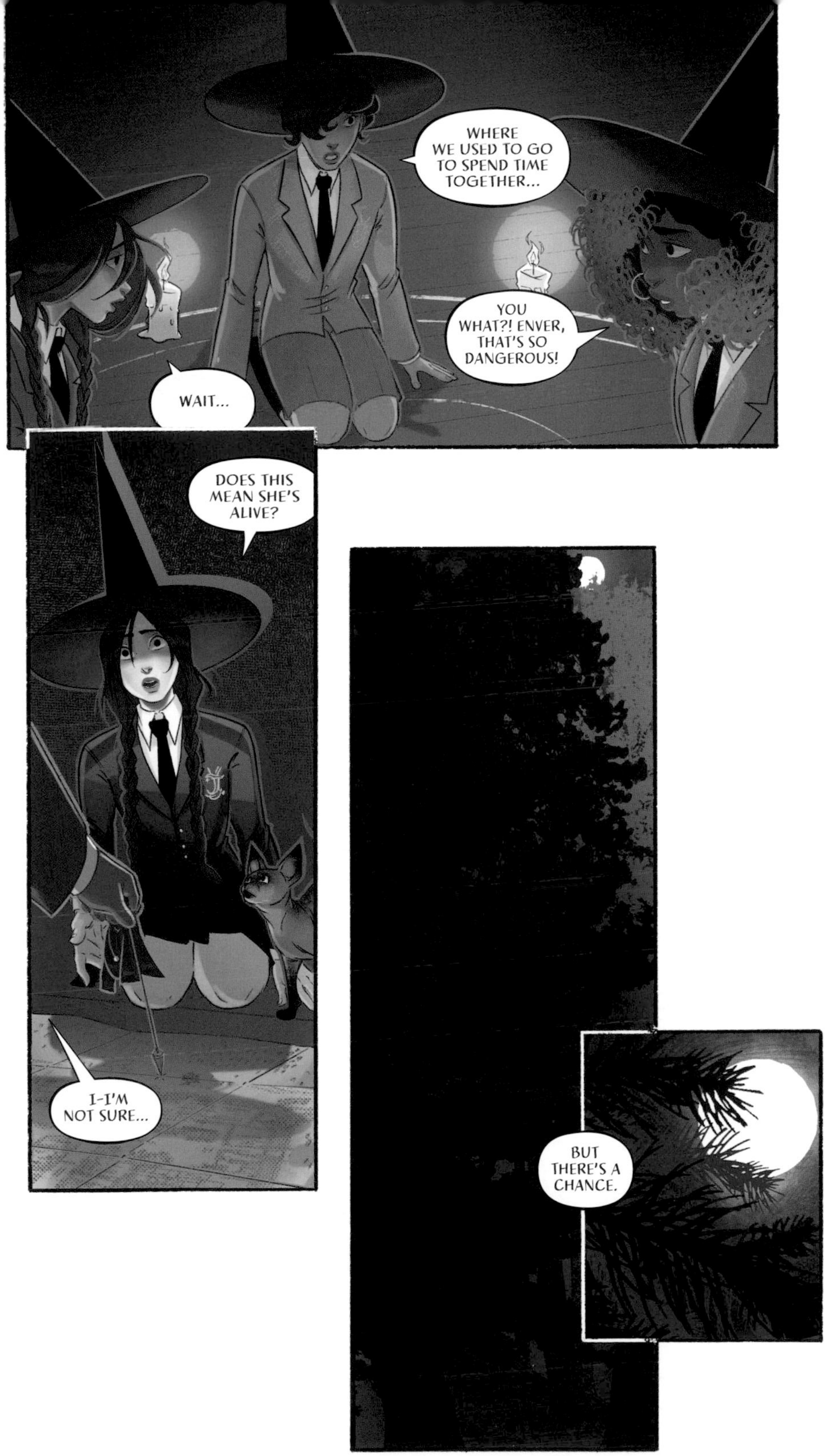
WHERE WE USED TO GO TO SPEND TIME TOGETHER...
YOU WHAT?! ENVER, THAT'S SO DANGEROUS!
WAIT...
DOES THIS MEAN SHE'S ALIVE?
I-I'M NOT SURE...
BUT THERE'S A CHANCE.

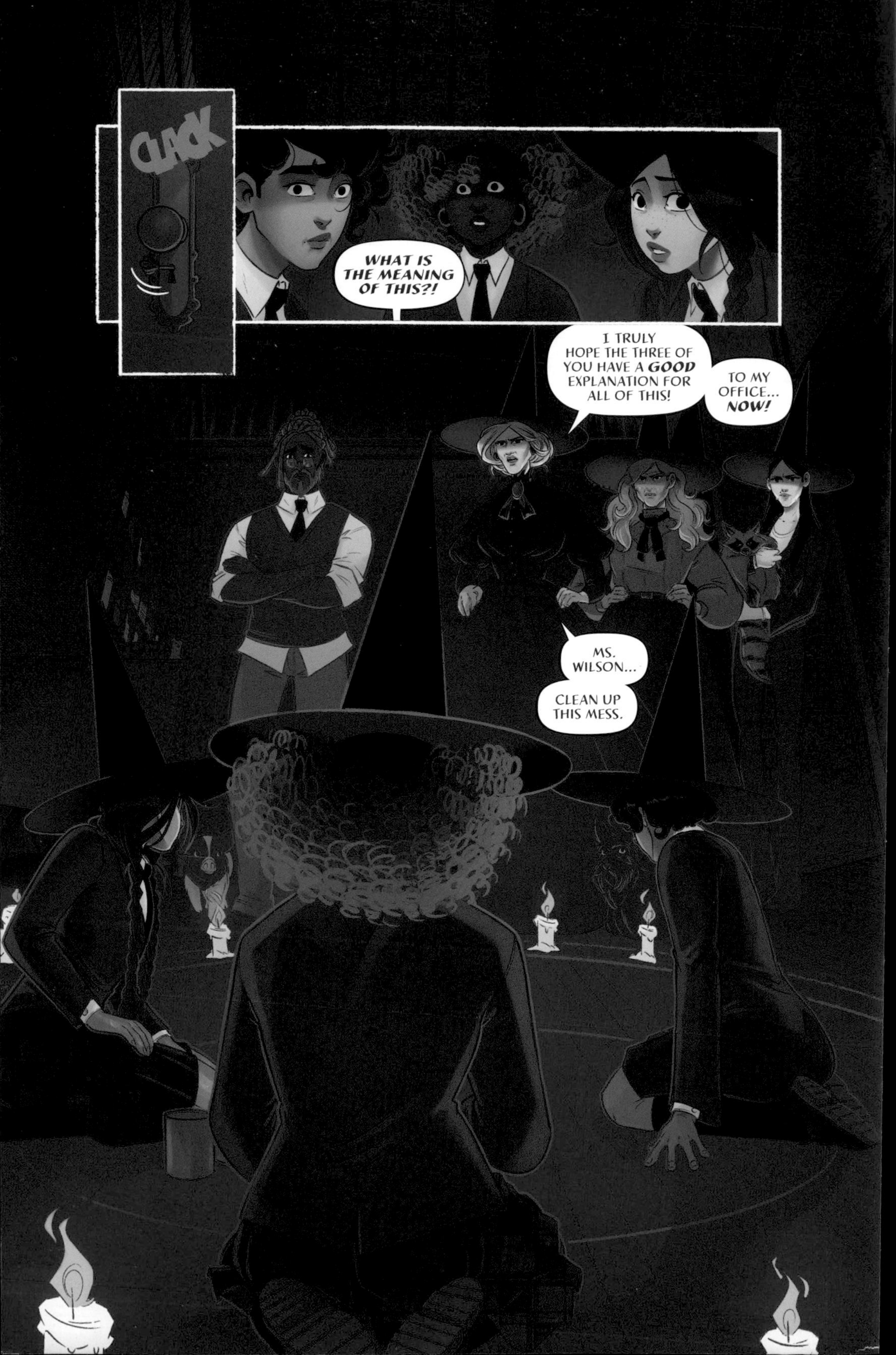
CLACK
WHAT IS THE MEANING OF THIS?!
I TRULY HOPE THE THREE OF YOU HAVE A **GOOD** EXPLANATION FOR ALL OF THIS!
TO MY OFFICE... **NOW!**
MS. WILSON...
CLEAN UP THIS MESS.

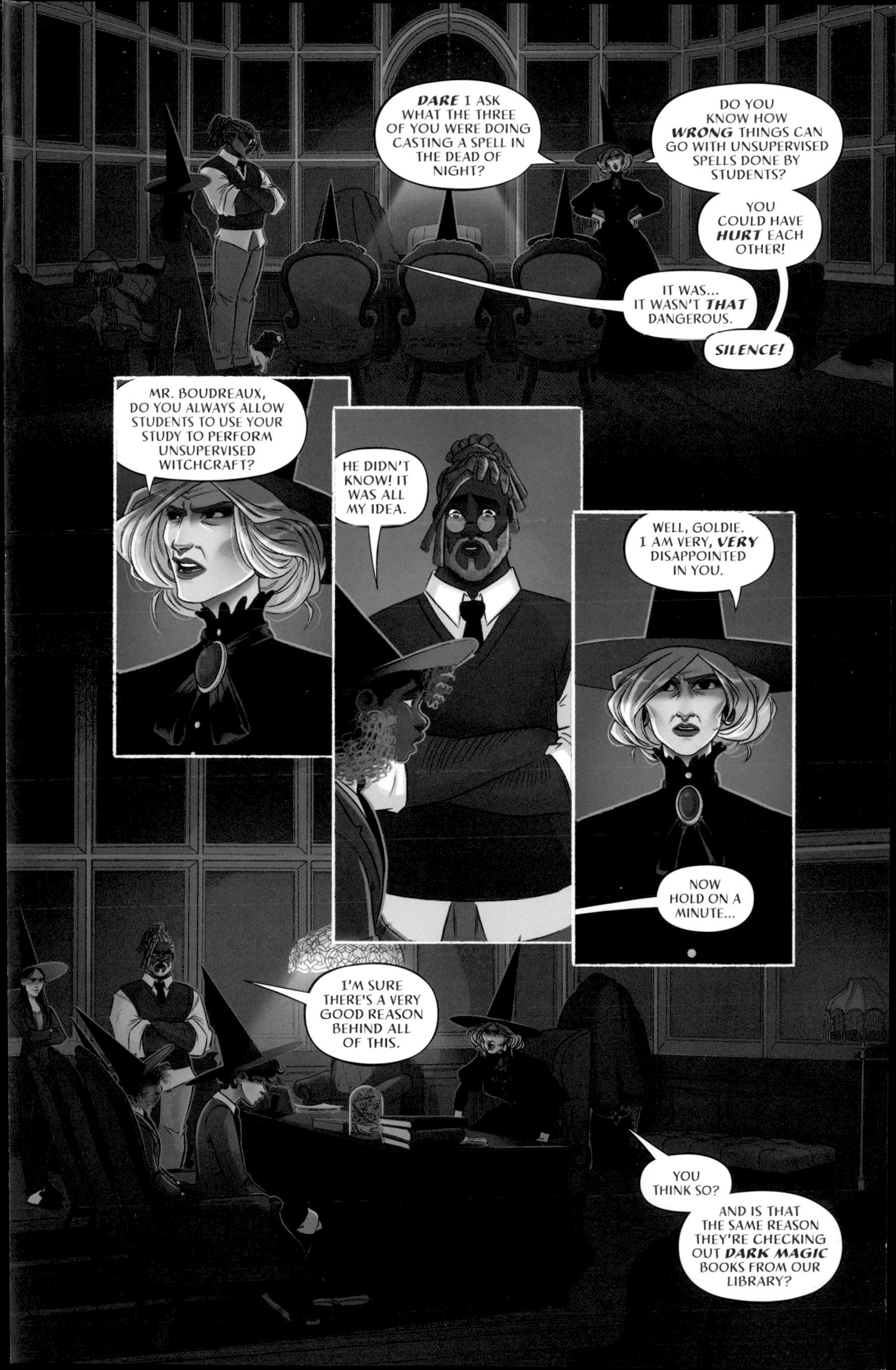
DARE I ASK WHAT THE THREE OF YOU WERE DOING CASTING A SPELL IN THE DEAD OF NIGHT?
DO YOU KNOW HOW WRONG THINGS CAN GO WITH UNSUPERVISED SPELLS DONE BY STUDENTS?
YOU COULD HAVE HURT EACH OTHER!
IT WAS... IT WASN'T THAT DANGEROUS.
SILENCE!
MR. BOUDREAUX, DO YOU ALWAYS ALLOW STUDENTS TO USE YOUR STUDY TO PERFORM UNSUPERVISED WITCHCRAFT?
HE DIDN'T KNOW! IT WAS ALL MY IDEA.
WELL, GOLDIE. I AM VERY, VERY DISAPPOINTED IN YOU.
NOW HOLD ON A MINUTE...
I'M SURE THERE'S A VERY GOOD REASON BEHIND ALL OF THIS.
YOU THINK SO?
AND IS THAT THE SAME REASON THEY'RE CHECKING OUT DARK MAGIC BOOKS FROM OUR LIBRARY?

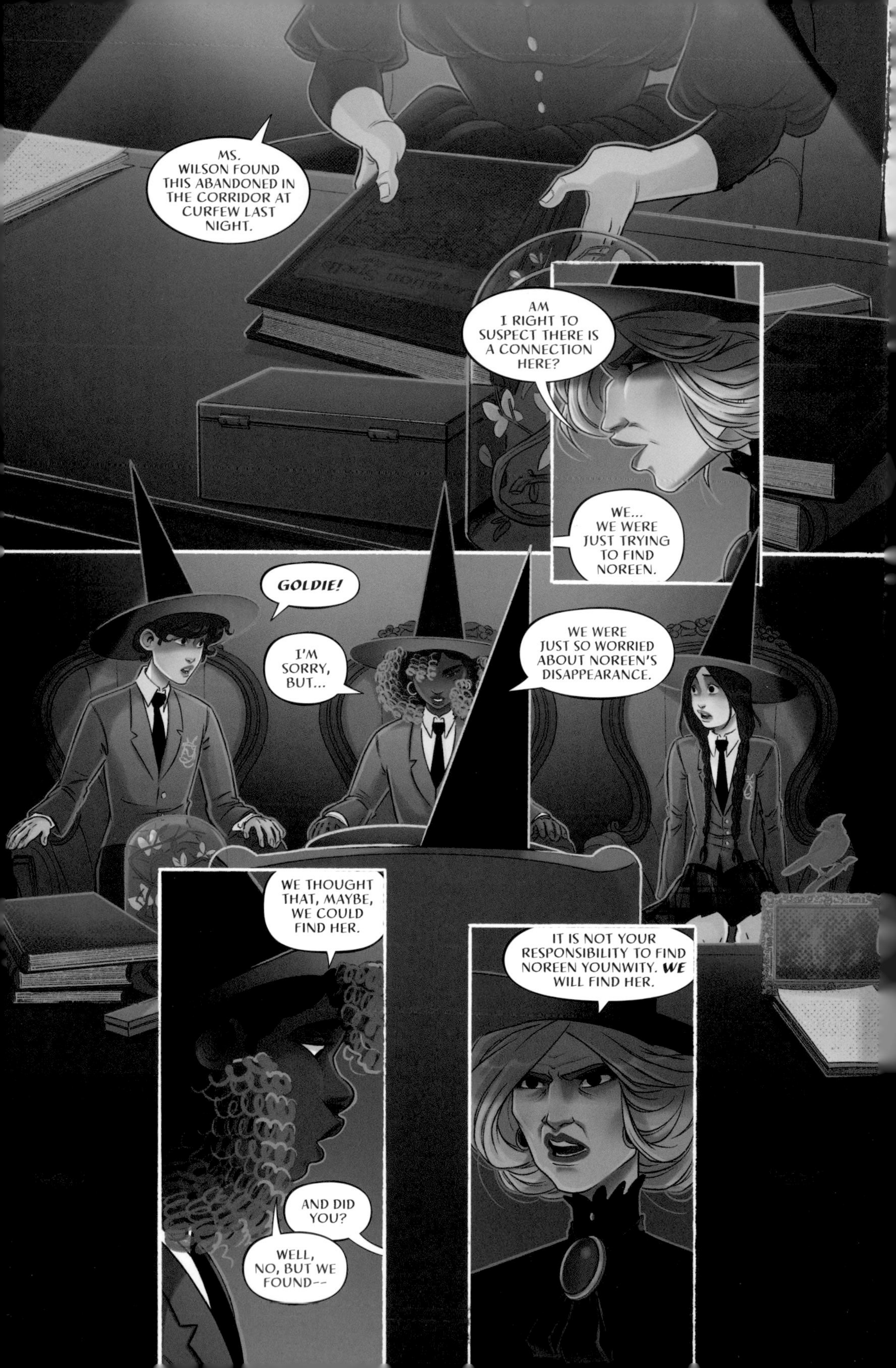

MS. WILSON FOUND THIS ABANDONED IN THE CORRIDOR AT CURFEW LAST NIGHT.
AM I RIGHT TO SUSPECT THERE IS A CONNECTION HERE?
WE... WE WERE JUST TRYING TO FIND NOREEN.
GOLDIE!
I'M SORRY, BUT...
WE WERE JUST SO WORRIED ABOUT NOREEN'S DISAPPEARANCE.
WE THOUGHT THAT, MAYBE, WE COULD FIND HER.
IT IS NOT YOUR RESPONSIBILITY TO FIND NOREEN YOUNWITY. WE WILL FIND HER.
AND DID YOU?
WELL, NO, BUT WE FOUND--

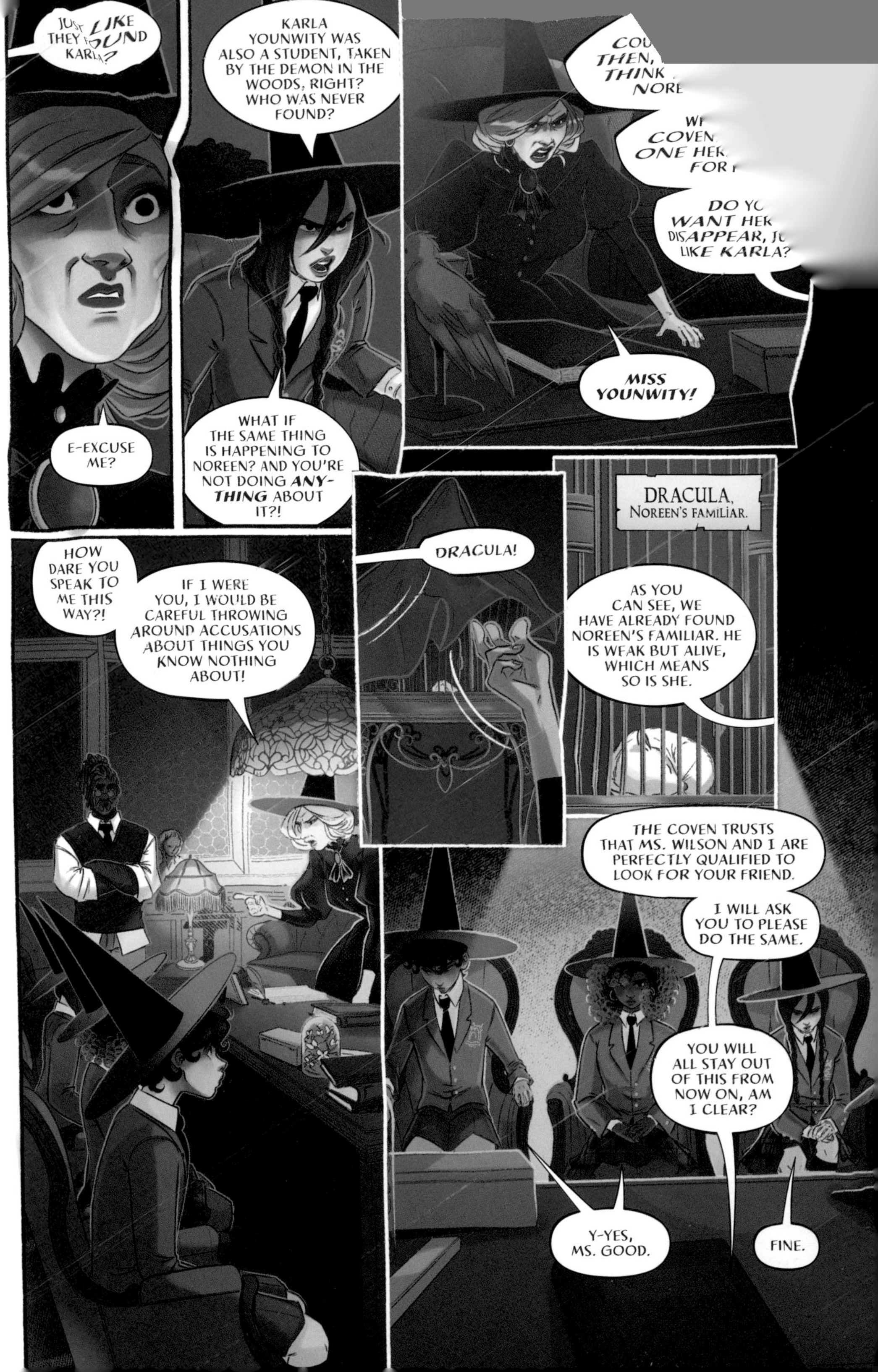
JUST LIKE THEY FOUND KARLA?
KARLA YOUNWITY WAS ALSO A STUDENT, TAKEN BY THE DEMON IN THE WOODS, RIGHT? WHO WAS NEVER FOUND?
E-EXCUSE ME?
WHAT IF THE SAME THING IS HAPPENING TO NOREEN? AND YOU'RE NOT DOING ANYTHING ABOUT IT?!
MISS YOUNWITY!
HOW DARE YOU SPEAK TO ME THIS WAY?!
IF I WERE YOU, I WOULD BE CAREFUL THROWING AROUND ACCUSATIONS ABOUT THINGS YOU KNOW NOTHING ABOUT!
DRACULA!
DRACULA, NOREEN'S FAMILIAR.
AS YOU CAN SEE, WE HAVE ALREADY FOUND NOREEN'S FAMILIAR. HE IS WEAK BUT ALIVE, WHICH MEANS SO IS SHE.
THE COVEN TRUSTS THAT MS. WILSON AND I ARE PERFECTLY QUALIFIED TO LOOK FOR YOUR FRIEND.
I WILL ASK YOU TO PLEASE DO THE SAME.
YOU WILL ALL STAY OUT OF THIS FROM NOW ON, AM I CLEAR?
Y-YES, MS. GOOD.
FINE.

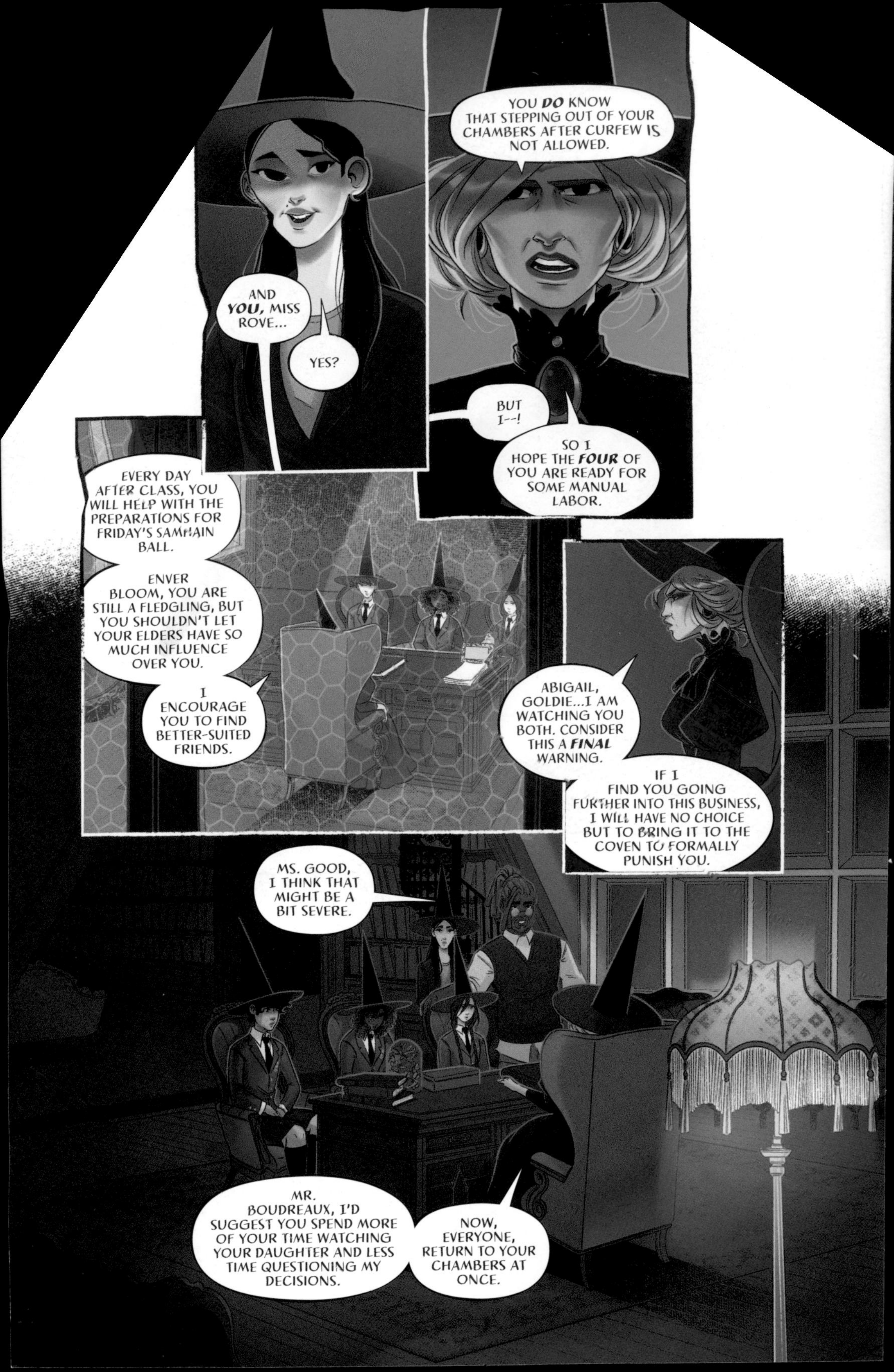
AND YOU, MISS ROVE...
YES?
YOU DO KNOW THAT STEPPING OUT OF YOUR CHAMBERS AFTER CURFEW IS NOT ALLOWED.
BUT I--!
SO I HOPE THE FOUR OF YOU ARE READY FOR SOME MANUAL LABOR.
EVERY DAY AFTER CLASS, YOU WILL HELP WITH THE PREPARATIONS FOR FRIDAY'S SAMHAIN BALL.
ENVER BLOOM, YOU ARE STILL A FLEDGLING, BUT YOU SHOULDN'T LET YOUR ELDERS HAVE SO MUCH INFLUENCE OVER YOU.
I ENCOURAGE YOU TO FIND BETTER-SUITED FRIENDS.
ABIGAIL, GOLDIE...I AM WATCHING YOU BOTH. CONSIDER THIS A FINAL WARNING.
IF I FIND YOU GOING FURTHER INTO THIS BUSINESS, I WILL HAVE NO CHOICE BUT TO BRING IT TO THE COVEN TO FORMALLY PUNISH YOU.
MS. GOOD, I THINK THAT MIGHT BE A BIT SEVERE.
MR. BOUDREAUX, I'D SUGGEST YOU SPEND MORE OF YOUR TIME WATCHING YOUR DAUGHTER AND LESS TIME QUESTIONING MY DECISIONS.
NOW, EVERYONE, RETURN TO YOUR CHAMBERS AT ONCE.

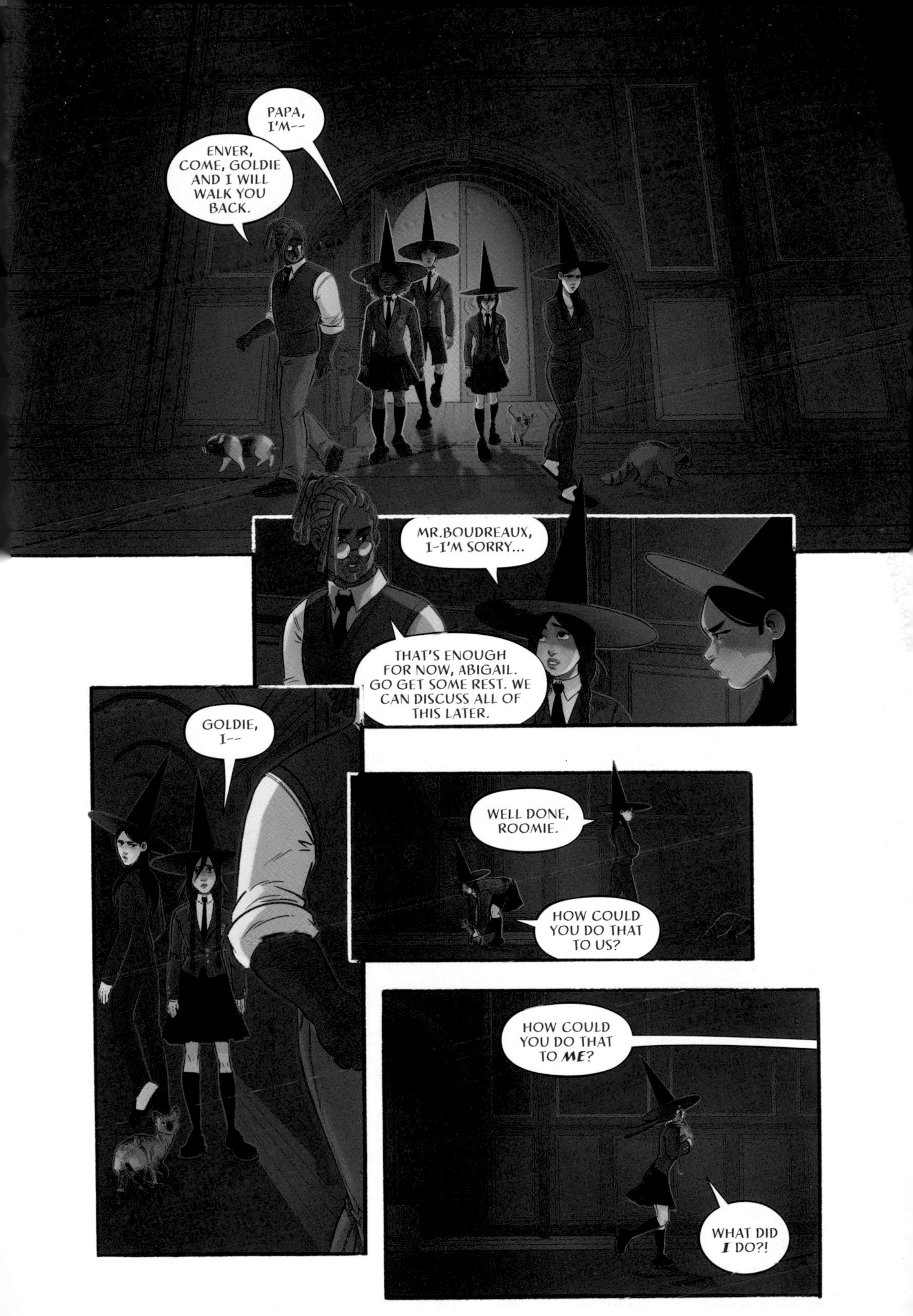
PAPA, I'M--
ENVER, COME, GOLDIE AND I WILL WALK YOU BACK.
MR.BOUDREAUX, I-I'M SORRY...
THAT'S ENOUGH FOR NOW, ABIGAIL. GO GET SOME REST. WE CAN DISCUSS ALL OF THIS LATER.
GOLDIE, I--
WELL DONE, ROOMIE.
HOW COULD YOU DO THAT TO US?
HOW COULD YOU DO THAT TO *ME*?
WHAT DID *I* DO?!

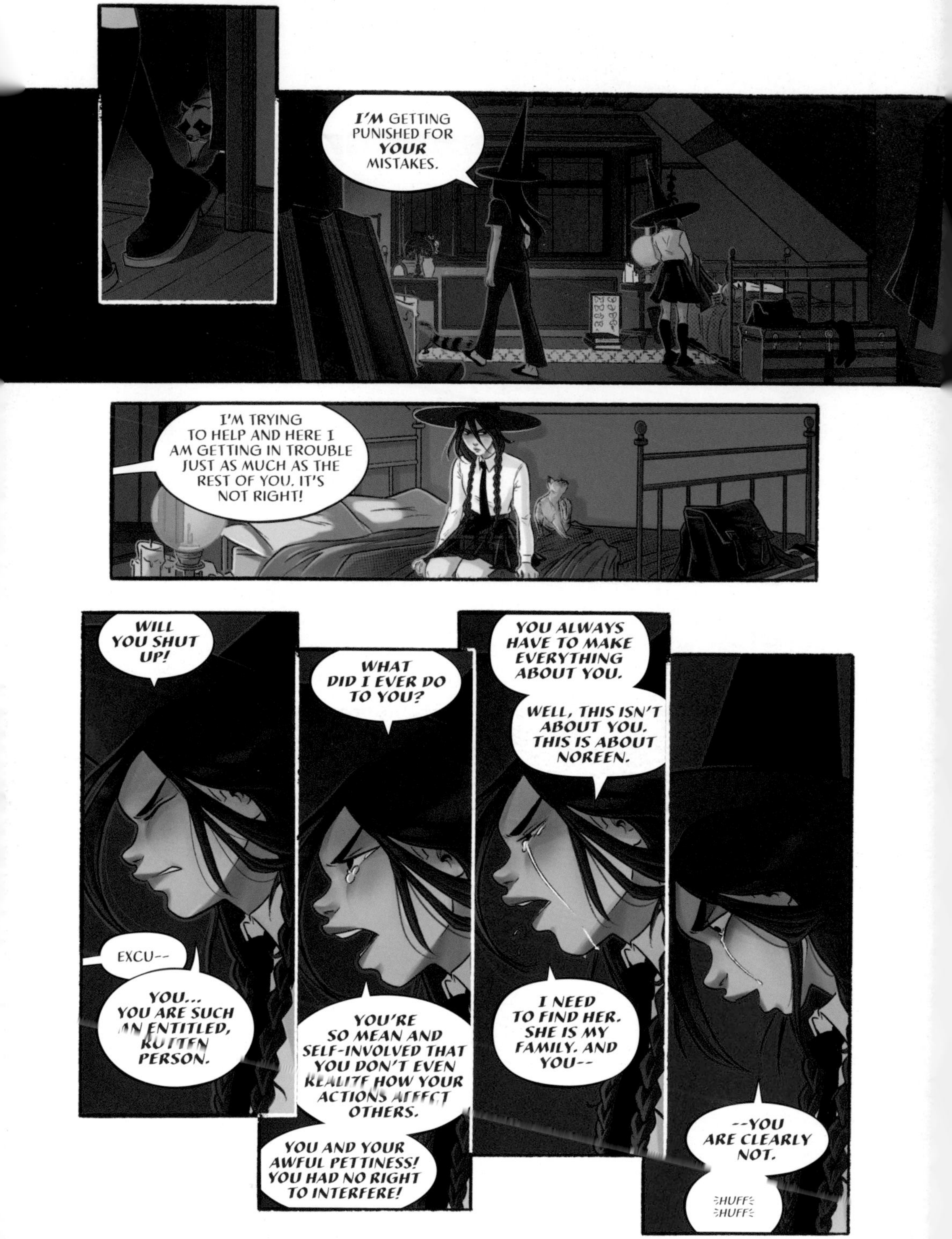
I'M GETTING PUNISHED FOR YOUR MISTAKES.
I'M TRYING TO HELP AND HERE I AM GETTING IN TROUBLE JUST AS MUCH AS THE REST OF YOU. IT'S NOT RIGHT!
WILL YOU SHUT UP!
EXCU--
YOU... YOU ARE SUCH AN ENTITLED, ROTTEN PERSON.
WHAT DID I EVER DO TO YOU?
YOU'RE SO MEAN AND SELF-INVOLVED THAT YOU DON'T EVEN REALIZE HOW YOUR ACTIONS AFFECT OTHERS.
YOU AND YOUR AWFUL PETTINESS! YOU HAD NO RIGHT TO INTERFERE!
YOU ALWAYS HAVE TO MAKE EVERYTHING ABOUT YOU.
WELL, THIS ISN'T ABOUT YOU. THIS IS ABOUT NOREEN.
I NEED TO FIND HER. SHE IS MY FAMILY. AND YOU--
--YOU ARE CLEARLY NOT.
HUFF HUFF

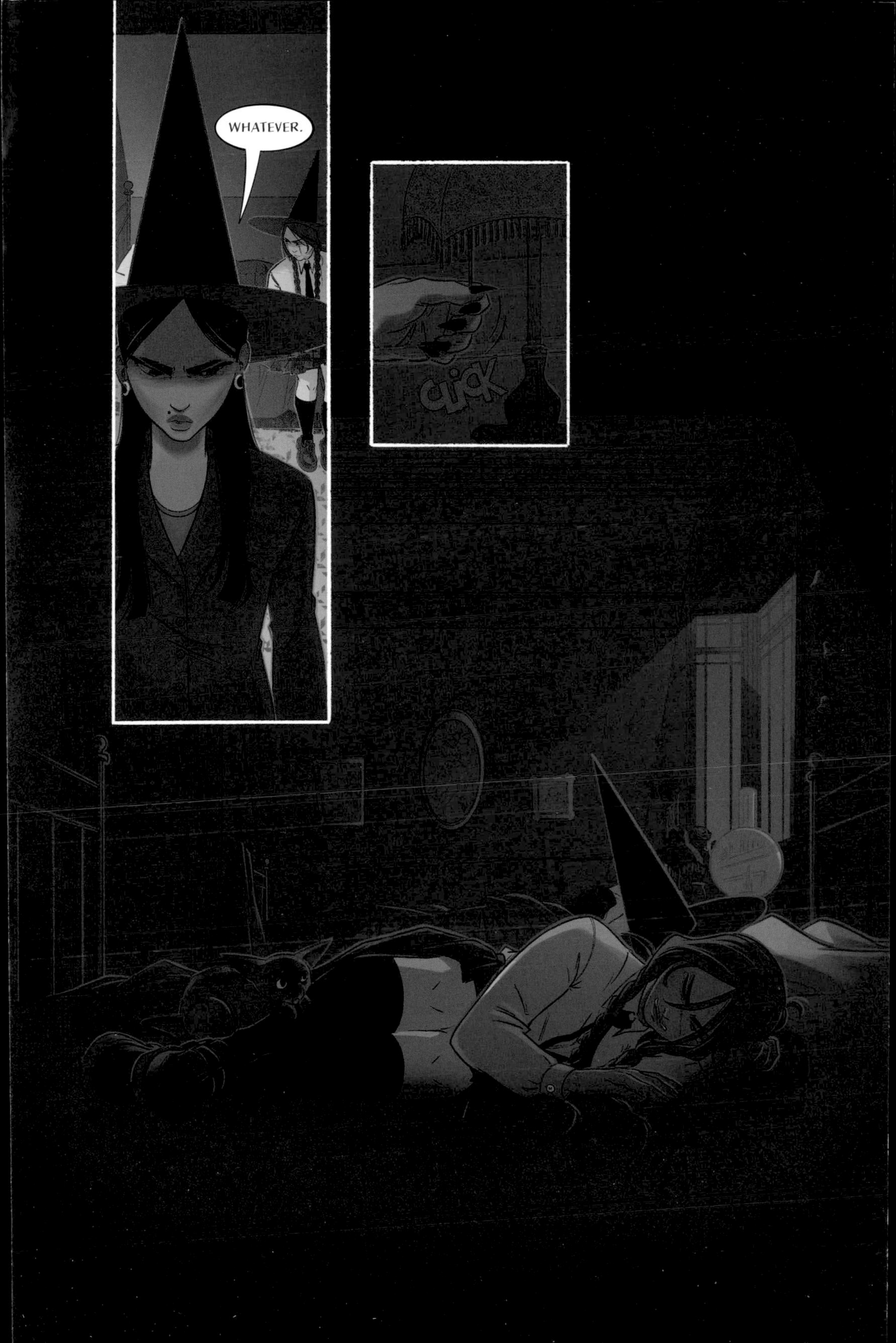
WHATEVER.
CLICK

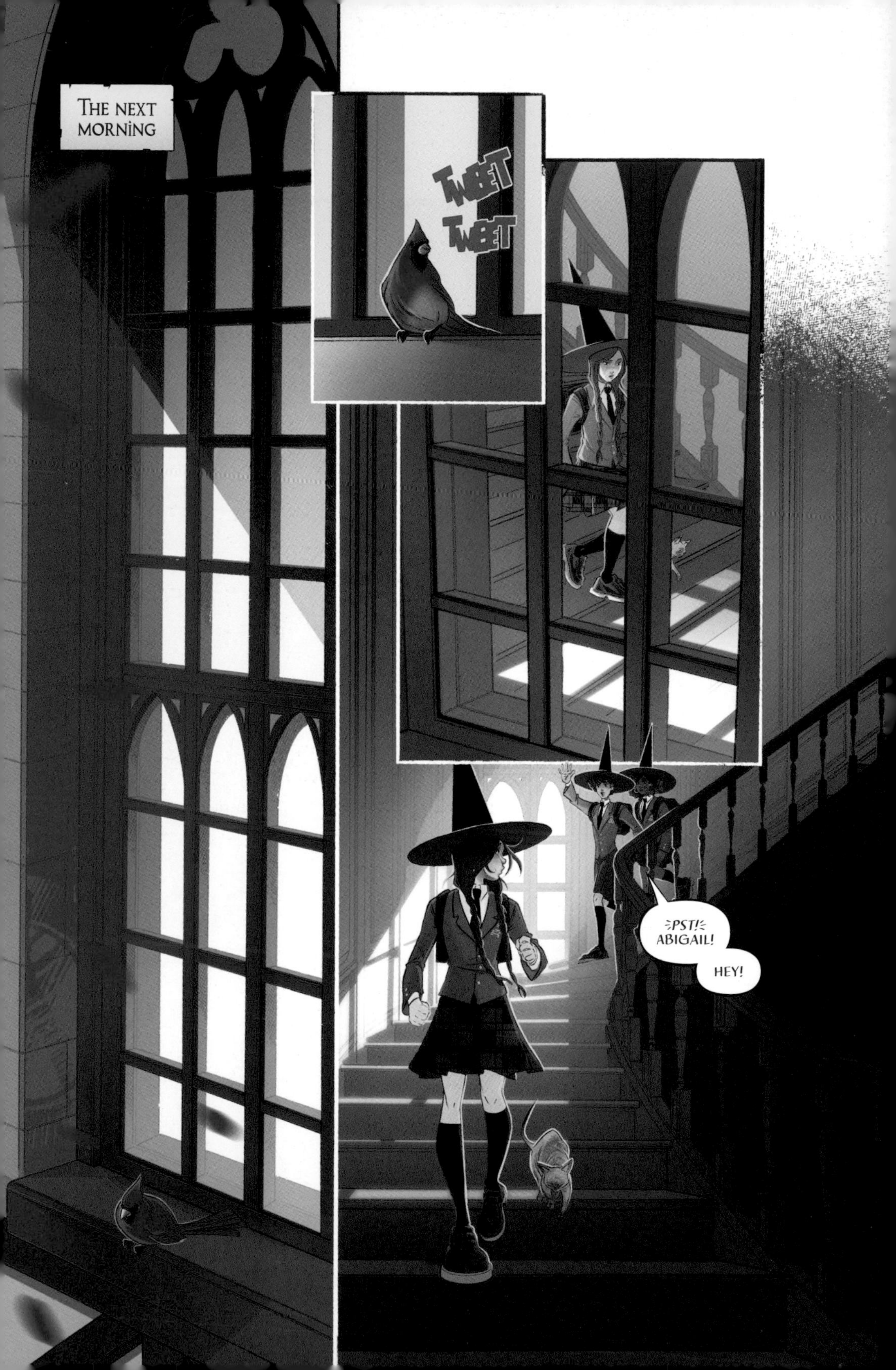
THE NEXT MORNING
TWEET TWEET
PST! ABIGAIL!
HEY!

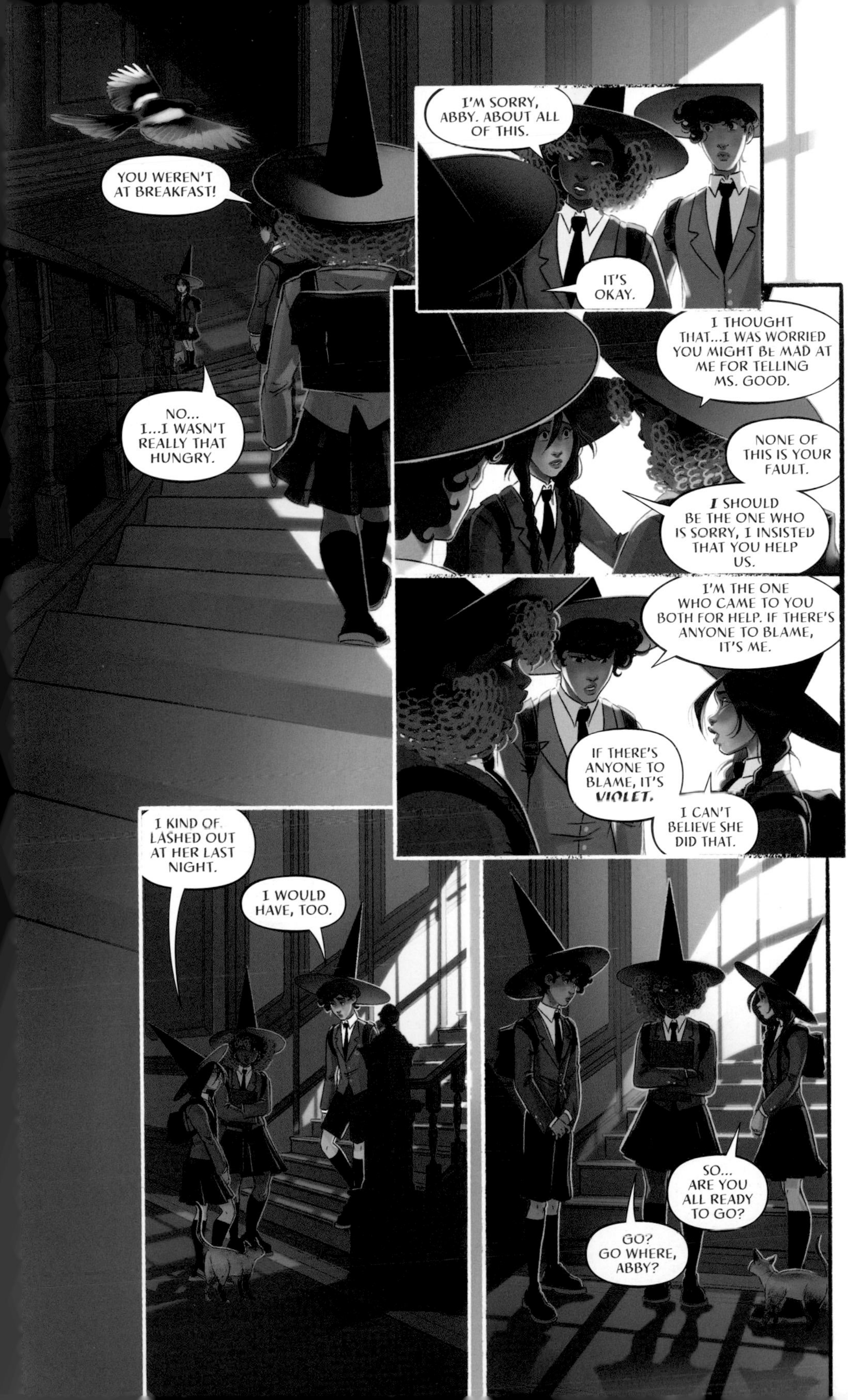
YOU WEREN'T AT BREAKFAST!
NO... I...I WASN'T REALLY THAT HUNGRY.
I'M SORRY, ABBY. ABOUT ALL OF THIS.
IT'S OKAY.
I THOUGHT THAT...I WAS WORRIED YOU MIGHT BE MAD AT ME FOR TELLING MS. GOOD.
NONE OF THIS IS YOUR FAULT.
I SHOULD BE THE ONE WHO IS SORRY, I INSISTED THAT YOU HELP US.
I'M THE ONE WHO CAME TO YOU BOTH FOR HELP. IF THERE'S ANYONE TO BLAME, IT'S ME.
IF THERE'S ANYONE TO BLAME, IT'S **VIOLET.**
I CAN'T BELIEVE SHE DID THAT.
I KIND OF LASHED OUT AT HER LAST NIGHT.
I WOULD HAVE, TOO.
SO... ARE YOU ALL READY TO GO?
GO? GO WHERE, ABBY?

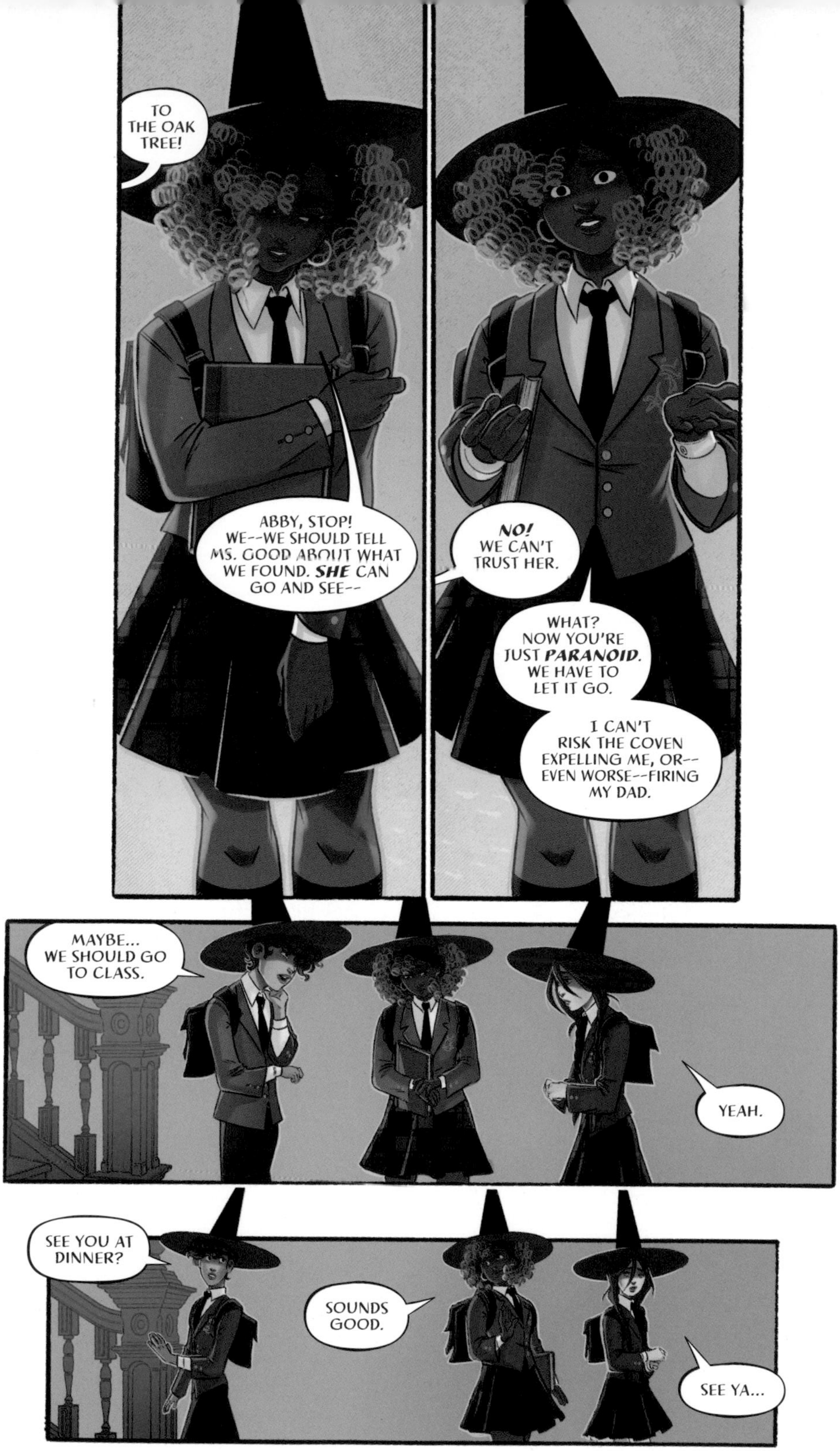
TO THE OAK TREE!
ABBY, STOP! WE--WE SHOULD TELL MS. GOOD ABOUT WHAT WE FOUND. SHE CAN GO AND SEE--
NO! WE CAN'T TRUST HER.
WHAT? NOW YOU'RE JUST PARANOID. WE HAVE TO LET IT GO.
I CAN'T RISK THE COVEN EXPELLING ME, OR--EVEN WORSE--FIRING MY DAD.
MAYBE... WE SHOULD GO TO CLASS.
YEAH.
SEE YOU AT DINNER?
SOUNDS GOOD.
SEE YA...

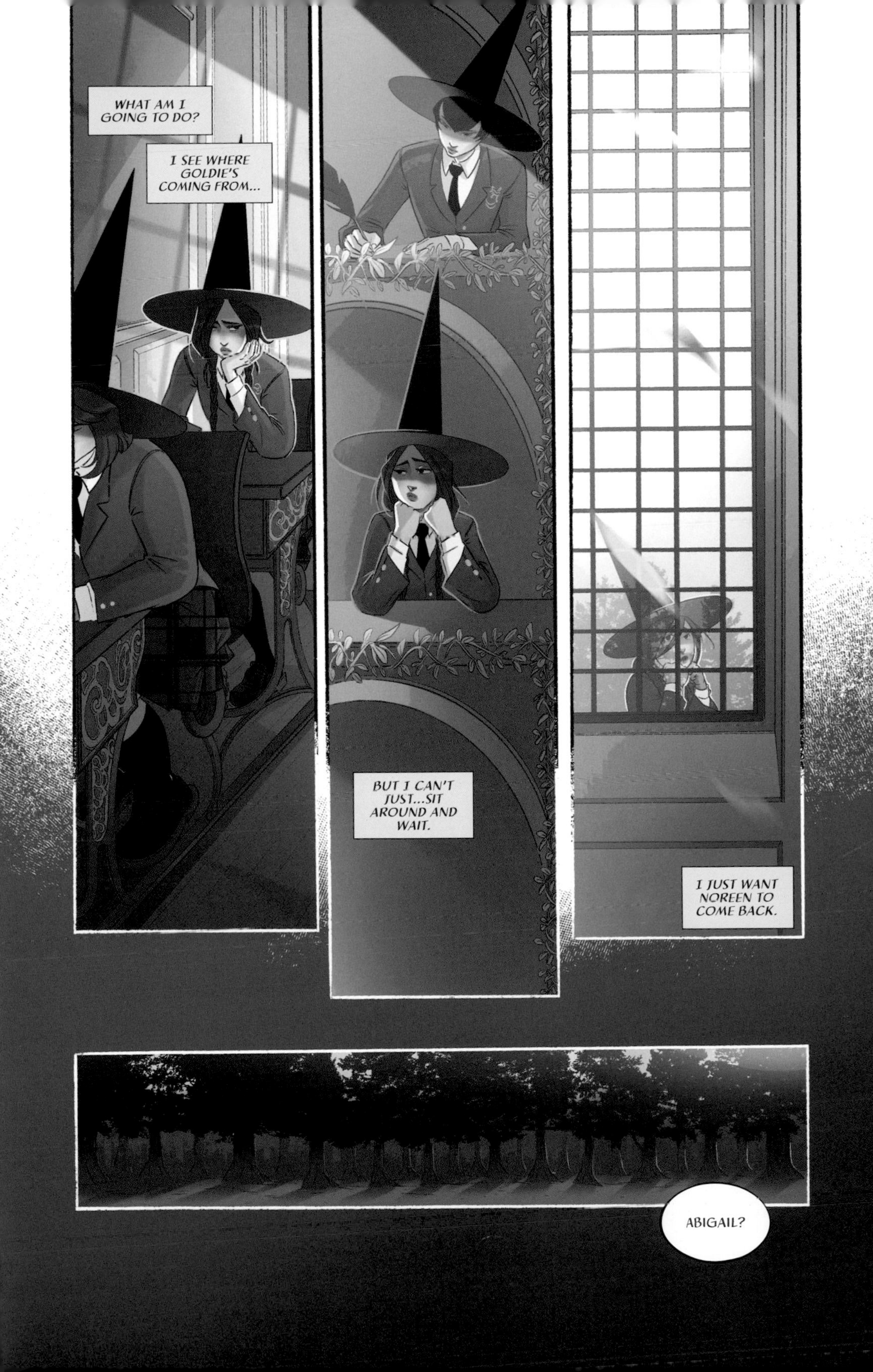
WHAT AM I GOING TO DO?
I SEE WHERE GOLDIE'S COMING FROM...
BUT I CAN'T JUST...SIT AROUND AND WAIT.
I JUST WANT NOREEN TO COME BACK.
ABIGAIL?

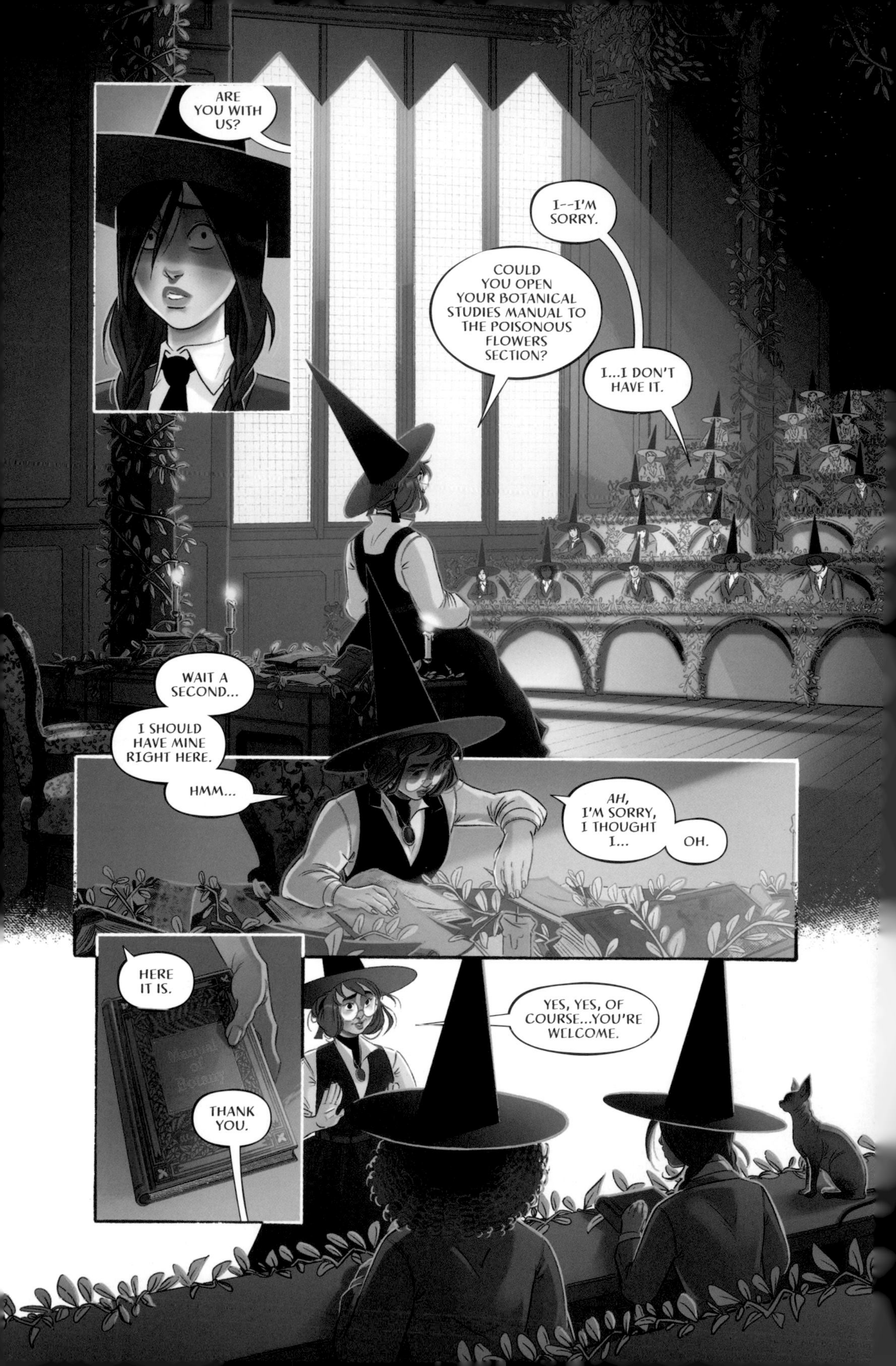
ARE YOU WITH US?
I--I'M SORRY.
COULD YOU OPEN YOUR BOTANICAL STUDIES MANUAL TO THE POISONOUS FLOWERS SECTION?
I...I DON'T HAVE IT.
WAIT A SECOND...
I SHOULD HAVE MINE RIGHT HERE.
HMM...
AH, I'M SORRY, I THOUGHT I...
OH.
HERE IT IS.
THANK YOU.
YES, YES, OF COURSE...YOU'RE WELCOME.

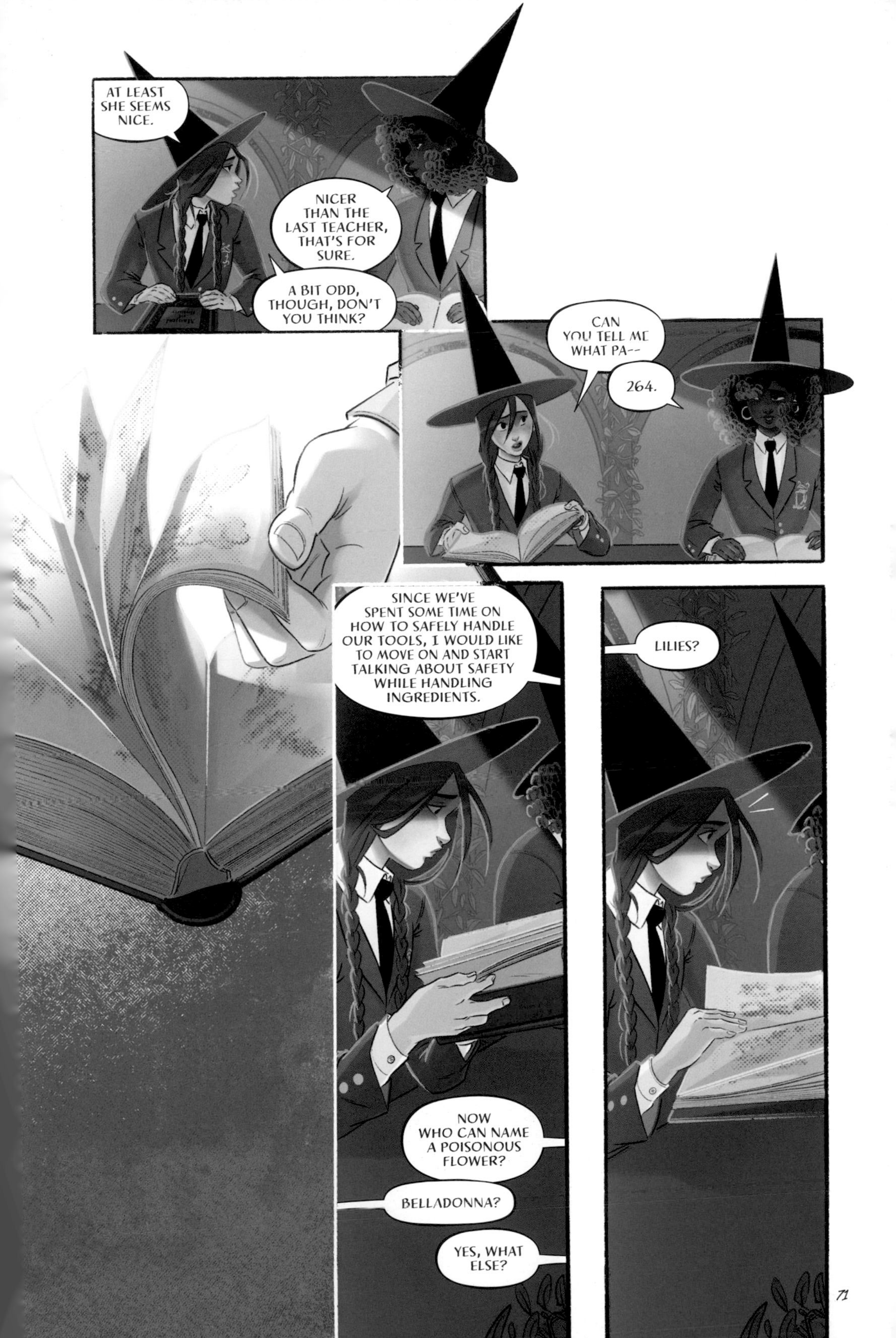
AT LEAST SHE SEEMS NICE.
NICER THAN THE LAST TEACHER, THAT'S FOR SURE.
A BIT ODD, THOUGH, DON'T YOU THINK?
CAN YOU TELL ME WHAT PA--
264.
SINCE WE'VE SPENT SOME TIME ON HOW TO SAFELY HANDLE OUR TOOLS, I WOULD LIKE TO MOVE ON AND START TALKING ABOUT SAFETY WHILE HANDLING INGREDIENTS.
NOW WHO CAN NAME A POISONOUS FLOWER?
BELLADONNA?
YES, WHAT ELSE?
LILIES?

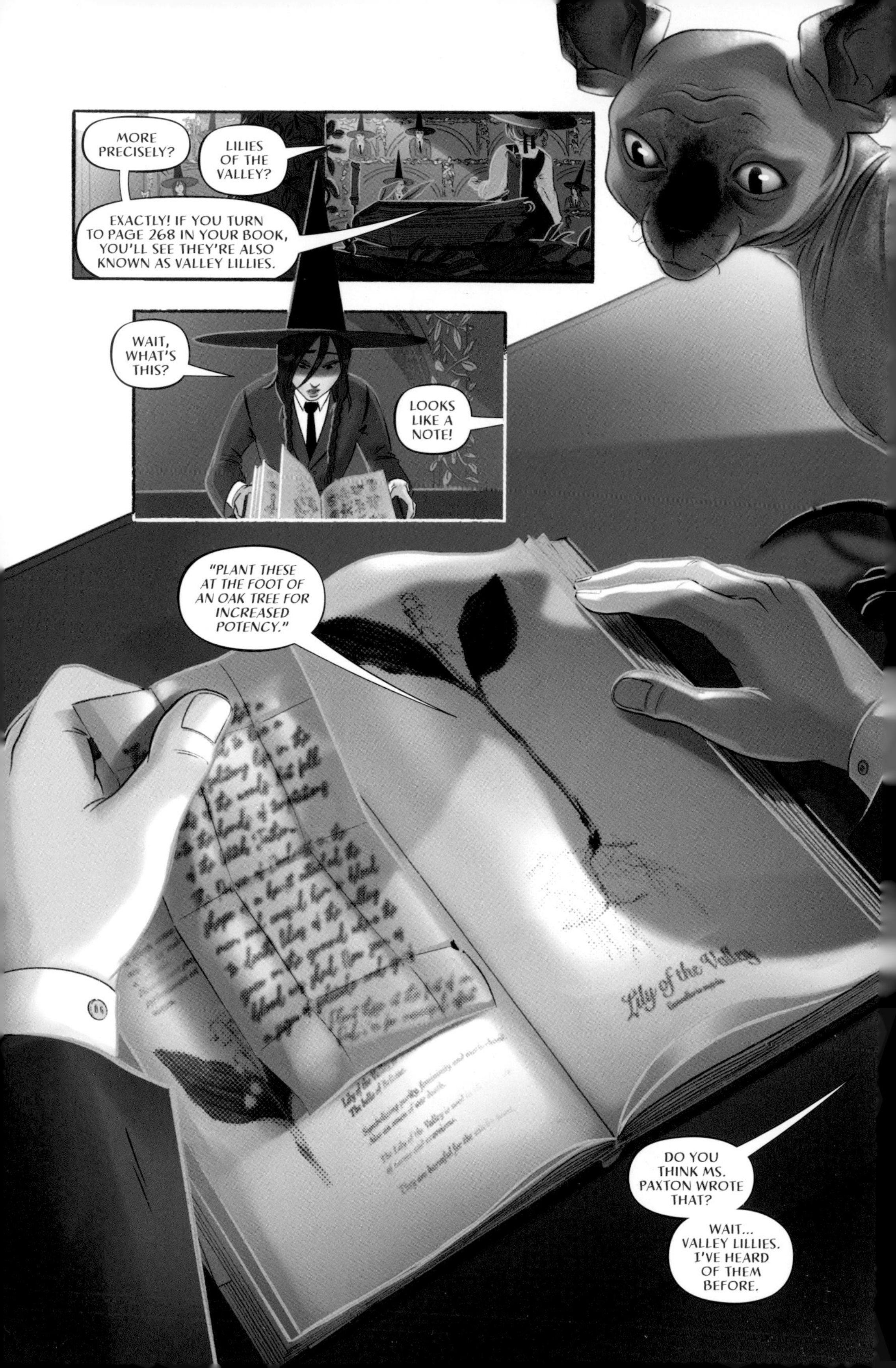
MORE PRECISELY?
LILIES OF THE VALLEY?
EXACTLY! IF YOU TURN TO PAGE 268 IN YOUR BOOK, YOU'LL SEE THEY'RE ALSO KNOWN AS VALLEY LILLIES.
WAIT, WHAT'S THIS?
LOOKS LIKE A NOTE!
"PLANT THESE AT THE FOOT OF AN OAK TREE FOR INCREASED POTENCY."
Lily of the Valley
DO YOU THINK MS. PAXTON WROTE THAT?
WAIT... VALLEY LILLIES. I'VE HEARD OF THEM BEFORE.

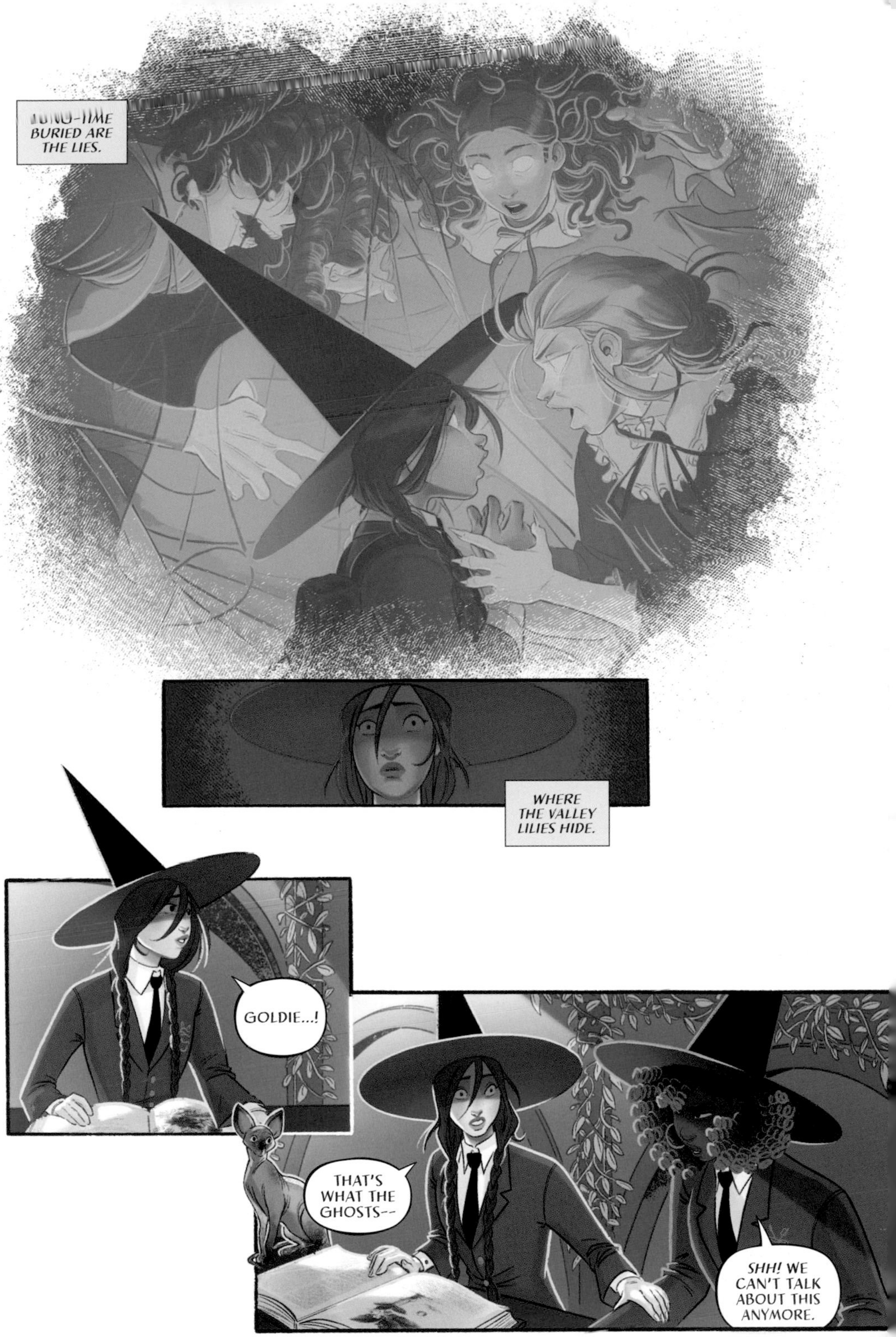
BURIED ARE THE LIES.
WHERE THE VALLEY LILIES HIDE.
GOLDIE...!
THAT'S WHAT THE GHOSTS--
SHH! WE CAN'T TALK ABOUT THIS ANYMORE.

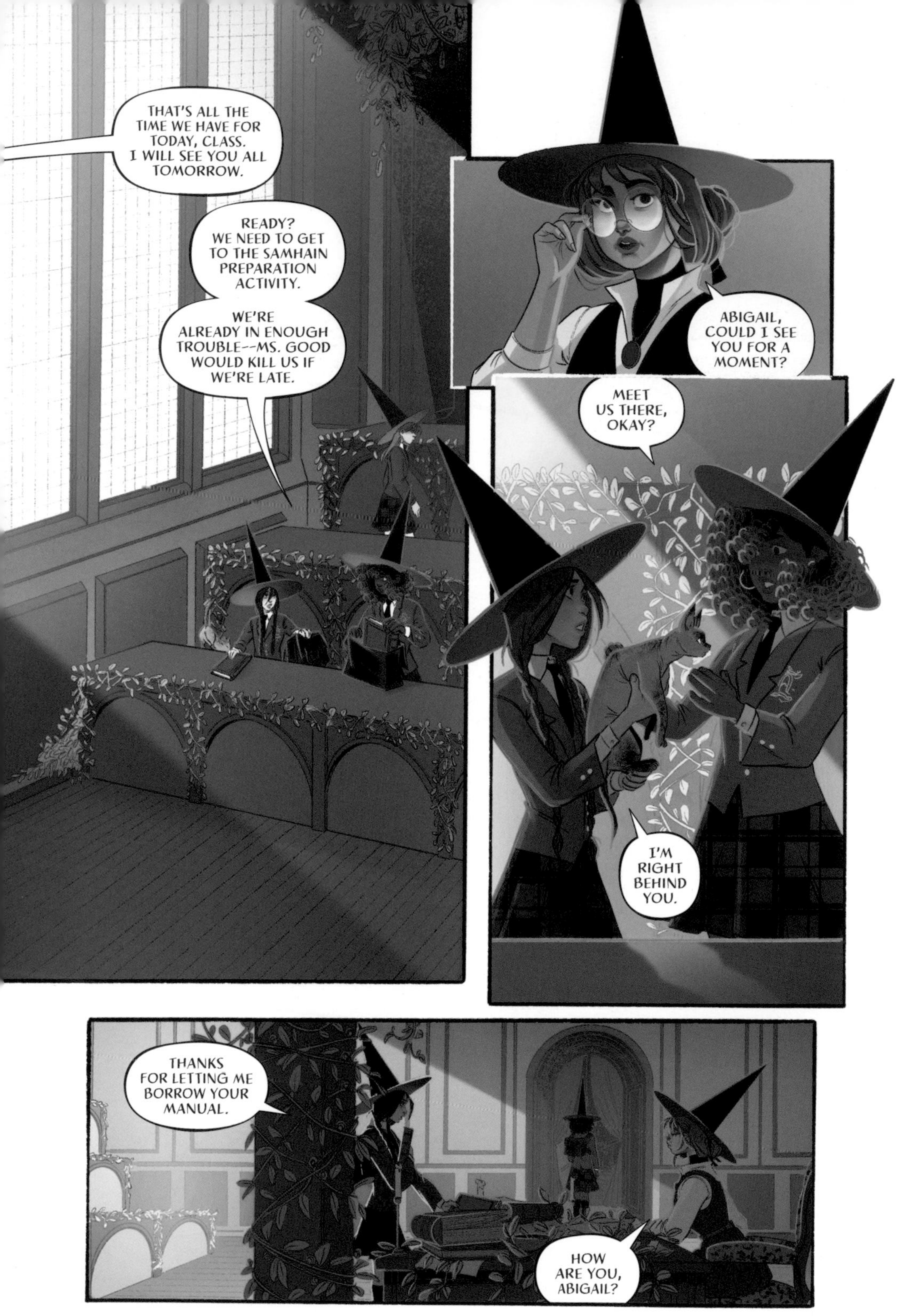
THAT'S ALL THE TIME WE HAVE FOR TODAY, CLASS. I WILL SEE YOU ALL TOMORROW.
READY? WE NEED TO GET TO THE SAMHAIN PREPARATION ACTIVITY.
WE'RE ALREADY IN ENOUGH TROUBLE--MS. GOOD WOULD KILL US IF WE'RE LATE.
ABIGAIL, COULD I SEE YOU FOR A MOMENT?
MEET US THERE, OKAY?
I'M RIGHT BEHIND YOU.
THANKS FOR LETTING ME BORROW YOUR MANUAL.
HOW ARE YOU, ABIGAIL?

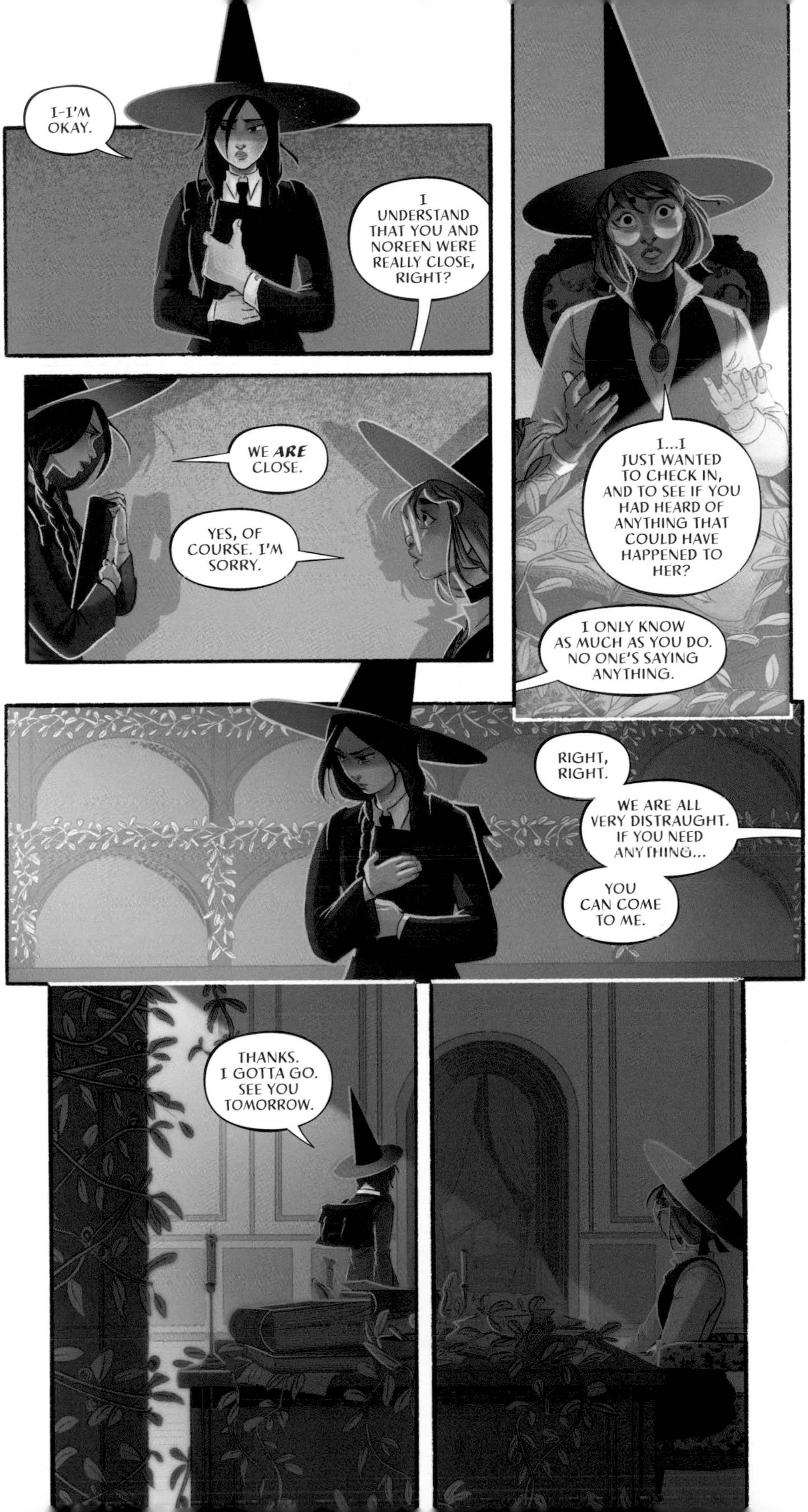
I-I'M OKAY.
I UNDERSTAND THAT YOU AND NOREEN WERE REALLY CLOSE, RIGHT?
WE *ARE* CLOSE.
YES, OF COURSE. I'M SORRY.
I...I JUST WANTED TO CHECK IN, AND TO SEE IF YOU HAD HEARD OF ANYTHING THAT COULD HAVE HAPPENED TO HER?
I ONLY KNOW AS MUCH AS YOU DO. NO ONE'S SAYING ANYTHING.
RIGHT, RIGHT.
WE ARE ALL VERY DISTRAUGHT. IF YOU NEED ANYTHING...
YOU CAN COME TO ME.
THANKS. I GOTTA GO. SEE YOU TOMORROW.

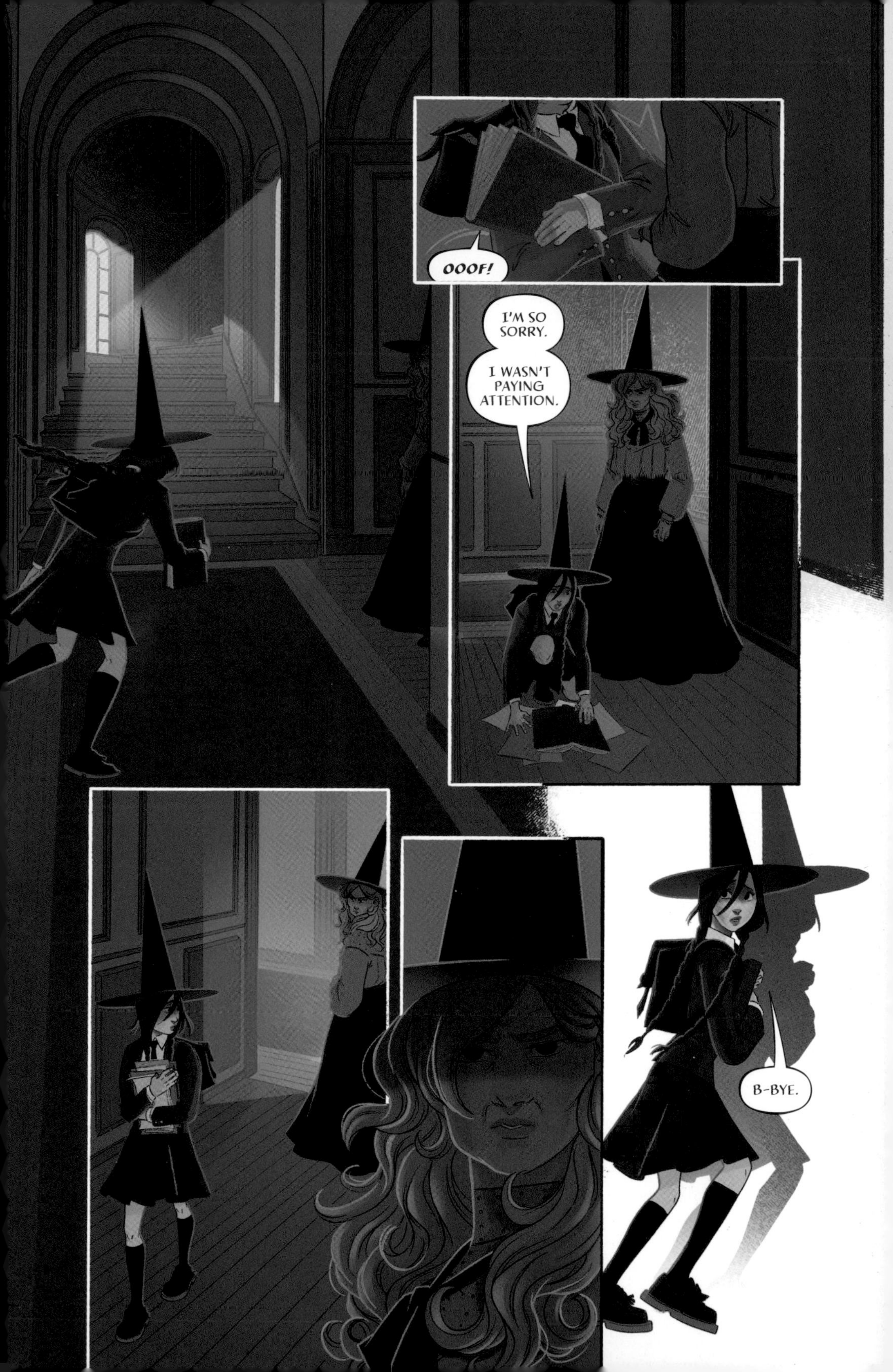
OOOF!
I'M SO SORRY.
I WASN'T PAYING ATTENTION.
B-BYE.

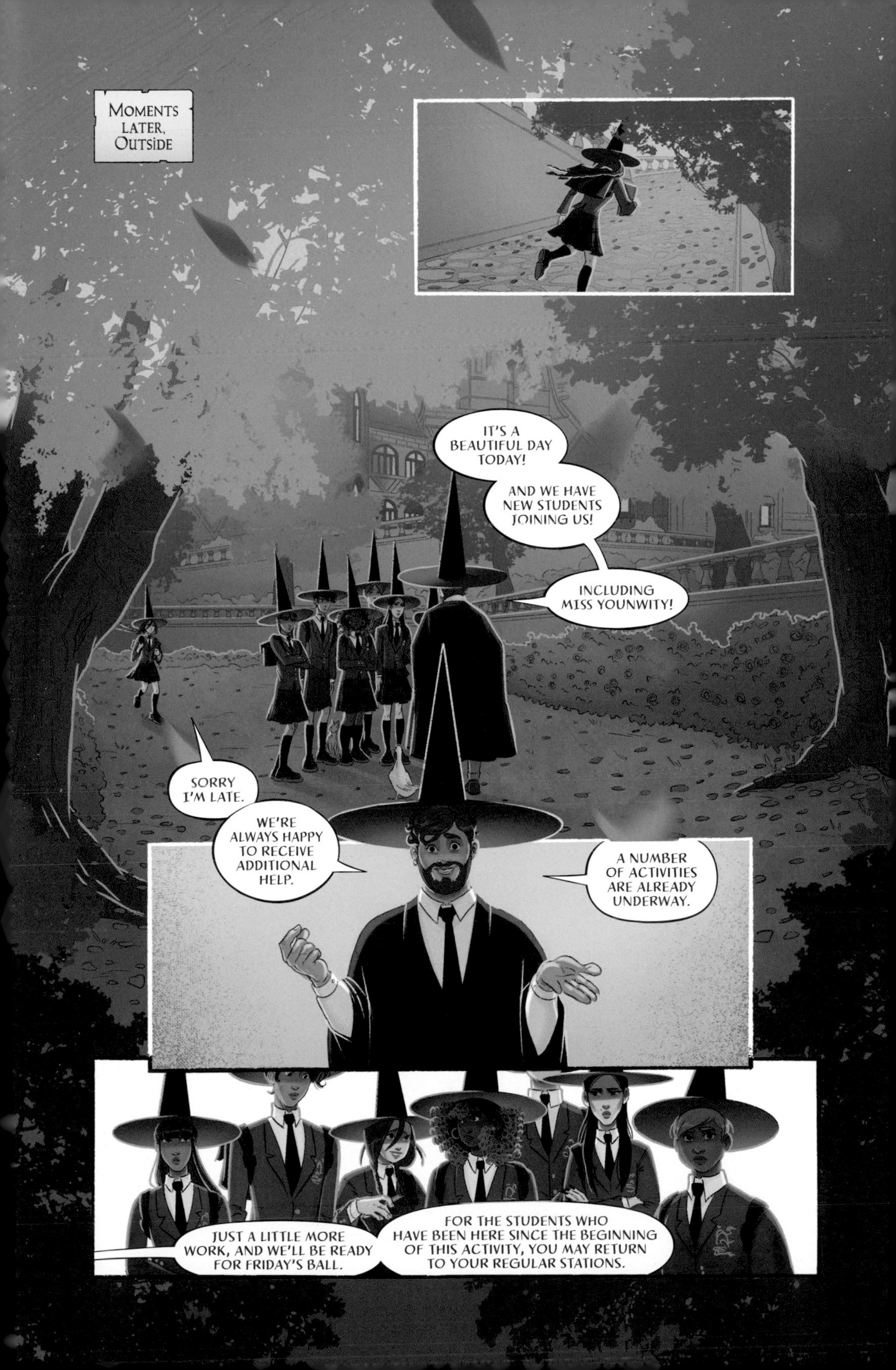
Moments later, Outside
It's a beautiful day today!
And we have new students joining us!
Including Miss Younwity!
Sorry I'm late.
We're always happy to receive additional help.
A number of activities are already underway.
Just a little more work, and we'll be ready for Friday's ball.
For the students who have been here since the beginning of this activity, you may return to your regular stations.

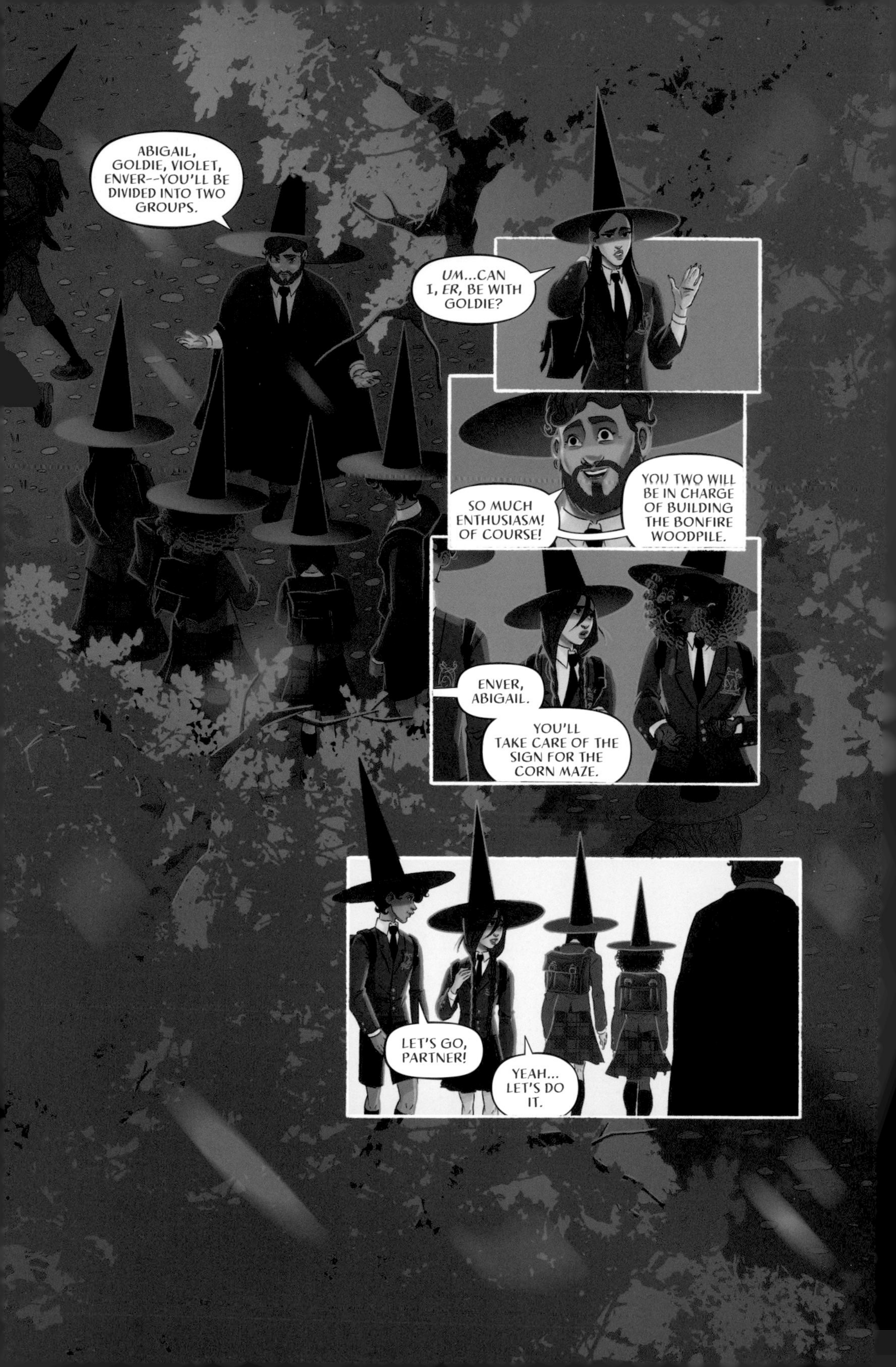
ABIGAIL, GOLDIE, VIOLET, ENVER--YOU'LL BE DIVIDED INTO TWO GROUPS.
UM...CAN I, *ER*, BE WITH GOLDIE?
SO MUCH ENTHUSIASM! OF COURSE!
YOU TWO WILL BE IN CHARGE OF BUILDING THE BONFIRE WOODPILE.
ENVER, ABIGAIL.
YOU'LL TAKE CARE OF THE SIGN FOR THE CORN MAZE.
LET'S GO, PARTNER!
YEAH... LET'S DO IT.

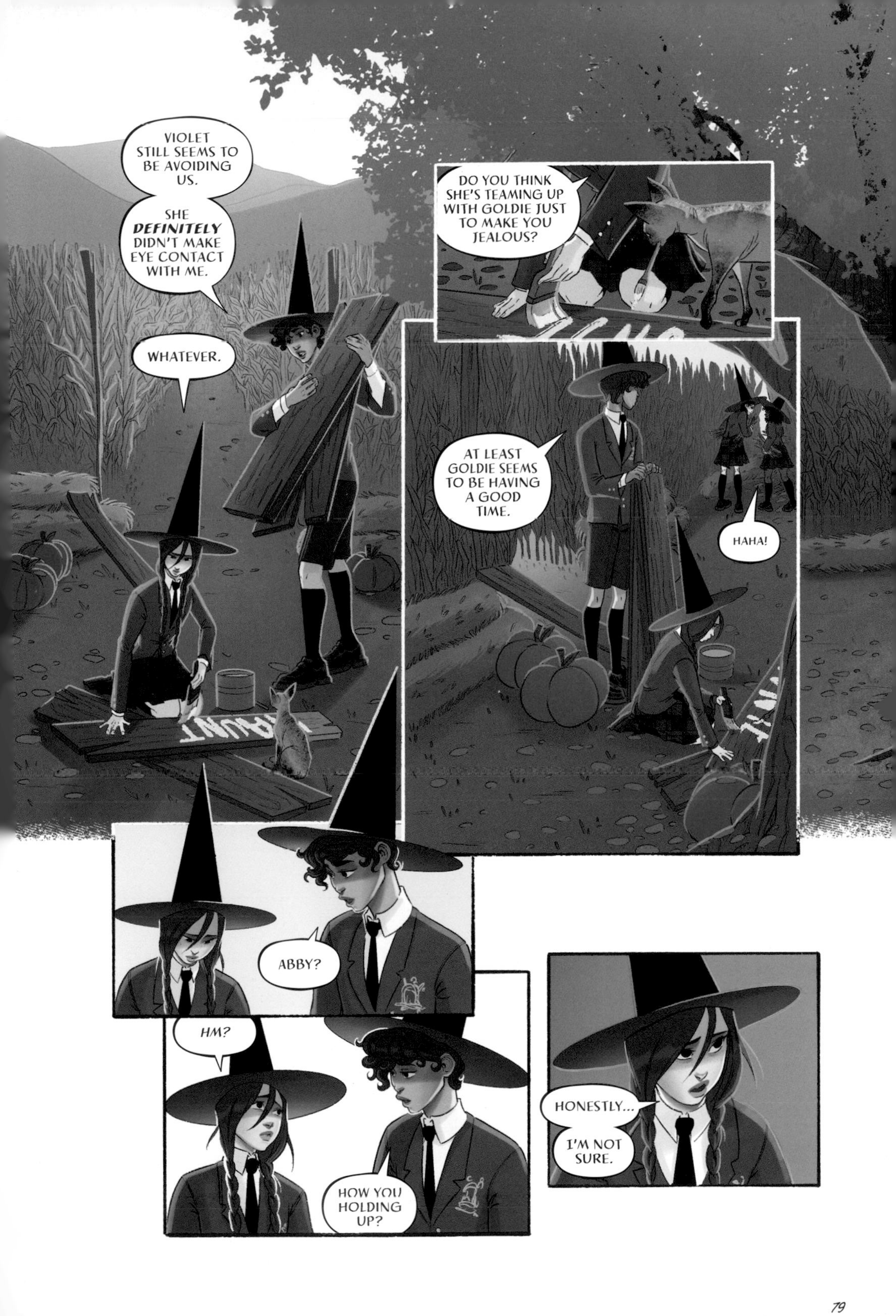
VIOLET STILL SEEMS TO BE AVOIDING US.
SHE *DEFINITELY* DIDN'T MAKE EYE CONTACT WITH ME.
WHATEVER.
DO YOU THINK SHE'S TEAMING UP WITH GOLDIE JUST TO MAKE YOU JEALOUS?
AT LEAST GOLDIE SEEMS TO BE HAVING A GOOD TIME.
HAHA!
ABBY?
HM?
HOW YOU HOLDING UP?
HONESTLY...
I'M NOT SURE.

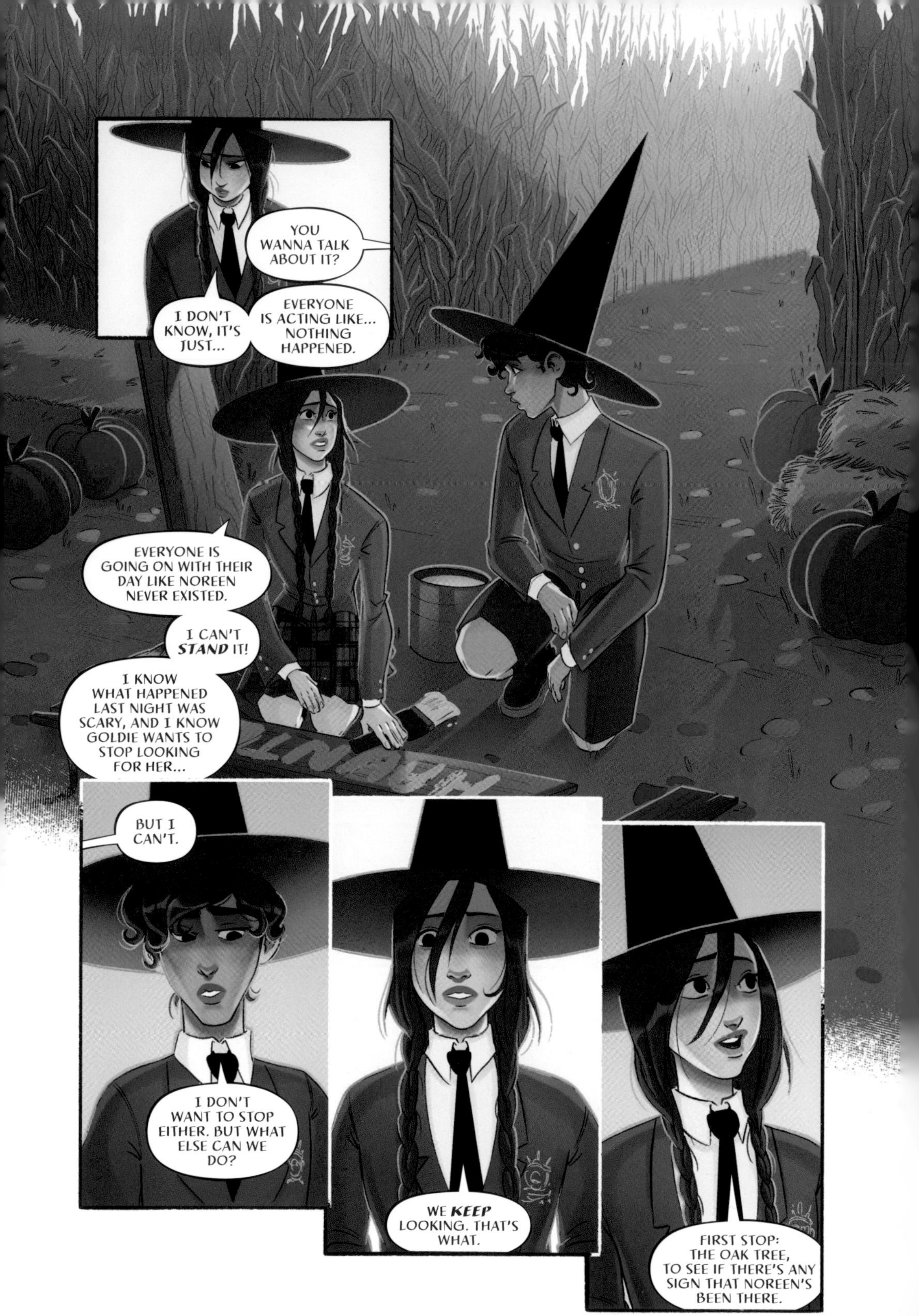
YOU WANNA TALK ABOUT IT?
I DON'T KNOW, IT'S JUST...
EVERYONE IS ACTING LIKE... NOTHING HAPPENED.
EVERYONE IS GOING ON WITH THEIR DAY LIKE NOREEN NEVER EXISTED.
I CAN'T ***STAND*** IT!
I KNOW WHAT HAPPENED LAST NIGHT WAS SCARY, AND I KNOW GOLDIE WANTS TO STOP LOOKING FOR HER...
BUT I CAN'T.
I DON'T WANT TO STOP EITHER. BUT WHAT ELSE CAN WE DO?
WE ***KEEP*** LOOKING. THAT'S WHAT.
FIRST STOP: THE OAK TREE, TO SEE IF THERE'S ANY SIGN THAT NOREEN'S BEEN THERE.

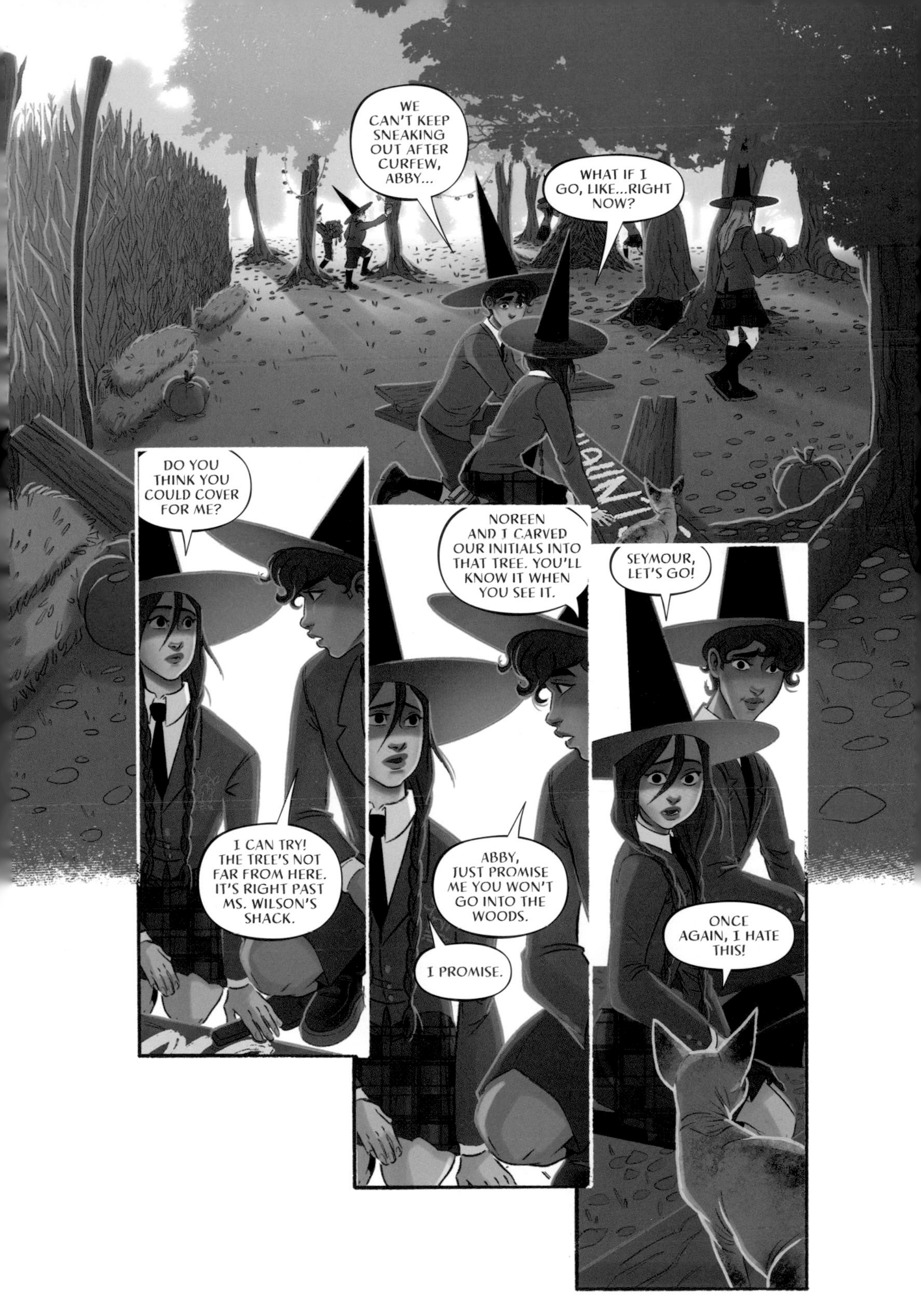
WE CAN'T KEEP SNEAKING OUT AFTER CURFEW, ABBY...
WHAT IF I GO, LIKE...RIGHT NOW?
DO YOU THINK YOU COULD COVER FOR ME?
I CAN TRY! THE TREE'S NOT FAR FROM HERE. IT'S RIGHT PAST MS. WILSON'S SHACK.
NOREEN AND I CARVED OUR INITIALS INTO THAT TREE. YOU'LL KNOW IT WHEN YOU SEE IT.
ABBY, JUST PROMISE ME YOU WON'T GO INTO THE WOODS.
I PROMISE.
SEYMOUR, LET'S GO!
ONCE AGAIN, I HATE THIS!

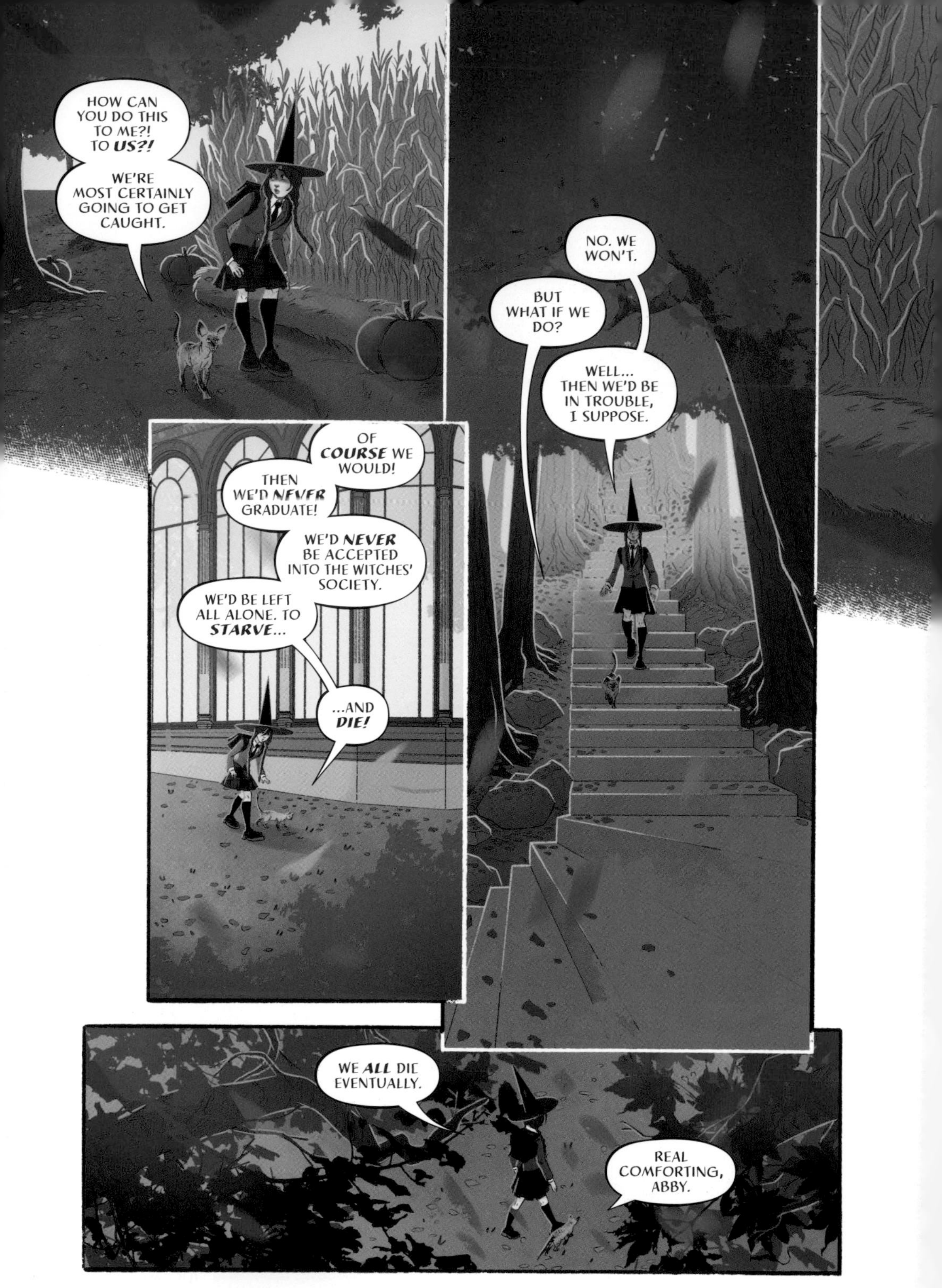

HOW CAN YOU DO THIS TO ME?! TO US?!
WE'RE MOST CERTAINLY GOING TO GET CAUGHT.
NO. WE WON'T.
BUT WHAT IF WE DO?
WELL... THEN WE'D BE IN TROUBLE, I SUPPOSE.
OF COURSE WE WOULD!
THEN WE'D NEVER GRADUATE!
WE'D NEVER BE ACCEPTED INTO THE WITCHES' SOCIETY.
WE'D BE LEFT ALL ALONE. TO STARVE...
...AND DIE!
WE ALL DIE EVENTUALLY.
REAL COMFORTING, ABBY.

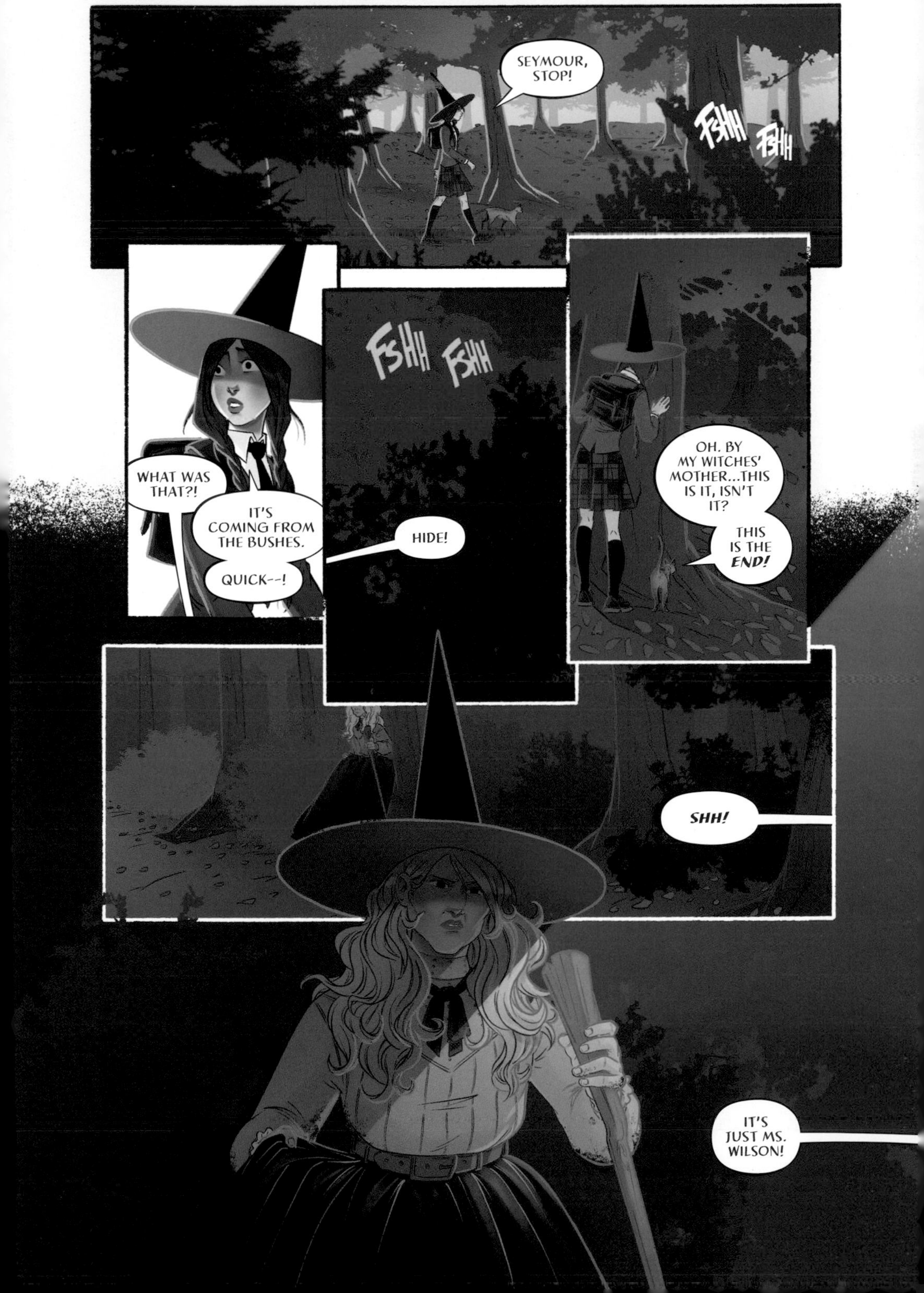
SEYMOUR, STOP!
FSHH FSHH
WHAT WAS THAT?!
IT'S COMING FROM THE BUSHES.
QUICK--!
FSHH FSHH
HIDE!
OH. BY MY WITCHES' MOTHER...THIS IS IT, ISN'T IT?
THIS IS THE *END!*
SHH!
IT'S JUST MS. WILSON!

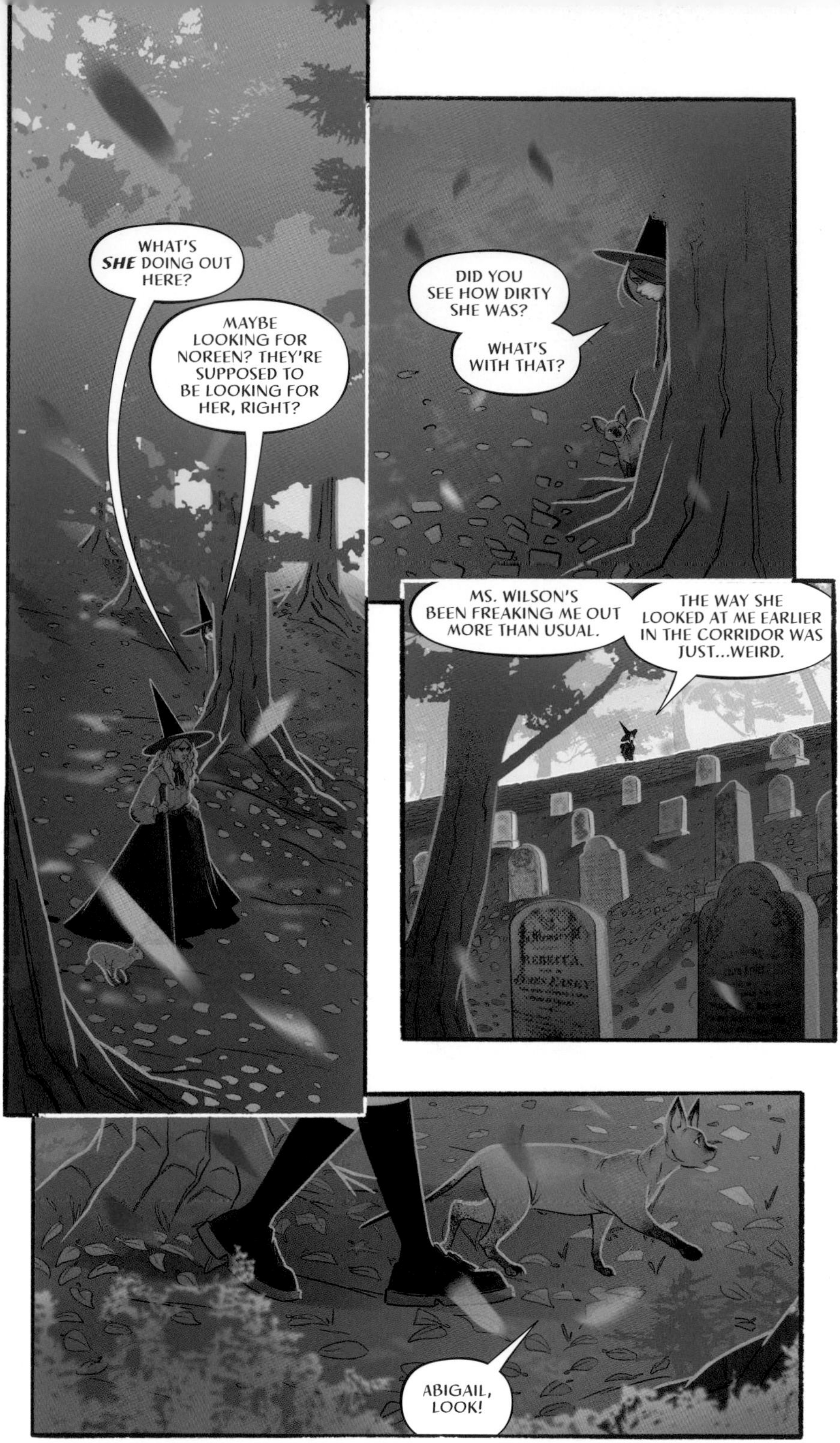
WHAT'S *SHE* DOING OUT HERE?
MAYBE LOOKING FOR NOREEN? THEY'RE SUPPOSED TO BE LOOKING FOR HER, RIGHT?
DID YOU SEE HOW DIRTY SHE WAS?
WHAT'S WITH THAT?
MS. WILSON'S BEEN FREAKING ME OUT MORE THAN USUAL.
THE WAY SHE LOOKED AT ME EARLIER IN THE CORRIDOR WAS JUST...WEIRD.
ABIGAIL, LOOK!

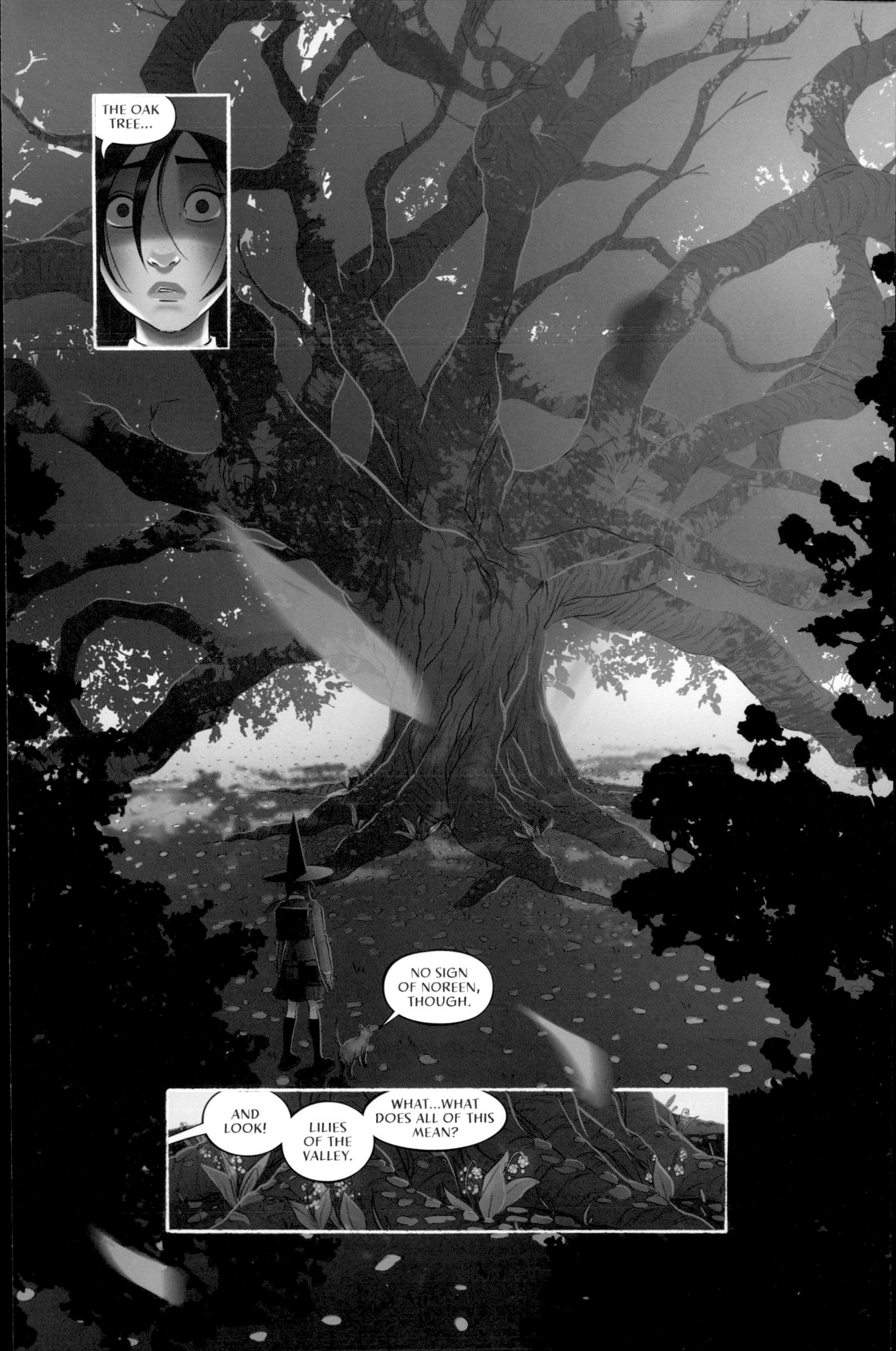
THE OAK TREE...
NO SIGN OF NOREEN, THOUGH.
AND LOOK!
LILIES OF THE VALLEY.
WHAT...WHAT DOES ALL OF THIS MEAN?

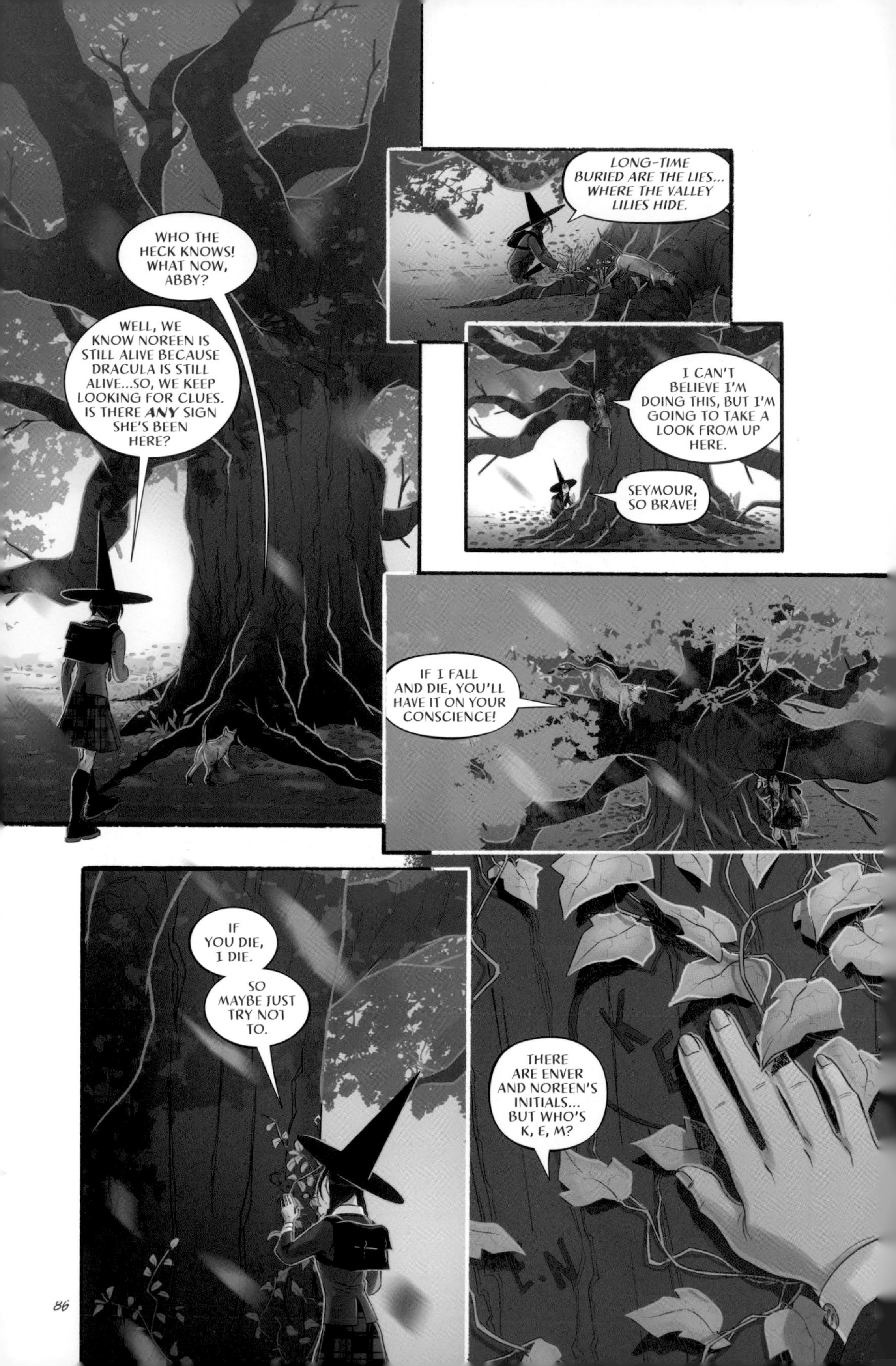
WHO THE HECK KNOWS! WHAT NOW, ABBY?
WELL, WE KNOW NOREEN IS STILL ALIVE BECAUSE DRACULA IS STILL ALIVE...SO, WE KEEP LOOKING FOR CLUES. IS THERE ***ANY*** SIGN SHE'S BEEN HERE?
LONG-TIME BURIED ARE THE LIES... WHERE THE VALLEY LILIES HIDE.
I CAN'T BELIEVE I'M DOING THIS, BUT I'M GOING TO TAKE A LOOK FROM UP HERE.
SEYMOUR, SO BRAVE!
IF I FALL AND DIE, YOU'LL HAVE IT ON YOUR CONSCIENCE!
IF YOU DIE, I DIE.
SO MAYBE JUST TRY NOT TO.
THERE ARE ENVER AND NOREEN'S INITIALS... BUT WHO'S K, E, M?

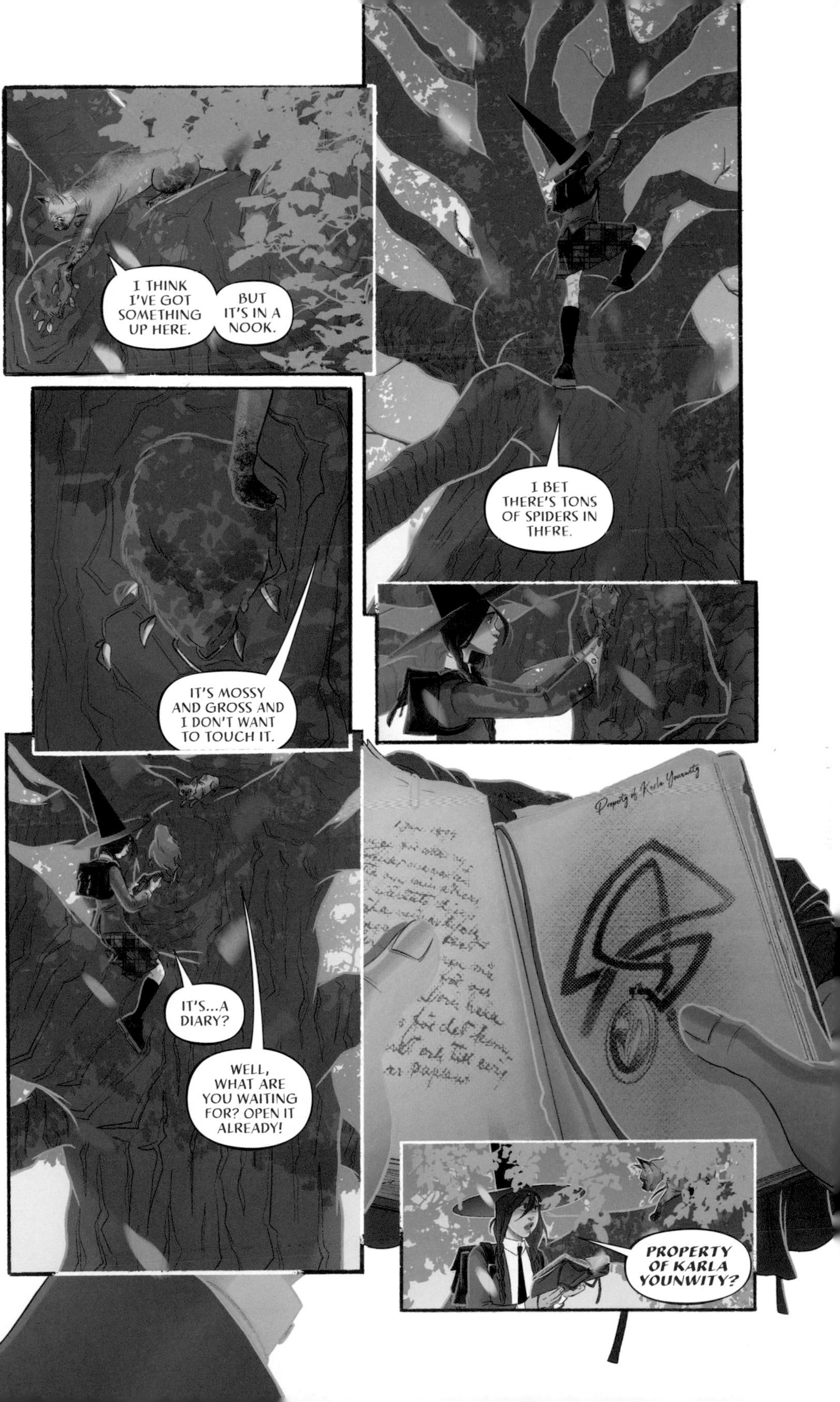
I THINK I'VE GOT SOMETHING UP HERE.
BUT IT'S IN A NOOK.
I BET THERE'S TONS OF SPIDERS IN THERE.
IT'S MOSSY AND GROSS AND I DON'T WANT TO TOUCH IT.
IT'S...A DIARY?
WELL, WHAT ARE YOU WAITING FOR? OPEN IT ALREADY!
Property of Karla Younwity
PROPERTY OF KARLA YOUNWITY?

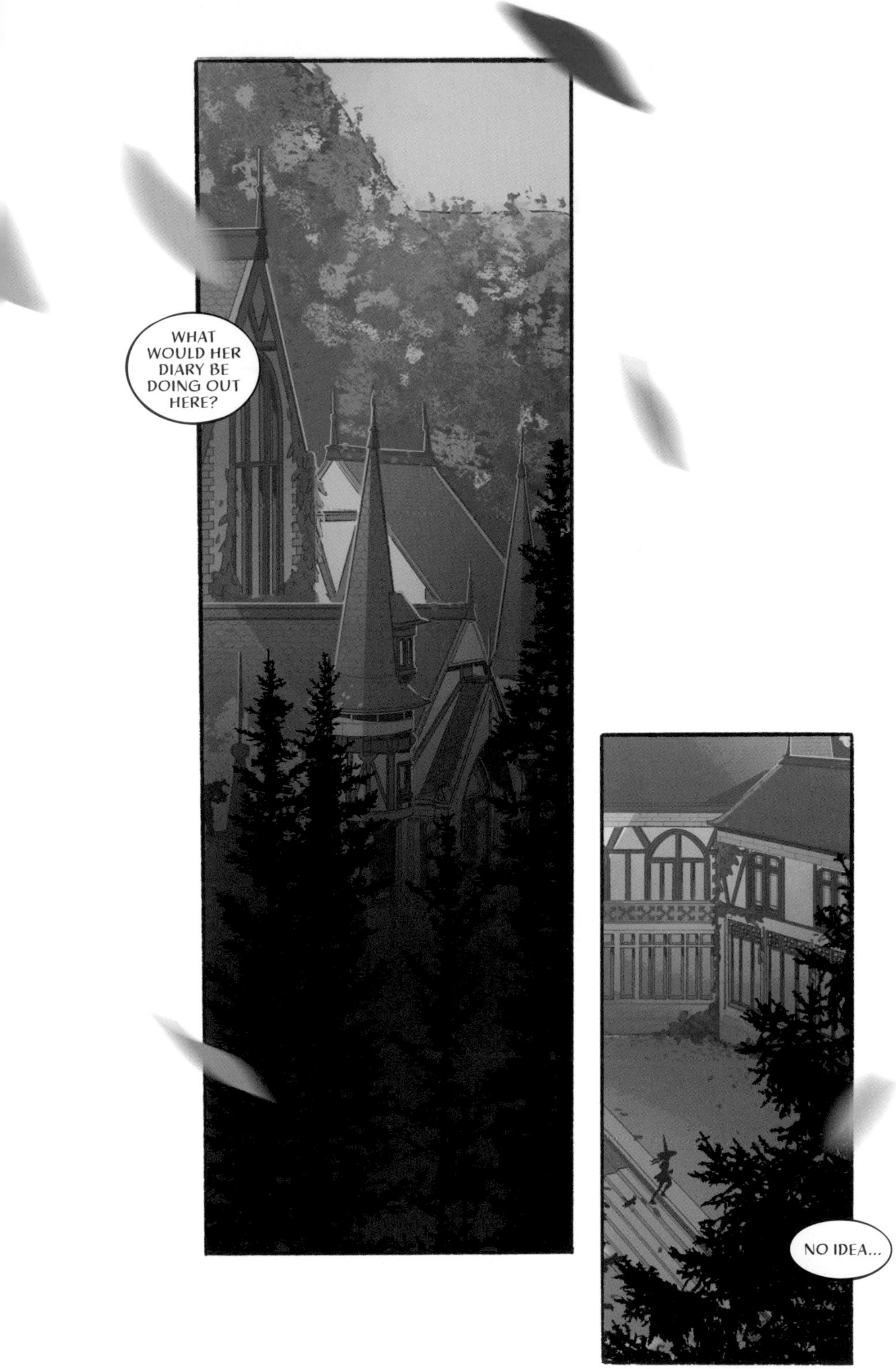
WHAT WOULD HER DIARY BE DOING OUT HERE?
NO IDEA...

CHAPTER III

Then -- in my childhood -- in the dawn
Of a most stormy life -- was drawn
From ev'ry depth of good and ill
The mystery which binds me still --

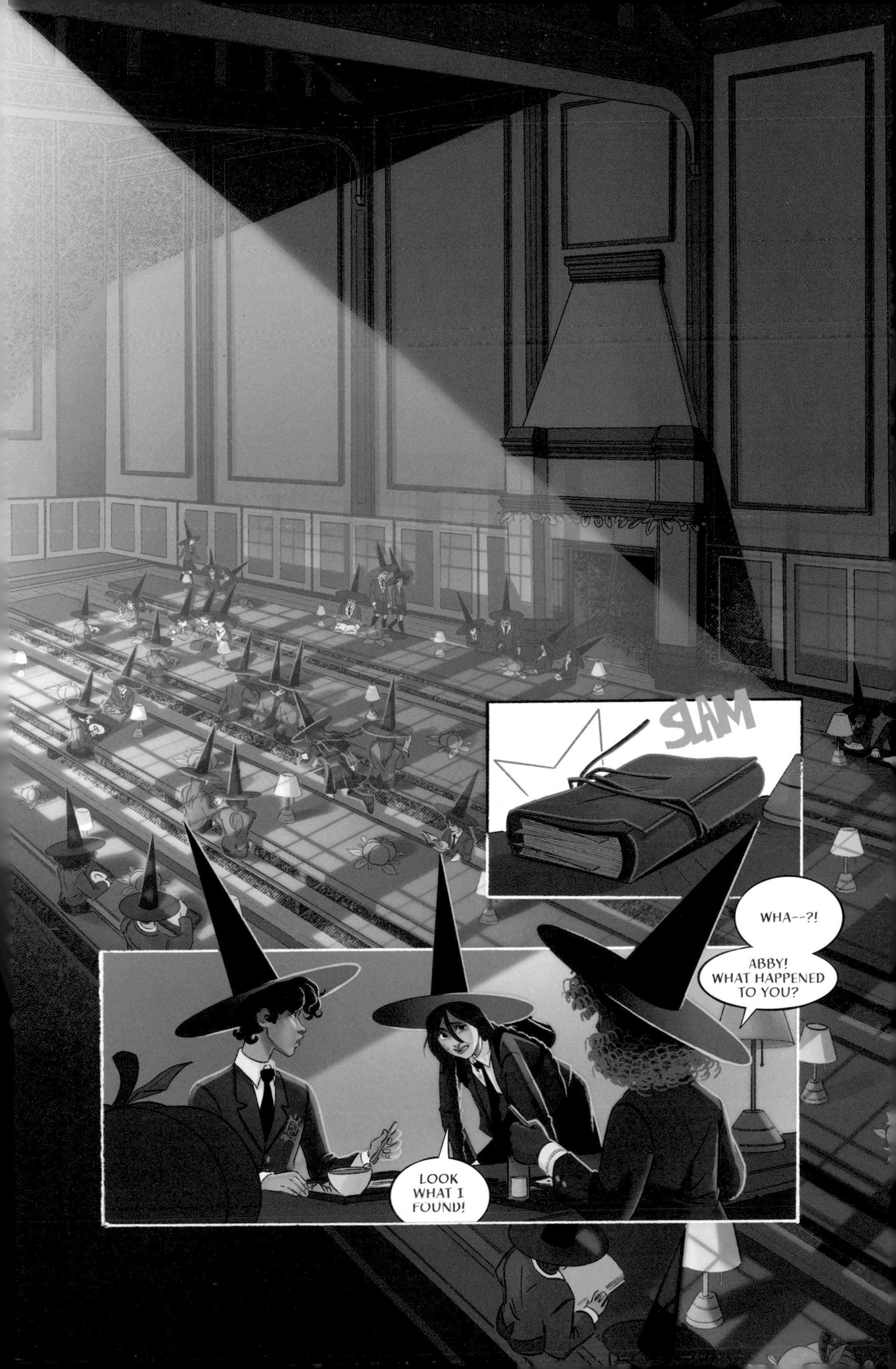
SLAM
WHA--?!
ABBY! WHAT HAPPENED TO YOU?
LOOK WHAT I FOUND!

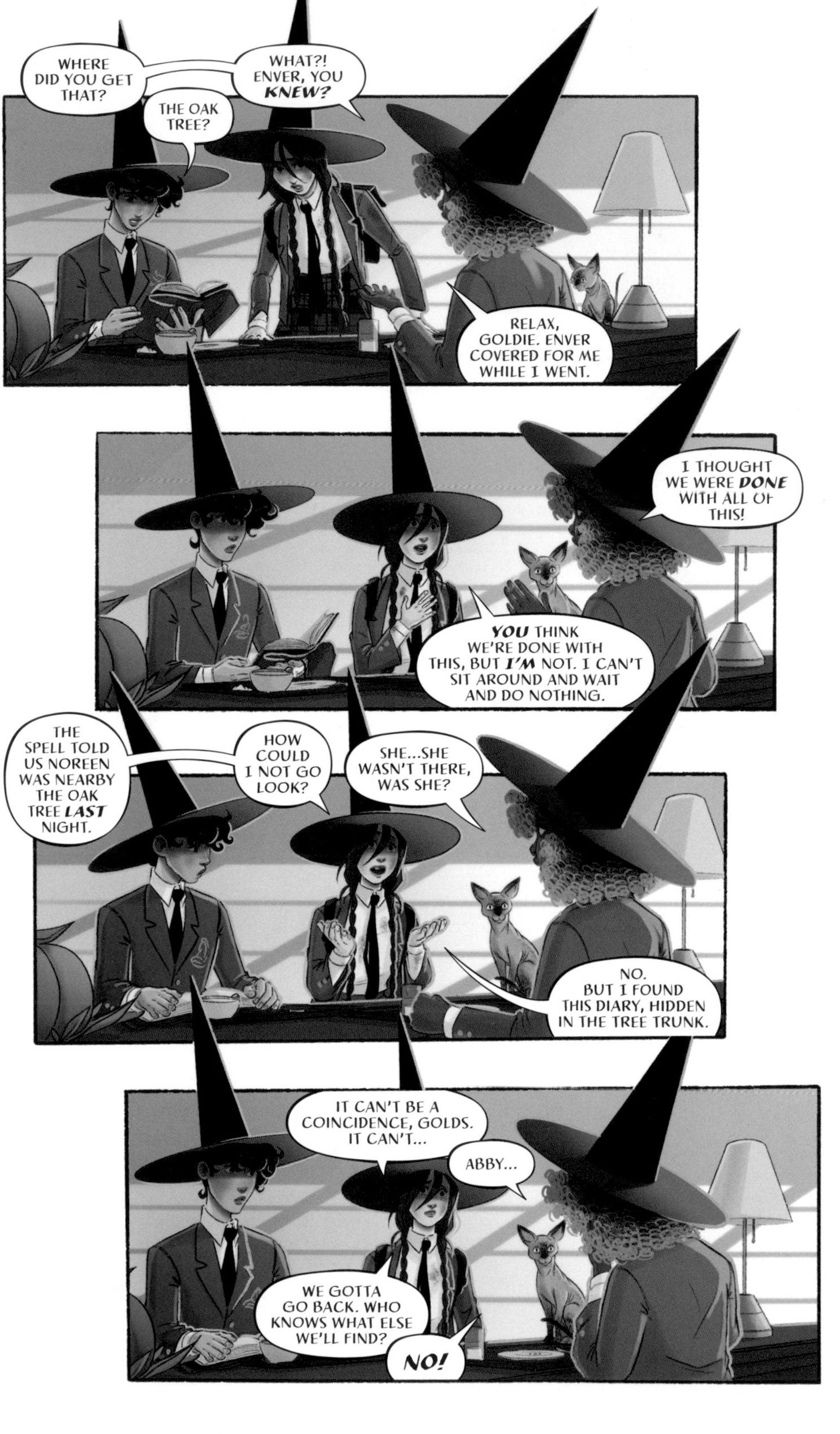
WHERE DID YOU GET THAT?
WHAT?! ENVER, YOU KNEW?
THE OAK TREE?
RELAX, GOLDIE. ENVER COVERED FOR ME WHILE I WENT.
I THOUGHT WE WERE DONE WITH ALL OF THIS!
YOU THINK WE'RE DONE WITH THIS, BUT I'M NOT. I CAN'T SIT AROUND AND WAIT AND DO NOTHING.
THE SPELL TOLD US NOREEN WAS NEARBY THE OAK TREE LAST NIGHT.
HOW COULD I NOT GO LOOK?
SHE...SHE WASN'T THERE, WAS SHE?
NO. BUT I FOUND THIS DIARY, HIDDEN IN THE TREE TRUNK.
IT CAN'T BE A COINCIDENCE, GOLDS. IT CAN'T...
ABBY...
WE GOTTA GO BACK. WHO KNOWS WHAT ELSE WE'LL FIND?
NO!

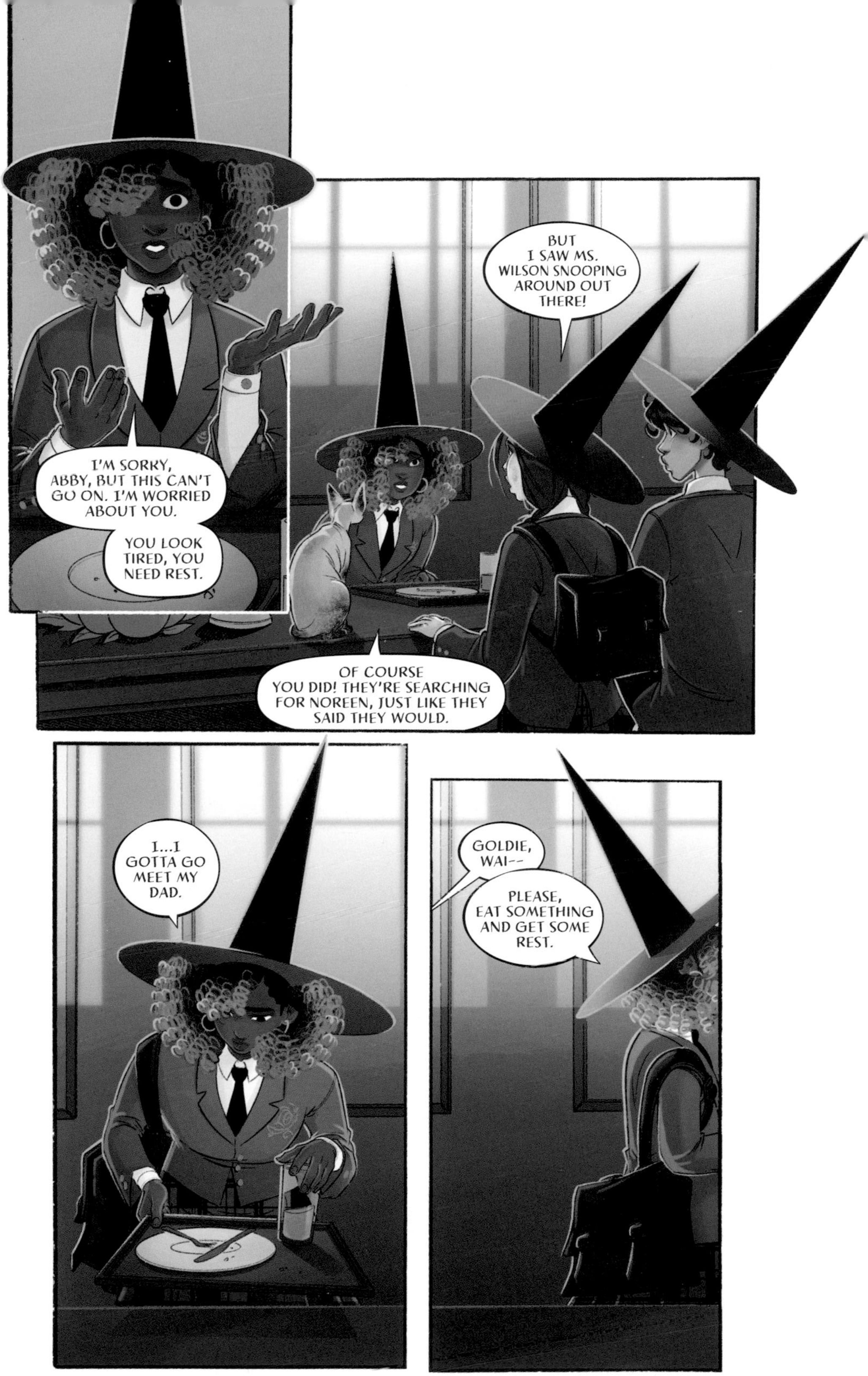
I'M SORRY, ABBY, BUT THIS CAN'T GO ON. I'M WORRIED ABOUT YOU.
YOU LOOK TIRED, YOU NEED REST.
BUT I SAW MS. WILSON SNOOPING AROUND OUT THERE!
OF COURSE YOU DID! THEY'RE SEARCHING FOR NOREEN, JUST LIKE THEY SAID THEY WOULD.
I...I GOTTA GO MEET MY DAD.
GOLDIE, WAI--
PLEASE, EAT SOMETHING AND GET SOME REST.

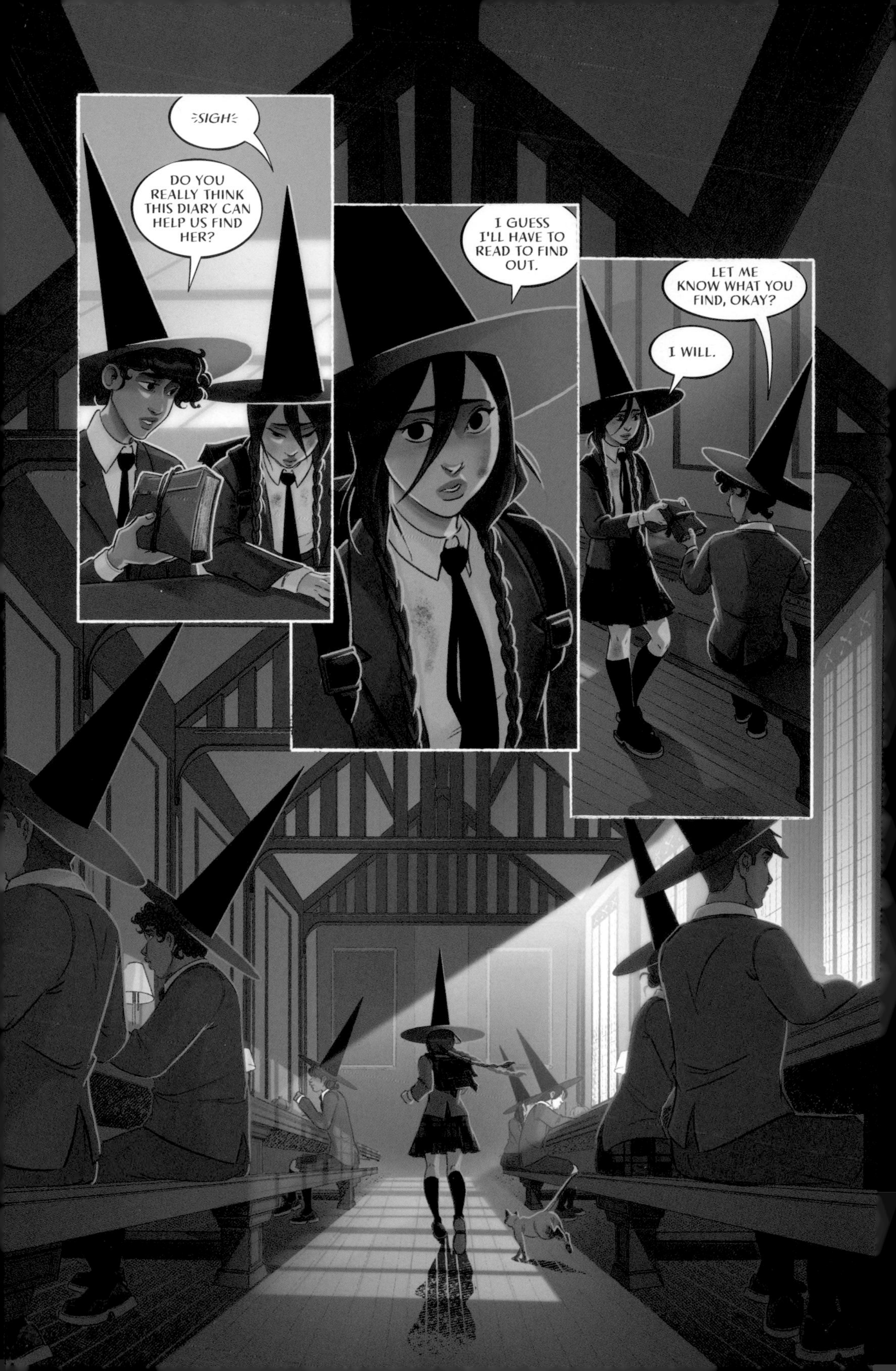

SIGH
DO YOU REALLY THINK THIS DIARY CAN HELP US FIND HER?
I GUESS I'LL HAVE TO READ TO FIND OUT.
LET ME KNOW WHAT YOU FIND, OKAY?
I WILL.

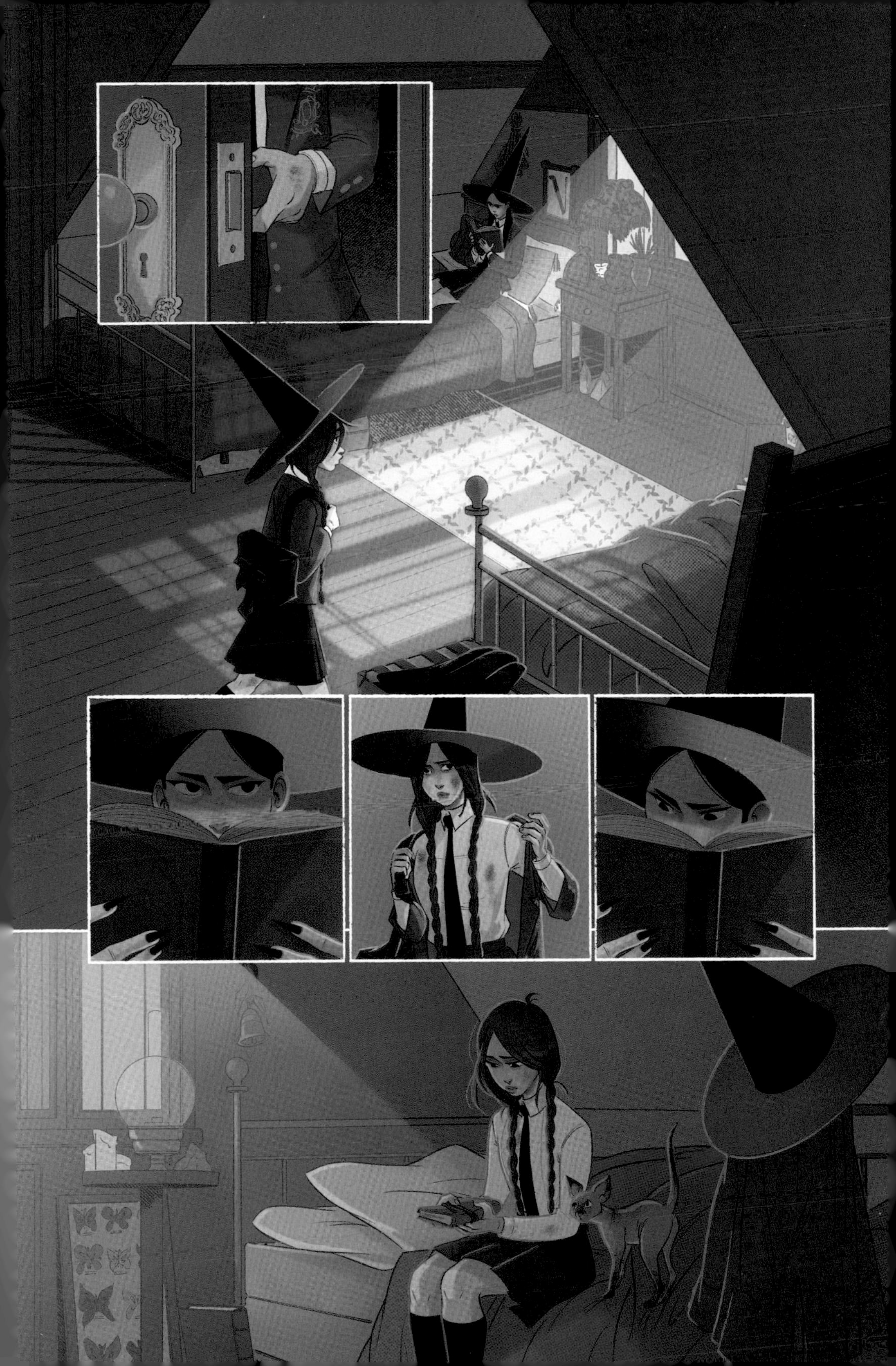

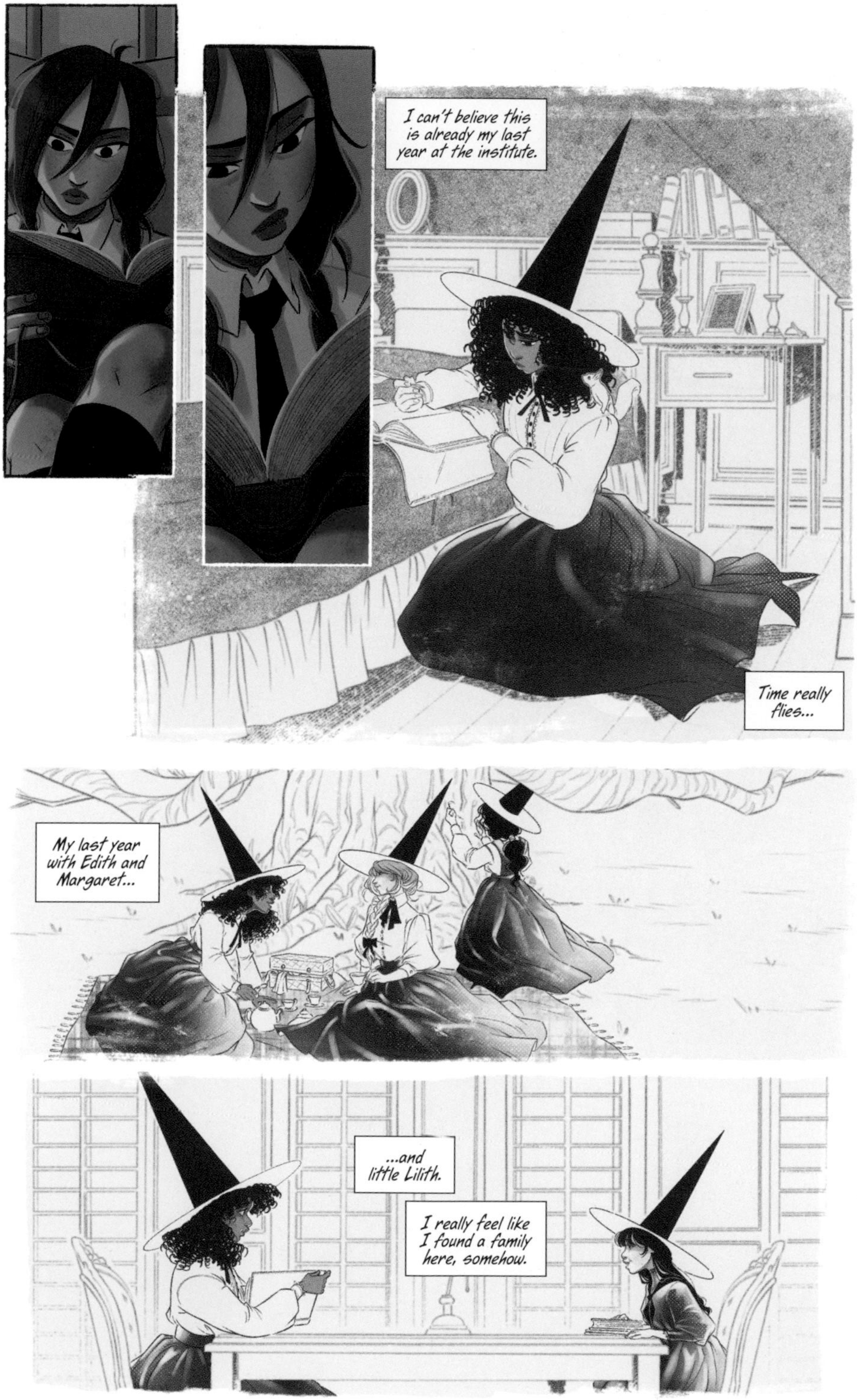
I can't believe this is already my last year at the institute.
Time really flies...
My last year with Edith and Margaret...
...and little Lilith.
I really feel like I found a family here, somehow.

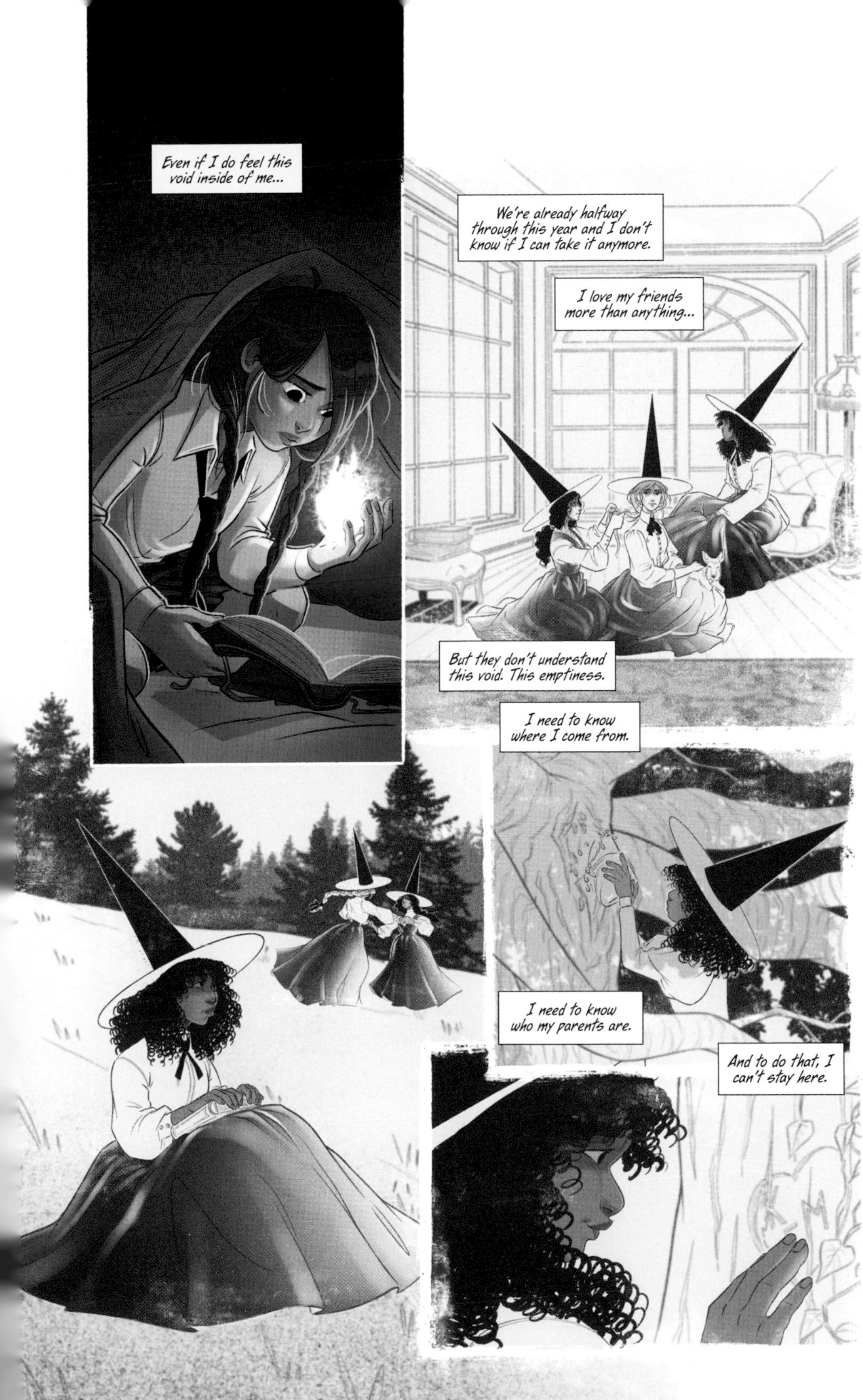
Even if I do feel this void inside of me...
We're already halfway through this year and I don't know if I can take it anymore.
I love my friends more than anything...
But they don't understand this void. This emptiness.
I need to know where I come from.
I need to know who my parents are.
And to do that, I can't stay here.

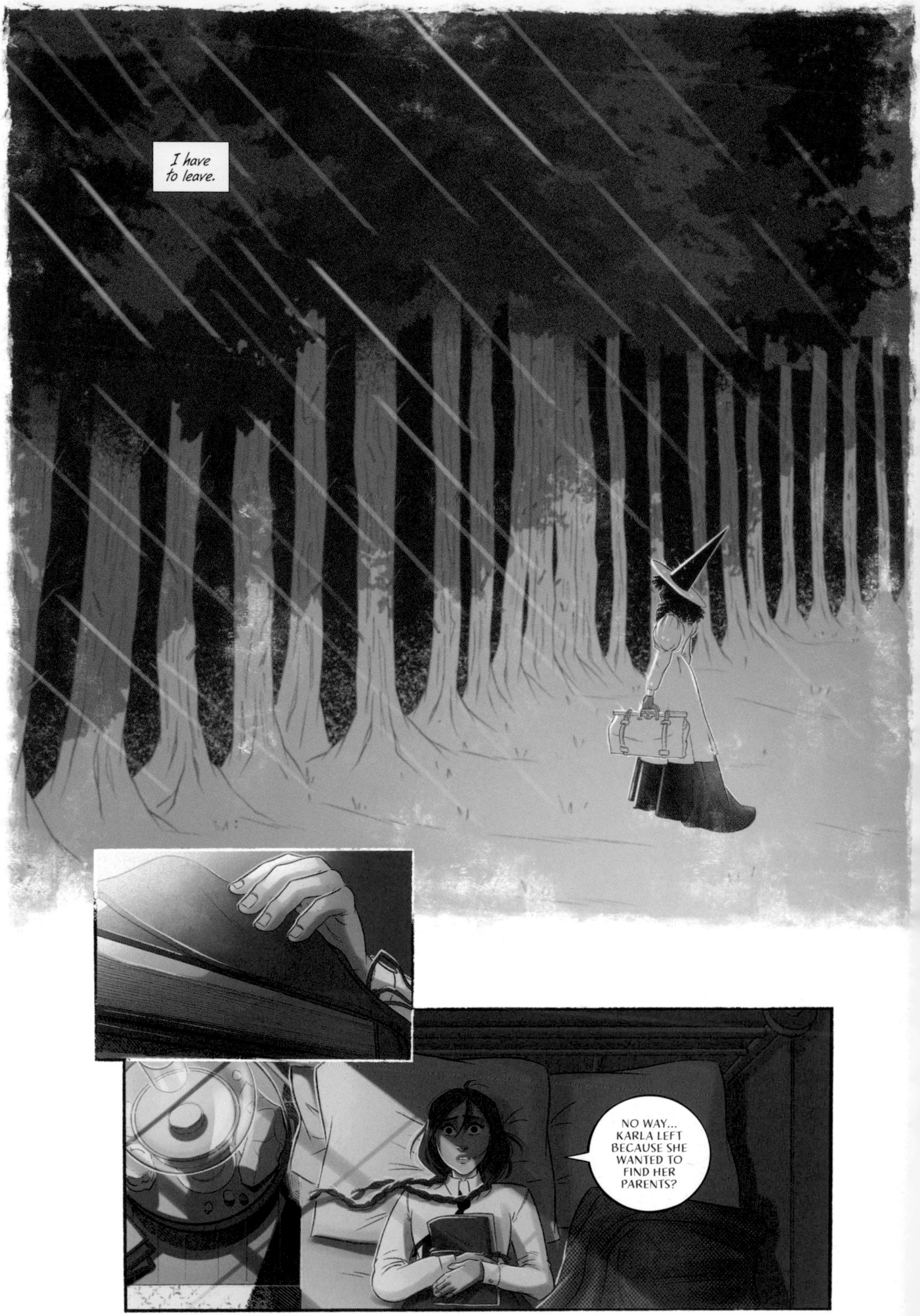
I have to leave.
NO WAY... KARLA LEFT BECAUSE SHE WANTED TO FIND HER PARENTS?

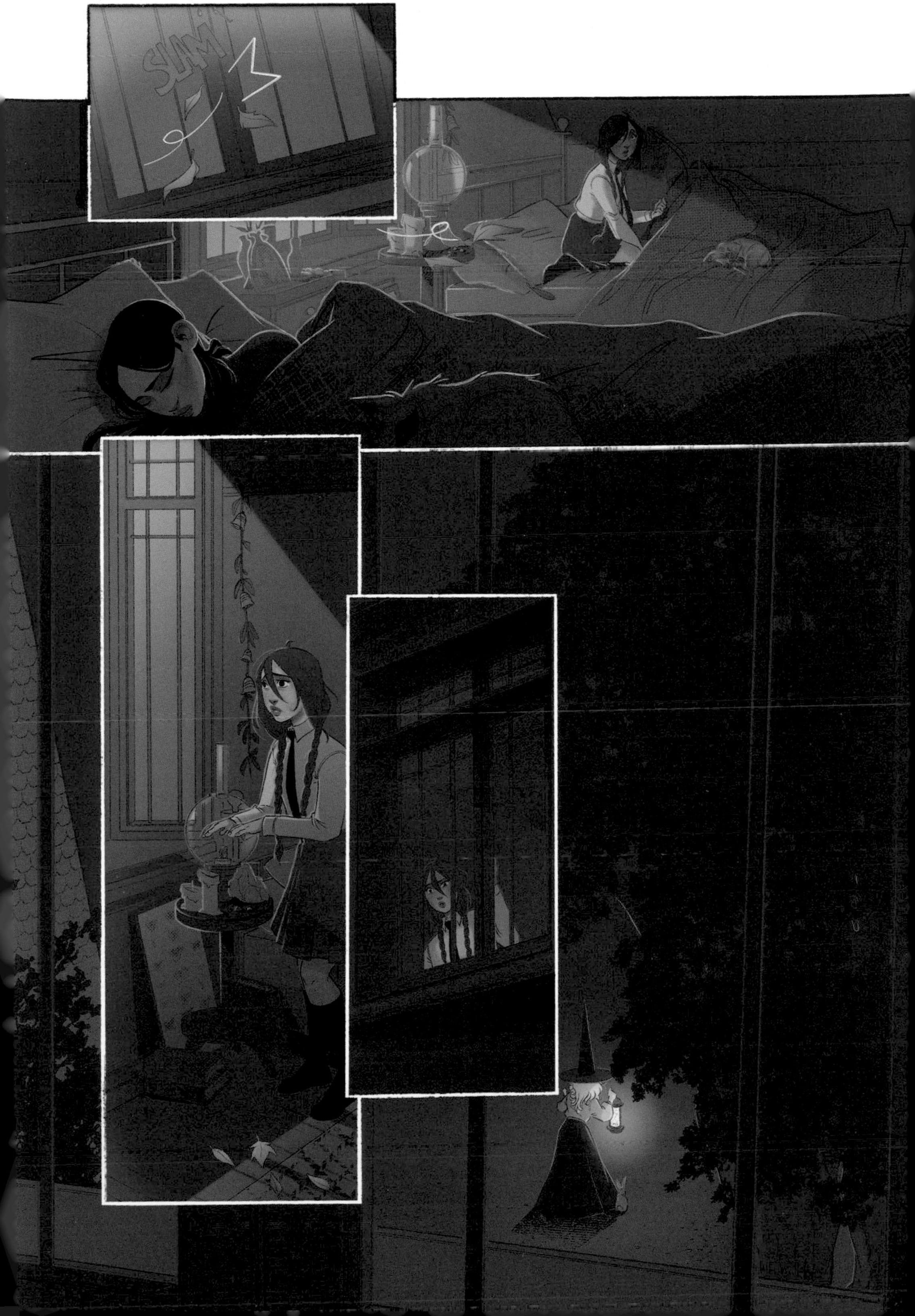
SLAM

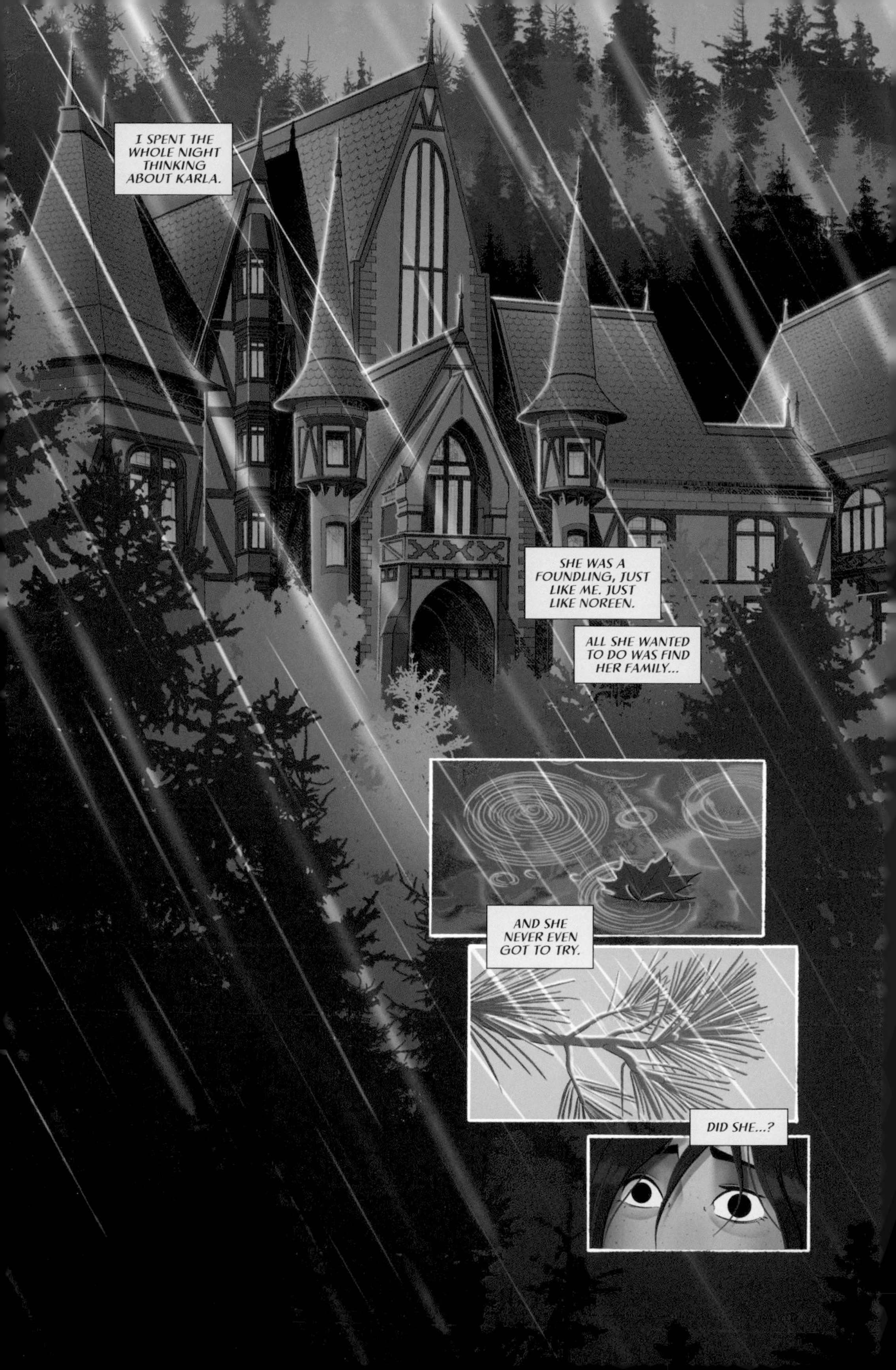
I SPENT THE WHOLE NIGHT THINKING ABOUT KARLA.
SHE WAS A FOUNDLING, JUST LIKE ME. JUST LIKE NOREEN.
ALL SHE WANTED TO DO WAS FIND HER FAMILY...
AND SHE NEVER EVEN GOT TO TRY.
DID SHE...?

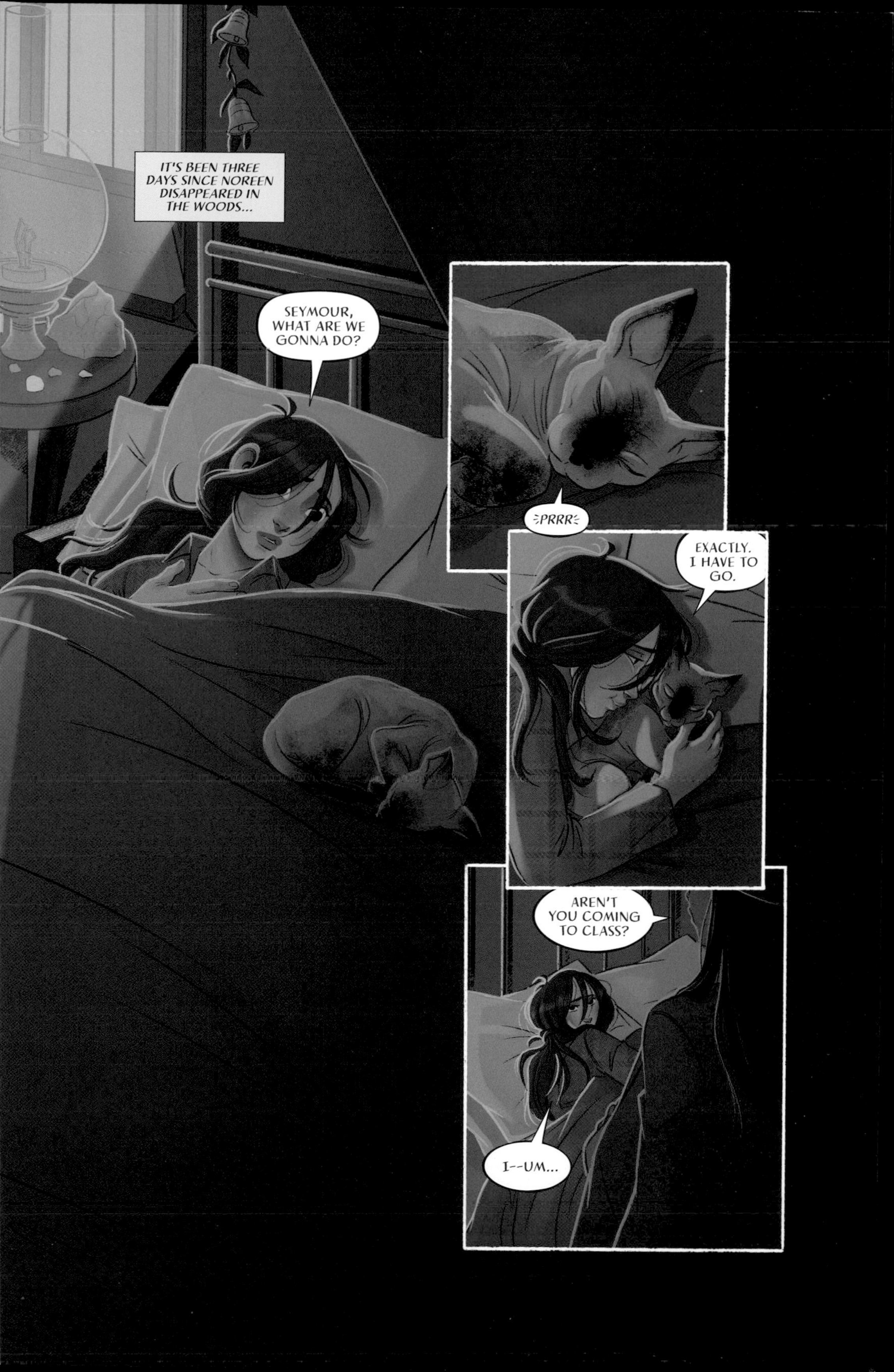
IT'S BEEN THREE DAYS SINCE NOREEN DISAPPEARED IN THE WOODS...
SEYMOUR, WHAT ARE WE GONNA DO?
PRRR
EXACTLY. I HAVE TO GO.
AREN'T YOU COMING TO CLASS?
I--UM...

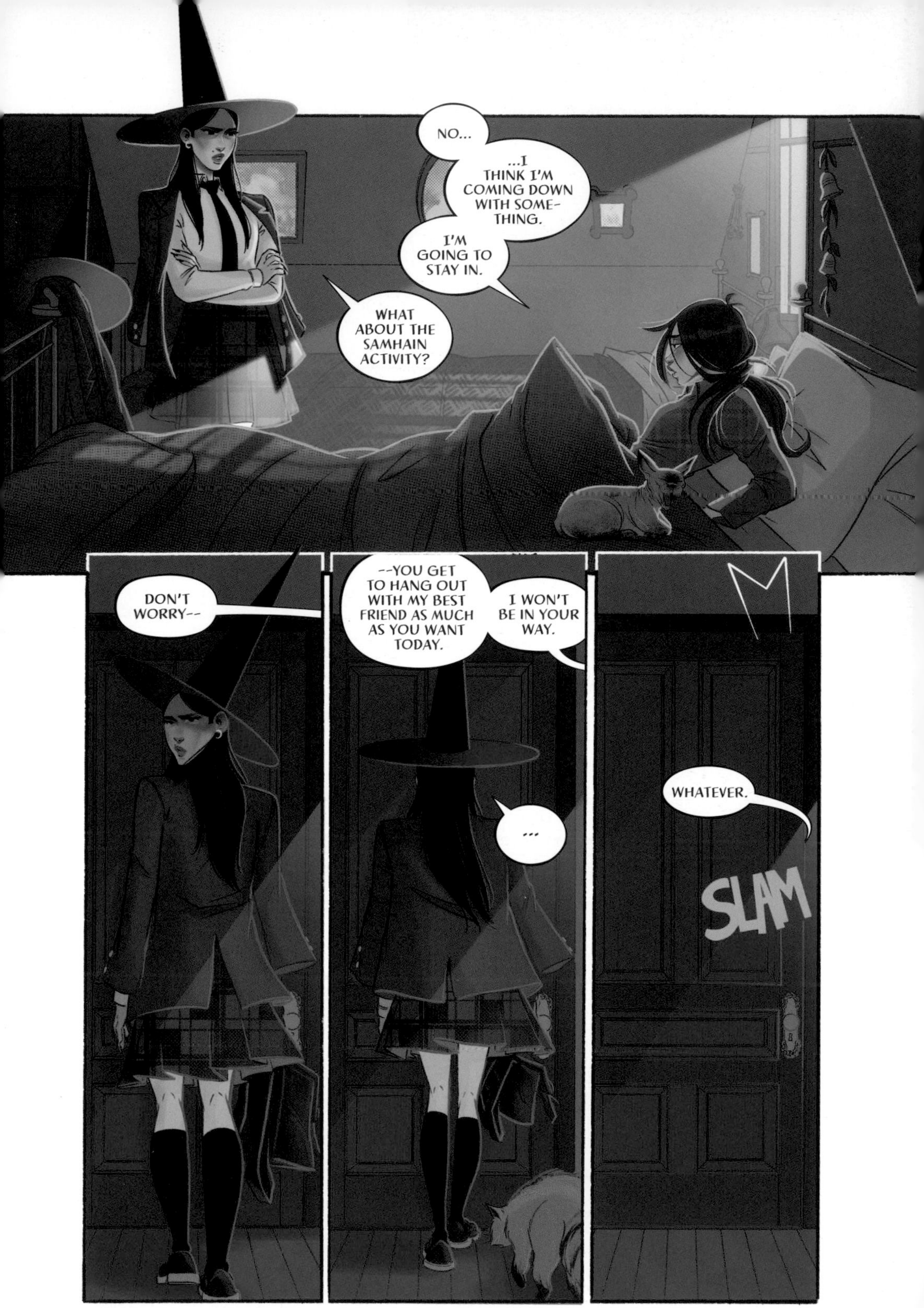
NO...
...I THINK I'M COMING DOWN WITH SOME-THING.
I'M GOING TO STAY IN.
WHAT ABOUT THE SAMHAIN ACTIVITY?
DON'T WORRY--
--YOU GET TO HANG OUT WITH MY BEST FRIEND AS MUCH AS YOU WANT TODAY.
I WON'T BE IN YOUR WAY.
...
WHATEVER.
SLAM

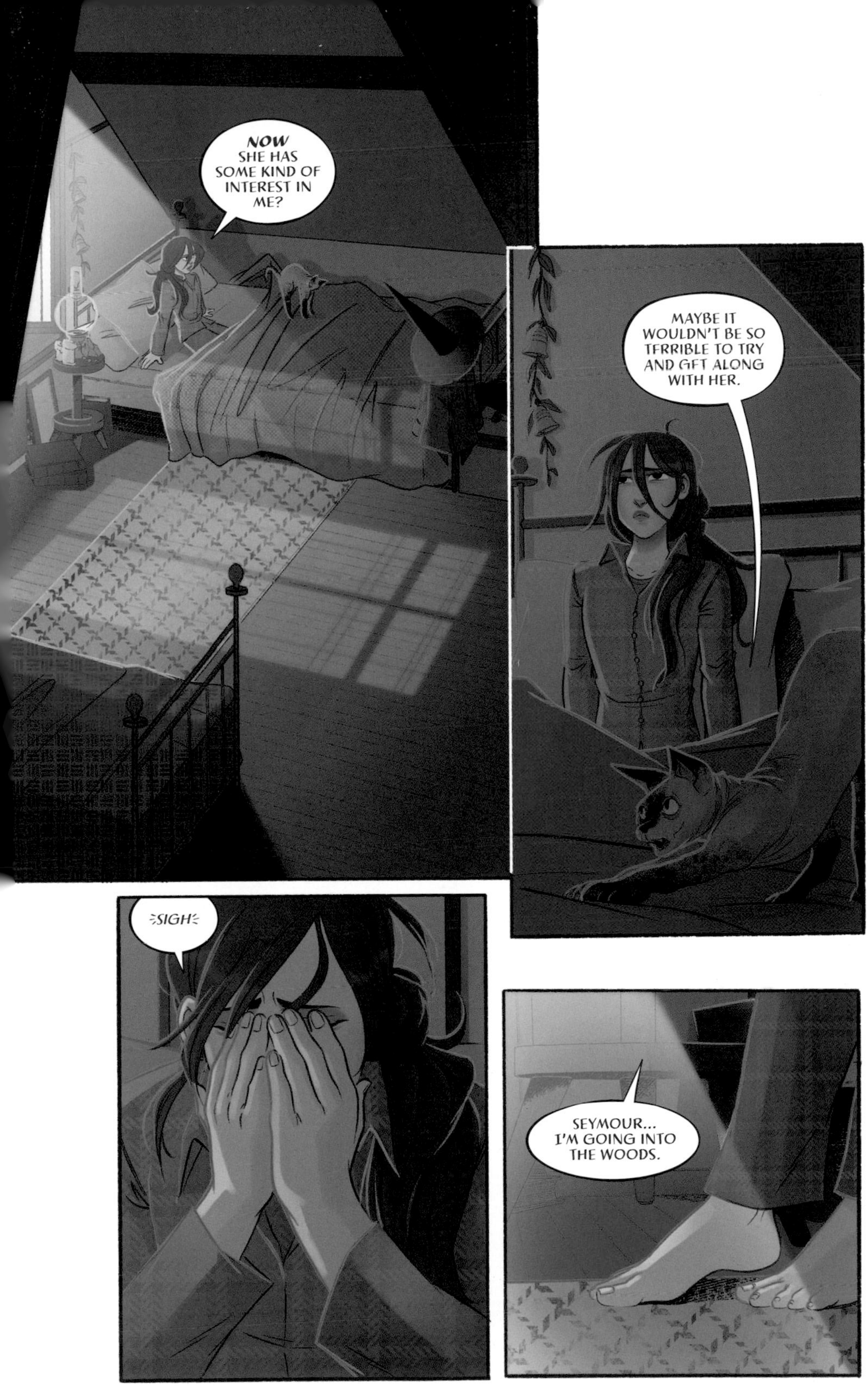
NOW SHE HAS SOME KIND OF INTEREST IN ME?
MAYBE IT WOULDN'T BE SO TERRIBLE TO TRY AND GET ALONG WITH HER.
SIGH
SEYMOUR... I'M GOING INTO THE WOODS.

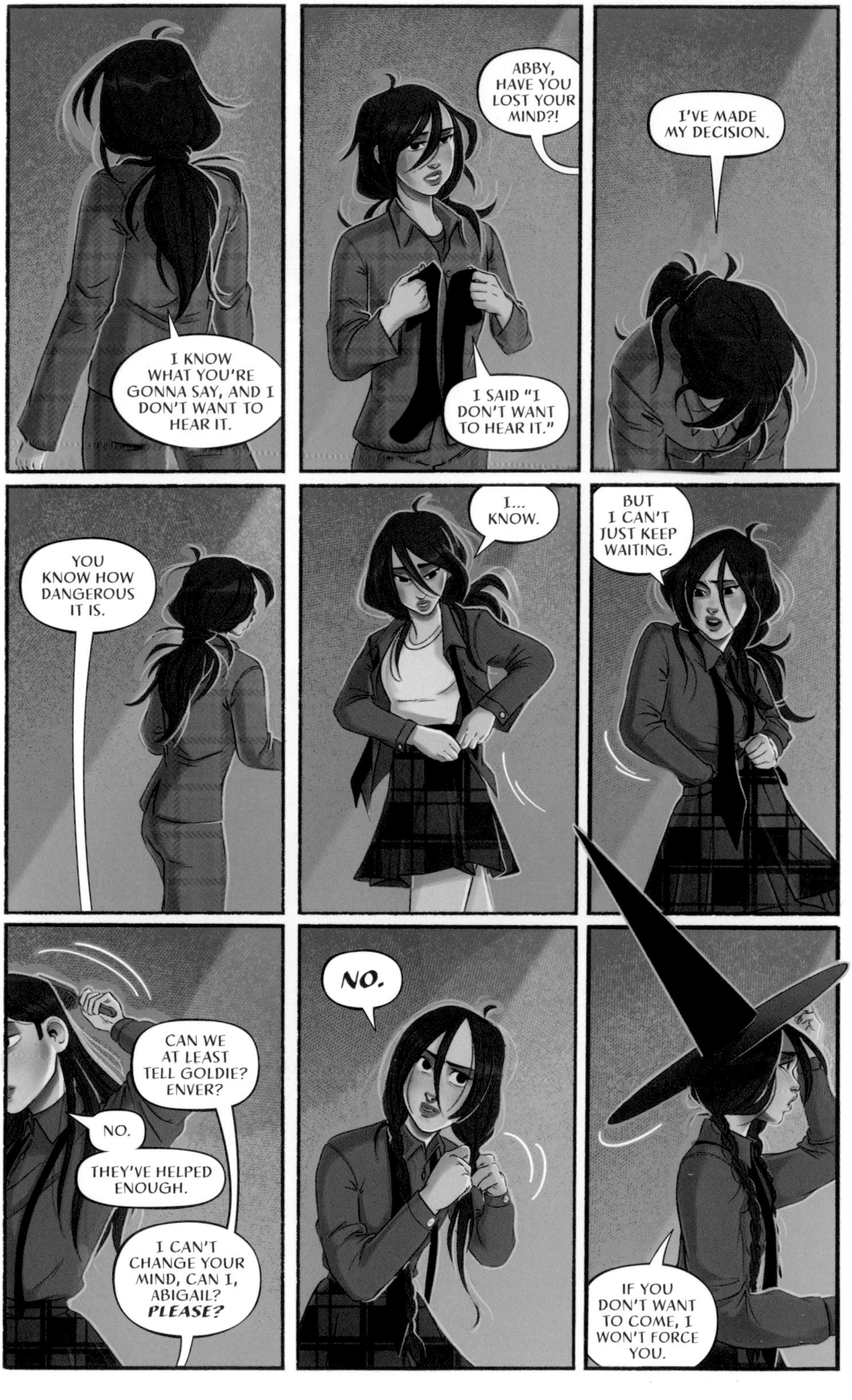
I KNOW WHAT YOU'RE GONNA SAY, AND I DON'T WANT TO HEAR IT.
ABBY, HAVE YOU LOST YOUR MIND?!
I SAID "I DON'T WANT TO HEAR IT."
I'VE MADE MY DECISION.
YOU KNOW HOW DANGEROUS IT IS.
I... KNOW.
BUT I CAN'T JUST KEEP WAITING.
CAN WE AT LEAST TELL GOLDIE? ENVER?
NO.
THEY'VE HELPED ENOUGH.
I CAN'T CHANGE YOUR MIND, CAN I, ABIGAIL? ***PLEASE?***
NO.
IF YOU DON'T WANT TO COME, I WON'T FORCE YOU.

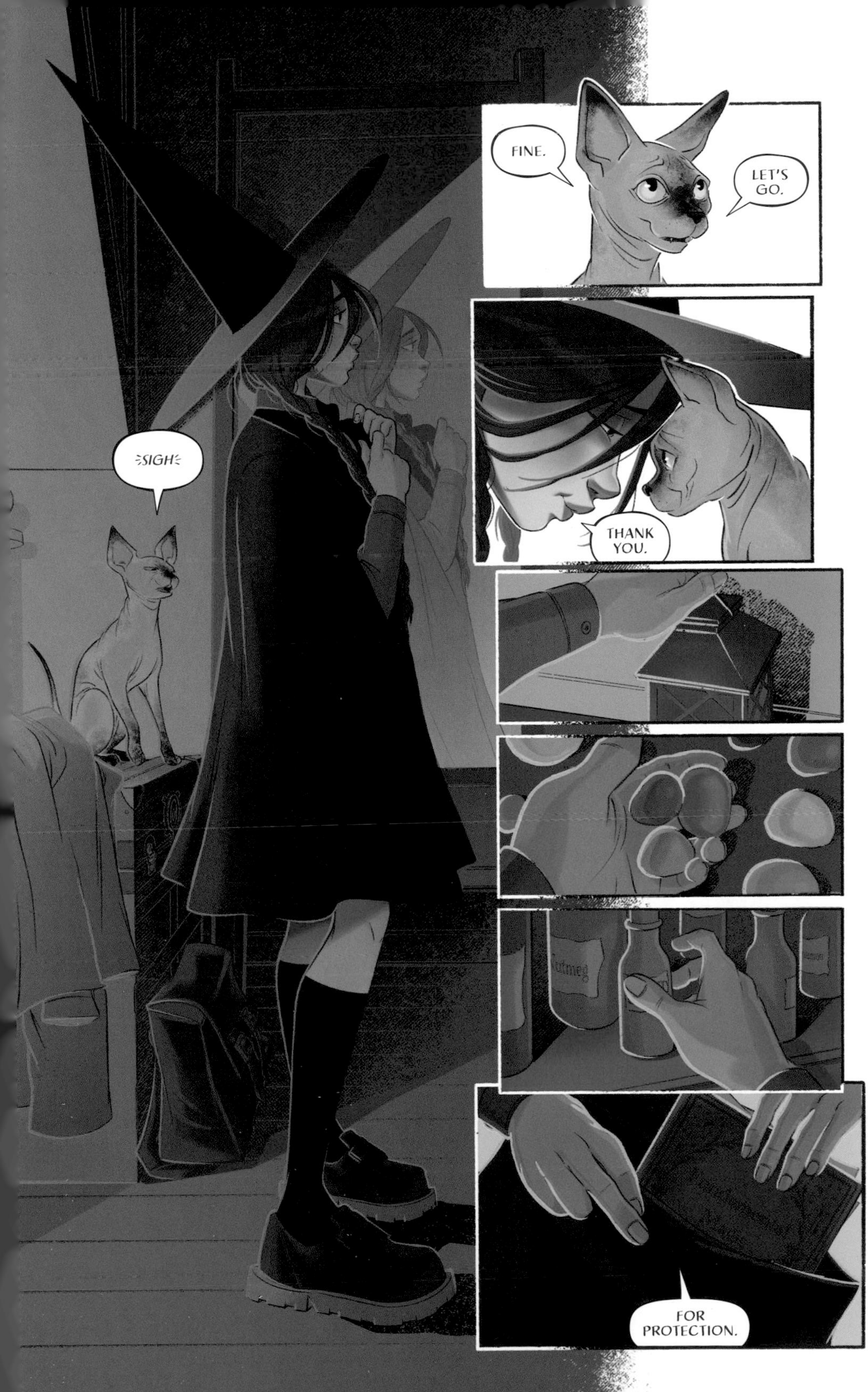
FINE.
LET'S GO.
SIGH
THANK YOU.
Nutmeg
FOR PROTECTION.

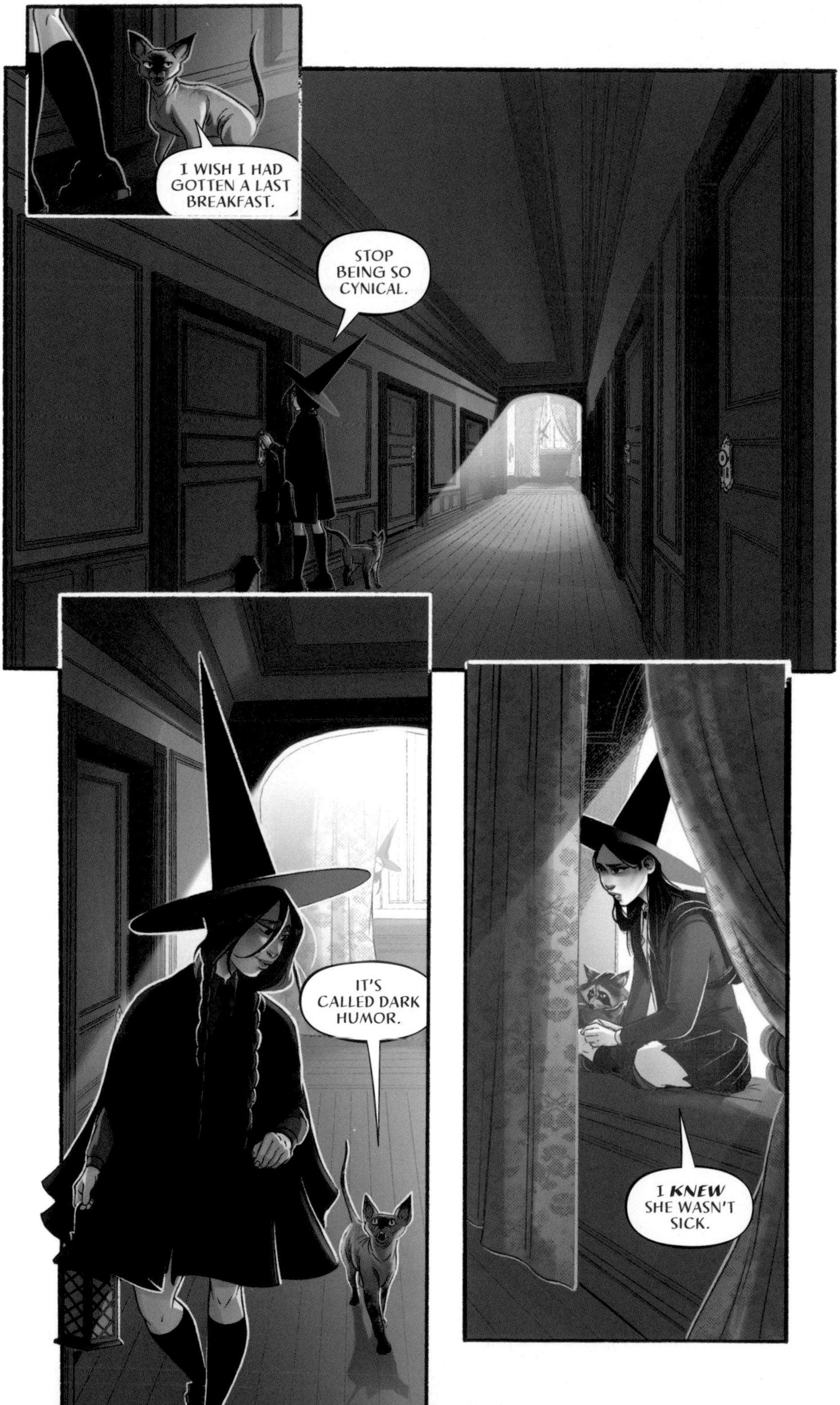

I WISH I HAD GOTTEN A LAST BREAKFAST.
STOP BEING SO CYNICAL.
IT'S CALLED DARK HUMOR.
I ***KNEW*** SHE WASN'T SICK.

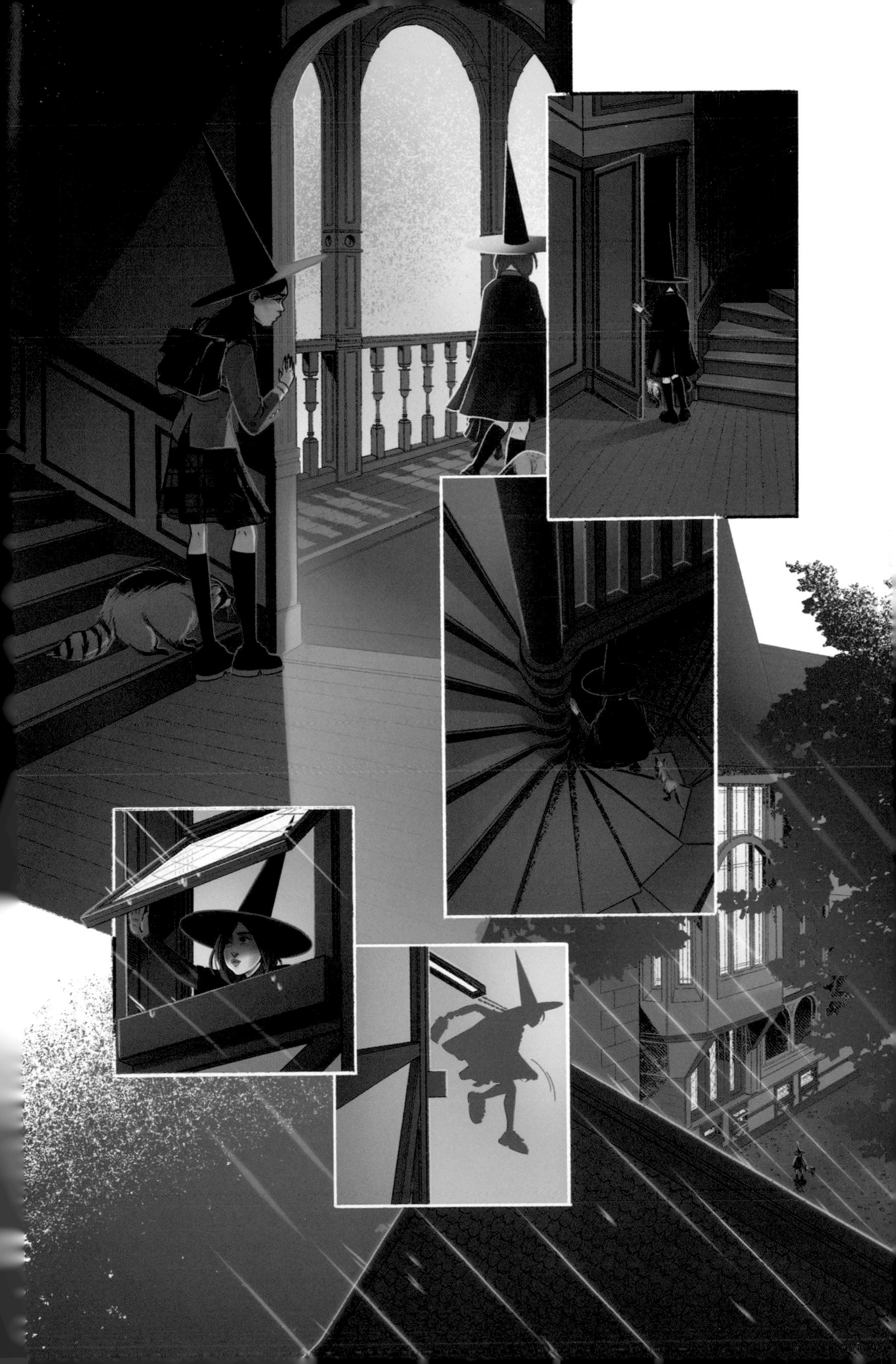

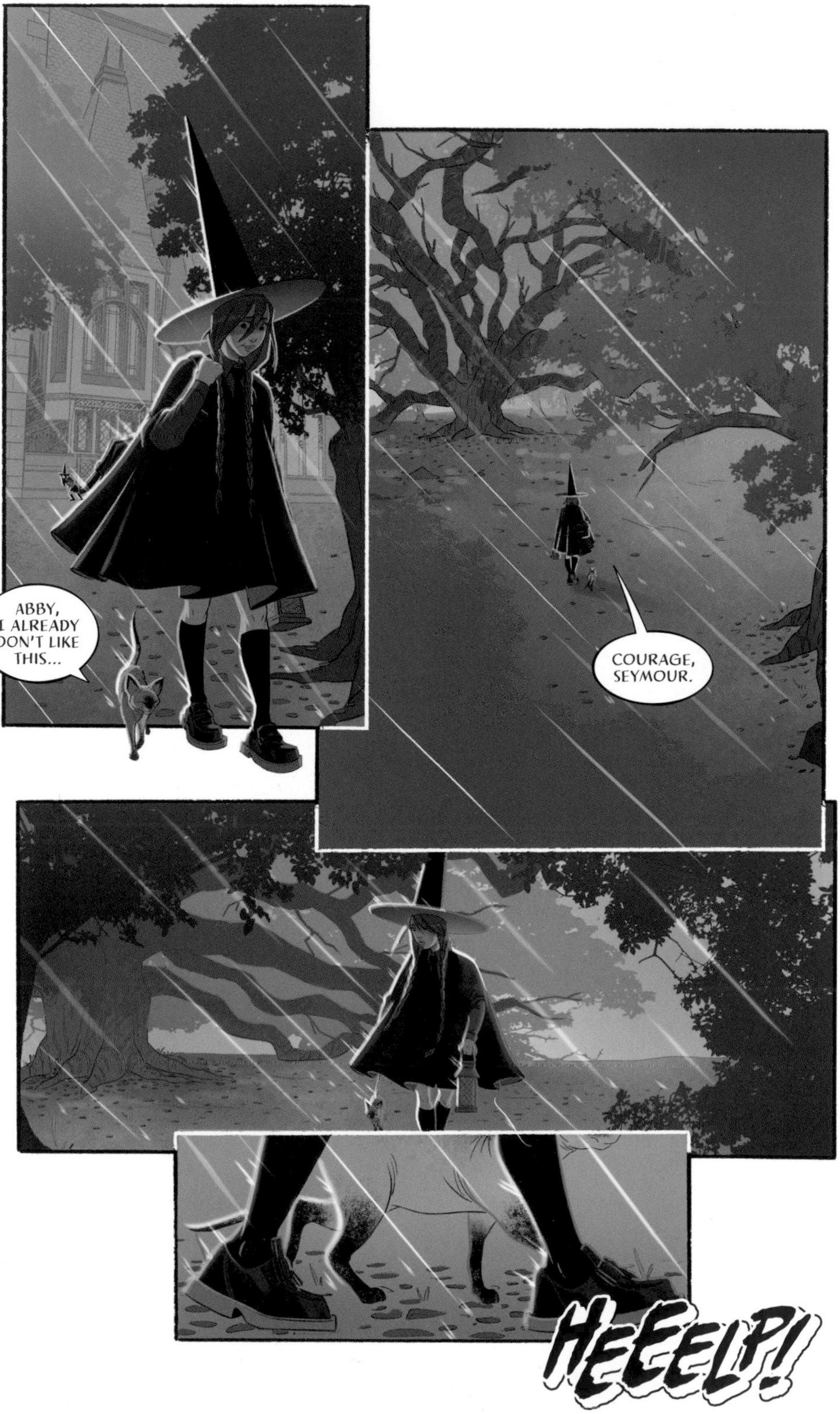
ABBY, I ALREADY DON'T LIKE THIS...
COURAGE, SEYMOUR.
HEEEELP!

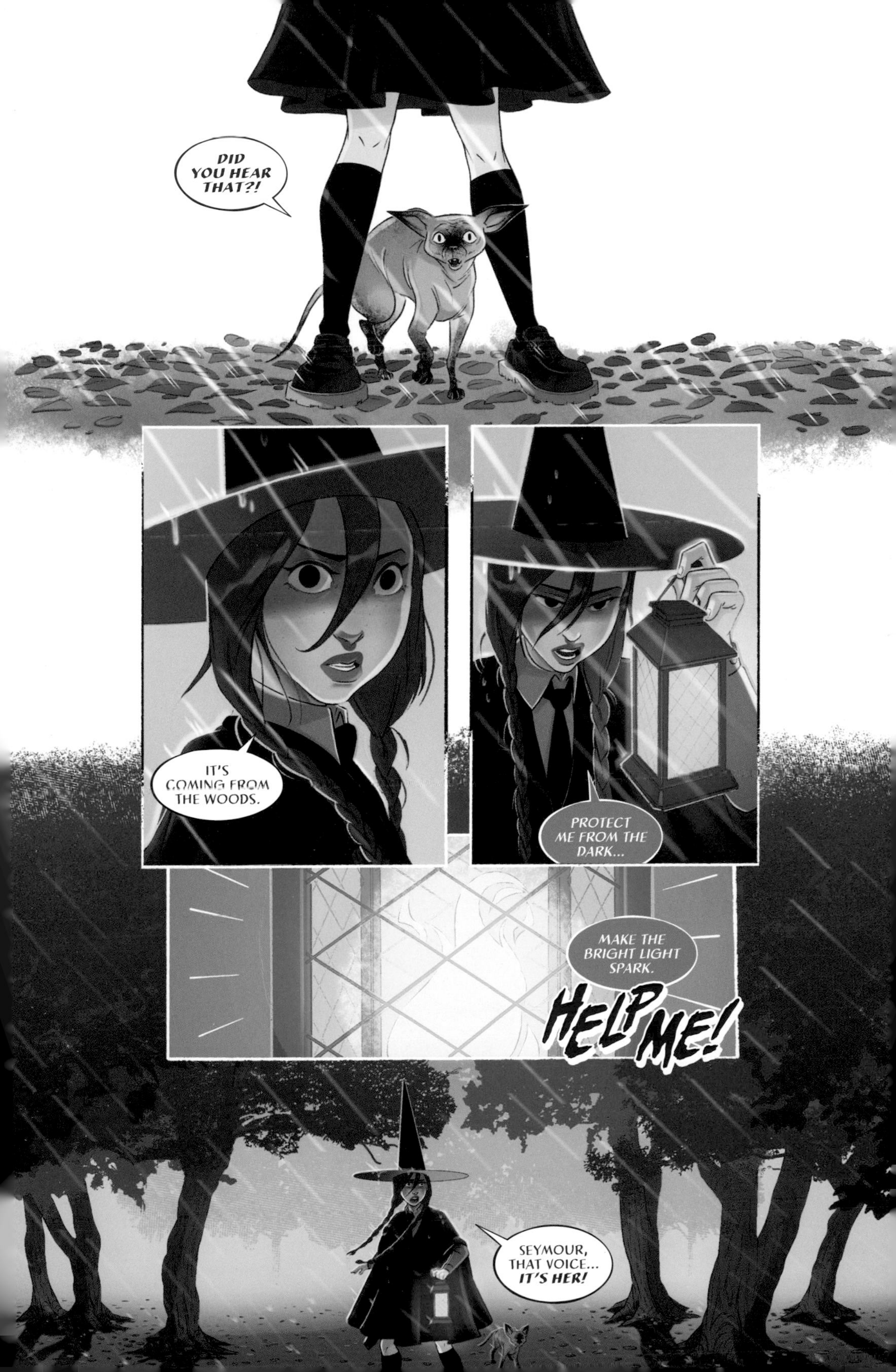
DID YOU HEAR THAT?!
IT'S COMING FROM THE WOODS.
PROTECT ME FROM THE DARK...
MAKE THE BRIGHT LIGHT SPARK.
HELP ME!
SEYMOUR, THAT VOICE... IT'S HER!

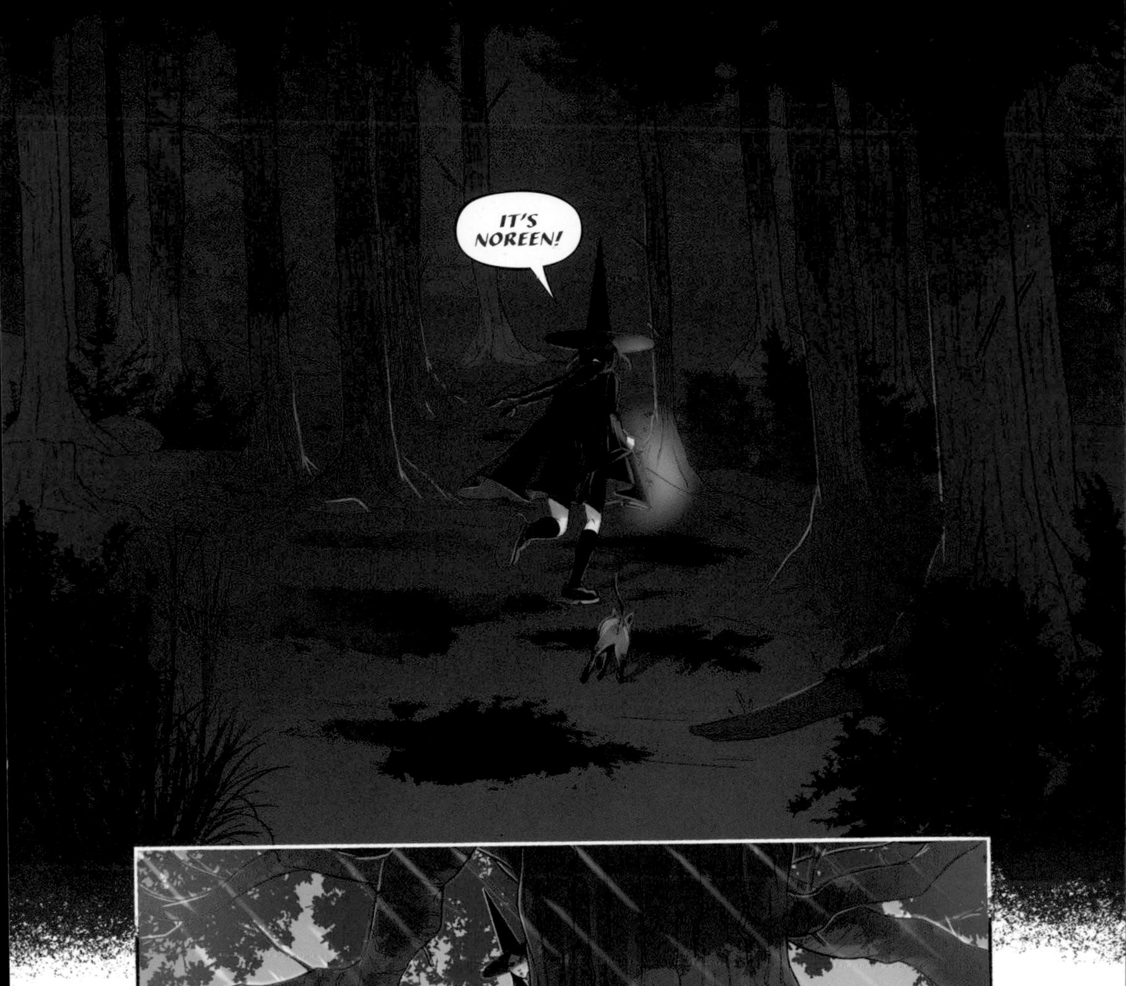
IT'S NOREEN!

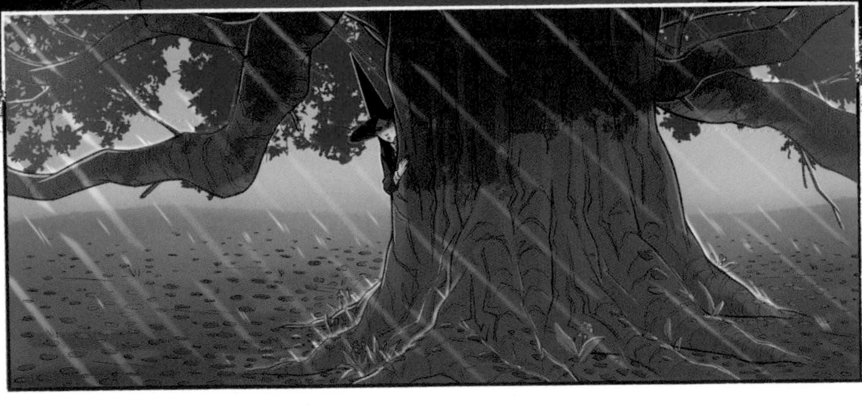

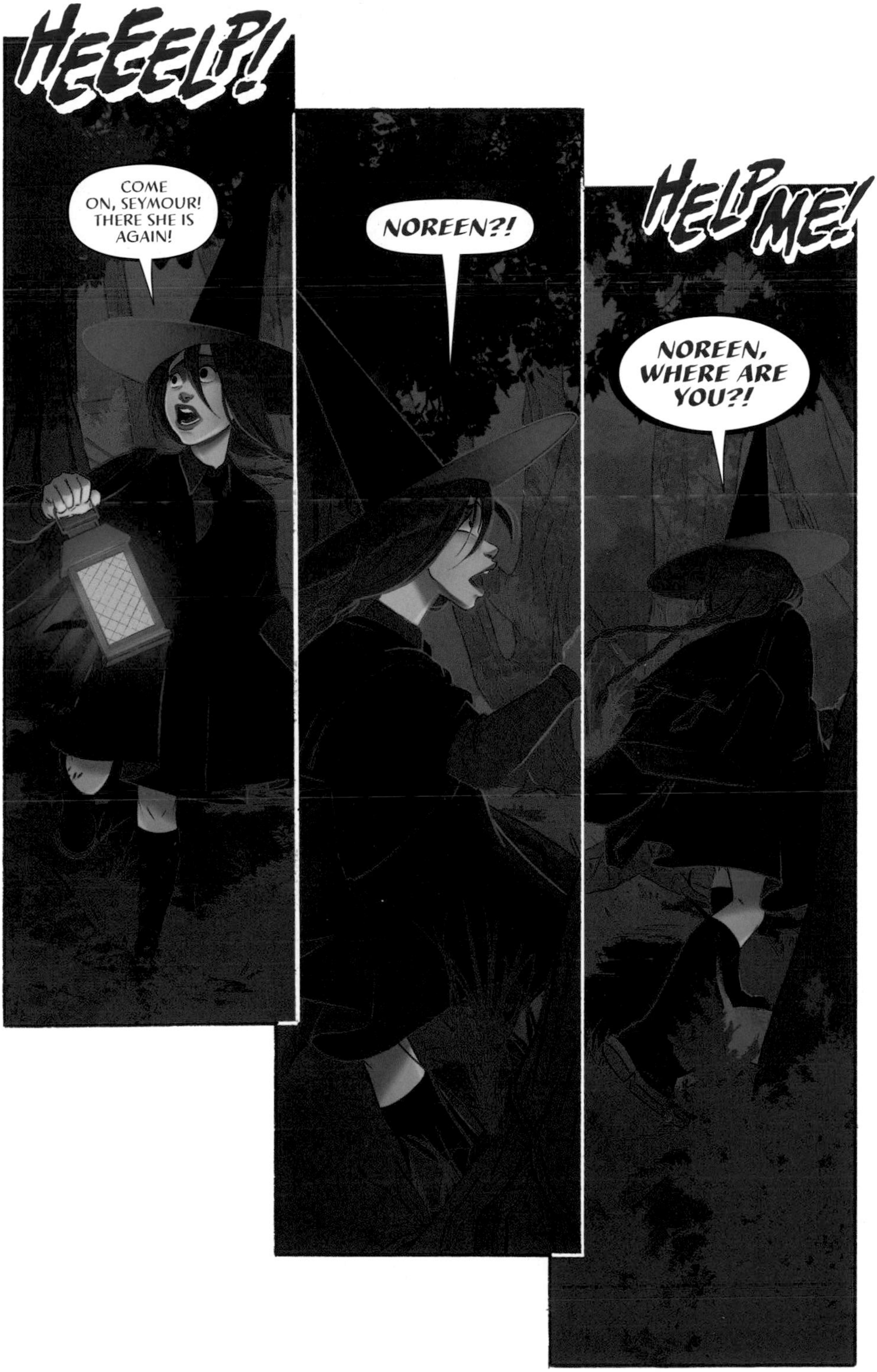
HEEEELP!
COME ON, SEYMOUR! THERE SHE IS AGAIN!
NOREEN?!
HELP ME!
NOREEN, WHERE ARE YOU?!

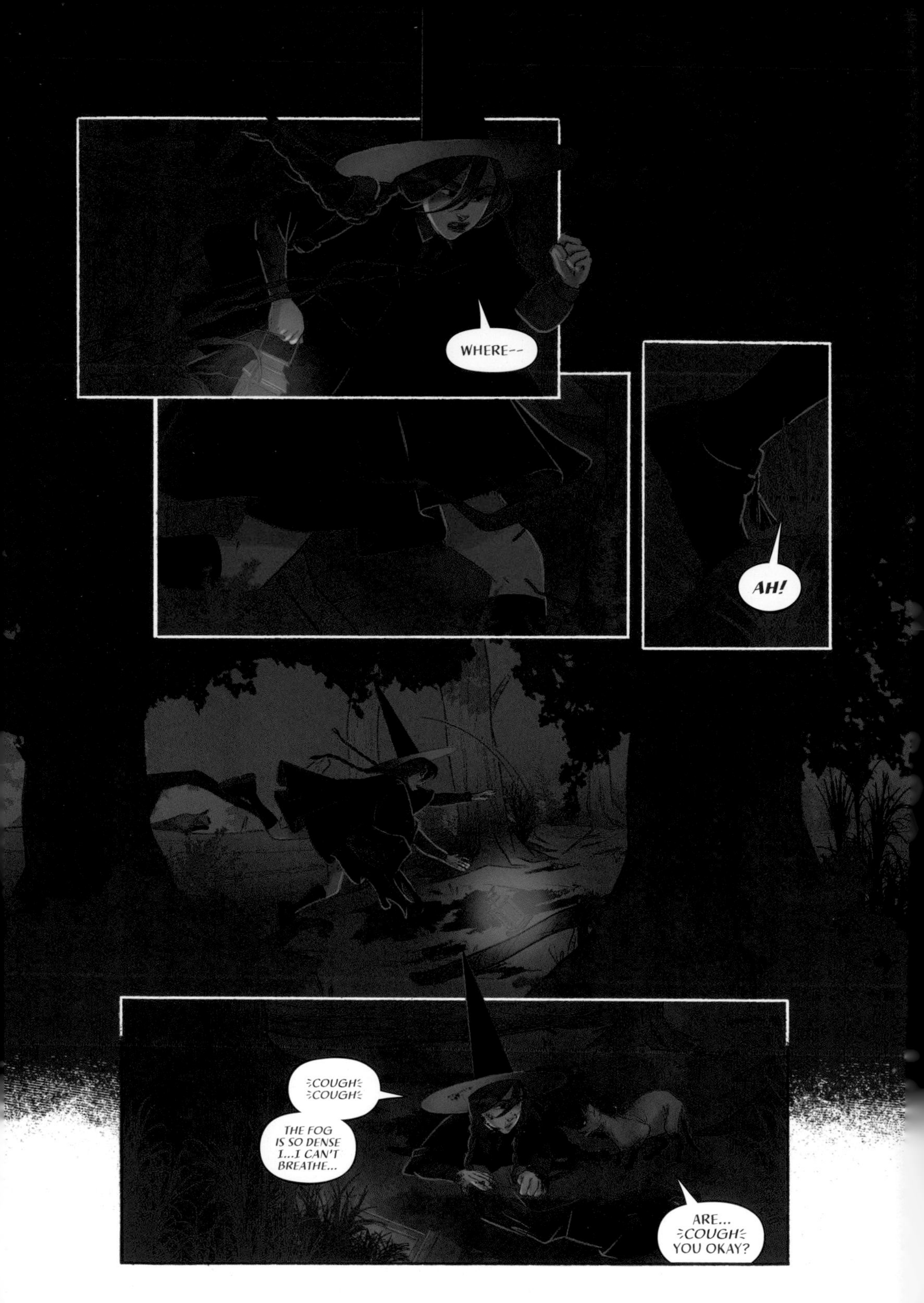
WHERE--
AH!
≈COUGH≈
≈COUGH≈
THE FOG
IS SO DENSE
I...I CAN'T
BREATHE...
ARE...
≈COUGH≈
YOU OKAY?

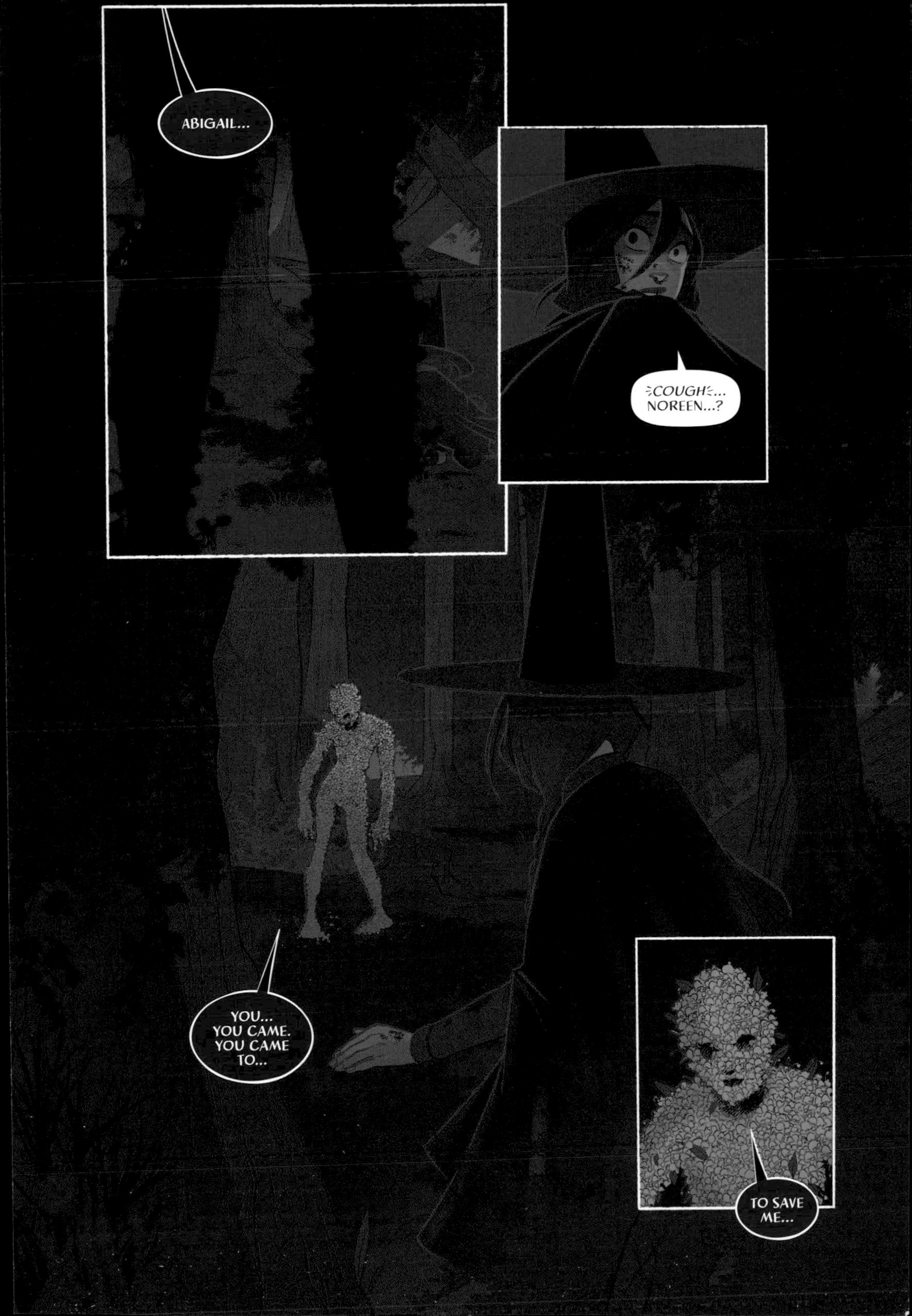
ABIGAIL...
⁝COUGH⁝...
NOREEN...?
YOU...
YOU CAME.
YOU CAME
TO...
TO SAVE
ME...

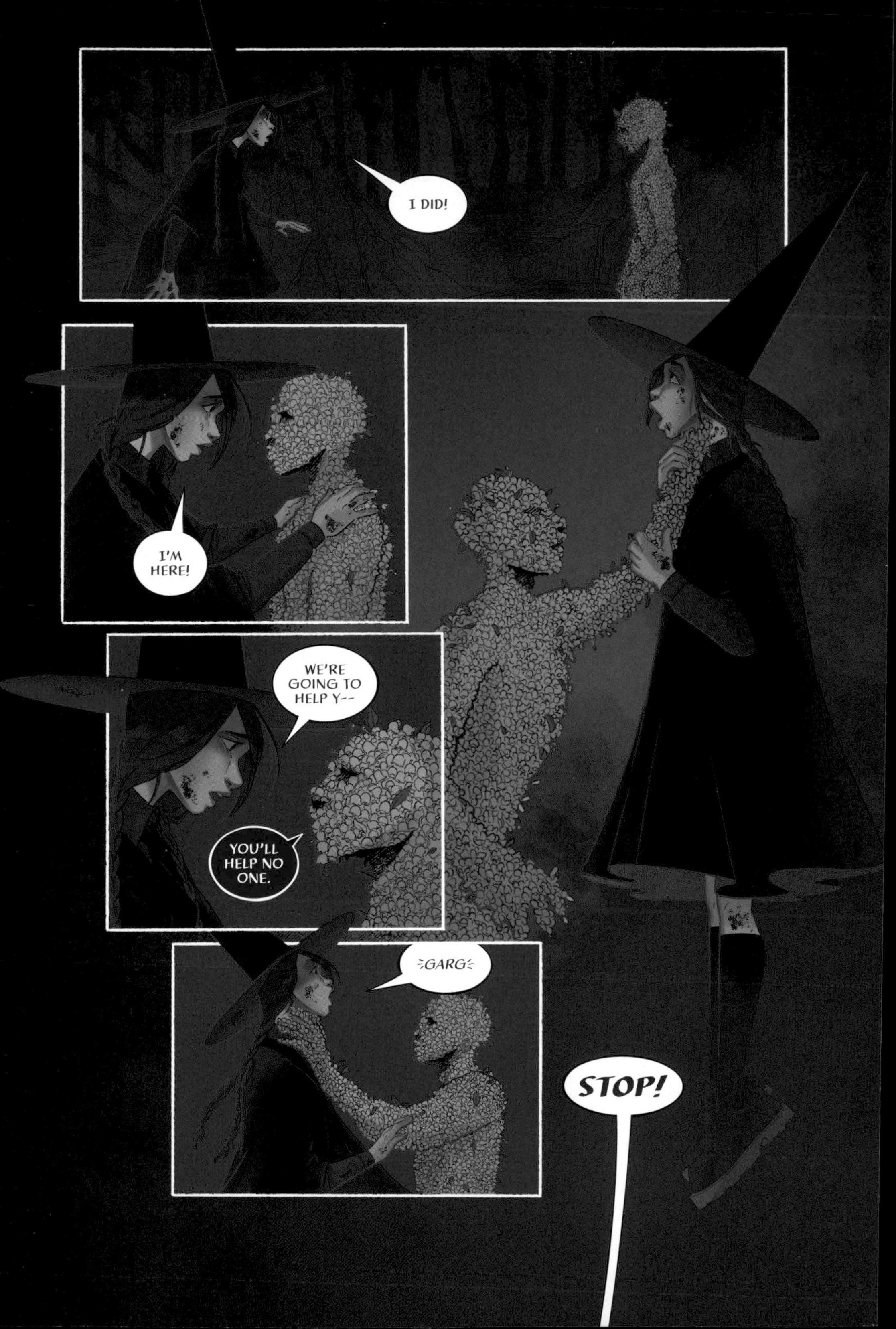
I DID!
I'M HERE!
WE'RE GOING TO HELP Y--
YOU'LL HELP NO ONE.
GARG
STOP!

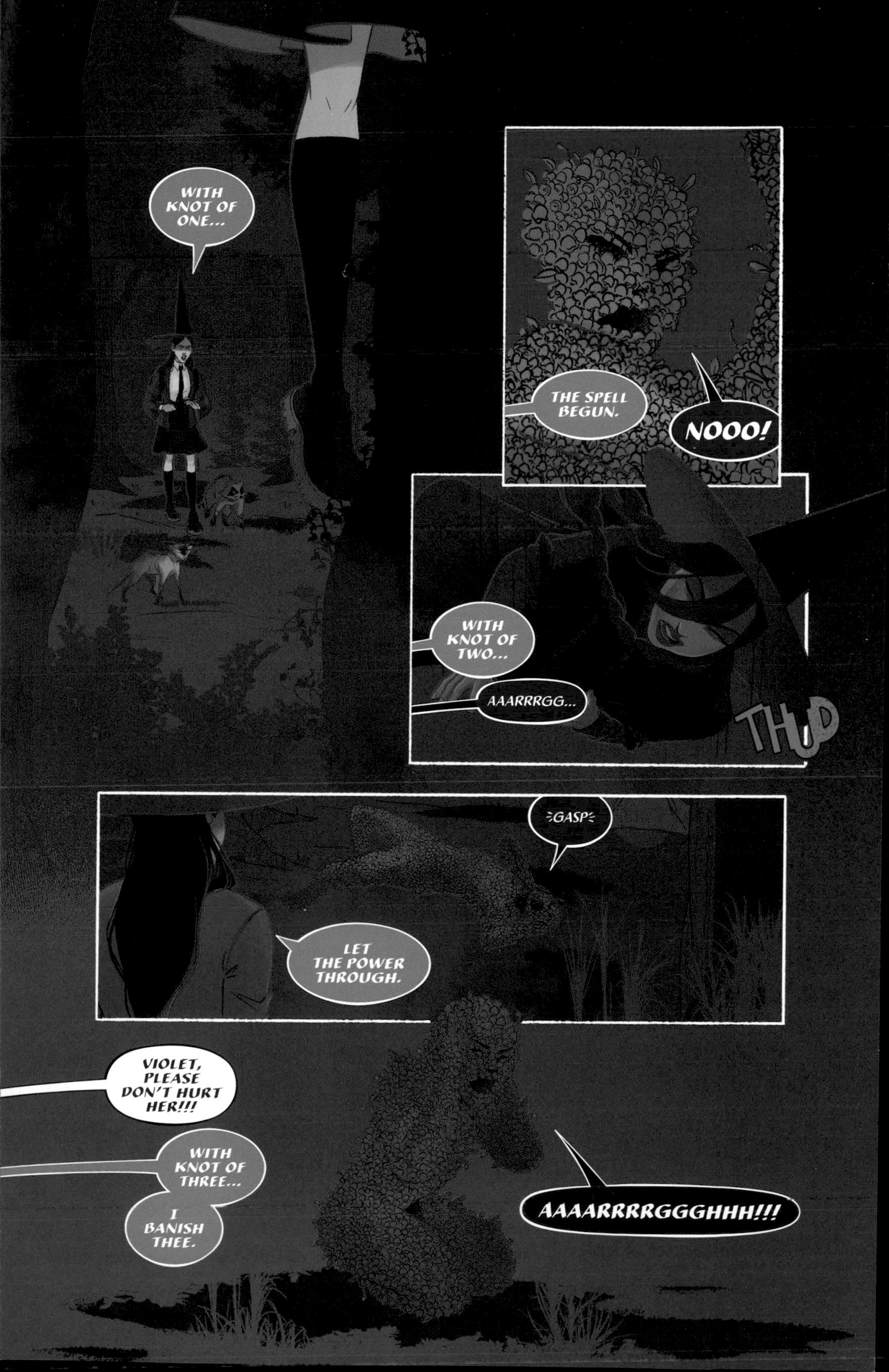
WITH KNOT OF ONE...
THE SPELL BEGUN.
NOOO!
WITH KNOT OF TWO...
AAARRRGG...
THUD
GASP
LET THE POWER THROUGH.
VIOLET, PLEASE DON'T HURT HER!!!
WITH KNOT OF THREE...
I BANISH THEE.
AAAARRRRGGGHHH!!!

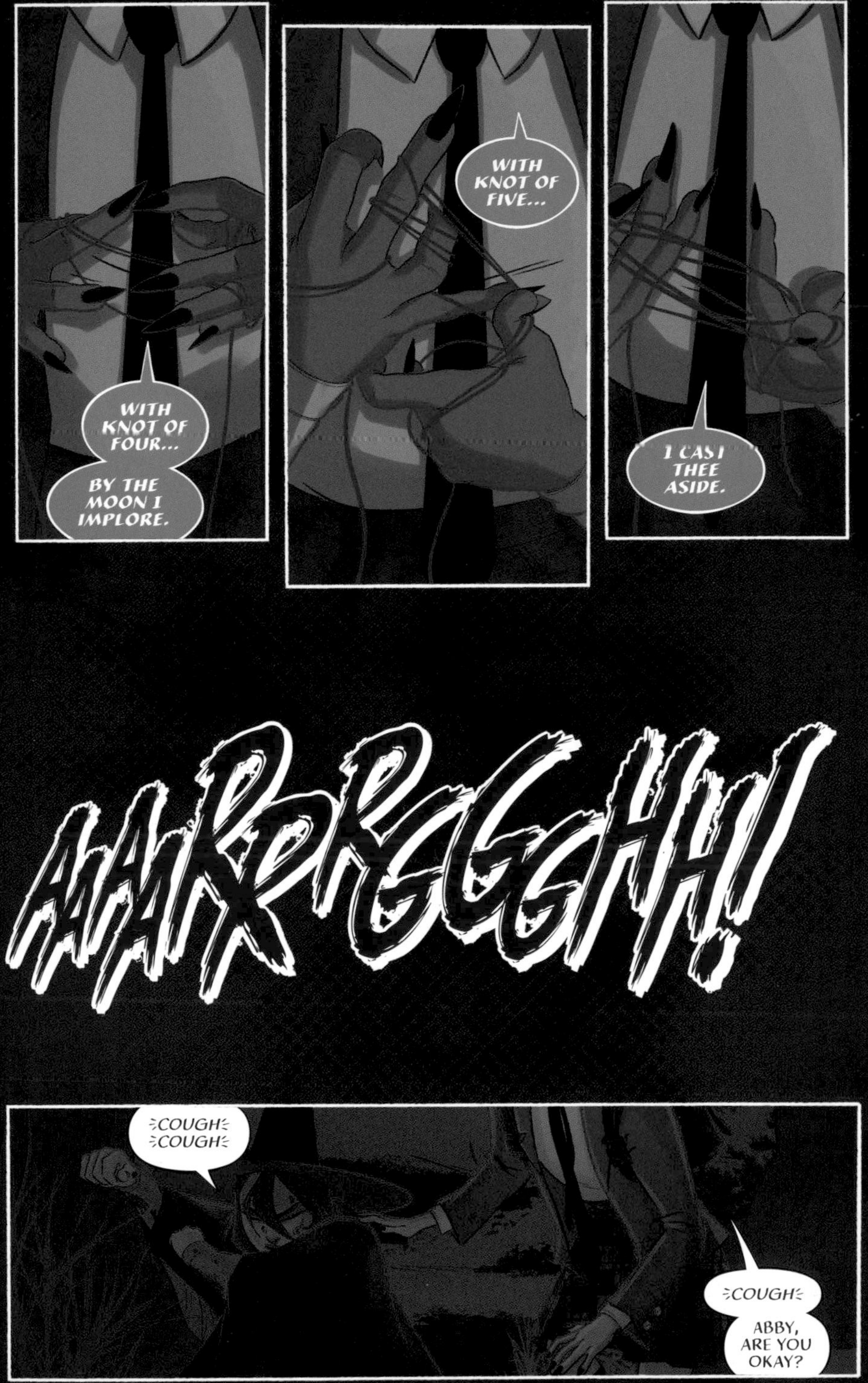
WITH KNOT OF FOUR...
BY THE MOON I IMPLORE.
WITH KNOT OF FIVE...
I CAST THEE ASIDE.
AAARRRGGGHH!
COUGH *COUGH*
COUGH
ABBY, ARE YOU OKAY?

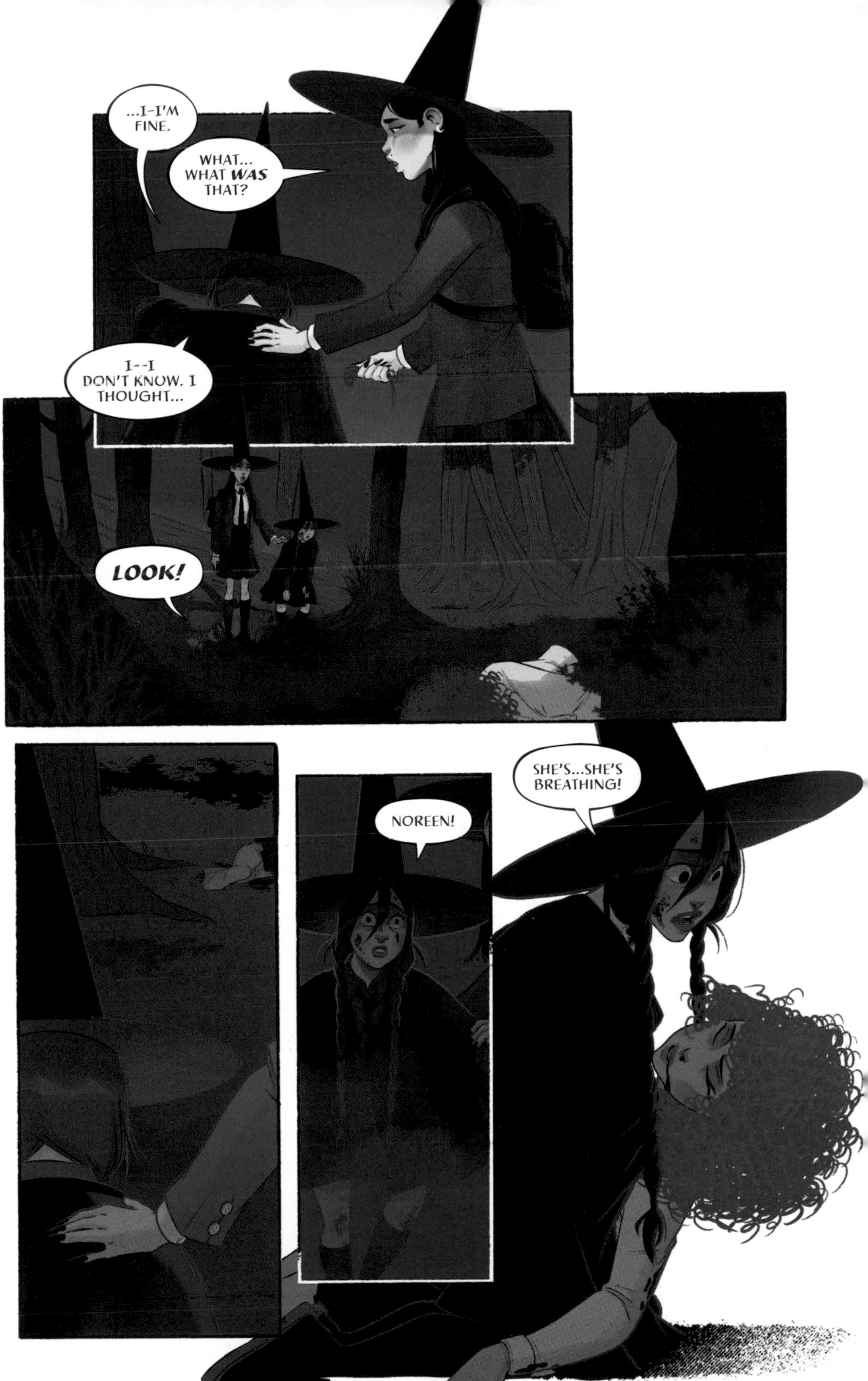
...I-I'M FINE.
WHAT... WHAT WAS THAT?
I--I DON'T KNOW. I THOUGHT...
LOOK!
NOREEN!
SHE'S...SHE'S BREATHING!

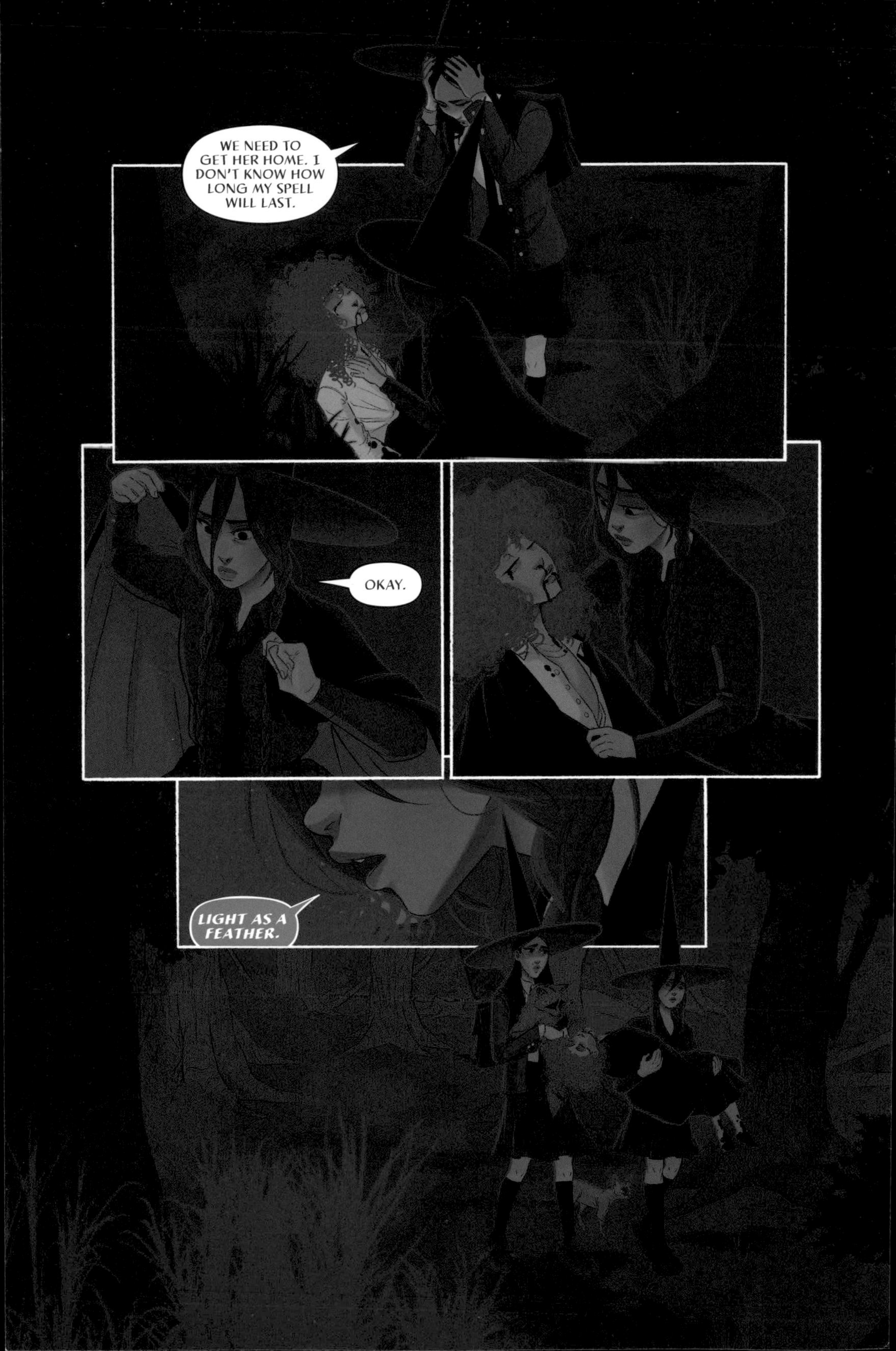
WE NEED TO GET HER HOME. I DON'T KNOW HOW LONG MY SPELL WILL LAST.
OKAY.
LIGHT AS A FEATHER.

CHAPTER IV

From the torrent, or the fountain --
From the red cliff of the mountain --
From the sun that 'round me roll'd
In its autumn tint of gold --

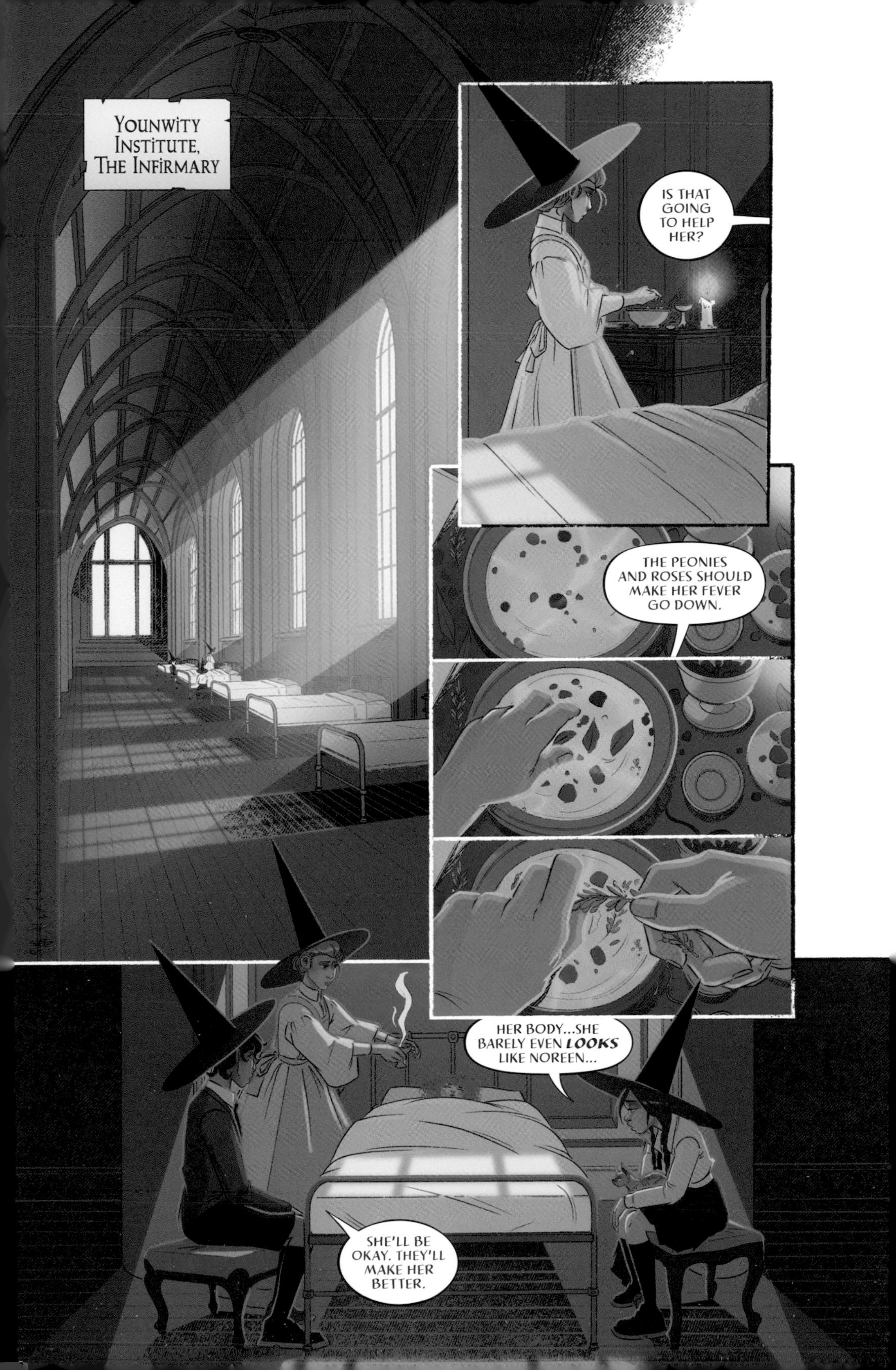
YOUNWITY INSTITUTE, THE INFIRMARY
IS THAT GOING TO HELP HER?
THE PEONIES AND ROSES SHOULD MAKE HER FEVER GO DOWN.
HER BODY...SHE BARELY EVEN ***LOOKS*** LIKE NOREEN...
SHE'LL BE OKAY. THEY'LL MAKE HER BETTER.

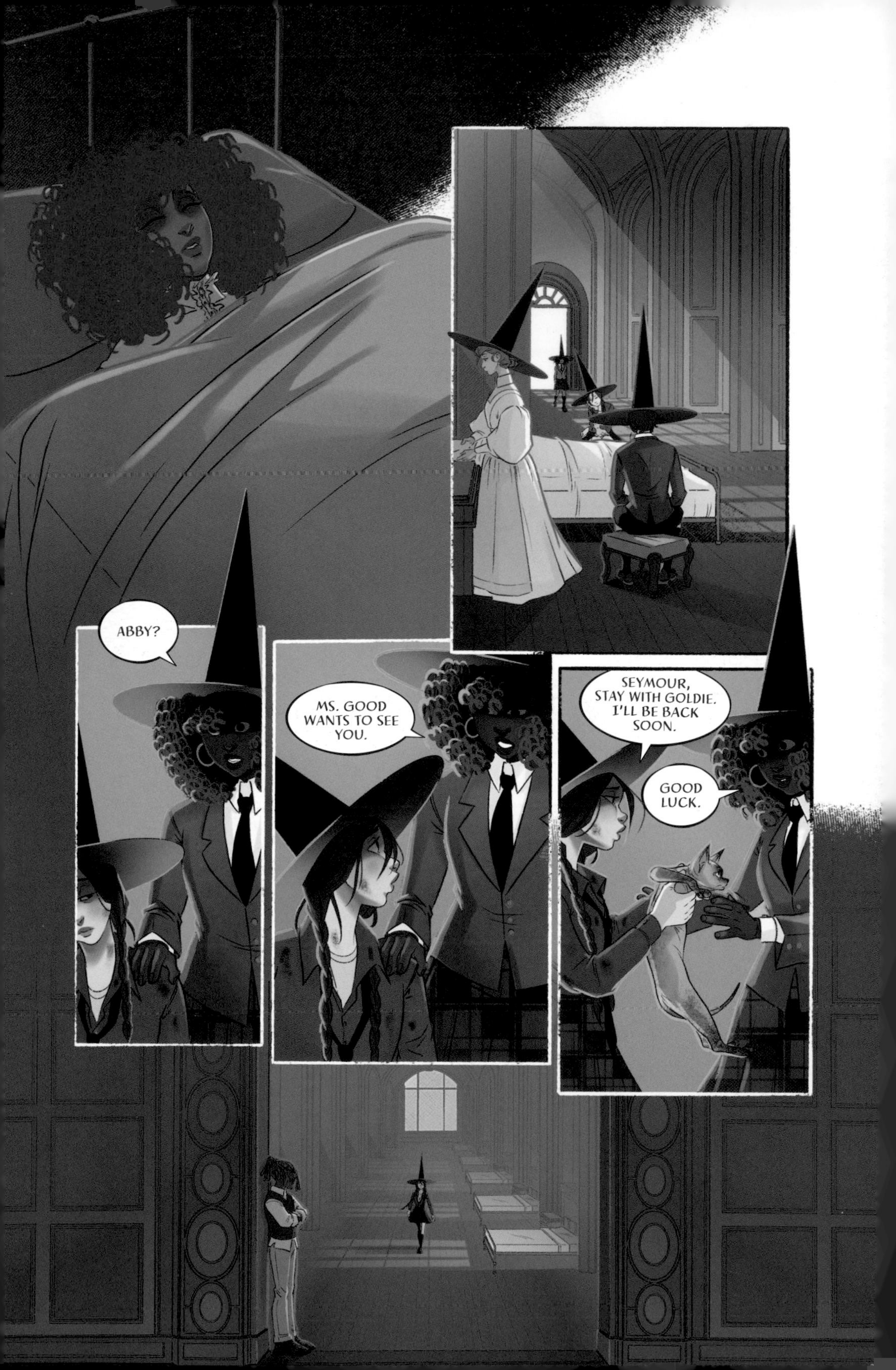
ABBY?
MS. GOOD WANTS TO SEE YOU.
SEYMOUR, STAY WITH GOLDIE. I'LL BE BACK SOON.
GOOD LUCK.

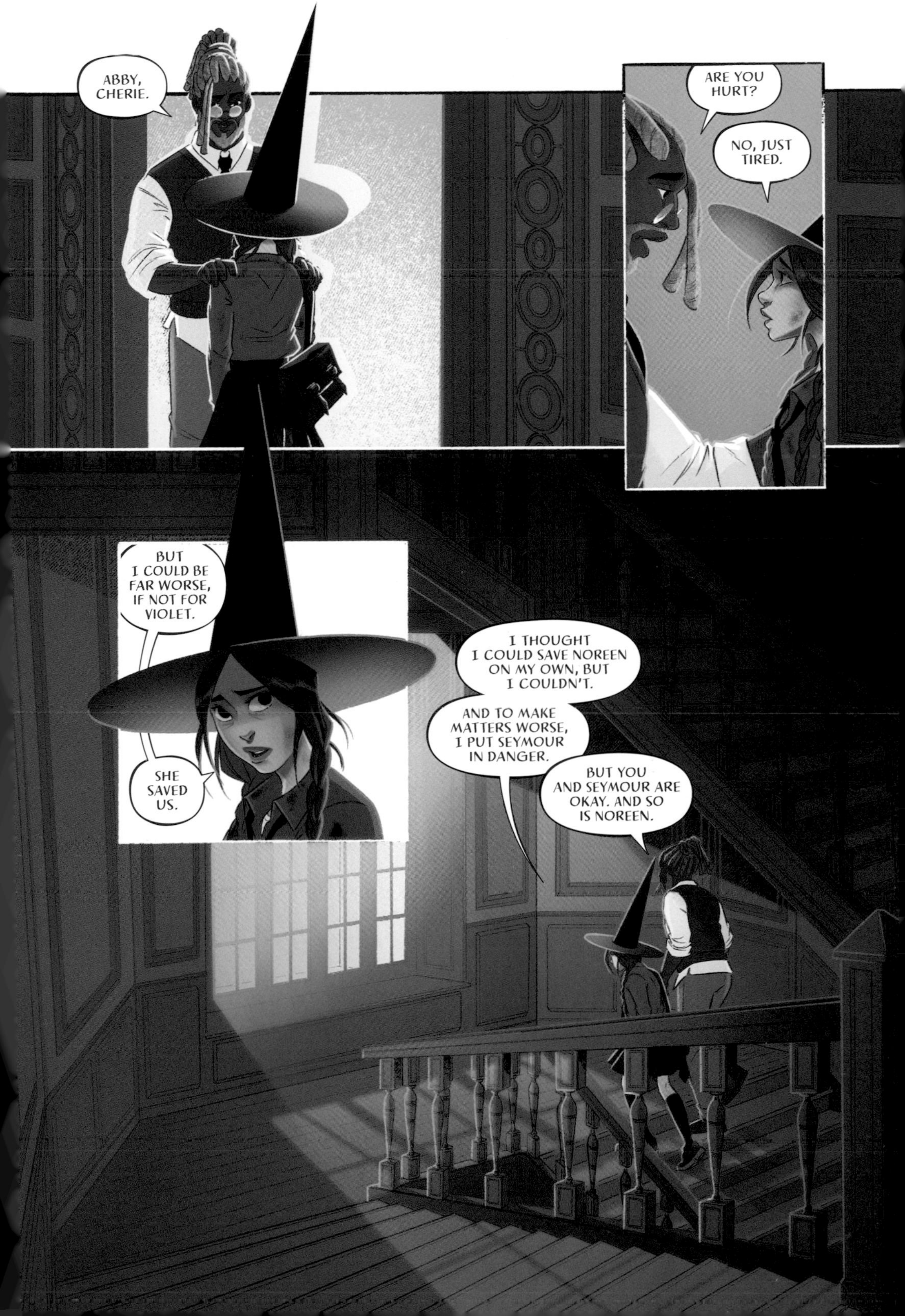
ABBY, CHERIE.
ARE YOU HURT?
NO, JUST TIRED.
BUT I COULD BE FAR WORSE, IF NOT FOR VIOLET.
SHE SAVED US.
I THOUGHT I COULD SAVE NOREEN ON MY OWN, BUT I COULDN'T.
AND TO MAKE MATTERS WORSE, I PUT SEYMOUR IN DANGER.
BUT YOU AND SEYMOUR ARE OKAY. AND SO IS NOREEN.

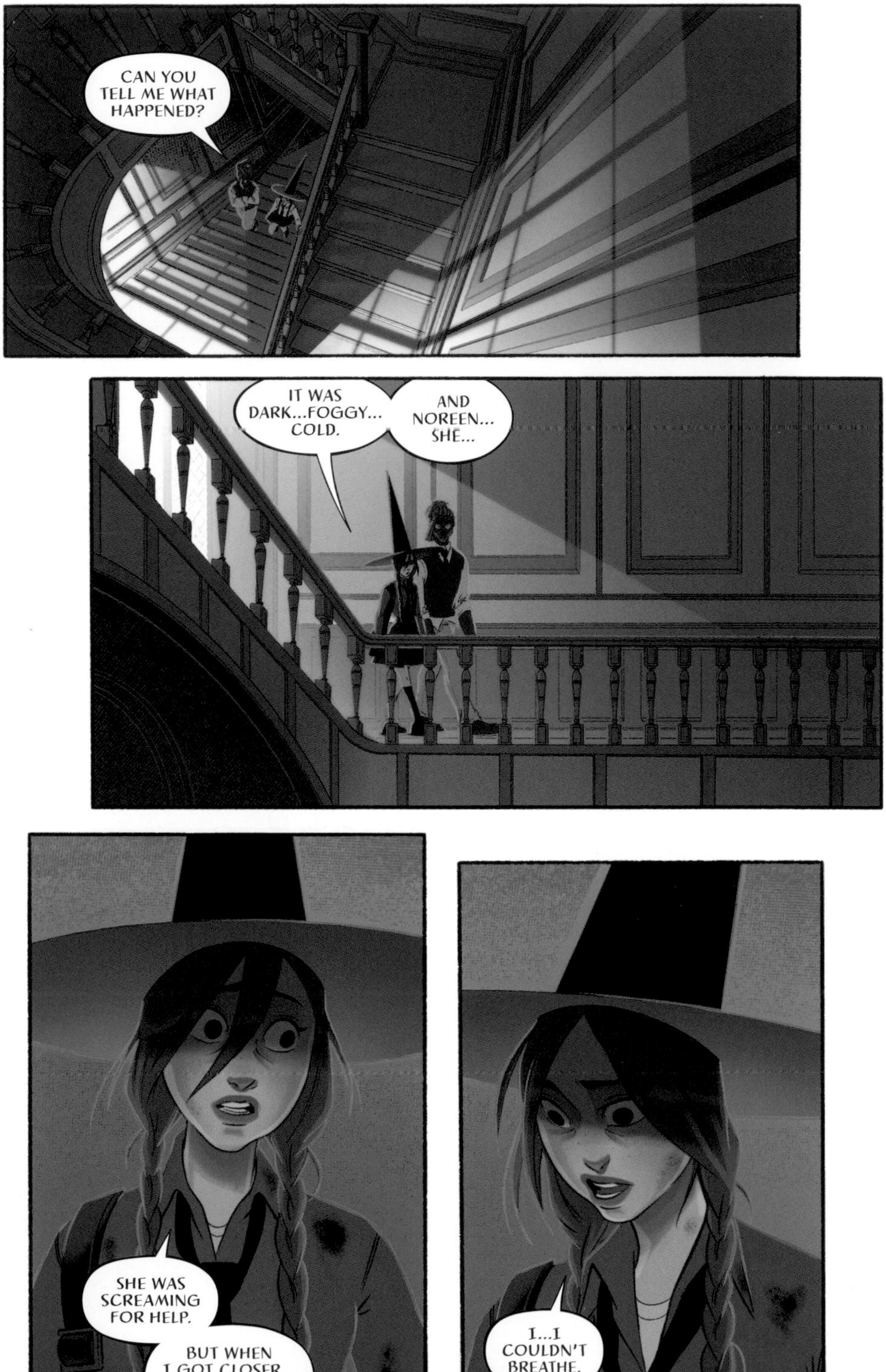
CAN YOU TELL ME WHAT HAPPENED?
IT WAS DARK...FOGGY... COLD.
AND NOREEN... SHE...
SHE WAS SCREAMING FOR HELP.
BUT WHEN I GOT CLOSER... SHE TRIED TO CHOKE ME.
I...I COULDN'T BREATHE.
AND, AND...

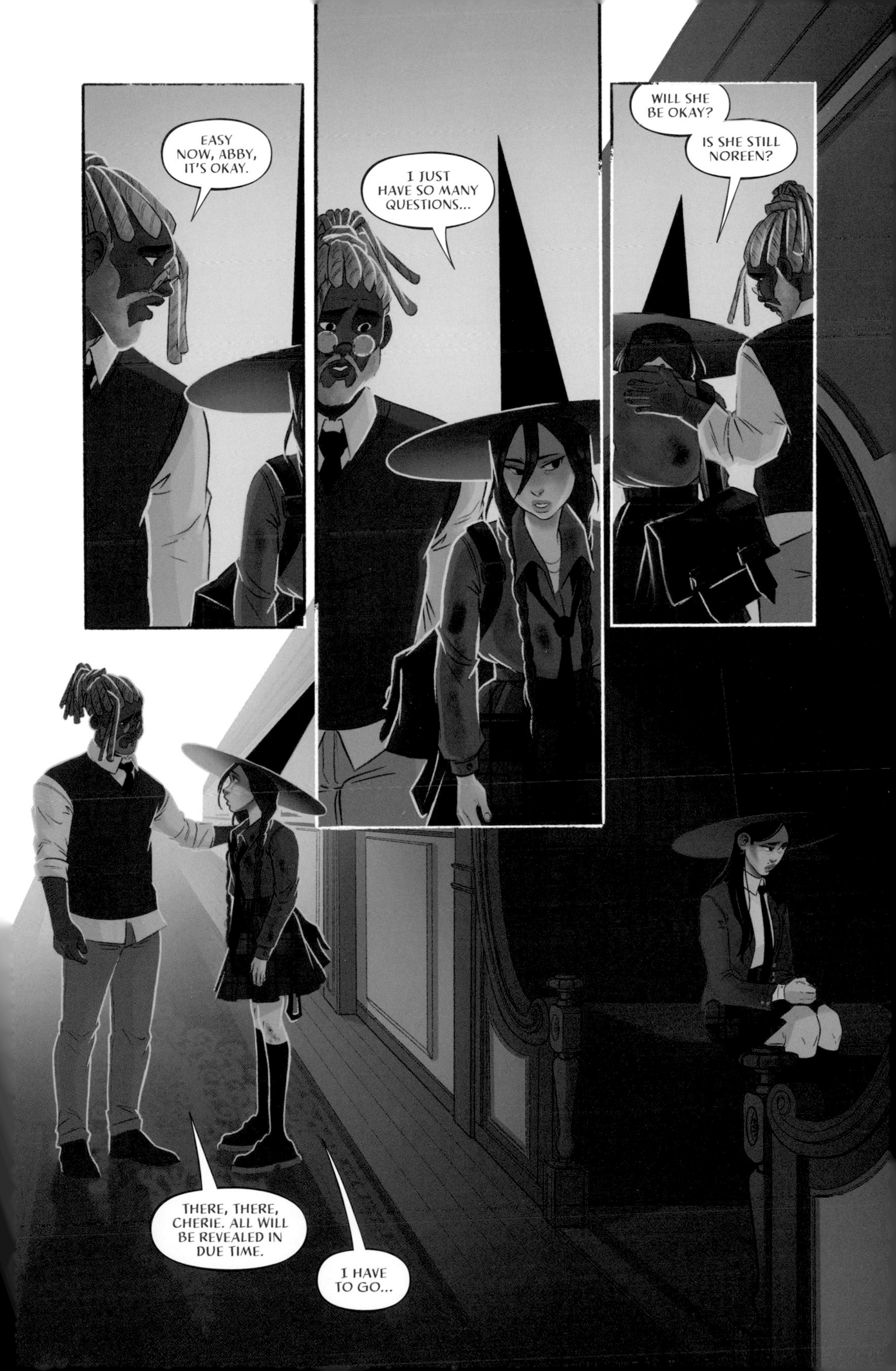

EASY NOW, ABBY, IT'S OKAY.
I JUST HAVE SO MANY QUESTIONS...
WILL SHE BE OKAY?
IS SHE STILL NOREEN?
THERE, THERE, CHERIE. ALL WILL BE REVEALED IN DUE TIME.
I HAVE TO GO...

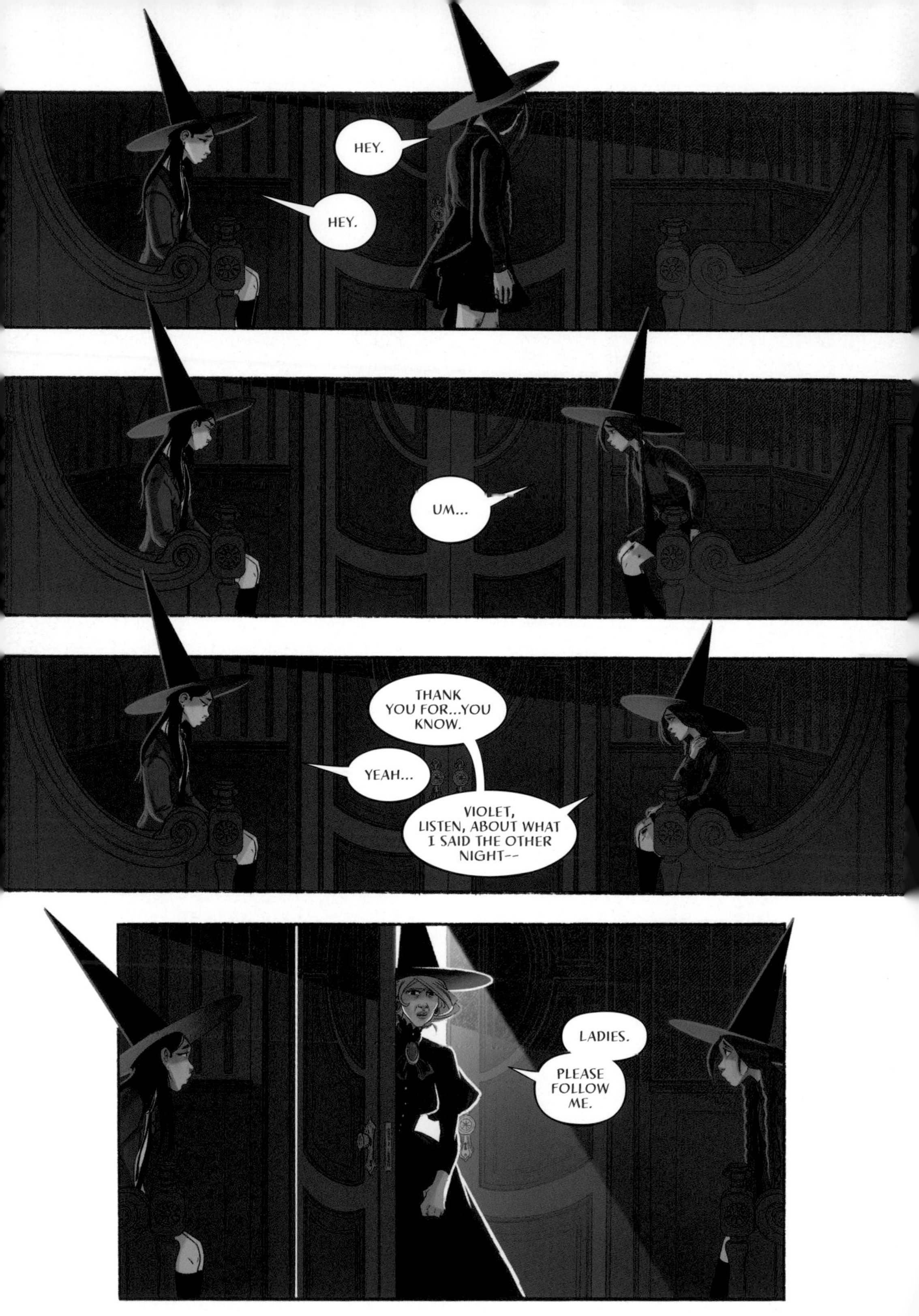
HEY.
HEY.
UM...
THANK YOU FOR...YOU KNOW.
YEAH...
VIOLET, LISTEN, ABOUT WHAT I SAID THE OTHER NIGHT--
LADIES.
PLEASE FOLLOW ME.

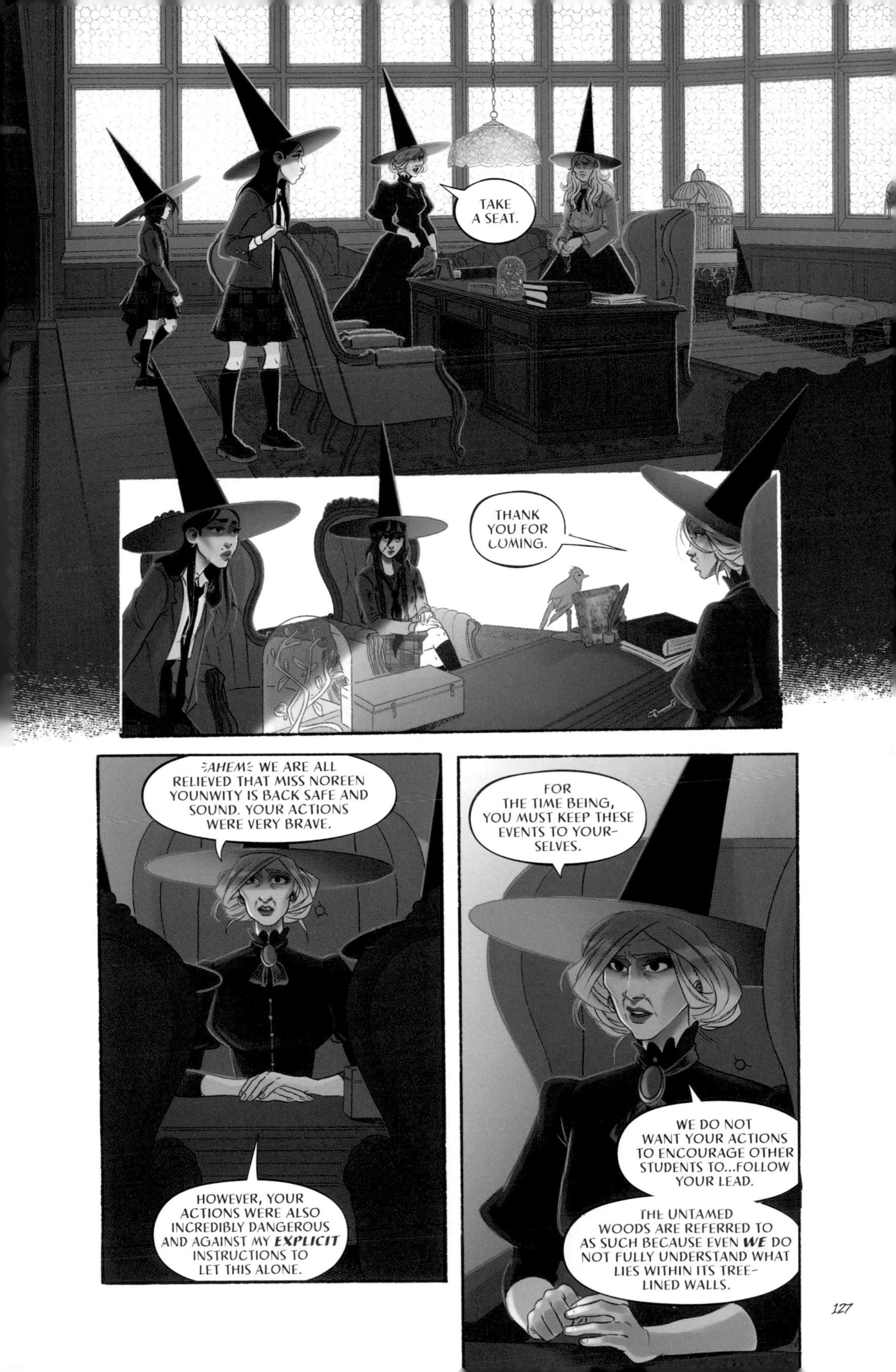
TAKE A SEAT.
THANK YOU FOR COMING.
AHEM WE ARE ALL RELIEVED THAT MISS NOREEN YOUNWITY IS BACK SAFE AND SOUND. YOUR ACTIONS WERE VERY BRAVE.
HOWEVER, YOUR ACTIONS WERE ALSO INCREDIBLY DANGEROUS AND AGAINST MY **EXPLICIT** INSTRUCTIONS TO LET THIS ALONE.
FOR THE TIME BEING, YOU MUST KEEP THESE EVENTS TO YOURSELVES.
WE DO NOT WANT YOUR ACTIONS TO ENCOURAGE OTHER STUDENTS TO...FOLLOW YOUR LEAD.
THE UNTAMED WOODS ARE REFERRED TO AS SUCH BECAUSE EVEN **WE** DO NOT FULLY UNDERSTAND WHAT LIES WITHIN ITS TREE-LINED WALLS.

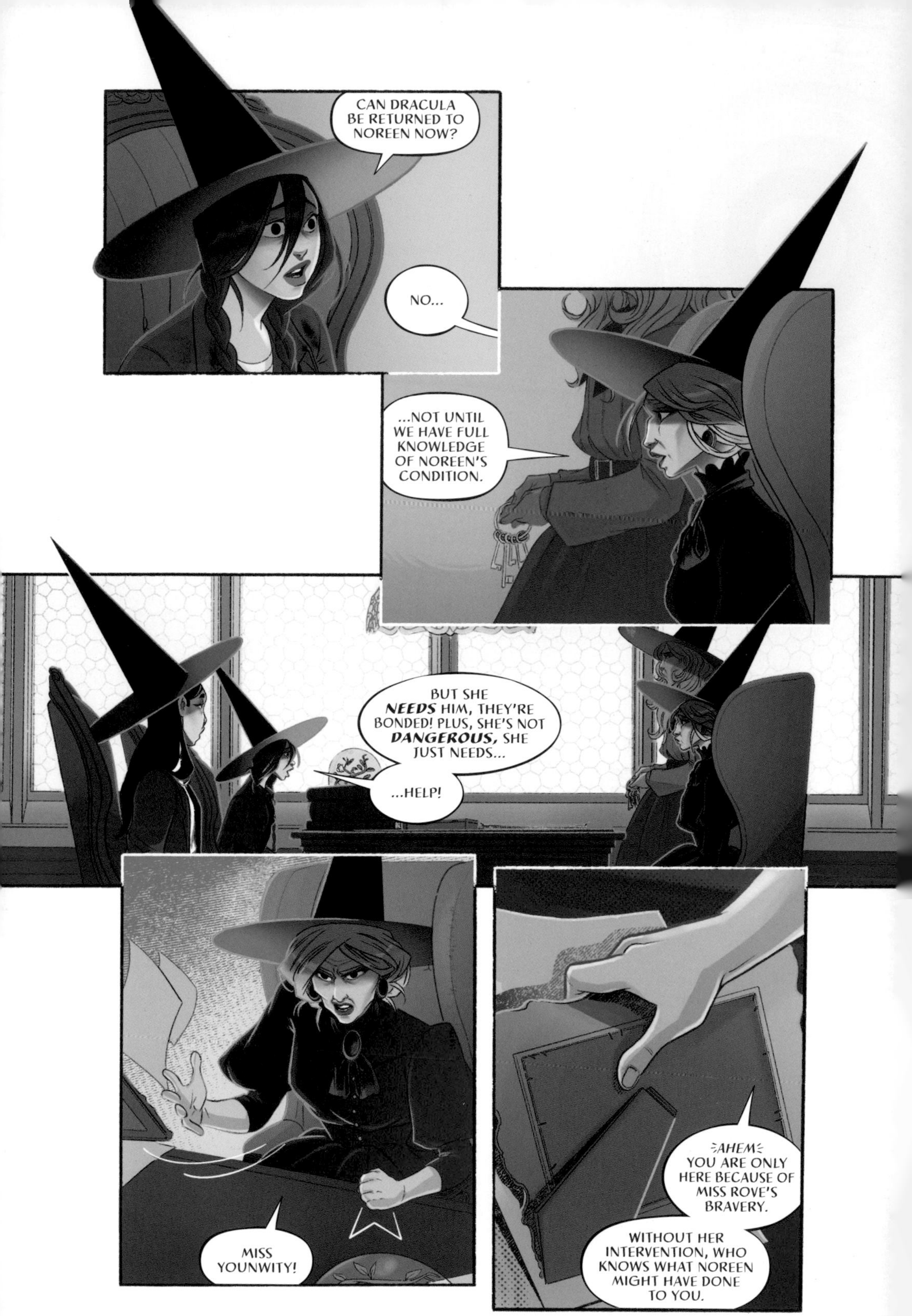
CAN DRACULA BE RETURNED TO NOREEN NOW?
NO...
...NOT UNTIL WE HAVE FULL KNOWLEDGE OF NOREEN'S CONDITION.
BUT SHE NEEDS HIM, THEY'RE BONDED! PLUS, SHE'S NOT DANGEROUS, SHE JUST NEEDS...
...HELP!
MISS YOUNWITY!
AHEM
YOU ARE ONLY HERE BECAUSE OF MISS ROVE'S BRAVERY.
WITHOUT HER INTERVENTION, WHO KNOWS WHAT NOREEN MIGHT HAVE DONE TO YOU.

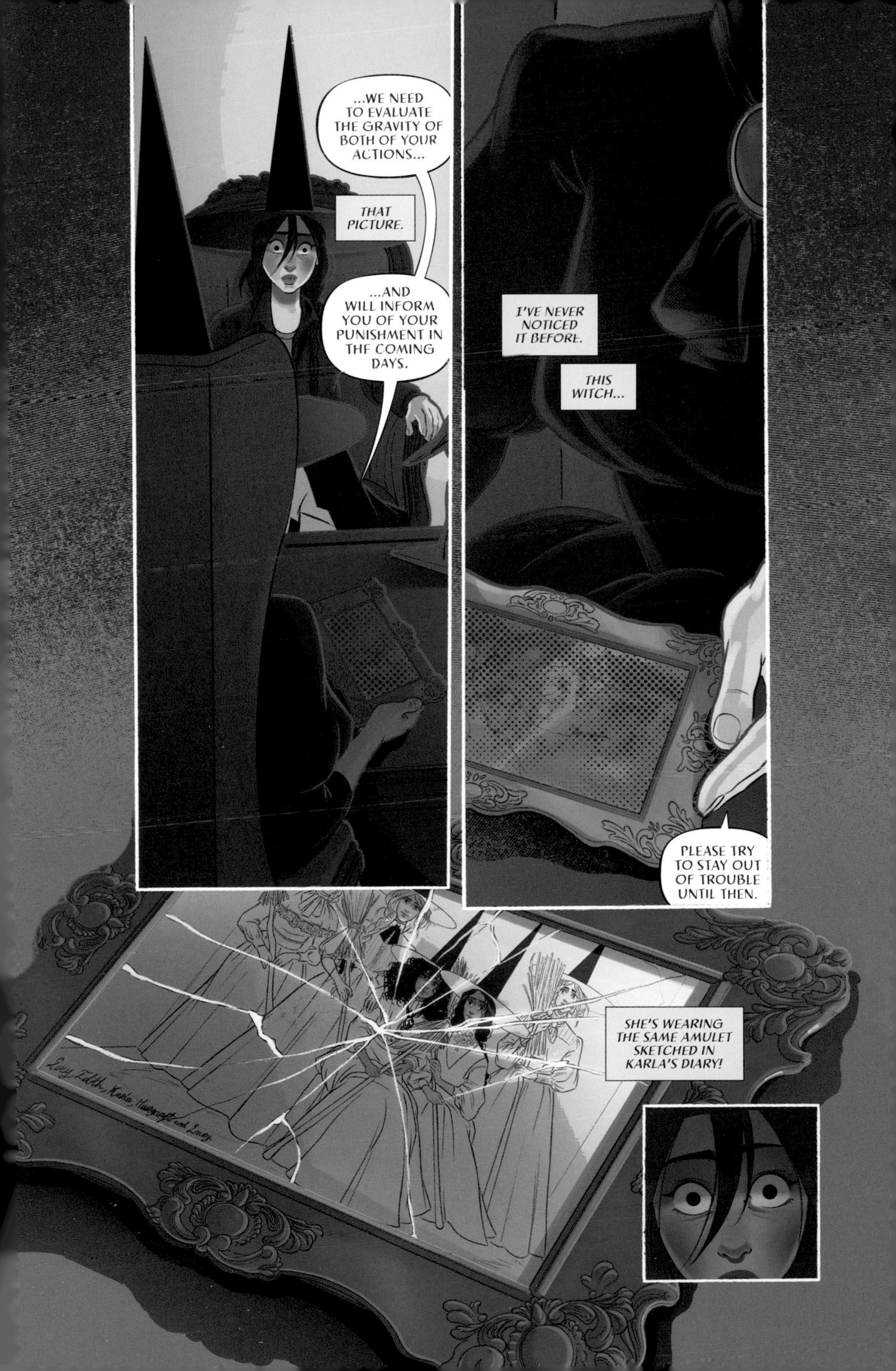
...WE NEED TO EVALUATE THE GRAVITY OF BOTH OF YOUR ACTIONS...
THAT PICTURE.
...AND WILL INFORM YOU OF YOUR PUNISHMENT IN THE COMING DAYS.
I'VE NEVER NOTICED IT BEFORE.
THIS WITCH...
PLEASE TRY TO STAY OUT OF TROUBLE UNTIL THEN.
SHE'S WEARING THE SAME AMULET SKETCHED IN KARLA'S DIARY!

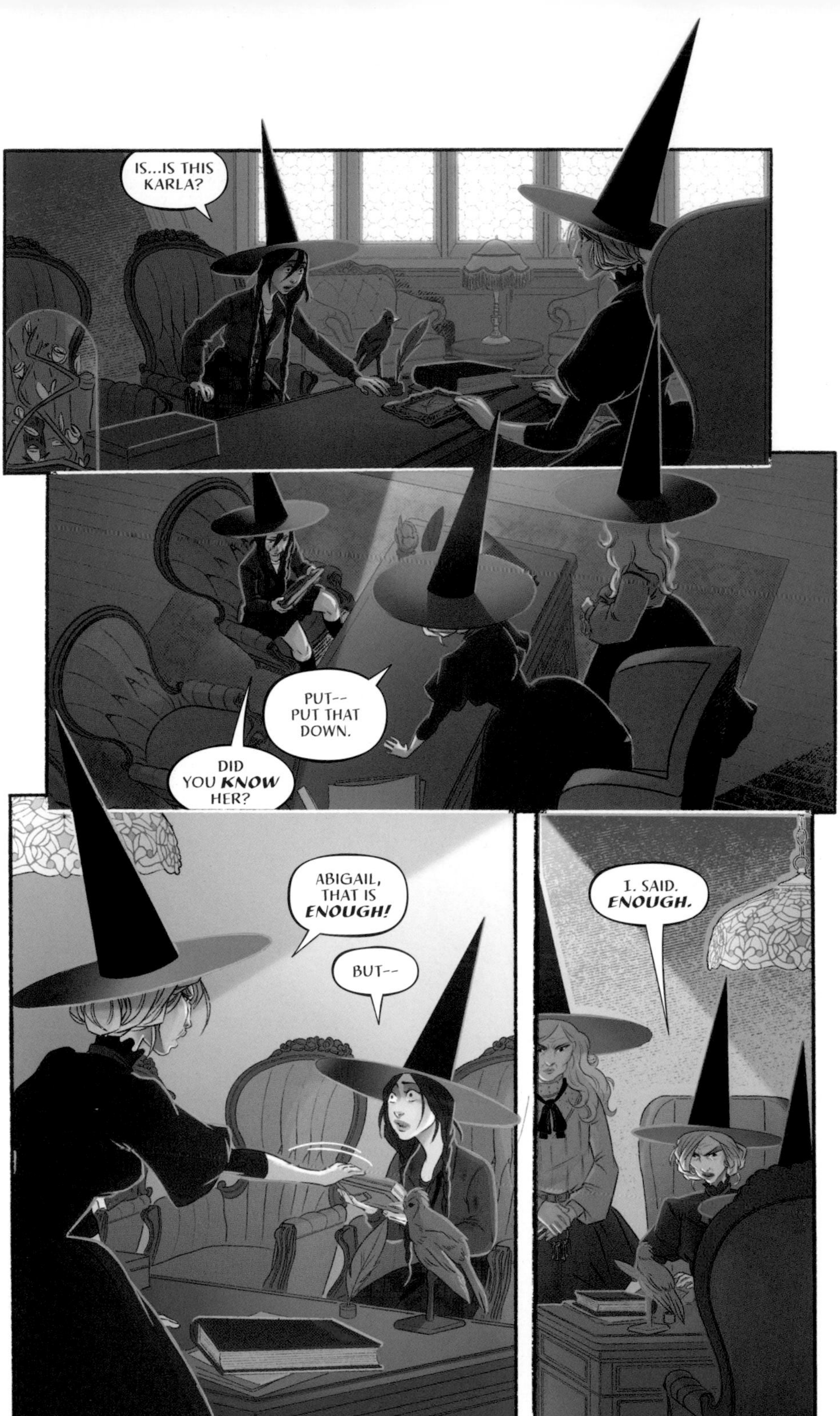
IS...IS THIS KARLA?
PUT-- PUT THAT DOWN.
DID YOU **KNOW** HER?
ABIGAIL, THAT IS **ENOUGH!**
BUT--
I. SAID. **ENOUGH.**

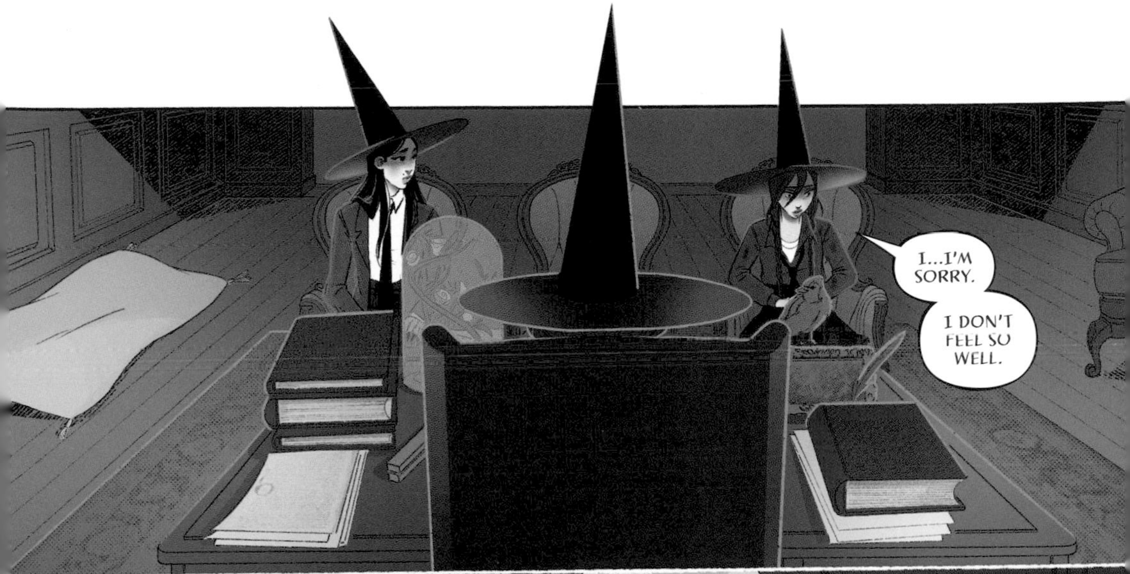
I...I'M SORRY.
I DON'T FEEL SO WELL.

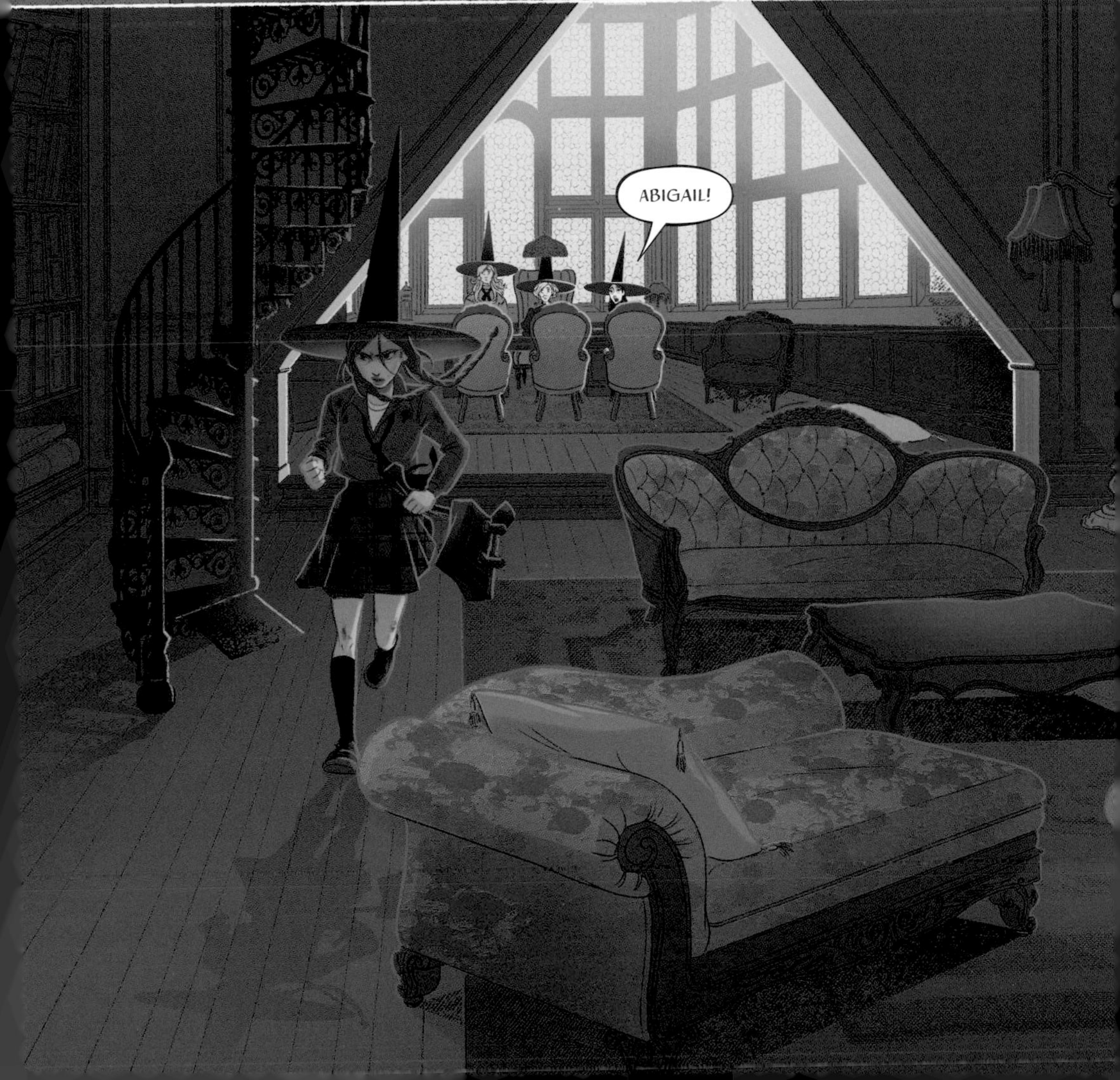
ABIGAIL!

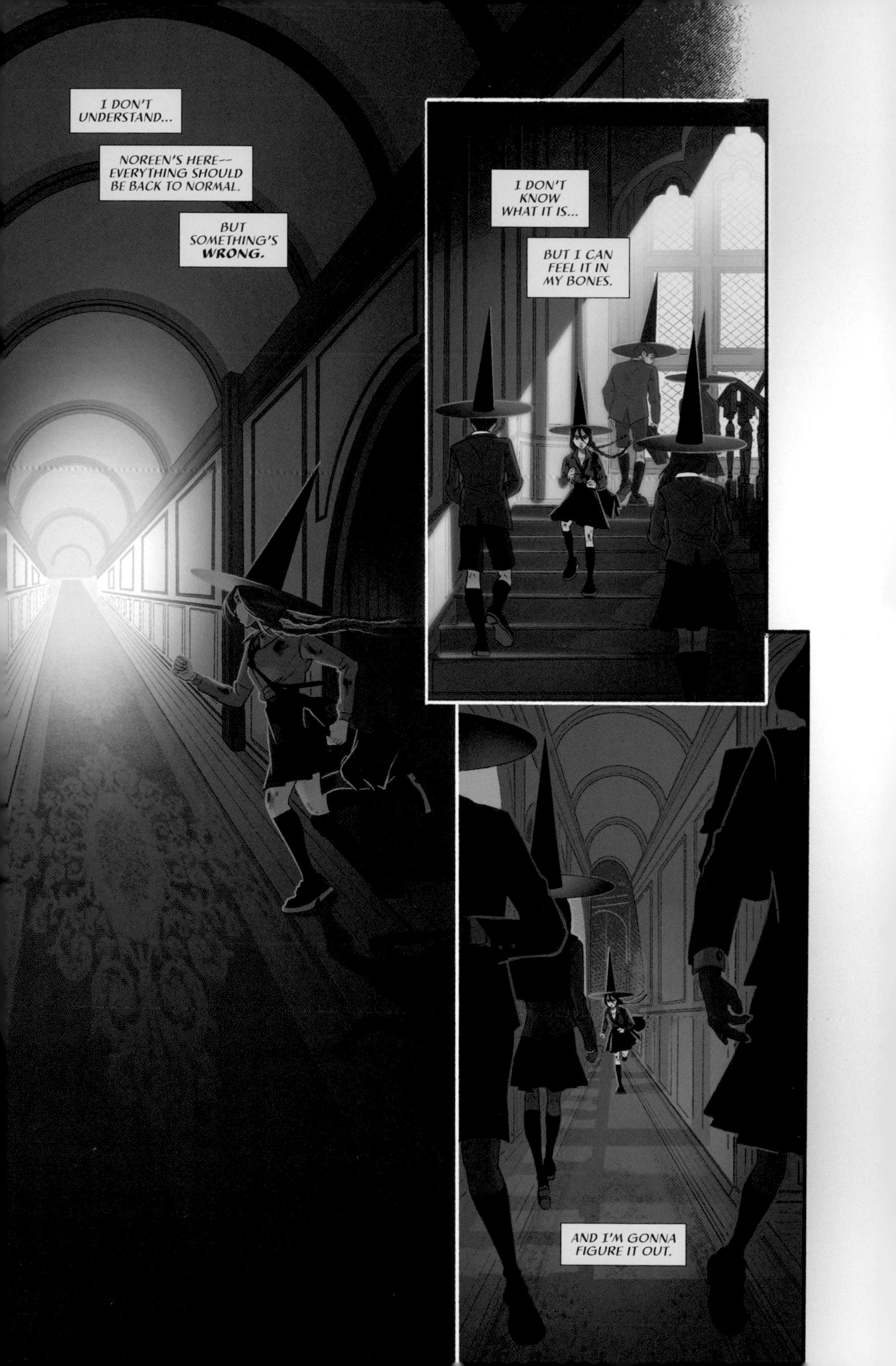
I DON'T UNDERSTAND...
NOREEN'S HERE-- EVERYTHING SHOULD BE BACK TO NORMAL.
BUT SOMETHING'S **WRONG.**
I DON'T KNOW WHAT IT IS...
BUT I CAN FEEL IT IN MY BONES.
AND I'M GONNA FIGURE IT OUT.

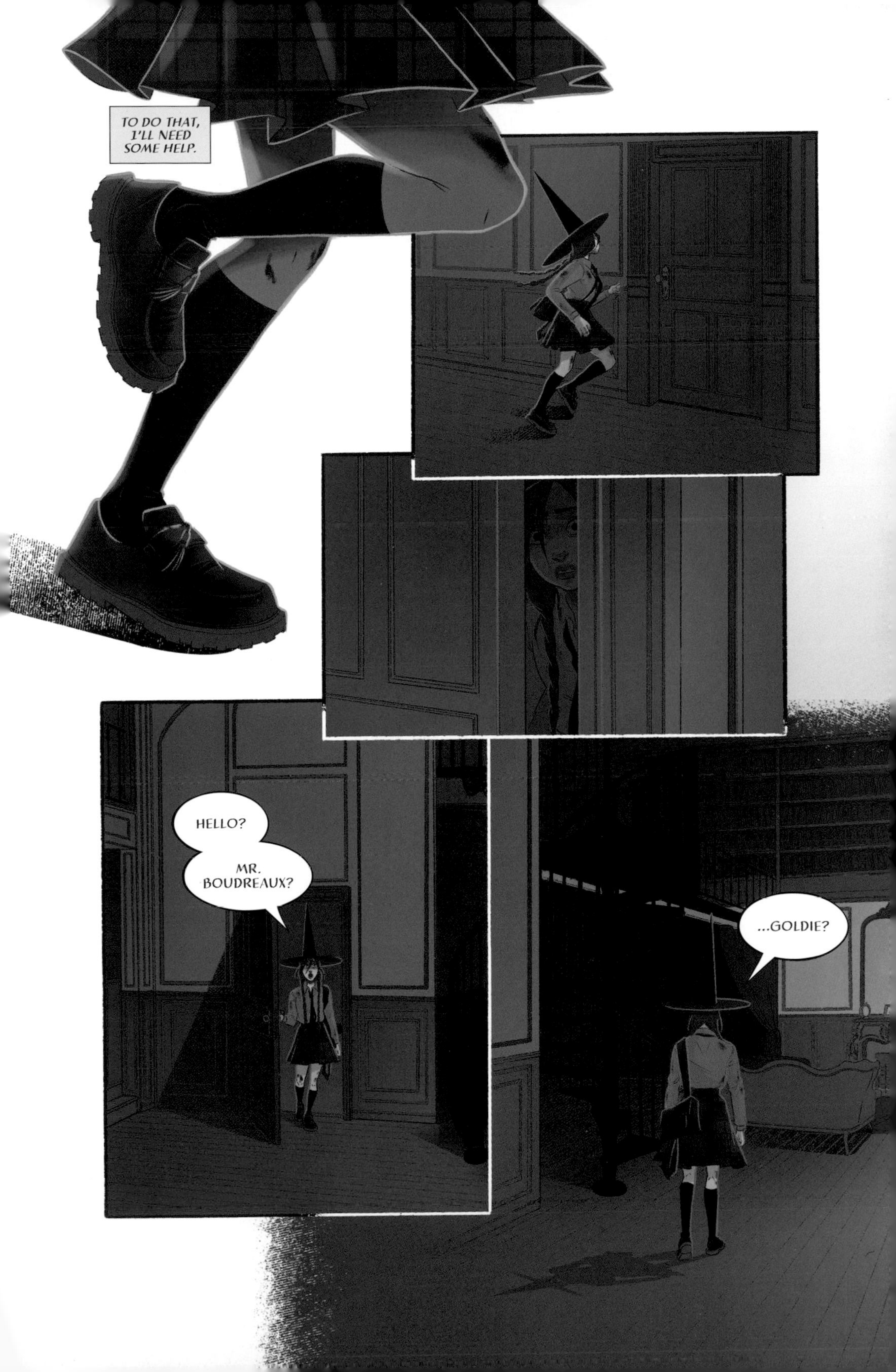
TO DO THAT, I'LL NEED SOME HELP.
HELLO?
MR. BOUDREAUX?
...GOLDIE?

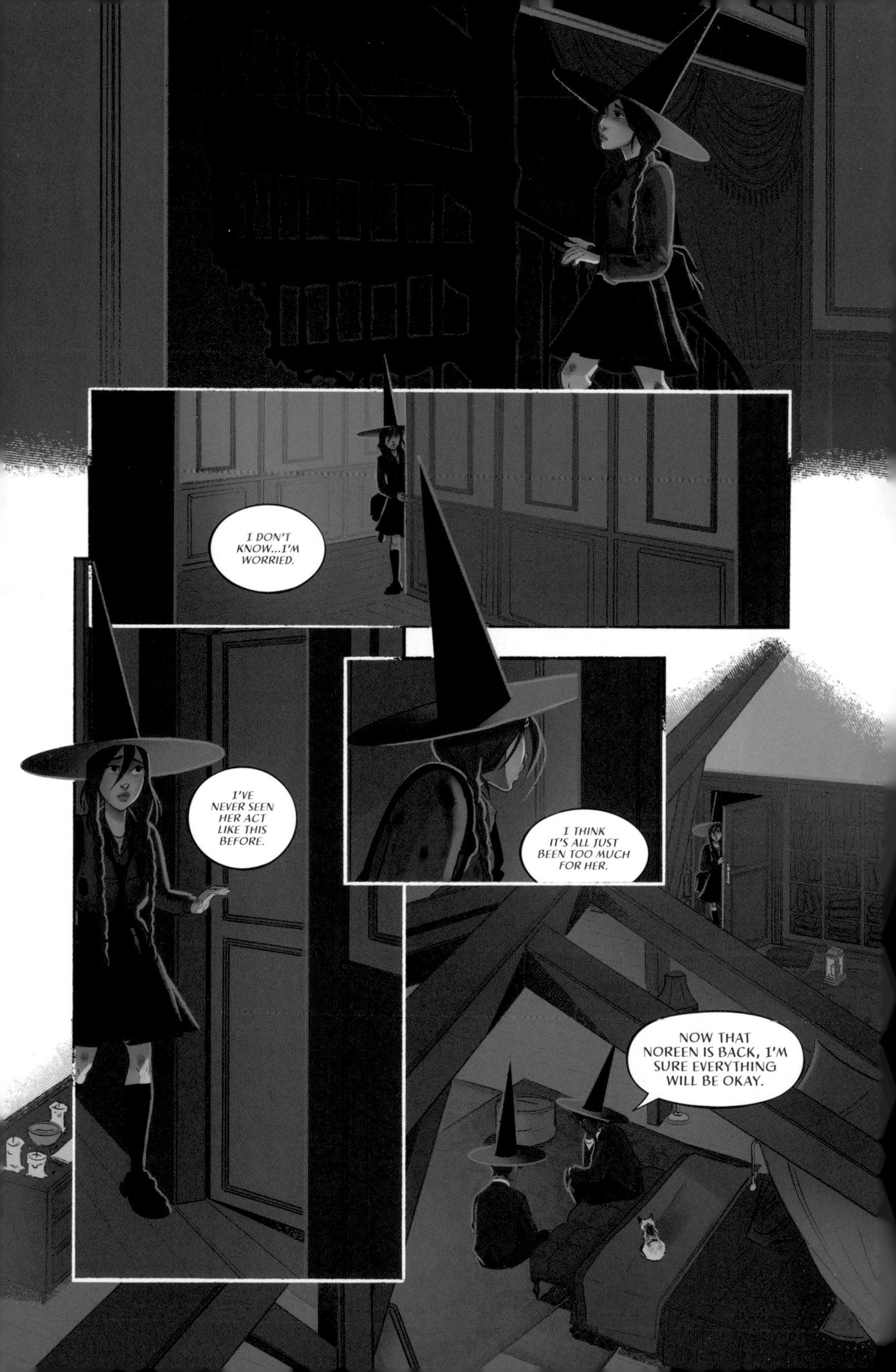
I DON'T KNOW...I'M WORRIED.
I'VE NEVER SEEN HER ACT LIKE THIS BEFORE.
I THINK IT'S ALL JUST BEEN TOO MUCH FOR HER.
NOW THAT NOREEN IS BACK, I'M SURE EVERYTHING WILL BE OKAY.

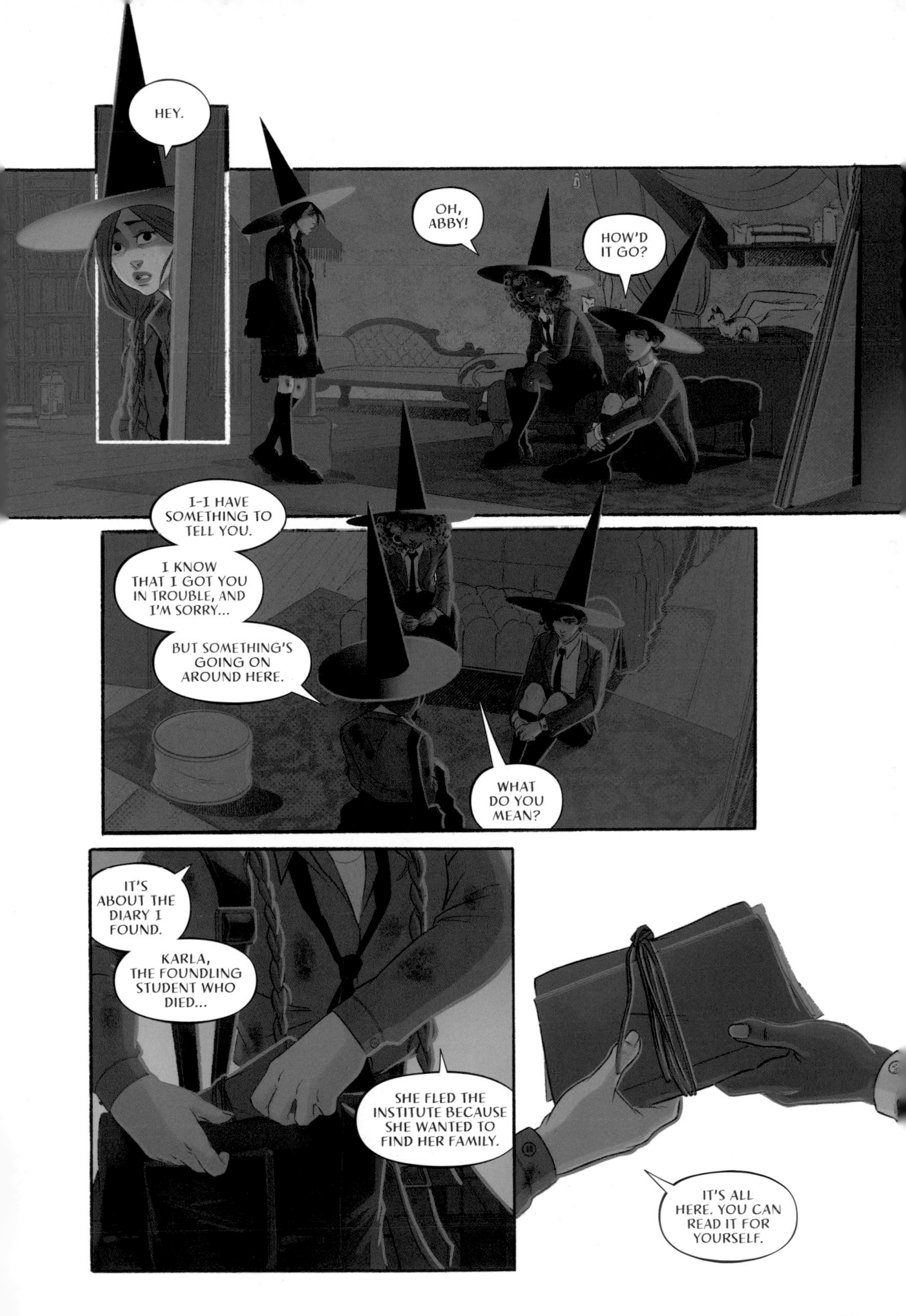
HEY.
OH, ABBY!
HOW'D IT GO?
I-I HAVE SOMETHING TO TELL YOU.
I KNOW THAT I GOT YOU IN TROUBLE, AND I'M SORRY...
BUT SOMETHING'S GOING ON AROUND HERE.
WHAT DO YOU MEAN?
IT'S ABOUT THE DIARY I FOUND.
KARLA, THE FOUNDLING STUDENT WHO DIED...
SHE FLED THE INSTITUTE BECAUSE SHE WANTED TO FIND HER FAMILY.
IT'S ALL HERE. YOU CAN READ IT FOR YOURSELF.

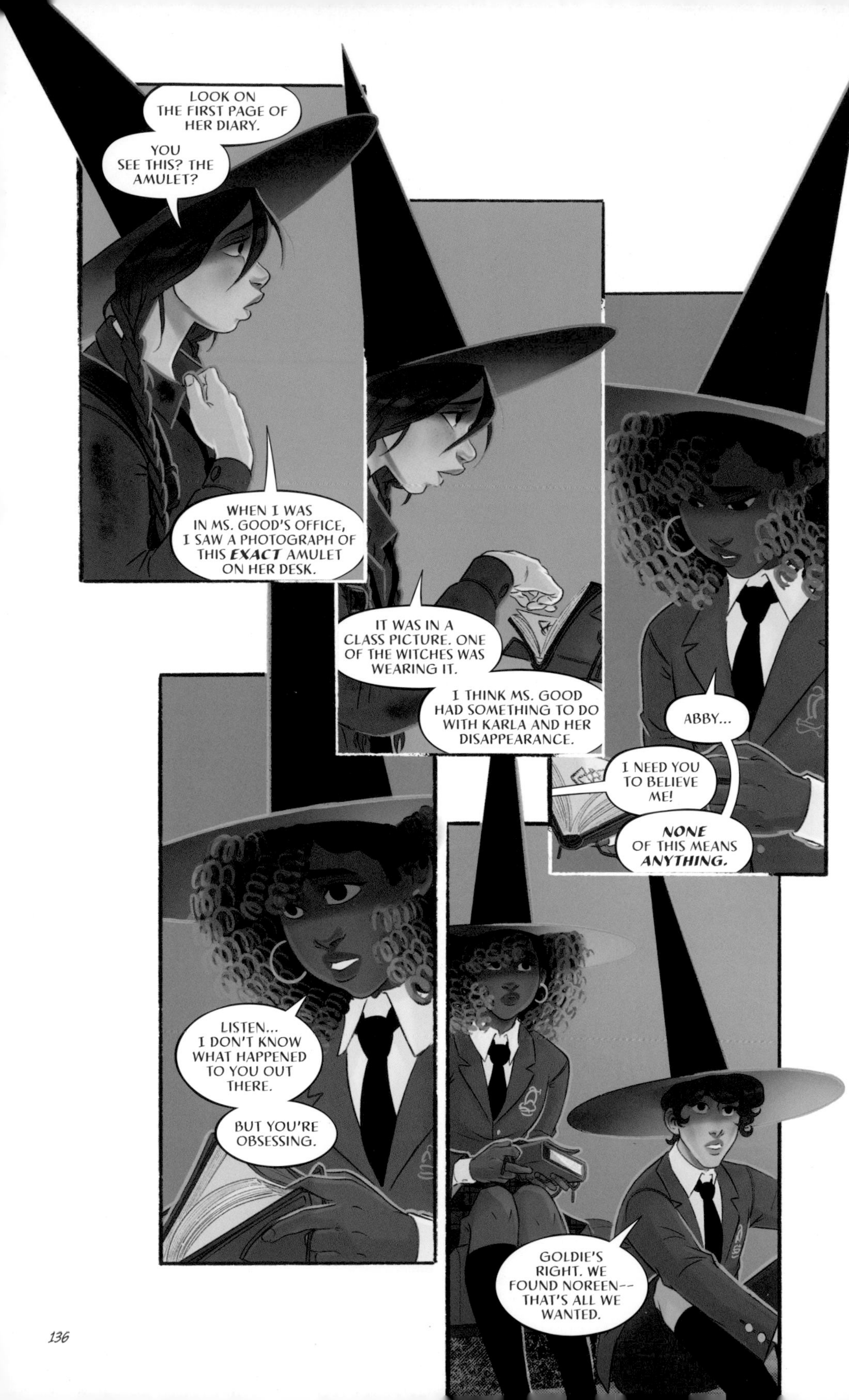

LOOK ON THE FIRST PAGE OF HER DIARY.
YOU SEE THIS? THE AMULET?
WHEN I WAS IN MS. GOOD'S OFFICE, I SAW A PHOTOGRAPH OF THIS *EXACT* AMULET ON HER DESK.
IT WAS IN A CLASS PICTURE. ONE OF THE WITCHES WAS WEARING IT.
I THINK MS. GOOD HAD SOMETHING TO DO WITH KARLA AND HER DISAPPEARANCE.
ABBY...
I NEED YOU TO BELIEVE ME!
NONE OF THIS MEANS *ANYTHING.*
LISTEN... I DON'T KNOW WHAT HAPPENED TO YOU OUT THERE.
BUT YOU'RE OBSESSING.
GOLDIE'S RIGHT. WE FOUND NOREEN-- THAT'S ALL WE WANTED.

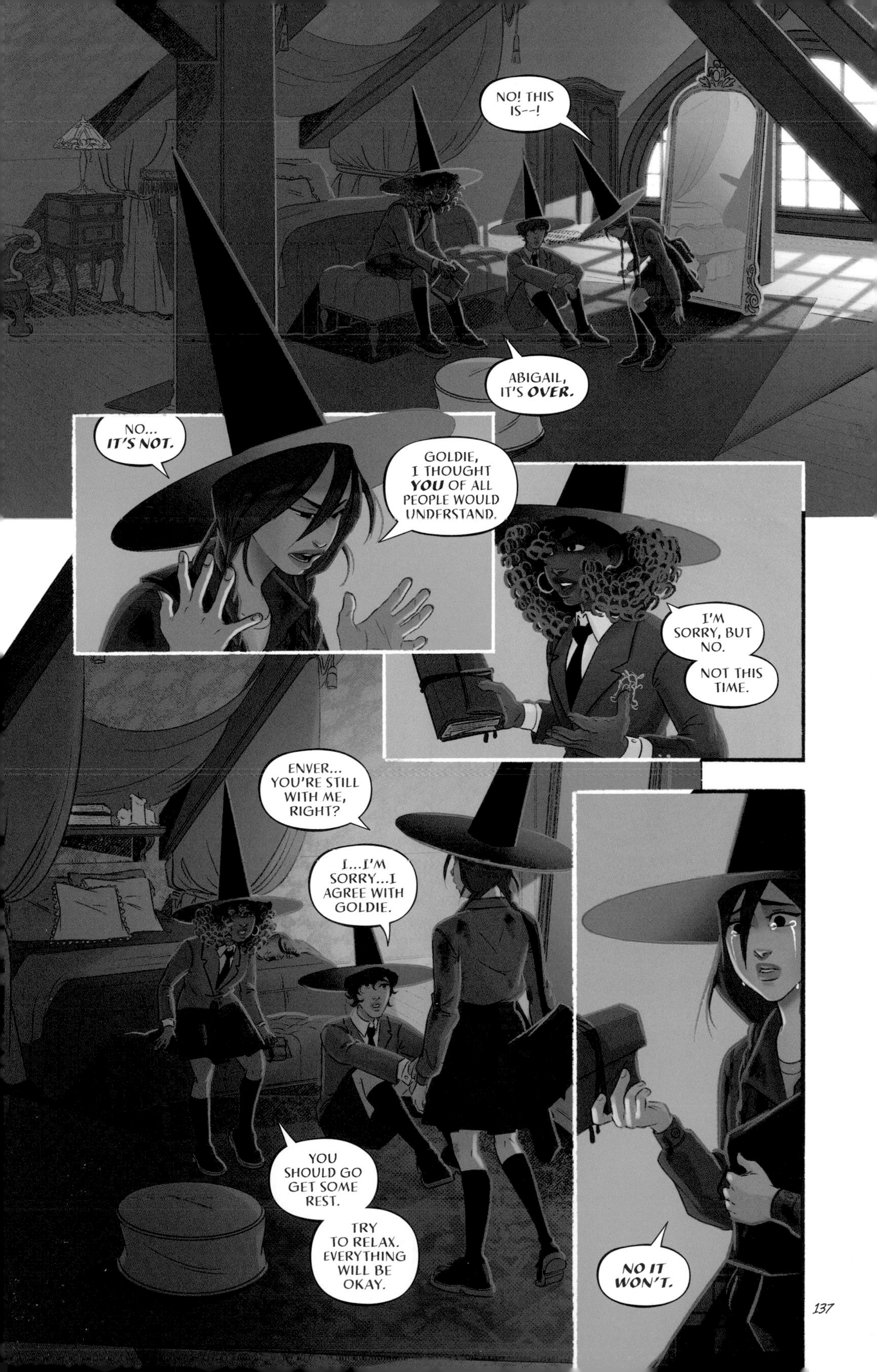
NO! THIS IS--!
ABIGAIL, IT'S OVER.
NO... IT'S NOT.
GOLDIE, I THOUGHT YOU OF ALL PEOPLE WOULD UNDERSTAND.
I'M SORRY, BUT NO.
NOT THIS TIME.
ENVER... YOU'RE STILL WITH ME, RIGHT?
I...I'M SORRY...I AGREE WITH GOLDIE.
YOU SHOULD GO GET SOME REST.
TRY TO RELAX. EVERYTHING WILL BE OKAY.
NO IT WON'T.

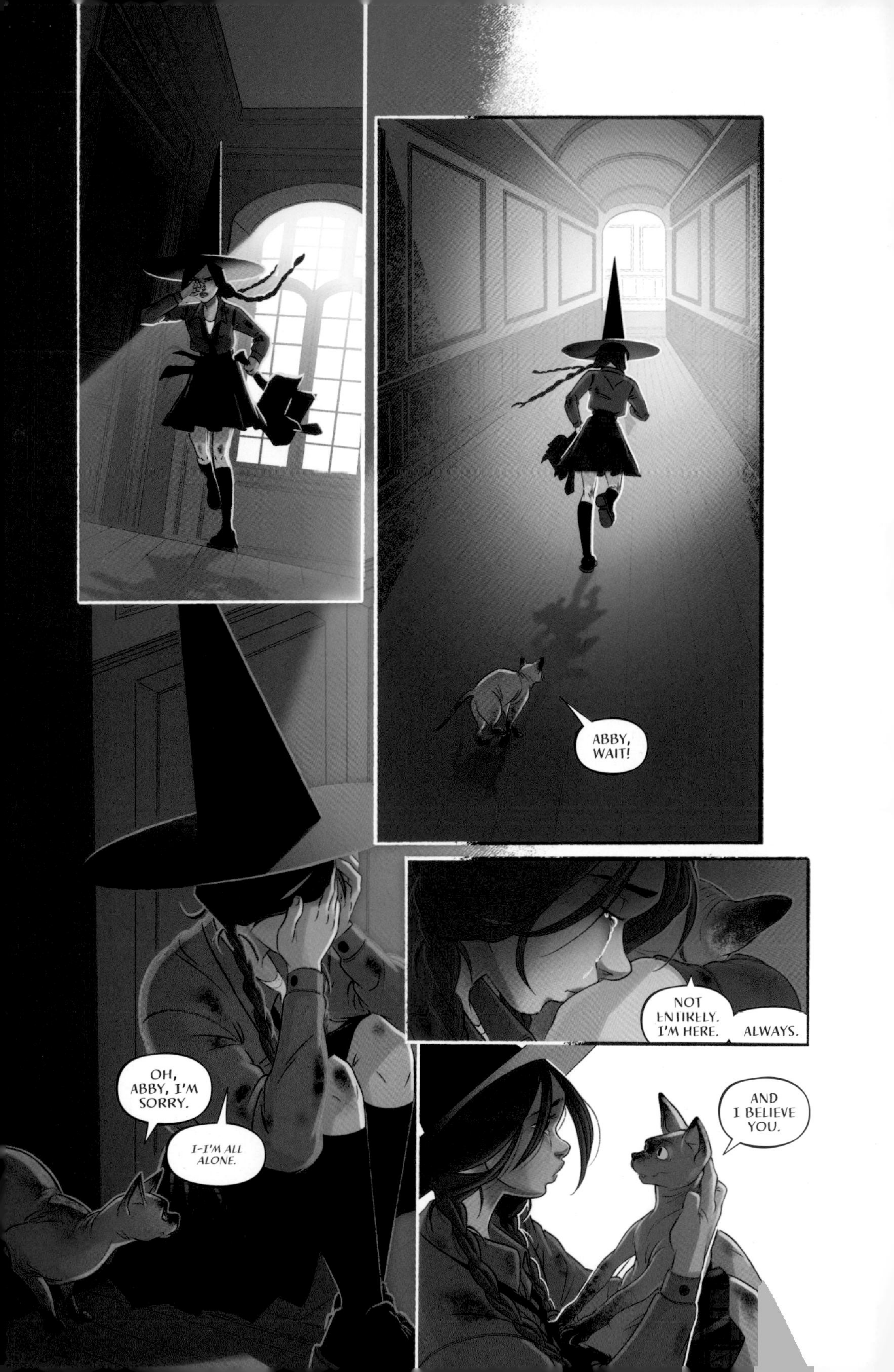

ABBY, WAIT!
NOT ENTIRELY. I'M HERE.
ALWAYS.
OH, ABBY, I'M SORRY.
I-I'M ALL ALONE.
AND I BELIEVE YOU.

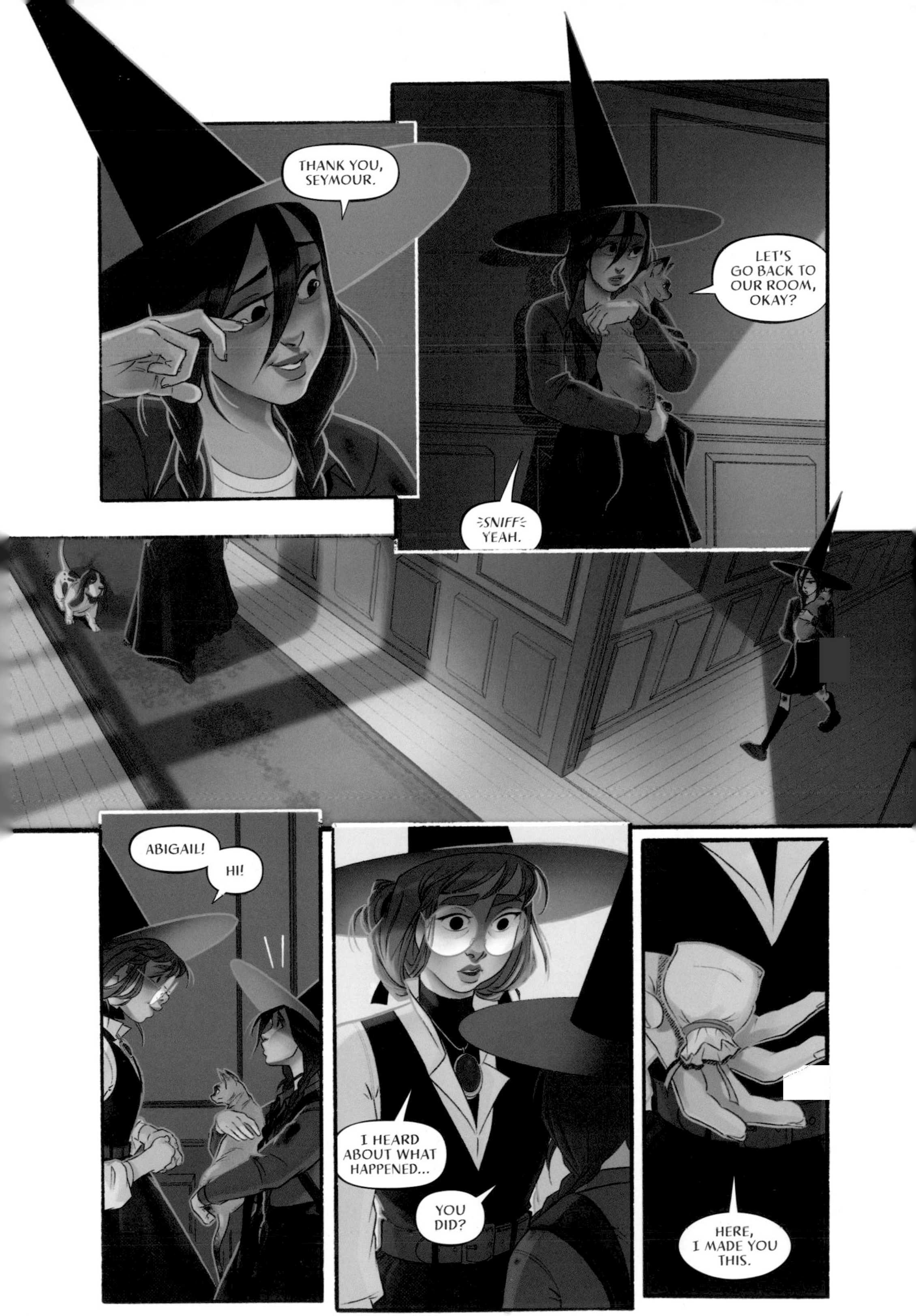
THANK YOU, SEYMOUR.
LET'S GO BACK TO OUR ROOM, OKAY?
SNIFF YEAH.
ABIGAIL!
HI!
I HEARD ABOUT WHAT HAPPENED...
YOU DID?
HERE, I MADE YOU THIS.

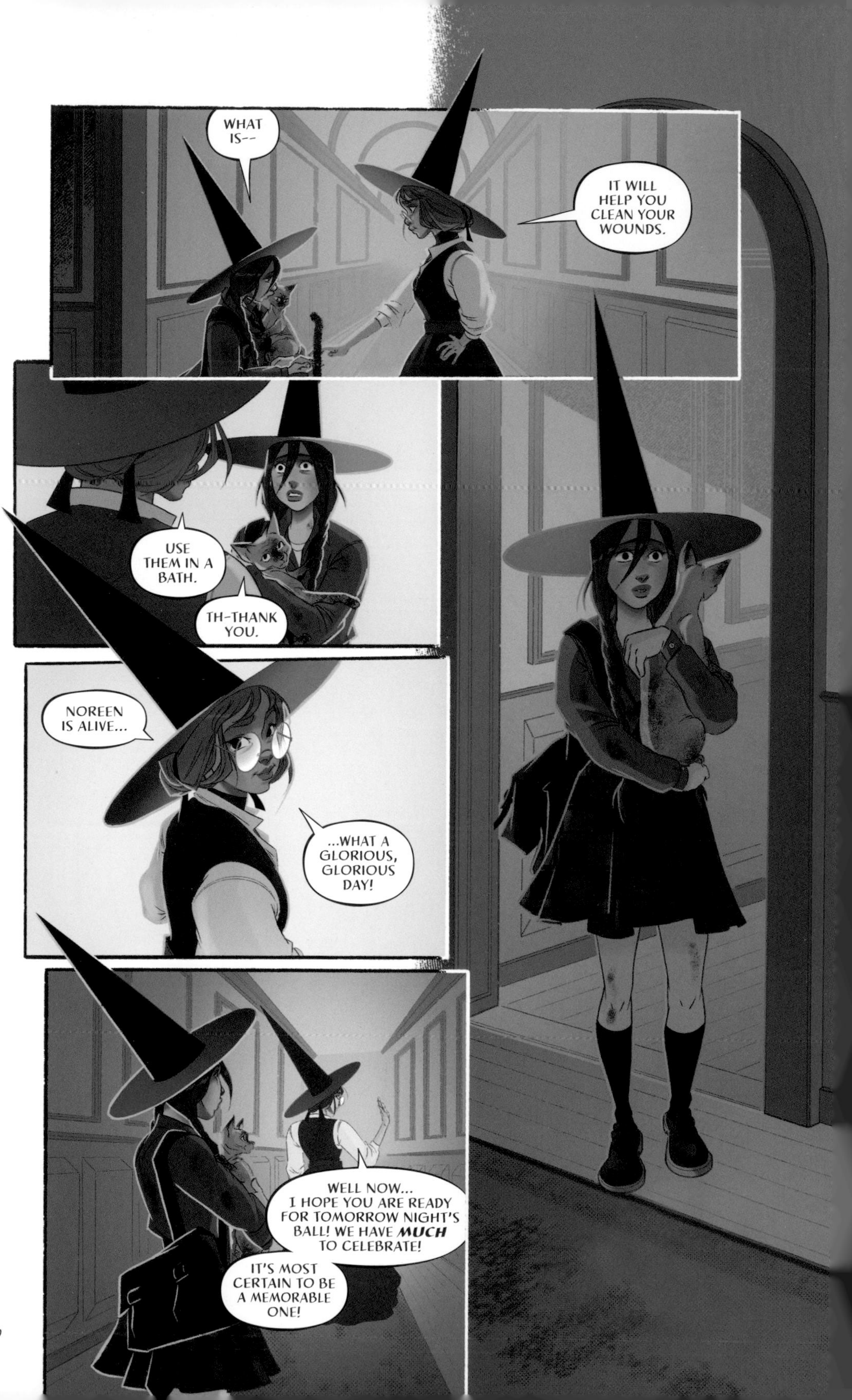
WHAT IS--
IT WILL HELP YOU CLEAN YOUR WOUNDS.
USE THEM IN A BATH.
TH-THANK YOU.
NOREEN IS ALIVE...
...WHAT A GLORIOUS, GLORIOUS DAY!
WELL NOW... I HOPE YOU ARE READY FOR TOMORROW NIGHT'S BALL! WE HAVE ***MUCH*** TO CELEBRATE!
IT'S MOST CERTAIN TO BE A MEMORABLE ONE!

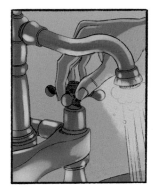

≳SIGH≲

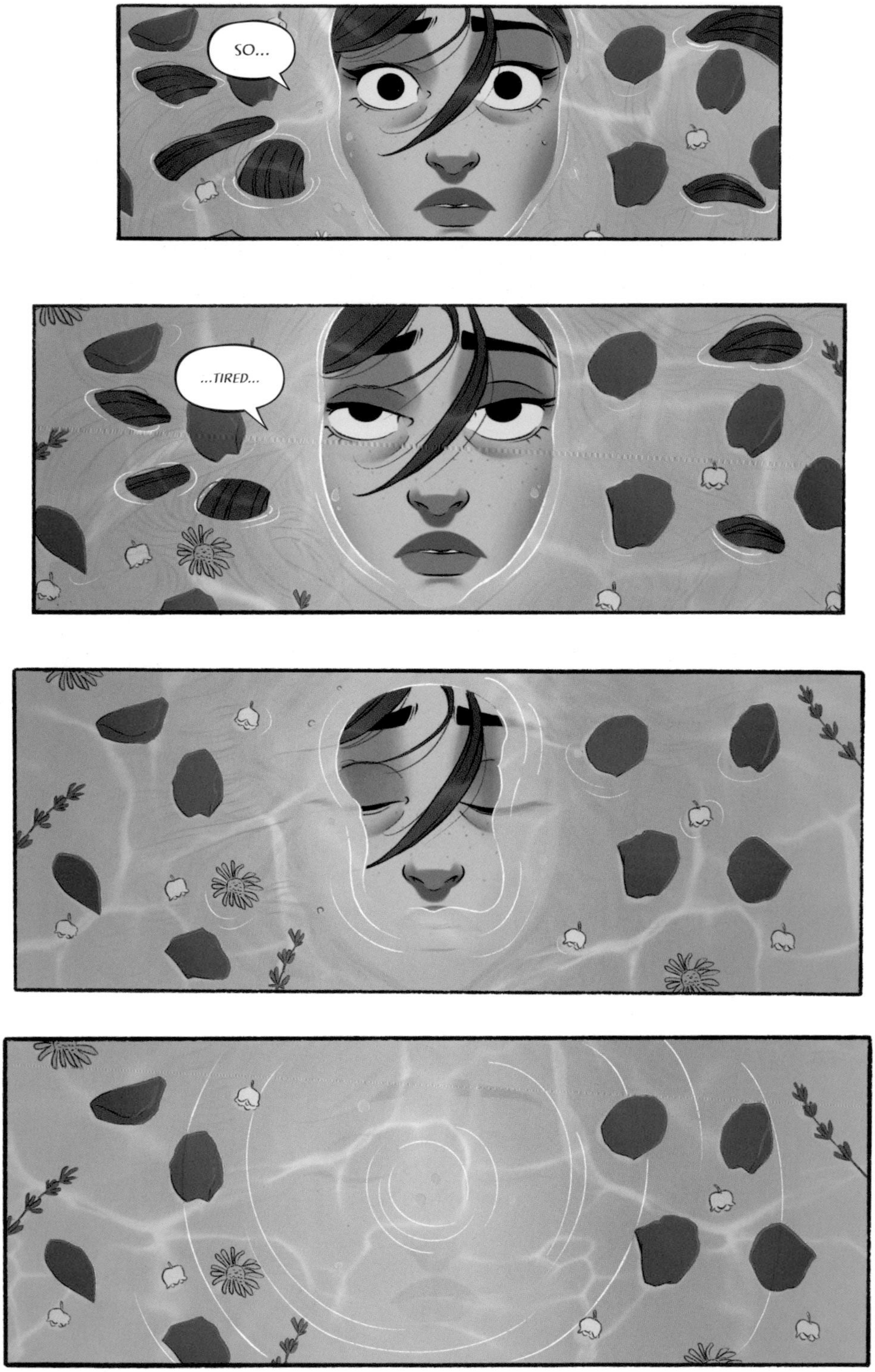
SO...
...TIRED...

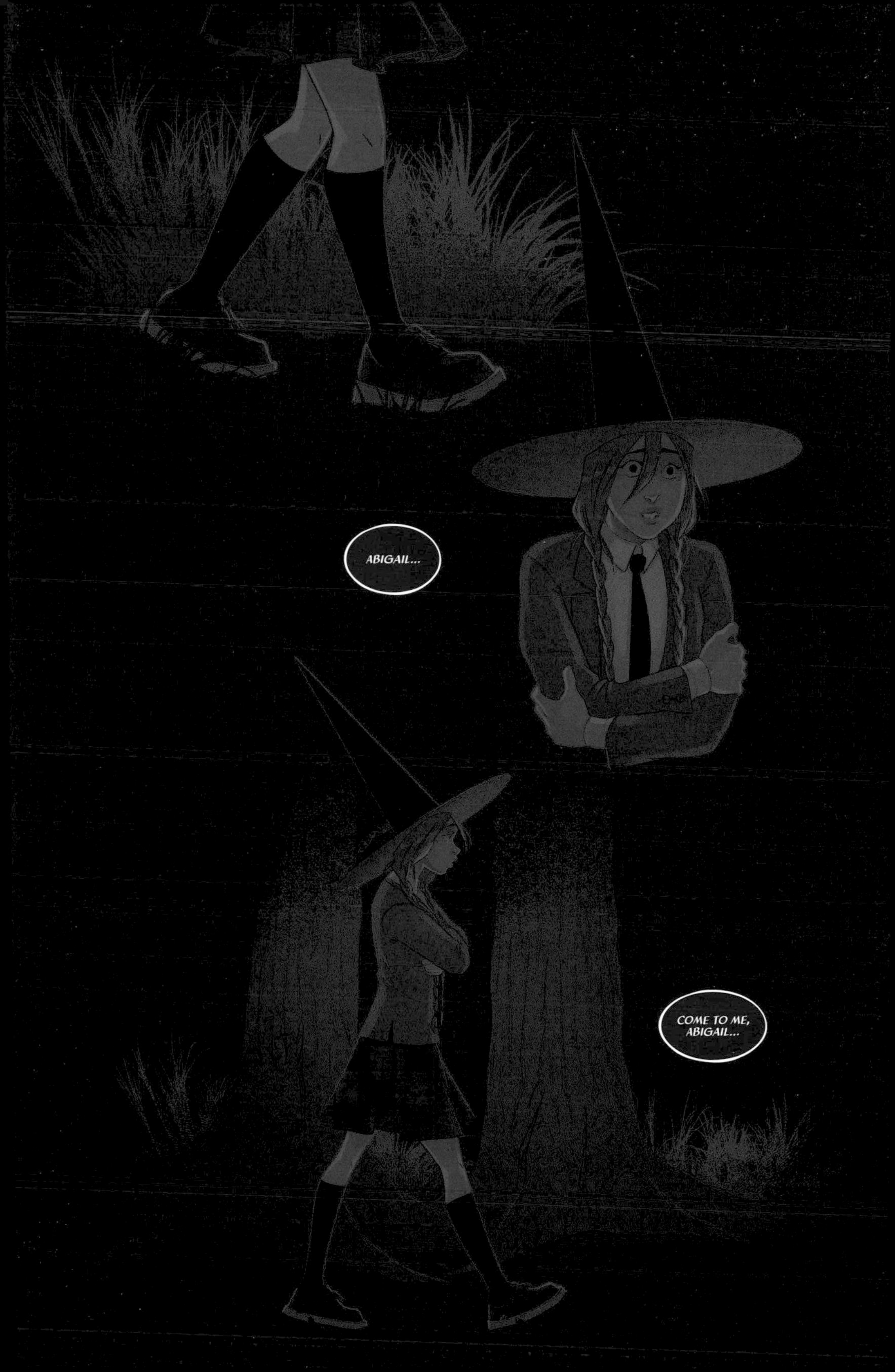
ABIGAIL...
COME TO ME, ABIGAIL...

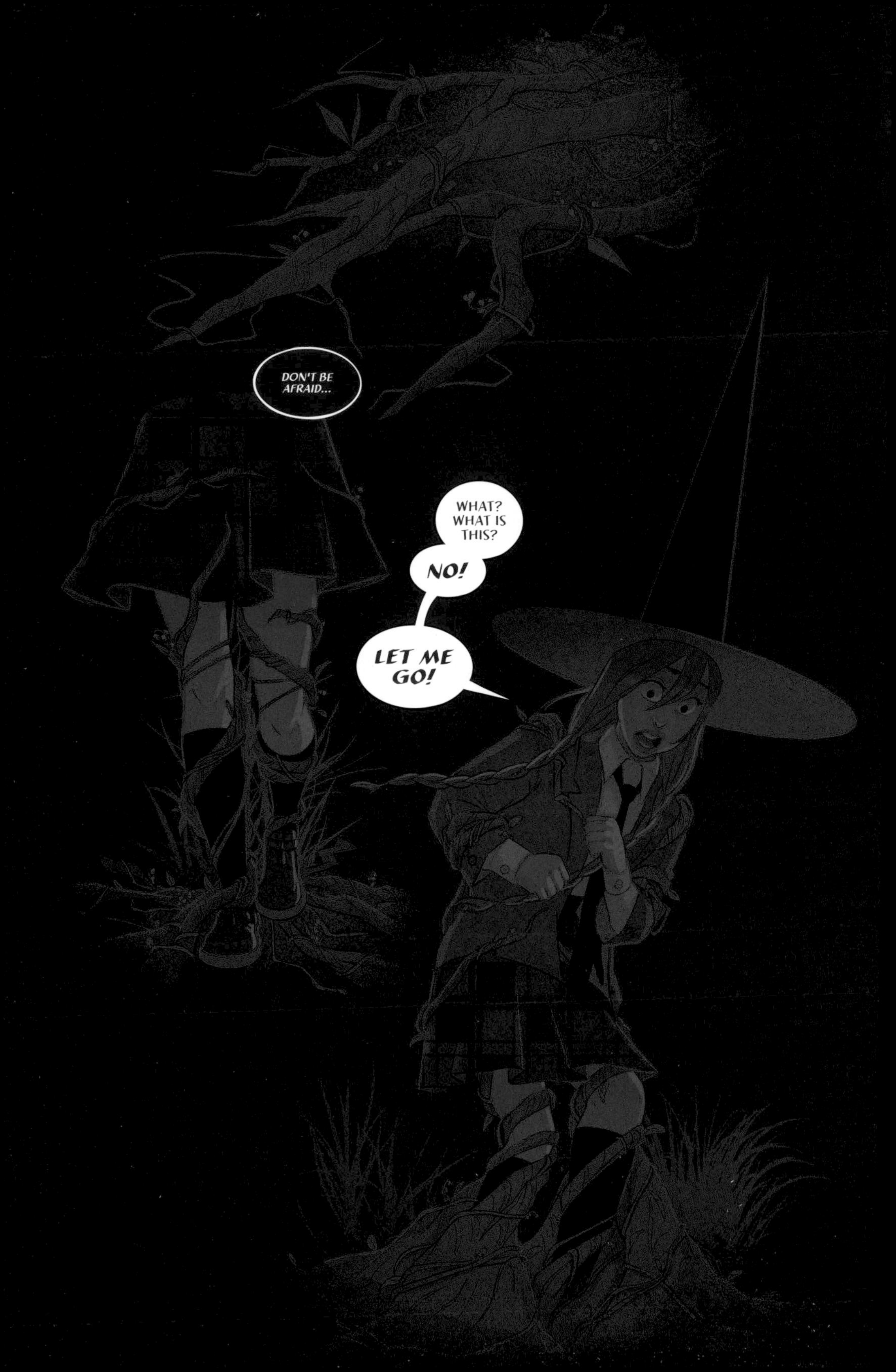
DON'T BE AFRAID...
WHAT? WHAT IS THIS?
NO!
LET ME GO!

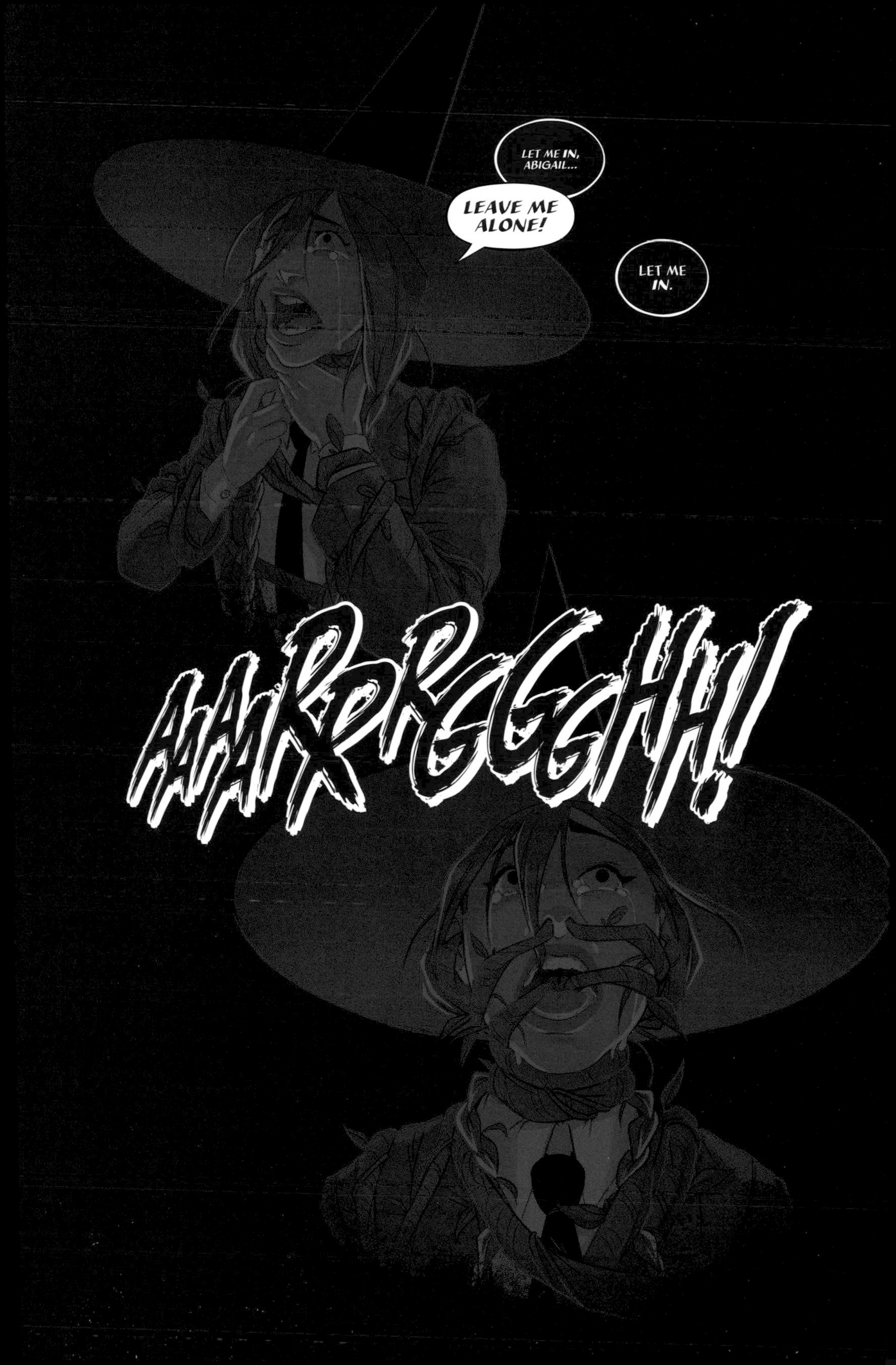
LET ME IN, ABIGAIL...
LEAVE ME ALONE!
LET ME IN.
AAARRRGGGH!

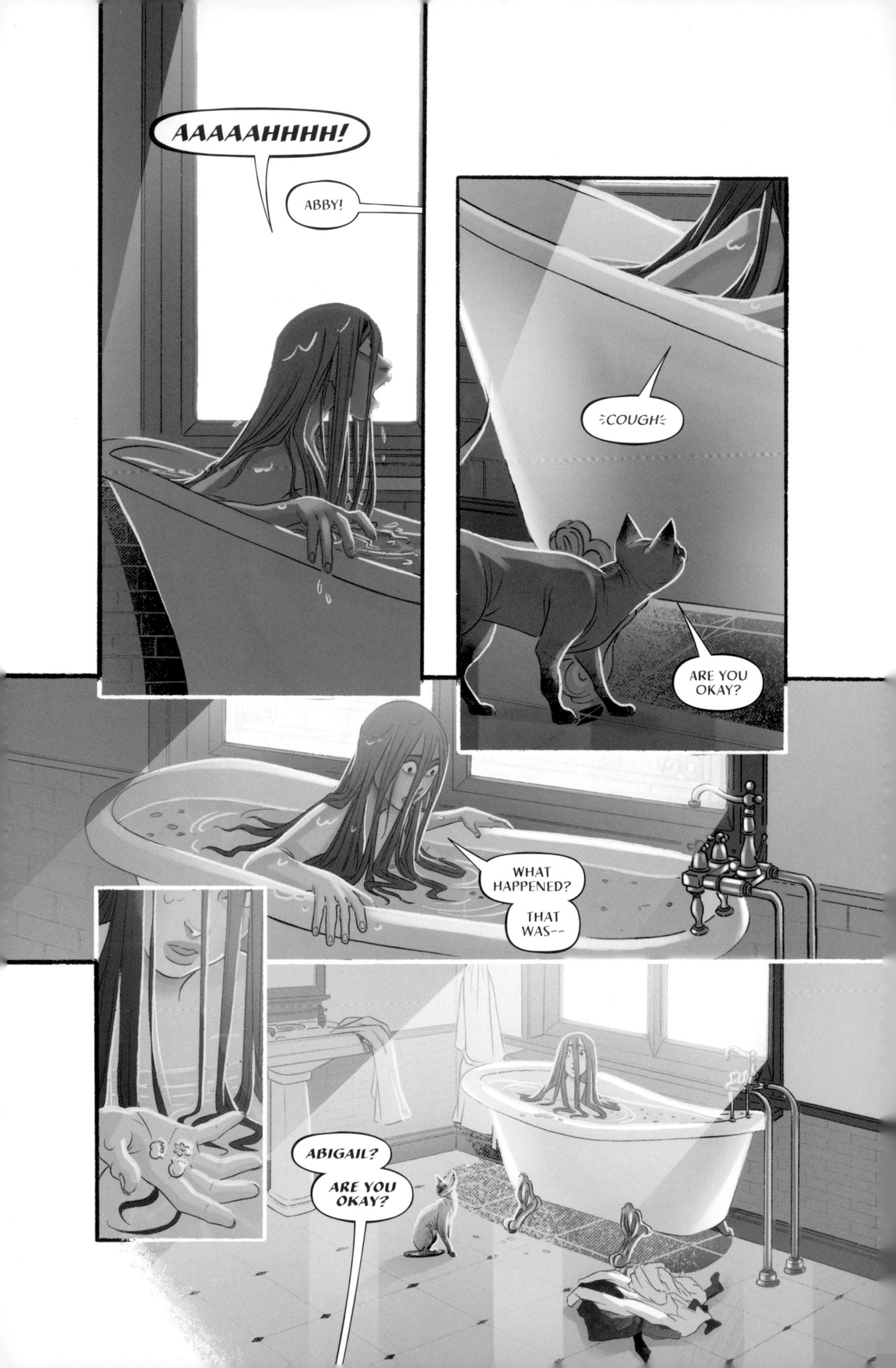
AAAAAHHHH!
ABBY!
COUGH
ARE YOU OKAY?
WHAT HAPPENED?
THAT WAS--
ABIGAIL?
ARE YOU OKAY?

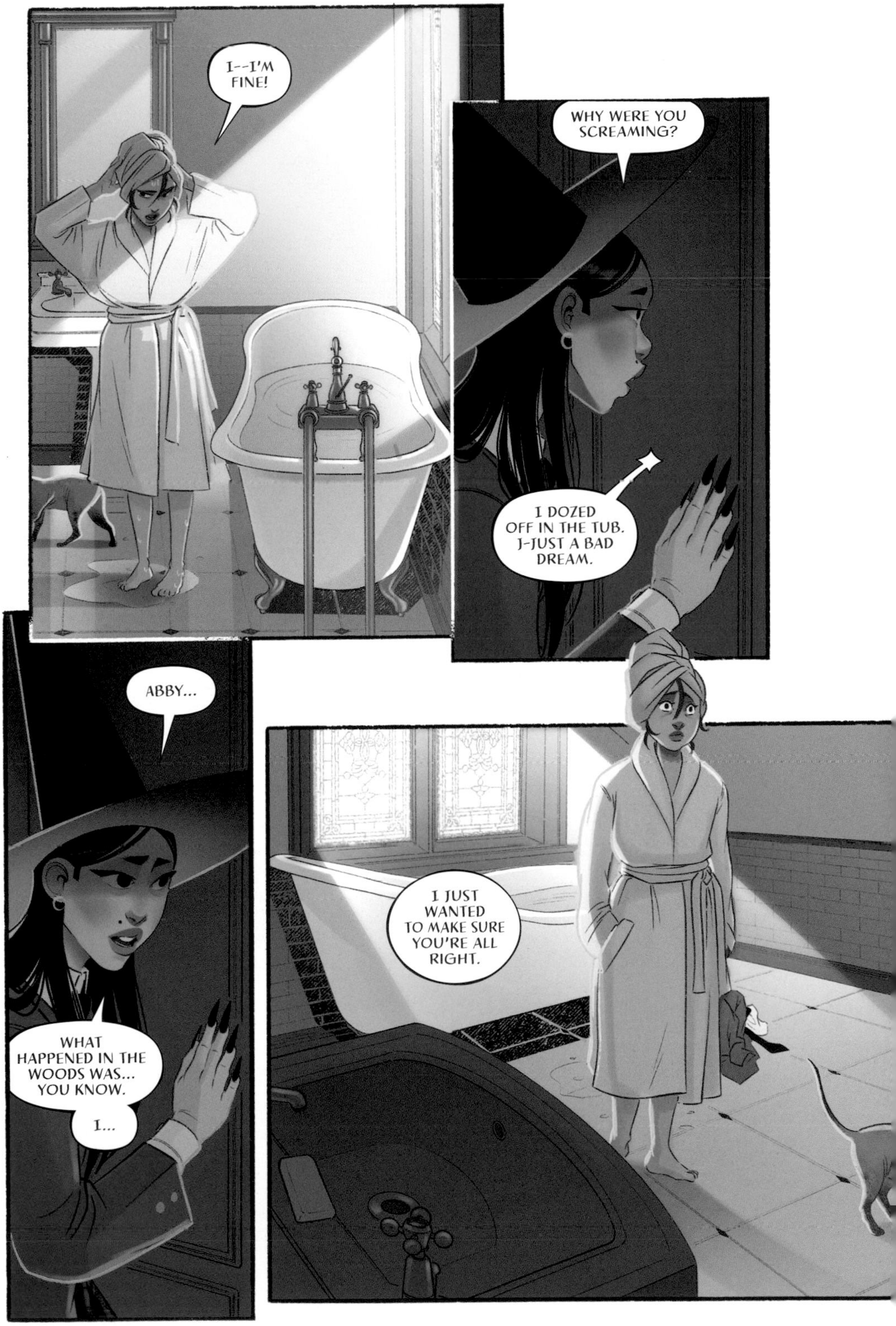
I--I'M FINE!
WHY WERE YOU SCREAMING?
I DOZED OFF IN THE TUB. J-JUST A BAD DREAM.
ABBY...
WHAT HAPPENED IN THE WOODS WAS... YOU KNOW.
I...
I JUST WANTED TO MAKE SURE YOU'RE ALL RIGHT.

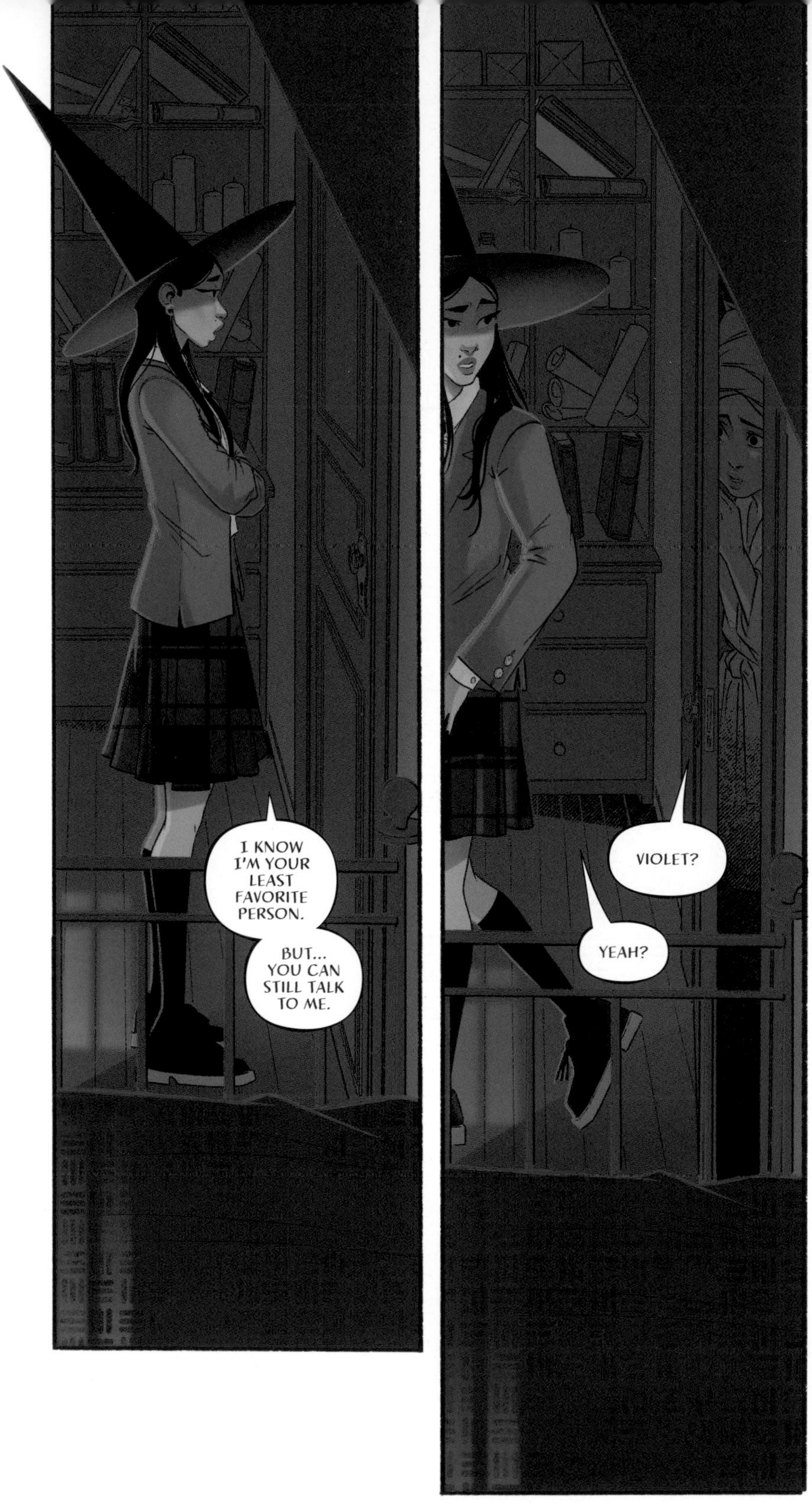
I KNOW I'M YOUR LEAST FAVORITE PERSON.
BUT... YOU CAN STILL TALK TO ME.
VIOLET?
YEAH?

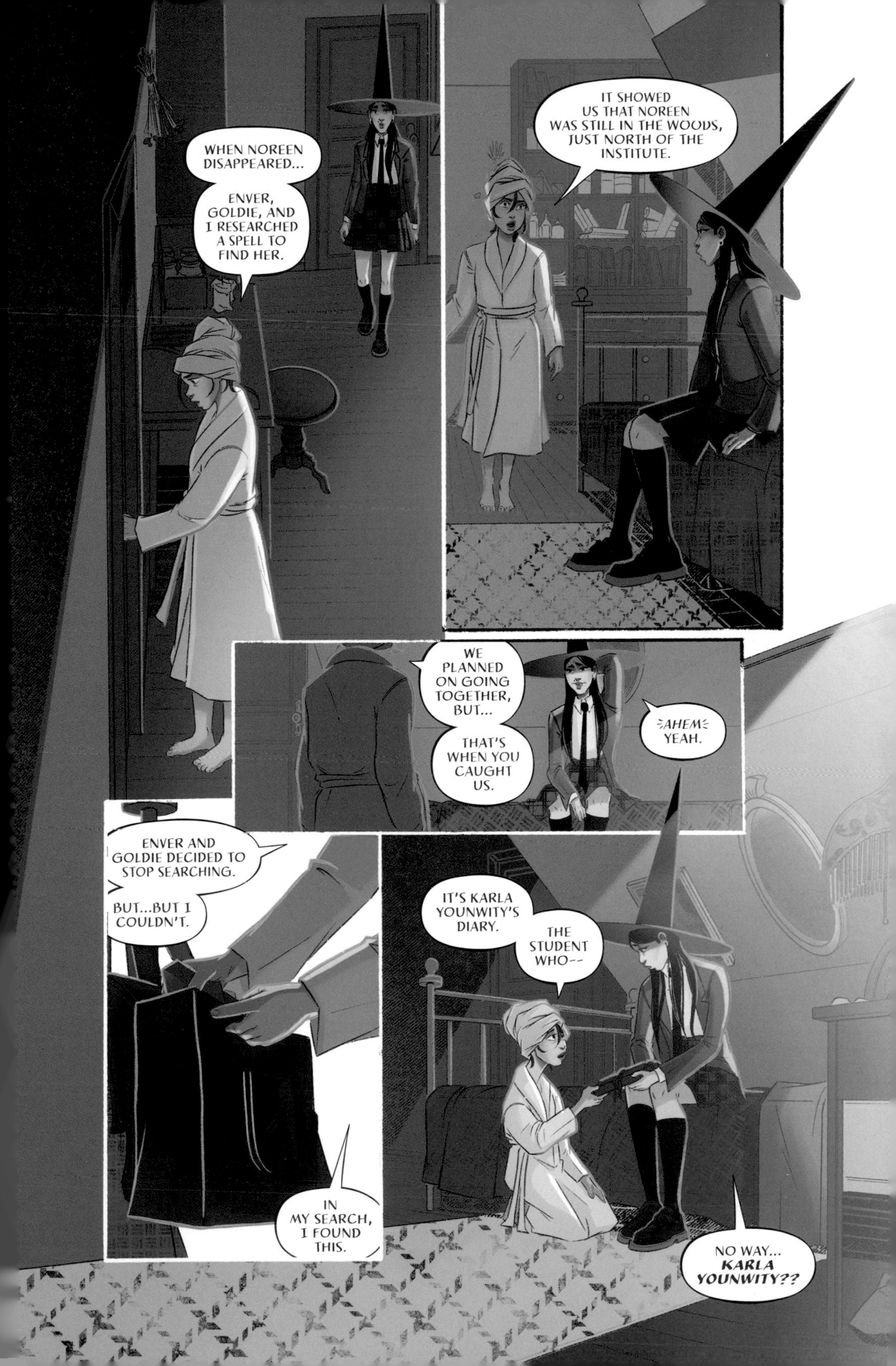
WHEN NOREEN DISAPPEARED...
ENVER, GOLDIE, AND I RESEARCHED A SPELL TO FIND HER.
IT SHOWED US THAT NOREEN WAS STILL IN THE WOODS, JUST NORTH OF THE INSTITUTE.
WE PLANNED ON GOING TOGETHER, BUT...
THAT'S WHEN YOU CAUGHT US.
AHEM YEAH.
ENVER AND GOLDIE DECIDED TO STOP SEARCHING.
BUT...BUT I COULDN'T.
IN MY SEARCH, I FOUND THIS.
IT'S KARLA YOUNWITY'S DIARY.
THE STUDENT WHO--
NO WAY... ***KARLA YOUNWITY??***

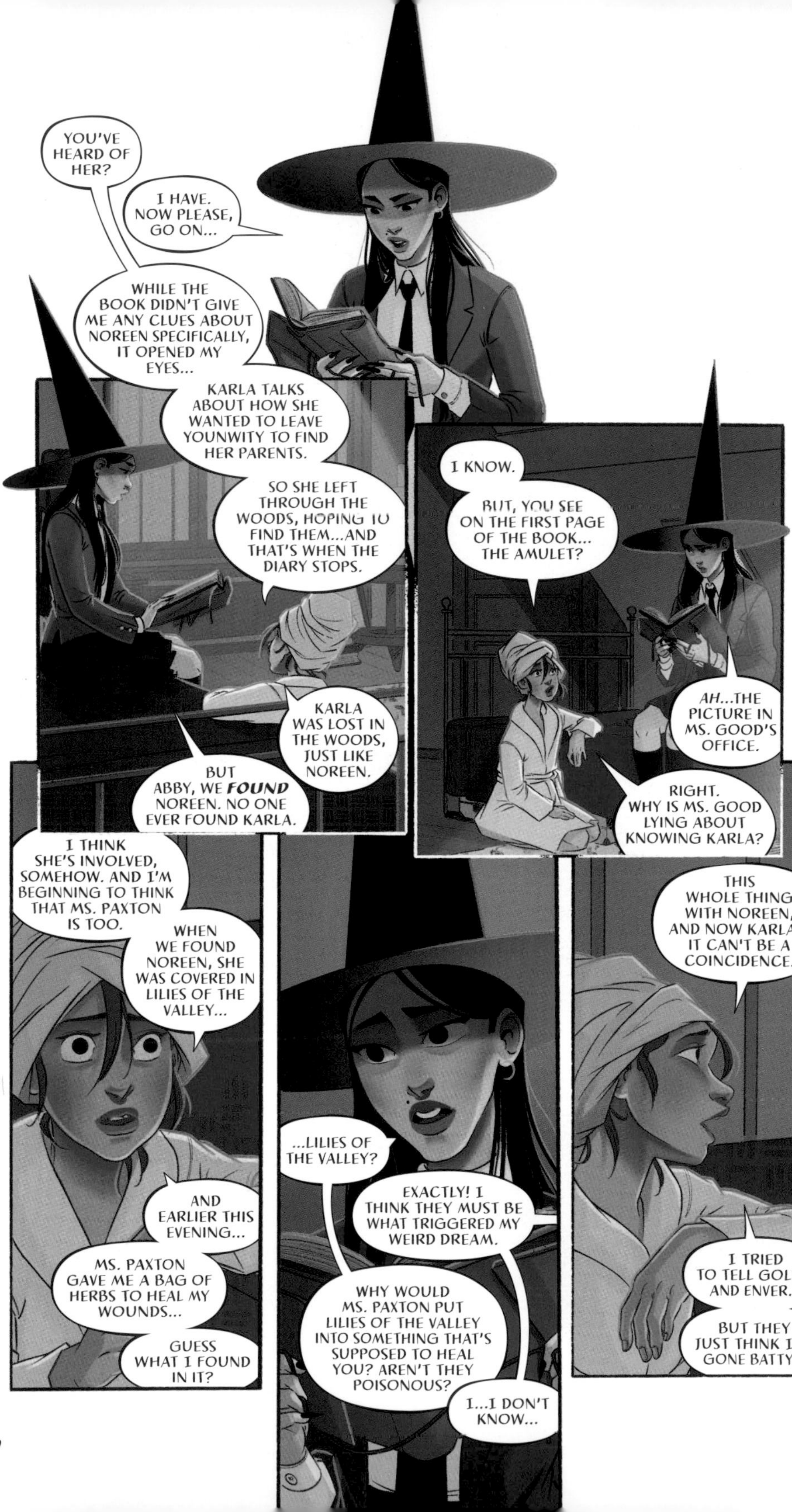
YOU'VE HEARD OF HER?
I HAVE. NOW PLEASE, GO ON...
WHILE THE BOOK DIDN'T GIVE ME ANY CLUES ABOUT NOREEN SPECIFICALLY, IT OPENED MY EYES...
KARLA TALKS ABOUT HOW SHE WANTED TO LEAVE YOUNWITY TO FIND HER PARENTS.
SO SHE LEFT THROUGH THE WOODS, HOPING TO FIND THEM...AND THAT'S WHEN THE DIARY STOPS.
KARLA WAS LOST IN THE WOODS, JUST LIKE NOREEN.
BUT ABBY, WE *FOUND* NOREEN. NO ONE EVER FOUND KARLA.
I KNOW.
BUT, YOU SEE ON THE FIRST PAGE OF THE BOOK... THE AMULET?
AH...THE PICTURE IN MS. GOOD'S OFFICE.
RIGHT. WHY IS MS. GOOD LYING ABOUT KNOWING KARLA?
I THINK SHE'S INVOLVED, SOMEHOW. AND I'M BEGINNING TO THINK THAT MS. PAXTON IS TOO.
WHEN WE FOUND NOREEN, SHE WAS COVERED IN LILIES OF THE VALLEY...
AND EARLIER THIS EVENING...
MS. PAXTON GAVE ME A BAG OF HERBS TO HEAL MY WOUNDS...
GUESS WHAT I FOUND IN IT?
...LILIES OF THE VALLEY?
EXACTLY! I THINK THEY MUST BE WHAT TRIGGERED MY WEIRD DREAM.
WHY WOULD MS. PAXTON PUT LILIES OF THE VALLEY INTO SOMETHING THAT'S SUPPOSED TO HEAL YOU? AREN'T THEY POISONOUS?
I...I DON'T KNOW...
THIS WHOLE THING WITH NOREEN, AND NOW KARLA... IT CAN'T BE A COINCIDENCE.
I TRIED TO TELL GOLDIE AND ENVER...
BUT THEY JUST THINK I'VE GONE BATTY...

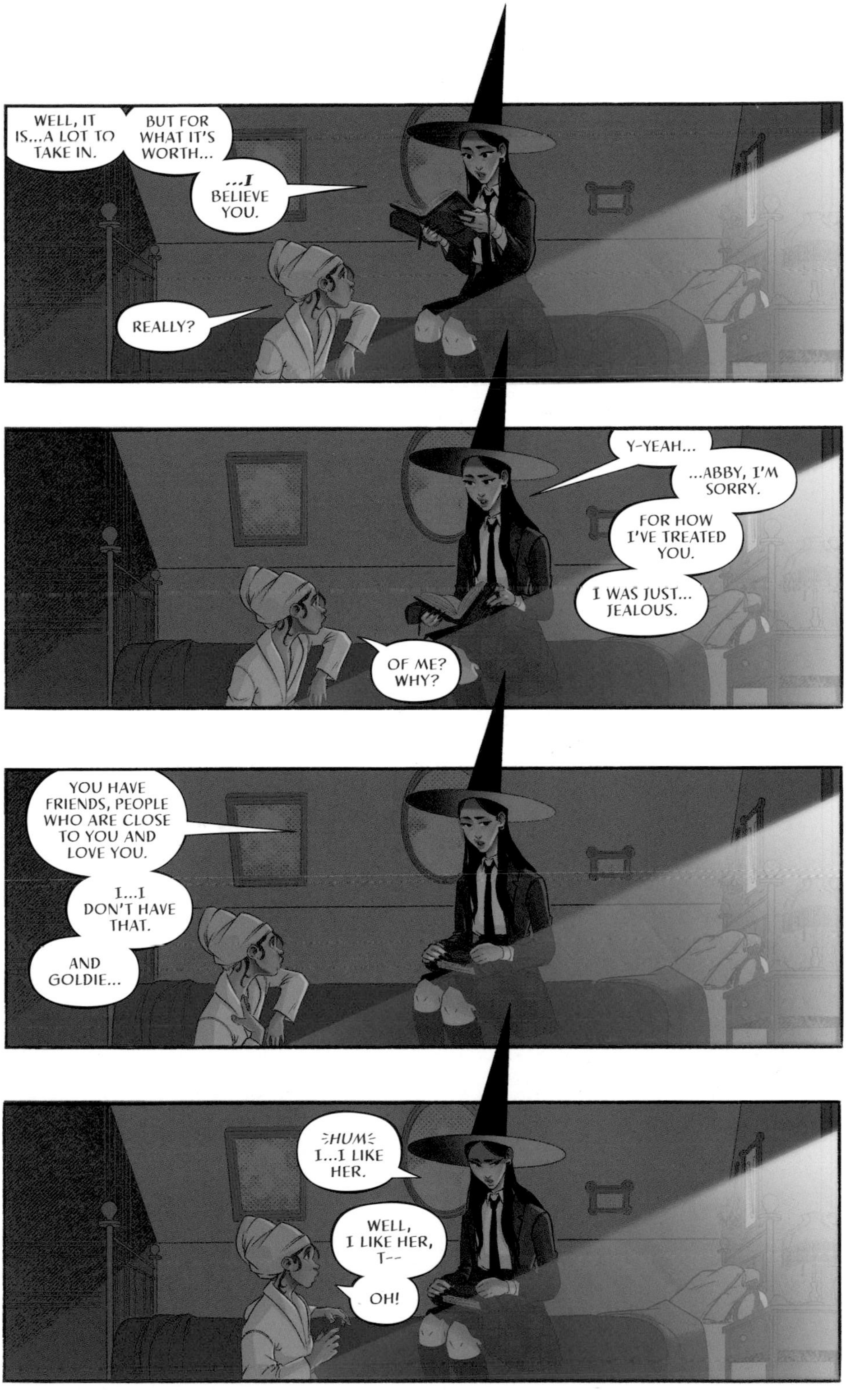
WELL, IT IS...A LOT TO TAKE IN.
BUT FOR WHAT IT'S WORTH...
...I BELIEVE YOU.
REALLY?
Y-YEAH...
...ABBY, I'M SORRY.
FOR HOW I'VE TREATED YOU.
I WAS JUST... JEALOUS.
OF ME? WHY?
YOU HAVE FRIENDS, PEOPLE WHO ARE CLOSE TO YOU AND LOVE YOU.
I...I DON'T HAVE THAT.
AND GOLDIE...
HUM
I...I LIKE HER.
WELL, I LIKE HER, T--
OH!

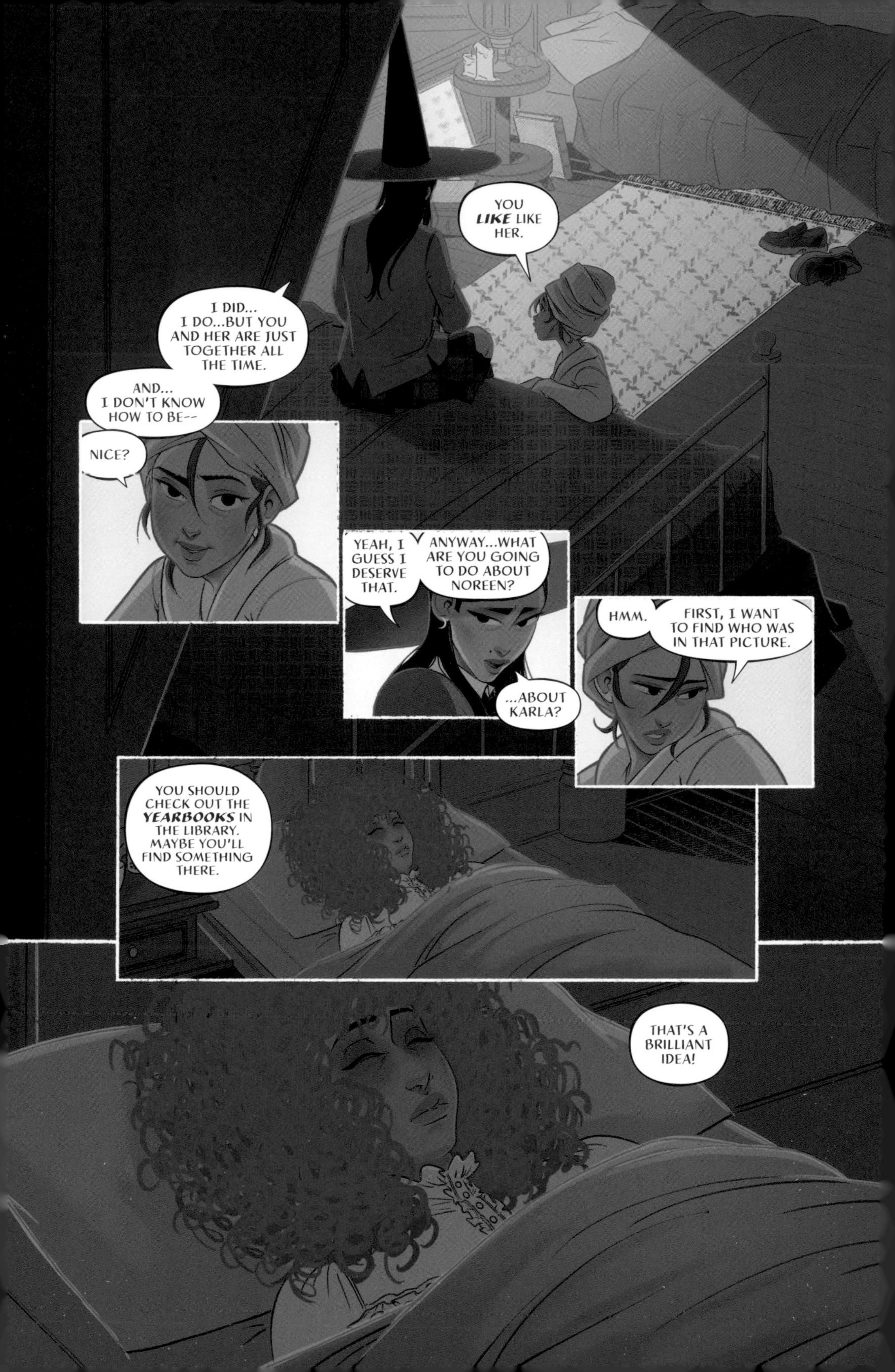
YOU LIKE LIKE HER.
I DID... I DO...BUT YOU AND HER ARE JUST TOGETHER ALL THE TIME.
AND... I DON'T KNOW HOW TO BE--
NICE?
YEAH, I GUESS I DESERVE THAT.
ANYWAY...WHAT ARE YOU GOING TO DO ABOUT NOREEN?
...ABOUT KARLA?
HMM.
FIRST, I WANT TO FIND WHO WAS IN THAT PICTURE.
YOU SHOULD CHECK OUT THE YEARBOOKS IN THE LIBRARY. MAYBE YOU'LL FIND SOMETHING THERE.
THAT'S A BRILLIANT IDEA!

CHAPTER V

From the lightning in the sky
As it pass'd me flying by --

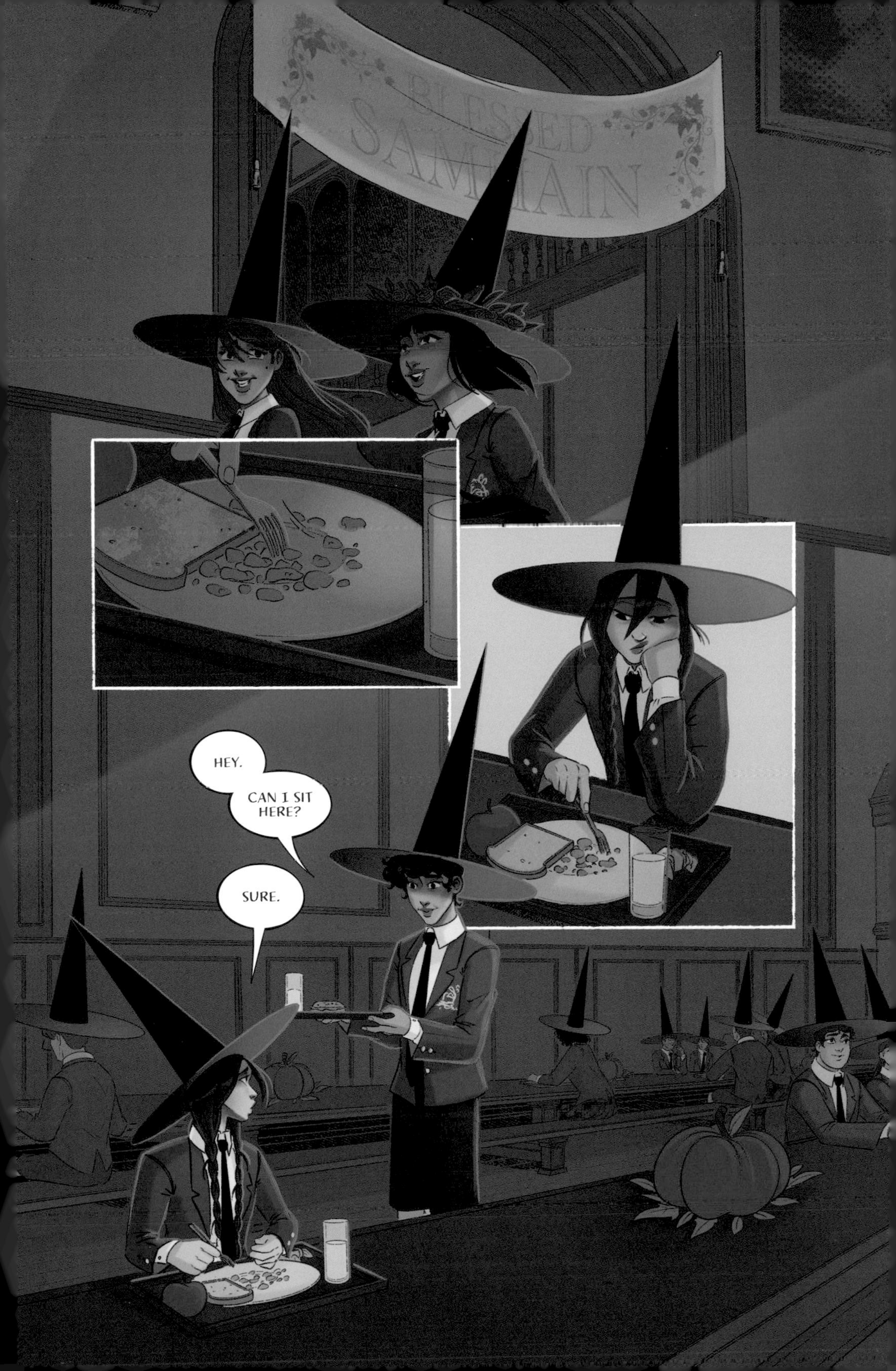
BLESSED SAMHAIN
HEY.
CAN I SIT HERE?
SURE.

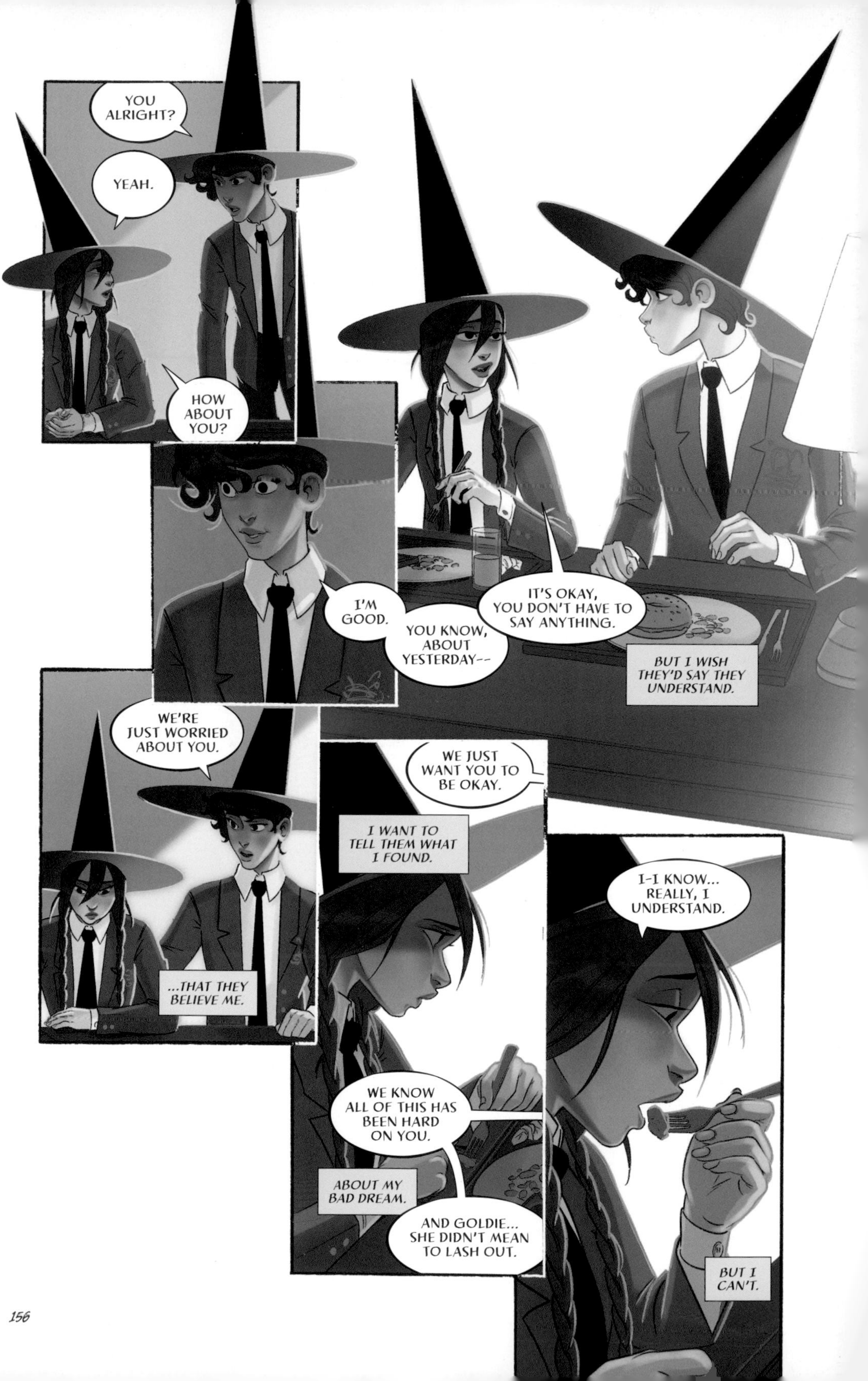

YOU ALRIGHT?
YEAH.
HOW ABOUT YOU?
I'M GOOD.
YOU KNOW, ABOUT YESTERDAY--
IT'S OKAY, YOU DON'T HAVE TO SAY ANYTHING.
BUT I WISH THEY'D SAY THEY UNDERSTAND.
WE'RE JUST WORRIED ABOUT YOU.
...THAT THEY BELIEVE ME.
WE JUST WANT YOU TO BE OKAY.
I WANT TO TELL THEM WHAT I FOUND.
WE KNOW ALL OF THIS HAS BEEN HARD ON YOU.
ABOUT MY BAD DREAM.
AND GOLDIE... SHE DIDN'T MEAN TO LASH OUT.
I-I KNOW... REALLY, I UNDERSTAND.
BUT I CAN'T.

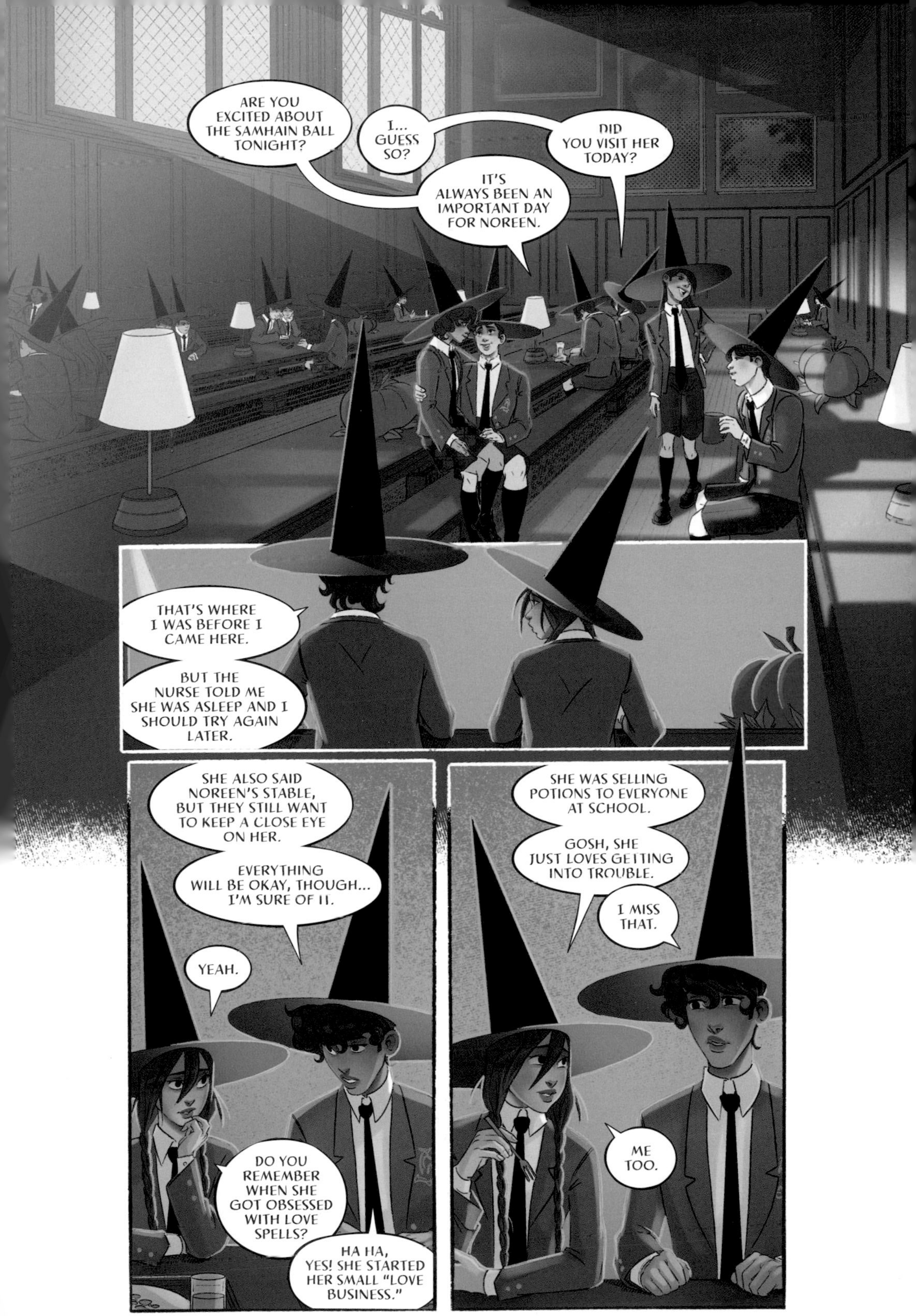
ARE YOU EXCITED ABOUT THE SAMHAIN BALL TONIGHT?
IT'S ALWAYS BEEN AN IMPORTANT DAY FOR NOREEN.
I... GUESS SO?
DID YOU VISIT HER TODAY?
THAT'S WHERE I WAS BEFORE I CAME HERE.
BUT THE NURSE TOLD ME SHE WAS ASLEEP AND I SHOULD TRY AGAIN LATER.
SHE ALSO SAID NOREEN'S STABLE, BUT THEY STILL WANT TO KEEP A CLOSE EYE ON HER.
EVERYTHING WILL BE OKAY, THOUGH... I'M SURE OF IT.
YEAH.
DO YOU REMEMBER WHEN SHE GOT OBSESSED WITH LOVE SPELLS?
HA HA, YES! SHE STARTED HER SMALL "LOVE BUSINESS."
SHE WAS SELLING POTIONS TO EVERYONE AT SCHOOL.
GOSH, SHE JUST LOVES GETTING INTO TROUBLE.
I MISS THAT.
ME TOO.

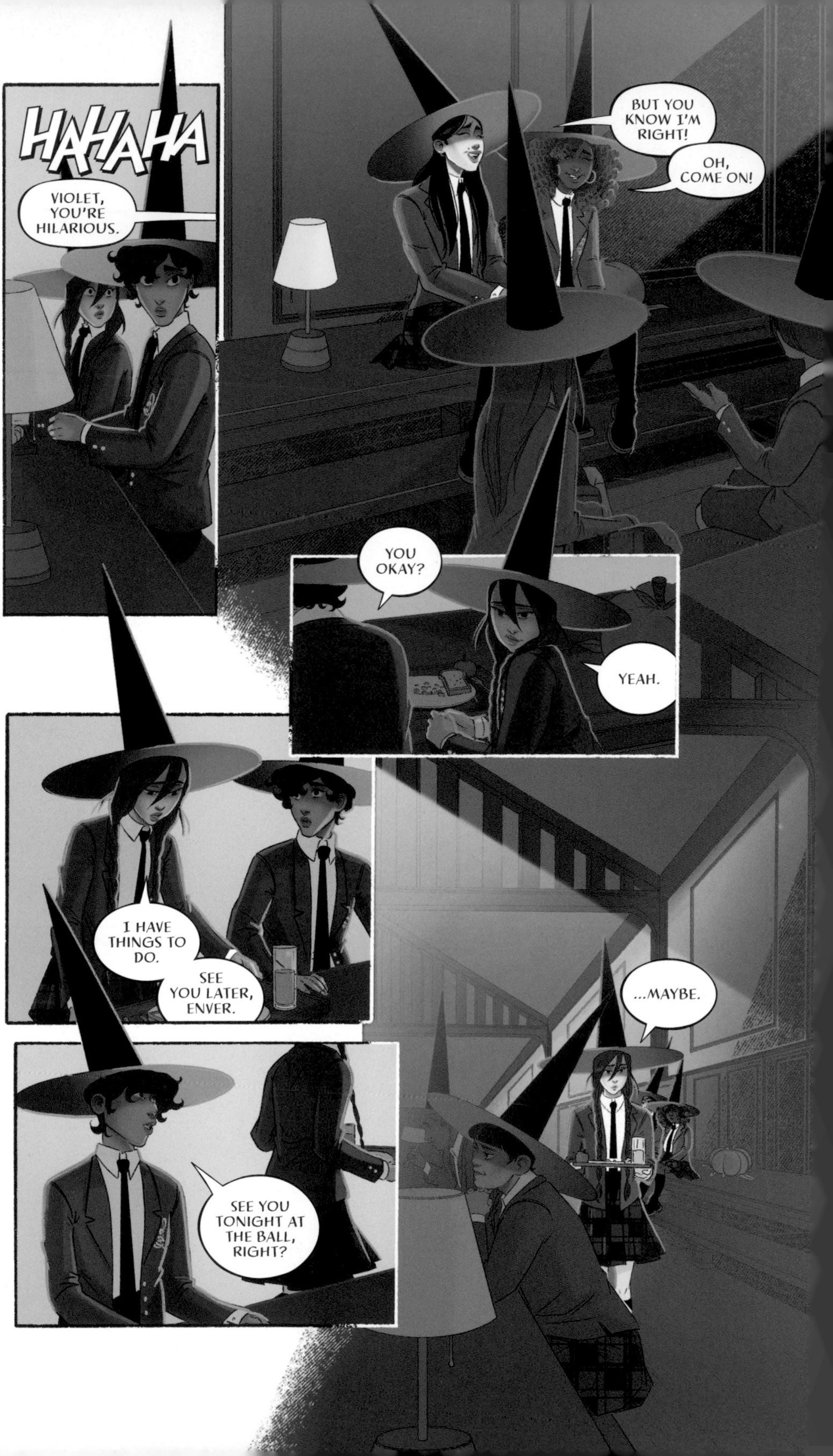
HAHAHA
VIOLET, YOU'RE HILARIOUS.
BUT YOU KNOW I'M RIGHT!
OH, COME ON!
YOU OKAY?
YEAH.
I HAVE THINGS TO DO.
SEE YOU LATER, ENVER.
SEE YOU TONIGHT AT THE BALL, RIGHT?
...MAYBE.

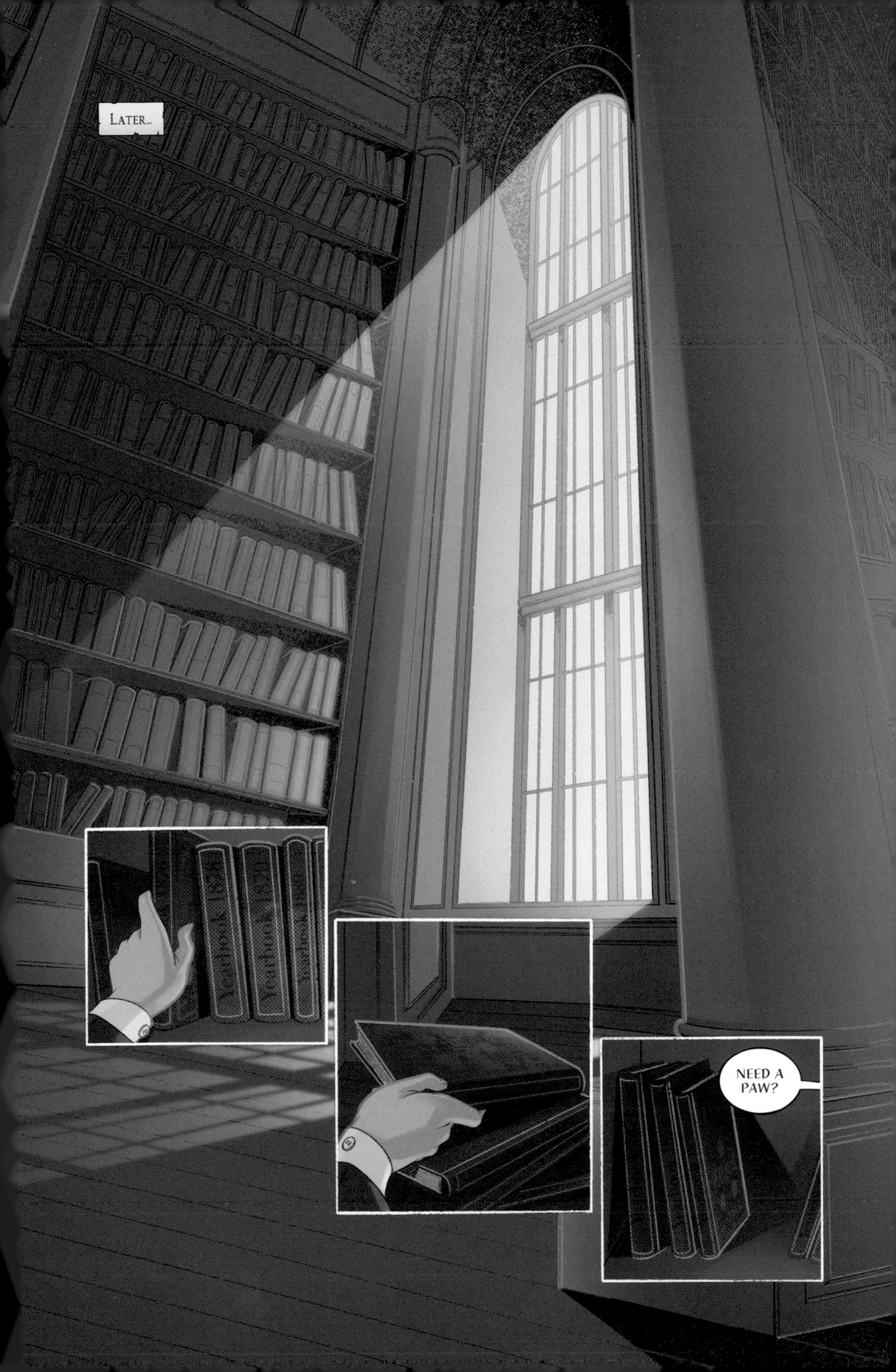
LATER...
NEED A PAW?

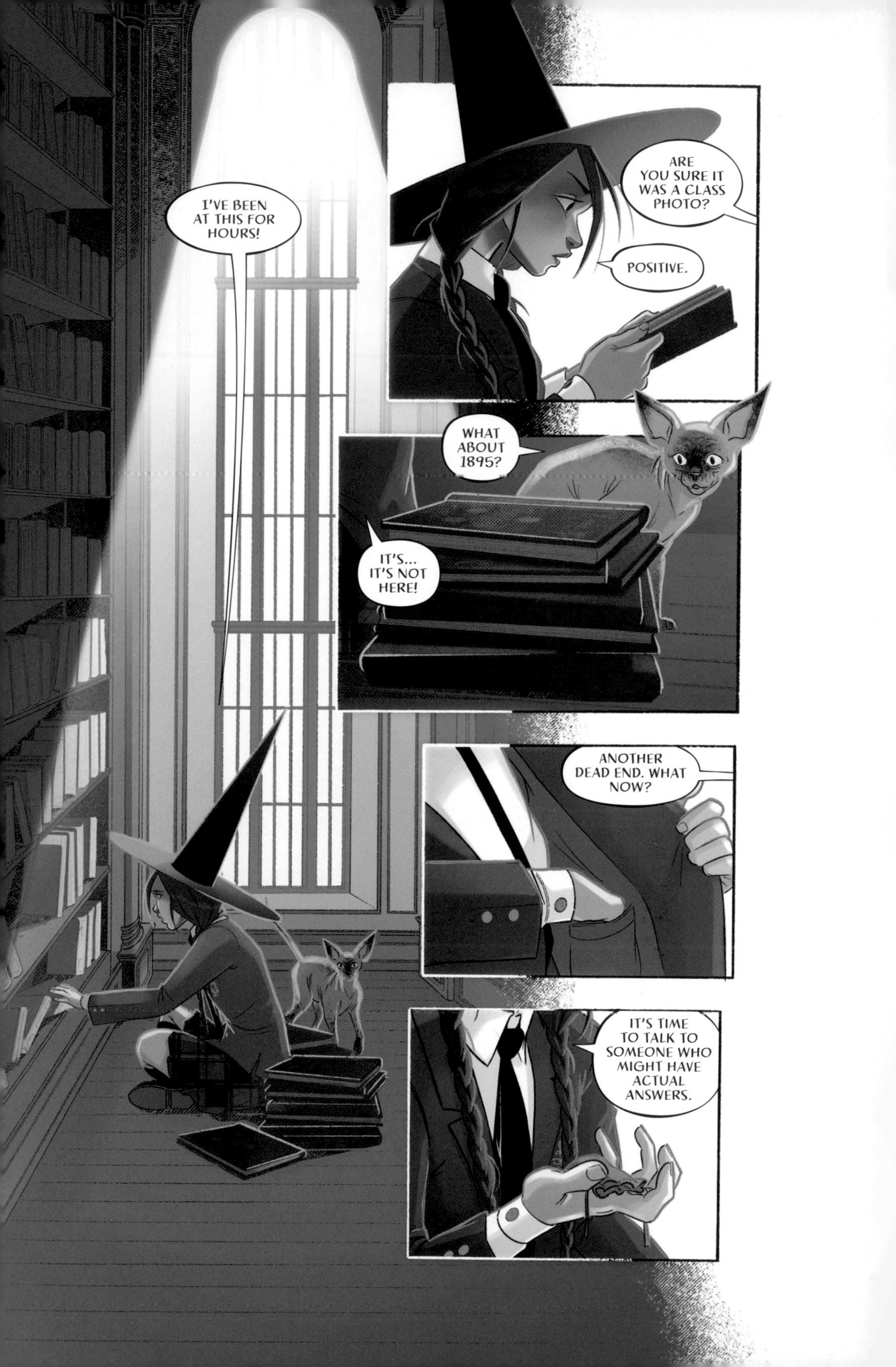
I'VE BEEN AT THIS FOR HOURS!
ARE YOU SURE IT WAS A CLASS PHOTO?
POSITIVE.
WHAT ABOUT 1895?
IT'S... IT'S NOT HERE!
ANOTHER DEAD END. WHAT NOW?
IT'S TIME TO TALK TO SOMEONE WHO MIGHT HAVE ACTUAL ANSWERS.

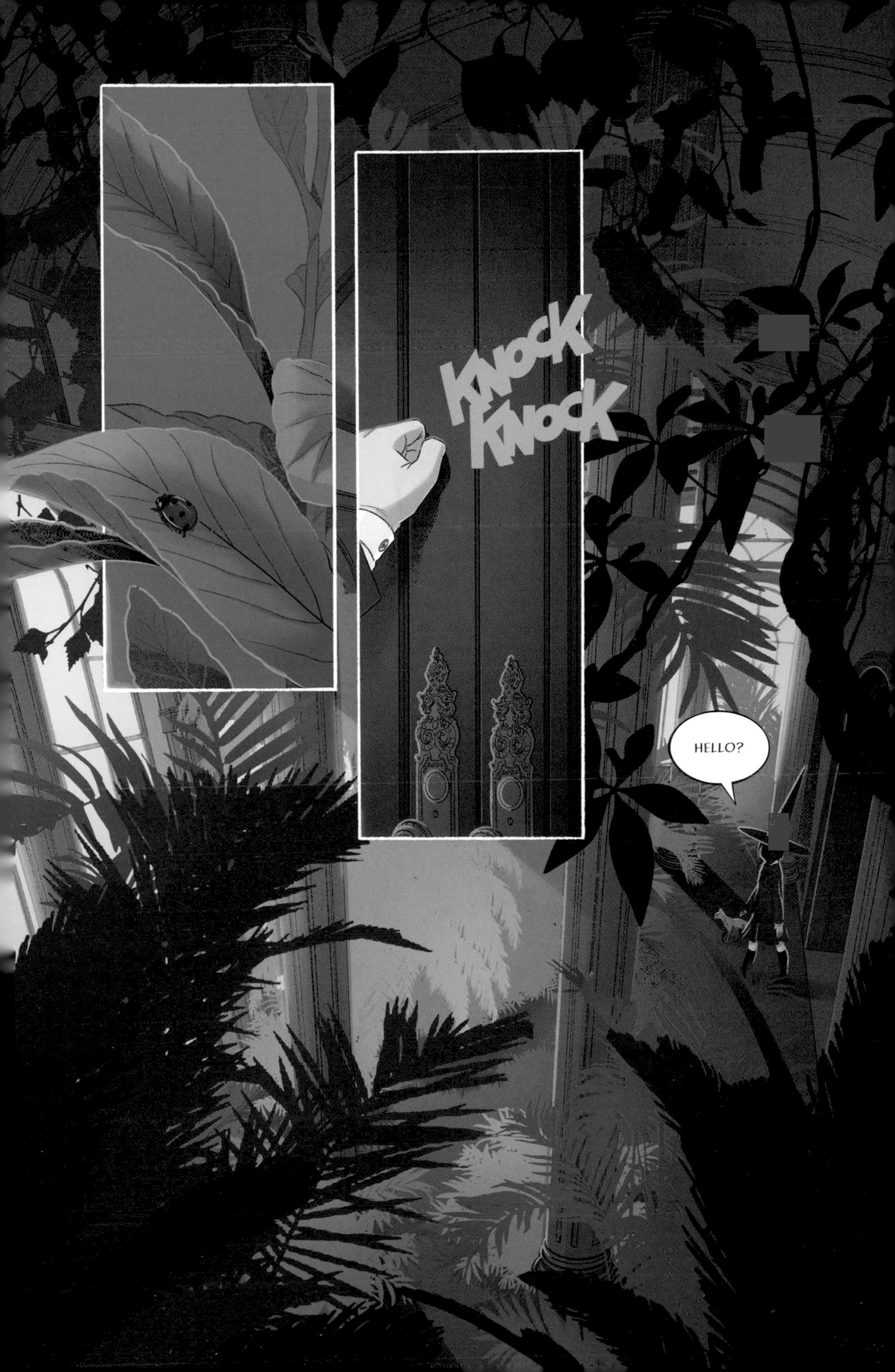
KNOCK KNOCK
HELLO?

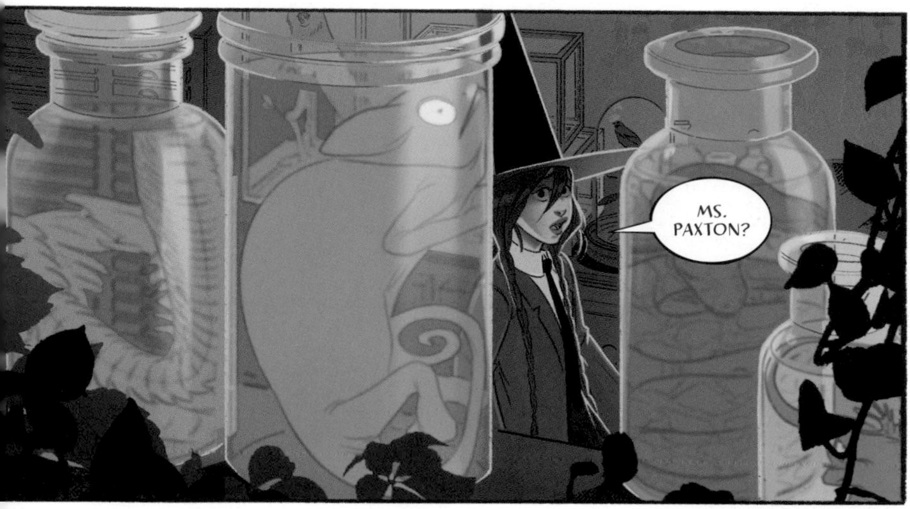
MS. PAXTON?

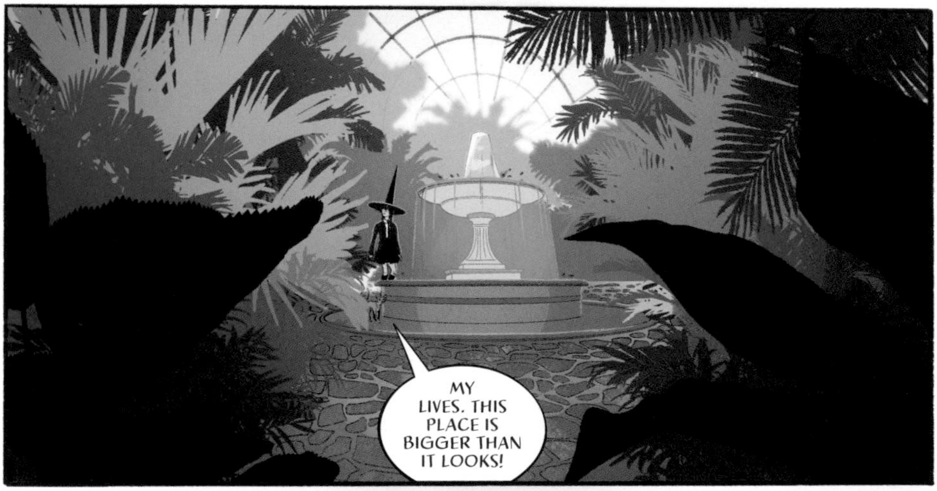
MY LIVES. THIS PLACE IS BIGGER THAN IT LOOKS!

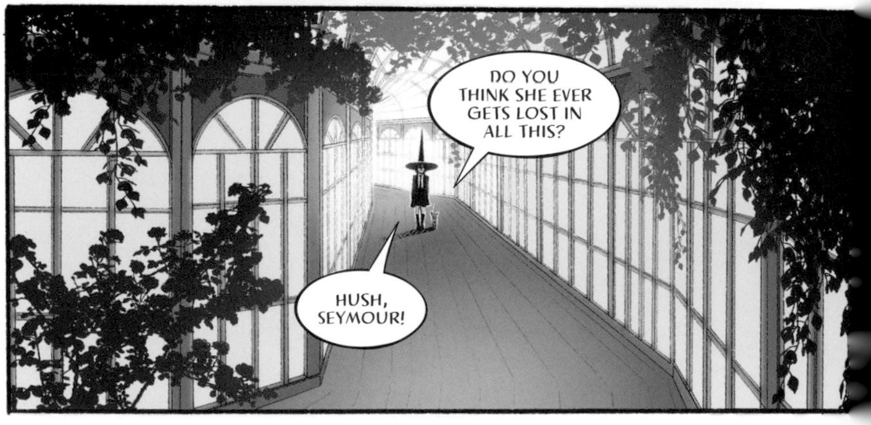
DO YOU THINK SHE EVER GETS LOST IN ALL THIS?
HUSH, SEYMOUR!

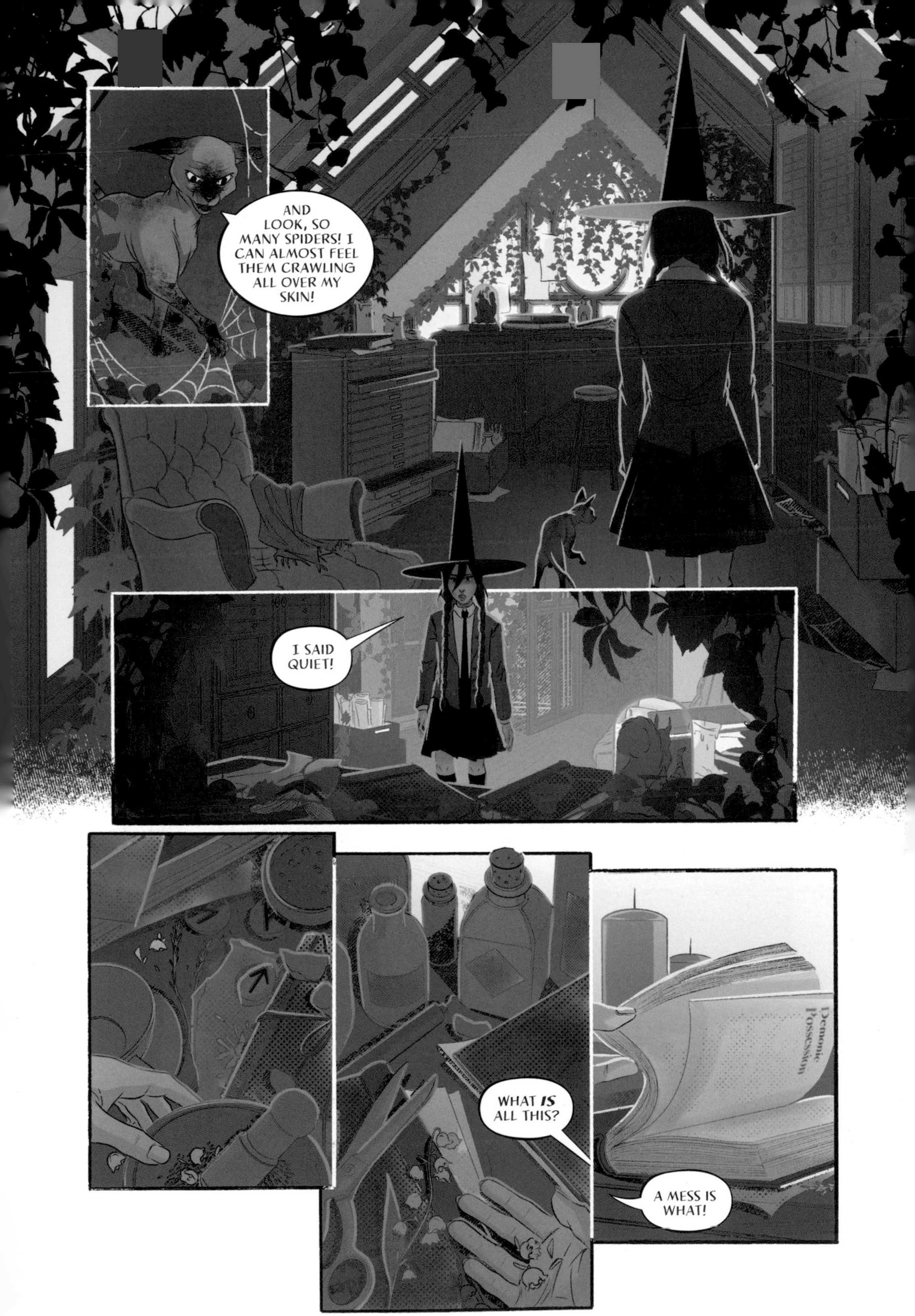
AND LOOK, SO MANY SPIDERS! I CAN ALMOST FEEL THEM CRAWLING ALL OVER MY SKIN!
I SAID QUIET!
WHAT IS ALL THIS?
Demonic Possession
A MESS IS WHAT!

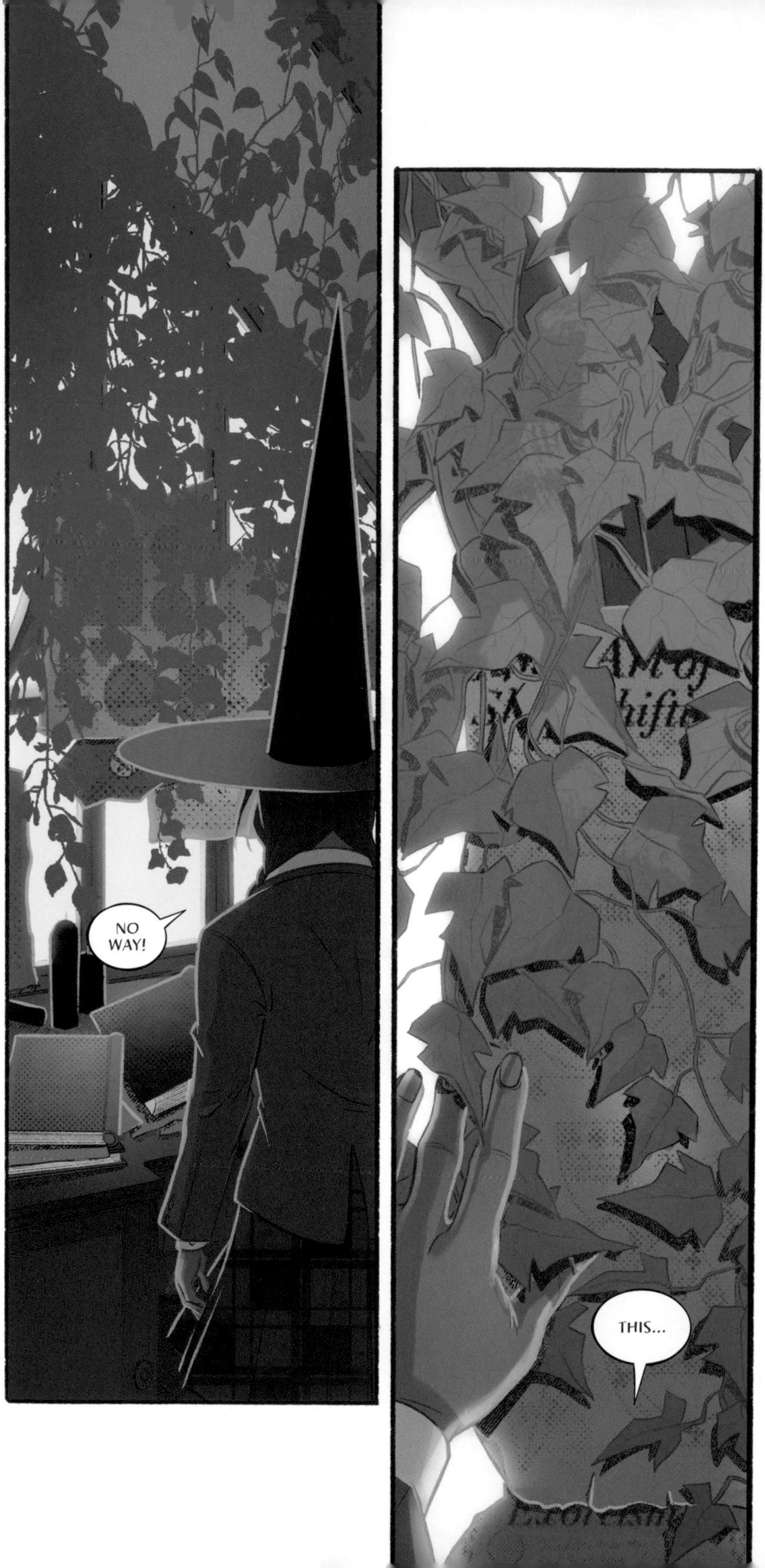
NO WAY!
THIS...

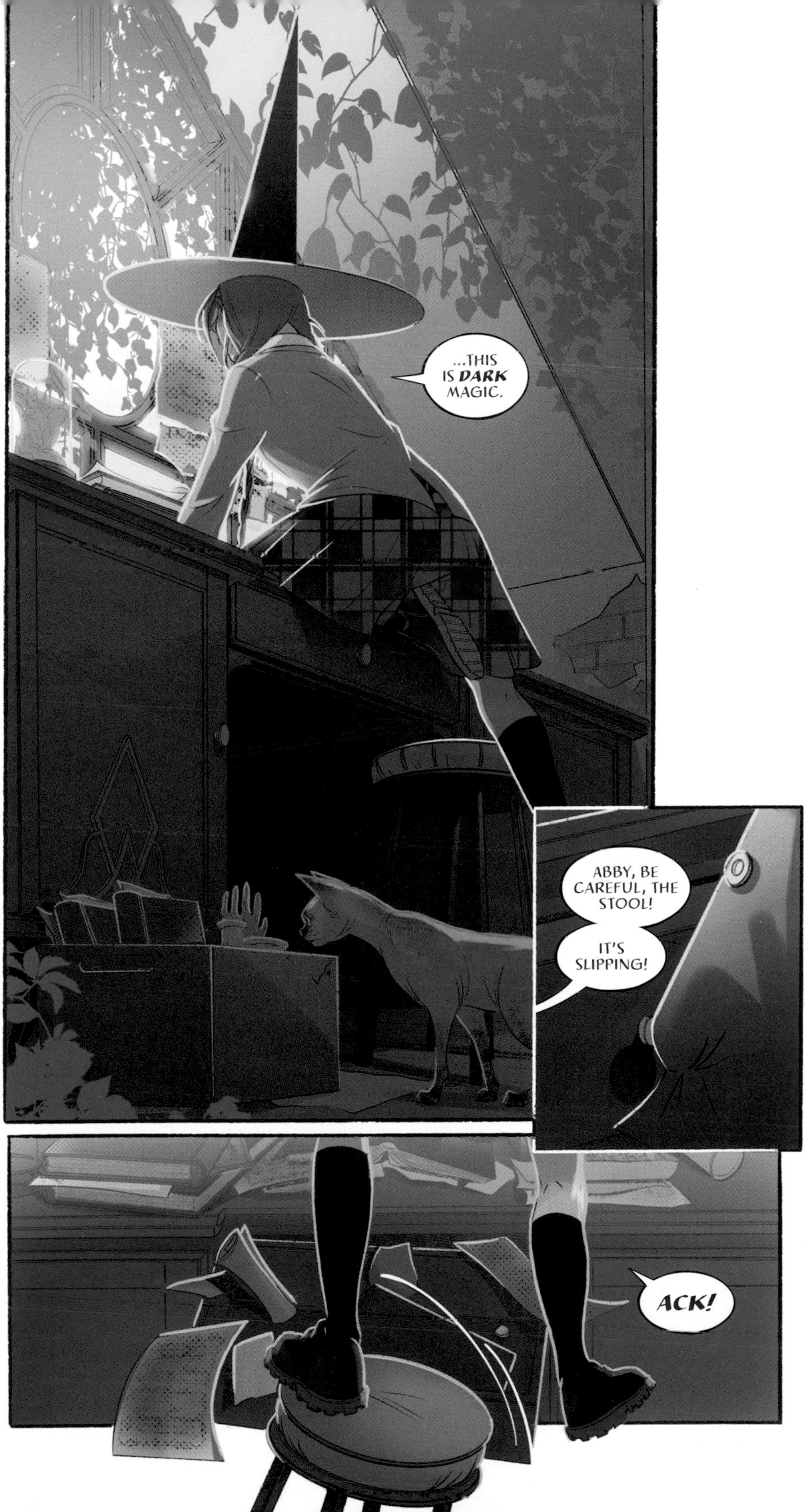
...THIS IS DARK MAGIC.
ABBY, BE CAREFUL, THE STOOL!
IT'S SLIPPING!
ACK!

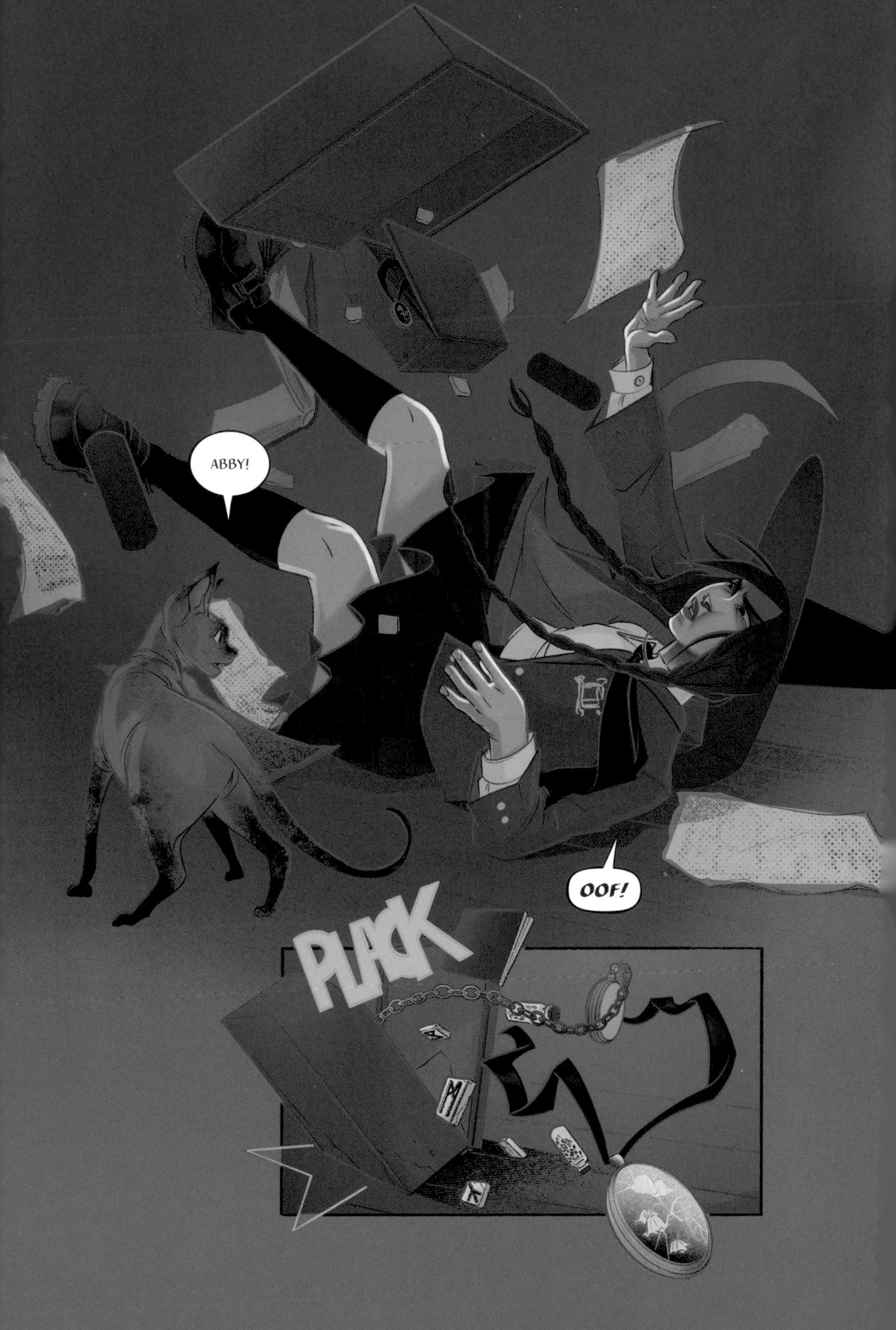
ABBY!
OOF!
PLACK

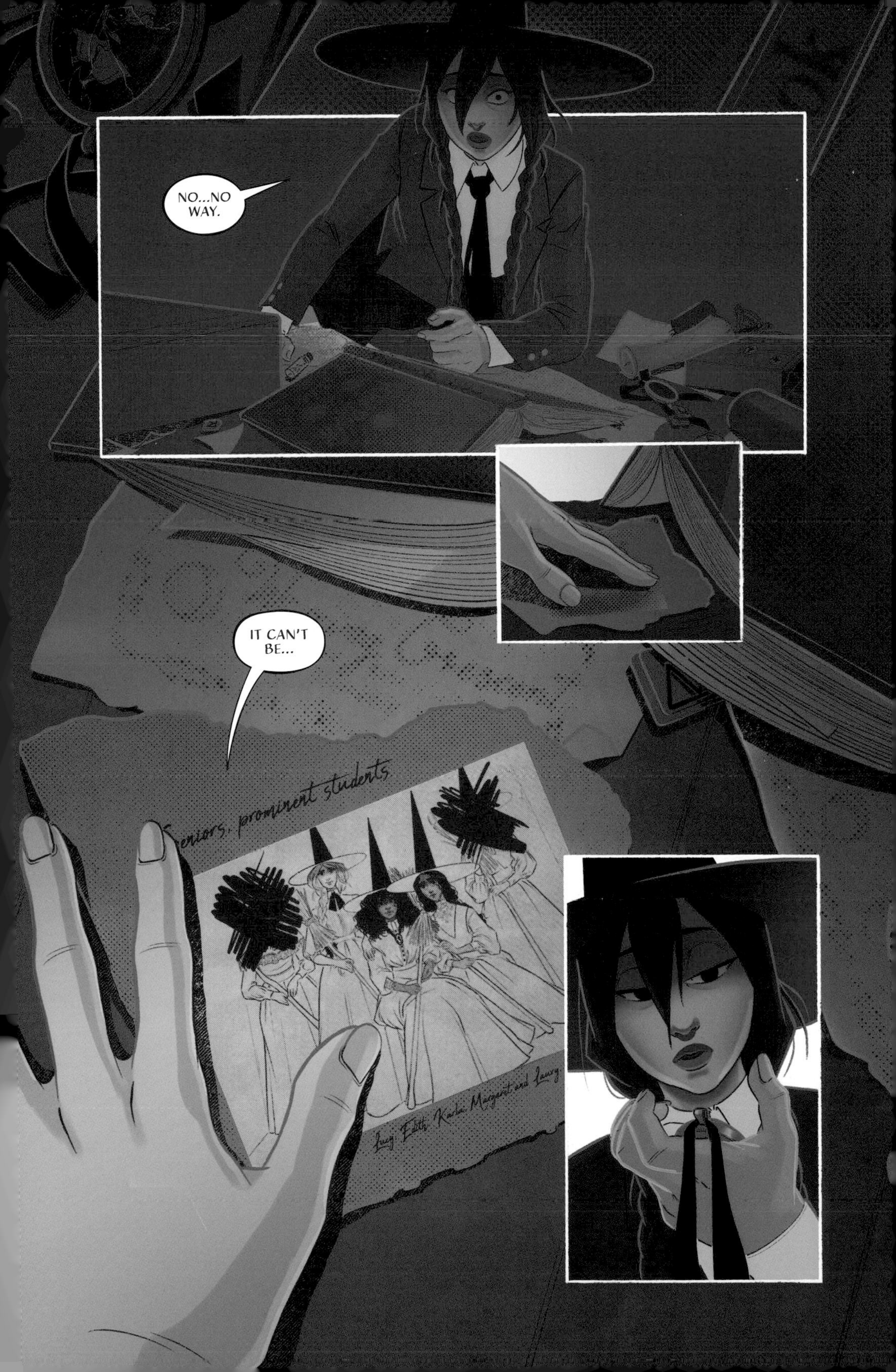
NO...NO WAY.
IT CAN'T BE...
eniors, prominent students.
Lucy, Edith, Karla, Margaret and Laury.

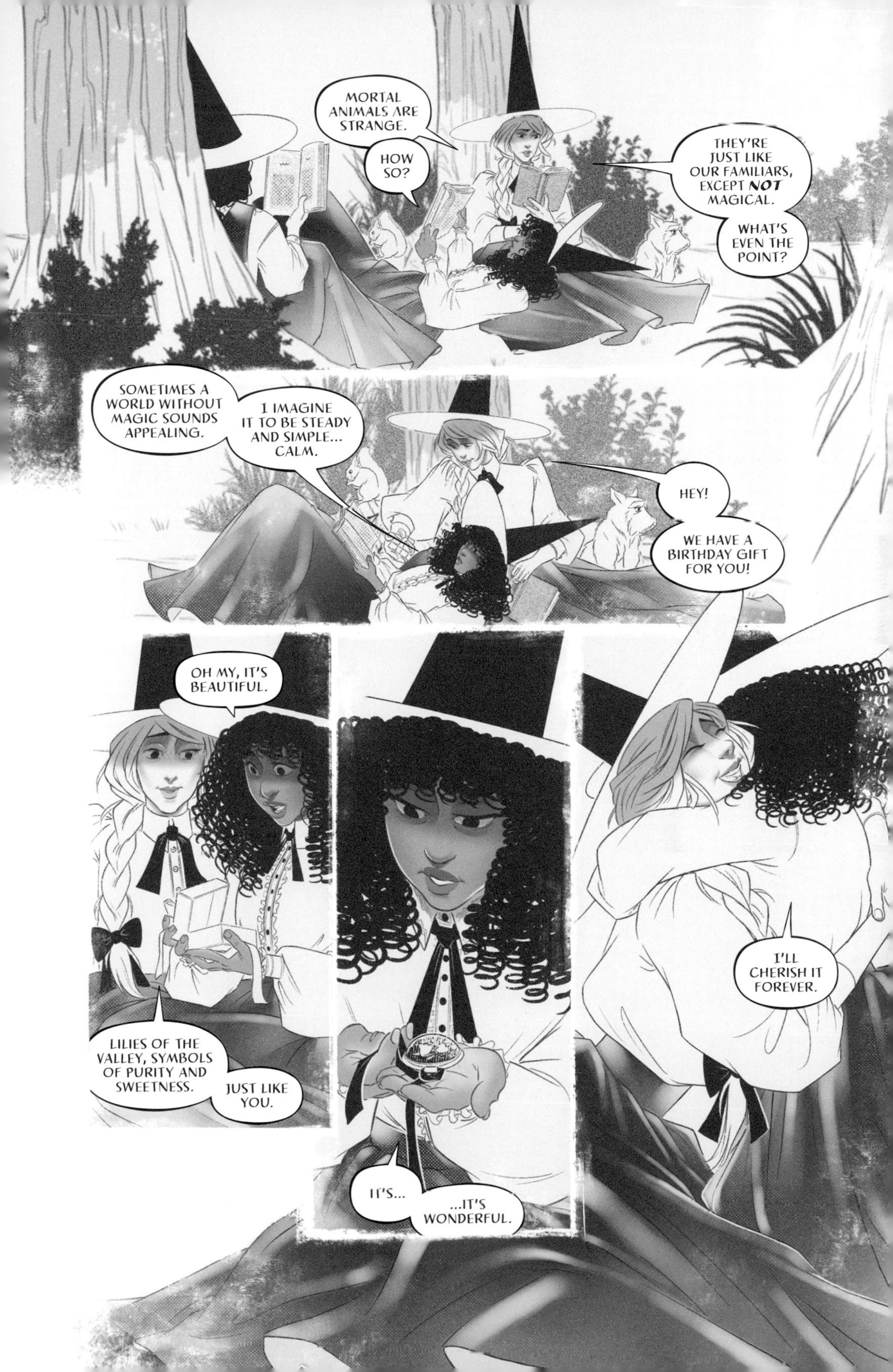
MORTAL ANIMALS ARE STRANGE.
HOW SO?
THEY'RE JUST LIKE OUR FAMILIARS, EXCEPT **NOT** MAGICAL.
WHAT'S EVEN THE POINT?
SOMETIMES A WORLD WITHOUT MAGIC SOUNDS APPEALING.
I IMAGINE IT TO BE STEADY AND SIMPLE... CALM.
HEY!
WE HAVE A BIRTHDAY GIFT FOR YOU!
OH MY, IT'S BEAUTIFUL.
LILIES OF THE VALLEY, SYMBOLS OF PURITY AND SWEETNESS.
JUST LIKE YOU.
IT'S...
...IT'S WONDERFUL.
I'LL CHERISH IT FOREVER.

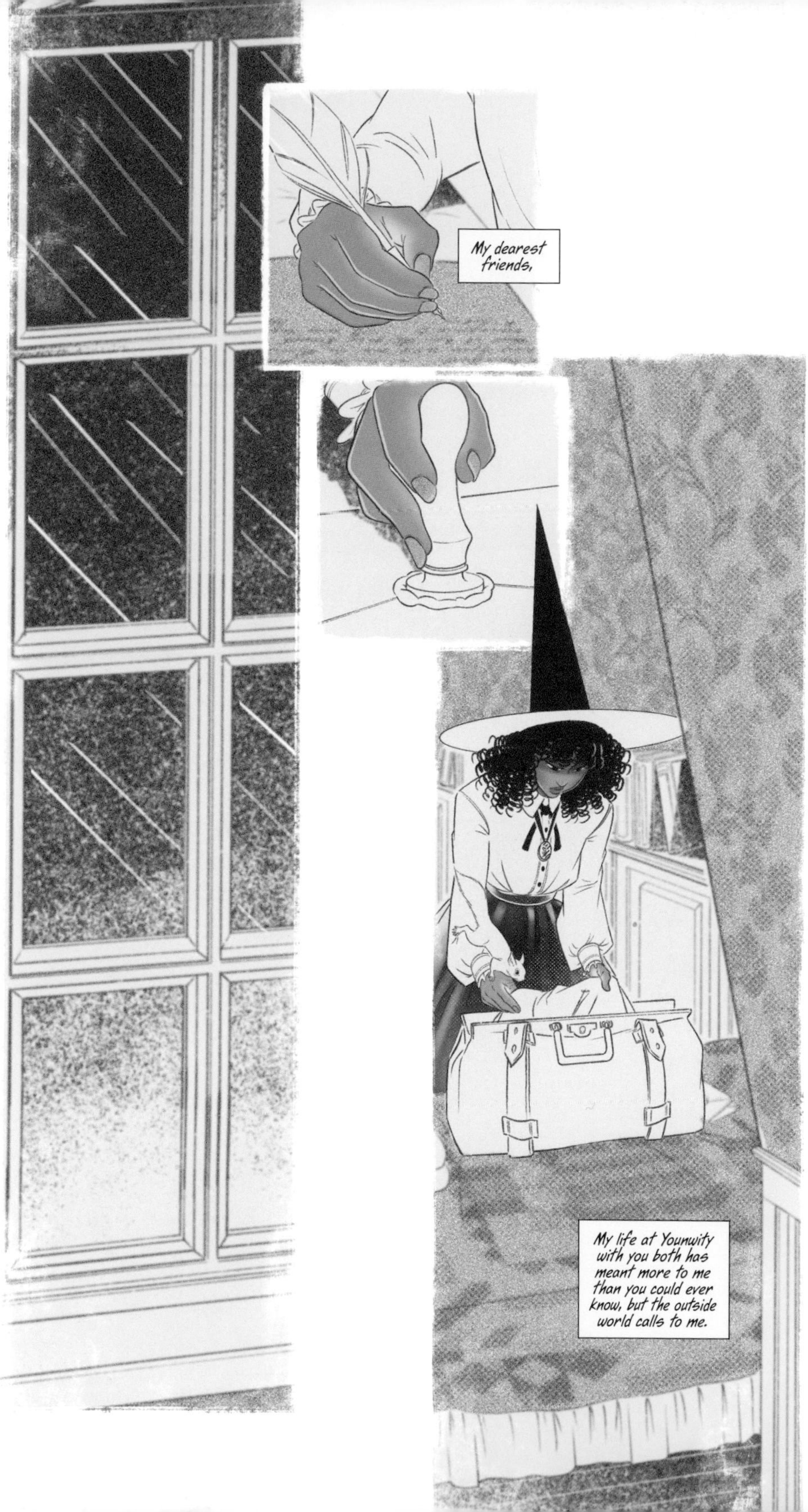
My dearest friends,
My life at Younwity with you both has meant more to me than you could ever know, but the outside world calls to me.

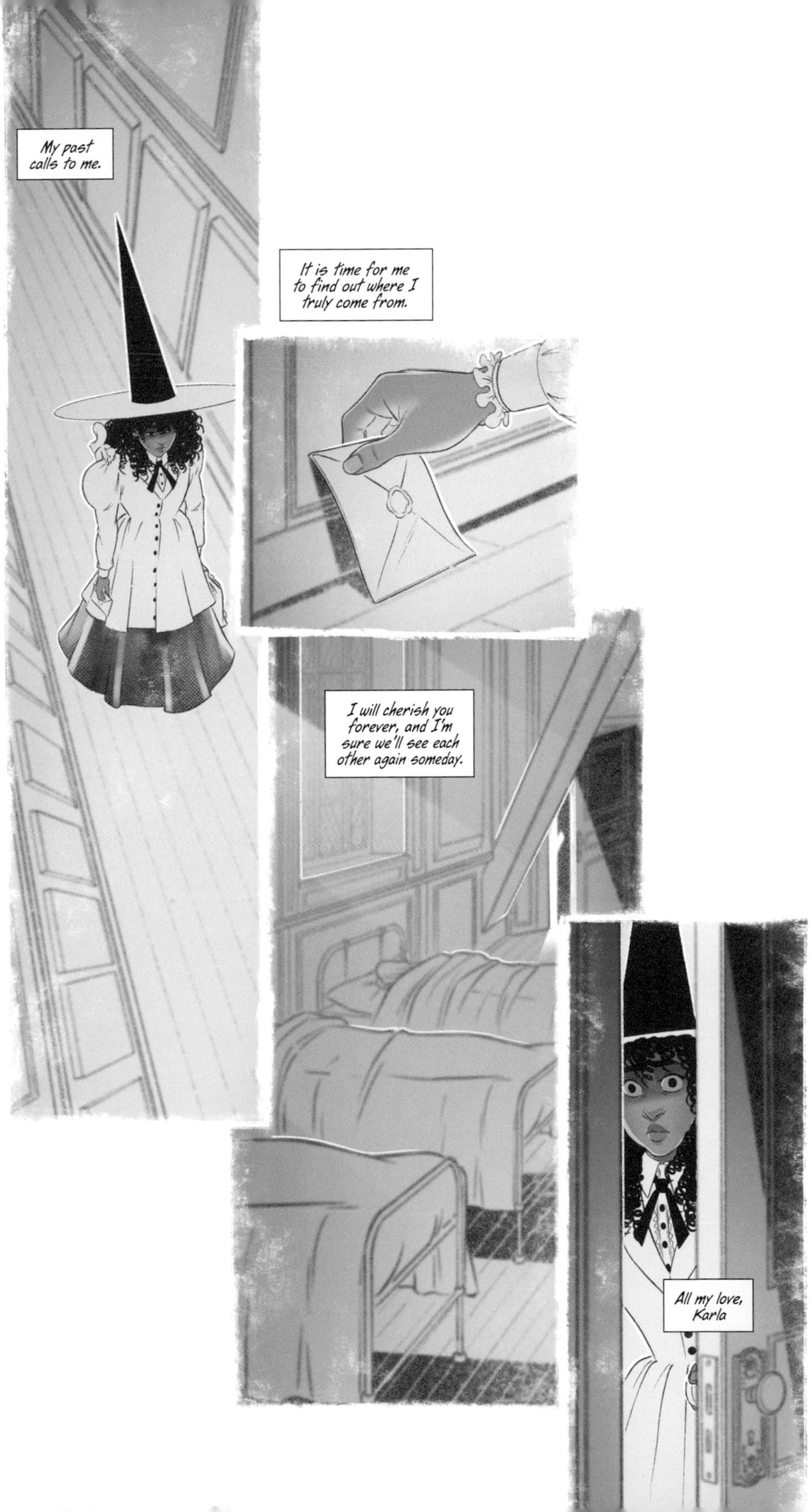
My past calls to me.
It is time for me to find out where I truly come from.
I will cherish you forever, and I'm sure we'll see each other again someday.
All my love, Karla

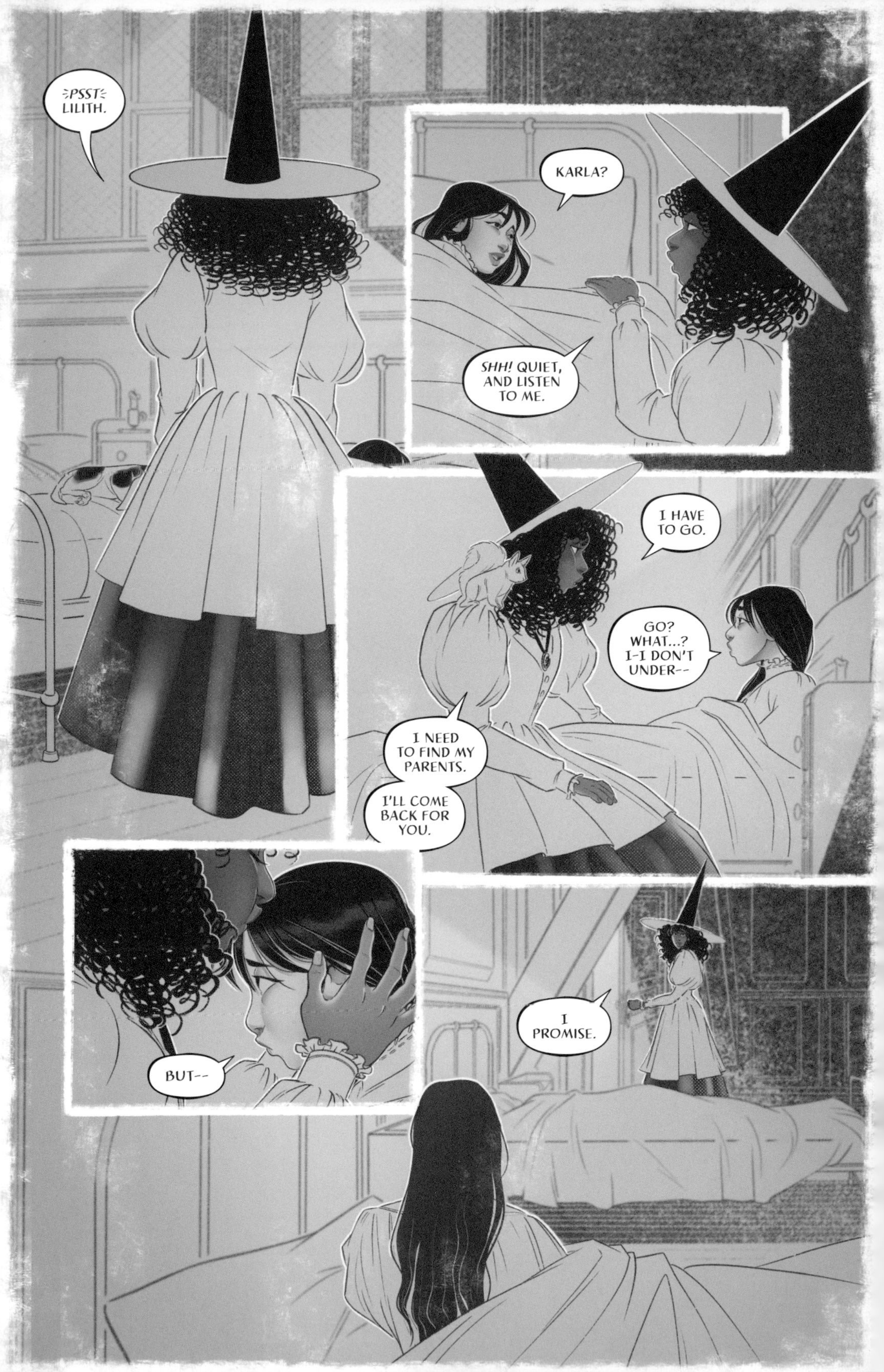

PSST LILITH.
KARLA?
SHH! QUIET, AND LISTEN TO ME.
I HAVE TO GO.
GO? WHAT...? I-I DON'T UNDER--
I NEED TO FIND MY PARENTS.
I'LL COME BACK FOR YOU.
BUT--
I PROMISE.

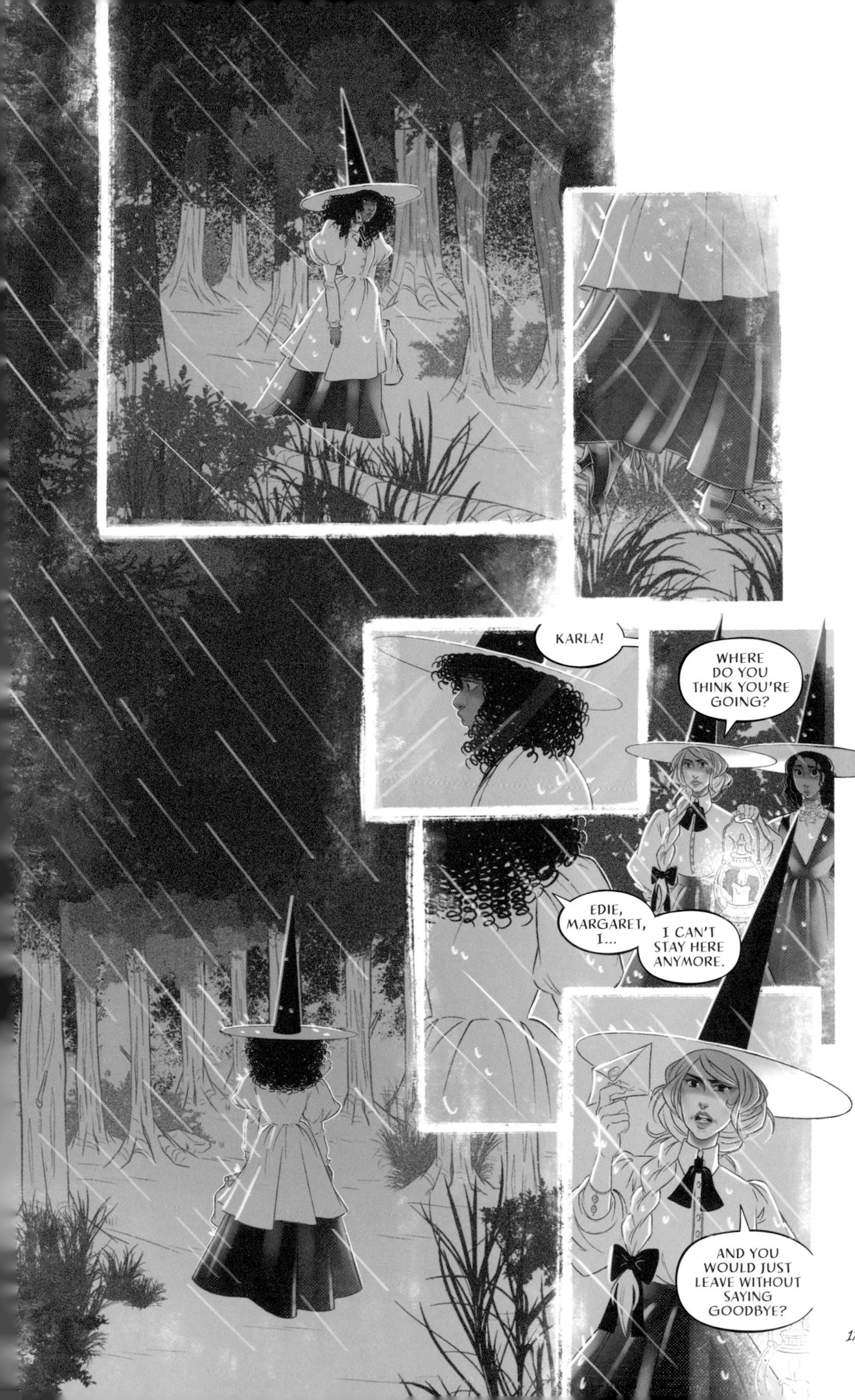
KARLA!
WHERE DO YOU THINK YOU'RE GOING?
EDIE, MARGARET, I...
I CAN'T STAY HERE ANYMORE.
AND YOU WOULD JUST LEAVE WITHOUT SAYING GOODBYE?

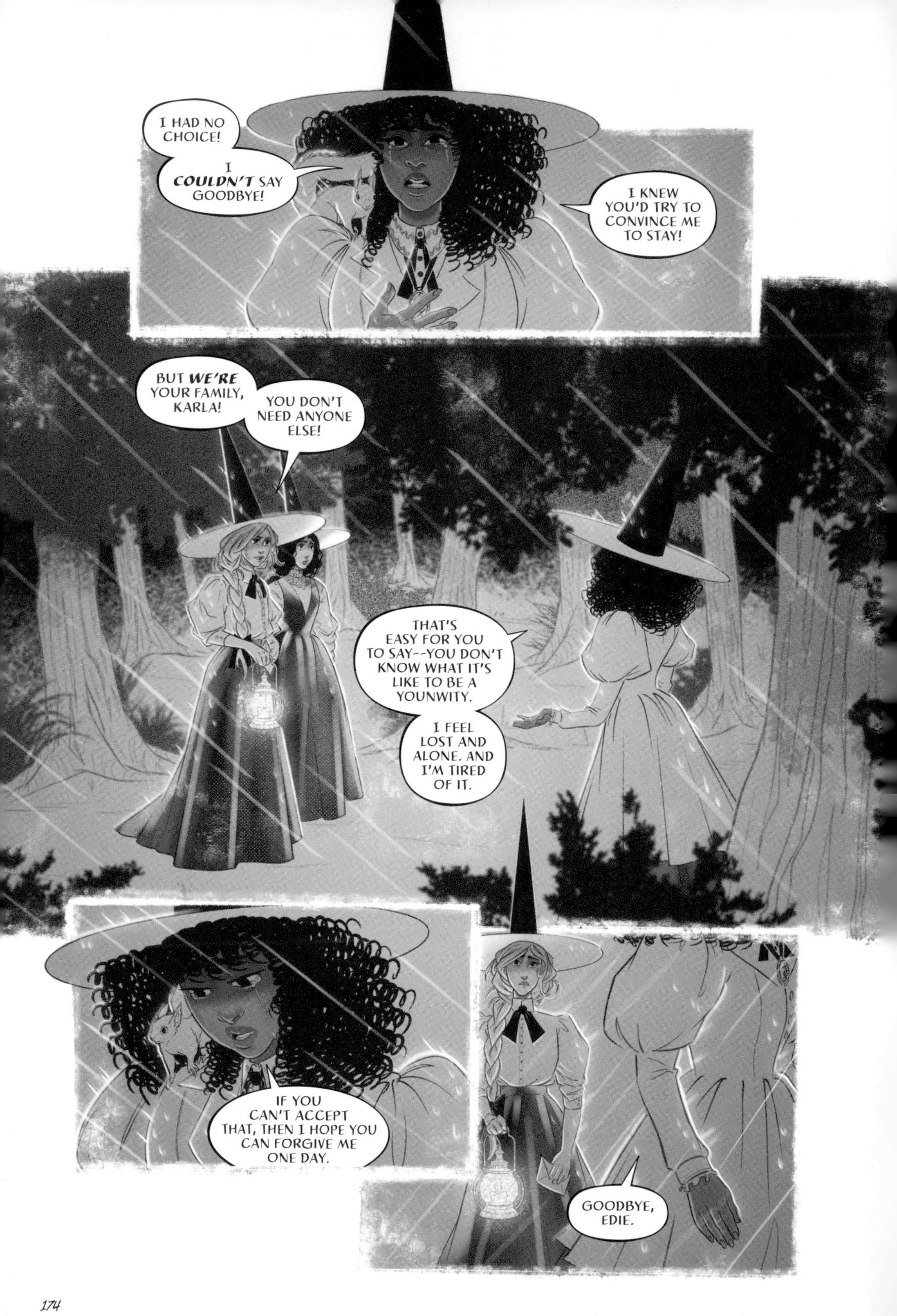

I HAD NO CHOICE!
I **COULDN'T** SAY GOODBYE!
I KNEW YOU'D TRY TO CONVINCE ME TO STAY!
BUT **WE'RE** YOUR FAMILY, KARLA!
YOU DON'T NEED ANYONE ELSE!
THAT'S EASY FOR YOU TO SAY--YOU DON'T KNOW WHAT IT'S LIKE TO BE A YOUNWITY.
I FEEL LOST AND ALONE. AND I'M TIRED OF IT.
IF YOU CAN'T ACCEPT THAT, THEN I HOPE YOU CAN FORGIVE ME ONE DAY.
GOODBYE, EDIE.

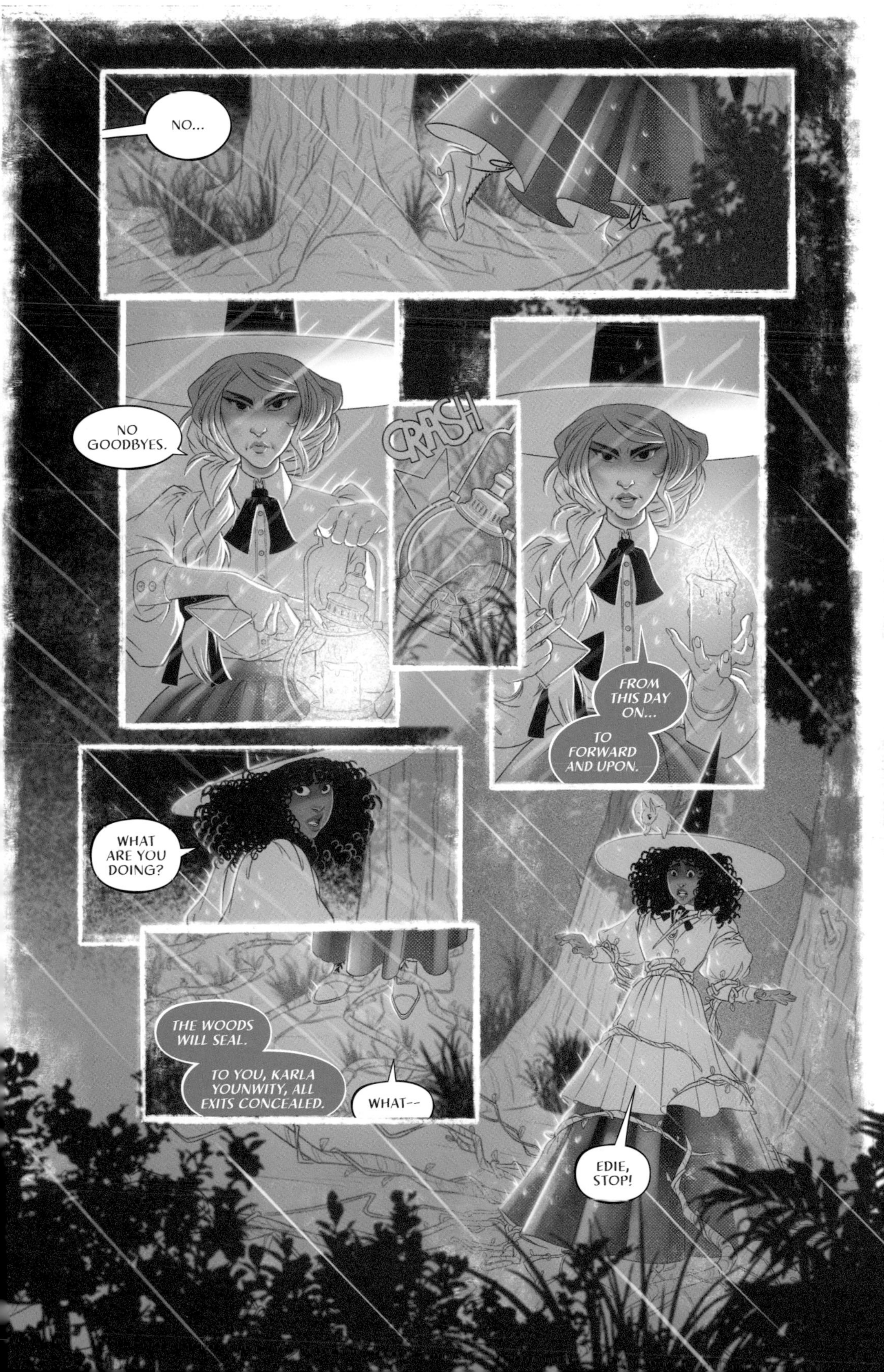
NO...
NO GOODBYES.
CRASH
FROM THIS DAY ON...
TO FORWARD AND UPON.
WHAT ARE YOU DOING?
THE WOODS WILL SEAL.
TO YOU, KARLA YOUNWITY, ALL EXITS CONCEALED.
WHAT--
EDIE, STOP!

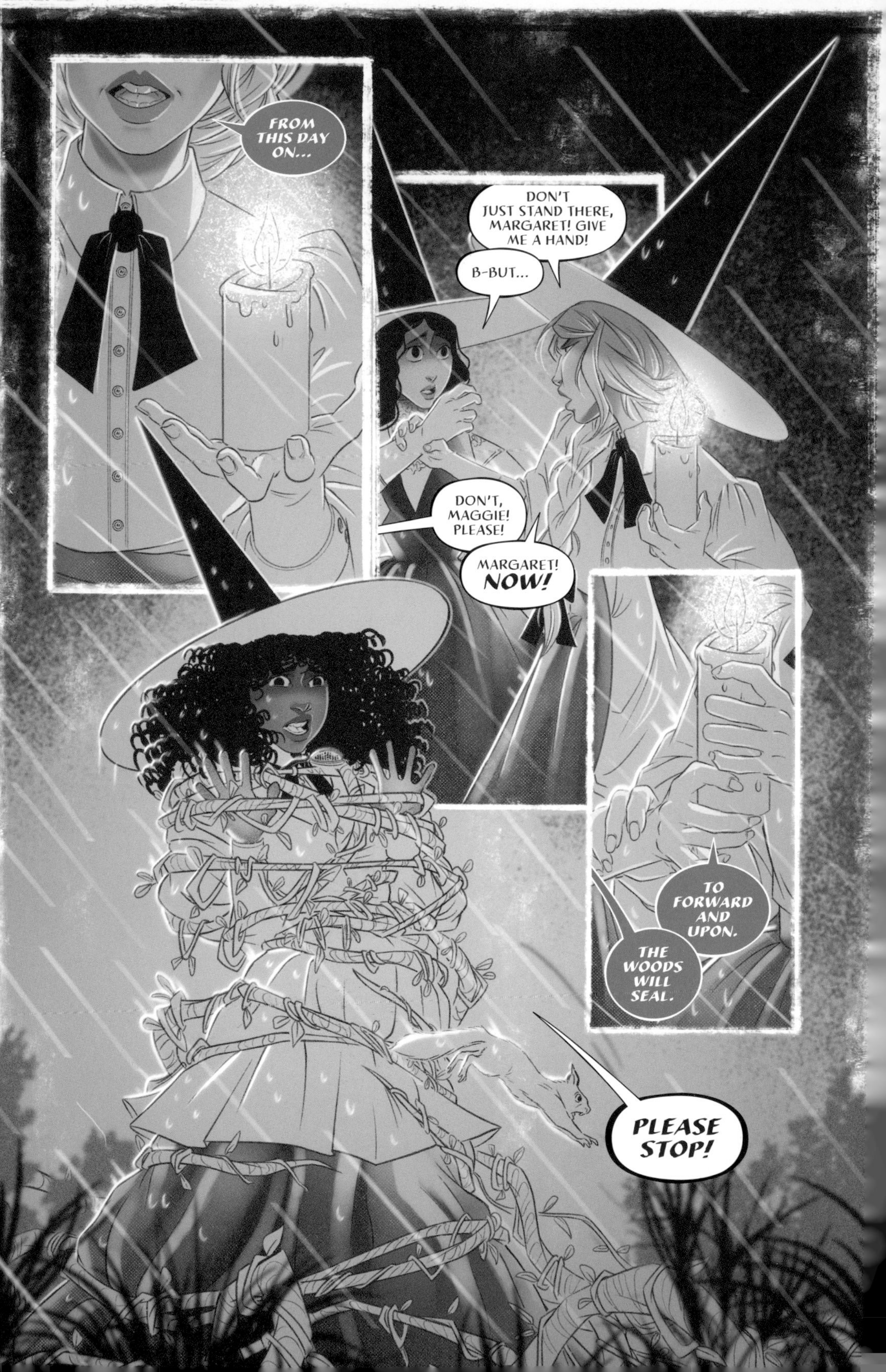
FROM THIS DAY ON...
DON'T JUST STAND THERE, MARGARET! GIVE ME A HAND!
B-BUT...
DON'T, MAGGIE! PLEASE!
MARGARET! NOW!
TO FORWARD AND UPON.
THE WOODS WILL SEAL.
PLEASE STOP!

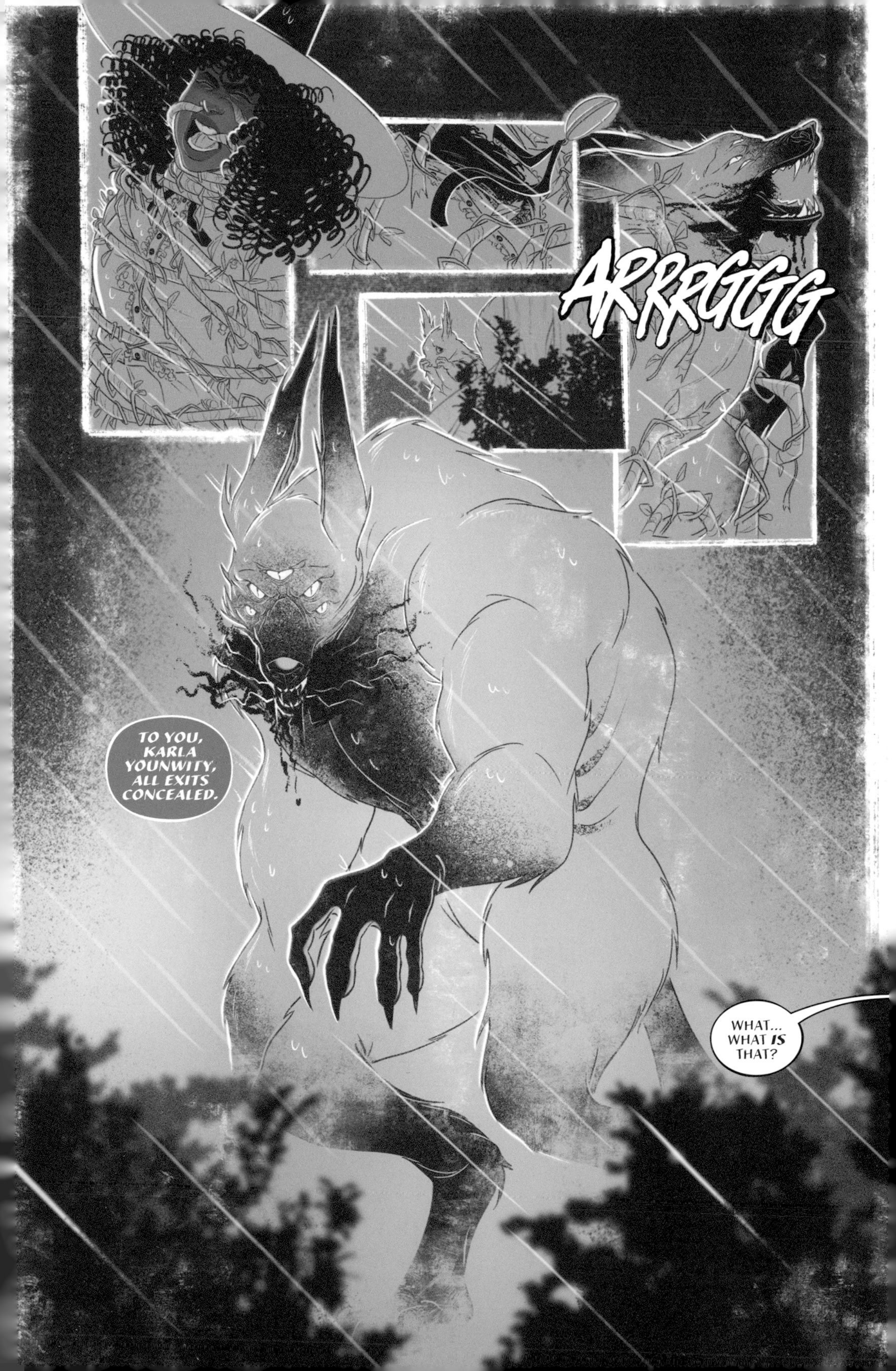
ARRRGGG
TO YOU, KARLA YOUNWITY, ALL EXITS CONCEALED.
WHAT... WHAT IS THAT?

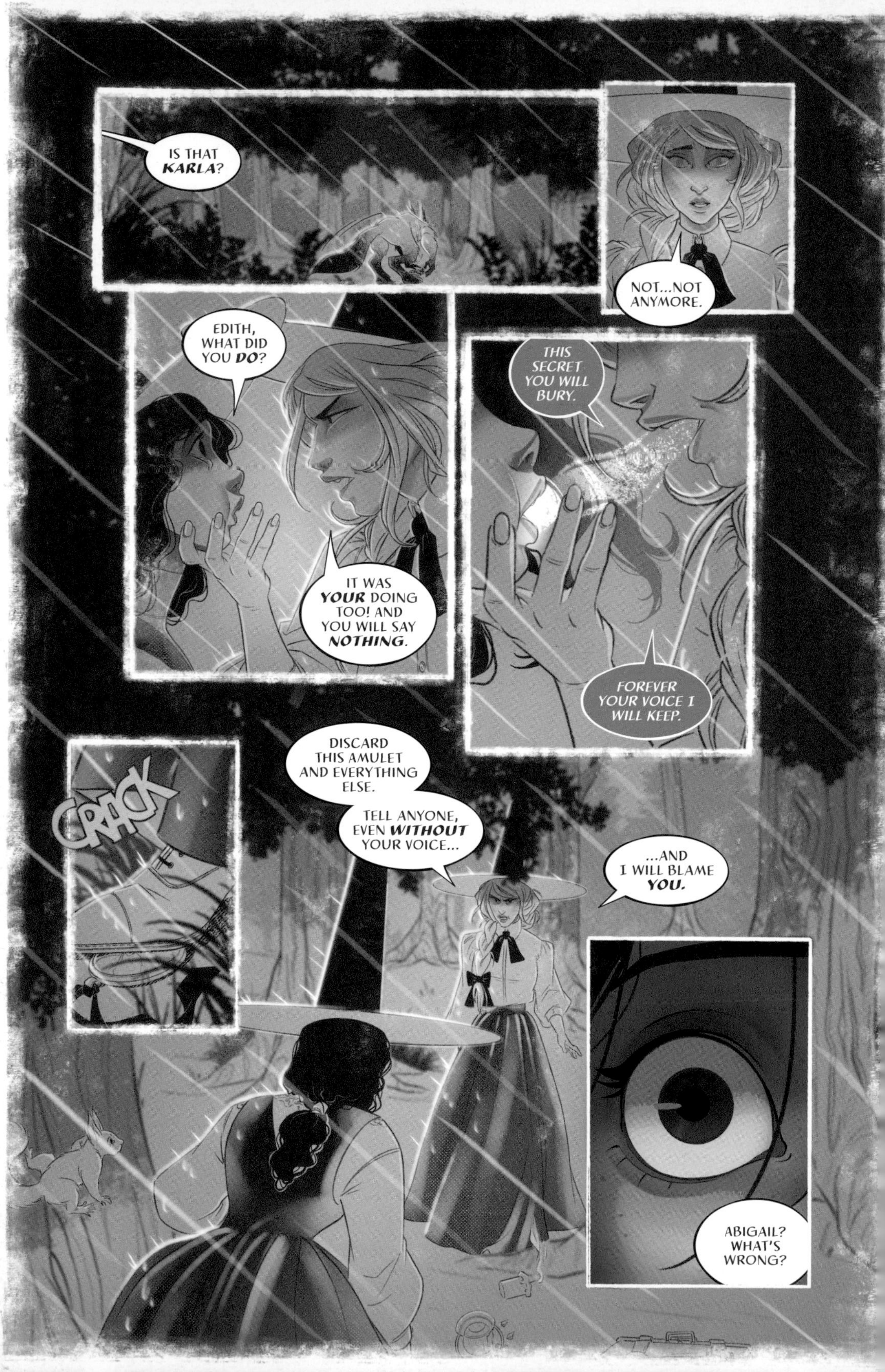
IS THAT KARLA?
NOT...NOT ANYMORE.
EDITH, WHAT DID YOU DO?
IT WAS YOUR DOING TOO! AND YOU WILL SAY NOTHING.
THIS SECRET YOU WILL BURY.
FOREVER YOUR VOICE I WILL KEEP.
CRACK
DISCARD THIS AMULET AND EVERYTHING ELSE.
TELL ANYONE, EVEN WITHOUT YOUR VOICE...
...AND I WILL BLAME YOU.
ABIGAIL? WHAT'S WRONG?

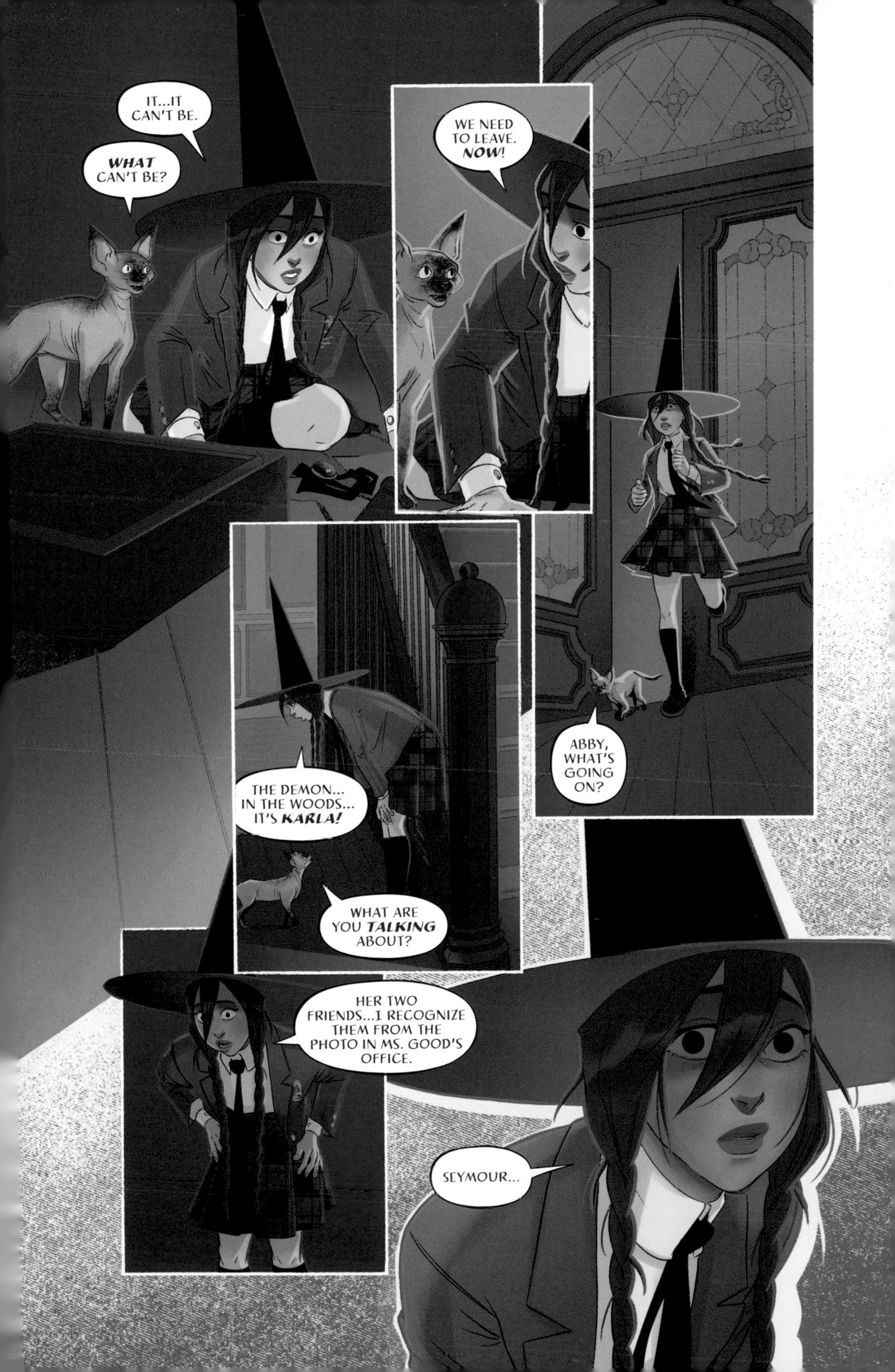
IT...IT CAN'T BE.
WHAT CAN'T BE?
WE NEED TO LEAVE. NOW!
ABBY, WHAT'S GOING ON?
THE DEMON... IN THE WOODS... IT'S KARLA!
WHAT ARE YOU TALKING ABOUT?
HER TWO FRIENDS...I RECOGNIZE THEM FROM THE PHOTO IN MS. GOOD'S OFFICE.
SEYMOUR...

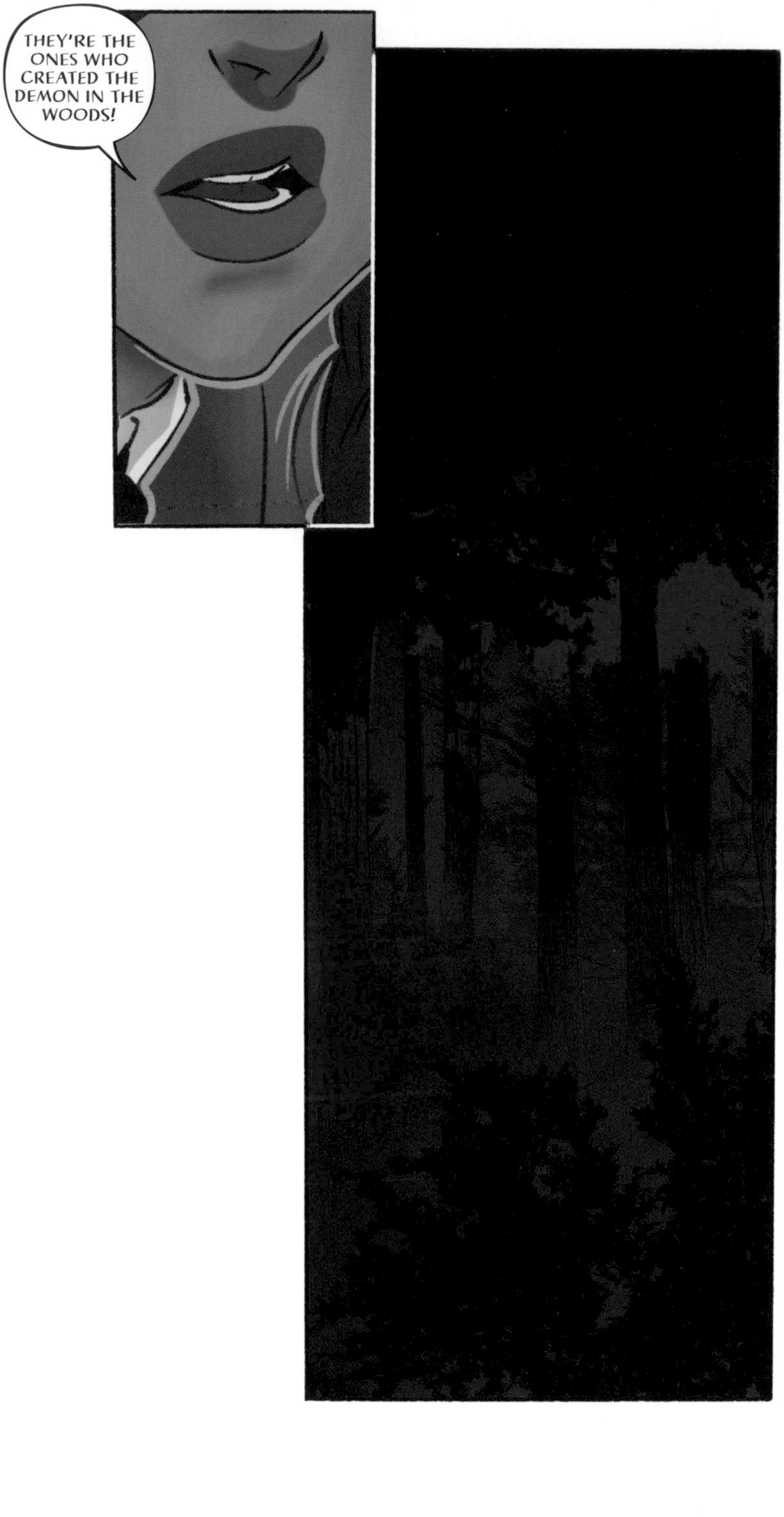
THEY'RE THE ONES WHO CREATED THE DEMON IN THE WOODS!

CHAPTER VI

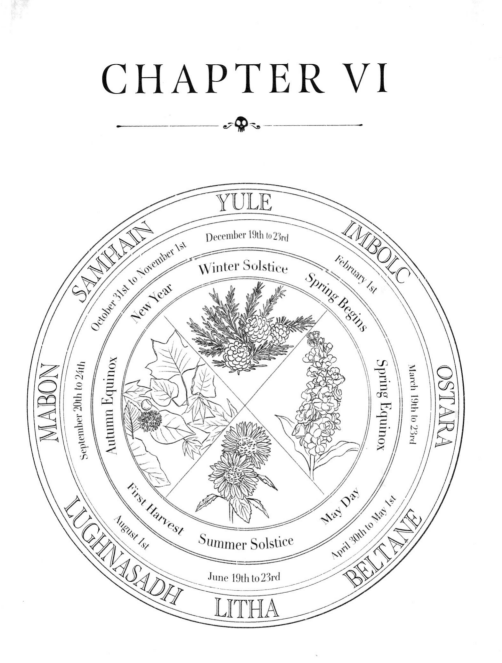

YULE

SAMHAIN

IMBOLC

December 19th to 23rd

October 31st to November 1st

February 1st

Winter Solstice

New Year

Spring Begins

MABON

OSTARA

Autumn Equinox

September 20th to 24th

March 19th to 23rd

Spring Equinox

First Harvest

May Day

August 1st

April 30th to May 1st

LUGHNASADH

Summer Solstice

BELTANE

June 19th to 23rd

LITHA

From the thunder and the storm --
And the cloud that took the form
(When the rest of Heaven was blue)
Of a demon in my view --

"Alone" by Edgar Allan Poe, 1875

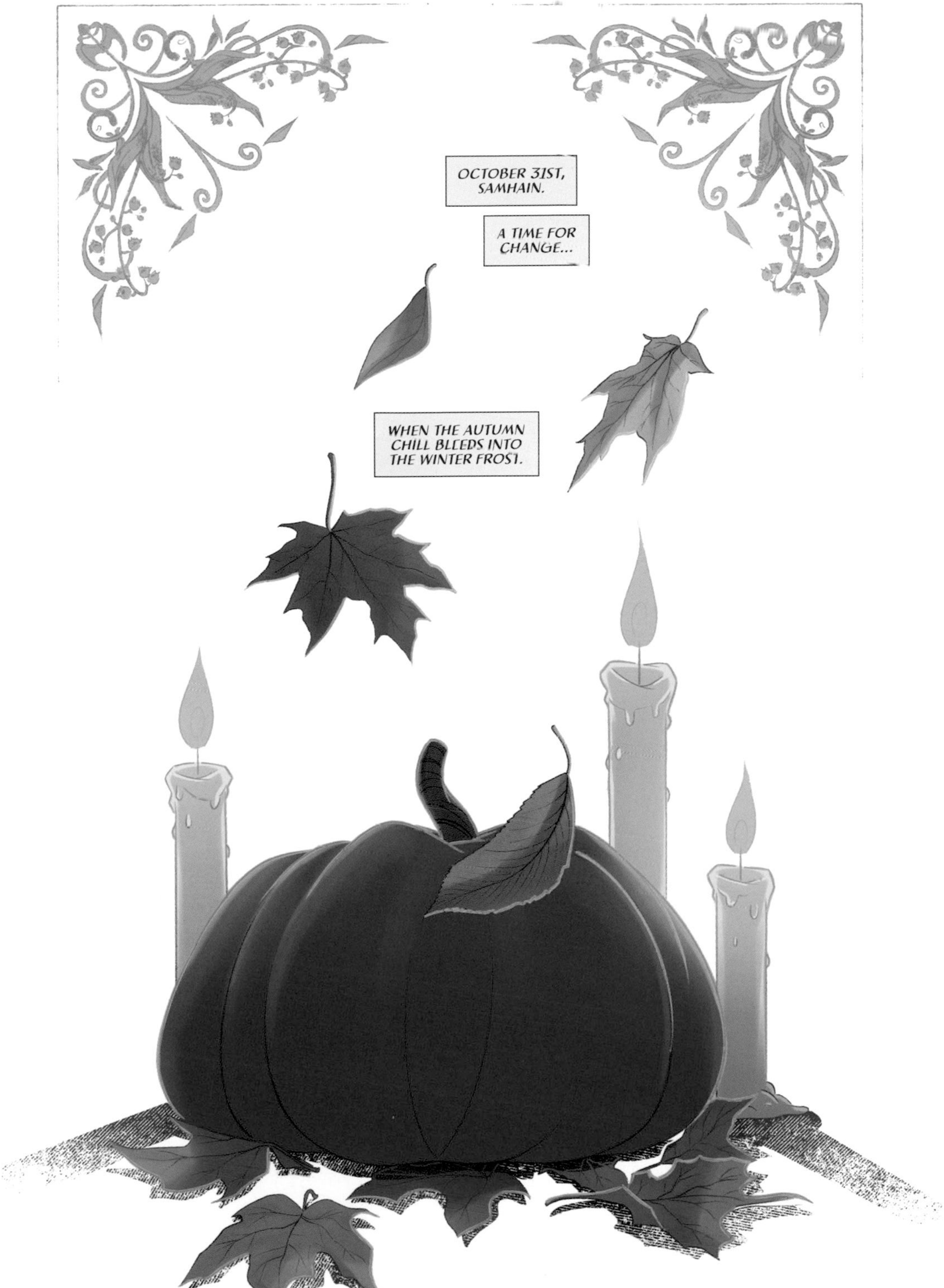
OCTOBER 31ST, SAMHAIN.
A TIME FOR CHANGE...
WHEN THE AUTUMN CHILL BLEEDS INTO THE WINTER FROST.

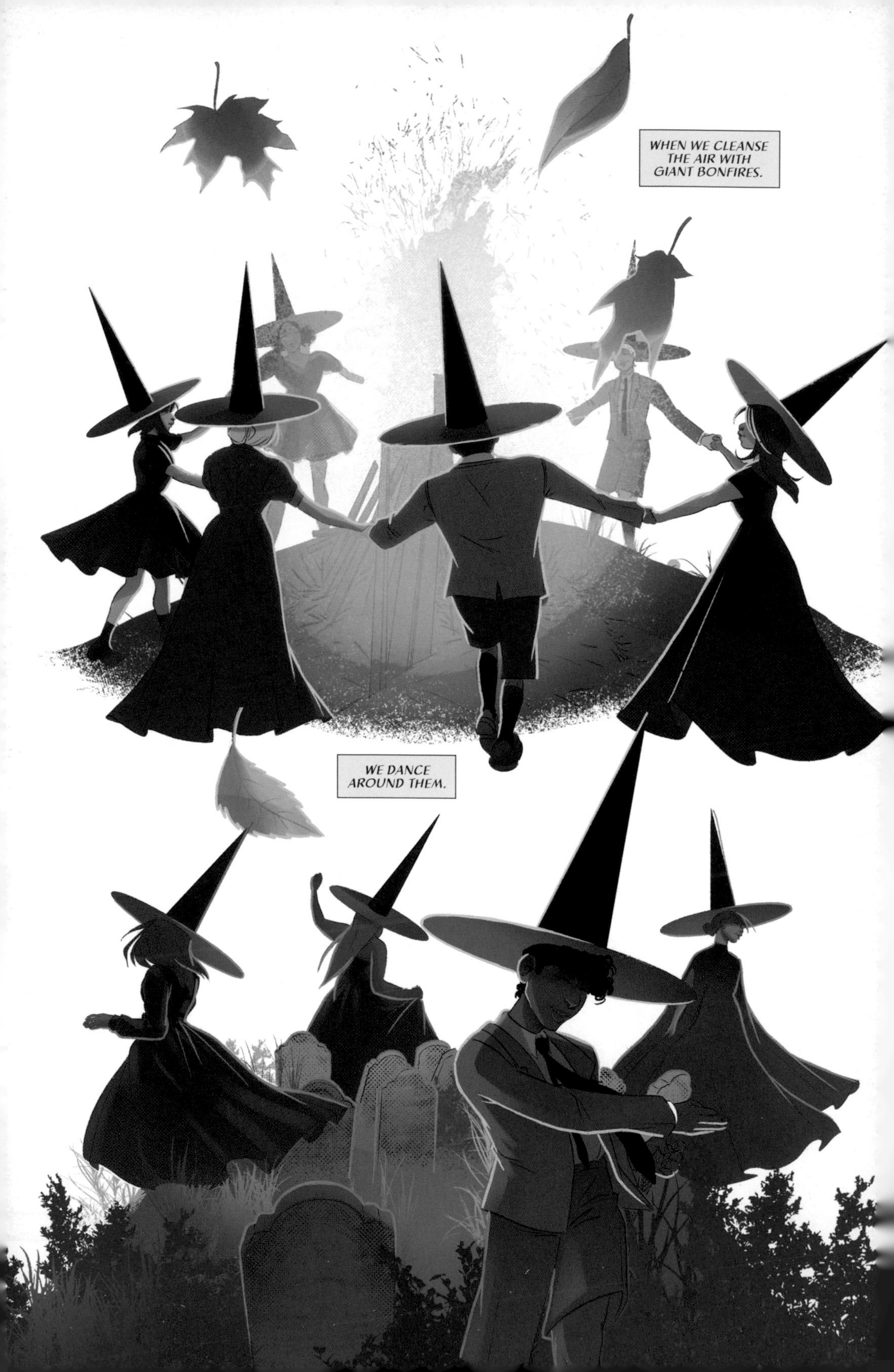
WHEN WE CLEANSE THE AIR WITH GIANT BONFIRES.
WE DANCE AROUND THEM.

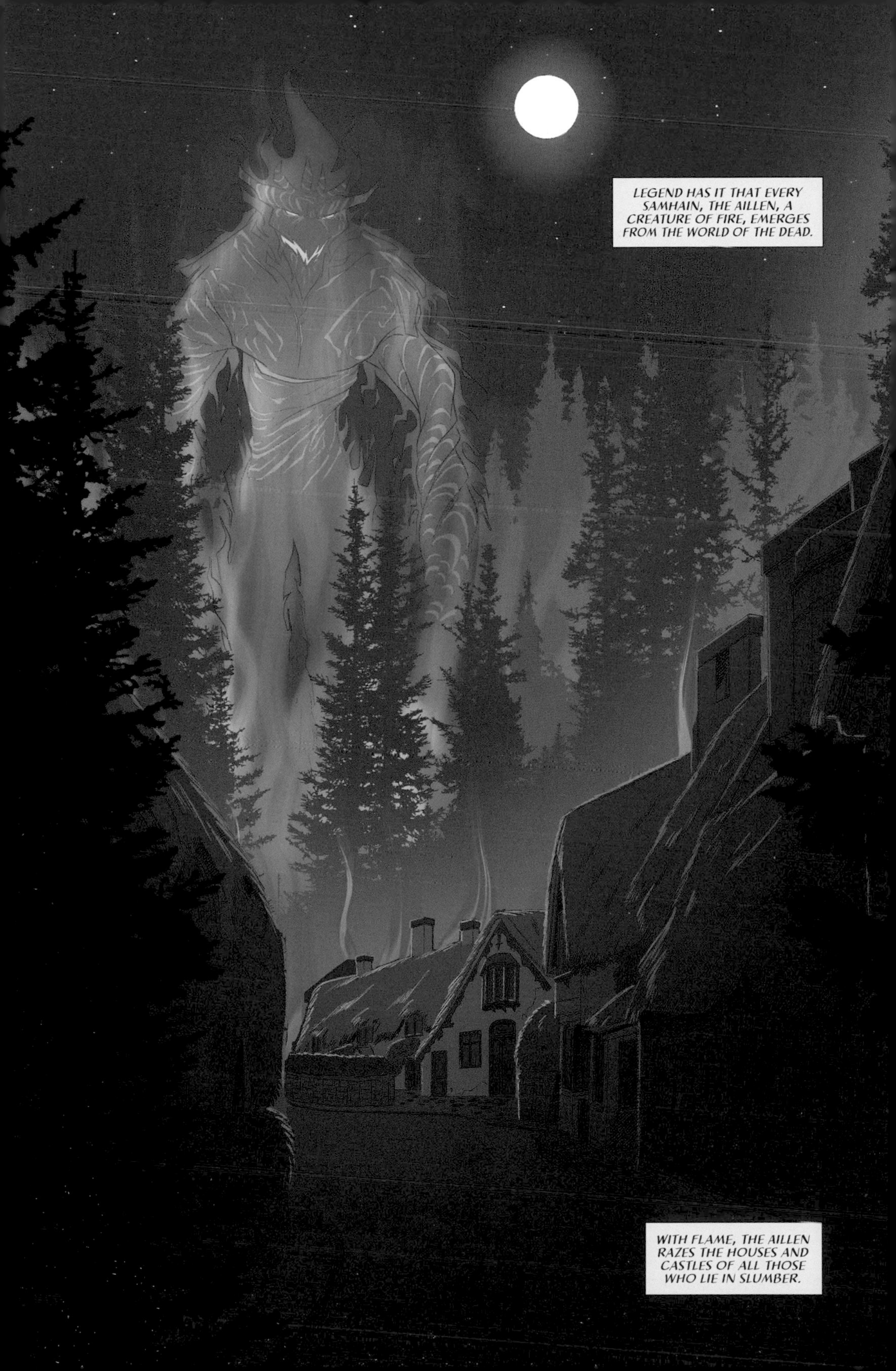
LEGEND HAS IT THAT EVERY SAMHAIN, THE AILLEN, A CREATURE OF FIRE, EMERGES FROM THE WORLD OF THE DEAD.
WITH FLAME, THE AILLEN RAZES THE HOUSES AND CASTLES OF ALL THOSE WHO LIE IN SLUMBER.

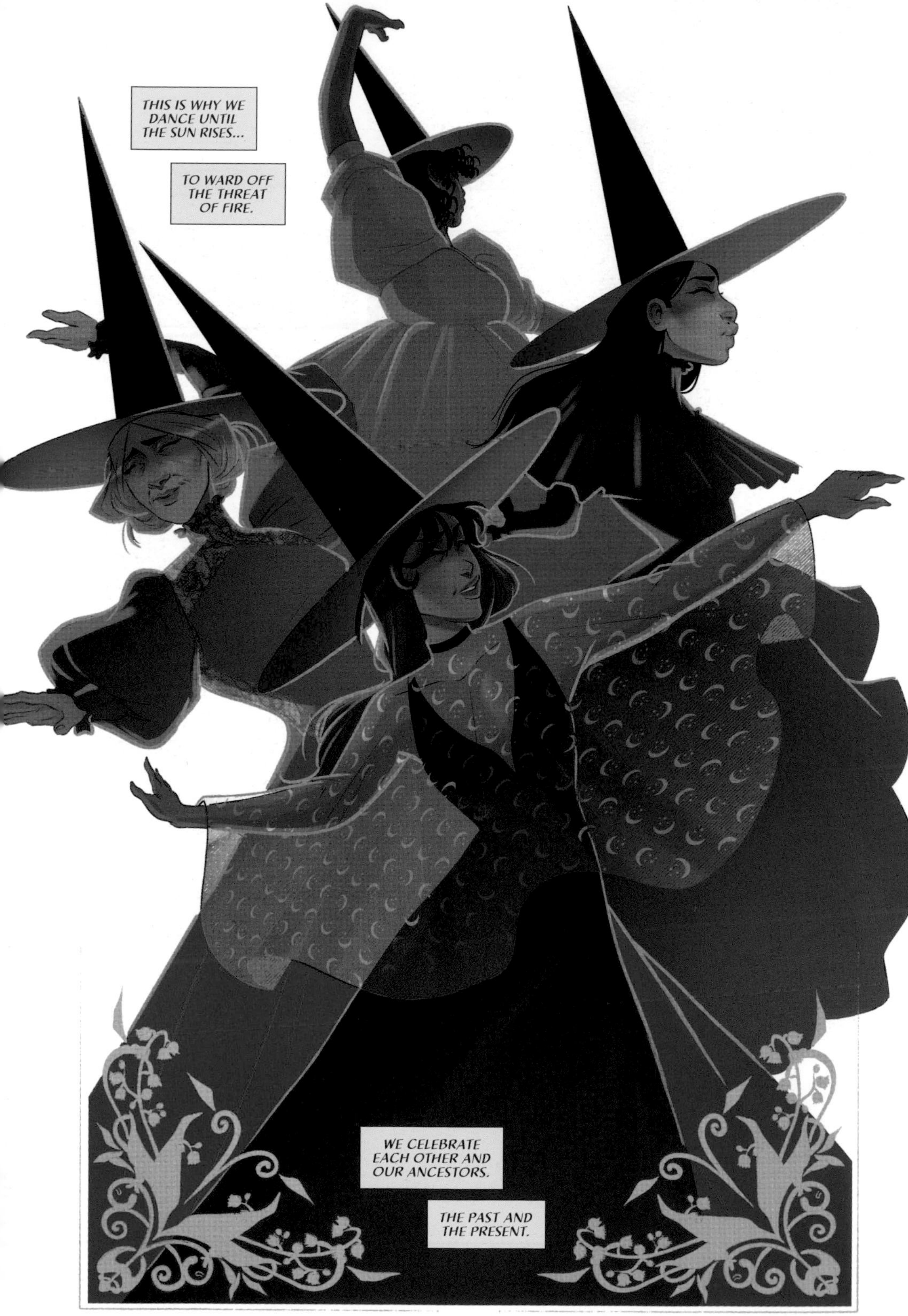
THIS IS WHY WE DANCE UNTIL THE SUN RISES...
TO WARD OFF THE THREAT OF FIRE.
WE CELEBRATE EACH OTHER AND OUR ANCESTORS.
THE PAST AND THE PRESENT.

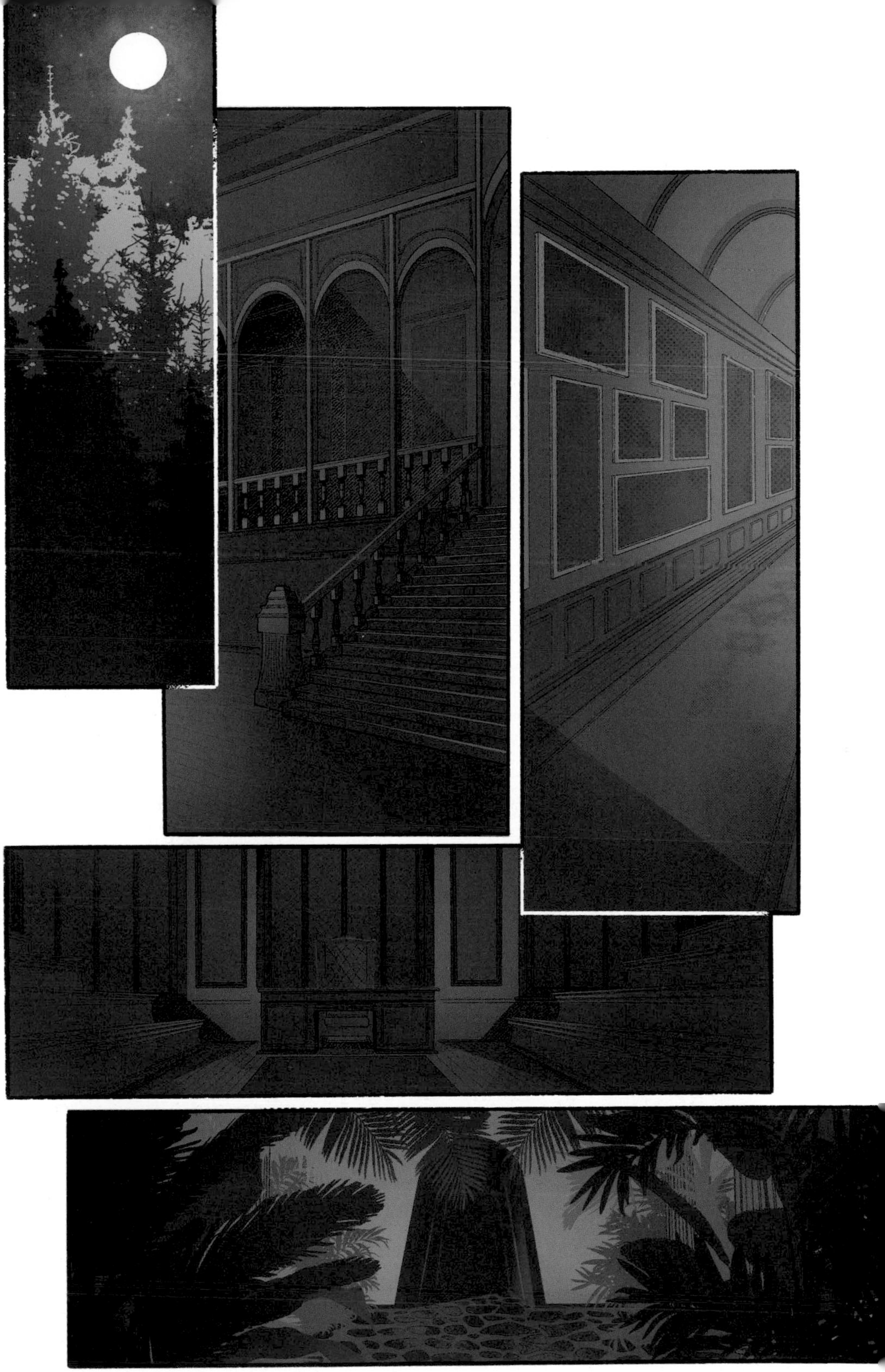

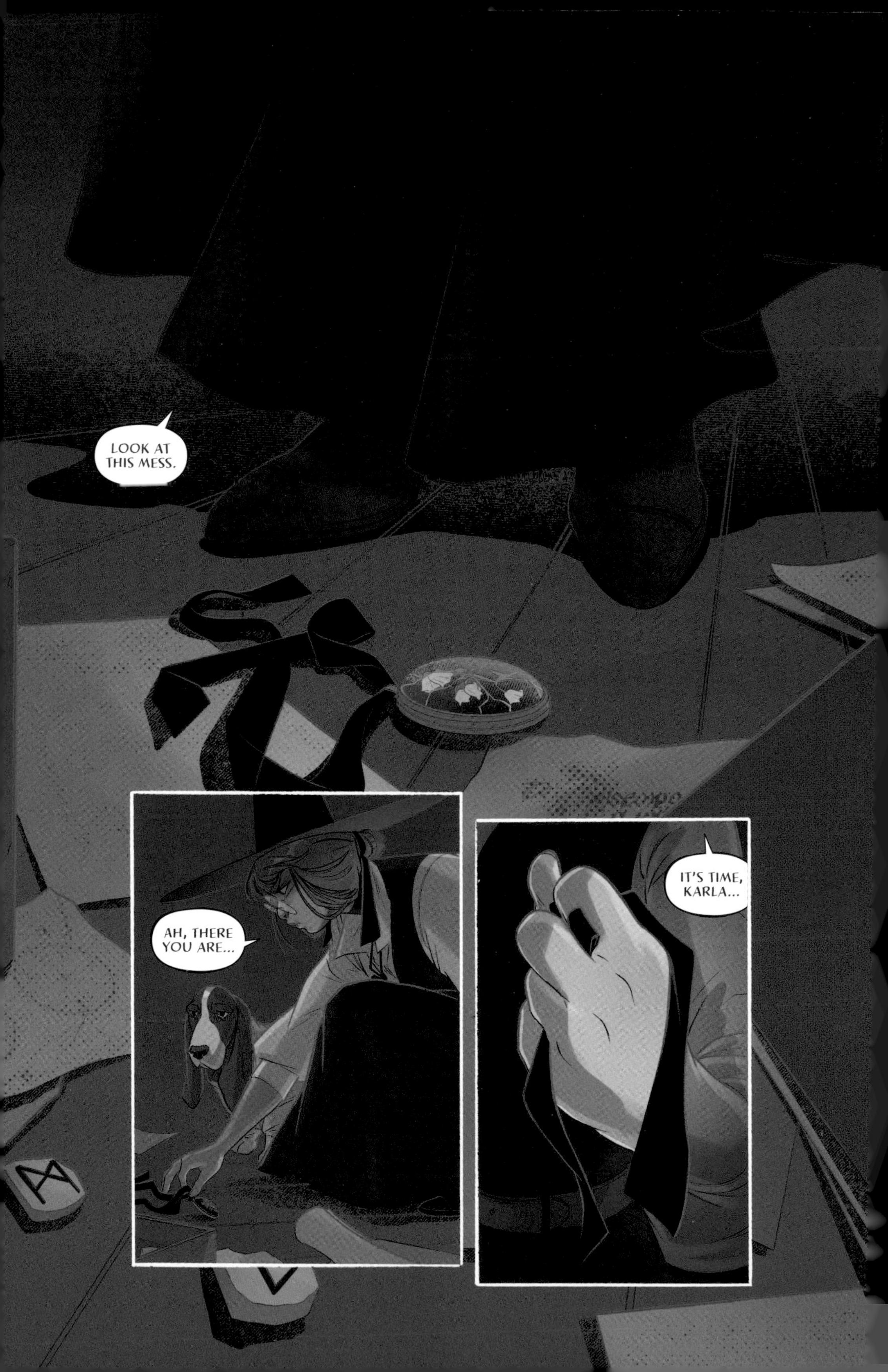
LOOK AT THIS MESS.
AH, THERE YOU ARE...
IT'S TIME, KARLA...

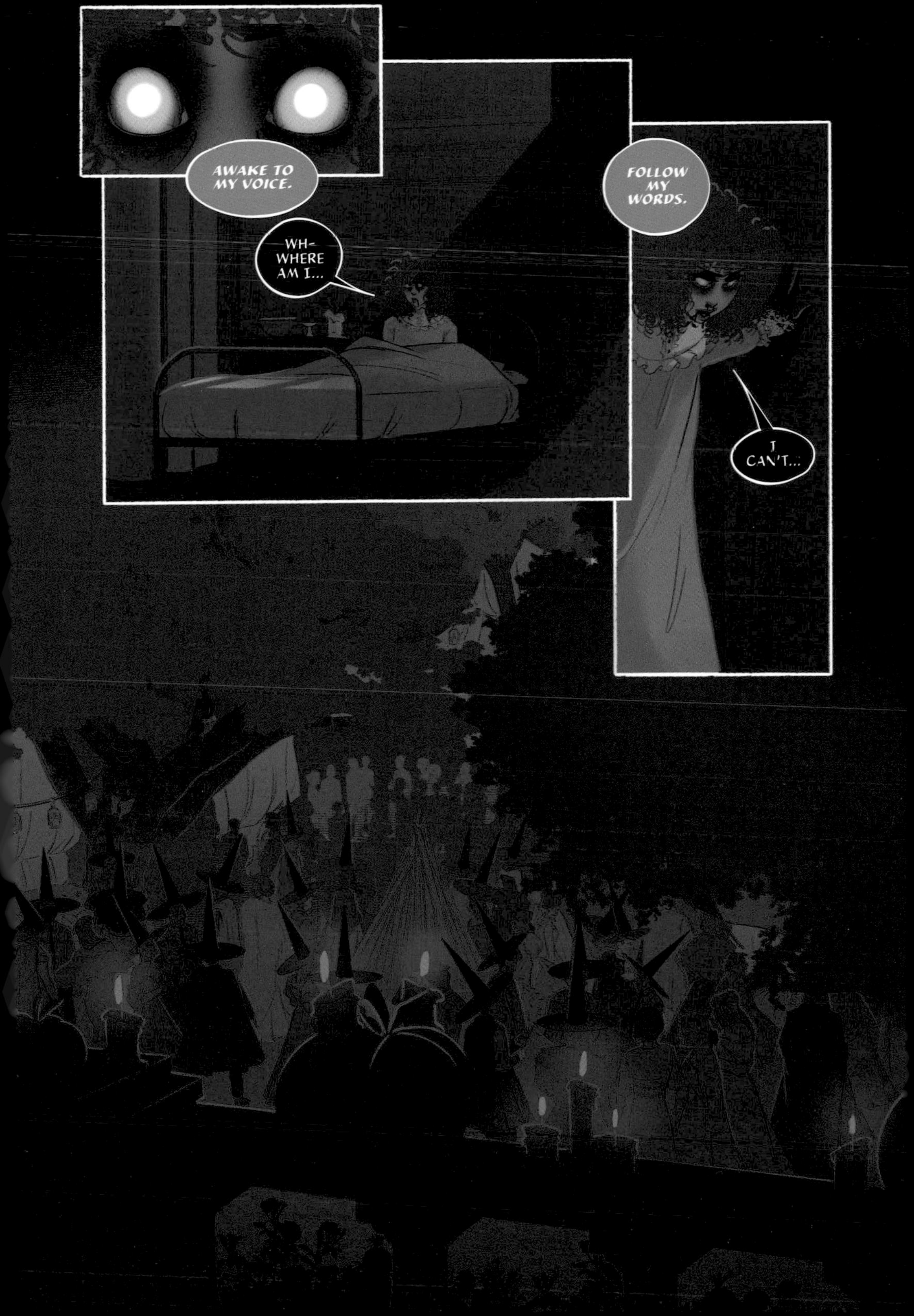
AWAKE TO MY VOICE.
WH-WHERE AM I...
FOLLOW MY WORDS.
I CAN'T...

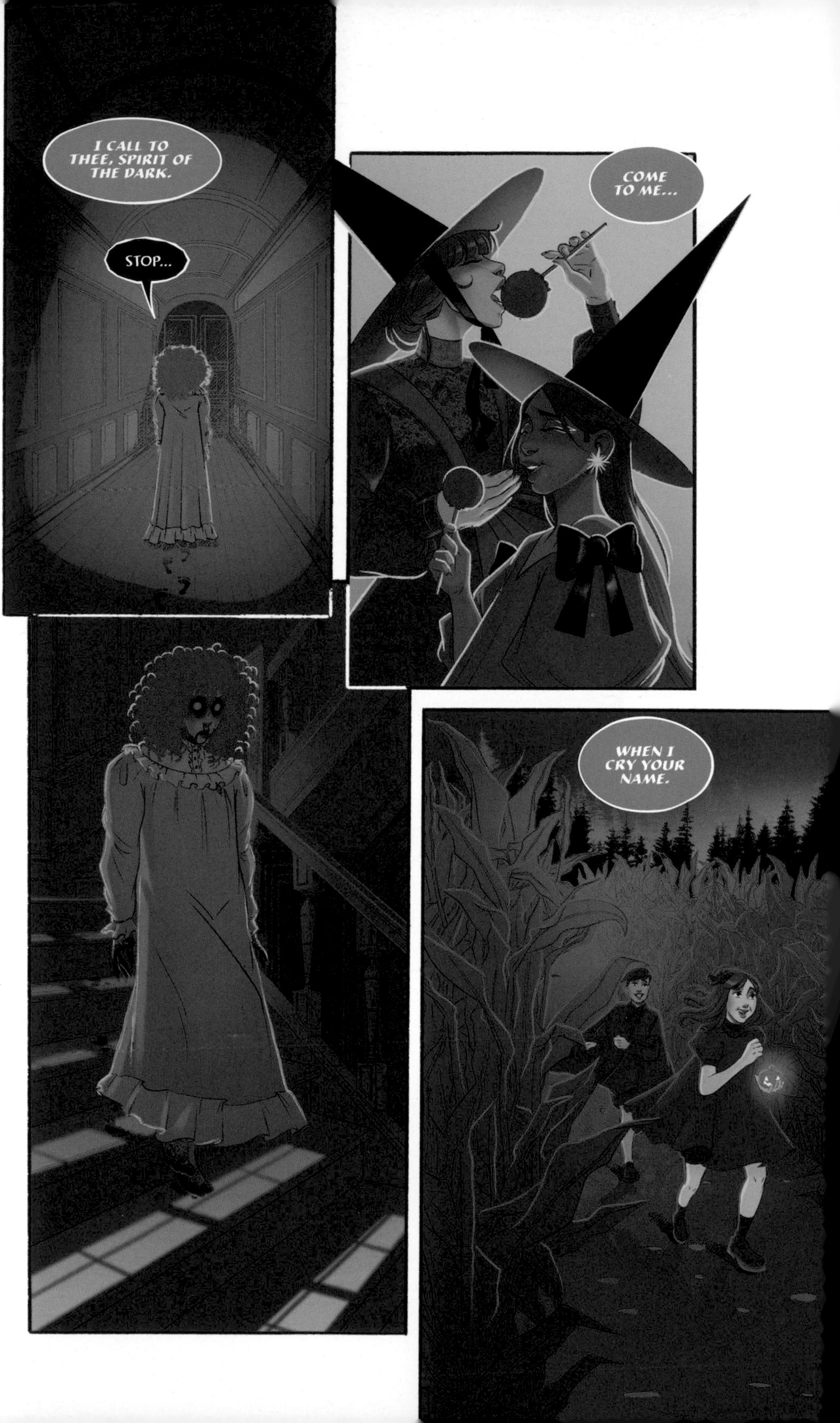

I CALL TO THEE, SPIRIT OF THE DARK.
STOP...
COME TO ME...
WHEN I CRY YOUR NAME.

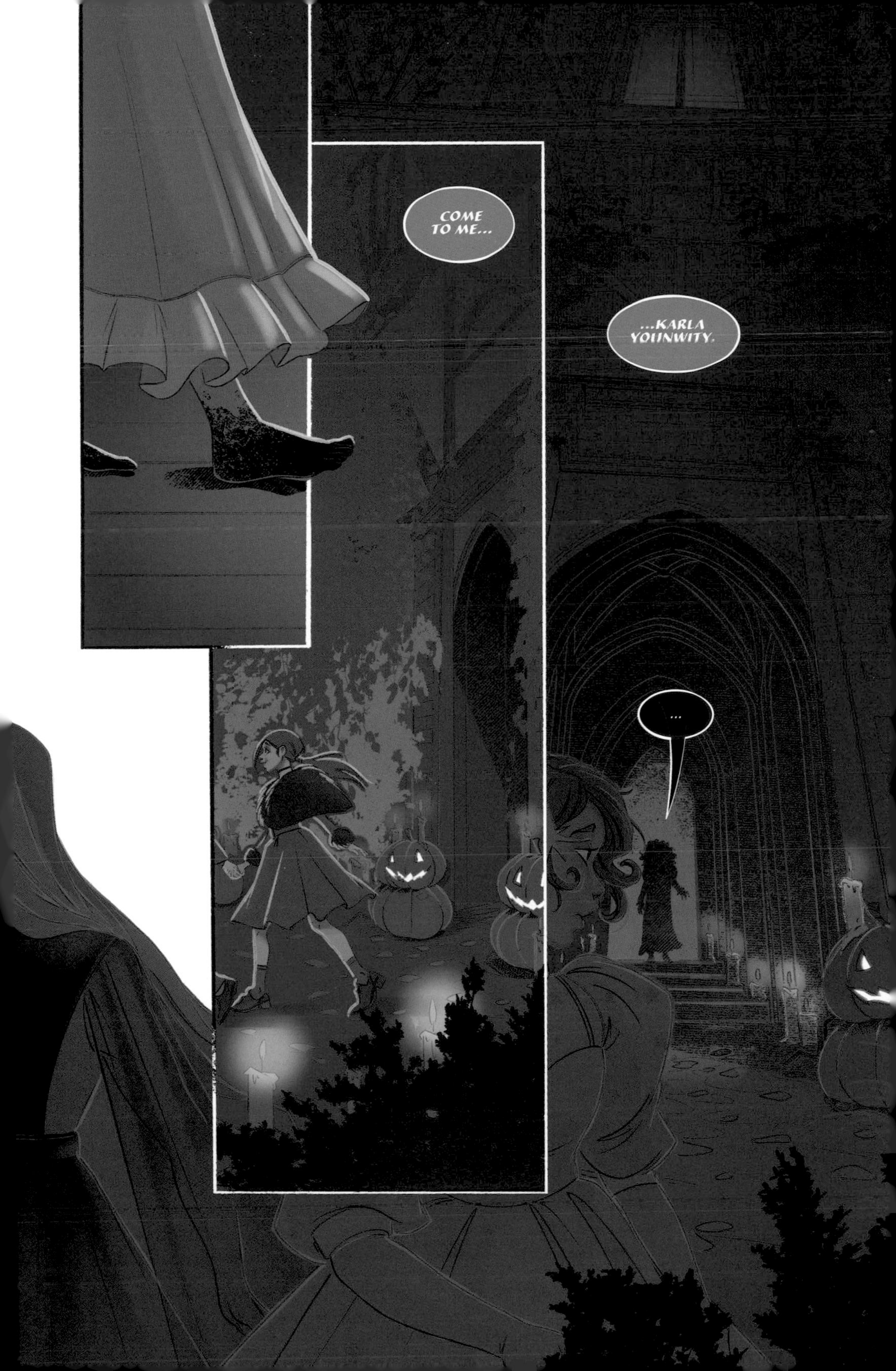
COME TO ME...
...KARLA YOUNWITY.
...

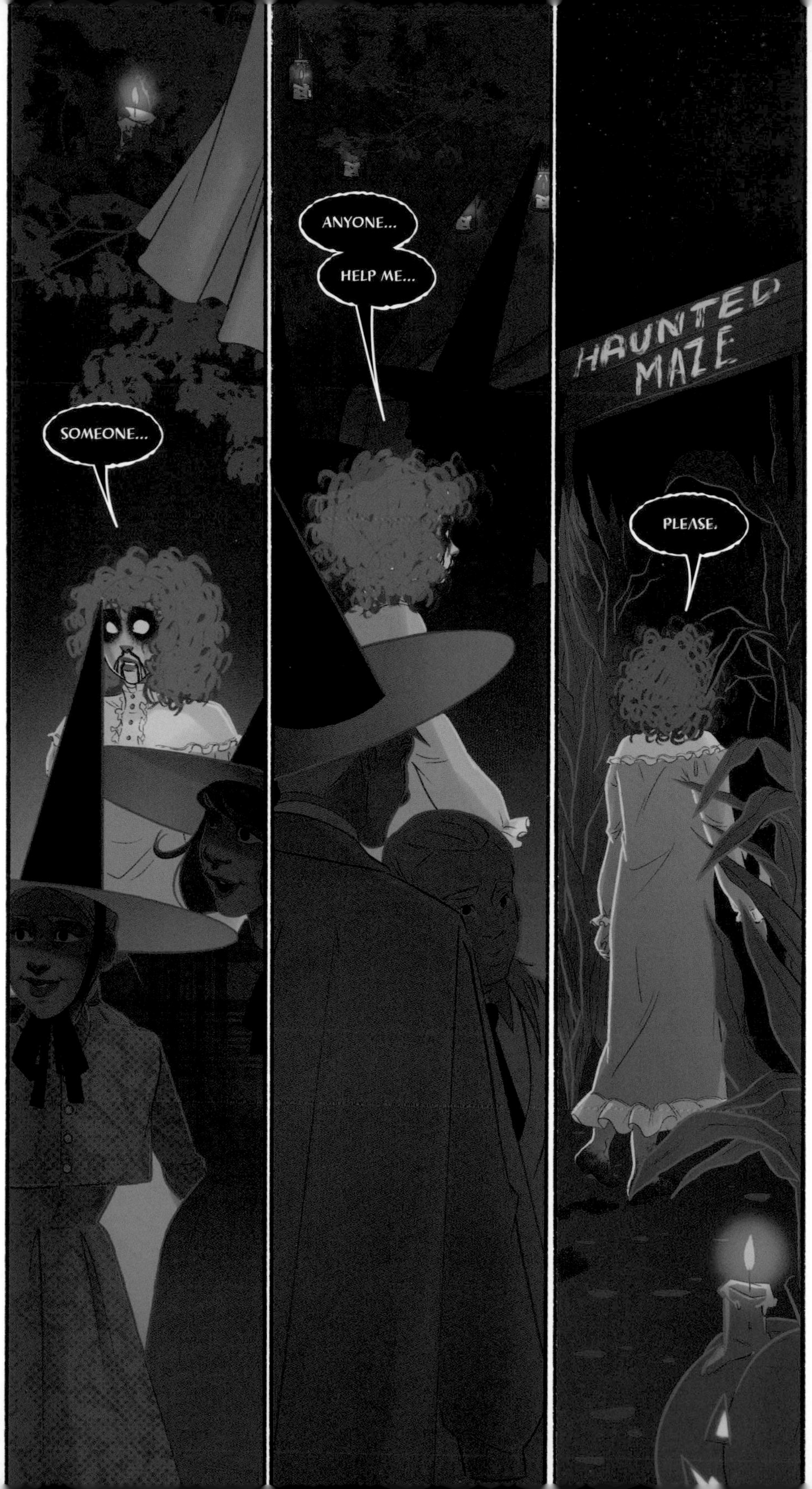
SOMEONE...
ANYONE...
HELP ME...
HAUNTED MAZE
PLEASE.

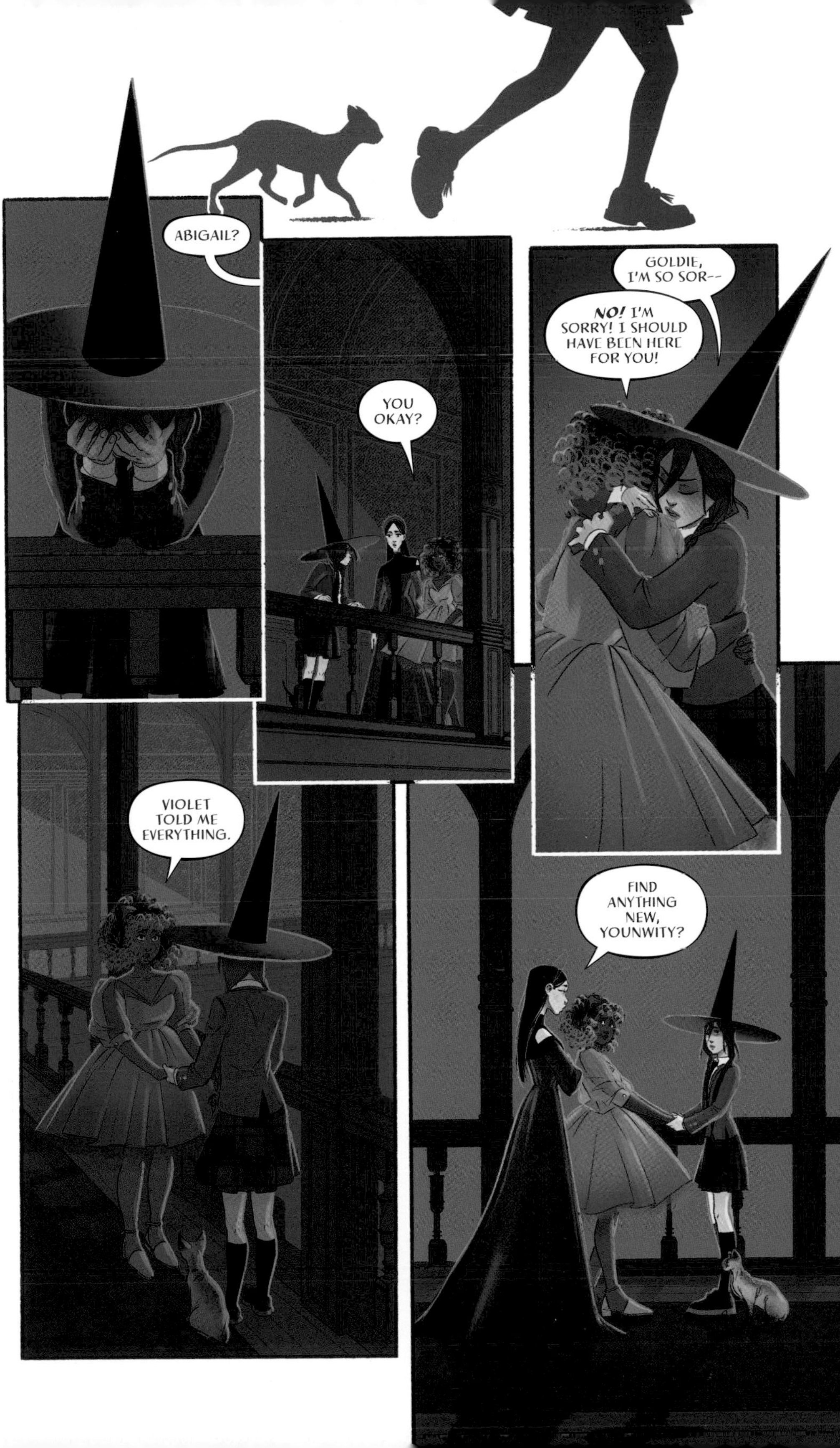
ABIGAIL?
YOU OKAY?
GOLDIE, I'M SO SOR--
NO! I'M SORRY! I SHOULD HAVE BEEN HERE FOR YOU!
VIOLET TOLD ME EVERYTHING.
FIND ANYTHING NEW, YOUNWITY?

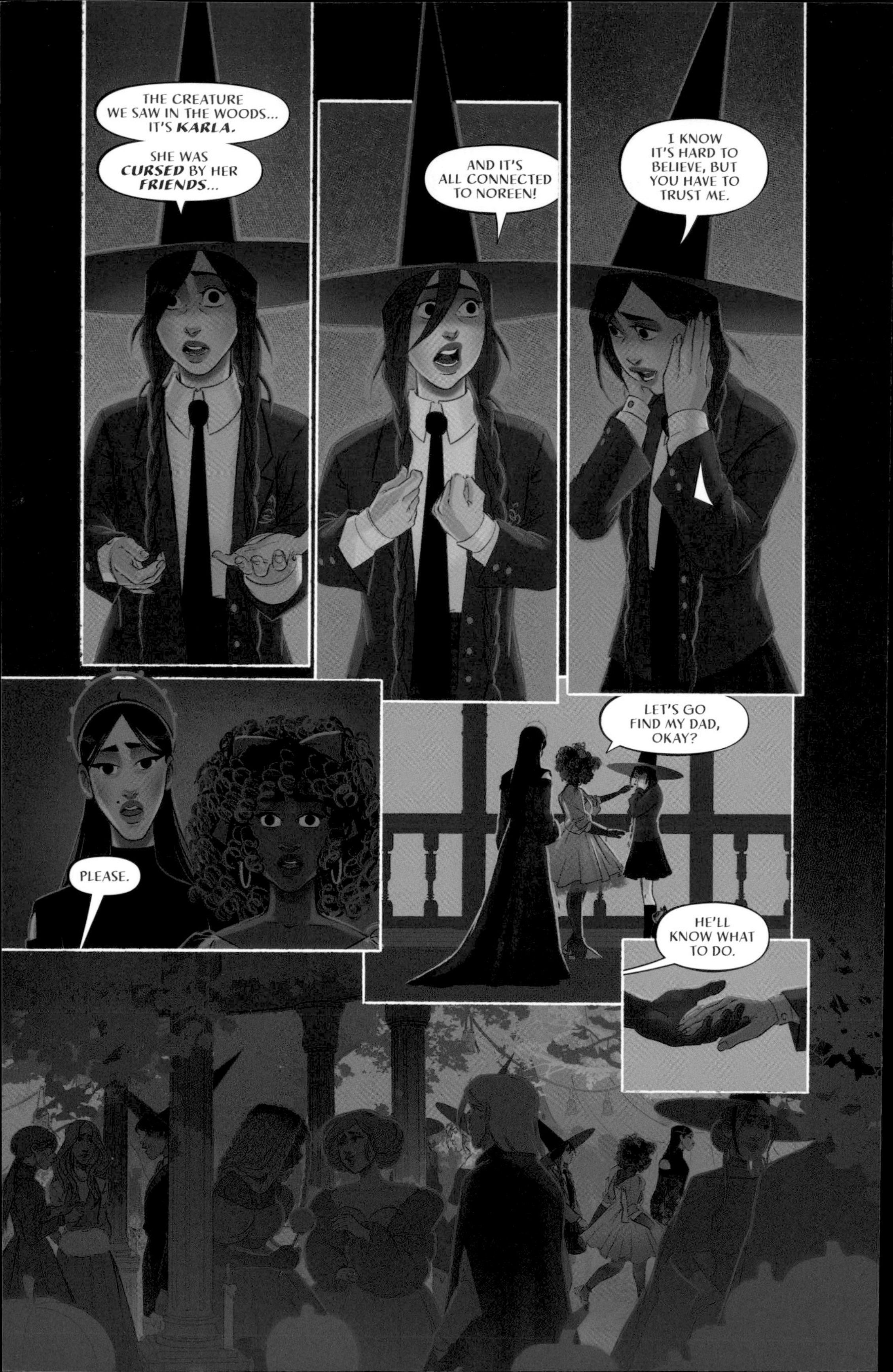
THE CREATURE WE SAW IN THE WOODS... IT'S *KARLA.*
SHE WAS ***CURSED*** BY HER ***FRIENDS***...
AND IT'S ALL CONNECTED TO NOREEN!
I KNOW IT'S HARD TO BELIEVE, BUT YOU HAVE TO TRUST ME.
PLEASE.
LET'S GO FIND MY DAD, OKAY?
HE'LL KNOW WHAT TO DO.

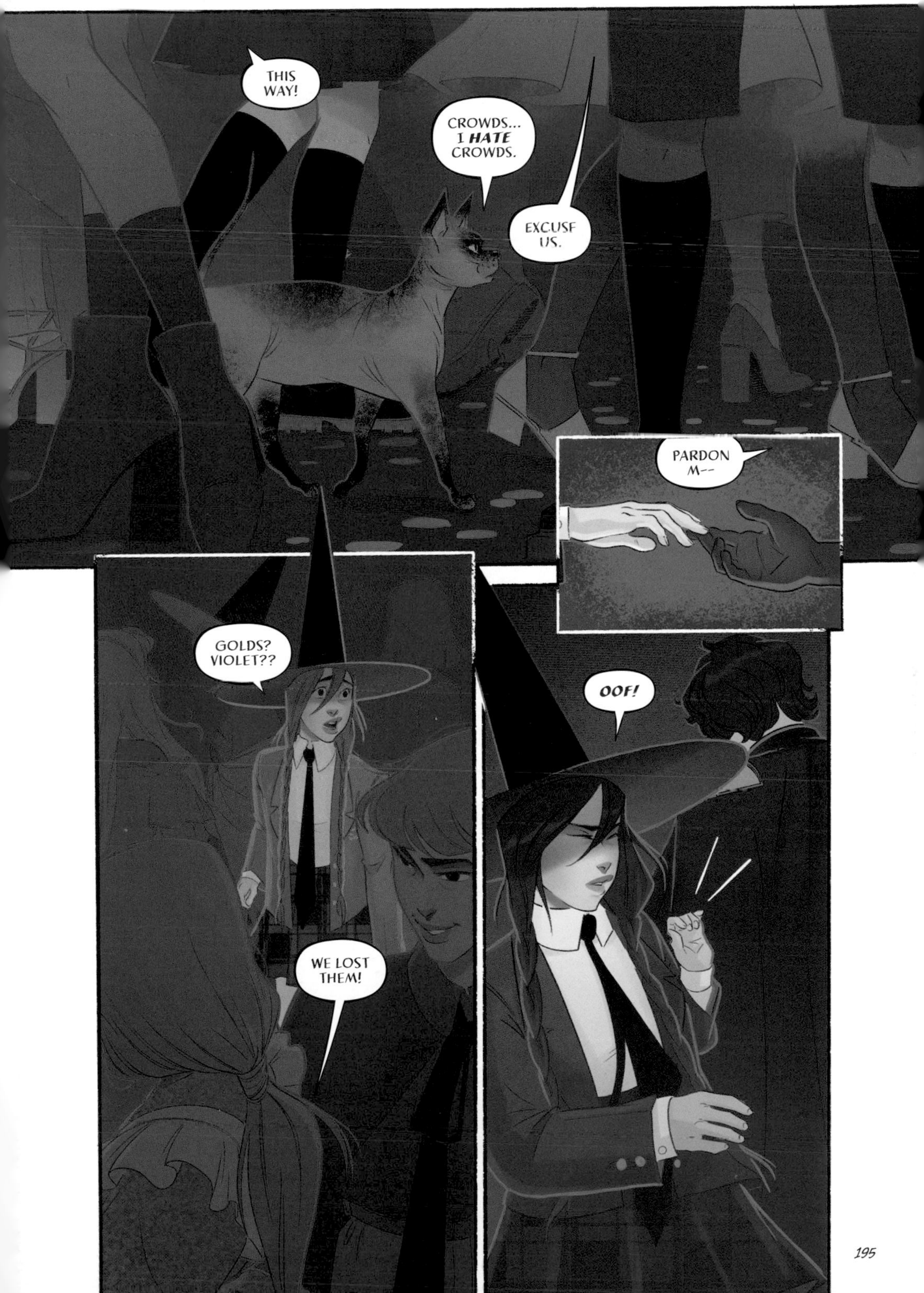
THIS WAY!
CROWDS... I *HATE* CROWDS.
EXCUSE US.
PARDON M--
GOLDS? VIOLET??
WE LOST THEM!
OOF!

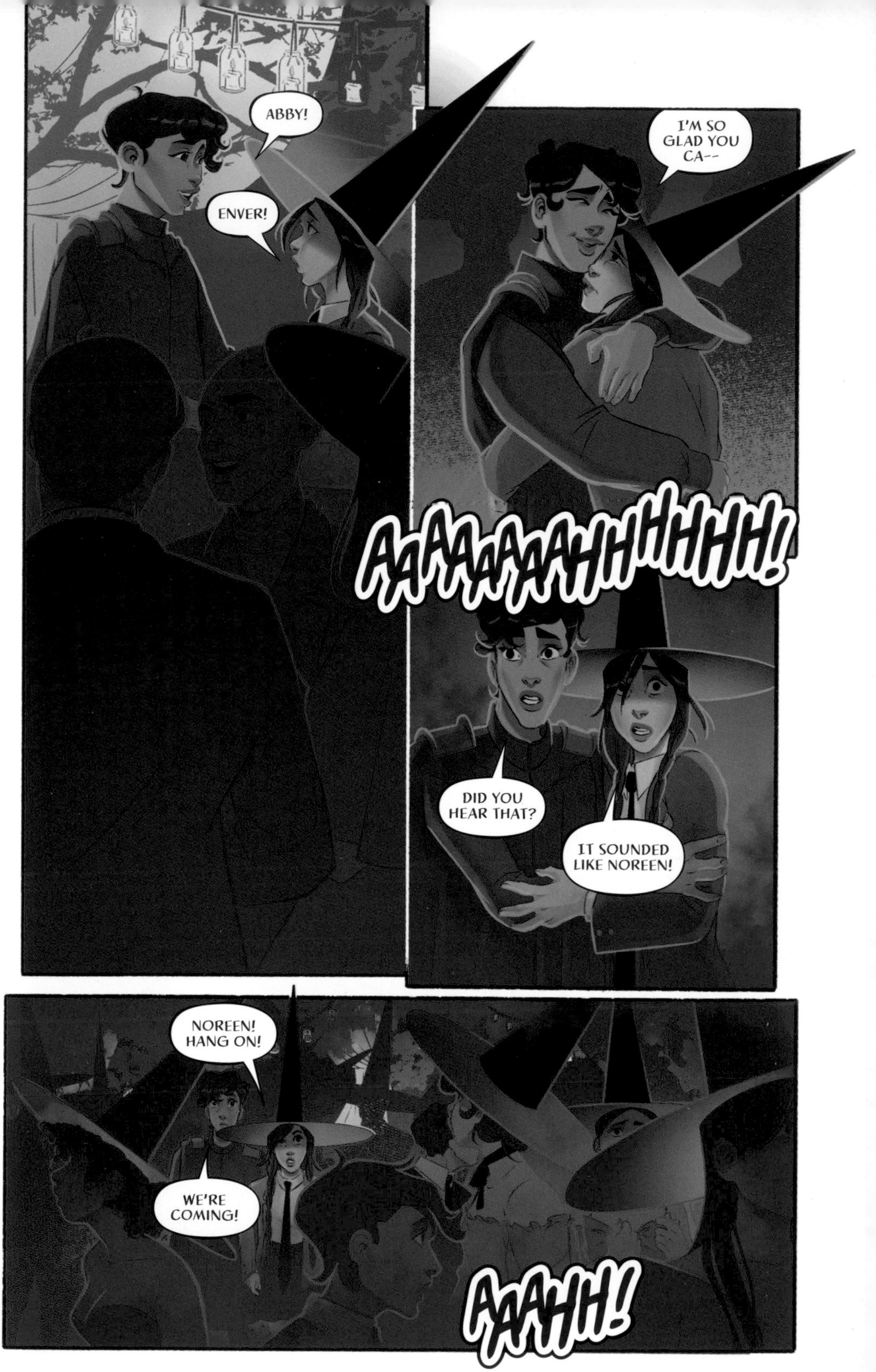
ABBY!
ENVER!
I'M SO GLAD YOU CA--
AAAAAAAAHHHHHH!
DID YOU HEAR THAT?
IT SOUNDED LIKE NOREEN!
NOREEN! HANG ON!
WE'RE COMING!
AAAHH!

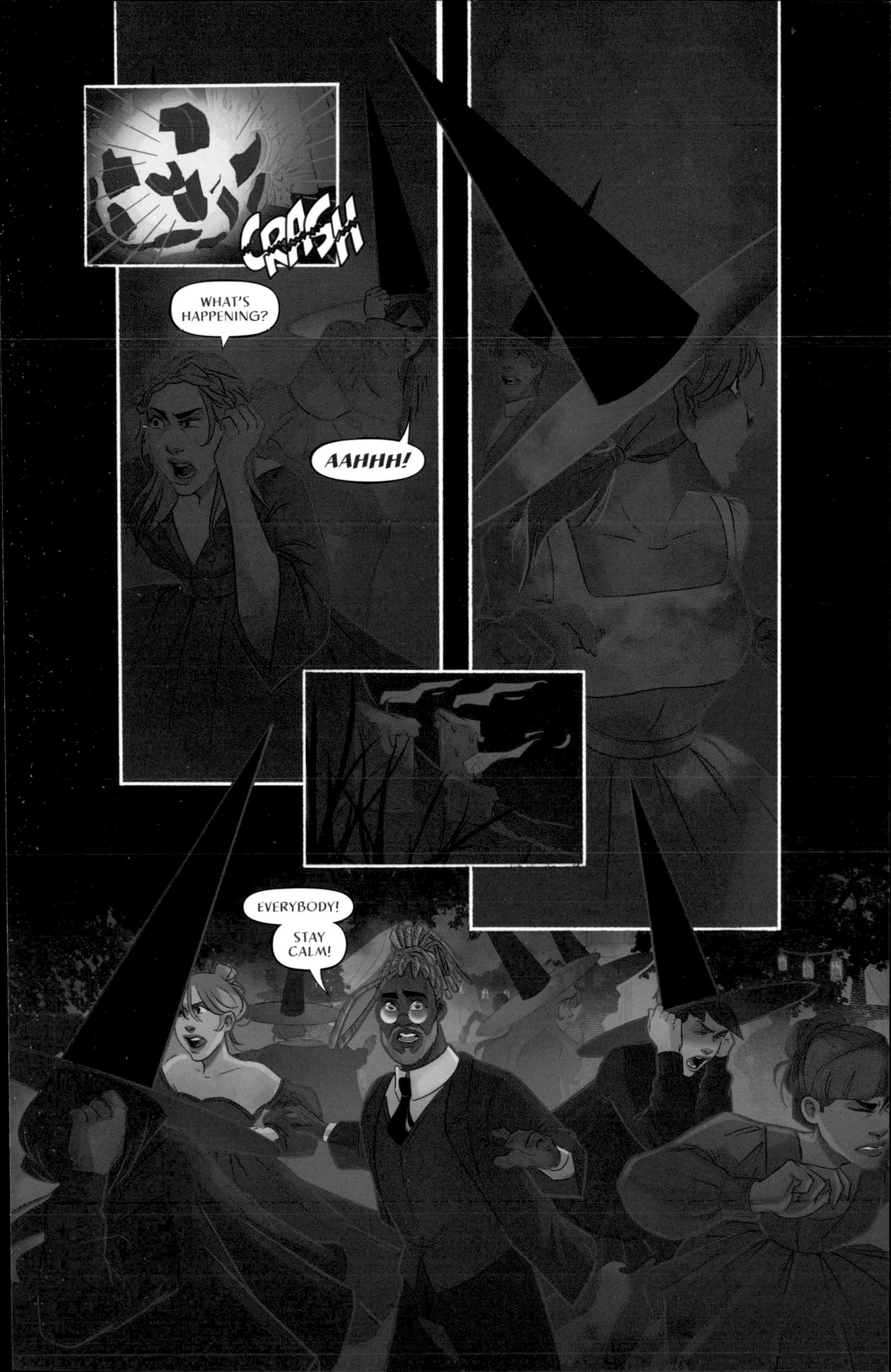
CRASH
WHAT'S HAPPENING?
AAHHH!
EVERYBODY!
STAY CALM!

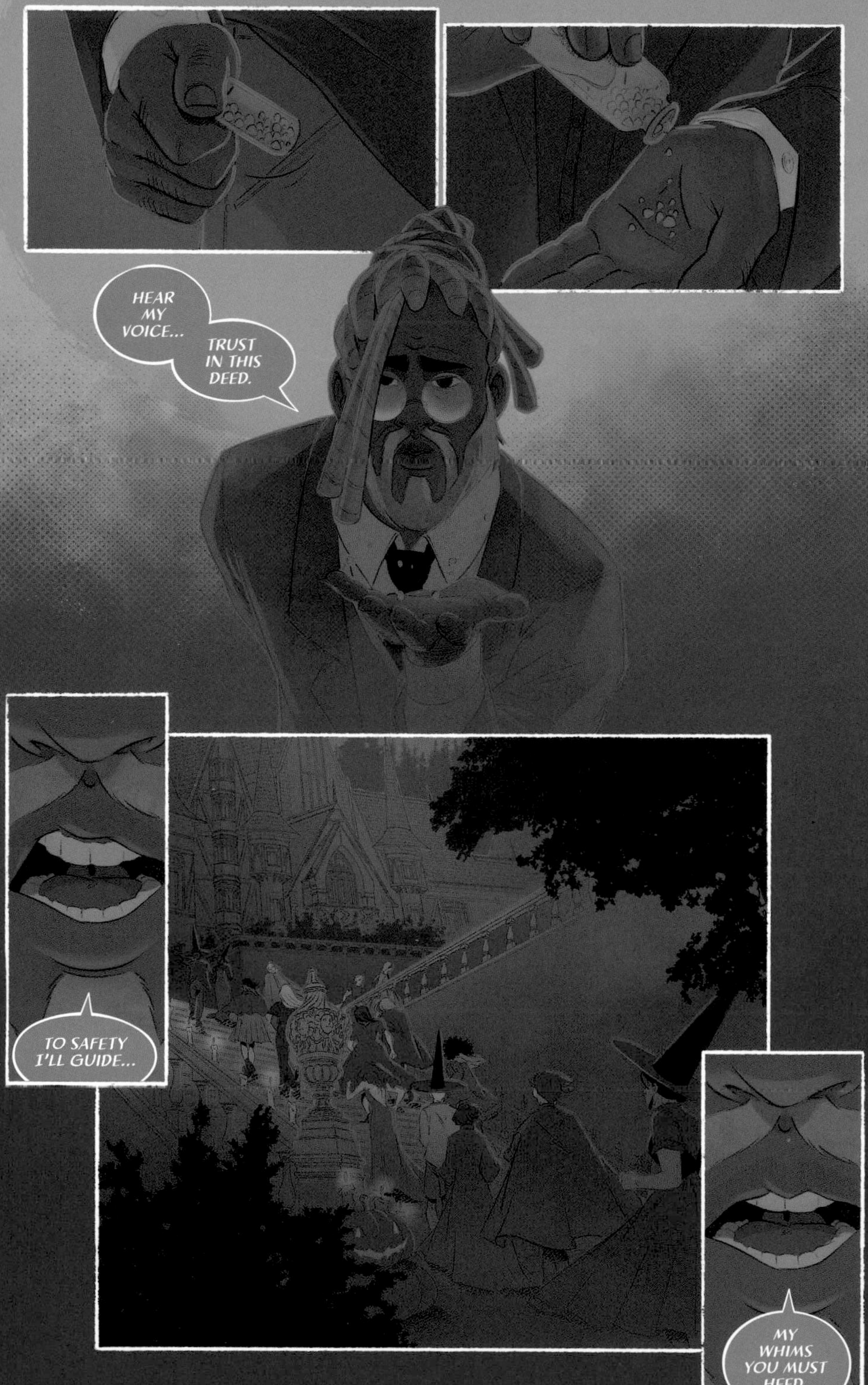
HEAR MY VOICE...
TRUST IN THIS DEED.
TO SAFETY I'LL GUIDE...
MY WHIMS YOU MUST HEED.

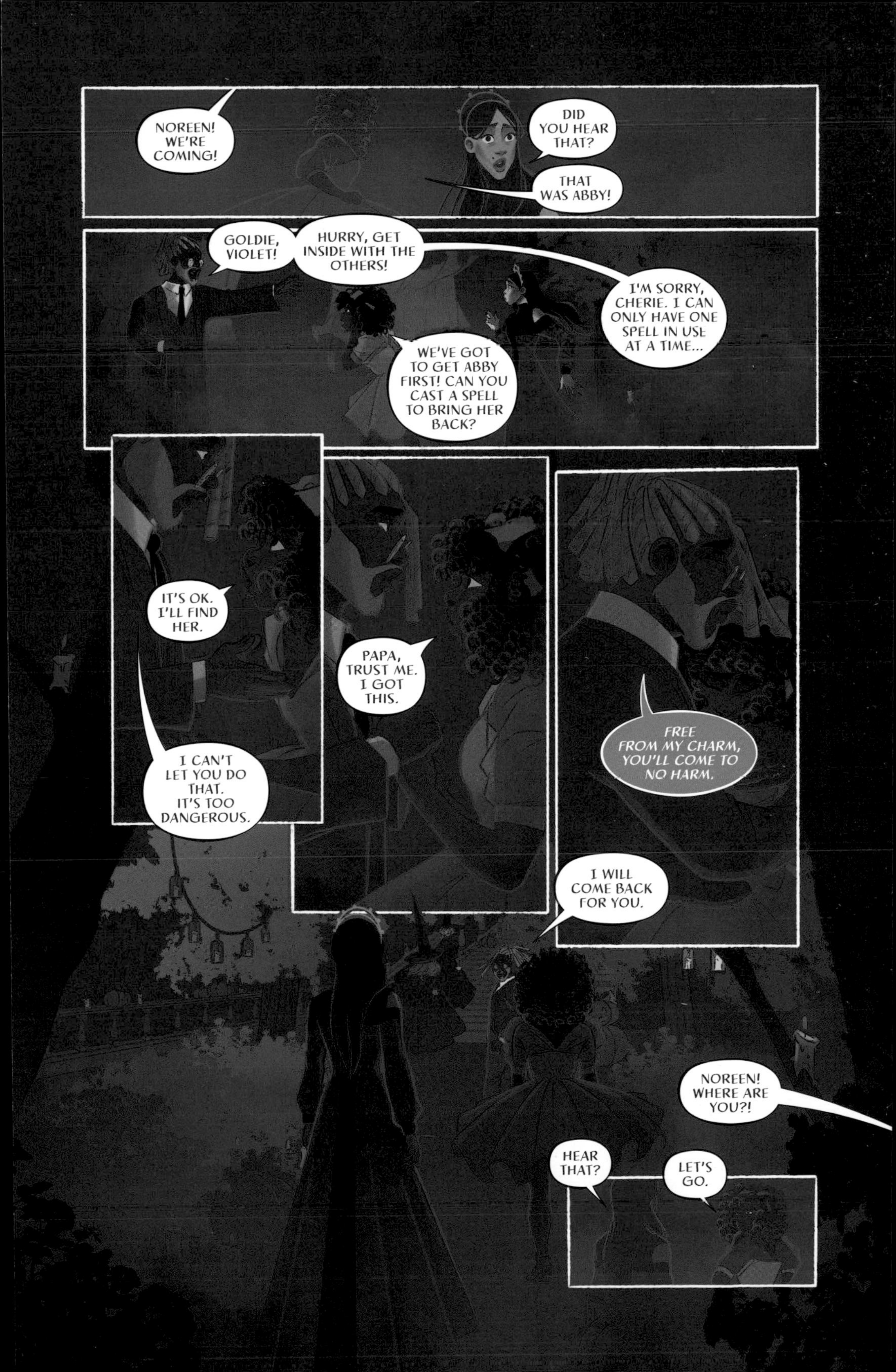

NOREEN! WE'RE COMING!
DID YOU HEAR THAT?
THAT WAS ABBY!
GOLDIE, VIOLET!
HURRY, GET INSIDE WITH THE OTHERS!
I'M SORRY, CHERIE. I CAN ONLY HAVE ONE SPELL IN USE AT A TIME...
WE'VE GOT TO GET ABBY FIRST! CAN YOU CAST A SPELL TO BRING HER BACK?
IT'S OK. I'LL FIND HER.
I CAN'T LET YOU DO THAT. IT'S TOO DANGEROUS.
PAPA, TRUST ME. I GOT THIS.
FREE FROM MY CHARM, YOU'LL COME TO NO HARM.
I WILL COME BACK FOR YOU.
NOREEN! WHERE ARE YOU?!
HEAR THAT?
LET'S GO.

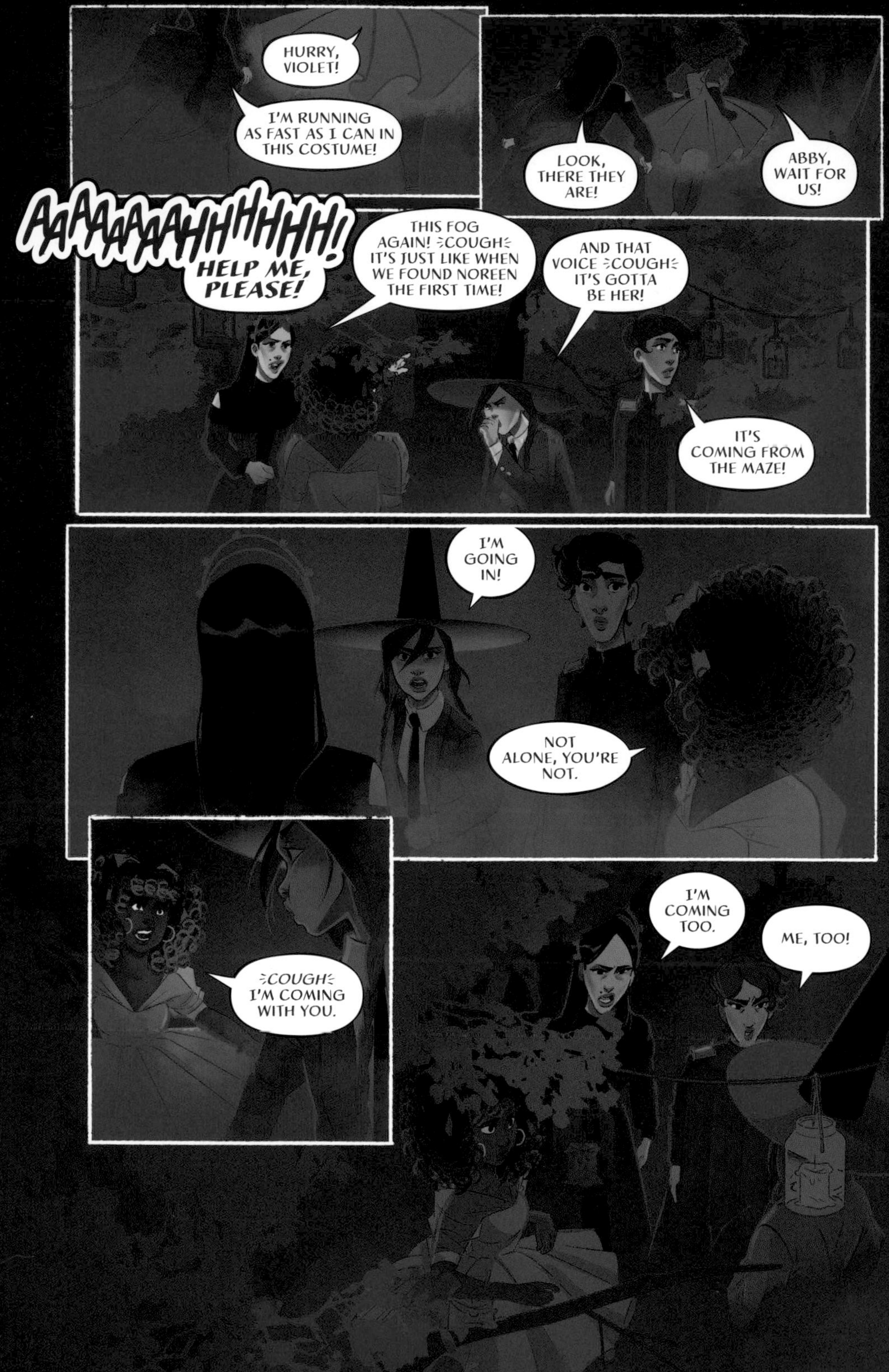
HURRY, VIOLET!
I'M RUNNING AS FAST AS I CAN IN THIS COSTUME!
LOOK, THERE THEY ARE!
ABBY, WAIT FOR US!
AAAAAAAHHHHHH! HELP ME, PLEASE!
THIS FOG AGAIN! COUGH IT'S JUST LIKE WHEN WE FOUND NOREEN THE FIRST TIME!
AND THAT VOICE COUGH IT'S GOTTA BE HER!
IT'S COMING FROM THE MAZE!
I'M GOING IN!
NOT ALONE, YOU'RE NOT.
COUGH I'M COMING WITH YOU.
I'M COMING TOO.
ME, TOO!

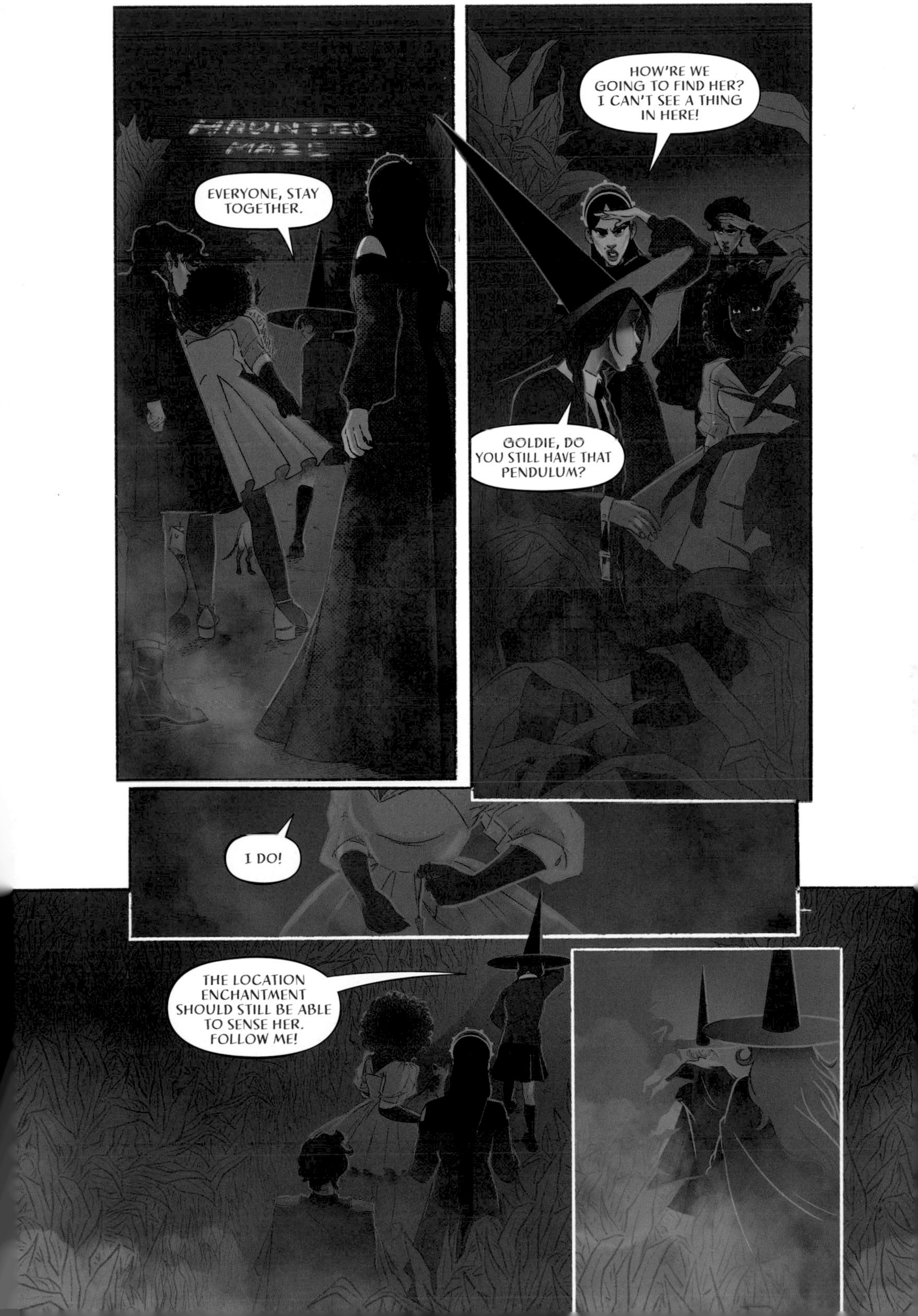
HAUNTED MAZE
EVERYONE, STAY TOGETHER.
HOW'RE WE GOING TO FIND HER? I CAN'T SEE A THING IN HERE!
GOLDIE, DO YOU STILL HAVE THAT PENDULUM?
I DO!
THE LOCATION ENCHANTMENT SHOULD STILL BE ABLE TO SENSE HER. FOLLOW ME!

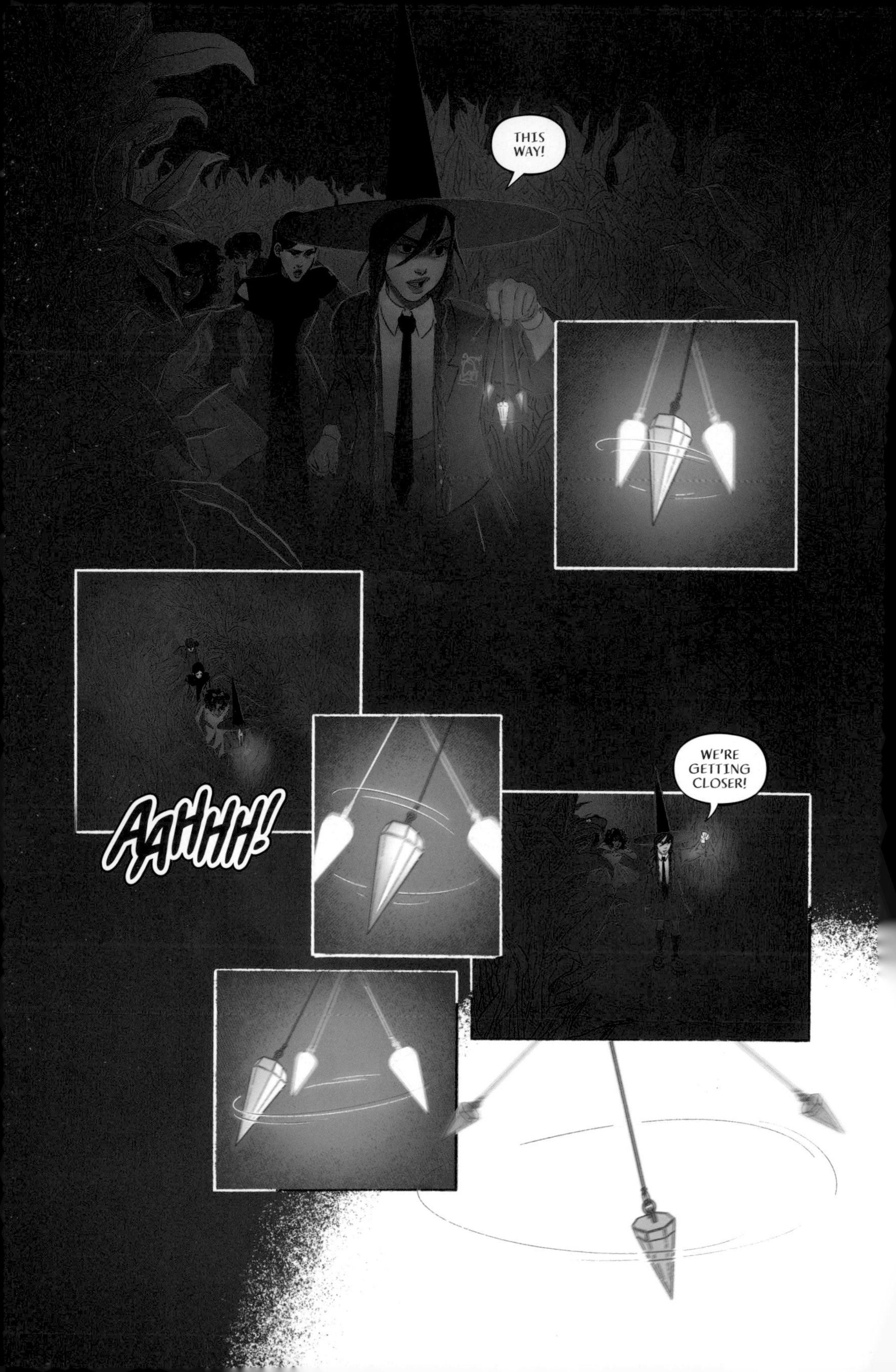
THIS WAY!
AAHHH!
WE'RE GETTING CLOSER!

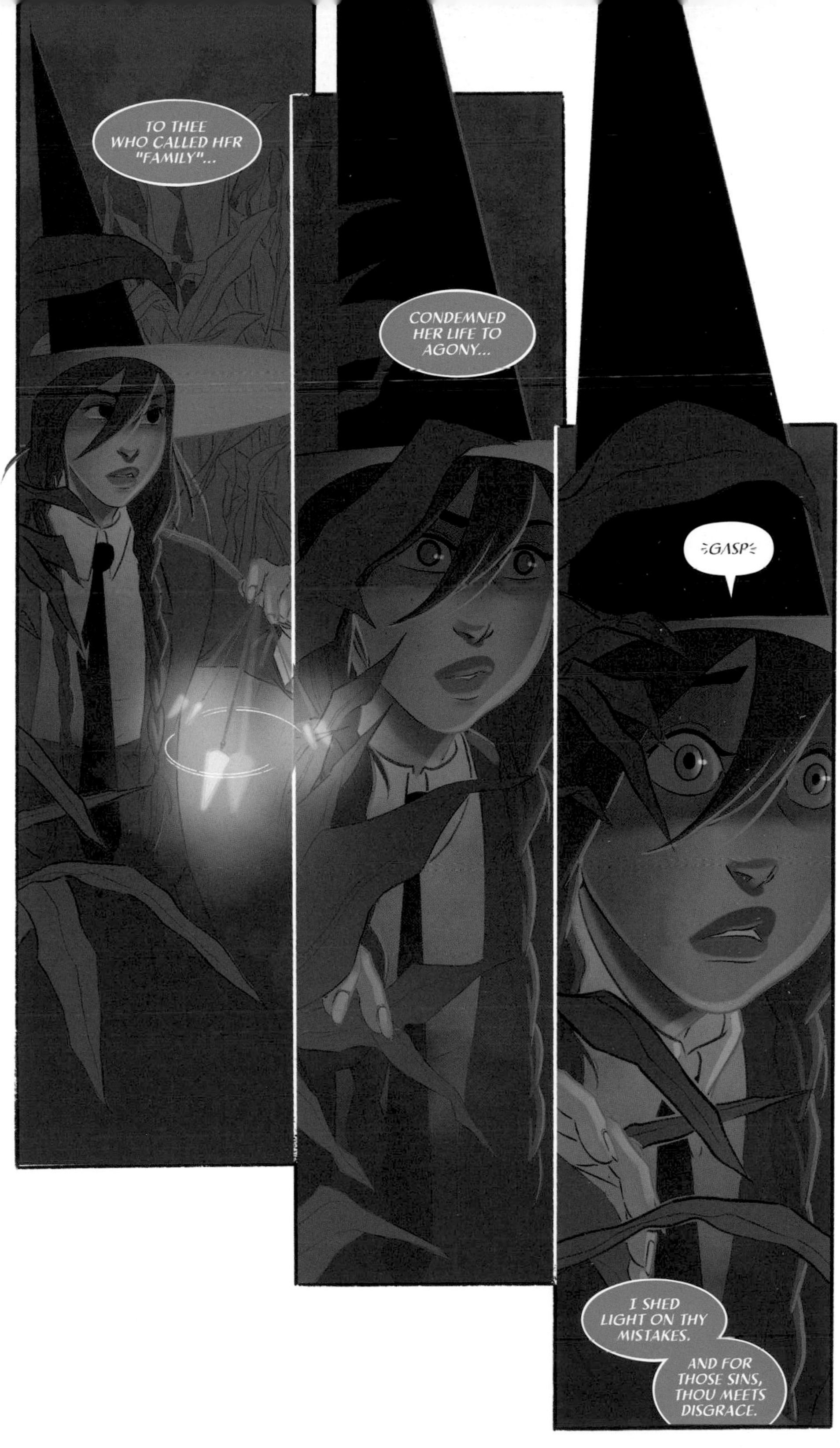
TO THEE WHO CALLED HER "FAMILY"...
CONDEMNED HER LIFE TO AGONY...
GASP
I SHED LIGHT ON THY MISTAKES.
AND FOR THOSE SINS, THOU MEETS DISGRACE.

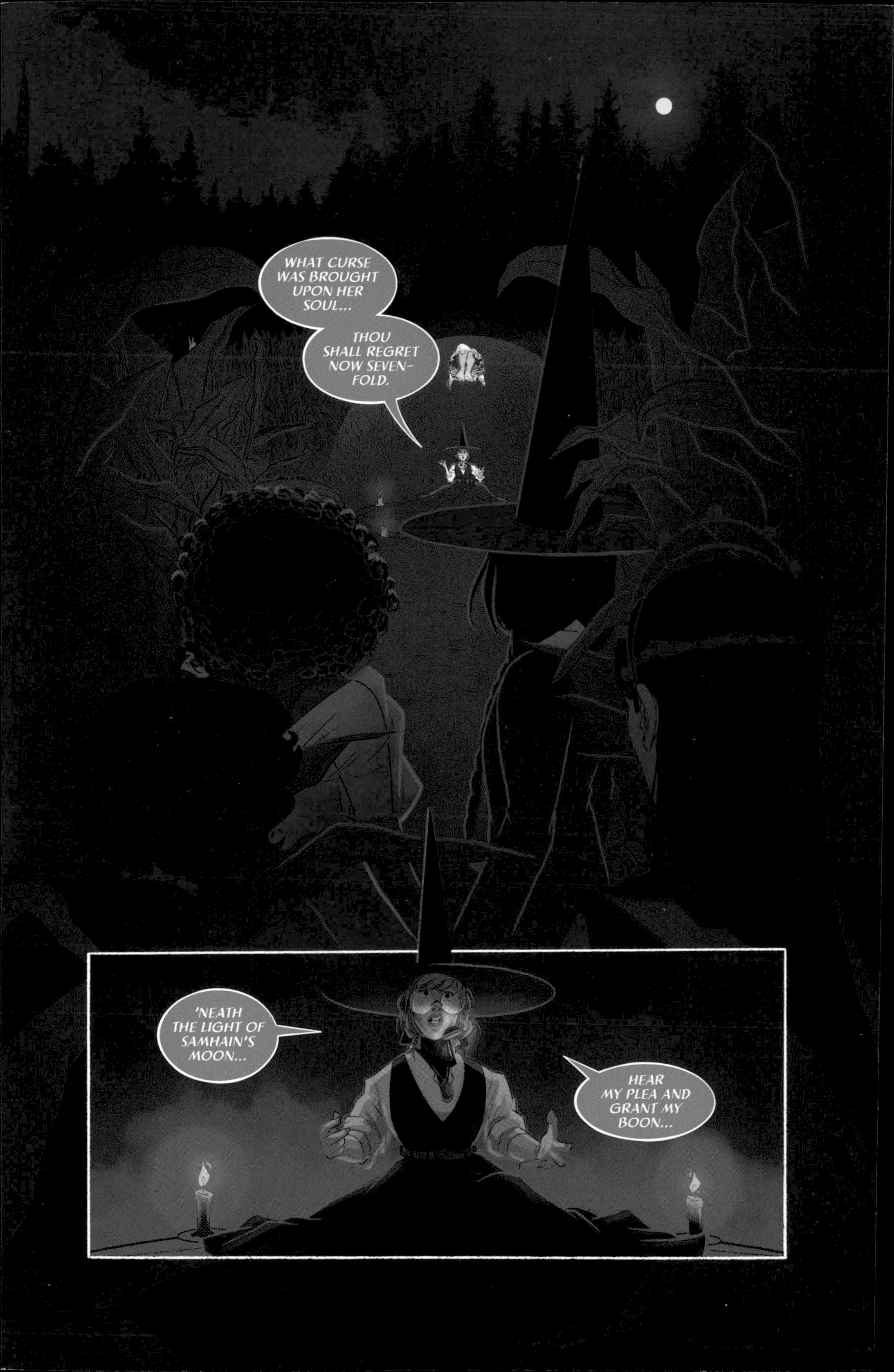
WHAT CURSE WAS BROUGHT UPON HER SOUL...
THOU SHALL REGRET NOW SEVEN-FOLD.
'NEATH THE LIGHT OF SAMHAIN'S MOON...
HEAR MY PLEA AND GRANT MY BOON...

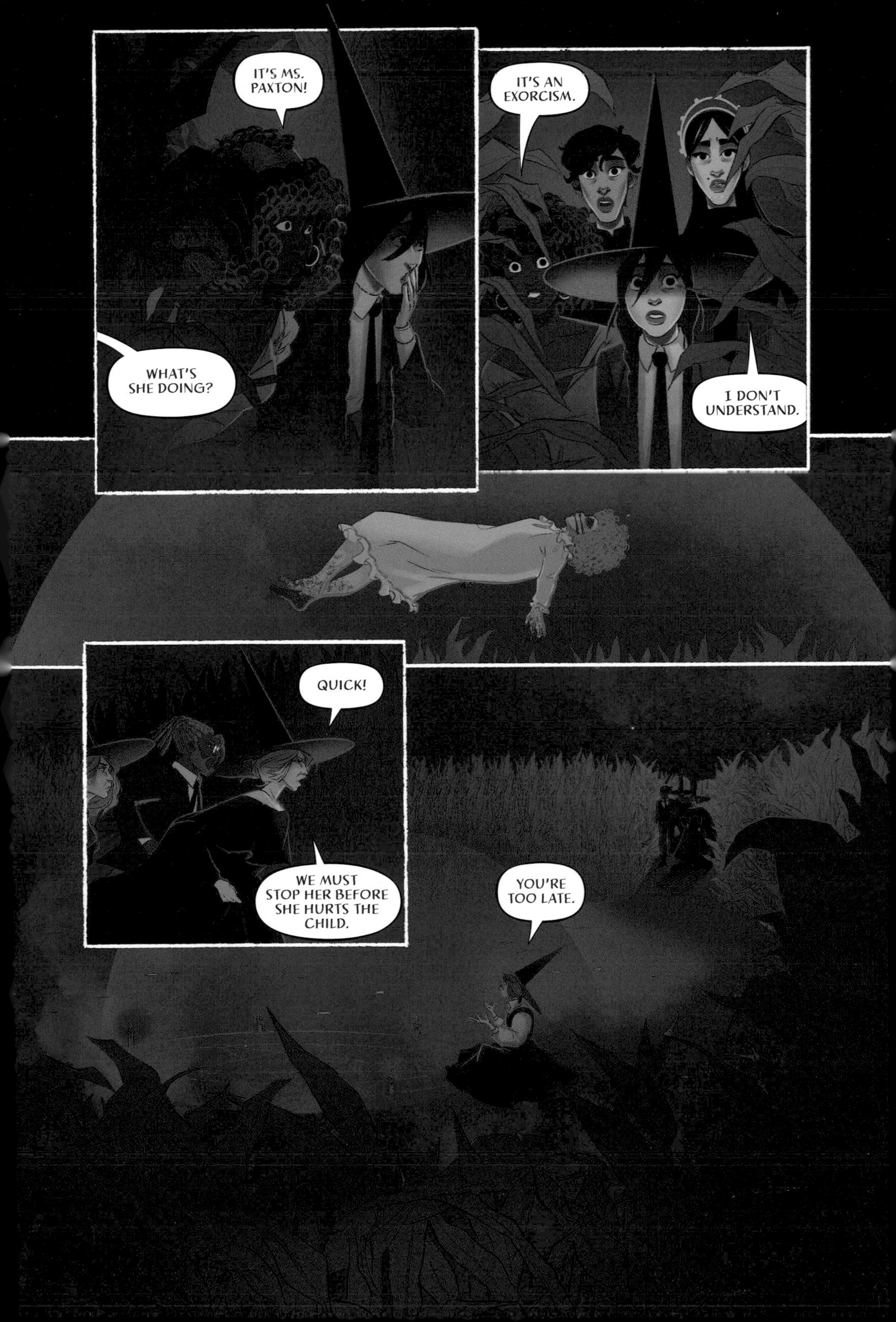
IT'S MS. PAXTON!
WHAT'S SHE DOING?
IT'S AN EXORCISM.
I DON'T UNDERSTAND.
QUICK!
WE MUST STOP HER BEFORE SHE HURTS THE CHILD.
YOU'RE TOO LATE.

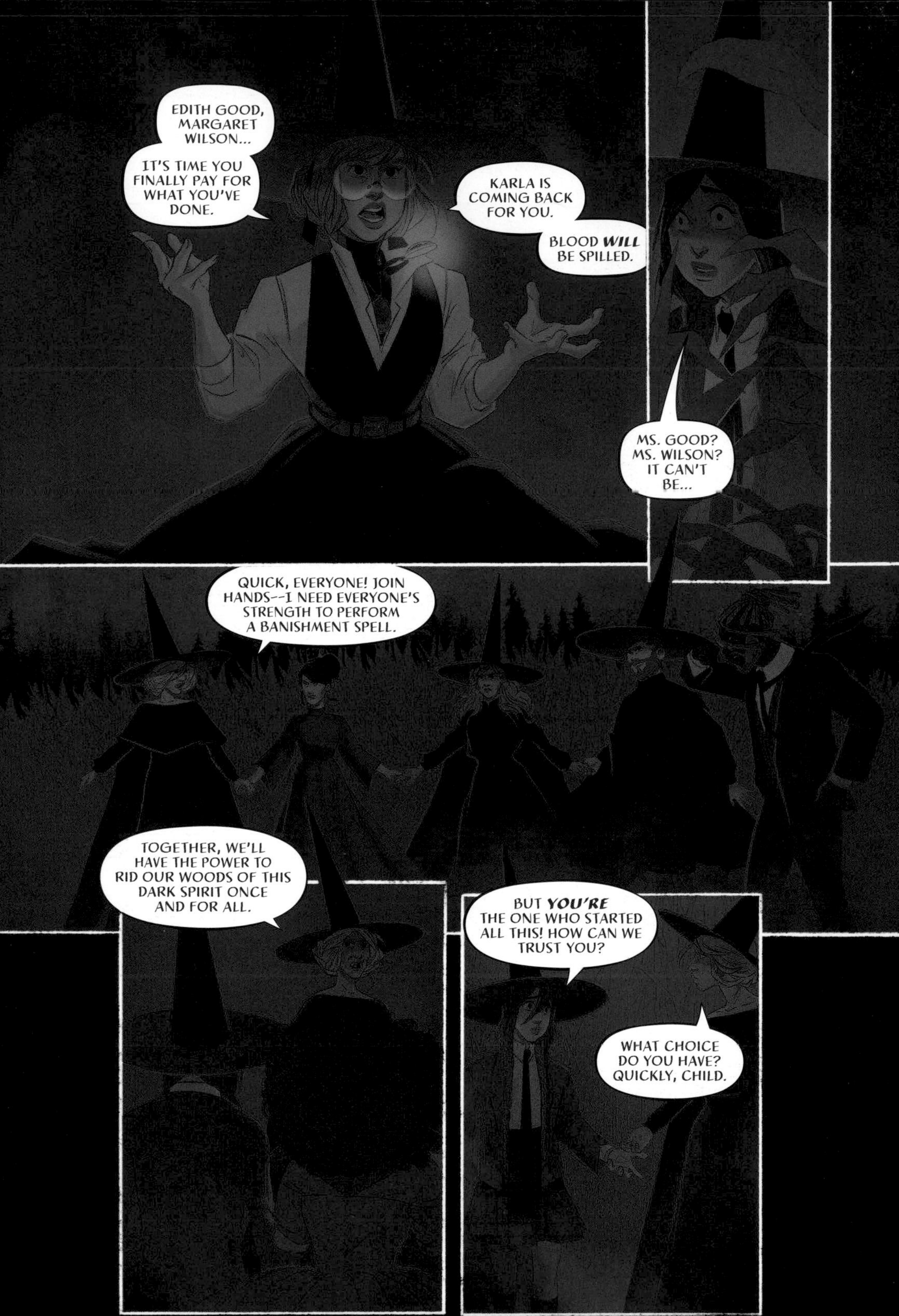
EDITH GOOD, MARGARET WILSON...
IT'S TIME YOU FINALLY PAY FOR WHAT YOU'VE DONE.
KARLA IS COMING BACK FOR YOU.
BLOOD *WILL* BE SPILLED.
MS. GOOD? MS. WILSON? IT CAN'T BE...
QUICK, EVERYONE! JOIN HANDS--I NEED EVERYONE'S STRENGTH TO PERFORM A BANISHMENT SPELL.
TOGETHER, WE'LL HAVE THE POWER TO RID OUR WOODS OF THIS DARK SPIRIT ONCE AND FOR ALL.
BUT *YOU'RE* THE ONE WHO STARTED ALL THIS! HOW CAN WE TRUST YOU?
WHAT CHOICE DO YOU HAVE? QUICKLY, CHILD.

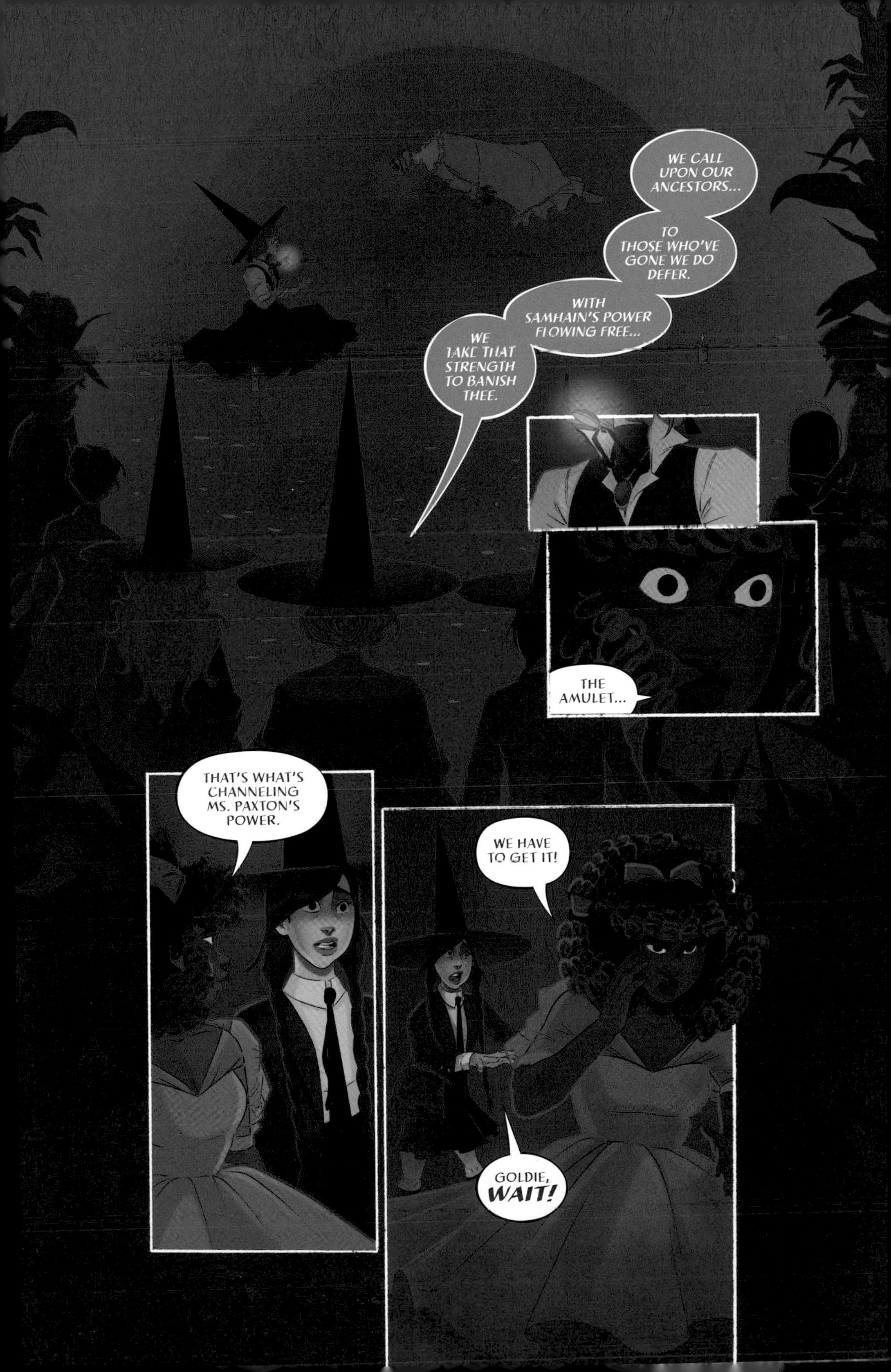
WE CALL UPON OUR ANCESTORS...
TO THOSE WHO'VE GONE WE DO DEFER.
WITH SAMHAIN'S POWER FLOWING FREE...
WE TAKE THAT STRENGTH TO BANISH THEE.
THE AMULET...
THAT'S WHAT'S CHANNELING MS. PAXTON'S POWER.
WE HAVE TO GET IT!
GOLDIE, WAIT!

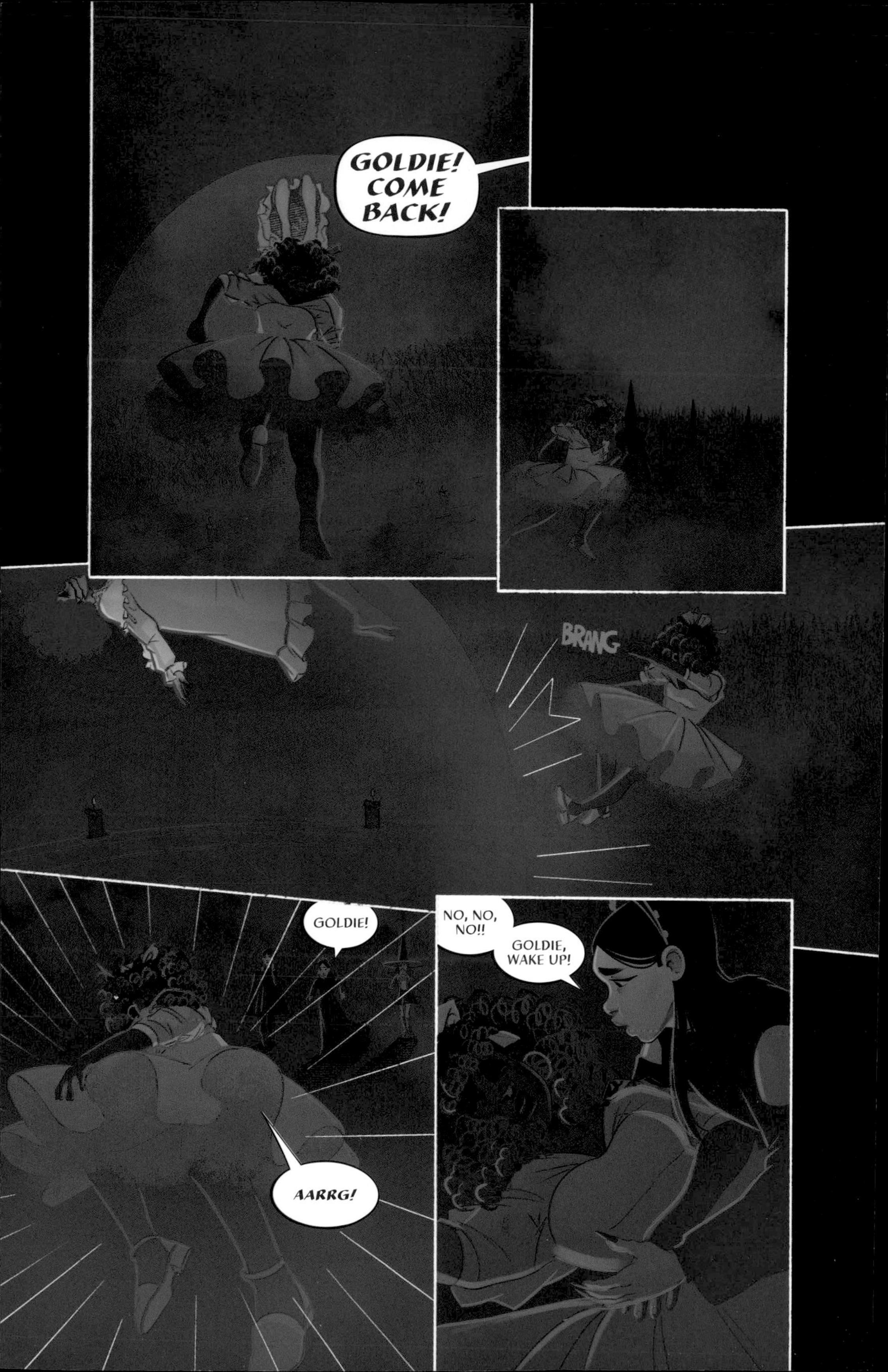
GOLDIE! COME BACK!
BRANG
GOLDIE!
AARRG!
NO, NO, NO!!
GOLDIE, WAKE UP!

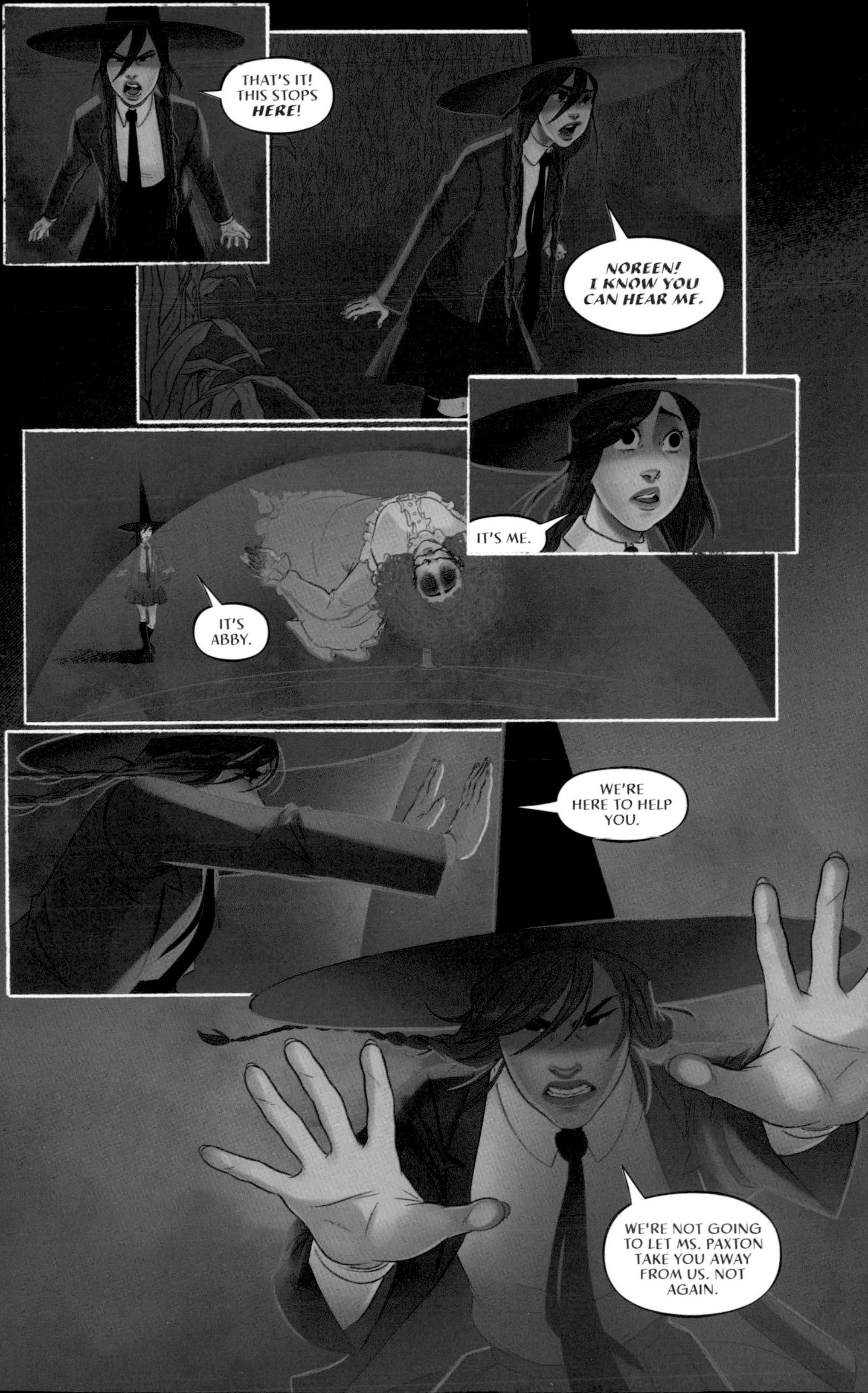
THAT'S IT! THIS STOPS *HERE*!
NOREEN! I KNOW YOU CAN HEAR ME.
IT'S ME.
IT'S ABBY.
WE'RE HERE TO HELP YOU.
WE'RE NOT GOING TO LET MS. PAXTON TAKE YOU AWAY FROM US. NOT AGAIN.

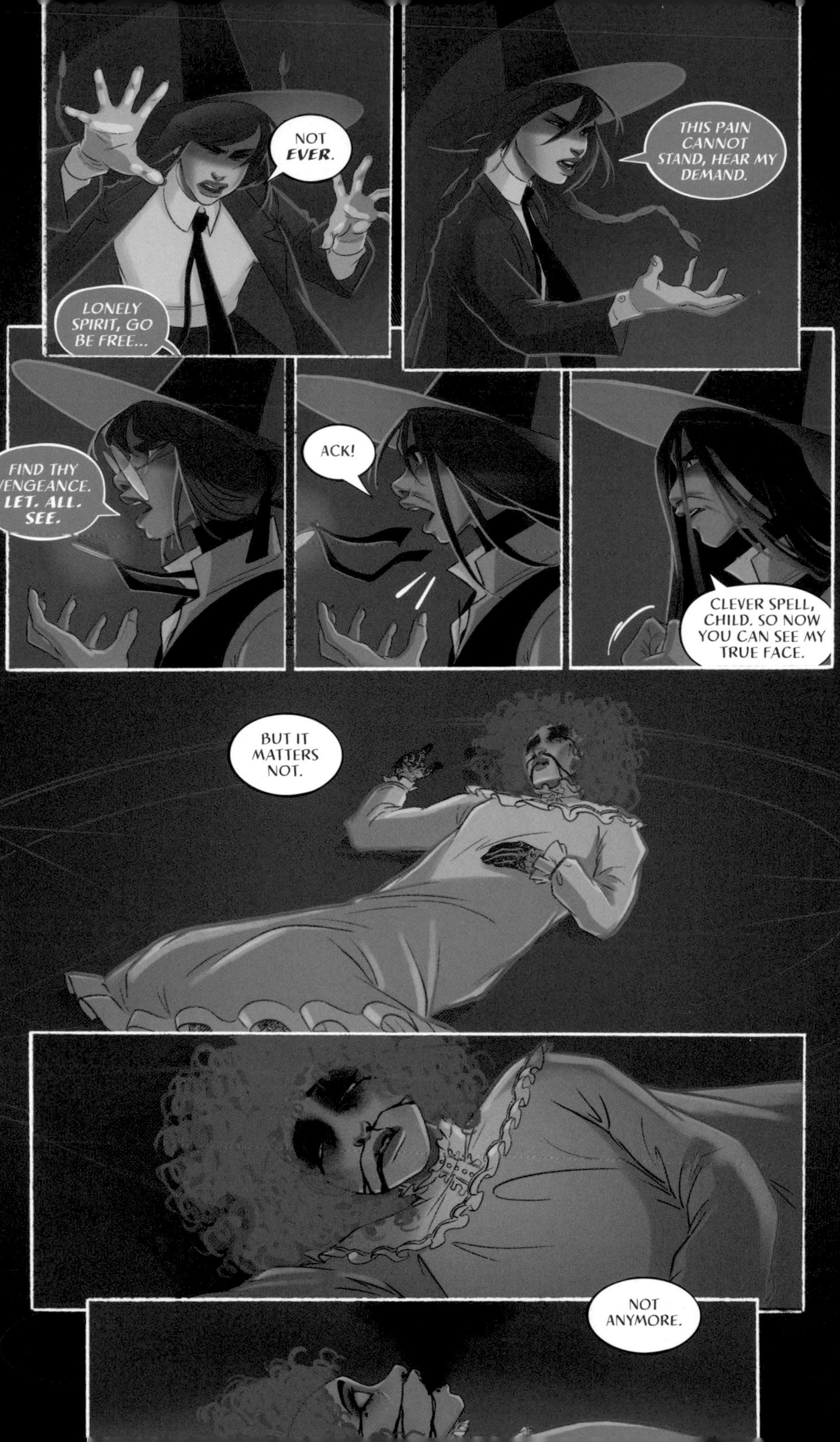
NOT **EVER**.
LONELY SPIRIT, GO BE FREE...
THIS PAIN CANNOT STAND, HEAR MY DEMAND.
FIND THY VENGEANCE. **LET. ALL. SEE.**
ACK!
CLEVER SPELL, CHILD. SO NOW YOU CAN SEE MY TRUE FACE.
BUT IT MATTERS NOT.
NOT ANYMORE.

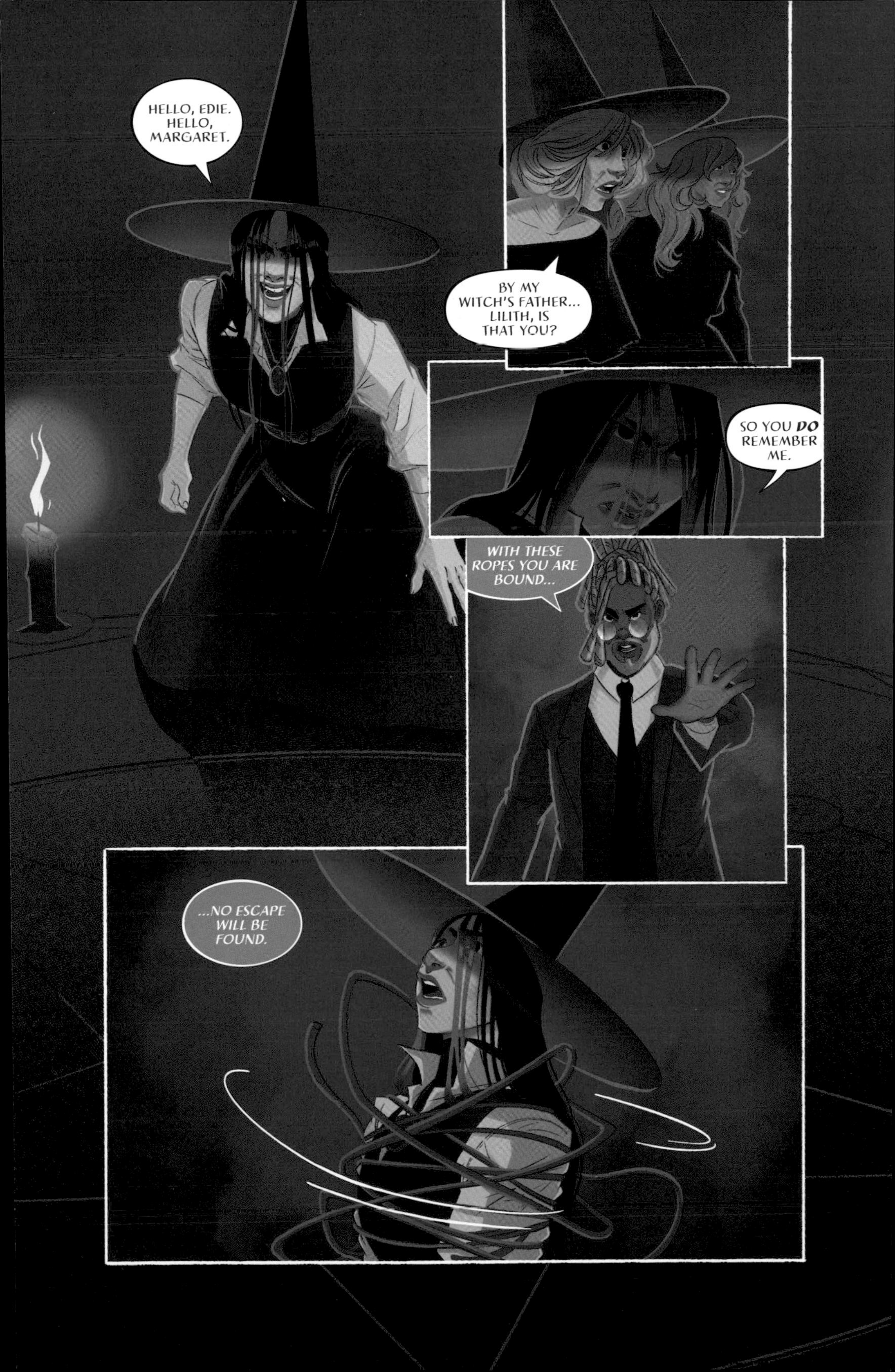
HELLO, EDIE. HELLO, MARGARET.
BY MY WITCH'S FATHER... LILITH, IS THAT YOU?
SO YOU ***DO*** REMEMBER ME.
WITH THESE ROPES YOU ARE BOUND...
...NO ESCAPE WILL BE FOUND.

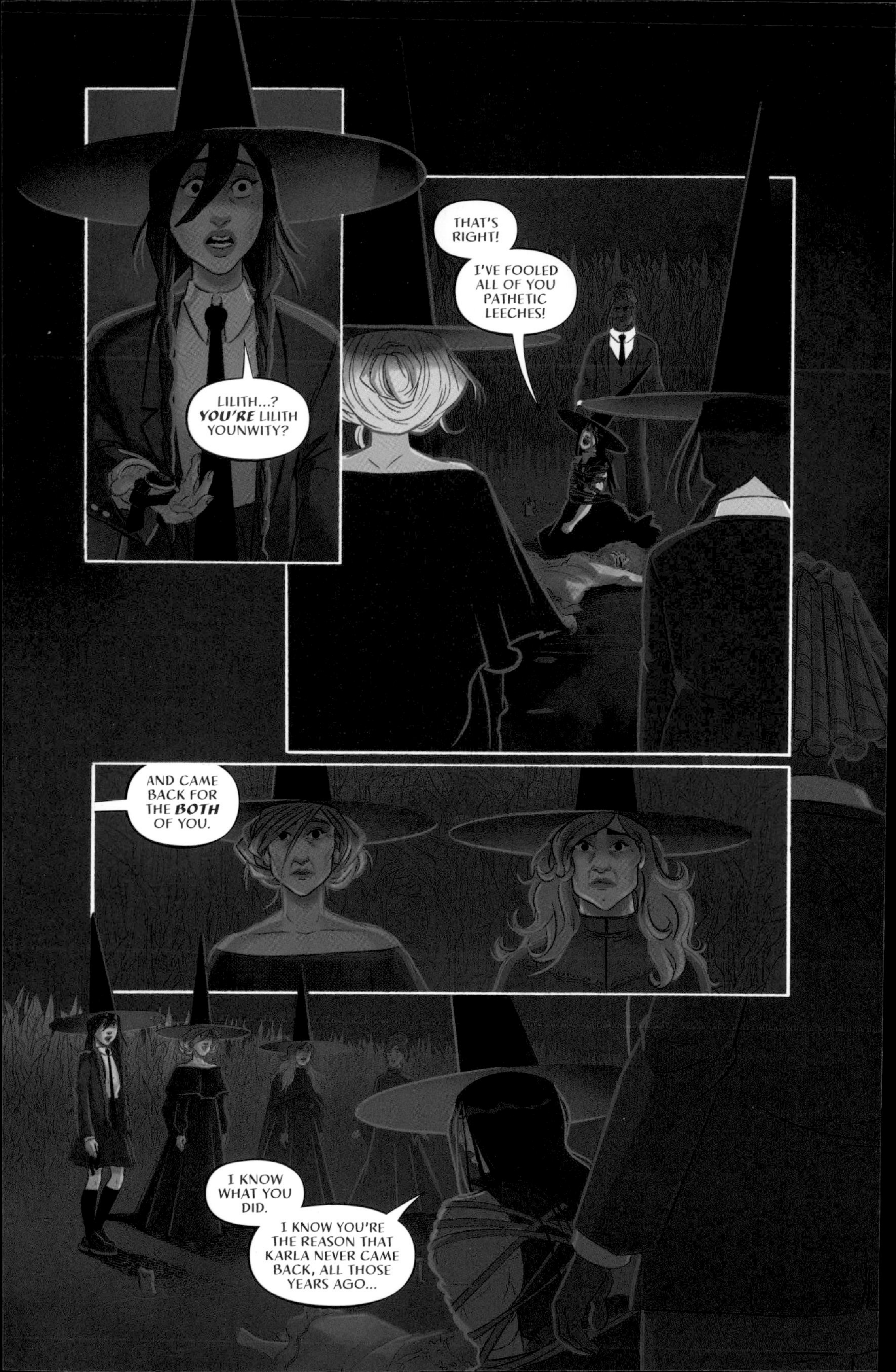
LILITH...? YOU'RE LILITH YOUNWITY?
THAT'S RIGHT!
I'VE FOOLED ALL OF YOU PATHETIC LEECHES!
AND CAME BACK FOR THE BOTH OF YOU.
I KNOW WHAT YOU DID.
I KNOW YOU'RE THE REASON THAT KARLA NEVER CAME BACK, ALL THOSE YEARS AGO...

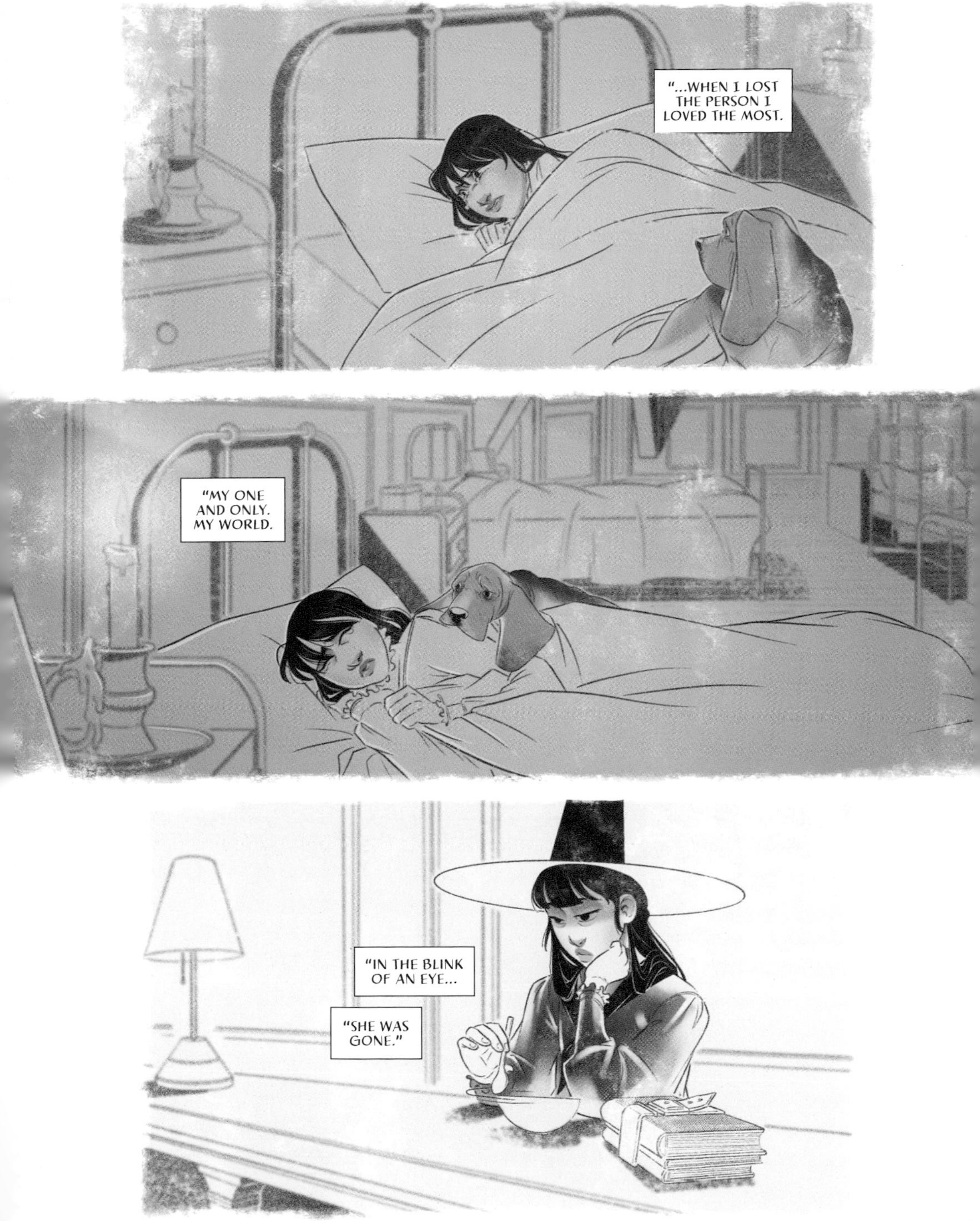
"...WHEN I LOST THE PERSON I LOVED THE MOST.
"MY ONE AND ONLY. MY WORLD.
"IN THE BLINK OF AN EYE...
"SHE WAS GONE."

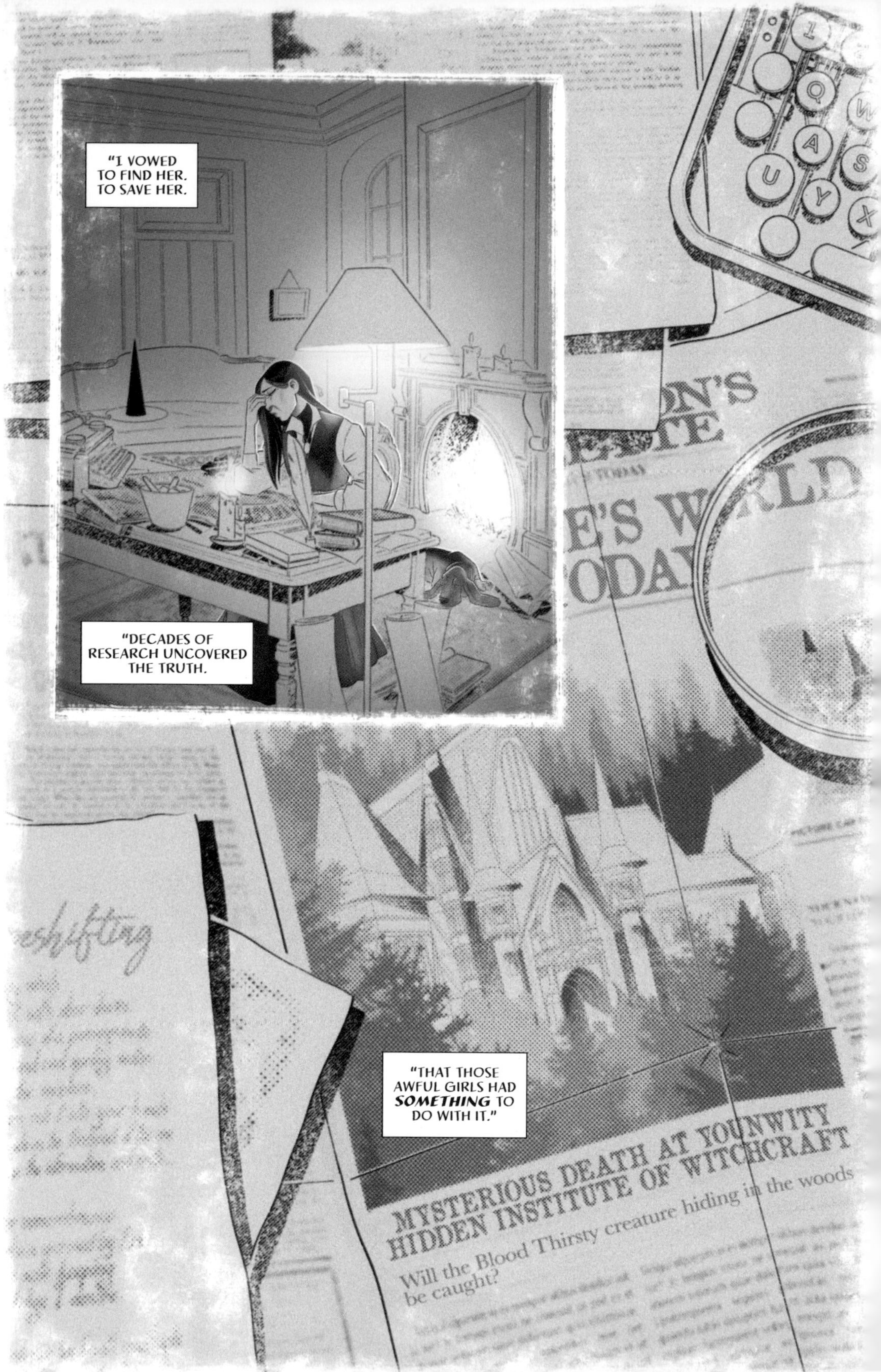

"I VOWED TO FIND HER. TO SAVE HER.
"DECADES OF RESEARCH UNCOVERED THE TRUTH.
"THAT THOSE AWFUL GIRLS HAD *SOMETHING* TO DO WITH IT."
MYSTERIOUS DEATH AT YOUNWITY HIDDEN INSTITUTE OF WITCHCRAFT
Will the Blood Thirsty creature hiding in the woods be caught?

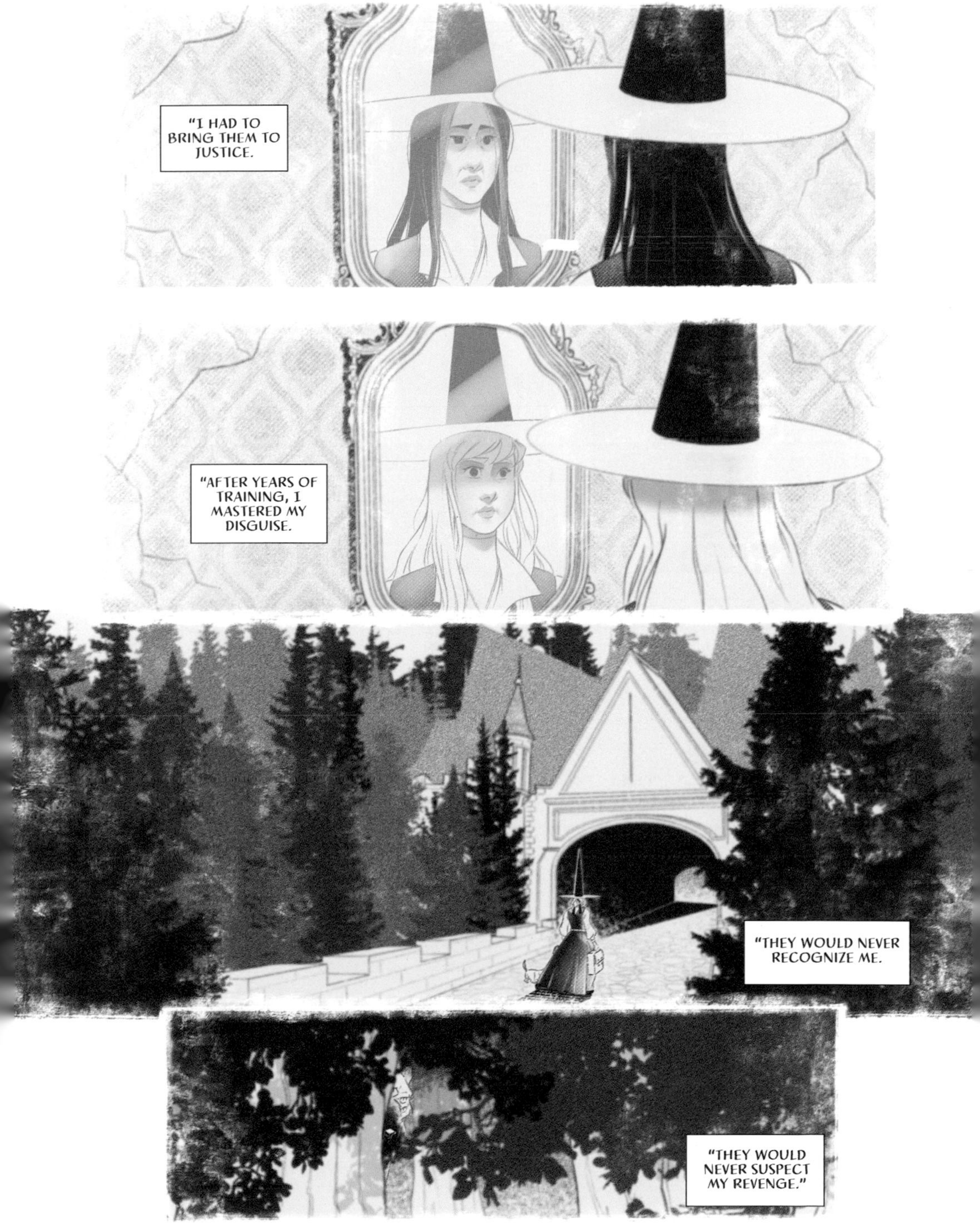
"I HAD TO BRING THEM TO JUSTICE.
"AFTER YEARS OF TRAINING, I MASTERED MY DISGUISE.
"THEY WOULD NEVER RECOGNIZE ME.
"THEY WOULD NEVER SUSPECT MY REVENGE."

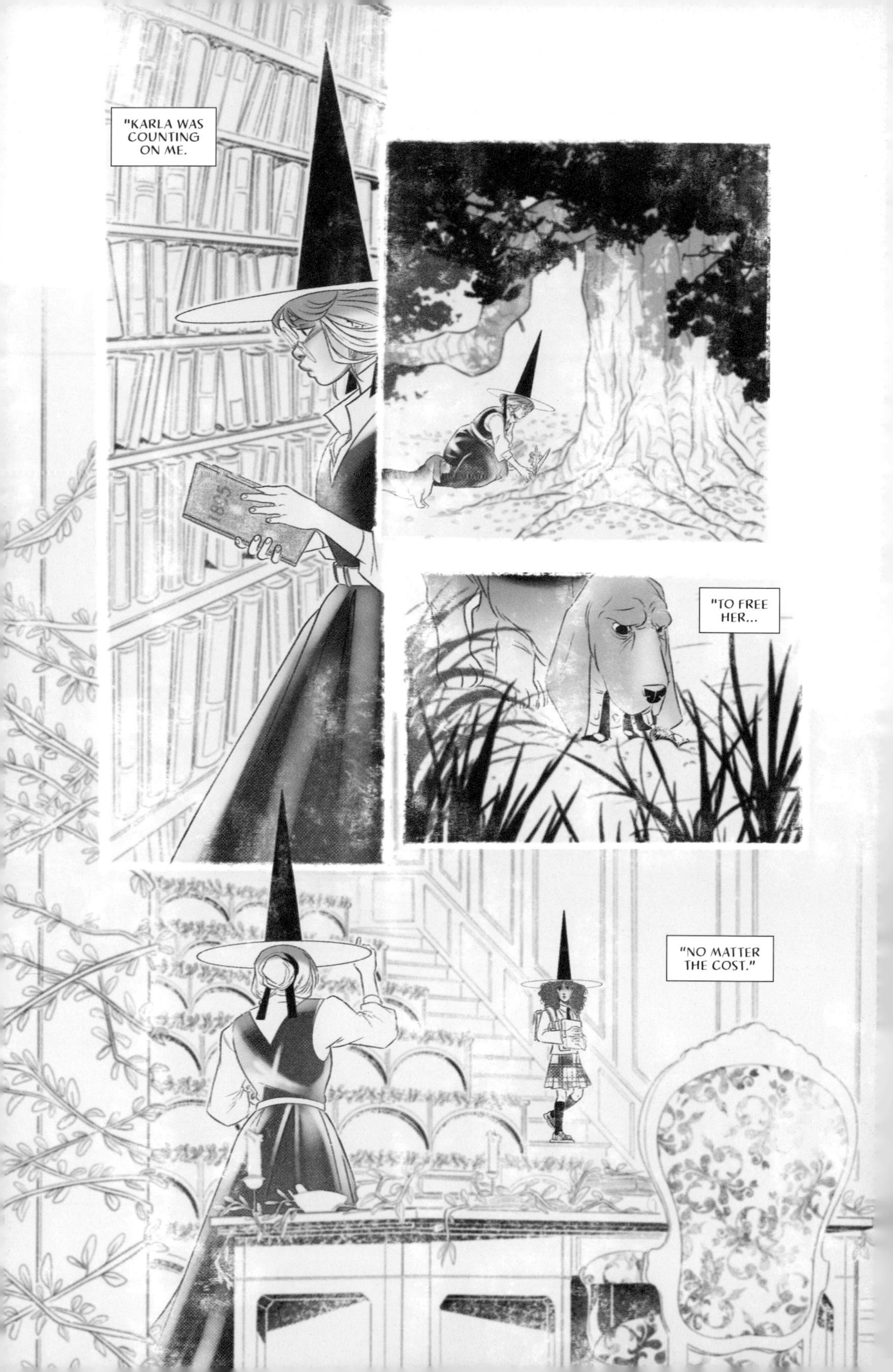
"KARLA WAS COUNTING ON ME.
"TO FREE HER...
"NO MATTER THE COST."

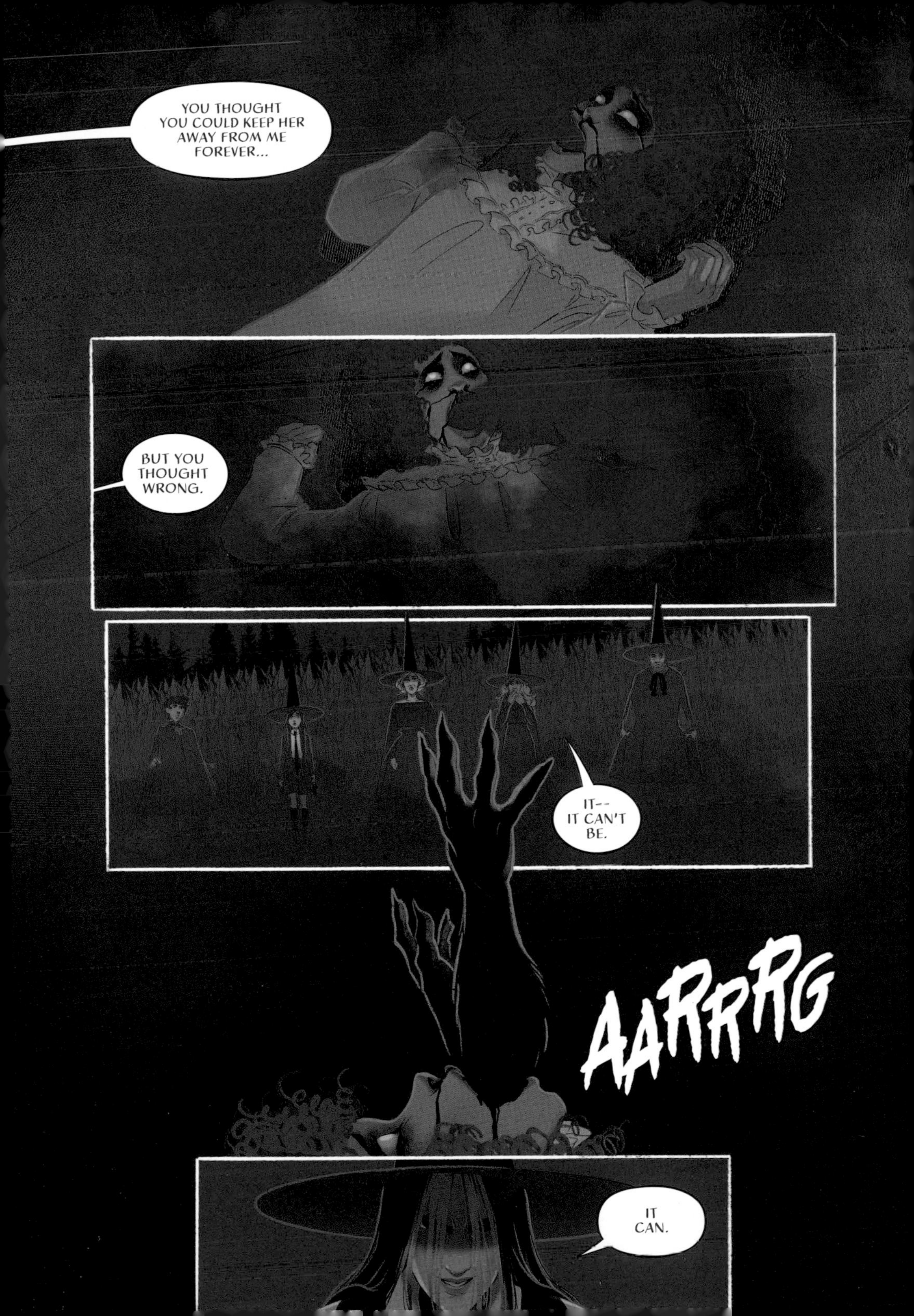
YOU THOUGHT YOU COULD KEEP HER AWAY FROM ME FOREVER...
BUT YOU THOUGHT WRONG.
IT-- IT CAN'T BE.
AARRRG
IT CAN.

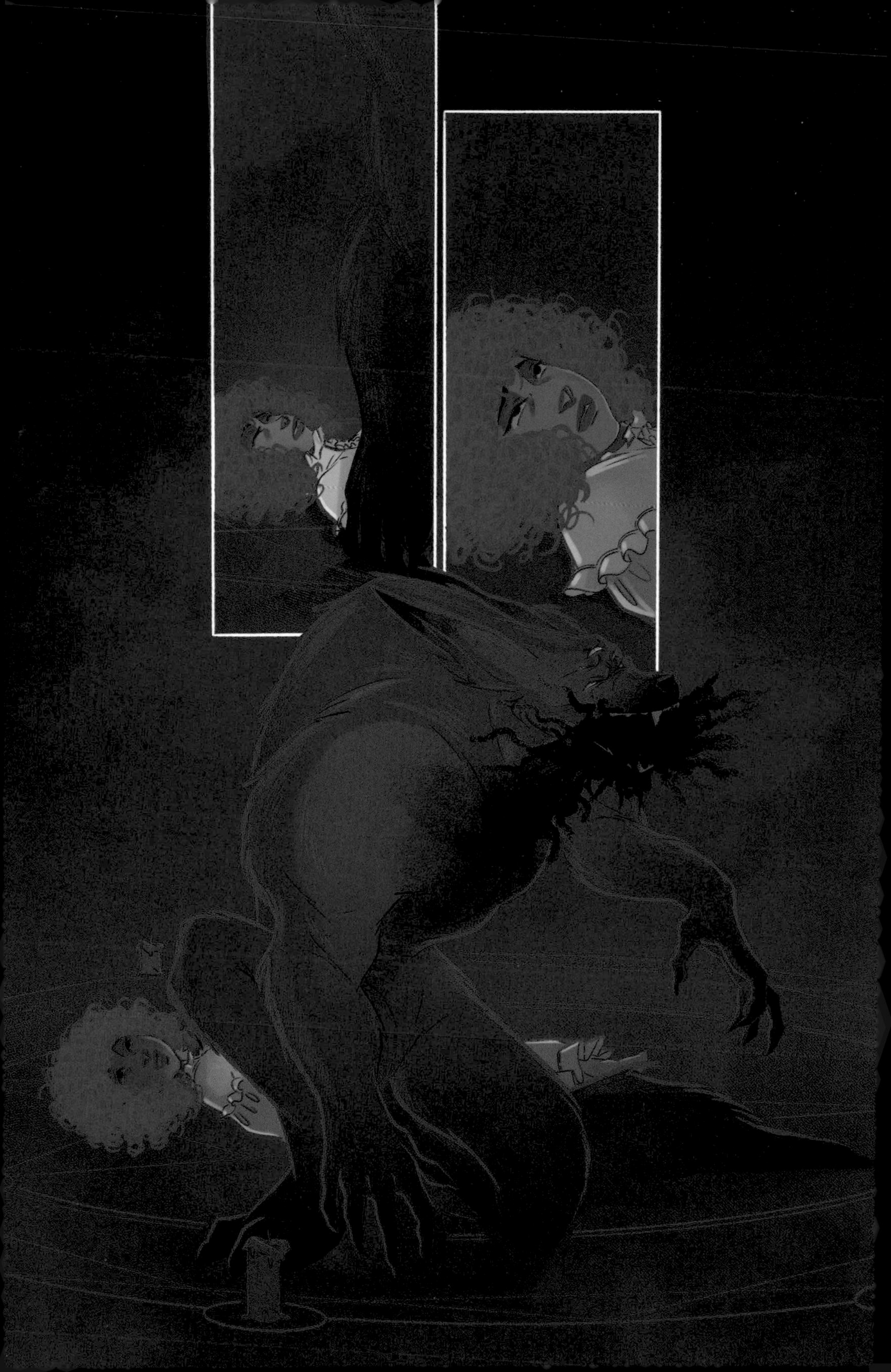

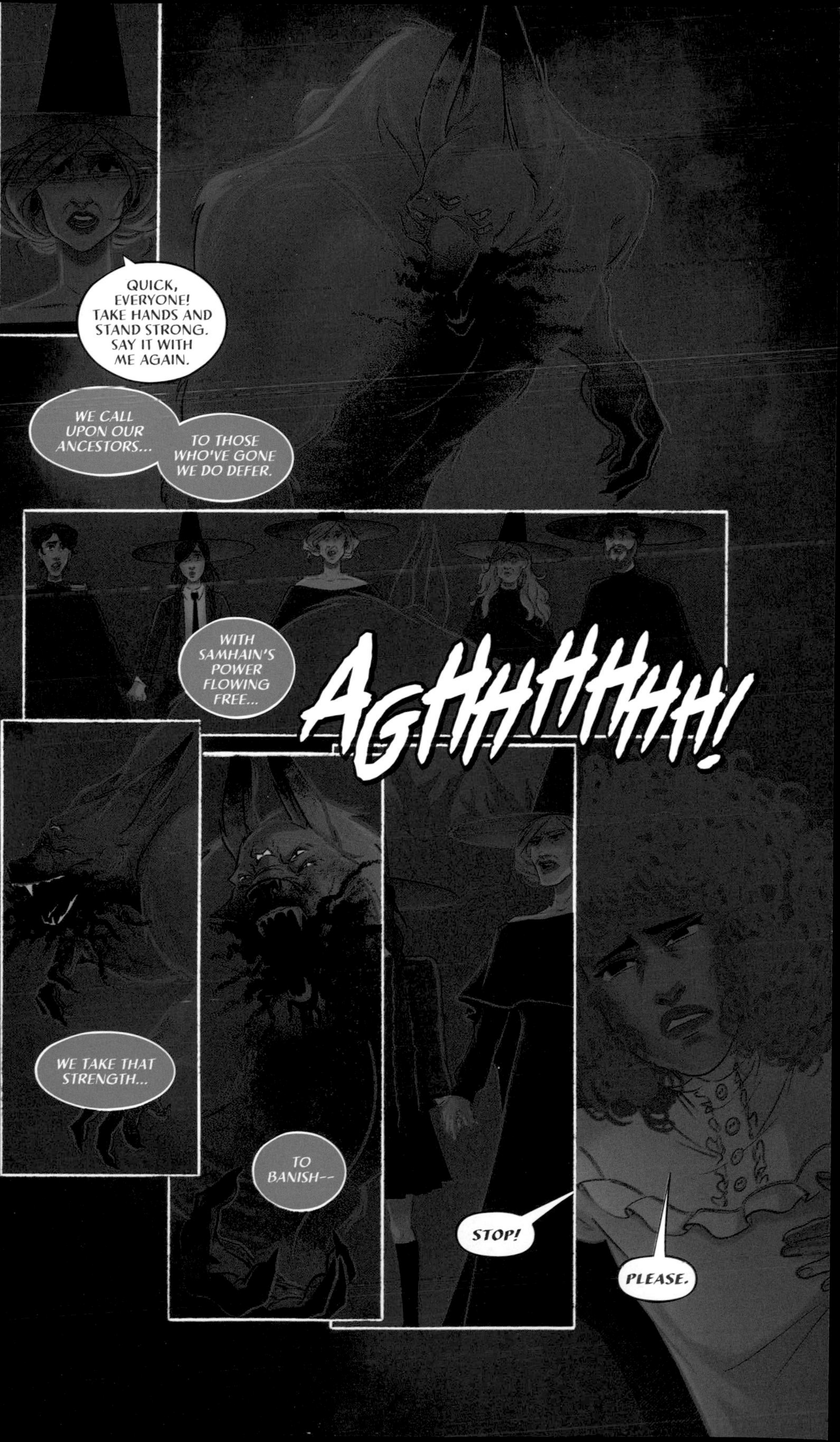
QUICK, EVERYONE! TAKE HANDS AND STAND STRONG. SAY IT WITH ME AGAIN.
WE CALL UPON OUR ANCESTORS...
TO THOSE WHO'VE GONE WE DO DEFER.
WITH SAMHAIN'S POWER FLOWING FREE...
AGHHHHHH!
WE TAKE THAT STRENGTH...
TO BANISH--
STOP!
PLEASE.

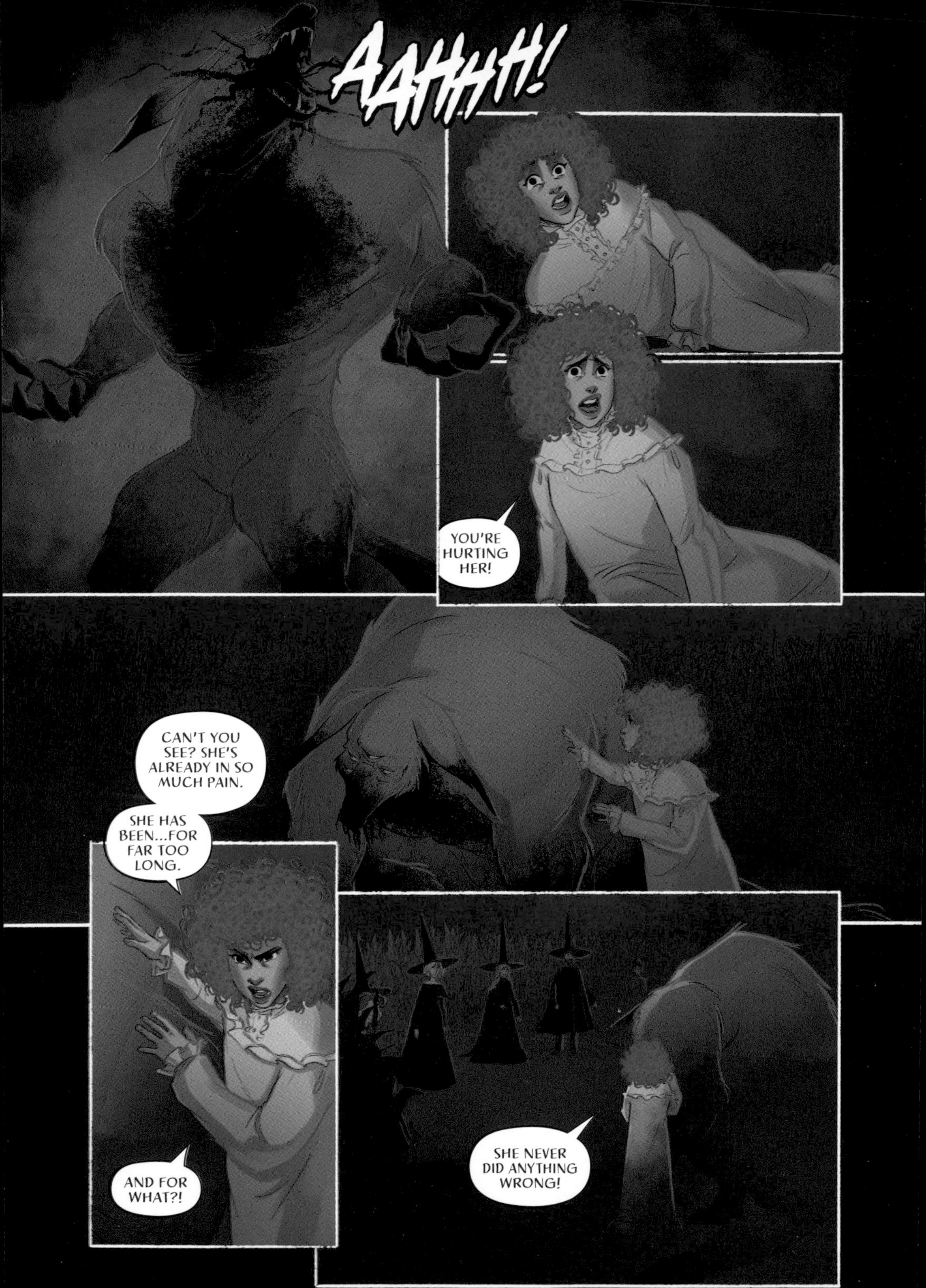
AAHHH!
YOU'RE HURTING HER!
CAN'T YOU SEE? SHE'S ALREADY IN SO MUCH PAIN.
SHE HAS BEEN...FOR FAR TOO LONG.
AND FOR WHAT?!
SHE NEVER DID ANYTHING WRONG!

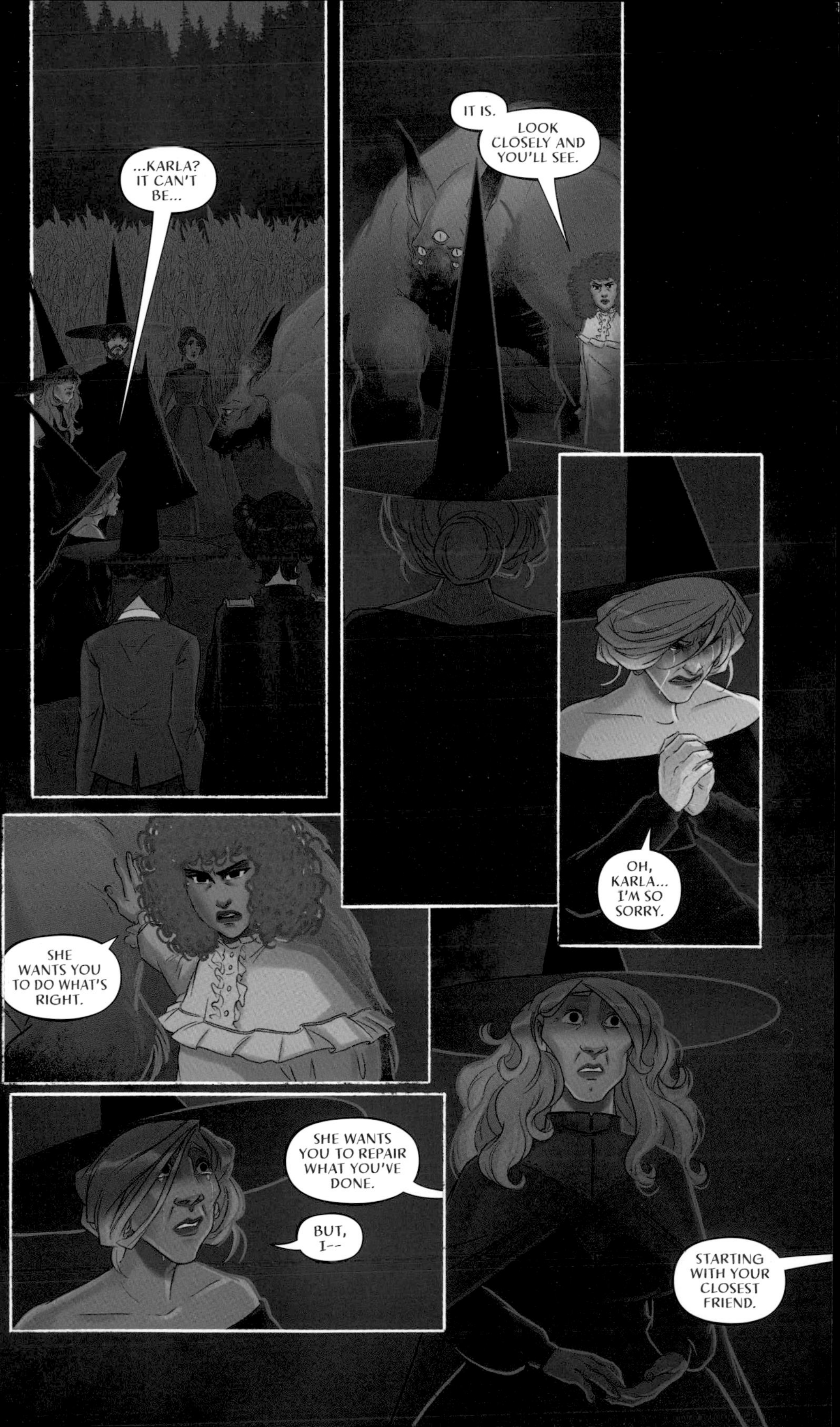
...KARLA? IT CAN'T BE...
IT IS.
LOOK CLOSELY AND YOU'LL SEE.
OH, KARLA... I'M SO SORRY.
SHE WANTS YOU TO DO WHAT'S RIGHT.
SHE WANTS YOU TO REPAIR WHAT YOU'VE DONE.
BUT, I--
STARTING WITH YOUR CLOSEST FRIEND.

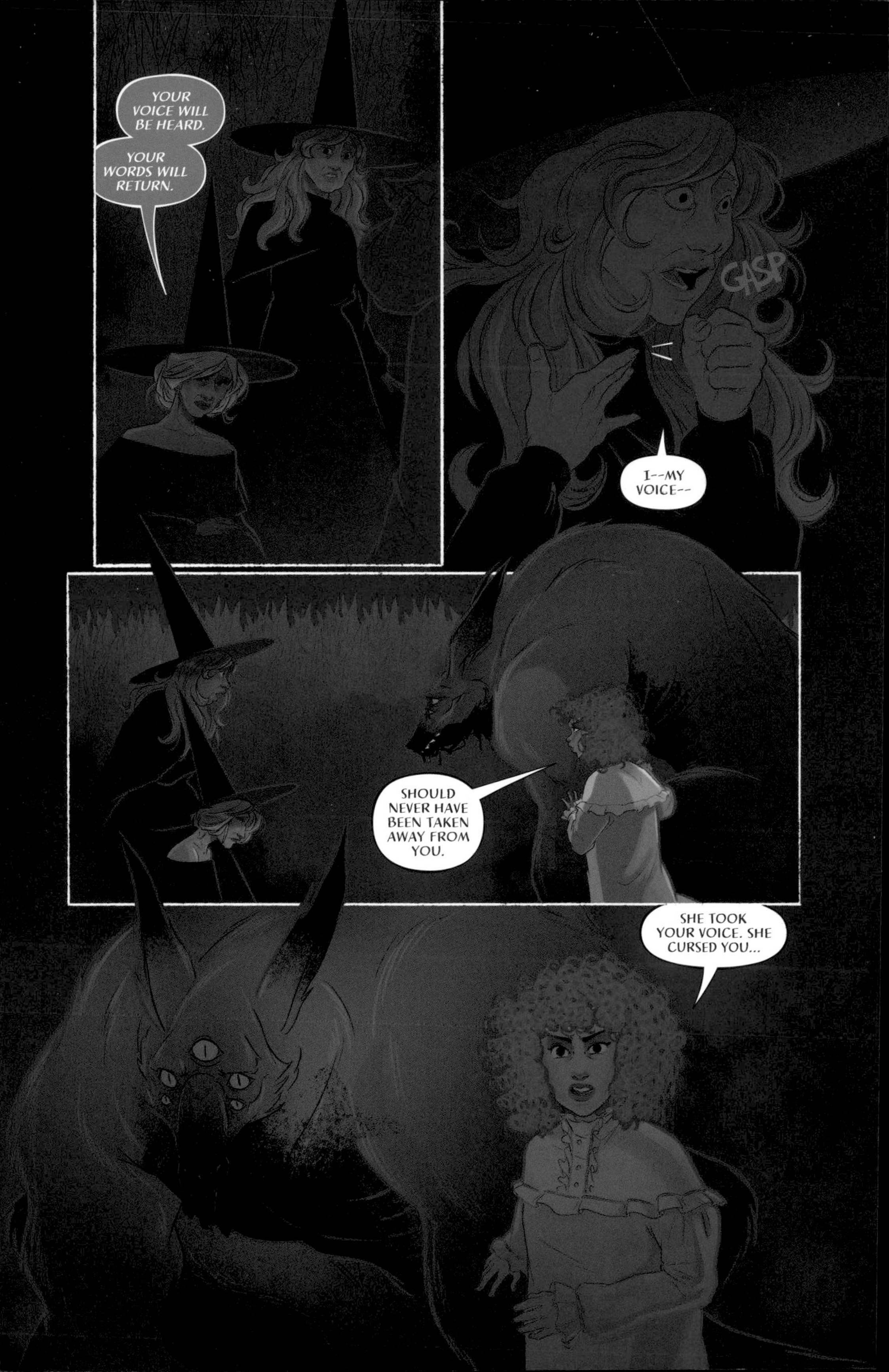
YOUR VOICE WILL BE HEARD.
YOUR WORDS WILL RETURN.
GASP
I--MY VOICE--
SHOULD NEVER HAVE BEEN TAKEN AWAY FROM YOU.
SHE TOOK YOUR VOICE. SHE CURSED YOU...

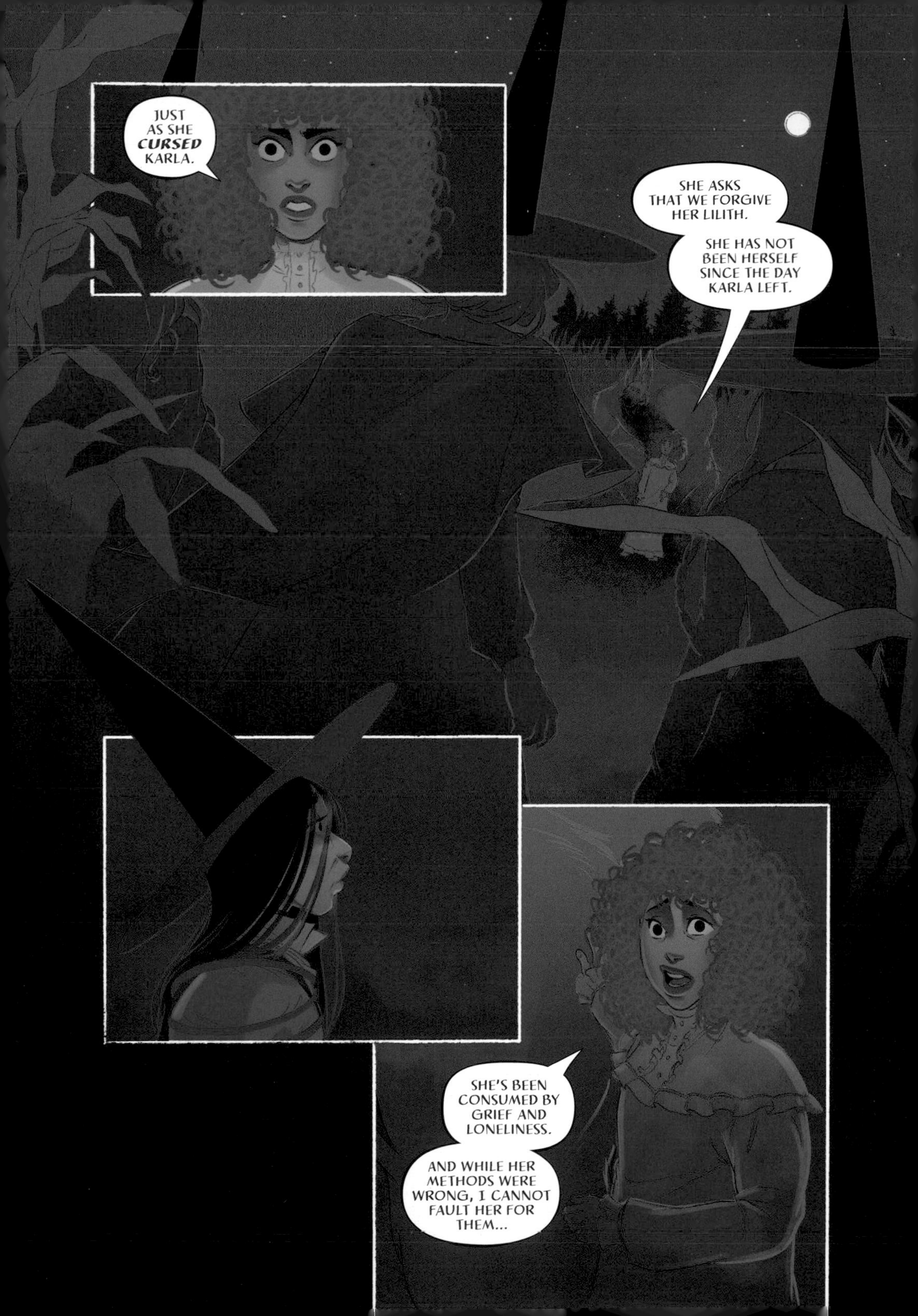
JUST AS SHE *CURSED* KARLA.
SHE ASKS THAT WE FORGIVE HER LILITH.
SHE HAS NOT BEEN HERSELF SINCE THE DAY KARLA LEFT.
SHE'S BEEN CONSUMED BY GRIEF AND LONELINESS.
AND WHILE HER METHODS WERE WRONG, I CANNOT FAULT HER FOR THEM...

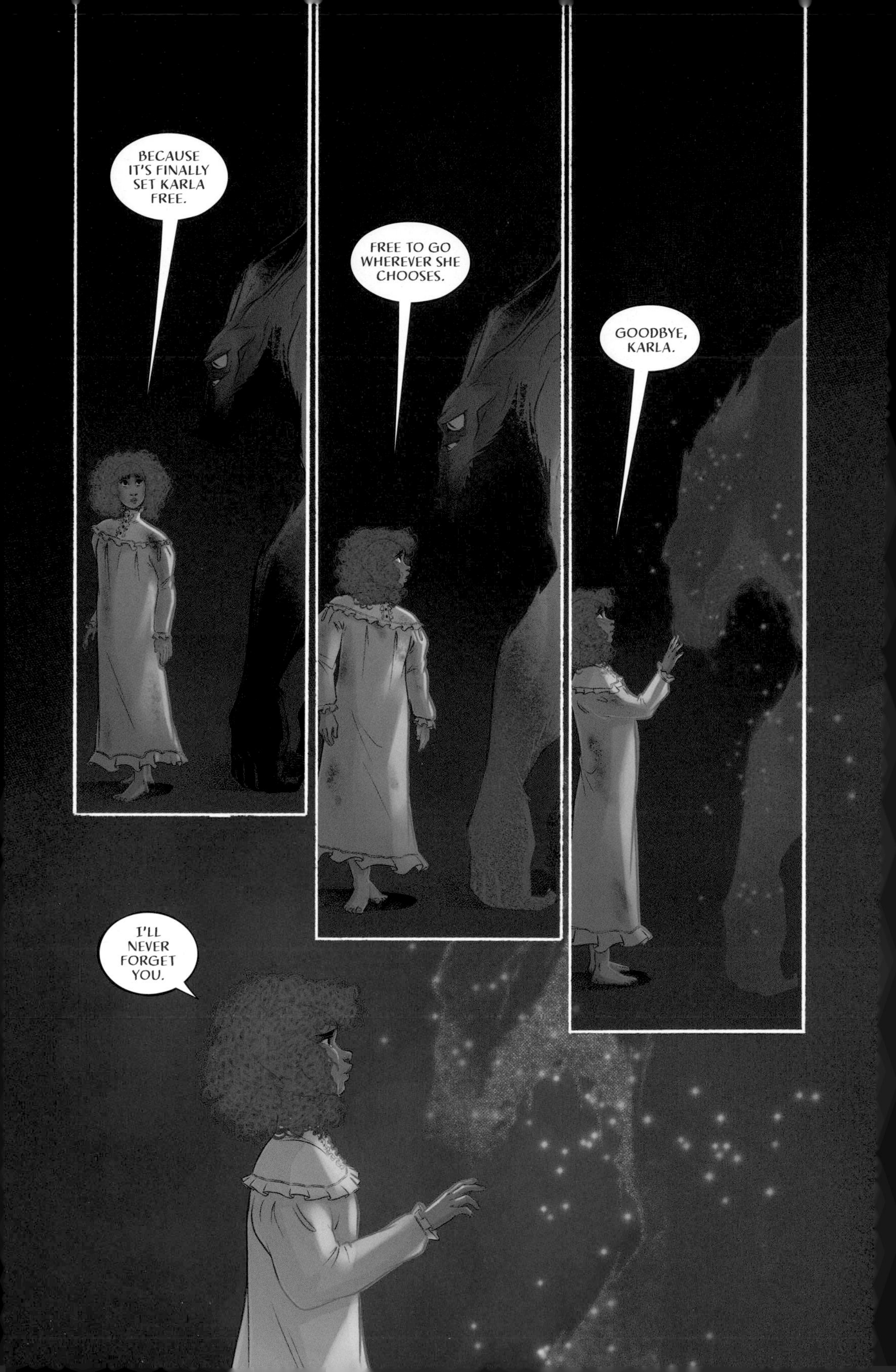
BECAUSE IT'S FINALLY SET KARLA FREE.
FREE TO GO WHEREVER SHE CHOOSES.
GOODBYE, KARLA.
I'LL NEVER FORGET YOU.

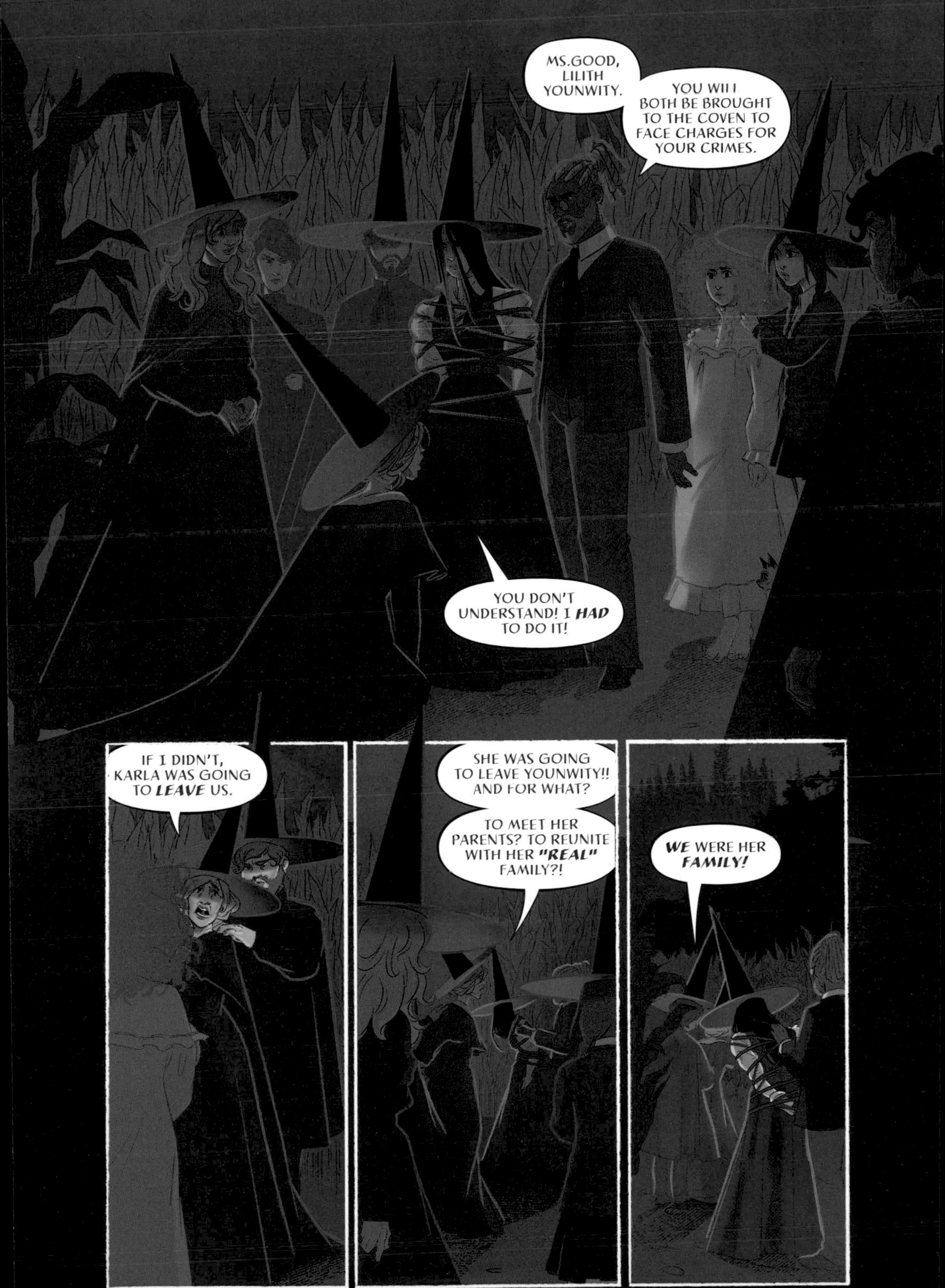
MS.GOOD, LILITH YOUNWITY.
YOU WILL BOTH BE BROUGHT TO THE COVEN TO FACE CHARGES FOR YOUR CRIMES.
YOU DON'T UNDERSTAND! I HAD TO DO IT!
IF I DIDN'T, KARLA WAS GOING TO LEAVE US.
SHE WAS GOING TO LEAVE YOUNWITY!! AND FOR WHAT?
TO MEET HER PARENTS? TO REUNITE WITH HER "REAL" FAMILY?!
WE WERE HER FAMILY!

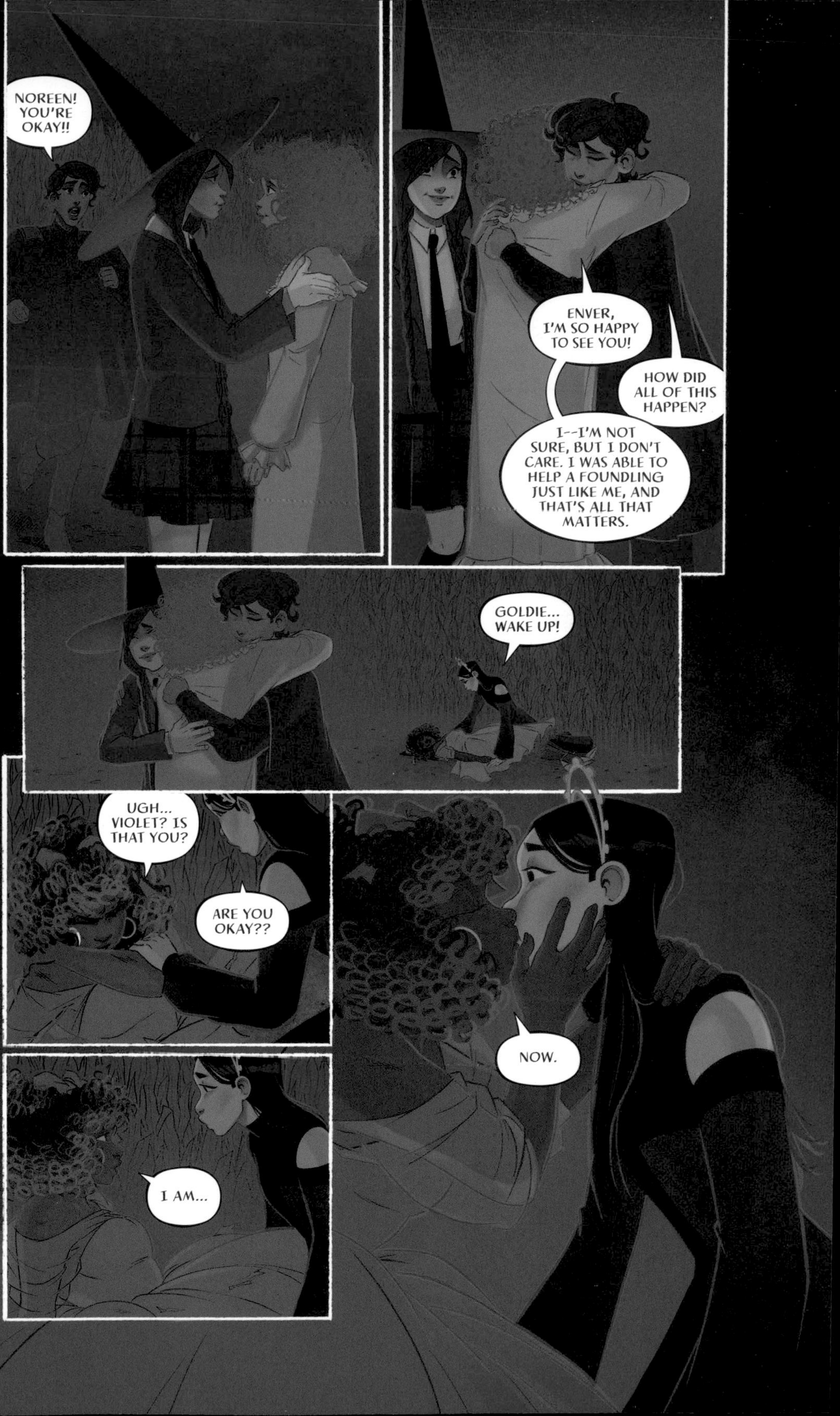
NOREEN! YOU'RE OKAY!!
ENVER, I'M SO HAPPY TO SEE YOU!
HOW DID ALL OF THIS HAPPEN?
I--I'M NOT SURE, BUT I DON'T CARE. I WAS ABLE TO HELP A FOUNDLING JUST LIKE ME, AND THAT'S ALL THAT MATTERS.
GOLDIE... WAKE UP!
UGH... VIOLET? IS THAT YOU?
ARE YOU OKAY??
I AM...
NOW.

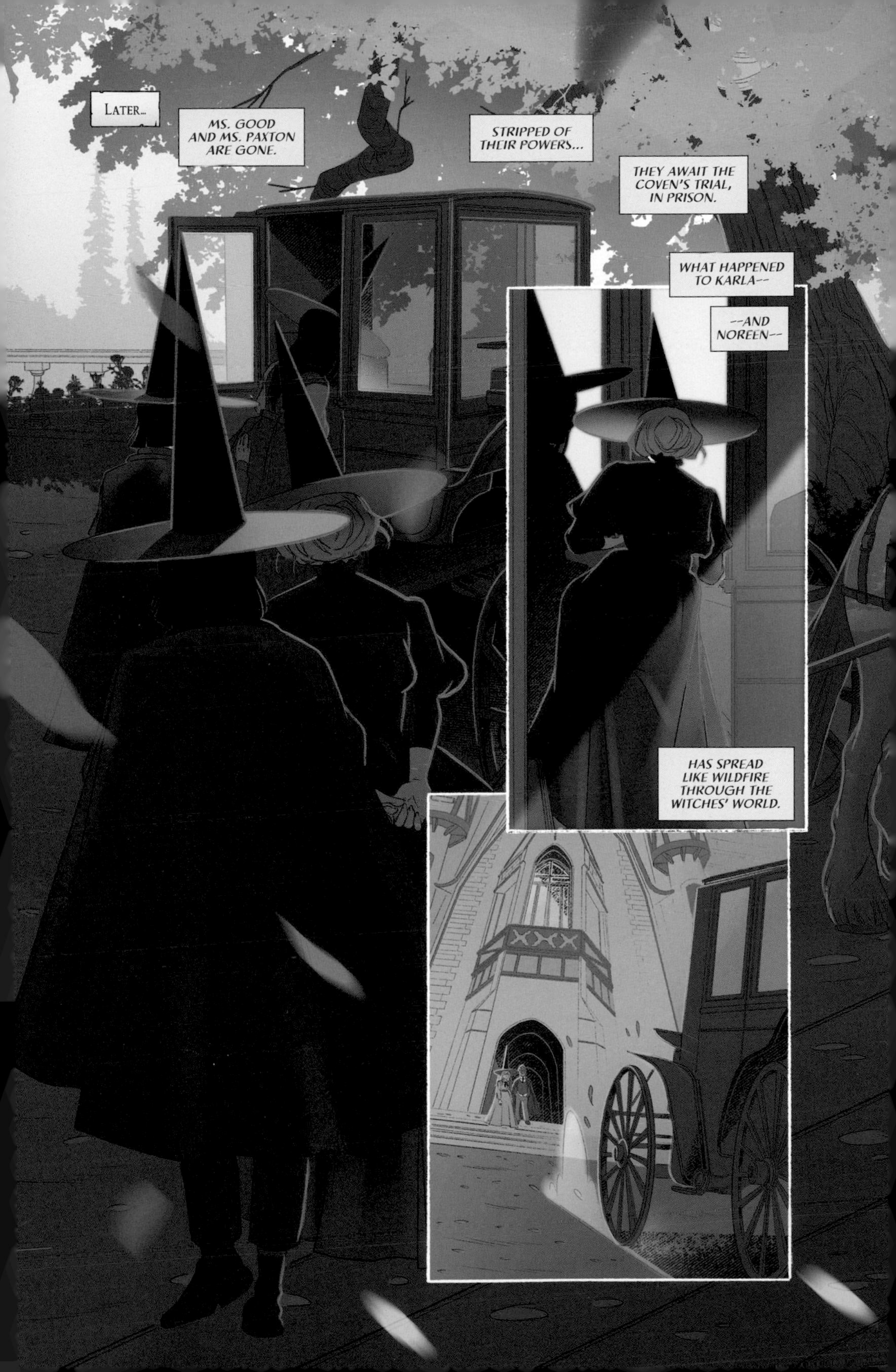
LATER...
MS. GOOD AND MS. PAXTON ARE GONE.
STRIPPED OF THEIR POWERS...
THEY AWAIT THE COVEN'S TRIAL, IN PRISON.
WHAT HAPPENED TO KARLA--
--AND NOREEN--
HAS SPREAD LIKE WILDFIRE THROUGH THE WITCHES' WORLD.

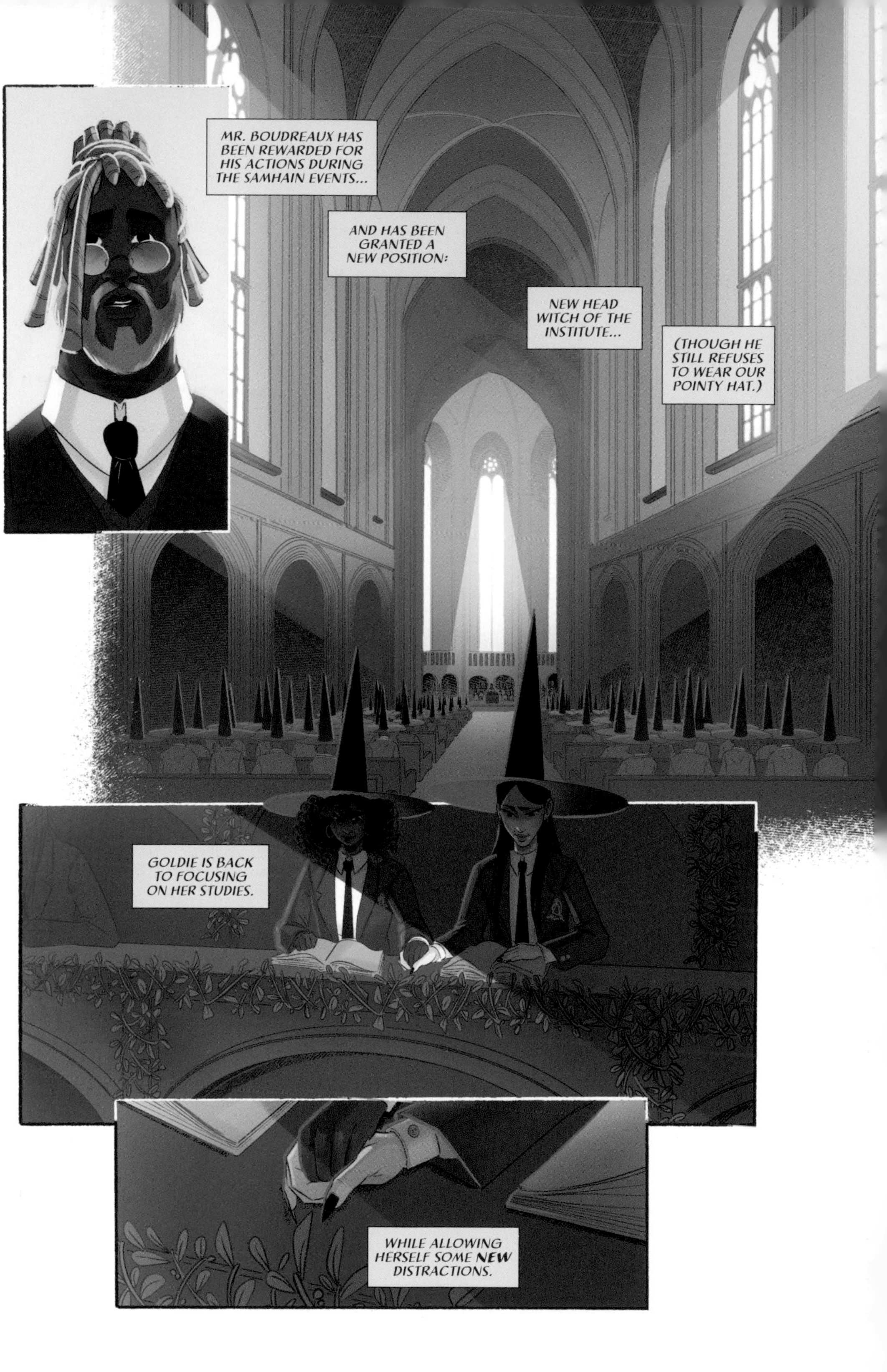

MR. BOUDREAUX HAS BEEN REWARDED FOR HIS ACTIONS DURING THE SAMHAIN EVENTS...
AND HAS BEEN GRANTED A NEW POSITION:
NEW HEAD WITCH OF THE INSTITUTE...
(THOUGH HE STILL REFUSES TO WEAR OUR POINTY HAT.)
GOLDIE IS BACK TO FOCUSING ON HER STUDIES.
WHILE ALLOWING HERSELF SOME NEW DISTRACTIONS.

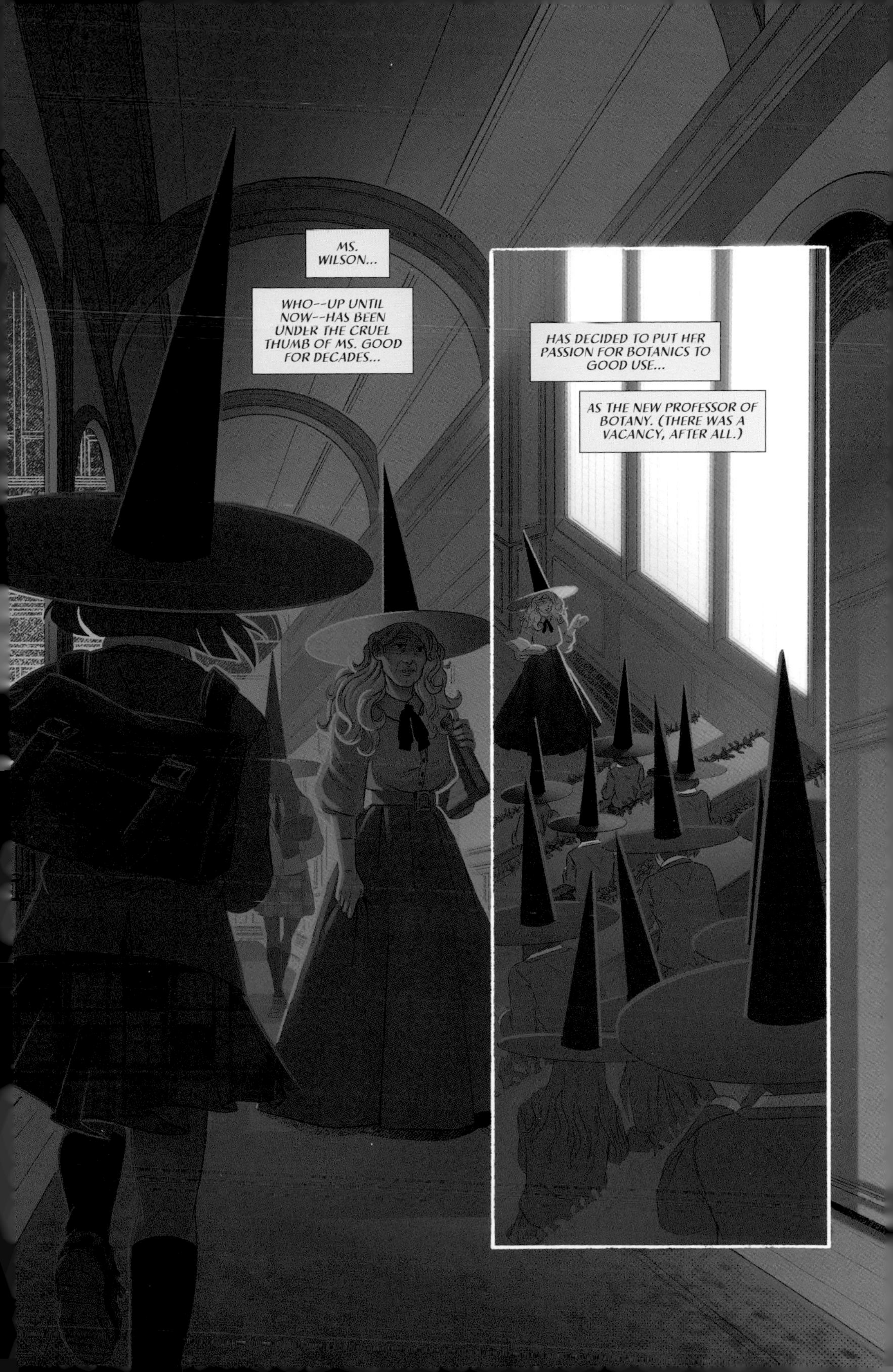
MS. WILSON...
WHO--UP UNTIL NOW--HAS BEEN UNDER THE CRUEL THUMB OF MS. GOOD FOR DECADES...
HAS DECIDED TO PUT HER PASSION FOR BOTANICS TO GOOD USE...
AS THE NEW PROFESSOR OF BOTANY. (THERE WAS A VACANCY, AFTER ALL.)

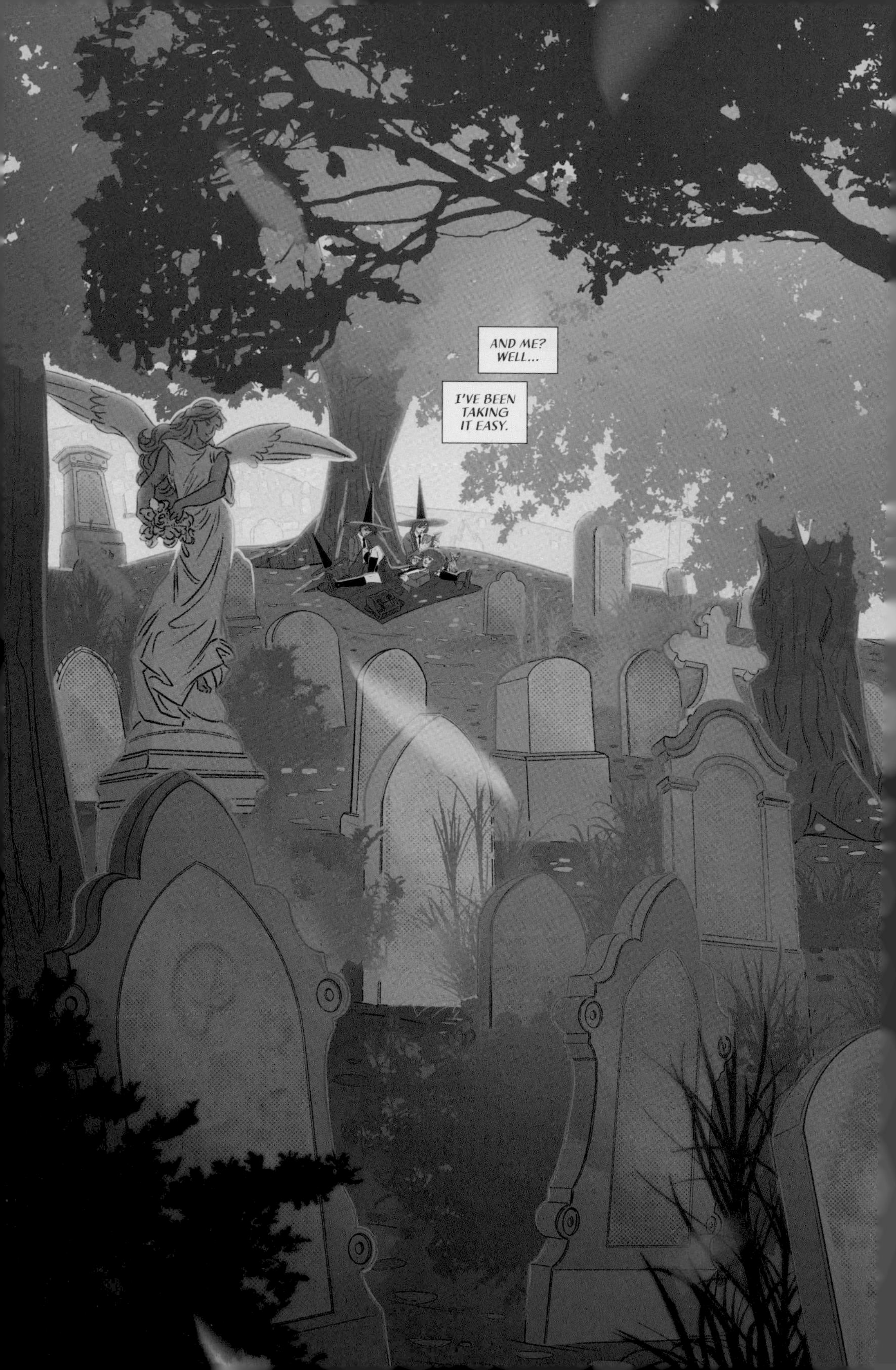
AND ME? WELL...
I'VE BEEN TAKING IT EASY.

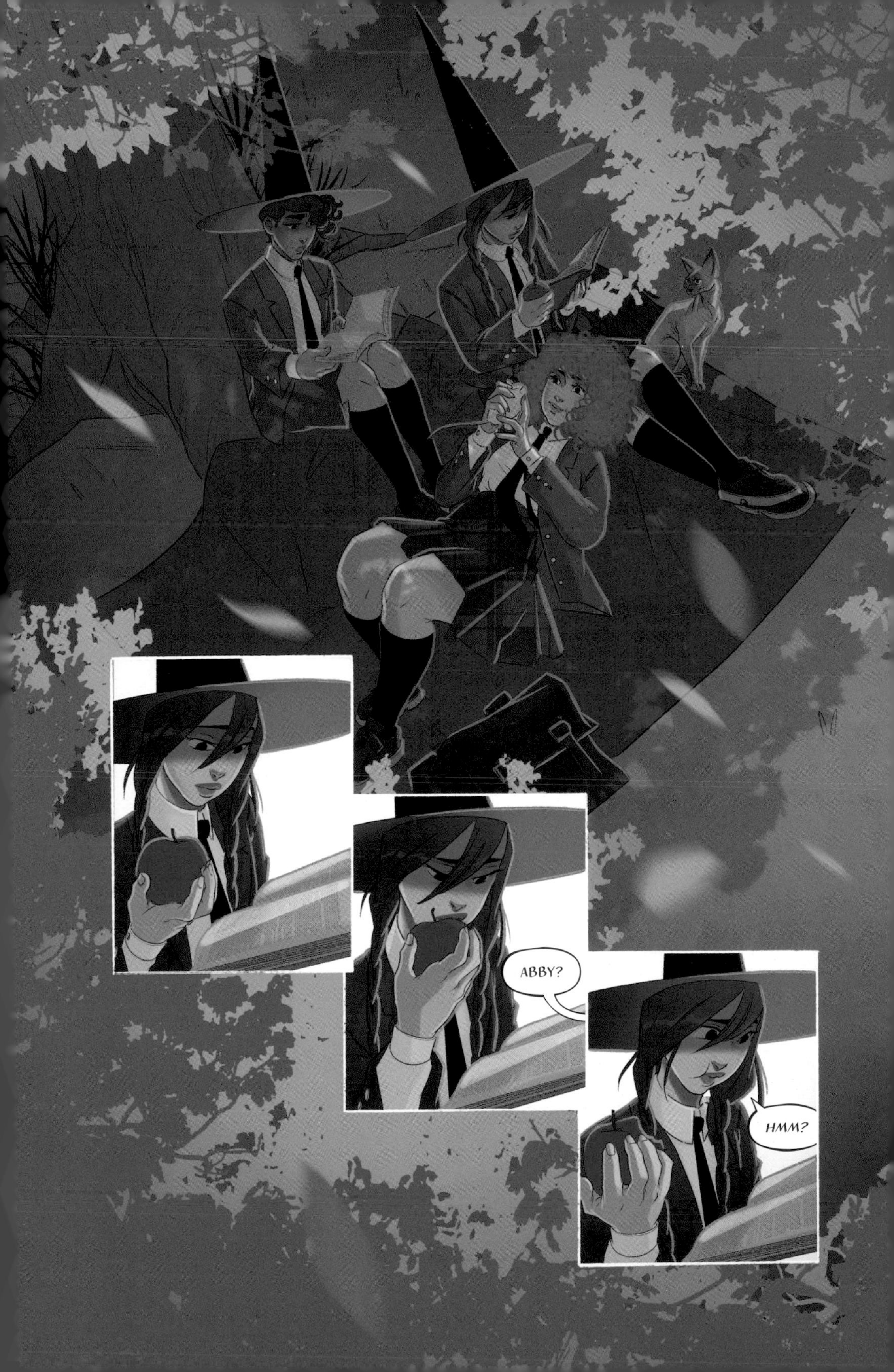
ABBY?
HMM?

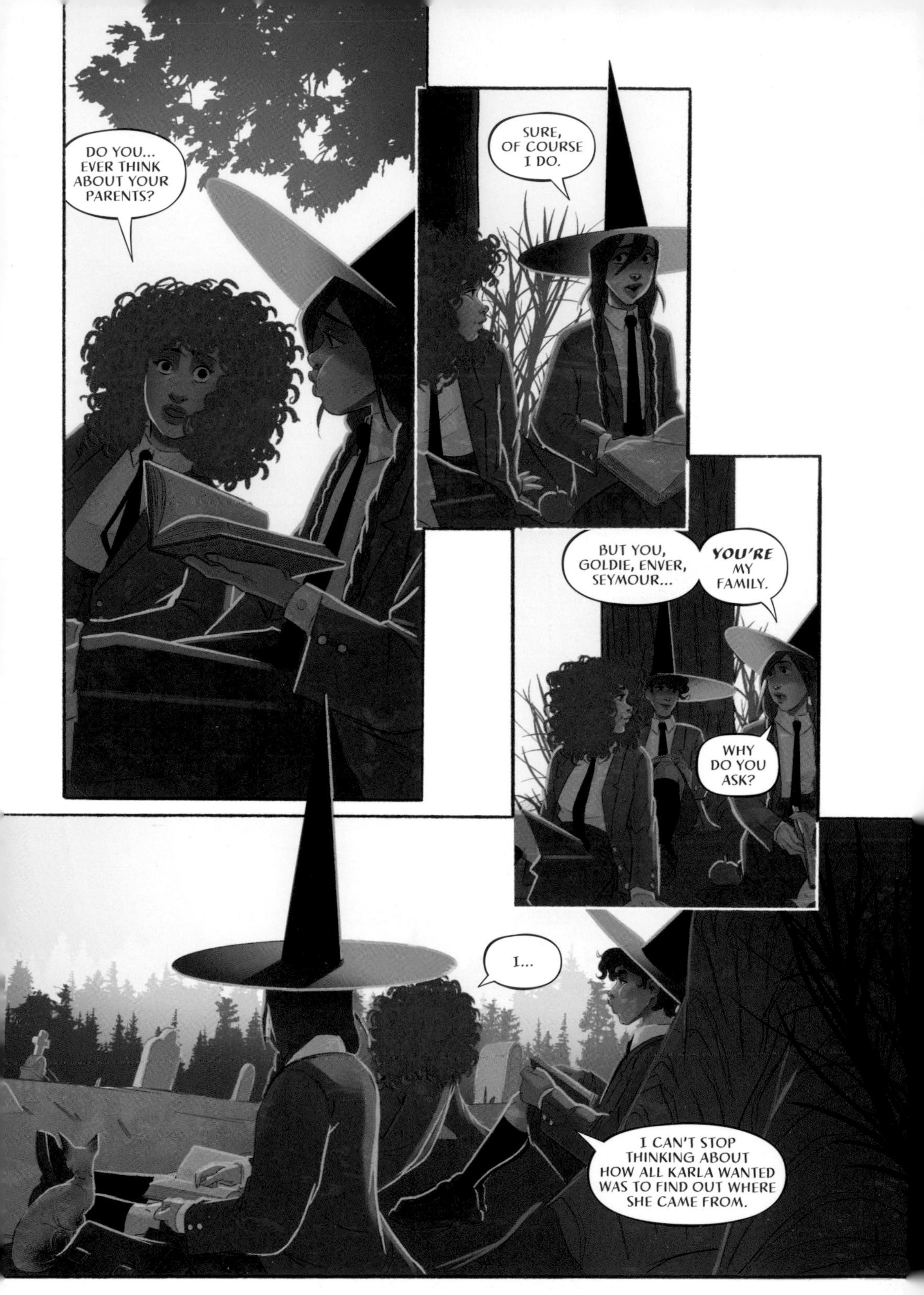
DO YOU... EVER THINK ABOUT YOUR PARENTS?
SURE, OF COURSE I DO.
BUT YOU, GOLDIE, ENVER, SEYMOUR...
YOU'RE MY FAMILY.
WHY DO YOU ASK?
I...
I CAN'T STOP THINKING ABOUT HOW ALL KARLA WANTED WAS TO FIND OUT WHERE SHE CAME FROM.

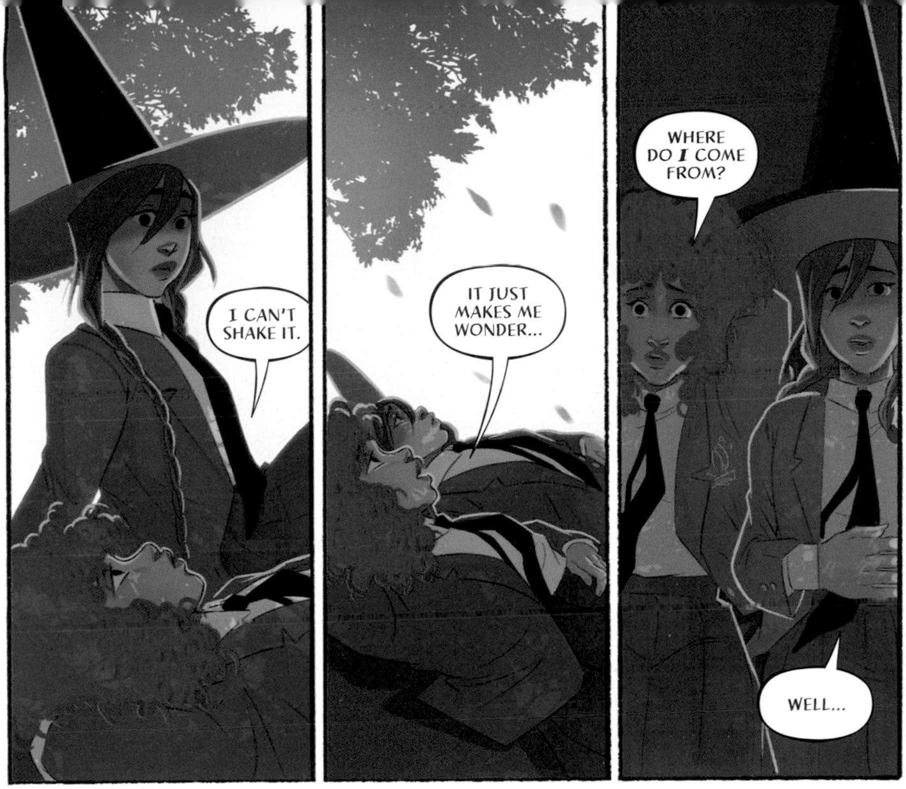
I CAN'T SHAKE IT.
IT JUST MAKES ME WONDER...
WHERE DO *I* COME FROM?
WELL...

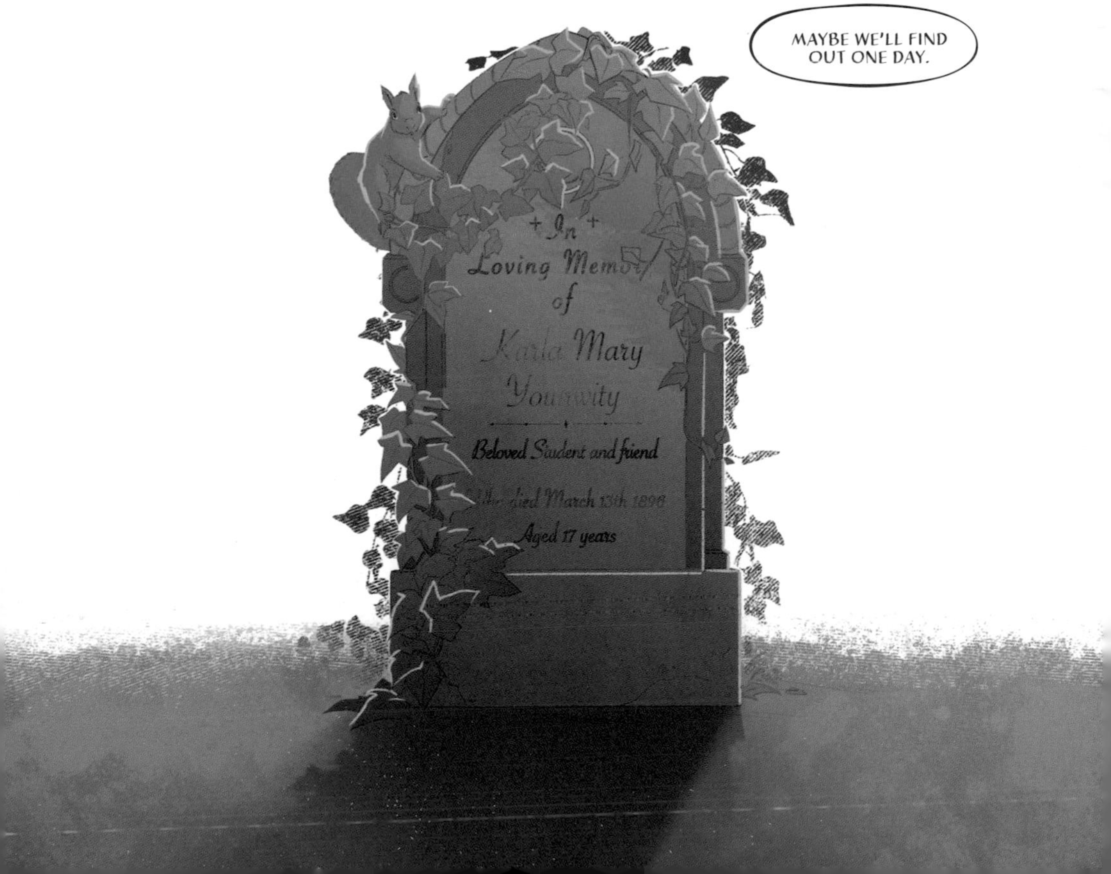
MAYBE WE'LL FIND OUT ONE DAY.
In
Loving Memor
of
Karla Mary
Beloved Student and friend
Aged 17 years

ACKNOWLEDGMENTS

To my partner, who's always next to me and supporting me, even when I work day and night, and our two lovely kitties that are the best emotional support anyone could ask for.

To my parents, for never questioning my passion and letting me do my own thing because I am too stubborn to do anything else.

For my readers and followers, for always being here for me; you are the reason I am here today. I am and will be forever grateful for you all.

To my wonderful agent Britt, who's been here for me since day one. I couldn't ask for anyone better to work with; thank you for putting up with my constant anxiety and being the best support!

To Andrew and Rose, thank you for believing in this project and for being so patient and supportive during the making of this book!

To DC, thank you for being part of this project. I loved working with you and hope to do it again and again!

To Avery, for being a LIFESAVER! Thank you for joining us and making this book so kick-ass, and for your professionalism and your efficiency; I couldn't have done it without you!

To the rest of the team at HarperAlley, thank you for helping, designing, and making this book so wonderful. I couldn't have dreamed of anything better!

To my friends who are still here, and the ones who are not. I cherish you, and I am grateful to you; thank you for being or having been my friend. I promise I will one day stop spending all my time working.

To Soo and the Crew, getting to know you all has been the bright light of this pandemic. I am in awe of your talent!

To Karl, Andy, Masao, Brendan, and Wes, the studio guys! Thank you for the time we spent at the studio, and for all your advice and for helping me shape up what became *Over My Dead Body*. I admire you all!

To all my high school teachers who thought I would never make it because I wasn't good enough in school. Look at me now!

This book is dedicated to everyone
who's incapable of putting boundaries
between work and personal time.

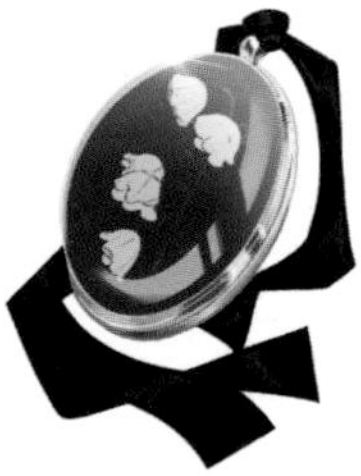

HarperAlley is an imprint of HarperCollins Publishers

Over My Dead Body
 For information address HarperCollins Children's Books, a division of HarperCollins Publishers, 195 Broadway, New York, NY 10007.
www.harperalley.com
Library of Congress Control Number: 2021953152
ISBN 978-0-06-305631-2 (hardcover) — 978-0-06-305630-5 (pbk.)

Colors by Avery Bacon and Sweeney Boo
Typography by DC Hopkins
22 23 24 25 26 GPS 10 9 8 7 6 5 4 3 2 1
❖
First Edition